TABLE OF CONTENTS

This book is dedicated to my sister Robyn, dedicated nurse, amazing cook and cake-decorator, and the reason Crabtree & Evelyn shares are a good buy.

Robyn was delivered to my parent's door in September 1966, just over a year after they took possession of me. The deliverer wasn't a stork but a Te Puke doctor – it's never been a secret to either of us that we were adopted, and it has never been a cause for drama or trauma. Under the wings of our adoptive parents' inspirational partnership, we've shared all that 'natural' siblings share, by which I mean we've at various stages played and argued, competed and collaborated, hugged and harangued, fought and made up. As adoptive children, our siblings could have been anyone – I'm glad, Robyn, that mine is you.

Praise for

THE MOONTIDE QUARTET

'Hair spins a satisfying fantasy that . . . is a sort of mashup of J.R.R. Tolkien and Henry Kissinger' *Kirkus*

'*The Scarlet Tides* is simply faster, better and even more satisfying than its prequel. So long for the difficult second book – Hair seems to handle these with ease' upcoming4.me

'Modern epic fantasy at its best' *Fantasy Book Critic*

'An excellent follow up to the first novel, continuing the tradition of vivid, dynamic characters and terrific world building . . . Readers of epic fantasy should definitely check out this series' BiblioSanctum

'Stellar pacing and vivid action . . . a ripping read' blackgate.com

'If you like your fantasy with a vast cast and a varied and intricate landscape then this is definitely for you' *British Fantasy Society*

'True epic fantasy. It has everything a fan could want . . . a compelling plot, and twists aplenty' abitterdraft.com

'Hair plays it right . . . a must read series' *Fantasy Review Barn*

'This story is so utterly *human* . . . Set in a world with religious and political struggles that wonderfully parallel our own, *Mage's Blood* depicts the good and bad of society and its obsession with power' *The Wishing Table*

'Makes for an outstanding start to a series which promises to recall epic fantasy's finest. This book could be huge – an honour I dare say David Hair deserves' Tor.com

90710 000 462 984

Also by David Hair

THE MOONTIDE QUARTET

Mage's Blood
Scarlet Tides
Unholy War

THE RETURN OF RAVANA

The Pyre

ASCENDANT'S RITE

THE MOONTIDE QUARTET BOOK IV

DAVID HAIR

Jo Fletcher
BOOKS

This paperback edition published in 2016 by
First published in Great Britain in 2015 by Jo Fletcher Books

Jo Fletcher Books
an imprint of
Quercus Editions Ltd
Carmelite House
50 Victoria Embankment
London EC4Y 0DZ

An Hachette UK company

A CIP catalogue record for this book is available
from the British Library

PB ISBN 978 1 78429 039 9
EBOOK ISBN 978 1 78429 038 2

This book is a work of fiction. Names, characters,
businesses, organizations, places and events are
either the product of the author's imagination
or used fictitiously. Any resemblance to
actual persons, living or dead, events or
locales is entirely coincidental.

10 9 8 7 6 5 4

Typeset by CC Book Production

Printed and bound in Great Britain by Clays Ltd, St Ives plc

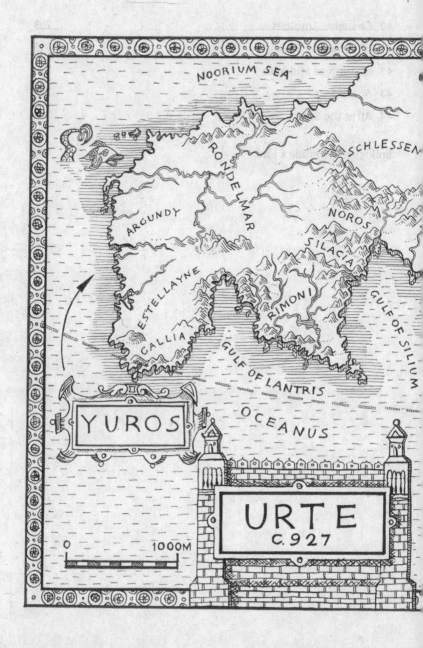

NOORIUM SEA

SCHLESSEN

RONDELMAR

ARGUNDY

NOROS

SILACIA

ESTELLAYNE

RIMONI

GALLIA

GULF OF SILIUM

GULF OF LANTRIS

OCEANUS

YUROS

0   1000M

URTE
C.927

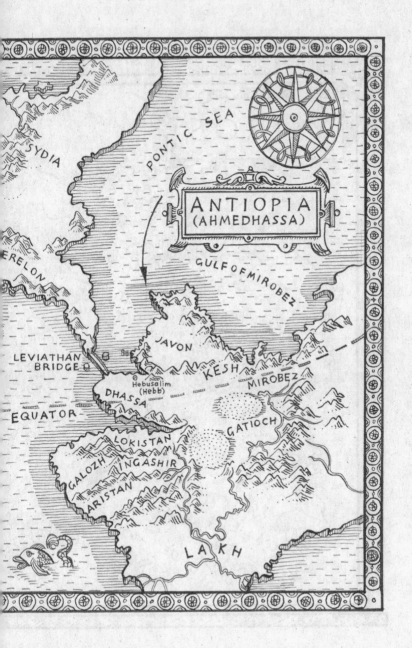

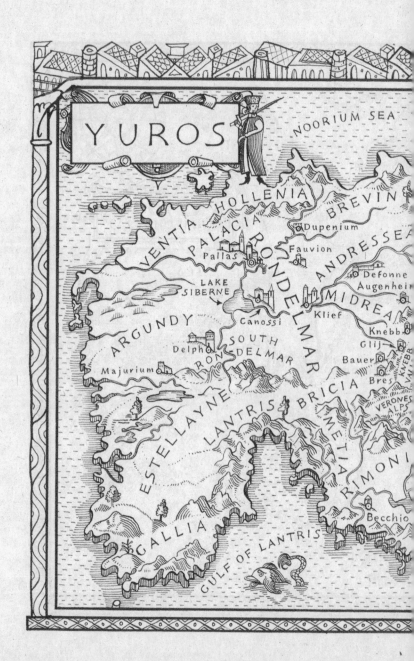

ICE WASTES

MIRODEAN ICE SEA

SCHLESSEN

SOUTH
SCHLESSEN
(BUNAVIA)

SYDIA

CEDRON
VALLEY

BREKAELLEN
VALLEY

Collistein

NOROS

Lukhazan

Dusheim
Spinitius

VERELON

Norostein

SILACIA

Cypinos

Thantis

GULF OF SILIUM

Pontus

Rym
Ruins)

Northpoint

0   500M

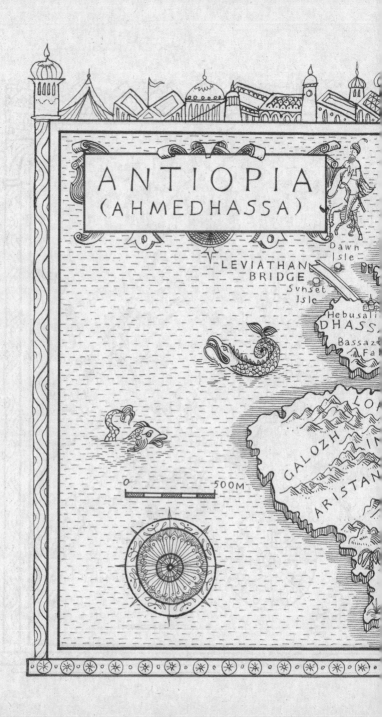

ANTIOPIA
(AHMEDHASSA)

LEVIATHAN
BRIDGE

Dawn
Isle

Sunset
Isle

Hebusali
DHASS
Bassaz
Fal

LO
GALOZH
IN
ARISTAN

0   500M

GULF OF MIROBEZ

Hytel

Lybis   Loctis
rochena
        Riban
        Forensa
AVON HARKUN
roz   Intemsa
  Krak   Hallikut
    Istabad
  Galataz
  Sagostabad   Shaliyah   Ghosh
    Peroz
edishar   Vida
bad   Barakabad
    Khotriawal
      Gujati
SITHARDH   GATIOCH   Ullakesh
DESERT
TAN
ASHIR   NIMTAYA
              ETERNAL
    Kankriti-   MOUNTAINS
    pur   Teshwallabad
BALAYAN
UNTAINS

    Tuklabad   Baranasi

  L A K H

sjidabad   Jeslamabad
      Dili

KESH MIROBEZ

EASTERN
KESH
DESERT

The Vexations of Emperor Constant
(Part Four)

Solarus Crystals

The Leviathan Bridge is the first piece of inanimate gnostic artifice that is entirely self-sustaining: it draws energy from the Sun and converts it to gnostic energy to sustain it against the immense forces of the ocean. The Sun's energy is harvested by giant clusters of special fused crystals in the domes of five great towers. They, more than the Bridge itself, point the way forward for the next developments in the craft of magic.

ORDO COSTRUO ARCANUM, PONTUS, 877

Pallas, Rondelmar
Summer, 927
1 Year until the Moontide

A frightened falcon perched on the chandelier above and shrieked at the corpse in the middle of the Inner Council room. The counsellors just gaped, speechless. Gurvon Gyle pressed back into his chair, distancing himself from what he'd just seen. It was one thing to plot the sacrifice of an army; it was quite another to see the emperor sanctioning illegal use of the gnosis – in this case, the taking of a human soul and placing it into the body of a beast. Even here in Pallas, where the pure-blood magi-nobility ruled supreme and mere humans were little more than chattels, this was surely without precedent.

I've just seen a Souldrinker perform a soul-stealing, and in the emperor's

1

own Inner Council Chamber! I must always remember this moment . . . though Kore knows who I could ever tell.

His eyes moved from the bird to the man who'd just demonstrated this horror: the Souldrinker or 'Dokken' introduced as Delta, named for the Lantric brand on his forehead – though Delta appeared to be more pawn than perpetrator: it was the Dokken's master, Ervyn Naxius, who'd truly done this. The old mage was cackling like a drunken grandfather in a Low Street tavern at the acclaim currently being heaped upon him. Gyle found his own hands applauding, his mouth spouting praise as if for a tourney victor, but his mind was reeling.

Beside him, Belonius Vult, his fellow conspirator, looked triumphant – as well he might: after all, this was his part of the plan for the conquest of Antiopia.

What else have you got up your sleeve, Bel?

Vult graciously accepted an appreciative nod from Mater-Imperia Lucia. The matronly former Empress – now a Living Saint – was effectively the ruler of the Rondian Empire; her opinion mattered even more than that of her son, Emperor Constant, who was staring into space, his sword-hand clenching and unclenching as if he might leap into the saddle and ride upon Antiopia this very instant. He might be an emperor, and in his mid-twenties, but few would deny – in private at least – that Constant had the demeanour of a spoilt squire.

The others present, some of the most powerful men in the Empire, also made great show of praising Naxius, though Gyle could detect wariness at all this acclaim being heaped upon another. Imperial Treasurer Calan Dubrayle, who'd sponsored Vult in bringing in Naxius, had the most reason to bask in the reflected glory. The great General Kaltus Korion clearly had his pleasure in anticipating new super-beasts for his armies tempered by seeing another's stock rise so dramatically. And Tomas Betillon, Governor of Hebusalim, looked no better pleased: his smile was sour, his praise muted.

The only person present who wasn't joining in the applause was Grand Prelate Dominius Wurther. The obese churchman lurched to his feet and denounced Naxius and his thrall in no uncertain terms. 'My Lord Emperor, this is *sacrilege*! This *abomination* that Naxius has demonstrated is a violation of the Book of Kore! I must protest!'

Emperor Constant looked away, but he showed no sign of repentance, so the Grand Prelate turned to Lucia, raising his hands beseechingly. 'Mater-Imperia, the Souldrinkers are our oldest enemies. This "Delta" must by our own law be put to death: his very existence is an affront to Kore. We must not allow ourselves to see virtue in this abomination.'

Lucia remained calm. 'Dominius, you are forever telling us that Kore has a reason for all He does, and all He allows in this world, are you not? So does it not follow that the Dokken must be part of His plan?'

Wurther's jowls wobbled. 'Mater-Imperia, that is one interpretation, but our theologists—'

'Please, don't let him bore us with theology,' Betillon groaned.

'Hear hear,' Kaltus Korion agreed. 'Since when has morality ever troubled you, you old windbag? The Church of Kore takes a percentage on every slave sold, as we all know. All you're worried about is that these new creatures might cause you to miss out on your cut.'

'Not all are as venal as you, Kaltus Korion! This deplorable proposal cannot be sanctioned – it is in every way a violation of Kore's Law!' Wurther pointed skywards to invoke Kore Himself. 'I can quote you every psalm that forbids such gnosis! The Church cannot support this.'

Gurvon was mildly impressed. He'd always believed the churchman to be utterly self-serving, but this display hinted at something resembling a moral compass. He was surprised such a thing had survived decades in the upper echelons of the clergy.

'I hear you, Dominius,' Lucia replied evenly, 'and I understand your reservations. Indeed, I am pleased you've voiced them. But I will remind you of the governing principle of this gathering: that what is agreed by the emperor becomes the will of us all, separately and collectively; we each of us champion my son's will when we leave this room.'

'But Mater-Imperia, there has to be limits – the Laws of Kore stand above us all!'

'But *we* are the Blessed of Kore,' Vult put in. 'We're the living expression of His will: so surely what we agree upon now must out-weigh a book written long ago and with no concept of the choices and threats that face us now.'

Gurvon glanced at Vult. *You could justify anything you like with that, Bel.*

'Not the "morality versus pragmatism" argument again,' Dubrayle sighed. 'Haven't we done it to death yet?'

'I don't think you should go back over our old disagreements on my or Bel's behalf,' Gurvon drawled. *As my father used to say: if you're going to blow with the wind, hoist your mainsail.*

Wurther threw him a dirty look, then sat down ponderously. 'You all know I respect the collegial nature of these meetings,' he grumbled. 'Of course I'll support the will of this group from the moment I leave this chamber, if it is the will of my Lord Emperor.'

'I support this proposal absolutely,' Constant declared, after a glance at his mother.

And so that's that.

The Dokken, Delta, bowed to the emperor, then turned and left, calling the falcon to his hand as he went. Naxius took a seat while a pair of guards bustled in and removed the body of the thief, their faces impassive.

So Naxius stays . . . ? Gurvon wasn't happy with that; this plan was his and Vult's; he didn't want that old snake stealing their glory.

'Make yourself comfortable, Magister Naxius,' Lucia said drily. 'You have been apprised of our intentions concerning Javon and the Duke of Argundy?'

'I have been briefed by Governor Vult, your Holiness,' Naxius replied obsequiously. 'I commend his plan wholeheartedly.'

Kaltus Korion raised a hand. 'A moment. What is he doing here? I have always held that a traitor is a traitor, even if that treachery benefits the empire. How can we trust him?'

Constant went to reply, but had no ready answer and as he stammered into silence Belonius Vult stepped in. 'Magister Naxius' knowledge of the Leviathan Bridge was vital. Gurvon found him, and I made the approach.'

'And that is enough for me,' Lucia said firmly, and the moment passed.

I don't like the man, but involving Naxius was unavoidable, Gurvon reflected. The plan required someone who knew the workings of the Bridge intimately but who hated the Ordo Costruo, and they'd not found anyone who filled those criteria who was not also committed to the East – except for Ervyn Naxius.

Twenty-three years ago, in 904, as the Leviathan Bridge rose from the sea, Constant's father Magnus had marched his armies across it to plunder Antiopia. Antonin Meiros, the founder of the Ordo Costruo, could have destroyed the Bridge then, but he'd hesitated and the moment was lost – for this, Meiros was reviled in the East. But few knew that Ervyn Naxius had been behind the founder's confusion.

Naxius was a gnostic researcher, once a humane man, but his centuries of research into the extreme possibilities of the gnosis had eroded his empathy; he had long since stopped paying any attention to the constraints of morality. He had fallen out with Meiros and the Order, and the First Crusade had presented him with an opportunity to gain a patron with almost bottomless resources. He threw in his lot with the emperor, misinformed Meiros about the troop build-up outside Pontus, then betrayed the Order to Magnus' Imperial Magi, enabling them to seize control of the Bridge. By the time Meiros had worked out what was happening, it was largely too late: the Crusade was proceeding, his reputation was destroyed and control of his Bridge was lost.

Naxius got his reward: Imperial approval to research without constraint. Gurvon had come across his handiwork during the Noros Revolt – some particularly vicious spells hidden in trinkets and talismans – and after the Revolt, he'd tracked down the source of these devices. The trail led in the end to Naxius' secret base, and eventually to this moment.

Gurvon turned his attention back to Vult, who was saying, 'Let's discuss the final part of our strategy. Provided all runs to plan, we'll have control of Javon and its resources, which will mean we'll be able to provision General Korion's armies in the field well beyond the end of the Moontide. Duke Echor of Argundy will be severely weakened, leaving him no choice but to retreat. Our new gnosis-beasts will ensure battlefield supremacy. So all that remains is to deal with the Bridge itself.'

Everyone sat up a little at his words. Though the Pallas Imperial Magi hated the Leviathan Bridge, the wider gnostic community were divided on the subject. Through the Bridge, the Merchant Guild had become fabulously wealthy, buying land, status and magi spouses, much to the annoyance of the Crown. Imperial control of the Bridge had not changed this: the boom-bust nature of the Moontide economy – two years of harvest and ten years of waiting – was worse than ever.

'We all know that the Second Crusade was a financial failure,' Vult went on. 'I understand this group debated whether to destroy the Bridge after that crusade?'

'The Bridge is a necessary evil,' Betillon growled. Hebusalim was the greatest city in western Antiopia, and his governorship had been *immensely* enriching. 'Destroying it would be cutting our own throats.'

Cutting yours, anyway, Gurvon thought.

Vult sailed on serenely, ignoring the choppy undercurrents. 'The objections to the destruction of the Bridge still apply. Though the Crusades grow more costly each Moontide, with less reward, they still paralyse trade, which hurts the merchants far more than the Crown. The Crusades allow us to dominate and weaken Antiopia. It isn't in our interests to let dangerous men like Rashid Mubarak grow more powerful.'

'Exactly,' Korion put in. 'We must keep our foot on their throats.'

'Quite,' said Vult, 'and thanks to Magister Naxius and his intimate knowledge of the Bridge, we have a new solution to propose.'

'Which is?' Betillon asked impatiently.

'Are you familiar with the concept that Urte is made up of massive landmasses called tectonic plates, a bit like an egg with a cracked shell?' He looked around, saw nodding heads and continued, 'And you know that the Leviathan Bridge is built upon an undersea ridge that runs from Pontus to the coast of Dhassa, yes? But what you might not realise is that the ridge is the remains of an isthmus that once linked Yuros and Antiopia. Well, the Ordo Costruo have studied the drowned isthmus. They believe that it was swept beneath the sea no more than two thousand years ago, when it was struck by a meteor, causing massive earthquakes and floods, something that is reflected in the mythology of both Dhassa and Sydia. The impact caused the isthmus to collapse into the sea and separated the two continents.'

'An Act of Kore,' Grand Prelate Wurther commented devoutly.

'Perhaps,' Vult agreed, 'but it is also an inconvenience. Rondelmar has the power to subjugate all of Antiopia, but the Bridge is open for only two years in twelve, and we don't have enough windships to supply an occupying army that is large enough to subdue the Noorish races, who outnumber us vastly. We can hold Hebusalim, and that is all. So you can see that it would be far better if the isthmus were to rise once more from the sea, enabling permanent access and occupation. My Lord Emperor would then be able to seize Antiopia and rule the known world.'

'You want to haul the isthmus up from the ocean depths?' Korion scoffed. 'You're mad! An Earth mage can lift a boulder: he can't lift mountains from beneath the ocean! You could assemble every mage on Urte and not have enough power to do such a thing—'

'On the contrary,' Naxius interrupted, his creaking voice oozing smugness, 'we do have such power. The Bridge itself has that power.'

'The Bridge? It's just a lump of stone—'

'Actually, General, the Leviathan Bridge is a repository for the greatest reservoir of gnostic power ever created,' Naxius replied. 'The five towers are each topped with massive clusters of the same crystal that you saw Delta use a few moments ago. They convert the energy of light, which we call *solarus*, to gnostic energy. That energy is required to keep the Bridge intact whilst it is under the ocean – if released, it could raze a city.'

Korion no longer looked dismissive. 'Is this true?'

'Everything we know supports it,' Vult replied.

'Then why aren't we building weapons using solarus crystals?' the general demanded.

Gurvon glanced at Dubrayle and Betillon, who were probably wondering how solarus could be used to make money. Wurther was likely speculating whether he could cook with it.

'It's a matter of logistics,' Vult replied. 'The crystals are only effective for short bursts unless clustered in masses too large to transport – on top of that, the materials are complex and rare, and using them is dangerous and debilitating – long-term use can be fatal without protection.'

'Magister Vult is correct,' Naxius agreed, 'but the solarus energy can be unlocked. The nexus where the power is gathered, stored and distributed is Midpoint Tower, halfway along the Bridge. It's controlled from thrones in each of the five Bridge towers. These are manned by senior pure-bloods of the Ordo Costruo, ensuring the flow of energy, converting solarus to Earth-gnosis, is maintained. Without it, the Bridge would be destroyed whilst it is submerged. It requires training and great power to control and maintain the flows – I myself have performed this duty,' he added, preening.

The counsellors were staring at the ancient magus with unease, until Lucia asked, 'So what exactly are you proposing, Magister Naxius?' as if she didn't already know.

Naxius showed some political instinct and handed the floor to his sponsor. 'That is for Magister Vult to relate, for it is his idea. I merely supplied my expertise, my knowledge of the Bridge and the land beneath.'

Smart enough to share the glory, Gurvon noted. *And, of course, the risk.*

Vult resumed eagerly, 'Those on the Tower thrones have the ability to rip the energy free of the Bridge and convert it to any form of the gnosis, though it can only be used within a narrow range. It could not, for example, be used to rain fire down on Hebusalim, three hundred miles away. But what we intend lies within its ambit: beneath Midpoint, wedged between the tectonic plates, is a rock the size of a hill: the heavenly body that destroyed the isthmus. If it were destroyed, the isthmus would rise again.'

Calan Dubrayle leaned forward. 'Say that again, Magister?'

'If the heavenly body were to be destroyed, the isthmus would rise again from the seas, permanently.'

'A new, permanent link between Yuros and Antiopia? A road from Pontus to Dhassa, always above water?'

'Allowing one empire to rule every known realm on Urte,' Lucia added in a soft voice. 'My son's empire – *our* homeland.'

Gurvon raised a hand. 'If we do this, there will be an earthquake like nothing ever seen before. It will destroy every building in Pontus and Dhassa, and likely cause damage all the way to the Brekaellen Vale in Yuros, and to the ranges dividing Dhassa and Kesh in the East. Tidal waves will swamp Dhassa and Pontus. It is unlikely that anyone in either place will survive. Millions will die, many of them people of Yuros.'

Even Kaltus Korion looked vaguely appalled at his words. *Good,* Gurvon thought. *You need to know and understand the full extent of what you are considering. These are the decisions that Gods make.*

And remember to pay my fee afterwards.

'Let's do it now,' grunted Betillon, who had never been accused of having a conscience.

Naxius shook his head. 'That is impossible: while the Bridge is beneath the waves, the solarus crystals are locked into sustaining it and are steadily drained of energy. They are virtually inert by the time the Moontide comes. Only when the Bridge is above water can the solarus energy reserves be rebuilt. We need that power to be at its zenith to be certain the meteor jammed into the tectonic fault-line is destroyed. That moment will come at the *end* of the next Moontide, Junesse 930, three years hence.'

Korion raised a hand. 'What of my army? Where will my forces be when the hammer falls?'

'My advice would be not return to Yuros at the end of the Moontide: if you remain east in Zhassi or Kesh, say – no further west than Ebensar Ridge – you will be on another tectonic plate and safe, barring some minor tremors. Provided your supply lines to Javon remain intact, you will be perfectly placed to weather the cataclysm and seize control of northern Antiopia afterwards.'

'Fair enough.' Korion frowned, then asked, 'What of Echor's army?'

'They will have been mauled by the Keshi, thanks to the other arrangements we have in place,' Gurvon answered. 'He'll probably be retreating across the bridge itself when we strike, or already in Pontus licking his wounds.'

'Until the sea washes them away.' Betillon guffawed.

'Then afterwards,' Vult added, 'there would be nothing to prevent Rondelmar from invading all of Antiopia, and this time staying permanently – in fact, my Lord Emperor could send his armies all over the known world. The only limits would be our manpower.'

'And after such destruction, and with the promise of untold plunder to come, I have no doubt our vassal states will be cowed into permanent submission,' Lucia concluded, a quiet smile on her face. 'At a stroke the Ordo Costruo will cease to matter, and the Merchants' ability to leverage the Bridge to their own benefit would be gone. All tribute and plunder will go through our Imperial Governors and the heathen will be utterly subjugated and brought to their knees before the throne of Kore. Rondelmar will rule all of Urte in a new and never-ending Golden Age.'

We don't make small plans, Gurvon reflected. *We're here to change the world.*

The Messiah's Murderess

The Murder of Corineus

Alas! One thousand times, Alas! How did we not see the snake which had nested amongst us, the evil viper in female form who had slithered into our midst and awaited the perfect moment to commit her crime. Imagine the Paradise on Urte that would have been, had Corineus but lived!

THE BOOK OF KORE

After five hundred years, we're no closer to understanding why, in the midst of the Ascendancy of the Blessed Three Hundred, Lillea Selene Sorades, known to the world as Corinea, murdered Johan Corin. She vanished before most were even aware of the crime, and she was never seen again. What happened that chaotic night to prompt her attack? We may never know.

ANTONIN MEIROS, ORDO COSTRUO, 880
(500TH ANNIVERSARY OF THE ASCENDANCY)

Teshwallabad, Northern Lakh, on the continent of Antiopia
Rami (Septinon) 929
15th month of the Moontide

Alaron Mercer sat on a muddy temple step, contemplating the waters of the Imuna River lapping his feet. A few feet away, the Zain monk Yash was playing with seven-month-old Dasra Meiros. Both little boy and young man were soaked, and gleefully happy.

'I'll look after him if you need a break?' he called to Yash. The young monk had spoken for them when he, Ramita and Dasra had arrived at the monastery seeking shelter.

Yash looked vaguely offended. 'Al'Rhon, this is the best time I've had since I got here.'

He'd never been the most spiritual of monks.

Alaron was glad to have someone else to keep an eye on the child. He couldn't look at Dasra without seeing his twin brother, Nasatya, stolen away by Huriya Makani and Malevorn Andevarion two days ago. Scrying had given no clues as to where they had gone, and his thoughts were full of self-recriminations.

I had Nasatya in my hands and I lost him.

I held the Scytale of Corineus in my hands, and I lost it.

I faced Malevorn, and I lost. Again.

He lowered his face into his hands, borne down by the weight of his failings.

After fleeing the mughal's palace in the wake of the carnage wrought by Ramita's former blood-sister and her Souldrinker followers, they had taken refuge in this Zain monastery, where his friend Yash dwelt. Outside in the city, Mughal Tariq hunted them. It felt as if they were outstaying their welcome.

Why Malevorn was helping Huriya was unfathomable: he was an Imperial Inquisitor and sworn to the destruction of all Souldrinkers. It made no sense. Despite that, they'd trapped Alaron and Ramita and with the babies held hostage, forced an exchange: one of Ramita's twins for the Scytale.

I let Ramita down . . . she must despise me!

What made his failure worse was how hopelessly in love with her he was. The realisation had struck at the worst possible time – in the midst of their battle with the Dokken – but it was now fact, as key to his being as water and air. It had been growing inside him during the months they'd spent together, training in the arts of the gnosis and sharing dangers and discoveries alike, and had crystallised as they faced death together. She was the drumming of his heartbeat. But he was pretty sure she didn't feel the same way; after all, she'd made him her adopted brother in a Lakh ceremony called rakhi, probably to ensure he didn't get any silly ideas. After all, she might have been born a lowly Aruna Nagar market-girl – but she was the widow of Antonin Meiros, one of the Blessed Three Hundred and greatest magician of the Age.

Who am I to dream so high?

Yash, his friend since they'd met at Mandira Khojana monastery and travelled together to Teshwallabad, had persuaded the Masters to take them in, but to stay much longer was to endanger their hosts. Having brought so much death and destruction, they owed it to the monks to leave soon.

He'd barely seen Ramita since they'd arrived; she had spent most of the last two days praying to her Omali gods in the temple. The Zains held all gods to be equal, but they had Lakh roots, so Omali shrines were maintained within their walls. So when her voice floated out of the temple door, quavering and uncertain, he was on his feet in an instant.

'Al'Rhon?' she called. 'Have you a minute?'

Something in her voice shouted danger. He swept up his kon-staff and kindled gnostic shields. 'Keep Das with you,' he told Yash. 'It may be nothing, but . . .'

But it might be Huriya and Malevorn, come back to finish the job.

'Vishnarayan-ji, Protector of Man, hear me! Aid me! Darikha-ji, hear me! Help me, Queen of Heaven! Hear me, Kaleesa-ji, Demon-Slayer! Come to my aid! Makheera-ji, Goddess of Destiny, alter your weaving to save my son!'

For the best part of two days, ever since the awful battle in the Mughal Dome, Ramita had been on her knees, beseeching the gods to undo the wrongs that had been done, begging for justice and mercy with her mind, calling with the gnosis, because surely the gods could hear a mage? Surely they would hear *her*. Surely they would lead her to her lost son!

But for two days the gods had remained silent.

They only help those who help themselves, her father had always said. Humbled, she gave up. Her knees unlocked painfully as she rose and turned towards the doors. Then she halted, petrified.

The statue of Makheera-ji, Queen of Fate, was stepping down from her pedestal, and Ramita's heart almost stopped. The life-sized icon was blue-skinned, with thick coils of hair like a nest of snakes. She held symbols of power and knowledge in her six arms, and her golden eyes transfixed Ramita where she stood.

'Makheera-ji?' Ramita gasped.

The goddess laughed, and changed form again . . .

Alaron paused at the small door and peered in. The temple was full of shadows and soft orange light flickering from the oil lamps and dancing over the faces of the Omali gods, some fierce, some wise, with their multiple arms and blue-painted stone skin. For a nightmare moment it was as if they were all alive, surrounding Ramita, who stood in widow's white in the middle.

'What is it?' he asked softly, his eyes piercing the gloomy interior.

'We have a visitor,' Ramita said in an odd voice. She usually sounded so certain about the world; what she didn't understand she placed in the hands of her gods. But right now her dark, serious face looked entirely mystified.

Alaron looked beyond her at a dark-robed figure standing at the edge of the light. She was slender and a little stooped, a Rondian woman with silvery hair, her skin fair, though darkened by the sun, her face a network of fine creases and faint wrinkles.

He raised his staff into a defensive position; though there was nothing in the least threatening about her posture or demeanour. But white-skinned women didn't come here, and she had a gnostic aura: she was a mage.

'Who are you?' he demanded.

'She is one of your Rondian gods,' Ramita said in a voice pitched between awe and disbelief. 'First she was a statue of Makheera-ji, then she changed.'

Alaron blinked. 'Rondians have only one god: Kore. He's a man.'

Disdain flickered across the woman's face. 'I didn't claim to be a god.'

'She wants to talk to us,' Ramita told him. 'She says her name is Corinea.'

14

Corinea! Dear Kore! Alaron's heart thudded painfully and he took an involuntary step backwards. 'Get behind me,' he told Ramita, his voice coming out thin and shaky. 'Ramita, she's—'

She's what – Hel's Whore? The Murderess of our Saviour?

He had been raised as a sceptic and didn't believe in any gods. His father maintained that Corineus had been just a man, and so too his sister Corinea . . .

How can this be her?

But Ascendant Magi can live a very long time, he reminded himself. *If it's really her, she's not a goddess, she's a mage: an old, very powerful mage.* He put himself between the woman and Ramita, trembling like a newborn colt and almost blinded by cold sweat. 'What do you want?'

'To talk. I don't mean you any harm.'

'Why would you want to talk with us?'

'Because I heard this young woman speaking of things that concern me. She prayed for you too, Alaron Mercer, and I have never before heard a Rondian name in the prayers of a Lakh woman.'

His eyes flickered to Ramita, who nodded, her face flushing a little, and for a moment his thoughts detoured as he wondered what she'd been praying about. *Concentrate, idiot!*

'Can you prove that you are who you say?'

Corineus' murderer. His lover and his sister.

'I don't suppose I can, very easily. Unless you'd like to link minds with me?'

He shivered at the casual offer. Unshielded mental links were dangerous, and the more powerful of the two magi involved controlled them.

'I will do it,' Ramita said firmly.

Alaron swallowed. 'No!'

'My husband told me I would be stronger than your Ascendant-magi,' the little Lakh girl reminded him.

'No one is stronger than an Ascendant,' Corinea said loftily.

'If she really is Corinea, then she's had almost six hundred years of using the gnosis!' Alaron protested. 'I'll do it. I'm expendable.'

'You aren't expendable!' Ramita said, suddenly alarmed. 'You are my brother. I refuse to let you.'

She really does have this whole brother–sister thing around the wrong way, Alaron thought. Even so, something inside him glowed.

'You are the widow of Antonin Meiros,' Corinea mused. 'He was the best of them; time has certainly proved that. But even he wouldn't see me.' She looked at Alaron. 'Even the Ordo Costruo, sworn to peace, tried to hunt me down.'

I'm sure they had good reason. Alaron glanced sideways at Ramita, then lowered his staff slowly; he was a quarter-blood, and it would do him no good against an Ascendant if Corinea chose to attack.

But we need to know . . . He made up his mind and stepped forward. 'Do it.'

Before Ramita could protest again, the Rondian woman had grasped his hand and images started crashing over him like a tidal wave: young people singing, holding torches aloft at twilight. A golden-haired man with a merry smile. That same man, standing on a platform, addressing an enraptured crowd chanting, 'Corin! Corin! Corin!' while hands were reaching out to him, and other young people were also clamouring for his attention. Then he saw frightened soldiers being pushed aside, flower garlands tangling in hair, a blur of tumultuous visions of love and dreams and death . . . A bloodied knife . . .

And behind the rush of images was the strong thread of identity present in any deep gnostic contact, which revealed that she was indeed exactly who she claimed to be. The shock of discovering that he was holding the hand of the most reviled woman in all of history was too much. He released her fingers and staggered away.

Ramita grabbed him, her eyes blazing. 'Bhaiya? Al'Rhon?'

'It's okay,' he panted, 'she didn't hurt me.' He marshalled his strength and straightened. 'It's her! Sweet Kore . . .' *She really is Corinea!*

Part of him expected her to burst into flame, grow horns or rip his heart from his chest, but instead she spoke perfectly normally, looking composed and patient. 'You asked your gods for guidance, Ramita Ankesharan. You asked aid in finding your son. You asked help in recovering the Scytale of Corineus. You begged for your remaining son to be kept safe, and this young man also. If you wish, think of me as the answer to your prayers.'

Ramita frowned disapprovingly at this blasphemy.

'What do you want of us?' Alaron asked fearfully.

'I want the Scytale.'

Of course: she wants to found a new Ascendancy, to take her vengeance on the magi.

Corinea shook her head as if in reply to his thoughts. He'd never been great at keeping his mind cloaked. 'No, Alaron Mercer, I don't wish to create a new Ascendancy. The first has caused quite enough misery; two factions of magi ripping at each other would destroy the world. No, I would use it to bargain for the opportunity to give my side of the story.'

'Your side?'

Bitterness filled her voice. 'Yes, my side of the story. I do have one, boy – and I promise you, it is not the one told in the *Book of Kore!*' She looked from him to Ramita and back. 'Will you hear it?'

Alaron swallowed and looked at Ramita. They both nodded hesitantly.

An hour later, they sat eating daal at a small table in the suite where the monks had housed them, two adjoining rooms with wooden beads hanging across the door frames. The air hung with incense and the spices in the curried daal, which they ate with rice and flatbreads, washed down with well-water. Corinea ate the Lakh way, rolling the curry and rice into balls then popping them in her mouth between sentences. She clearly spoke Lakh fluently, but used Rondian for Alaron's benefit – Ramita was more proficient in Alaron's tongue than he was in hers. After examining Corinea doubtfully – he'd not seen a white woman before – Yash had taken Dasra to the refectory for dinner. Her name meant nothing to him, and he'd taken Alaron's assurance that all was well at face-value.

'Who is your ancestor among the Blessed?' Corinea asked Alaron. All Rondian magi could trace their ancestry to someone in the Blessed Three Hundred.

17

'Berial.'

'I recall Berial: Brician woman, brown hair.' She studied Alaron. 'You have her nose.'

'My father told me Berial died three hundred years ago. But her grandson got a woman of the human Anborn family pregnant. It's the family scandal, although I never did understand why – surely that's how all the half-blood lines started.'

The name Anborn clearly meant nothing to Corinea. 'I fled Rondelmar immediately after the death of Johan Corin, and came to Ahmedhassa the year the Ordo Costruo discovered the continent. I've lived hidden here ever since. I have very little up-to-date knowledge of Yuros.'

'Where did you live?' Ramita asked curiously.

'Many places; I've travelled from the north of Mirobez to the south of Lakh.'

'My family is from Baranasi,' Ramita declared.

'I knew you were an Aruna Nagar girl!' Corinea smiled faintly. 'I can hear it in your voice, and see it in the way you wrap your sari. I know Baranasi well. It's my favourite place in Lakh.'

Alaron wasn't pleased to see Ramita beam at the compliment. *The Big Question* was hanging in the air, and he could no longer leave it unasked.

'Lady,' he said gruffly, 'I must ask: why did you *murder* Corineus?' The word wiped the smile from the lips of both women.

Corinea's face became reflective. 'I will tell you,' she said softly. 'You know what Sertain said about me, but you've never before heard the *truth*. So listen, and withhold your judgement until afterwards.'

Alaron nodded cautiously, wishing these monks distilled some kind of liquor, because he could see he was going to need a strong slug of something any minute now.

'I was born Lillea Selene Sorades,' Corinea began. 'I come from a small town in Estellayne, but my mother was Argundian.'

'So you weren't Johan Corin's sister?' Alaron interrupted. The *Book of Kore* said she was.

'Not I! If he had been my brother, he couldn't have been my lover, could he? We're not Sydians! No, no, my Argundian mother married my Estellan father during a period of peace, then they had to flee when war came again and we settled in West Bricia. That's where I first heard Johan speak. I was sixteen and betrothed to a Brician farmer who was fifteen years older than me and poor as the dirt he tilled. Johan and his band of forty followers, as it was then, came to our little village a month before my nuptials.' Her voice softened and her eyes half-closed. 'It was summertime, hot and humid, and the air was filled with bees and buzzing insects, the fragrance of flowers and ripe fruit and crushed berries, and passion.

'Johan's friends were mostly young men who'd run away from their homes because there was no future except soldiering or farming if they stayed. They were mostly from well-off families with too many heirs, and they were all well-educated – they read poetry aloud and debated ethics and morality and slept with anyone who smiled at them – they had a retinue of young women who were wild and free in a way that I had never even dreamed of. I would creep out to hear Johan speak – he used to stand on the edge of the village well and preach that freedom was our birthright! His friends filled the local pub, drinking the beer and dancing and flirting with the prettiest of the local girls. My fiancé was one of the village men who took cudgels to them, and that made me feel sorry for them, so I ran away and joined them.'

Alaron frowned. The *Book of Kore* spoke of young men filled with holy zeal, preaching in the name of Kore, not a drunken mob of lechers staggering from town to town.

Corinea preened. 'I was young then, and very pretty, with a dewy dark complexion, different to the milkmaid-white girls who'd been following Johan around. I caught his eye and he took to dancing with me, and then he taught me how to dance beneath the blankets.' She sighed softly. 'It was a magical time. I was infatuated with everything he did and said – I loved this word "freedom", to say and do what you liked, without priests or nobles telling you not to. To marry who you chose, and not the person your parents picked. And most of all, to be able to do everything a man was permitted ... oh, we were all besotted with freedom, and we wanted all the world to be like us. We wanted to remake the empire with love.' She laughed softly. 'Oh, stupid, foolish youth.'

'Was my husband there?' Ramita asked.

'Antonin? He joined us in Lantris. He was very intelligent, with the most piercing eyes and a really earnest manner. He was a sweetie.' She fixed Ramita with a knowing smile. 'I remember making love with him on starry nights, when Johan had taken another girl to bed.'

Alaron was shocked at this casual promiscuity among those who would become the moral guardians of the empire. He presumed Ramita's discomfort was more personal, even though it was hundreds of years before she even met Meiros, let alone married him.

'I had most of his inner circle,' Corinea went on, careless of their disapproval, 'because that's what freedom meant to me: doing what I liked with whomever I liked. Half the girls got pregnant, with no idea at all who'd fathered their children. I was marginally more sensible: I took precautions, even though Johan wanted me to bear his child. In those days I went by Selene, my Argundian middle name, because Estellayne was in revolt against the Rimoni. By the time we reached southern Rondelmar, there were more than a thousand of us, including some nobles like Baramitius and Sertain – I didn't like them; I was sure they were there for the wrong reasons. They were ambitious, for a start, and Baramitius kept coming up with increasingly new and unpredictable drugs. But Johan was close to them – he liked to sleep with women, but it was to the men that he really talked.' She paused, regret on her face. 'We should have talked more, he and I.'

'Then what happened?' Alaron asked, caught up in the story despite himself.

'As we travelled north, Johan became more and more outrageous – he'd already started calling himself Corineus, and though we looked nothing alike he called me Corinea and told people I was his sister and lover – just to shock them! But as we became more extreme, some of our own followers started leaving, and there were huge arguments. Meiros and his friends tried to get Johan to tone things down, lest the authorities turn on us, but that just made Johan act up even more. And Baramitius was becoming completely obsessed with his alchemy – he started boasting that he was on the verge of distilling a potion that would grant eternal life – it was an old myth of the Kore.'

Ramita frowned. 'But is not your Corineus the same god as this Kore?'

Corinea laughed in amusement. 'Good Heavens, no! Kore was a Rondian god, had been since time immemorial. Remember, this was the time of the Rimoni Empire, and Rondelmar was just a province. People spoke Rimoni as well as their native tongues, and the only gods who could be worshipped openly were Sol and Luna, the Sun and Moon of the Sollan faith. Kore's worshippers had been driven underground.

'Then Baramitius told Johan that he'd found the key, and by then his drugs had us all enthralled – we might have thought his ravings about eternal life were just symptoms of his insanity, but we were addicted, physically and mentally, to his potions and powders. He spent days measuring us and writing all these notes, as if research-ing every part of us, then he produced this special potion, with each measure tailored to the individual recipient. We were warned that it was potent, and that we would be sent into a dream-state for some hours.'

Alaron struggled to reconcile this account with the words of the *Book of Kore*, which told of a night of solemn purpose and destiny. He might be a sceptic, but questioning something he'd grown up half-believing in was hard.

'We'd heard whispers that a legion was coming to arrest us,' Corinea went on. 'Baramitius wasn't the only one of us to sense that our untrammelled freedom – and for him, the opportunities to experi-ment freely – were ending, but it drove him to take risks. Even so, that potion – the one now called "ambrosia" – well, it exceeded his wildest dreams. We all fell into a dream-state, which he'd told us to expect, and I remember my senses intensifying. I was sure I was dying – my body was wracked with shooting pains; I've never forgotten, even through all these years – but strangely I wasn't afraid. My mind began to open up, and just went on opening. I felt like I was passing through room after room in a bewildering palace filled with glowing people and treasures, lights and scents and beautiful textures, laughter and crying, sweetness and fulfilment. I felt connected to everything and everyone, as if we were climbing toward a transcendent bliss, as if Paradise were seeping into our world and changing it for ever.

'And most of all, I felt close to Johan. We were wearing nothing but white shifts and flowers, passed out on blankets with our food and wine spilled everywhere. Our hands were joined, and our every thought was shared, an intimacy that grew in intensity with every passing second. I felt like we were as one: the most profound communion I have ever experienced. Then the visions began.'

Corinea took a sip of water to calm herself. Her voice, which had started to become impassioned, even feverish, softened again. 'I know now that the ambrosia was taking our bodies to the threshold of death while freeing our souls – normally the soul is confined until death, but the ambrosia allowed those who survived to access powers we now call the gnosis, the Secret Knowledge. Most of us gained simple things, like the ability to manipulate water or fire, but the more intellectual among us gained more complex powers. Johan was a visionary, of course, and in some ways so was I; with our minds entwined, we both dreamed of what was to come, a world in which the gnosis ruled . . .

'Then Johan tried to kill me.'

Her final sentence was like being doused suddenly in iced water. Alaron clutched Ramita's hand and they both squeezed.

'In the vision Johan and I shared,' Corinea continued, 'I became a Seeress, and the future I saw was without him – because he, like so many in our group, was not destined to fully gain the gnosis. His body partially rejected the ambrosia, so he would only become a Souldrinker . . .'

Alaron swallowed. This was the greatest heresy he'd ever heard: an inconceivable renunciation of all that the post-Corineus Church taught. In the *Book of Kore* – which had of course been revised by Bar-amitius! – Corineus was the Saviour, the one who sacrificed himself to gain the gnosis for his brethren. Corineus a Souldrinker?

Surely not!

'Our minds were linked,' Corinea repeated in a hushed voice, as if she could hardly bring herself to say the words out loud, 'and of course he saw what I'd foreseen, a future in which I was empress, blessed with a gnosis that he could only gain by killing. He saw himself demonised, alongside all those similarly tainted, and at first all I felt was his panic, and my own horror – because I truly loved him; I worshipped him beyond life itself, and I couldn't bear what we both foresaw.

'Then his mind seized on other potential futures in which he would kill me and trigger his own powers that very night, then show those others who were afflicted as he was to do the same, by killing their neighbour and draining their souls – so they would be the only ones to survive that night: there would be an Ascendancy, yes: an Ascendancy of Souldrinkers, led by Corineus, for no one else with these new powers would last until the dawn.

'With that plan in mind, he took up his hunting knife and tried to kill me . . .'

'What did you do?' Alaron asked in a husky voice.

'I fought back – I might have been in love, but my mother was Estellan and I knew how to use a knife. In the time it takes to tell you this, I had caught his wrist, twisted it and jammed the blade backwards, even as his other hand found my throat. As his weight settled on me, he fell onto the blade and it slid between his ribs and into his heart. By the time I rolled him off me, he was dead, but others were waking and some had seen what had happened – or at least, what they *thought* had happened. Baramitius was the first to have awakened and he started shouting that I had murdered Johan, so I ran.' She looked sad. 'I might have killed others, one or two who tried to stop me, but even now the rest of that night remains a blur. And I've never really stopped running.'

Alaron tried to take it all in: Corineus, the messianic figure of the

23

Church of Kore, doomed to be a Souldrinker emperor, prevented from reigning only by his lover . . . 'Why didn't you tell them?'

'Tell them what?' Corinea asked sharply. 'How could I have proven anything? And why would they listen? Corineus was our leader, and beloved by all, not just me. My crime was unforgivable. Anyway, I wasn't thinking rationally! I wanted – I *needed* – to flee that terrible place. I'd just killed the man I loved and idolised! By fleeing, I proved my guilt.'

Alaron stared at her. *Holy Kore, is anything I've been taught true?* 'What happened next?'

'I escaped,' Corinea said, 'because people were only just coming round and there was a lot of confusion. By the time the legion attacked at dawn and the magi awoke to their new powers and destroyed them, I was long gone. Afterwards, the leadership had other concerns, like conquering Yuros. Baramitius revised the *Book of Kore* as a rallying point against the Rimoni emperor, casting Johan as the Son of Kore and me as a tool of the Lord of Hel, and I have been reviled ever since.'

'If this is true . . .' Alaron began to say, then stopped. This *was* true. Not a word of it struck him as anything less than gospel – not a holy gospel of the Kore, but truth nevertheless. He floundered at the enormity of it all.

'It's true, every word,' she replied, as if reading his mind. 'I once convinced a Kore priest in Verelon, but that got him burned as a heretic and I barely escaped. I tried to tell Antonin Meiros, but he had loved Johan as deeply as the rest of us and wouldn't receive me. At the time he was hunting a Dokken Seeress called Sabele, and I think he believed Sabele was my tool. I had to flee again. That's when I went into Lakh.'

Ramita looked at Alaron, her expression way beyond confused. 'Why do you think we can help you?' she asked.

'I don't know that you can,' Corinea replied, 'but you're my last chance. You see, I'm dying: my body is deteriorating in ways too complex for me to heal. Time is finally defeating me. I don't wish to have my candle blown out without one final effort to tell my tale. I was travelling north after hearing of Antonin Meiros' death, to see if those who succeeded him might heed me – then I heard Ramita's prayers, her mind speaking aloud of all you've been through, and I learned that she was married to Antonin Meiros, that she has borne his children and lost one, that you've both held the Scytale of Corineus, the one treasure so valuable that I could use it to bargain with. I have seen the way you treat each other, that you are good-hearted people, and so I'm hoping you will help me.'

Ramita leaned forward. 'And if we do, what will you do for us?'

Kore's Blood, she's bargaining with Corinea!

The ancient woman cackled grimly. 'You are indeed a daughter of Aruna Nagar market, Ramita Ankesharan. A price for anything, and anything for a price.' She smiled ruefully. 'Such is this world, is it not? Well, perhaps it would interest you that I know the master ingredient to the ambrosia? Yes, I know of the notes you still carry, and that you are missing that key fact.'

With huge effort Alaron put that thought aside and asked, 'How could we tell anyone your story? We're outlaws, wanted by both sides of the war.'

'I know this,' Corinea replied tersely. 'I've been listening to your minds for the past day and a half, ever since I detected you here. You are a failed mage with dangerous ideals, Alaron Mercer. You, Ramita Ankesharan, are the widow of poor Antonin and part of the Ordo Costruo. More than that: if you both regain the Scytale and create a new order of magi, you will have the authority to speak to the world. All I ask is that when you do, you champion my tale.'

They looked at each other, then Ramita said, very formally, 'Lady Corinea, Al'Rhon and I must speak alone.'

'Of course. I will wait outside.'

'No, no, we will go,' Ramita said quickly, surprising Alaron, until he remembered that Dasra was outside with Yash.

Ramita almost ran to the river. She took her son from Yash and hugged him hard, ignoring his soaked clothing dampening her sari.

Alarmed at her visible distress, the young Zain asked 'What is wrong? Shall I summon help?'

DAVID HAIR

'No!' Alaron said quickly. 'No, could you just ... er, give us a moment?'

Yash looked perplexed, but he bowed in acceptance and backed out of earshot. Ramita looked up at Alaron, her face now full of protective resolve. 'This is the woman who killed your god, if we believe the story she has told us.' She didn't mention Corinea's claim to have slept with her husband and Alaron decided it was probably politic to forget that bit of her tale. 'Does she really want to help us? Or does she just want the Scytale for herself?'

How would I know? He'd never been good at dealing with duplicity. 'I *think* she's being honest,' he said after a moment. 'Everything she said sounds real and true to me, but I really wouldn't know. If she is Corinea, she's been very successfully hiding from the most powerful magi in the world for five centuries. Everyone thinks she's dead. If she wanted the Scytale I don't think she'd need our help, or our permission.'

'But why would she need our help to tell her side of the story?'

'Well, it could be as simple as she says: she needs someone to open the doors for her. But Hanook told us the Ordo Costruo were destroyed at the start of the Crusade. I don't think she knows that.'

'If we refuse her, what happens?'

'That would depend on her,' Alaron replied. 'But if we do agree to help her, she says she knows the key ingredient for the ambrosia ...'

'What are you thinking, bhaiya?'

'Well ... remember when we were trying to figure out how the Scytale worked? We used some of the monks as research subjects, to try out our ideas about the recipe variations? I've still got all those notes; all I'm missing is that key ingredient. If she tells us what it is, if we can make up the recipe, perhaps we could return to Khojana Mandira and see if the monks are willing to become Ascendant magi and help us fight Malevorn and Huriya.'

Ramita's eyes went round as saucers. 'But they are *Zains*! They are sworn to peace!'

Alaron dropped his voice. 'Shhh. I know. But Yash would do it, for one – we know he wanted to be a mage before he wanted to be a monk.'

26

'But Huriya and Malevorn have the Scytale – they could make *hundreds* of magi.'

'That's true, but don't forget they'd run the risk of losing control of the Scytale if they did that. I suspect they'll have the same problem we had: they won't know how to use it, and there's no one they can trust to help them decode it. I reckon we've still got time to hunt them down before they use it, but we're going to need help.'

Ramita stroked Das' head, then said decisively, 'Let us do so then.'

Sweet Heaven above, we're about to make a deal with Hel's Whore herself . . .

Ramita seized his hand. 'Alaron, I've not had the chance . . . *Thank you*. You gave up the Scytale for my son, and I'll never forget that, bhaiya, not for as long as I live. You are a true brother to me.'

He dropped his gaze. 'No. I failed you.'

'No, bhaiya,' she told him earnestly, 'that you most certainly did not!'

2

The Emperor's Great Prize

The Ambrosia

The greatest secret of the Empire is the formula for the ambrosia, the potion used to raise the Blessed Three Hundred to the gnosis. It is encrypted into the Scytale of Corineus, which was devised by Baramitius. It is said that the ambrosia will either kill you, or raise you to the ultimate gnostic power, but a third fate exists. Some become Souldrinkers, which is another form of death.

ORDO COSTRUO COLLEGIATE, PONTUS, 772

Northern Lakh, on the continent of Antiopia
Rami (Septinon) 929
15th month of the Moontide

The slope below Malevorn Andevarion fell toward a barren plain somewhere north of Teshwallabad, where small herds of cattle wandered seeking water or shade, neither of which were evident to his eye. With Huriya's Dokken, he'd fled the city after the battle for the Scytale of Corineus – *the battle I won*, he crowed silently as he moved his left hand to stroke the travel-worn leather satchel containing the artefact, reassuring himself it was still there. His right hand remained firmly on his sword-hilt as he ran his eye over his travelling companions.

A dozen or more shapeshifters had entered the Mughal Dome, but only he and Huriya had emerged alive to join the six or seven who had been standing guard outside, led by the Lokistani archer-woman Hessaz, now the only other female left. Her hair was barely a stubble, and she was bony with dark, leathery skin. Lokistan was a mountainous land that bred hard, insular people like her. She was freshly widowed, and Malevorn pitied whatever man was stupid enough to go near her next. These few were all who remained of a hundred-strong Dokken shapeshifter pack, and they looked shattered, both physically and mentally.

Huriya Makani was sitting in their midst: a tiny Keshi girl with the Ascendant-strength gnosis she'd gained by drinking the soul of the Dokken seeress Sabele. She might look like a sexy little bint – even if she was a mudskin – but as he had discovered to his cost, looks could be deceptive. She was the only one of the pack he feared. She was holding an infant, one of the twins of Antonin Meiros and his Lakh peasant wife. Mercer had the other, traded for the Scytale.

The weak-minded fool! I'd have fought to the death to keep the Scytale.

It was nightfall, but the temperature remained hot and oppressive, making his costume – he was armed and armoured in the style of a Keshi mercenary – even more uncomfortable. The sun had darkened his visage, and with his new beard and ragged hair he looked the part. But beneath his armour, his skin was pearly-white, unlike the Dokken, who were all darker-skinned, of Vereloni, Sydian or Ahmedhassan descent. *Inferior blood – as the fighting at the mughal's palace proved. They might have strong gnosis, but they've got no idea what to do with it. Even Alaron Mercer was too much for them.*

But I've got the Scytale now, Mercer, and what have you got?

It was a pity he'd left Mercer still alive, but he doubted that situation would have lasted: even as he and Huriya were escaping, the mughal's soldiers had been pouring into the Dome, and with gnosis-use suppressed in there, surely Mercer had been captured. *I'll bet he's screaming on a rack even now*, he thought, grinning at the image.

He looked calmly about the ring of dirty, dark faces. Hessaz was fingering her bow, and it didn't need a visionary to see she was longing to use it on him – she hated him, as they all did, although he wasn't to blame for their predicament; after all, it was Huriya who'd drawn them from their pathetic lives in the wild into the chaos of the hunt for the Scytale. Admittedly, most of the pack had died at the hands of an Inquisition Fist, and Malevorn himself had been responsible for a good number of those deaths. They'd punished him by forcibly turning him into one of them; they still saw him as an enemy.

I wonder how many of these fools I'll have to kill before the end?

'Malevorn?' He looked round as Huriya gave the infant to Hessaz and walked over to him. She put out a hand for the leather case, tense, as if she thought he'd refuse.

'Of course, "Heart of my Heart",' he said mockingly.

Scowling at his reference to the heart-bind spell that linked their lives – if he died, she did too, and vice versa – Huriya pulled the tooled leather case from the satchel, took off the cap and drew out the legendary artefact. It was a cylinder of metal and ivory, inscribed with runes and studded with domes. The top end had four leather straps attached, with eight domes on each, clearly made to attach to the cylinder in certain configurations.

She turned the Scytale over and over in her hands, her eyes narrowed, her lips moving, and he watched with interest. He wondered belatedly what Sabele – whose memories Huriya now owned – knew of the Scytale, but it couldn't be much, not judging from the way she was frowning. Reluctantly, she passed it back to him and he peered at the runes himself. He recognised a few, but not many. The tutors at the Arcanum had never talked much of the Scytale, but they'd all agreed that it required specialised knowledge to decipher. He twisted the cylinder's head thoughtfully, saw the runes change as it swivelled, and began to realise just how little he actually knew.

'What's happening?' one of the Dokken males asked. 'When will you cure us?'

There it was: the promise that had led them into danger and destruction. Sabele had told the tribe that the Scytale of Corineus could 'cure' a Souldrinker, turn them into a normal mage, one who did not have to ingest souls to renew their powers. That was the dream that had led hundreds of them across half the continent and into battle against magi and Inquisitors.

'How does it work, Inquisitor?' Huriya asked, interrupting his reverie.

'I don't know,' Malevorn confessed.

'What? You told me—'

'I told you that it required special learning. I don't have that learning.'

One of the males, a bulky Sydian named Tkwir who favoured a boar's head when in battle, sprang to his feet. 'You lying glob of pus! I'll—!'

Tkwir stopped and stared at the curved scimitar that had flashed into Malevorn's hand, the point of which was now resting against his belly. The others erupted with fury, but the threat of the blade kept them in check.

Hessaz still held the infant, and didn't appear at all moved by the men's aggression.

Malevorn kindled blue fire in his left hand. 'I don't know how to use the Scytale,' he said. 'There are probably fewer than two dozen people in the world who do. But I know one of them.'

'Who?' Huriya demanded.

'Adamus Crozier, the man who led the hunt.'

. . . *and sacrificed me, Raine, Dominic and Dranid. I'll destroy him for that.*

'He'll still be hunting us. Perhaps it's time he found us: on ground of our own choosing.'

He watched Huriya consider, while Tkwir and the other men backed away.

'How many men will this Adamus Crozier have?' Huriya asked.

'A Fist: ten Inquisitors.' *More than enough to deal with your rabble.*

'Can he be separated from them?'

'Potentially. We have no chance if we can't.'

'Our current weakness isn't permanent,' Huriya said. 'We have other kindred, other packs. Can you find him?'

'Yes, provided I can use a relay-stave to contact him.'

'You know we don't have the skill to make such trinkets.'

'But I do,' he said pointedly. 'I need living wood, two feet long, three inches wide, the straighter the better. Are there any trees at all in this Kore-forsaken land?'

'There are forests on the slopes of the Nimtaya Mountains, northeast of here,' Hessaz replied, 'tall trees that are always green.' Her harsh voice took on a wistful tone he'd not heard before. 'Also in the highlands of my country.'

'We're not going to rukking Lokistan,' one of the men grumbled.

'There is a pack of our Brethren in Gatioch, in the forests south of Ullakesh, near the Valley of Tombs,' said another man, a greasy-haired Vereloni named Toljin. 'My sister is mated to one. I could lead us there.'

'I know the pack,' Huriya replied. 'Or Sabele did. If we go there, how long would it take you to create this relay-stave, Inquisitor?'

'Two weeks? It's exacting work, you know. But it's the only way a non-clairvoyant can reach another mage over long distances.'

'And you really can't decipher this thing yourself?'

'In time, perhaps, but I'd need access to an Arcanum library. Have you got one?'

Huriya scowled at him. For a pretty face, it could pull a lot of ugly looks. 'Then we must go to Gatioch. Tomorrow. Tonight we rest.' She surveyed the men, appearing to come to the same conclusion as Malevorn: that she'd been left with the dregs of the pack.

'What of this child?' Hessaz asked, holding up Nasatya.

Malevorn tried to work out what that *something* was in her voice, then remembered Hessaz had lost a child as well as a husband.

'We keep him,' Huriya said. 'Knowing we have him will keep Ramita in her place. And he will have strong gnosis when he grows into it: that will be a valuable bloodline for us.' She patted the infant's head uncomfortably. 'You tend him. I want nothing to do with the whining thing.' She lost interest and sashayed away.

Huriya really isn't the mothering kind, Malevorn noted. But Hessaz didn't look displeased as she clutched the infant to her and hurried after Huriya.

Malevorn was left eyeing up the six men, gripping the hilt of his scimitar. 'Well?' he challenged. 'Try me, if you think you're up to it.'

'Go rukk yourself, Inquisitor,' Tkwir muttered as they backed away.

I might as well; there'll be no other fun to be had amongst this lot.

They travelled northeast, skirting the immense mountains from which rose the springs that fed the Imuna. They raided the few villages they found for food, striking the thatched mud-brick huts like a hurricane; their gnosis meant they had no fear of pursuit or retribution. In two weeks they reached the highlands south of Ullakesh, the chief city of Gatioch. It was a rugged, arid landscape, where spaden trees clustered in sheltered places between the stark ridges – like hairy armpits, Toljin joked.

It took another two days for Malevorn to find the perfect tree, one whose trunk was long and straight enough to make a decent relay-stave.

Certain gnostic actions – 'spells', as the layman called them – were enhanced by using a specially created tool, and using Clairvoyance to contact a known person was one such. At the Arcanum, they'd described it as 'astral harmonics'. Naturally, Malevorn had been the most skilled in his class, even better than his pure-blood friends, and far ahead of Alaron Mercer.

Thinking of that fool Mercer reminded him of something troubling: at one point in the fight at the vizier's house in Teshwallabad, Mercer had used Illusion to disable and almost kill three Dokken – but Malevorn *knew* that Mercer had no affinity as an Illusionist. He shouldn't have been capable of using the gnosis like that . . .

Was it really Mercer? Or has he been possessed by something? But possession didn't work that way, which left the uncomfortable thought that Mercer had somehow changed. *He's had the Scytale for months – surely he couldn't have used it?* But no, Mercer hadn't been unusually *strong* during the fight, just *competent* . . . and with unexpected powers.

What did it matter? Mercer was probably dead by now, and hopefully his Lakh peasant was too . . . *Ramita*, Huriya's once-friend. She'd also been able to use her gnosis under the Mughal Dome. Huriya's strength was equivalent to an Ascendant, which made Ramita just as strong. Pregnancy manifestation, where a human who bore magi children developed the gnosis, had never been recorded at more than pure-blood level. Another puzzle.

Perhaps Mercer and his bint did escape – and perhaps they are still hunting us.

It didn't worry him overly and he turned his attention back to his relay-stave. While he worked, the surviving Dokken found their own amusements – hunting and sleeping, mostly. Huriya and Hessaz shunned the males, leaving them moody and violent – and stinking; only he and the two women were inclined to wash in the icy streams running from high up the slopes. Neither approached him, and he had no desire to get close to a mudskin woman, even Huriya, who had a certain dusky beauty to her. The heart-bind spell they shared was said to have emotional effects, but none had yet manifested. Unfortunately, the spell was nigh on impossible to negate.

He buried himself in his task: paring the selected wood into strips, then rebinding them as if creating a recurved bow, only perfectly straight. He sanded it while attuning it with sylvan-gnosis. As a non-Clairvoyant, his call wouldn't have great range, but his knowledge of Adamus would help.

It wasn't until the New Moon rose in Octen, while Toljin and Huriya were away negotiating aid from the local shapechanger pack, that he was finally able to climb to a high point, gripping the stave, and begin his call.

<*Adamus Crozier!*>

You betrayed Dom and Dranid, you bastard.

<*Adamus Crozier!*>

And for selling Raine into death, I'll gut you.

<*Adamus Crozier! I need your help, Master!*>

'You must kill the Inquisitor,' Hessaz told her, over and over, but Huriya refused to listen.

I can't. Not with that damned binding spell that links us. My heart is his heart: if he dies, I die.

She couldn't tell Hessaz that, though. 'He's useful,' she replied, avoiding the Lokistani's burning eyes.

The two women had spent much of the last few weeks together, but it wasn't an easy companionship. Hessaz was a brooding mass of resentments, jilted by the man she desired and disappointed by the mates she'd settled upon instead. But Huriya was discovering there was another side of Hessaz. She'd been raised in unforgiving Lokistan and she was both inured to hardship and committed to family and clan, because you couldn't survive alone. Those values shaped her loyalty to the Souldrinker pack. She was a soldier in the long war against the magi, and she was willing to give her life to the struggle. And she fussed over Ramita's baby as if he were her own.

Hessaz lives for this pack, Huriya reflected, *but I can't see why she gives a damn about these wretches.*

The contrast between the two women couldn't have been stronger: Hessaz was lean and muscular without an ounce of spare flesh; her skin was dark and hard, her face like leather stretched over bone, framed by close-cropped black hair. Huriya was small and lush and curvaceous, her face soft and pouting, her every movement sensuous. Neither liked the other, nor pretended to, but they were dependent on each other now and both knew it.

'Does the Seeress still speak inside you?' Hessaz asked.

Huriya shuddered. The Seeress Sabele did indeed still linger inside her: they were at war for her body and soul, a war neither was winning. Sabele's essence had saved her on occasion, giving her wisdom she didn't have. But her presence frightened Huriya beyond anything else.

'Yes, she's in me still.'

Hessaz gripped her hand. 'Huriya, make peace with her. Let her guide you. We need her, you and I.'

And lose myself for ever? She snatched her hand away. 'No, Hessaz, I will *not* become just another body for her to inhabit. I will not give in! I deserve a life of my own!'

'The moment the Inquisitor solves that artefact, that . . . *Sk'thali* . . . he will betray us, you know this.'

Yes, I do know it.

'Embrace Sabele, please Huriya! She always worked for the Brethren – she devoted all her lives to our cause. Yet now when we need her most, she is lost inside your mind.'

Huriya rose abruptly. 'No! And don't ask again!' she snapped, and stalked away.

35

3

The Return of the Queen

The Rimoni of Javon

After the opening of the Leviathan Bridge, many Rimoni, outcasts in their own lands since the fall of the Rimoni Empire and the rise of the Rondian magi, crossed into Antiopia and settled in Javon. Rival Houses were forced to cooperate if they were to survive: Kestria, Nesti, Gorgio, Aranio and others, whose feuds are enshrined in the annals of the Rimoni, buried their rivalries – but they still simmer, even today.

RENE CARDIEN, ORDO COSTRUO, HEBUSALIM 873

*The Kiskale, near Lybis, Javon, on the continent of Antiopia
Rami (Septinon) 929
15th month of the Moontide*

Cera Nesti, Queen-Regent of Javon, wrapped anonymously in a bekira-shroud, waited nervously on the steps of the inner keep of the Kiskale Fortress, watching the plaza filling up with people and wishing the approaching scene was already done so she could take her little brother home. Not that that was likely, not imminently. Beside her, Elena Anborn whispered to her Keshi lover, Kazim Makani. Cera didn't know Kazim, and her own relationship with Elena was ... *troubled*. They had been as close as sisters until Gurvon Gyle had found a way to tear their bonds apart, and she was desperate to find a way to rebuild that trust. She had missed Elena, in so many ways.

Mekmud, the Emir of Lybis, had retreated here after a maniple of

Endus Rykjard's mercenaries had seized Lybis. The Kiskale – the White Keep – had been built high up in the mountains, above the winter snowline, and even the well-equipped and experienced Rondians were leery of attacking the fort. The approaches were commanded by bastions from which flaming oil and boulders could be dropped, and heavy ballistae guarded the approach. So for now an impasse reigned: Mekmud couldn't get out, and Rykjard's men, encamped below on the plains, couldn't get in.

She laid a hand on Timori's shoulder. *Only nine years old, and he's been through so much* ... He was eagerly watching the plaza fill with a great crowd of the emir's people: Mekmud had promised a great revelation and the air buzzed with speculation.

If this goes badly, there will be a riot.

A trumpet blared and the emir's herald stepped forward. 'The Emir of Lybis, Mekmud bin al'Azhir, wishes to announce the presence of great allies, who have joined him here to take the fight to the enemies of Ja'afar!'

This caused a stir among the crowd. As one everyone pressed forward: the wealthy men at the front, the poorer men in the middle and even some women at the back, all tried to get a better view.

The herald's voice boomed as he announced, 'Emir Mekmud welcomes to his realm a new ally and friend of Lybis ... Lady Elena Anborn!'

The name sent a shiver of interest through the gathered Jhafi, nobles, soldiers and commoners alike, and drew muted cheers from the latter. The noblewomen peered intently through their veils while the men stared more openly, respectful, but wary. They all knew who Elena was: Alhana, the White Shadow, once bodyguard to the Queen-Regent Cera Nesti, more recently a ghost stalking the northern roads killing Rondians. Cera saw approval, but there was fear too, and more than a few evil-eye gestures.

She is magi. No matter how much she gives this kingdom, some will always suspect her.

'The emir also welcomes Lord Kazim Makani of Baranasi,' the herald shouted.

37

Cera studied the Keshi as he lowered his hood. He was a young man, but tall and well-muscled, and he looked every inch the warrior-lord, despite his rough clothing. In fact, he was no aristocrat at all, but a title was needed if the Jhafi nobles were to give him any credence. Elena went to Kazim's right side, prompting a murmur of interest, as that was where a wife would stand.

And now, at last, came the moment she'd prayed and ached and suffered and almost died for. *How will they react?* she wondered.

'And Emir Mekmud is *most honoured* to welcome Timori Nesti, Crown Prince of Javon,' the herald shouted. His eyes bulging with pride, he cried, '*LYBIS WELCOMES OUR FUTURE KING!*'

Cries of shock went through the plaza and people spilled forward, all crying out the boy-king's name. The crows in the towers rose, their beaks clacking at the sudden clamour below, as if they too honoured their sovereign. Cera thought she would burst with emotion as the slender boy walked to the top of steps as he'd been coached, dropped his hood and waved his hand. The soldiers began to hammer their spear-butts against the stonework, a rhythmic thumping that echoed off the peaks.

Welcome to public life, little brother. May it be merciful.

Of course, Timori had been presented to crowds before, but not in these circumstances. He had been a prisoner of the Rondians for more than a year, but he was free now. The Nesti needed all Javonesi, Rimoni and Jhafi both, to rise to his command if they were to be restored and the Rondians driven out.

The emir, his iron face grave, raised a hand for silence and signalled for the herald to go on.

'And finally, Emir Mekmud welcomes Princessa Cera Nesti, Queen-Regent of Ja'afar.'

A hush fell as Cera lowered her veil. For a moment she was almost overwhelmed, feeling all those eyes piercing her like spear-points. But she too had been bred for public life: she *belonged* to these people. Though most had never seen her in person, they *knew* her: they had sung hymns to her and gossiped about her, judged every known deed, from defying the Rondians to capitulating and marrying one – and speculated on others that were only rumour. When they heard she'd been stoned as a safian, some would have believed, others not.

What would they do if they knew the truth? she wondered for a moment, then drove that thought away; right now the heart of the matter was this: she, Cera Nesti, was supposed to be dead.

They mourned me for days on end. They thought me condemned and shamed, stoned and cremated.

There was a long moment of utter silence, the fullest silence Cera had ever felt. She held her breath and clutched Timori's hand for courage.

It's much easier to love a martyr than a living person.

Perhaps, left to human nature alone, it might have gone badly: the crowd might have believed her to be an imposter, put forward by the emir to rally the people for war. The serious-faced girl in the plain shift was surely too imperfect to be their princessa, because everyone knew princessas were special, creatures of beauty, not bookish and plain. But leaving things to chance had never been Elena's style. Cera had spent the morning being made up, her hair washed and combed, and she was dressed as a supplicant, come to appeal for forgiveness. The dark circles beneath her eyes, like her other imperfections, had been concealed. Elena wanted her to look like she'd stepped down from on high.

Cera recognised the faint look of concentration on Elena's face even as her white dress began to glow, the effect so subtle it looked entirely natural, just as if the light shone slightly brighter on her than on mere mortals. On a roof above, a single white songbird fluttered its wings and broke into song.

Then a woman in the front of the crowd burst into a loud, joyous wail of thanks to Ahm and sank to her knees, and slowly, the rest did the same, a wave of homage that swept backwards through the plaza.

Cera almost fell to her knees herself, bowled over by relief, but she kept her legs straight, locked in place, her eyes gazing into space, as Elena had instructed: this was only the first step, and there were so many more to take.

Kazim Makani sipped a peach sharbat and wished the evening would end as yet another kohl-eyed Jhafi lady glided up and enquired, ever so subtly, if it was indeed the case that he, a Keshi lord, was wed to a Rondian mage. He wasn't married, but that was not because of any lack of commitment, which went deeper than anyone here could imagine. He was a Souldrinker, but he no longer had to kill to maintain his power, for their bond of love had become a gnostic bond, replenishing him as if they were one being. It was far easier to gravely assure the noblewoman that he was indeed married to Lady Alhana, and that Ahm had been generous to give him such a wife, blessed as they *both* were with the gnosis. He had to restrain himself from laughing as the woman scrabbled to get away, all but poking his eye out with a gesture against the evil eye.

It's either laugh or go mad.

The hardest part of the evening was still to come: dinner. Elena had been drilling him on table etiquette among the nobility, and though it sounded simple enough there was much to remember. Eat with the right hand – slowly! – and don't finish everything on your plate. Sip your drink; don't eat when someone talks to you; take your time and lots more besides.

'You can always eat in your room afterwards,' she'd said. 'It's not really a meal; think of it as more like a conversation with nibbles.'

But it was the nuances that were confusing him; like what to do with his left hand, and how to remember all these accursed titles. He was deeply regretting leaving Elena's side, but right now she was in earnest conversation with a Jhafi lord on the other side of the room. Her shining blonde hair marked her out in this sea of glossy black hair and dark skin. Her face was tanned but recognisably Yurosian, with crow's feet around her eyes that gave away that she was much older than him. He didn't care: she was a mage, and would enjoy a long and vigorous life. With him.

'Lord Makani?'

He turned, and found the one person in the room he'd been avoiding: Cera Nesti, a young woman with thick black hair plaited around her head, deep-set eyes and a grave manner. Elena had exchanged

Cera and Timori for the life of the Rondian spymaster Gurvon Gyle, and he still doubted they'd got the best of that deal. Timori might make a good king one day, but this Cera Nesti seemed untrustworthy – she'd already betrayed Elena once. Was she truly worth losing the ferret-faced Rondian? He was someone who could turn the tides of war with a single knife-thrust – and he was Elena's former lover. Not that he was jealous of the man; far from it; he just knew he'd sleep easier if Gyle was dead.

He turned his attention to Cera, who'd been waiting patiently for him to acknowledge her. He sketched a bow. 'My Queen,' he said politely, though she wasn't his queen at all.

'I've been wanting to meet you,' Cera said, 'ever since the news came to Brochena that Elena and an unknown Keshi had been attacking Dorobon soldiers. I've been wondering who you were.'

Kazim had never been a shy youth, or modest – but that was before he'd become a Hadishah assassin, killed Antonin Meiros, the most famous mage in the world, and discovered he was a Souldrinker. Now he'd rather talk about almost anyone other than himself. 'My parent was Ordo Costruo,' he lied, giving the agreed story. 'There's not much more to tell.'

Cera looked sceptical. 'Were you raised in Dhassa? Your accent is unusual.'

'Er, no . . . in Lakh.'

'Really? Teshwallabad?'

'No, Baranasi.'

'Ah – but your parents were Keshi, yes?'

'Yes.' *This much is true.* 'My father was severely wounded in the First Crusade and taken in by a Lakh trader. He took my parents south to Lakh so he could care for him.'

'That was a great kindness.' Cera studied him frankly, but not in the way that women usually did. He was used to women looking at him speculatively, but her eyes were cool and distant. She'd been condemned as a safian, and though it was clear most Jhafi thought it a lie concocted by the Rondians to justify ridding themselves of a troublesome young woman, Elena believed it to be true. It felt odd to

41

be in the company of such a one. There had sometimes been gossip in his youth about this or that girl liking her female friends far too much, but he'd never met someone he actually knew was . . . *that*. It left him unsure how to react.

'How did you come to return to the north?' Cera asked.

'I heard the call for shihad,' he said after a moment. That too was at least part of the whole story. 'I should join Elena—'

'Wait! Would you please tell Elena that . . . that I won't let her down again. I swear it.' Cera looked up at him, her dark eyes full of pain.

'Can't you tell her yourself?'

'I don't think I can,' she admitted. 'Not in a way she'll believe. I was so stupid to listen to Gyle – but I was scared, and . . . I thought I was protecting Timori.'

Elena hadn't told him the details of what had happened – she had to come to that in her own time. But he thought his lover did want to find a way to forgive. 'I'll tell Alhana what you said,' he promised. *And it is time for her to tell me what happened, so I will know the signs if it happens again.*

She turned away, then stopped. 'Does Elena have a plan to get us out of here?'

He grinned, despite his wariness. 'Most certainly, yes.'

Elena Anborn tied down her pack and buckled on her sword belt, then looked around the room where she and Kazim had spent the past week. She was thankful to be able to cast aside the bekira-shroud and courtly manners and get back to being who she really was: a mage and a warrior.

Beside her, Kazim flexed and stretched, as impatient as she to be moving. For a week they'd been laying plans with Mekmud, Cera and those of Mekmud's advisors he really trusted. Lybis was no place to try and start a war from, not when the Nesti's main strength was in Forensa, on the far side of the kingdom, and Mekmud accepted this, though he clearly wanted Elena and Kazim to stay. The best he'd been able to wrangle from Cera, who'd grown into a shrewd negotiator despite her youth, were unspecified promises of aid. Once they'd gone, Mekmud would fight on regardless, and hope the Rondians withdrew once open war broke out.

'Where is Gyle now?' Kazim asked.

Elena sighed. 'I don't know. He might be in Lybis town, just a few miles away, or he might be back to Brochena by now. But if I were him, I'd be trying to pen us in here, and that's why we need to get out.'

'I can't wait,' he said fervently.

In her gnostic sight, Kazim's nature was clear: she could clearly see the tainted aura of the Souldrinker, the tendrils embedded in her own aura, but they were so entwined now that the further she and Kazim were apart, the more it hurt; even a few hundred yards was hard. They were Mage and Dokken in love, bound together in unprecedented ways, with nothing in history or legend to guide them – they were making it up as they went.

'Then let's go,' she said firmly.

As they left the room together, her eyes lingered over the stone latticed windows where they'd sipped coffee and watched the sunset from a tangle of pillows and blankets. It had been a beautiful interlude.

They descended a spiral stair, emerging on battlements overlooking the valley. The dawn air was cool, for all that it was summer. Elena's eyes were drawn upwards to two small Rondian windskiffs circling high above. Was Gurvon Gyle up there, or Rutt Sordell? Neither, she hoped.

A mental touch nudged her consciousness and she responded, then signalled to the waiting group below to join her. Cera and Timori were among them, dressed in travelling clothes and rubbing bleary eyes.

A sentry shouted as a large windship swam into view from around a bluff. Its sails bore the emblem of the Holy Inquisition of Kore: a scarlet Sacred Heart impaled on the Dagger that slew Corineus. Alarm bells clanged wildly in the gate-tower and men began to pour from the barracks.

Elena pursed her lips as the two windskiffs darted toward the ship, no doubt sending greetings back and forth. The next few moments would tell her whether this was going to go smoothly or not. She gripped the stone wall, watching as the skiffs ran up alongside the Inquisition vessel. Beside her, the emir's men peered anxiously upwards.

There were only half a dozen sailors visible on the warbird, which was some fifty yards long, with swivel-mounted ballistae fore and aft. The rough-clad captain was exchanging words with the nearest skiff-pilot, though they were too far off for Elena to make out what they were saying.

Suddenly shapes rose from concealment on the Inquisition ship and the ballistae, giant crossbows on swivel-mounts, swung round. She saw fire ignite as the crew set alight the bundles of rags that had been tied behind the spearheads – then the bolts went searing across the sky like comets.

The nearest skiff was swatted sideways as the bolt slammed into the mast and sent the little ship spinning over and over. Arms and legs flailed in vain as the pilot fell towards the ground just as his craft burst into flames. But he was the fortunate one. The other mage-pilot was convulsing wildly as he was pinned to the mast by the bolt, engulfed by the flames that roared up his sails. Without his gnosis to move it, his craft lost impetus and just hung, burning, in the air.

On the walls, the soldiers were bewildered: enemies fighting enemies in the skies above was quite beyond their experience. Elena frowned as the falling pilot engaged Air-gnosis and soared away down the valley, arms spread and robes flapping madly. He wasn't as fast as a skiff, and he'd not be able to get far, but she'd hoped to kill both men.

She looked to the warbird, calling mentally, <BRING HER IN! BRING HER IN!>

The emir's officers had succeeded in reassuring the soldiers that the incoming windship was friend, not foe, and when the trumpeter blared a few notes, the call to attention, and the noise in the courtyard barely lessened, Emir Mekmud shouted, 'Be still!' When his men were once again silent and giving him their full attention, he called, 'No matter what you now see, keep your hands from your weapons!'

'What's happening?' Timori asked loudly.

'The windship does indeed belong to the Rondian Inquisition –
but it has been stolen by friends!' Mekmud shouted. He was greeted
by cheers which died away as he added, 'Those onboard are allies of
Lady Alhana – and *they are not human.*'

The onlookers gasped, and as one the eyes of the soldiers flashed
as they stared at Elena. This would be as near to a demon as any
of these men would ever see, and she hoped they would be able to
keep calm. 'The ship is piloted by men,' she called in Jhafi. 'But the
fighters aboard are Naga!'

A palpable sense of superstitious awe was generated by her words:
though the emir's people were Amteh, most would know something
of Omali mythology and the tales of the snakemen who helped the
gods to create the world – though she doubted any here would ever
have believed in them.

And quite rightly, she added wryly to herself. *Well, they're in for a
surprise now!*

The windship sailed right to the walls and came about, silhouetted
by the rising sun against the glorious pink and gold dawn sky. She
heard cries of wonder as a shape swarmed up the masts and furled
the sails, moving with incredible agility – thanks to the massive
snake-tail he had instead of legs. As the creature came into sight
the watching Jhafi could see that his skin was scaly and green, and
a crest like a rooster's adorned his skull. Others appeared on deck,
equally inhuman – and heavily armed.

Though Elena had called them 'Naga' so the Jhafi would know what
to expect, these creatures named themselves 'lamia', from Lantric
legend – although that was no more accurate, for they hadn't been
created by gods, but constructed by magi, illegally using Animagery
to blend men and reptiles in a bid to make better soldiers.

*I still can't believe my wayward nephew is responsible for me having an Inqui-
sition windship full of escaped constructs at my beck and call,* she thought,
and offered up a heartfelt, *Thank you, Alaron!*

'Lady Elena?' the largest male 'Naga' called as ropes were thrown
down and lashed to stanchions along the wall.

'Kekropius – you're right on time!'

The emir's men stared in fear and fascination: few had even seen windships this close, let alone creatures straight out of myth, and they backed away as the lamia Elder flowed down a rope to the battlements. Kekropius had a human upper body broad enough to rival even Kazim's, but the length of his thick, lithe snake trunk made him a giant. Though his face was almost human, his slitted amber eyes, skin tones and musculature made him look utterly alien.

Elena swept into a respectful bow. Kekropius might not pick up the nuances of the greeting, but the men watching would certainly understand her open acknowledgement of friendship and equality.

Hopefully that will be enough to prevent any of Mekmud's men from panicking and doing something stupid. 'Welcome, welcome, and thrice welcome,' she cried aloud in Rondian, seizing Kekropius' right hand with both of hers. 'It is very good to see you, my friend!'

'And you, Elena,' the lamia replied, before embracing Kazim, causing murmurs of wonder among those watching. 'The kin of Alaron our Guide has only to ask and we will come.'

I wonder if I'll ever get to tell my nephew about all this . . .

Elena turned to Mekmud. 'Kekropius, this is Emir Mekmud bin al'Azhir. This is his keep, the Kiskale.'

Kekropius straightened, then bowed – not deep enough by Jhafi standards, but Mekmud had been forewarned that these creatures didn't know their ways, so took no offence – no doubt a creature such as this bowing to him at all would hugely elevate his standing.

'My people thank you for the bequest you have given us,' Kekropius said solemnly, and Elena translated his words. The distant river valley where the lamiae had settled might have been uninhabited, but it was part of the emir's lands. 'In return' – Kekropius signalled to the waiting windship and six more lamiae began writhing athletically down the ropes – 'these six will serve you, Lord Emir, for the period of this war, and if any fall, they will be replaced.'

Elena couldn't quite hide her wince, though she had helped broker the deal; six males was a significant number for the lamiae, for the tribe numbered barely sixty, and that included the females and children.

By now everyone in the keep had found a perch to watch, and as it became apparent that the six lamiae were going to stay, eyes widened with wonder and excitement and they scarcely noticed the baggage being hoisted into the windship.

Elena went down on one knee to Mekmud and let him draw her back to her feet and kiss both her cheeks in farewell. 'They are swift learners,' she reassured him. 'They'll pick up your tongue very quickly. They do have the gnosis – it's part of their very being and they use it instinctively – but they don't have the deep training of a Rondian mage, nor experience in war. Use them sparingly, I beg you.'

'I cannot protect them from all danger, Alhana,' the emir replied, 'but I believe Gyle will leave once he learns that you've gone. I shall then retake my city, and afterwards harass the Rondians as I can.'

She clasped his hands. 'You have our sincere thanks. Once we've made Forensa, I'll be in contact.'

'Sal'Ahm, Alhana. I will instruct the Godsingers to offer up prayers to you.'

She laughed. 'I doubt an Amteh cleric will ever pray for a heathen mage, my lord!'

'They'll do what I tell them,' Mekmud bristled.

No doubt they will, if they know what's best for them. She bowed in thanks again.

Timori led the way up the rope ladders, moving with all the gangly fearlessness of a child. His sister followed more awkwardly, and Elena and Kazim brought up the rear. Kazim signalled they were all safely aboard and lamiae rushed to loose the anchor ropes and hoist the sails as one of their number released energy from the keel and sent the craft into the air again.

As the emir and his men raised their arms in farewell, the windship turned majestically and set sail for the east, and Forensa.

Lybis, Javon, on the continent of Antiopia
Rami (Septinon) 929
15th month of the Moontide

Gurvon Gyle slouched on the Emir of Lybis' ornate but deeply uncomfortable throne at the head of a long council table. He drained his wine goblet, then crushed it in a gnosis-strengthened hand. It was pewter, but dipped in gold, beautifully engraved with hunting scenes and decorated with gems, a rare and valuable piece – but right now he didn't give a *rukking shit* about that. 'You're telling me they've *escaped* the Kiskale?'

The soot-stained, battered and bruised young mage standing before him cringed. He'd flown the ten miles from the Kiskale to Lybis on Air-gnosis after his skiff was shot from the skies, and he was almost out on his feet. 'It was an Inquisition ship . . . we thought they were friends . . .'

'We don't have any bloody friends in the Kore-bedamned Inquisition!' Gyle erupted. 'We're *mercenaries*, you rukking *imbecile*! What on Urte possessed the two of you to pull alongside and blow kisses to them?'

The pilot glanced at his captain, Endus Rykjard, but got no sign of support. He hung his head, as well he might: they'd lost not just his fellow wind-pilot, but two valuable skiffs to that piece of stupidity.

'Sir, I'm sorry – I won't . . . I mean, I'll be more . . .'

'Get out!' Gurvon bellowed. 'Before I throw you out the window!'

The pilot fled to the sound of sniggers from Rutt Sordell, the other man in the room. Rutt had always enjoyed seeing bright young mages being put in their place.

Gurvon was becoming sick of Rutt's bitterness. The Argundian complained incessantly that his senses were failing. That was the price of no longer being a full human: the real Rutt Sordell was a Necromantic scarab burrowed into Guy Lassaigne's head, controlling Lassaigne's body. But Rutt was nothing if not loyal, clinging tenaciously to his 'life' so he could continue to serve Gurvon. At least Lassaigne was a pure-blood, as Rutt had been before losing his body.

Worryingly, in the way of pets coming to resemble their masters, Lassaigne's body now bore a real resemblance to the original Sordell: the once toned, healthy-looking courtier was now florid, anxious and flabby. And he was drinking far too much.

'Gurv, it wasn't Marklyn's fault,' the Hollenian snapped, protective of his man – once he wasn't around to hear.

'Then is it your fault, Endus?' Gurvon shouted. 'If you hadn't been spending all day screwing Jhafi whores, maybe you'd have been able to brief them better? Or maybe you'd have even been there!'

Rykjard's affable face hardened. 'Don't you tell me how to run my lads! Marklyn and Jesset knew their business. But an Inquisition ship, Gurv? Who knew—? Did you?'

'Of course not!' Gurvon snarled. He hurled the crushed goblet into the corner of the room, and was abruptly thirsty again. '*Shit!* I wanted Elena locked up in that damned fort! I wanted her *contained!*'

Rutt raised a cautious hand. 'We've only got eight more skiffs – there's no way we could have stopped a warbird, Gurvon. And those snakemen . . . well, you know what they can do.'

Gyle shuddered. These impossible creatures Elena had somehow magicked up had not just ambushed a full maniple of Rykjard's men, but killed them all – every single soldier: *five hundred men!*

He seldom lost his temper, but he could feel himself fraying at the edges as the stakes rose. With an effort he cooled down. 'I'm sorry, Endus. I misspoke. Marklyn did well to get out alive. Tell him I said so.'

'It's hard to nail Elena down,' Endus said. 'You know that better than anyone.'

Meaning that I was nailing her for twenty years and still couldn't control her. 'I do,' he conceded. 'I presume she'll make for Forensa.'

'We can't stop her,' Rutt put in, 'but perhaps others can? Betillon has a few warbirds in Brochena.'

Gurvon grimaced at the mention of the Governor of Hebusalim. While he'd been Elena's prisoner Mater-Imperia Lucia had lost confidence in him and sent Tomas Betillon to Javon to fix things. Yes, the Crusade depended upon supplies from Javon, so he could *just about* understand Lucia's concerns. But Gurvon had little reason to love Betillon: they'd been on opposite sides of the Noros Revolt twenty years ago and seeking his help tasted bad. But Rutt's idea had some merit.

'We'll give it a try, I suppose. If he can intercept that damned warbird and bring it down, so much the better. We can't afford a three-way conflict.'

'Sure, but what next?' Endus asked. 'The rest of my legion are marching up from Baroz; they'll get here in a few days. Do we still plan on taking that hill fort, what's it called – the Kiss-my-cock?'

'Kiskale,' Rutt replied, prissy as ever. 'We should teach that emir a lesson at the very least,' he added. He'd been in Lybis when the emir had revolted, and he took such things personally.

'Pointless. The emir can keep his Kore-forsaken hole for all I care.' Gurvon got up and went to the map, unrolled on the table and weighted down by a selection of priceless goblets and decanters. He poured more wine and poked the map. 'Betillon is in Brochena with a legion of Kirkegarde, and presumably now controls the Dorobon legions, some fifteen thousand men. We've got twenty-five: Adi's legion at the Krak, your lot in Baroz, Staria with her ten thousand at the Rift Forts and Hans Frikter's legion near Riban. Plus we can bring the Gorgio legions down from Hytel, provided they don't throw in with Betillon.'

Rutt blinked owlishly. 'Haven't I told you? I scryed Hytel last night: the Gorgio family are falling apart: Alfredo's bastards are at war with each other. They're all vying for control.'

Gurvon stared. 'What? But Alfredo Gorgio—'

'—is dead,' Rutt interrupted. 'On the day Portia Tolidi gave birth to Francis Dorobon's son, Alfredo rode to the cliffs and hurled himself into the ocean. They never recovered his body.'

'*Rukka mio*, I was only gone for a month!' Gurvon downed the wine and poured another. 'Is Constant still emperor? Is Mater-Imperia still a bitch? Does Luna still float in the heavens?'

'They say the whole Gorgio court is in terror of Portia Tolidi.' Endus licked his lips. 'She has the gnosis now – through pregnancy manifestation – and no one to teach her how to use it. By the sound of it she's completely out of control. Send me up there, Gurv. I'll straighten her out.' He sniggered like a college boy. 'The hard way.'

'No, Endus. Hytel is irrelevant. They've no magi.' Gurvon studied the map thoughtfully. 'Let Betillon worry about them. Anyone he sends to bring them into line will be away when we strike. I'm more concerned about the Jhafi – there are more than five million natives in Javon. I know most have no military value, but the Rimoni-dominated cities of Riban, Forensa and Loctis worry me, especially if they act in concert. Dealing with Cera and Timori Nesti is *crucial*.'

Endus Rykjard looked at him ironically. 'You let them go, Gurv.'

'I'm lucky I had them as a bargaining chip, or I'd not be here,' he replied, while inwardly acknowledging that Endus was absolutely right. He tapped the map. 'Endus, I'm sorry, you urgently need to turn your men round and send them back to Baroz. We *must* control the trade routes. Can you leave immediately?'

'Of course.' Rykjard stood and finished his wine. 'Keep me posted, Gurv.' He gave a sloppy salute and swaggered out.

A good man, but he spends too much energy on whoring and drinking.

He turned to Rutt. 'I want you to pull everyone we can spare out of Yuros and fly them here, to Javon.' It was a chilling thought that of all the magi-agents he'd brought to Javon, Elena had killed them all except Rutt, who'd be dead too if he wasn't a Necromancer.

'But boss,' Rutt replied, looking worried, 'everyone left in Yuros is in deep. Some of those plays you've had running for years.'

'Rutt, this is a *kingdom* we're talking about. Those swindles I've got running in Rondelmar are nothing compared to this. Right now we need our people, badly.'

'But most of them aren't fighters, boss: they're thieves and courtiers and assassins. And you'll still need ears in Pallas.'

He's right: I'm overreacting. But the nagging feeling that this was going to get worse before it got better persisted. He'd have to compromise.

'All right, let's bring those outside Pallas at least: I want Sylas, Brossian, Veritia, and their apprentices. And Drexel too: he was apprenticed to Elena for a time – perhaps he can get close to her where others can't. That's what, eleven magi? Tell them I'll double their money.' He added, 'You too, Rutt. Double the money, backdated to the start of the Moontide.'

'I don't do this for the money, Gurvon. You know that. But I'll take it, of course,' Rutt added, with a faint smile. 'I'll find some staves and contact them immediately.'

'Bring me one too, will you? I suppose I'd better speak to Betillon.'

Brochena, Javon, on the continent of Antiopia
Rami (Septinon) 929
15th month of the Moontide

Tomas Betillon had been enjoying such an excellent morning that it was only to be expected that the day would go downhill in the afternoon. Nothing good lasted in this Kore-forsaken place. Radiant heat throbbed up from the stones and down from the skies. In the distance the dried-up salt-lake, which was apparently full for only a few months after the annual rains, was eye-blisteringly white.

He'd been presiding over an execution: some crime-lord that Gyle had been pussy-footing around in one of his usual highly suspect games of cat and mouse. Betillon didn't have the patience for any of that; he just had the man brought in and racked. Mustaq al'Madhi was a fat, balding man who looked like a shopkeeper but apparently ran half the crime in the city. He'd had him and his male kin publically hanged and displayed them on the city wall. Examples had to be made.

By way of spreading his favours, he'd given the criminal's women to the rankers to screw, apart from one, a skinny little maid who looked girlish enough to stir his own blood. She was roped up in one of the bed chambers awaiting his pleasure – *his* pleasure, not hers.

The Grandmaster of the Kirkegarde legion who had come with him to Javon, a scar-faced mage-knight named Lann Wilfort, leaned against the nearest pillar, picking his teeth. He'd just been expounding on the need to go north and knock some Gorgio heads together. 'I'll bring back the Tolidi bint for you to break,' Wilfort was saying. 'The Hytel mines are vital.'

'I don't care about this Tolidi woman,' Betillon replied with a wave of the hand. He preferred unbled virgins, the younger the better, and the famed beauty of Portia Tolidi held little attraction, especially not when she'd so recently given birth – what an ugly mental image *that* was. *She'll be fat and stretched and ugly now, not to mention amply used by Francis Dorobon, they say. Why would I want that?* 'Forget Hytel. We can't afford to send anyone, not until Gyle comes to heel.'

'But the mines . . .' Wilfort rubbed his scar, which ran from his right eye to the remaining stump of his ear. 'They provide this wasteland with all its iron.'

'Irrelevant for now: it's food the Crusade needs. We've got to take the Krak in the south or Kaltus' legions are going to starve.'

Wilfort whistled softly. 'The Krak di Condotiori . . . defended by a mercenary legion . . . I'd call that nigh on impregnable.'

'Not from the north. The Krak's main defences face south.' Betillon scratched his crotch and thought about the skinny Jhafi girl tied up in his suite. Was she scared enough yet? She'd be ripening nicely, but he could let her stew a little longer.

Or maybe not . . . The stench of the bodies was becoming unpleasant and he began to rise when a familiar gnostic contact nudged against his awareness. He fed the link, and shuffled into the shade of a wall, away from prying ears. <*Gyle? What in Hel do you want?*>

<*I've got information for you.*> Gurvon Gyle sounded tense, as well he might.

<*Sure you have. Lies and misdirection, I'm sure. But say on . . .* >

<*This is truth: there is an Inquisition windship sailing from Lybis to Forensa. It'll pass the northern reaches of Brochena inside two days. You must intercept it.*>

<*Really? Inquisition? What are those bastards doing here?*>

<*It's not piloted by Inquisition: it's been stolen.*>

<*Stolen? Who by, Gyle? You?*>

<*No. By Elena Anborn.*>

Tomas rocked back on his heels, momentarily discomforted. Gyle had supposedly been Anborn's captive, but perhaps they were colluding – they had been lovers, after all . . . perhaps they still were.

<Really? She stole it? From where? There haven't been Inquisitors operating in Javon throughout this Crusade.>

<Look, she's got one, all right?> Gyle snapped, unusually brittle. <You must intercept!>

<Why should I?>

<Because it's got Cera Nesti and Timori Nesti onboard.>

This sounded ever more far-fetched. <Cera Nesti is dead.>

<She isn't. I faked her death, and exchanged her life for mine. She's alive, and she's more dangerous than Timori or Elena. She could rouse the whole of Javon.>

Gyle faked Cera Nesti's death? Betillon almost laughed. Sweet Kore, the man spins in strange circles! But even if this was true and not some ruse to divert his attention, he was unmoved. <I'm not scared of Noories, Gyle. Even if I believed you, scouring the skies for one windship just isn't practical. Let her rouse the kingdom: I'm planning on making an example of Forensa anyway.>

<You underestimate the danger—>

<No, you over-estimate it. Listen to me, Gyle. You've run out of friends. Lucia might have liked your plan, but she's lost patience with you. Get out of the nursery while you can: the grown-ups are here now, and your toys are about to be crushed.>

<You're not the big boy here, Tomas,> Gyle retorted. <Three legions to my five, and most of yours are Dorobon conscripts. It's you who should be getting out. And if you don't intercept Elena, you'll regret it, I promise you.>

<Fuck off, Gyle.> He broke the connection with a savage burst of energy, vindictively burning out Gyle's relay-stave. I hope I seared your fingers, you arsehole.

He re-ran the conversation in his head, then shrugged. I'm not going to jump at his behest. He doubted there was any windship; more likely it was some trick. Gyle was right about their relative strength, though, and that troubled him. He needed more men. Perhaps I need to woo that damned Tolidi bint in Hytel after all . . .

He waved offhandedly at Wilfort. 'Finish this,' he growled, gesturing to the line of men still waiting to be executed. He surveyed the crowds below: skinny, unwashed Jhafi, staring up at the scaffolding bearing the broken prisoners, their faces sickly and frightened. *Look and learn, mudskins.*

He waved his personal aide forward. Mikals, a portly Hollenian, shared his taste for young flesh. 'Let's go and see about the afternoon's entertainment. Have you had her washed?'

'She's had her Noorie stink rinsed off, my lord. I left Pendris to oil her.' Mikals rubbed his hands together. 'A feisty bint, this one. She should be entertaining.'

They strode together through the palace, past the Kirkegarde sentries at each door, reaching the inner bailey just as a skinny Jhafi boy wearing the Betillon livery skittered out. He glanced after the boy, a little puzzled to see a native in his livery, but Mikals was talking, describing a furnace he'd found, perfect for disposing of the girl's body after they'd done with her.

'Pendris better not have done more than oiled her,' he growled, clapping Mikals on the shoulder. 'I want first flower – she is a virgin, I trust?'

'Not this one, Lord,' Mikals replied. 'Well used, I deem – everyone knows Noorie women can't keep their legs together. But even so, she is young and nubile enough to please you.'

His anticipation soured a little. 'I suppose a virgin was too much to hope for,' he acknowledged. This one had caught his eye during the capture of Mustaq al'Madhi – she'd put up quite a fight, and that would make her conquest all the sweeter. They climbed the stairs to the royal suite, to the room he'd set aside for his pleasure. He paused at the door, grinned at Mikals and pushed open the door.

A river of blood flowed down the middle of the floor. Its wellspring was young Pendris' throat, which had been laid open ear to ear. The young man was lying on his back in the blood, naked and paling as he bled out. Untied ropes were turning scarlet, soaking up the blood. The girl was gone.

Betillon clenched his fists, suppressing the urge to immediately immolate this whole tableau. Mikals blanched and fell against the wall: the unlucky Pendris was his only son. Slowly his hand raised, pointing at something scrawled in blood on the wall.

ALHANI.

Betillon growled. 'What is that word? Is it her name?'

Mikals shook his head. 'No. Her name was Tarita.'

'Then what does "Alhani" mean?'

'It doesn't mean anything . . .' He paused, his face almost as white as his son's. 'Well, except . . . I've heard that the Jhafi called Elena Anborn "Alhana", so maybe "Alhani" would be like a plural of that? Or a collective noun, maybe?'

Betillon stared. *Fuck! Has Elena Anborn been here?*

Then he remembered the skinny boy in his own livery, going the other way unchecked, because of course the guards only questioned those entering. He hammered his fist into the wall.

Alhani . . .

'Bring the rest of the women from al'Madhi's house,' he ordered. 'And the chief torturer. I want to know all there is to know about this *Tarita*.'

4

Broken Bridges

The Leviathan Bridge

Symbols are powerful things. They inspire us all, which is another reason why we must build this bridge: not just to facilitate trade and understanding and improve the lives of millions, though those benefits are clear. This bridge will become a symbol, a link between East and West, tangible proof that two continents which once were joined may be so again, to the benefit of all. This Bridge will be a sign of hope, of better days to come. Bridges link us, allowing us to bypass obstacles and reach places we otherwise could not go. Let this one be the greatest of all.

ANTONIN MEIROS, CONSTRUCTION PROPOSAL IV,

PONTUS, 702

*Near Vida, Southern Kesh, on the continent of Antiopia
Rami (Septinon) 929
15th month of the Moontide*

Getting out of Shaliyah had been a desperate situation, and so too breaking into Ardijah. But this camp could be the worst of all, because getting out might require fighting their own people, and Ramon Sensini wasn't sure the Lost Legions were ready for that.

They'd marched into the East for many reasons, these rankers from Noros and Argundy and the other provinces of the Rondian Empire: some because they truly believed that Kore had commanded them to fight the infidel; some for loyalty to the empire, or to their liege-lord. But for most, the motivations were more prosaic. Unless you were a mage or a merchant, life in Yuros offered little more than a plough or a pick, scratching a living from the earth, with nothing to look forward to but a mug of ale at the end of the day. The Crusades offered a chance to get out of the endless cycle of poverty. And no one cared much about the rights and wrongs; they just wanted to return to their farms and villages alive and with as much coin as they could scrounge.

Ramon's own motives were more complex: he'd been born to a serving girl who'd been raped by a Rondian mage. His mother, barely thirteen when she gave birth, had been taken in by the head of the Retia familioso in Silacia – not that there'd been any kindness in the deed, only Pater-Retiari's desire to secure control of a mage-child. As Ramon grew older and harder to manage, the threat of violence against his mother had kept him in line. Revenge was what motivated Ramon, against both true and adopted fathers, and freedom for his mother: these needs underpinned everything he did.

He'd entered this Crusade with a plan. Trying to get twelve thousand legionaries safely home had never been part of that, and yet here he was – along with thirty wagon-loads of gold he'd acquired along the way. All carefully concealed, of course.

How in Hel can I get us all across that damned river?

'Any ideas?' Seth Korion muttered quietly as they surveyed the Tigrates. The river was one of the main arteries of northern Antiopia, and over a mile wide. On the opposite bank, shimmering like a mirage, was a dark mass of stone: the fortress-town of Vida, which presided over the one bridge for hundreds of miles – except there was no bridge now, only the stumps of the support pillars, blackened by fire. The rainy season was a month past but the waters were still in spate, making the Tigrates an impassable barrier to a force without boats or windships.

Ramon had left the birthing bed of his first child and ridden four hours through the desert to be here, on the banks of the river. It was pre-dawn, the eastern glow behind him heralding another scorching day to come.

'I just got here,' he grumped at Korion. *Try thinking for yourself,* he didn't add. Seth was no strategist or tactician, and it was Ramon himself who'd practically forced him into being the titular head of their small force. He could hardly complain about the tool he'd chosen to use.

At least the Korion name still had power. Ramon was amazed at the sanguine reaction of the soldiers to this latest setback. They'd escaped Shaliyah and been penned in Ardijah and still they held together, with calm belief that those in charge would find a way back. At least part of that was the power of that magical word *Korion*. Since Shaliyah, Seth had added his own deeds to the lustre of his father's illustrious career: the rankers believed in him too, now.

This could break their hearts, though.

'Have we any word from the other side?' he asked.

'Nothing – it's like they don't want to acknowledge we're even here.' Seth was blond and handsome enough, in a weak-chinned way, though his face was hardening, starting to slough away its youth. Ramon had known him for years – they'd both been educated at Turm Zauberin, the Norostein Arcanum. They'd loathed each other then, but a better person was emerging from the sulky, uncertain boy Seth had been.

War surely does change people . . . Hel, look at me: I'm a father now . . .

As if sensing the drift of his thoughts, Seth said, 'By the way, Sensini, congratulations. I'm told it's a girl?'

'Julietta,' Ramon replied. 'It's a Rimoni name, but it's common in Rondelmar too.'

'A good compromise,' Seth approved. 'Severine is well?'

'She's complaining about everything, and wants her mother.'

Severine Tiseme: the last person Ramon would have thought would be his lover, let alone have a child with. Severine was a highborn Rondian of Pallas, and as preening, self-absorbed, prissy and arrogant as that background implied. Even her rebellious spirit had manifested itself in ways typical of such circles: culminating in disgrace for penning snide poetry against the Sacrecours. But though that was the limit of her rebelliousness, her loathing for injustice and slavery was honest and passionate. Such idealism was odd to Ramon, a pragmatist of shifting morality, but he liked it in her; he felt like a better person when he was with her. Well, some of the time anyway. She was no saint, and neither was he; daughter or no, he had no idea if their relationship would survive the Moontide.

'It sounds like she's recovering fast, then,' Seth remarked, smiling. But he sobered as he stared across the dark waters. 'I'm thinking of sending Prenton across in the skiff at dawn to find out what's going on.'

Ramon considered that. He was convinced that the massacre of the Second Army at Shaliyah had not been a fluke but a carefully planned sacrifice by Emperor Constant: to the emperor, Duke Echor of Argundy, the commander of the Southern Army, had been a bigger threat than the Sultan of Kesh. There was too much evidence that the Keshi had been lying in wait at Shaliyah for months preparing their defences, and that suggested collusion to him: Shaliyah had been a victory for both Emperor Constant *and* Sultan Salim.

It was a mindboggling, treasonous thought.

So how welcome would we survivors of Shaliyah be in Vida? he asked himself.

His suspicions about Shaliyah weren't the only dangerous notions he had: on their trek in and out of eastern Kesh they'd seen the Inquisition and the Kirkegarde, the military arms of the Church of Kore, engaged in slave-taking on a massive scale, using unprecedented and utterly illegal methods. He'd found them rounding up native Ahmedhassans and not just enslaving them or killing them, but something far worse: forcing their souls into animals and construct-creatures to be used by Kaltus Korion's army. And they'd been using captive Souldrinkers wielding strange crystals to do the deed – when Souldrinkers were supposed to be abhorred by the Church and killed on sight. It was heresy on a grand scale, a crime that ought to be shouted from the rooftops . . . except that it was clearly sanctioned at the very highest levels.

So now Ramon tried to work out if sending Baltus Prenton, currently their only pilot-mage with Severine still in her birthing-bed, to talk to the commander at Vida was sensible or stupid. The commander of the Vida garrison might have been under instructions to destroy the bridge anyway, but far more likely he'd had orders from the Inquisition to trap Seth's force on the eastern shore, with the sultan's army only days behind them.

'I don't think Prenton would be permitted to come back,' he told Seth gloomily. 'Where's your father's army?'

'How would I know?' Seth replied bitterly. 'I last talked to my father almost two years ago. As far as I know, the Northern Army were marching on Hall'ikut, then retreating through Istabad. The Moontide ends in nine months so they should be beginning to pull back. Armies can march about ten miles a day, but in this heat they can't sustain that pace, so he'll move early. They'll have to be at Southpoint by the end of Maicin for the crossing, so I'd say they'd be near Istabad by now. I don't think he'll help us, if that's what you're thinking.'

'If he found out someone had deliberately cut you off, he'd—'

'He'd what?' Seth interrupted sourly. 'Does he care? I don't know. He put me in Echor's army . . .'

. . . *knowing it was marching into disaster* . . . Ramon grimaced. 'Have you sent scouts looking for other crossings?'

'Of course, north and south. The river widens as it goes south, while to the north it's narrower but still impassable. The land is flat as a table, except for a few low ridges at a place Coll found two days north of here.'

'Defensible?'

'Marginally – but there are no fords, so we'd still be better off going south.'

'The men are exhausted, Seth. We were pushing hard to get here, and Salim isn't far behind us.'

'Perhaps we can parley with them?' Seth ventured.

Ramon frowned; he didn't trust Seth's judgement where the Keshi threat was concerned, not since Seth's friendship with the Salim impersonator they'd held as hostage for a time. 'No, we've played that card: Salim told us we had until the end of Septinon to cross the Tigrates or he'd have no choice but to attack, and that's two days away – and we've got no way to cross the river.'

'Yes, but when we agreed those terms . . .'

'*Rukka mio*, they're *Keshi*, Seth! They aren't our friends!'

'But Salim—'

'That *wasn't* Salim! That was Latif, who spends his life pretending to be someone else!'

'So he said. I think it really was Salim,' Seth said mulishly.

'Well, how would we *know*? You never let us probe him.'

'That would have been wrong, Sensini! It could have broken him.'

'He was an enemy!' Ramon's eyes narrowed. 'Do you have any idea what it looked like, you and him spending every waking hour together? To the men, you were fraternising with an enemy.'

Seth waved a dismissive hand towards the tents. 'We've got two thousand Khotri and Dhassan women in our baggage train – all *I* did was talk! Latif was better company than anyone in this army!' He looked away, and changed the subject. 'If we can't cross by the end of Septinon we need to find a defensible position.'

'Well, at least we agree on that. It probably is too late to find a crossing. We need to think about defence. It'll take days to dig in, wherever we go.'

'But we're magi. Surely we can cross a river—?'

'Sure, *we* can! But our men? Think about it, Seth: the Tigrates is a mile wide, deeper than a three-storey building and flowing fast and hard as a mountain stream. And there are Inquisitors on the other side!'

Seth fretted quietly, then made up his mind. 'Then we'll march north to the place Coll found and dig in.'

'That's our only real option right now. Chin up, Lesser Son!' He regretted using the old jibe even as he spoke it. One old philosopher had written, 'Great men breed lesser sons', and Ramon had gleefully picked up on it at college. He and his best friend Alaron Mercer had used the term to denigrate Seth Korion whenever they could, as revenge for the physical and mental bullying they'd endured from him and his cronies. But he knew Seth better now. 'Truly,' he added, 'the rankers respect you, and so do I.'

Seth accepted that. 'You get some sleep. I'm going to see if I can at least ask the commander in Vida what's going on. And ... Sensini, thank you for coming. I know you'd rather be with Severine and your daughter.'

They both started yawning; the sun would be rising soon and the men would be looking to their commanders to extricate them from this latest predicament, but Ramon had spent the previous day waiting to see if Sevvie would deliver and live, whether the child would come out bawling, or silent and cold. Right now, everything was just a little bit too much to deal with. So he stumbled back to his horse, Lu, who was being rubbed down by a groom, found his bedroll and looked for a quiet place on the far side of the corral, wrapped himself in a blanket and closed his eyes.

When he woke next it was noon, the air was hot, past breathing comfortably, and someone was shaking his shoulder. 'Wake up, sir. We're on the move.'

Seth Korion wandered away from the river, seeking his fellow magi. This close to the river, the air was sultry, and half the rankers hadn't even erected tents, sleeping instead beneath the stars. Here and there dark-skinned women slept among them, dusky creatures with pinched faces and bony limbs, some shockingly young, all refugees from their own kind, gambling their lives on the affections of an enemy soldier far from his own home. He wondered what it would be like to be that desperate. Did they love the man beside them, or was he just the last toss of a weighted dice?

Despite being a pure-blood mage, his whole life had been ruled by fear – not of death or destruction, but more existential dreads: fear of failure, of falling short in his father's eyes. Fear that his House's fortunes would falter under his aegis. The name of Korion ranked high in the empire. The price of failing to consolidate and enhance that legacy would be subtle but terrible, and he'd never felt worthy of that burden.

Winding his way through the churned sandy ruts that were the paths between the tents, he passed drowsy sentries and men stumbling to the trenches to piss, some saluting, others too tired to realise or care that they had just bumped into their commander. The air was thick with sweat and damp bodies, a sweat-sour miasma that was unpleasant to inhale. He found Baltus Prenton's tent, shoved the flap open as he bent over and pushed in. 'Baltus! Wake up! I need you to— Oh—'

He flushed scarlet as a white blob in the semi-darkness resolved itself into buttocks with a pair of skinny legs, just as white, wrapped about them. The tangle of sheets and bodies fell still and two faces turned toward him: Baltus Prenton, the Brevian Air-mage, and Jelaska Lyndrethuse, the Argundian Necromancer, who was probably twice his age.

'Sorry! Sorry! I'll wait outside!'

'We won't be long,' Prenton stammered.

'We'll be as long as we like,' Jelaska disagreed. 'Rukk off, General.'

Seth stumbled back out, tripped on a tent-peg and ended up on his arse. A sentry peered over at the commotion, then looked away as Seth stood, dusted himself off and went looking for fresh air.

Ten minutes later, Prenton and Jelaska found him at the riverbank. Both were still flushed from their exertions, and maybe a little embarrassment. They were both wearing Dhassan long-shirts and leggings.

'Morning sir,' Prenton grinned sheepishly, saluting. He was a career battle-mage and liked to keep things at least a little military.

Not so Jelaska, who regarded all this saluting and the like as nothing more than men stoking each other's egos. 'What's so important you just barge into someone's tent?' she demanded.

Most considered Prenton a brave man when he'd started what Seth euphemistically termed 'seeing' Jelaska – for Jelaska's partners had an unfortunate tendency to die, so much so that she considered herself cursed, even though curses didn't actually exist; the gnosis didn't work that way. But belief in curses was as old as belief in gods, and Jelaska didn't get many suitors, though she was not unattractive, despite being gaunt and severe-looking; her world-weary face was shrouded in a tangle of softly ruffled grey hair. Her voice was husky, with a sultry timbre and for all her age, she had an enviable lust for life and living, which was ironic, considering she was a renowned

Necromancer. Baltus Prenton, though, had a blithe confidence in himself, and he too enjoyed life to the full. If anyone was going to disprove the curse . . .

'We need to open up negotiations with the commander of the Vida garrison,' Seth told them. 'They're ignoring gnostic communication, so it'll have to be face to face.'

'Sure,' Prenton said brightly. 'Who's going to talk to them?'

'I am,' Seth replied firmly.

'Why you?' Jelaska asked bluntly. She was a pure-blood too, and regarded herself as matriarch of the army.

'Because I'm the one person we can send who the garrison commander won't dare to arrest.'

Prenton scowled. 'Unless Siburnius has got to him. That rukking Inquisitor . . .' His voice trailed off and Seth tried to hide his shudder at the thought of Ullyn Siburnius, Commandant of the Twenty-Third Fist of the Inquisition, and his tame Souldrinker Delta; what they'd been doing to the Keshi and Dhassans they'd captured was both astounding and disturbing. And Siburnius had fled directly to Vida.

'That's a risk we'll have to take,' he acknowledged. 'We need to find out what's happening – we've had no news for nine months, not since Shaliyah.'

'I'd like to know where your father is in all this,' Jelaska agreed.

'Exactly.'

'I'll come too.'

'No – you're our strongest battle-mage. I want you here, with Ramon. I'm leaving him in charge.'

Jelaska grunted in a most unladylike way. 'Has Severine pushed out the baby yet?'

Seth grinned. 'A girl: Julietta.'

'Good. Hopefully that'll help keep him focused on getting us all home.' She laid a proprietary hand on Prenton's shoulder. 'Make sure you bring my man back, General. Or you'll have me to answer to.'

Wind rushed through Seth's hair as the skiff banked a hundred feet above the river and the walls of Vida. It was an hour past dawn, the best time of the day, and the walls were bathed in golden light. He sat in the fore-deck of the skiff, concentrating on the nearest tower where he could see a small cluster of men, mostly clad in red or black-and-white; legion or Church. Seth focused his sending on a tall man in the purple of senior Imperial service.

<*I repeat, my name is Seth Korion and I am ranking General of the Southern Army. I wish to parley with the garrison commander.*>

They circled again, Prenton using Air-gnosis to keep wind in his sails.

Finally the aether crackled. <*Battle-mage Korion,*> the voice responded, pointedly ignoring his claimed rank. <*I am Arch-Legate Hestan Milius of the Imperial Revenue. I authorise you to land in the courtyard beneath this tower.*>

Imperial Revenue? What are they doing here? An arch-legate was someone even his father would be wary of. They only got to such lofty ranks through purity of blood and absolute loyalty to the emperor.

But by belittling Seth, Milius was belittling Seth's men.

<*Greetings, Arch-Legate Milius. I repeat: I am the General of the Second Army, and demand acknowledgement of this, or I cannot parlay with you,*> he replied, marvelling at his own daring.

There was a vexed pause, then Milius replied tersely, <*Acknowledged, General. Your safety and freedom are guaranteed.*>

This seemed as much aimed at those with him as Seth himself. *I bet Siburnius is down there, urging him to have me locked up.*

Prenton took the windcraft down with practised ease, clearing the walls and dropping into a slate-stone courtyard. Seth climbed briskly from the hull and faced the trio who came to meet him. Introductions were made: Ullyn Siburnius was indeed present, together with the garrison commander, a half-blood noble named Bann Herbreux, who was promptly ignored. Here, only Arch-Legate Milius mattered.

Milius was a tall and impressive-looking man with a flowing grey beard and shoulder-length salt-and-pepper hair. He was clearly cultivating a look of eternal wisdom. 'General Seth Korion, a pleasure to make your acquaintance,' he boomed, striding forward and offering his hand: a conciliatory gesture as if among equals, even if Seth's claim to general's rank was flimsy – 'by acclamation' was still legal, but it hadn't happened since the First Argundian War.

'Arch-Legate,' Seth replied evenly, reminding himself that he had twelve thousand men and three thousand camp followers relying on him. 'You're far from Pallas.'

'The needs of the empire are many,' Milius replied. 'I'm told you've led your men out of Shaliyah? A great feat, worthy of your illustrious name.'

So, flattery first . . . 'It was a team effort, Arch-Legate. We all pulled together. But we aren't safe yet.' He indicated the river, invisible beyond the buttress walls behind him. 'We had thought to cross here, but we find the bridges down.'

'The orders to retreat behind the Tigrates and destroy the bridges came some time ago. The timing is unfortunate, but I'm sure we can ferry your magi and officers across before any enemy arrive.'

While my rankers and their women can rot in Hel, eh? 'I have fifteen thousand souls in my care, Arch-Legate. I will see them all safe, not just those of rank.'

Milius clearly regarded this as noble tosh. 'Our windborne scouts report that the Keshi are less than thirty miles from here. You will likely see their mounted advance guard by tomorrow evening, if the weather holds. I doubt there is time to bring everyone across.'

Kore's Blood, are they that close? 'Then my request that the bridge be repaired is all the more urgent. You should have sufficient timber and wood for the Earth- and sylvan-magi to work with. We can cross where the pillars stood and proceed to a staging ground south of the city.'

Milius looked into the sky, as if studying the movement of the clouds for omens. 'It might be possible,' he acknowledged, 'but we've insufficient stores to feed your soldiers, and much less can we accommodate your camp followers.' His clear eyes met Seth's briefly. 'You must leave your Noorie whores behind, General.'

'Wives,' Seth replied. 'They are wives.' *Well, mostly.* The ceremonies had been performed by his chaplain, Gerdhart, a priest of Kore, which made them legitimate. 'We don't leave our people behind.'

Milius looked down his nose, but dropped the subject. He turned to face Seth fully, as if to emphasise the importance of his next words. 'You have a battle-mage: one Ramon Sensini. I have a warrant for his arrest. Hand him over, and we can prepare an evacuation of your men to this side of the river.' He thrust some papers at Seth, who took the sheath of parchment.

He wasn't really surprised; it was Ramon who'd been investigating whatever Siburnius was up to, and if he was right, it was ghastly – so of course Siburnius would want him silenced. *And he's got an Arch-Legate to help him . . . But why someone from the Imperial Revenue?*

The papers were indeed an arrest warrant, and carried the right seals. What surprised him was that they all related to fraud, impersonating a Treasury official or issuing false Imperial debt papers. It was bizarre, especially when put up against what Siburnius and his cronies were doing. *I'd have suspected Sensini of a lot of things, but this?* Slow anger kindled in his gut, the same anger he'd felt two weeks ago when he drove Siburnius from the refugee camp. *Rukk you. Sensini might be a damned nuisance, but he's one of us.*

He threw a cold look at the Inquisitor, standing there all relaxed and confident. 'Sensini has been with the legions since the Moontide began. Are you sure he's the right man?'

Milius looked at him gravely. 'The evidence is clear. Battle-mage Sensini has misused Imperial documentation in his role as Logisticalus of the Thirteenth Pallacios to create illegal promissory notes.'

'So what if he has?' Seth replied. 'His tactical skills have saved the army several times, and he has unearthed an Inquisition plot that violates the laws of Kore. I refuse to put that aside for a few piffling promissory notes.'

Milius cocked an eyebrow, then quite deliberately dropped his voice. The air suddenly crackled around them as he shielded their words from being overheard, even by Siburnius, just a few feet away. 'Seth – may I call you that? I think you fail to understand the extent of the issue. Ramon Sensini and his criminal confederates have fooled a group of investors into pouring money into the Crusade in unprecedented levels, in return for monopoly control of opium out of South Dhassa. *Opium*, Seth: a killer of families, the ruination of lives. The level of investment has contributed to severe inflation in Yuros, pushing basic commodities beyond the price of most men.

People are starving in Yuros, Seth! Bread is now seventeen foli in Bricia! Seventeen!' His face was aghast, as if he were revealing signs of Kore's Purge and the Day of Returning, not the price of a loaf.

Seth had understood about one word in three. 'There is no opium in our column. Never has been.' He turned his thoughts away from the rumour that Ramon had saved them all at Shaliyah by dumping opium powder in the path of the enemy and setting it alight. 'As for the promissory notes: what proof is there?'

Hestan Milius looked like a parent forced to explain something complicated to a child. 'It is commendable that you defend your underlings, General, but his guilt is clear. Your only responsibility in this matter is to surrender him to justice, so that we can concentrate on the more urgent matter: the safety of your army.'

Seth searched his memory of law classes from college, which he'd always enjoyed. *Yes, that's what I need!* 'To issue a warrant of arrest, someone must have submitted proof to the issuing Justiciar.' He looked at the papers again. 'That's you. I'd like to see that proof. Otherwise I must suspect that Commandant Siburnius has misled you to protect himself.'

'The integrity of a servant of the Inquisition isn't for even a general to question,' Milius said heavily. 'Your youth excuses you in part, Seth, but you must learn to trust the institutions you serve.' Any pretence of friendliness was gone. Seth could feel Prenton twitching nervously; he might not be able to hear, but the anger on the Arch-Legate's face was easy to read.

'I want to see proof,' he repeated firmly. 'For my own peace of mind.' He wondered if he might have to fight his way out. *I'd get about two feet.*

Milius sighed, reached into a pocket and produced another piece of paper. 'Here, *General.*'

It was an Imperial Promissory of the sort that Seth had seen floating about the legion, especially in the early months, usually in lieu of cash when settling gambling debts. They were mostly used by the logisticalus of each legion to facilitate transfer of supplies. He focused on the signature: illegible, but familiar. 'It's not Sensini's signature.'

But it's his handwriting, I'll give you that. The seal wasn't actually of the Imperial Treasury either: it was a heraldic crest of the sort the noble Houses used in Pallas. He recognised it, too; who wouldn't?

'Do you recognise the crest?' Milius asked.

Seth nodded mutely. 'Is it . . . genuine?'

'Of course not! He got hold of it somehow – stolen, most likely. We'll recover it when we arrest him.' He held out his hand for the papers and the promissory note. 'Now, can we agree to this, General, and get on with saving your men?'

Seth bit his lip, looking about him without focusing on anything. *My father boasts of never leaving a man behind, but then he's never lost a battle, so it's probably never come up . . . And Ramon, the little shit, has been the one who got us out of Shaliyah, and into and out of Ardijah . . . I can't just hand him over on their say-so. I saw that death-camp too . . .*

But he had fifteen thousand lives to protect.

Damn this . . .

Southern Kesh, on the continent of Antiopia
Rami (Septinon) 929
15th month of the Moontide

Cymbellea di Regia was curled up in a foetal position when the ground began to tremble. The vibrations shook her back to awareness, though she'd not really been asleep. Part of her was amazed that she still lived and breathed. She'd been helpless in the care of these women for days, too ill and weak from blood-loss to move, her heart torn in two and her brain too numb to grasp the weak straws of consciousness that flowed past.

She looked up at a wizened face so deeply brown it was almost black, one of several women who'd been shielding her from the clamour of the camp. Bunima, a widow from South Dhassa, had held her down, hugged her and whispered calm into her ears while the others pierced her womb and scraped out her unborn child. They'd protected her since, though she was not just of Yuros but a mage;

she'd been sure they would just cast her outside the women's camp to where the circling men were calling for her death. Stones had been hurled into the cluster of women, an indiscriminate rain of rock that had taken lives and broken bones, but the men had not actually dared to enter the women's camp – she didn't know why, and she didn't know why the women were shielding her either. But Bunima with her smattering of Rondian had become her protector and carer, though they couldn't hold more than a basic conversation.

Only one man had entered: *Zaqri*, the father of her child. Her dead child. She could still hear his anguished cry as he realised what she'd done: the wail of a sinner cast into Hel. She'd seen him just once since, when he'd told her that he would wait for her recovery, then they would continue their hunt for the Scytale of Corineus. She wondered if he was still holding to that promise. Aborting a child among her people was not unusual; it carried little stigma – but here, it was a deadly sin, though of course it still happened. She knew her action had wounded Zaqri deeply, just as she'd also intended – but there was another reason, equally as pressing: their child was half Dokken, and no one knew what it might have been.

Pater Sol! Mater Lune! Tell me I've done the right thing . . .

But as always, there was no answer. *Silence is the Voice of God*, she'd once heard a priest say.

The old woman said a few words, of which Cym picked out 'soldiers' and 'sultan' and 'here'. She did understand that she was in danger if she stayed.

Irrationally, she just wanted to see Zaqri again. The Dokken packleader had saved her, protected her, loved her, and in her mind's eye he still shone like a god among mortals – but he was a Souldrinker: a cursed demon, and he'd killed her mother. Even though it had been in combat, Rimoni law demanded retribution: she'd killed his child so she wouldn't have to kill him. It had felt right and just at the time, but now she couldn't move without feeling the wounds inside her body and her soul.

Pater Sol, Mater Lune, why did you make me want him so?

Her father would have told her that *done is done. Life must go on.*

71

Clinging to that thought, she rolled into a sitting position, then tried to stand. She was still clad in her bloodstained chemise, with a thin blanket draped about her. She staggered, but a dozen hands caught her and she clung to them gratefully until she got her balance and could stand on her own two feet.

Bunima was right: there were mounted soldiers coming down the long slope to the east, columns and columns of them, all wearing the pointed steel helmet of the Keshi. They had lances and circular shields, and bows in sheaths lashed to their legs. The man at the head of the column rode bare-headed, his thick black hair oiled and gleaming in the afternoon sun: a prince of men. He rode with lordly grace to greet a group of ragged men from the male camp to the south. She watched with a vague feeling of concern. *They'll take me to their breeding-camps and rape me and force me to bear mage-children until I die . . .*

Even that thought couldn't shake the lethargy from her limbs. She was too ill and exhausted to care.

Then she saw *him*: blond hair and beard catching the light, his huge frame towering above the Ahmedhassans as he shouldered his way through the men and into the women's camp. He exchanged words with one of Bunima's colleagues and then he was before her, like a hero of legend come to her rescue. Even after all that had passed between them, all the ugliness and deception, it was to the tender moments that her mind always returned.

I wish I could just reach out and erase the blood that lies between us . . . Impossible, of course.

Zaqri allowed her a moment, despite the urgency, to say farewell to those who'd tended her. Bunima and the other women pressed about her, a sea of faces and outstretched hands, work-hardened, but gentle on her face. It made her feel almost like she was home in her father's caravan, wrapped in a cocoon of love.

'Bunima, thank you—'

'Cym must go. Hurry now. Soldiers come.' Bunima kissed her cheeks with chapped lips. She smelled of sun-bleached bones. 'Go now. Sal'Ahm, Cym.'

'Why help me?' Cym whispered.

'We are woman,' Bunima replied. 'We know.' She touched Cym's belly. 'We understand. Men don't choose. Gods don't choose. Is our choice only.' She pointed to the sky. 'Life is circle. All souls return, again and again. Life finds a way.' That sounded more like Omali beliefs than Ahm, but South Dhassa was a strange intersection of cultures. Whatever the reason, she was grateful that Bunima's world view could find a way to forgive her.

She was passed down the line of women, hugging her and blessing her in a mix of tongues, then, suddenly wobbling on coltish legs, she was standing in front of Zaqri. He caught her and held her erect. She inhaled his scent and regained some steadiness.

'Can you ride?' he whispered. 'I've prepared a camp for us, not too far away. Can you manage?'

'I think so. If it's not too far?' She glanced at the princely Keshi leader and his cavalry entering the camp.

'It is close. I've picked out a place south of the march of the army. I thought we had a few more hours, but it won't matter. These are just scouts and outriders.' Zaqri looked worried. 'Are you strong enough?'

She still felt wrung-out, but they couldn't stay here. 'I'll manage.'

He didn't look convinced, but said, 'I need to get to the Dokken in Salim's army without being noticed; I'll ask them to get me an audience with Sultan Salim. We'll need help if we're to find your friend Alaron and the Scytale.'

'The Dokken won't care about Alaron or Ramita,' Cym whispered. 'They will just want the Scytale for themselves.'

'Perhaps, but the Scytale represents salvation for my kind: for us, it is more important than the war itself. I will persuade the Dokken here to aid us, Cymbellea. They will *beg* to help us find your friends.'

She was struck by a sudden sense of foreboding so strong she almost choked, but she pushed it away. The Keshi cavalry were getting closer and they had to go. 'Then let's get out of here.'

5

The Key to Empire

Zain Monks

We of the Zain faith don't learn to fight: we learn to defend ourselves. The distinction is important. Our aim is not to commit violence but to prevent it. We're sworn not to kill, when maiming is sufficient, not to maim when stunning is sufficient, and not to stun when deterring is sufficient. It is a hard path, requiring courage and judgement, but what righteous path is ever easy?

MASTER GURAYAD, MANDIRA KHOJANA,
LOKISTAN, 766

So we corners this little beggar in orange, an' all he's got's a stick, right? Easy picking, you'd think. 'cept he's not, cos he wields that stick like it's Bullhead's Hammer. He taps Myro and Sim afore they can e'en blink, an' then he comes for me. I jus' bloody ran for it!

LONN BRINDIU, PALLACIAN RANKER,
SECOND CRUSADE, 918

Aruna Nagar Market, Baranasi, on the continent of Antiopia
Shawwal (Octen) 929
16th month of the Moontide

Ramita Ankesharan pulled her dupatta tighter about her head, concealing her face deeper in the folds. This was how every modest young Lakh woman dressed in public; no one looked twice at her. That was a good thing here in her home town.

Baranasi. Aruna Nagar. The words sang inside her. She had come *home.*

Aruna Nagar market was an assault on the senses. There were great swathes of colour everywhere you looked – the bright stall awnings; the women's vivid saris, contrasting with the men's dirty white robes; the pungent spice piles, their fragrant scents mingled with the acrid stinks of untold numbers of people and beasts in a head-swimming brew. Animals brayed and barked and yowled amidst the clamour of the sellers and buyers, the buzz of chatter and negotiation rising and falling as each deal, however humble, was beaten like copper coins into its final shape. Each look and word told a tale of prosperity or desperation; each transaction was a duel. Just being here sent a tremor through her bones: this was the place where she'd been born, where she'd grown up, where she'd first fallen in love. It was where she'd laboured from the day she was old enough to pass her father goods to sell, the place where she'd giggled and gossiped with the other girls, eyed the boys, argued with other stallholders and dreamed of better things. Tears stung her eyes. *This is my home.*

But it didn't feel quite the same and she knew the difference was in her, not the bellicose thrum of the market. She'd passed the house where she'd been born and raised, one of many fragile-looking piles of bricks leaning against each other and relying on the neighbours' properties to stay up. It looked so *small* now; it would have been swallowed up by even one wing of Antonin Meiros' house in Hebusalim. How had they all fit, she and her parents and her many brothers and sisters – and the Makanis, too? But it wasn't even her family's home any more, and knowing that left a bubble of emptiness in her gut.

Alaron and Corinea were waiting with the windskiff outside the city, but Ramita wasn't alone; Yash was following her, discreetly – it wouldn't be fitting for a Zain monk to be seen travelling with a woman. She'd claimed that only in Aruna Nagar would they find all the ingredients they'd need for the Scytale potions; maybe that wasn't entirely true – no doubt Teshwallabad, Kankritipur or any of a dozen other cities would have the same things – but she needed to come here, perhaps to see if her parents really were gone, perhaps just to show Dasra, bundled in her arms, the city she called home, although he was so young she knew he'd never recall this day.

She needed a bulk dealer, so naturally she sought out Vikash Nooradin, who'd been her father's closest business ally – but he wasn't in his usual spot, and when she'd asked a trader where to find him today, the man looked frightened and his response was brusque, just, 'He is gone, girl.'

She tugged at the trader's sleeve. 'What do you mean, gone?'

The man clearly didn't recognise her, though her family had worked just a few stalls away from his for years. He snapped, 'Chod! I'm busy, girl!'

'Ram Sankar, talk to me!' she snapped back, and the man blinked and peered into her gauzy dupatta. 'Who are—? *Ramita*? Ramita Ankesharan?' He dropped his voice and his face turned ashen. He started looking left and right, but Aruna Nagar Market was its usual chaotic self and his just one voice in thousands. No one had noticed them. He touched her shoulder. 'Little Ramita? Is that really you?'

She could remember her father Ispal and Ram Sankar laughing together so many times, at the massive wedding celebrations that filled the autumn months in Aruna Nagar, and the time they'd found a snake in a carpet consignment and the panic it caused . . .

She swallowed heavily. 'Yes, it is me.'

Ram went to hug her, then stopped. Ramita had left with mysterious strangers, after which her whole family had vanished. Then he forgot his wariness and hugged her anyway. 'Dear girl, it is so good to see you! But we cannot talk here – come to my home. Sunita would love to see you!'

'Thank you, Ram Sankar-ji. But I must make some purchases first,' Ramita told him. 'I will need a buyer, as there will be too much for me to carry.' She steeled herself for the worst, and asked, 'Where has Vikash Nooradin gone?'

Ram shook his head sadly. 'Later, Mita. Not here.'

Sweet Parvasi, what has happened?

'Will you be my buyer?' she asked, and at his emphatic nod, gave him her list and a pouch of coins and agreed to meet at his house in an hour or so. That left her free to wander down to the bathing ghats and immerse herself in Imuna's healing waters. The wide stone steps were filled with clothes-washers now that the morning pooja was done, soaking their laundry in the muddy water and beating the cloth against the flat rocks before leaving them drying on the hundreds of lines that had been strung from every high place. No one stole – there was no point; no one had anything of quality to wash here. The rich had their own places inside their palaces. Once Ramita had wondered what that would be like, but now she knew: palaces were dangerous traps. They marked you out as a target and left you isolated from those you loved. Antonin Meiros had died in his palace. No one was safe.

All along the ghats hump-backed cattle sacred to the Omali wandered freely. Many were in the river, no doubt pissing and shitting in the same water that people used for drinking and cooking. The pandits said Imuna was the cleanest water in the world, but that was a different kind of cleanliness – spiritual, not physical – and she knew the difference now.

There were girls just like her, clustered or alone, fetching water, washing clothes or praying, bombarding the gods with prayers asking for money or status or a good husband, for love or children or blessings on their family.

It is well that there are so many gods to pray to.

She left Dasra on the steps playing with the lapping waters, knowing Yash was watching, and waded until she was waist-deep. The thick silt on the bottom steps oozed through her toes. She put aside her foreboding and prayed to Sivraman and Parvasi. They represented the wilder part of humanity, attuned to nature and the passionate emotions; her life had been so beset by turmoil and strife that only Parvasi could see her through. But there was more: she and Alaron had learned new ways to use the gnosis, symbolised by a statue of Sivraman and Parvasi conjoined; they held the keys to all powers. The Omali taught that there were many gods, but they were all an aspect of one, Aum; each person found their personal divinity through identification with one of the many aspects of Aum. Parvasi was her gateway.

And Alaron's gateway is Sivraman. He might not know this yet, but it is so.

It was a pleasing thought, that the earnest young Rondian was slowly opening his eyes to Aum, but it was also troubling, for Sivraman and Parvasi were husband and wife. She knew Alaron cared for her, that he wanted her – the danger and their shared trials had bound them close. She knew the rhythm of his heartbeat from the nights pressed to his chest, trying to sleep in the cold wilds. And now that her prospective marriage to the mughal could not happen, she was free to follow her heart.

Parvasi, Mother, she prayed, *is it right to give him my love? It feels too soon after the loss of my husband. One of my twins is missing, the world is at war and we hunt a deadly treasure. What room is there for love?*

Fear that giving in to his desires – and hers, she reluctantly acknowledged – might weaken them both when they so desperately needed to be strong, paralysed her emotions. They had to rescue Nasatya, and recover the Scytale. And yet . . .

I miss the good things that love brings, she admitted.

She lost track of her prayers, asked for forgiveness, then sloshed back up the ghats and sat in the baking sun, watching the people and the cows and the goats and the elephants and all the rest of the world as they drank and washed and prayed. She fed Dasra with the last dregs of her breast milk; she was becoming dry. She missed her other son.

An hour bell rang. It was time to learn what had happened to Vikash Nooradin.

Afterwards, she wished she hadn't.

They'd hidden the windskiff in the broken lands some two hours' walk from Baranasi. Now Alaron Mercer filled the waiting hours practising different aspects of the gnosis. His new way of wielding it meant he had theoretical access to every Study, far more than he yet knew how to use, but theory was different to practise. He needed to master each equally, and that was an ongoing struggle.

It was hard to concentrate when he was alone with the Queen of Evil. Not that Corinea had done anything even remotely evil since they'd met her. Up close she was just like someone's grandmother:

an old white woman with a serene face and long silver hair. She was disconcertingly ordinary, but that didn't banish his fears.

If all went well, Ramita and Yash would be back by dusk. Apart from a herd of cattle below them, tended by a scrawny old man with a matted beard to his waist who'd spent most of the day asleep, they had seen no one. Sunset was perhaps two hours away.

Setting his worries aside, Alaron focused on a new exercise: scrying through different media, using water, stone, flame and even the air before him. Earth had been his first affinity and he had to fight to keep the other bonds as strong, which took all his concentration. Scrying was delicate work, not something he'd used much since he learned this new path as he'd concentrated on more combat-oriented gnosis. So he called up a close up image of a distant tree, first conjuring it in a stone, then a pool of water, then a flame and finally in the empty air before him. He clenched a fist triumphantly when he managed Water, the most difficult for him.

'How is it that you can do all this?' Corinea said, snapping Alaron out of his reverie. The ancient woman had been silent since dawn, apparently lost in her own trance of memory and regret, and for a while he'd forgotten she was here.

'Do what?'

Her brow furrowed. 'I've seen you using every element and almost every one of the Sixteen Gnostic Studies in the past four hours. Most magi can only use two or three well, and another two or three at all. How can you do that?'

In their solitude Alaron had forgotten that what he was doing would be considered impossible by most magi – including Corinea, clearly. That was a weird feeling, to know more than such a legendary person.

'It's a new training technique,' he admitted after some thought. 'It's taken a lot of work to get this far.'

'Interesting.' She studied him, clearly with her gnostic sight engaged. 'I had to teach myself, of course. Air and Water, and Sorcery . . . those were what I found my affinities to be. I spent a lot of time spying on other mages and trying to duplicate what they did.'

'Was it dangerous?'

'Of course: everyone knew what I'd done – or what they *thought* I'd done – and there was a king's ransom on my head. I became very good at hiding and disguise. I didn't have living teachers, but I found other ways to learn – when people started writing things down and I could steal books, that made it easier.'

'It must have been lonely, to be in hiding for so long,' Alaron commented, hoping not to cause offence.

'Oh, I was seldom alone. I was a needy person, once I got over mourning for Johan. The hard part was trying to learn the gnosis while concealing my skills from whoever I was with.' She sighed reflectively. 'I've been married eight times, and had many lovers.' She looked at him frankly. 'Some as young as you.'

He blushed. 'I'm ... um ...' *Is she flirting with me?*

She laughed drily. 'Don't worry, boy, you're not my type. And I'm not blind: you only have eyes for one person, and she isn't me.'

'Oh.' His colour deepened. 'No, that's just ... No, you're right. It's just that there's so much happening to us, and I won't take advantage of her, not when she's still grieving for her husband, and for Nasatya. Her needs come first.'

'Well, well ... And you're how old? I've met few grown men with the maturity to see beyond their own appetites. Well spoken, Master Mercer.'

'Thank you.' He ducked his head and changed the subject. 'I didn't recognise the ingredients of the base compound that you wrote down for Ramita ...'

She smiled indulgently. 'They're mostly poisons – in the wrong quantities they'll stop your heart. But there is also senaphium, which Baramitius called "jolt-root" because he said it could restart the heart if given in the right quantities.'

'So the ambrosia kills and then revives you ... and that's how the gnosis is freed?'

'The objective is not to kill but to *almost* kill, then pull the drinker back from the brink. The rest of the ingredients, the ones that are personalised, are designed to moderate the poisons and awaken those parts of the brain conducive to gnostic use. Without them, the potion is just a poison. With them, it almost always works.'

'Then why did so many of those given the ambrosia the first time die or get twisted into Souldrinkers?'

'Because these refinements came later – that first potion was just poison, senaphium and a couple of extra herbs – what Baramitius did that night was reckless, almost insane. But that was Baramitius.'

'But how did you know that you would gain the gnosis?' he asked curiously.

'We didn't! We had no idea – even Baramitius didn't know: he thought he was transporting us *bodily* into Paradise! We thought we were all going to sprout wings and turn into angels! The gnosis was all an accident, a fluke. Yet afterwards, Baramitius swore he received "visions from Kore"!' She sighed reflectively. 'They were mad days. I lost everyone I cared about that night, and had to kill the love of my life to escape. If I could go back I'd knife Baramitius and burn his rukking research to ash.'

Alaron couldn't imagine a life without his own gnosis – it hadn't always been easy, being a quarter-blood mage, but he knew he really was blessed. 'But you're still willing to allow a new Ascendancy?' Suddenly the idea of drinking a cup of mixed poisons brewed by this woman felt a lot more frightening.

She looked at him intently. 'You know what I want: a platform to tell my side of the story. In the end, all we have is our reputation, and I want mine cleansed. So yes, I will help you. The gnosis has been unleashed on the world, Master Mercer, and there is nothing I can do to change that; we are now blessed and cursed to live with it. I promise you, I will brew the ambrosia honestly.' Her mouth curled bitterly. 'I only hope that your Zain monks are as angelic as you think they are, or they'll be just as monstrous as the Pallas magi.'

'They aren't like that.'

'Power will change them, Alaron Mercer. I'll warrant that in a few years you won't be able to tell your monks from any other mage who thinks himself semi-divine.'

That was another worry Alaron really didn't need. 'We don't have any choice,' he said firmly. 'They're the only ones we've notes for – unless you'd rather I just chose a random village and poisoned their well?'

'No, Master Mercer, you're playing the only game you can, given the state of the tabula board. And I've met worse people than Zains to gift the gnosis to.'

'They've got to be better than whoever Malevorn and Huriya give the ambrosia to, right?'

'Probably.' She frowned at him. 'Tell me more of this Huriya Makani . . . there's something familiar about her . . . I distantly sensed her gnosis in Teshwallabad, and it had the same taste as an old Soul-drinker, Sabele. I sometimes encountered that one's touch when divining the future.'

The name Sabele meant nothing to Alaron. Then he noticed a small cluster of dark shapes emerging from the haze less than half a mile across the plains. He immediately scryed, and Ramita's face appeared before his. <*Did you get everything?*>

Her face looked strained, but she wagged her head in that characteristic Lakh way. <*Everything. My father's friend Ram Sankar-ji has provided it all. He is with me.*>

Minutes later he was greeting them in the flesh. Ram Sankar was a bony grey-haired man with a scrawny son leading two pack-mules bearing Ramita's purchases – not just the ingredients, but new clothes for them all too. Alaron noticed the quizzical expression when he was introduced as 'Al'Rhon, my rakhi-bhaiya' – he couldn't follow the rapid-fire conversation in Lakh that followed, but it was pretty clear the old man didn't approve.

'Did anyone notice you both?' Alaron asked Yash quietly.

The young Zain shook his head, and Alaron knew the monk was streetwise enough to have spotted a tail. He relaxed just a little.

Corinea checked the supplies carefully, making sure they had precisely what was required – errors could be fatal, she warned them. In the end she declared herself satisfied, and the old trader had a final low conversation with Ramita before collecting his son and the mules and setting off back towards the city.

Alaron waited until the trader had gone before asking Ramita what had happened.

Tears ran down her face as she repeated Ram Sankar's story of the horrific torture and murder of Vikash Nooradin and his family and friends by Huriya and her pack. 'They were killed because of *me*,' she concluded, her eyes bleeding tears.

'No, Ramita,' Alaron replied quietly. 'They were murdered because Malevorn and Huriya are killers. You know that, and you can't blame yourself.' He'd been through this anguish when Malevorn's Inquisitors destroyed a Rimoni camp he'd been sheltering in. 'I'm so sorry,' he added, 'but it's their deed, not yours.'

His words appeared to reach her. 'Sivraman will grant us retribution,' she murmured, then took Dasra from Yash. 'I'll hold him while you pack.' Her voice was still a little unsteady. 'I think we should go. Better we fly by night rather than risk witnesses.'

The *Seeker* wasn't a big skiff and with passengers, gear and goods was heavily weighed down, but there was no help for it. Fortunately, all three magi could use Air-gnosis to keep the craft aloft.

As the windskiff rose into the skies, Ramita stared back toward her home city, tears once again running down her cheeks.

'You'll come back, one day,' Alaron told her, but he wasn't sure she heard him.

Mandira Khojana, Lokistan, on the continent of Antiopia
Shawwal (Octen) 929
16th month of the Moontide

Corinea and Yash made the return journey to Mandira Khojana far easier; the old woman claimed to have crossed the desert many times, and she certainly knew the shape of the land. And Yash had walked into the mountains to find Mandira Khojana, and knew the landmarks to look for, invaluable knowledge as a week after crossing the Sithardha Desert they found themselves amongst the massive, maze-like peaks of Lokistan. Alaron recalled his first arrival at the monastery: a crash-landing that all but wrecked the *Seeker*; he wasn't at all keen to repeat that experience.

The air became thin and frigid, and they shared the sky with massive vultures with ten-foot wingspans that preyed on the mountain goats and kine that nimbly roamed the slopes and sheer valleys below. The knife-edged peaks that constrained their route glistened with ice, forcing them to fly lower, and constantly tack, a wearying task in a badly overloaded vessel with little room to manoeuvre, inside or out.

They were all unwashed, itchy, cold and increasingly irritable. The young men were sharing the aft deck, with the two women at the fore. Alaron and Yash were used to each other, and though they complained half-jokingly about each other's farting, they got along.

The women were far less amicable. Alaron found it fascinating to watch them, for both were interesting to him, for different reasons. He adored Ramita, of course, the whole diminutive, fierce, self-contained, capable and adaptable being that she was. *An ignorant Rondian mage might just see an uneducated peasant*, he admitted to himself, *but her practical knowledge and insight always amazes me . . . and as for her raw gnostic power . . .* Of course, she'd borne twins to not just a pure-blood but an Ascendant, which was unprecedented. *Even so*, he thought proudly, *her gnostic skill's becoming more intuitive*. He grinned to himself as he thought, *She's like a plum: dark and sweet on the outside, with a core that hammers couldn't crack.*

Corinea was another thing entirely.

As the days passed, the woman of legend slowly emerged. That Corinea had been a force of nature, a dancer, a singer. The Kore Church had her strutting about half-naked all the time, flowers tangled in her hair, fornicating with anyone who desired her, faithless, promiscuous and conniving. In the *Book of Kore*, she was Corineus' blind spot. Now, watching her, hearing her stories and the gradual revelation of her character, Alaron began to think that whilst the Church might have embellished the stories for their own use, they had been rooted in truth: perhaps she wasn't the demoness of legend, but it was clear she was far from a saint.

She complained bitterly of the cold and the cramped skiff. She bitched about Ramita's cooking, Yash's ignorance and Alaron's piloting. She moaned about the smell of Dasra's swaddling and Ramita's breast milk. Even the even-tempered Yash looked harassed when she started a rant. All in all, Alaron was heartily sick of her by the time they reached inner Lokistan, living legend or not. How Ramita put up with her he didn't know, because in the fore-deck she bore the brunt of it.

'A group of emasculated eunuchs hiding from the real world,' was how Corinea sneeringly dismissed Zain monks. It was their fourth night in the mountains after a trying day riding the fast-shifting winds through the rugged peaks.

'I don't think you know anything about it,' Alaron retorted, tired past caring about manners. At least Yash was away looking for firewood; he might have felt the need to leap to the defence of his order otherwise. Ramita was preparing to cook and he'd been lashing down the sails for the night while, as usual, Corinea waited like a princess for them to set up the camp, doing nothing herself. 'I'm Arcanum-trained and they can whack the Hel out of me,' he added.

'You?' She arched an eyebrow. 'You're slow, skinny and soft. You'd not last five minutes in a real fight.'

'I've fought Inquisitors and Souldrinkers, and I'm still here. You've not even been in an Arcanum. So shut your ignorant mouth, *your Highness*.'

'Oh, temper!'

You bet. The Anborn line is famous for it. 'Perhaps you could be useful for once and prepare the meal?' he suggested with *that much* sarcasm.

'Each to what they're best at, dearie. I'll do the thinking and leave the labouring to those born to it.'

Alaron picked up a pail and stalked toward her. 'Why don't you fetch the water? It's time you did something, you lazy old biddy.'

'I don't think so, shop-boy,' She scoffed, but her eyes had gone flinty.

He refused to be intimidated. *She's not a demoness from the* Book of Kore. *She's just an old strumpet with an attitude problem.*

And Ascendant-level gnosis.

He thrust the pail and a bag of food into her lap. 'Stop being a bitch and do your share for once.'

'Or what?'

'Or the deal's off.' He put his hands on his hips. 'Listen, *Lillea Sorades*. You've given us what we need from you, so thanks and all that. I can make the ambrosia now – maybe not as well as without you, but we'll manage. So what exactly do we need you for, anyway?'

She blinked, and her voice dropped to a reptilian dry rasp. 'Boy, you forget yourself.' Behind that voice came the perception of her gnosis, a reservoir of power deep and wide, dwarfing his tiny pool. *Ascendant gnosis.*

If I back down now I'm nothing in her eyes . . .

'No. I remember who you are: some arrogant, preening witch in a book. The Kore are going to love you: you're going to justify every preconception they've got. If you want to stand in front of the world and convince them you're something other than an entitled bitch, why don't you stop behaving like one?'

Her eyes went round, her lips pulled back from her teeth and for an instant he really thought that the next moment would see him buried by some bone-crushing spell. He was peripherally aware that Ramita was on her feet, but this was his fight.

She's primarily Air and Sorcery. The opposite is Earth-gnosis . . . and she's sitting on a rock . . . He prepared a spell, wondering if it was the last thing he'd ever do.

Corinea let out her breath in a low hiss. 'I haven't cooked for decades, boy.'

'Then it's time you got some practise.' He deliberately turned his back and walked away, trying to slow his heartbeat to something less than a gallop.

To his faint surprise, she did what he said, all of it, with far more skill than she'd led them to believe she had. For once she stilled her litany of whining, and as they all went to sleep, he wrapped himself in his blanket with a sense of satisfaction. They all stayed close to the fire, their breath frosting in the night air. Mater Luna was edging toward her full face and shone silver and bright in the darkness.

Sometime in the night, a little bundle of womanhood wriggled against him. Ramita laid her head on his chest, holding Dasra between them, sharing her blanket and heat. 'You did right,' she whispered, making him glow.

He inhaled the soft, oily fragrance of her thick black hair. He liked her smells, all spicy and earthy. He murmured and fell asleep again, warmer already.

As distances that would have taken weeks to traverse on foot melted beneath them in hours, Alaron reflected that flying was in some ways the most incredible magic of all the gnostic feats. *We travel like gods*, he reflected, then reflected that gods probably travelled far more comfortably on their winged steeds and chariots and the like. *Lucky sods.*

'We're here!' Yash cried aloud, mid-afternoon on their sixth day in the mountains, as a distinctive green slope dotted with red poppies came into view, followed by the buttress of sheer stone, hewn into lines and planes: Mandira Khojana, huge, sprawling – and almost inaccessible. It was wholly manmade too, without any Earth-gnosis.

Alaron grinned at the young monk. 'You're home!'

'This was never really my home,' Yash muttered. Of all the young acolytes Alaron had befriended here, Yash was the least suited to monastic life. 'Let's not stay too long,' the young acolyte added fervently. He pulled a face and said, not for the first time, 'I doubt you'll find many takers for the ambrosia.'

Of course, Alaron thought, *even if any of the Zains are willing to drink the ambrosia, I wonder how many will survive the experience? We could be sending many of them to their graves.*

But what choice have we got?

Alaron and Ramita had hoped their return to Mandira Khojana would be a joyous occasion. They'd been happy here, and it was only a few months since they'd left, believing that by delivering the Scytale – and Ramita herself – to Vizier Hanook was the right path forward. Instead, they'd not just brought down death upon the vizier and his son, and so many others, they'd lost the Scytale.

DAVID HAIR

Nevertheless it was a genuine pleasure to bow before Master Puravai as they stepped from the windskiff onto the courtyard.

'Brother Longlegs, welcome back.' The old Zain addressed Alaron
gravely. His skull was freshly shaven and his beard plaited. His robes
of dark grey were the only sign of his rank. He looked Alaron up
and down, then ran his eye over the rest of the group. Yash was still
bowing deeply. 'Come,' he said, 'all of you. I see you've a tale to tell,
so let us go somewhere more private.'

He ignored the curious crowds, the monks and novices in saffron
and crimson, and the villagers from settlements further down the
valleys who'd all found reason to be in the courtyard as the windskiff
descended. Mandira Khojana was the heart of several communities
spread over more than thirty miles of rugged terrain, providing
spiritual and physical succour for thousands of precarious lives.
Although the Order was agnostic about both religions and gnostic
powers, the Ordo Costruo had a relationship with this and other Zain
monasteries that stretched back hundreds of years.

Master Puravai gestured to a group of novices loitering near the
skiff and set them to work unloading the baggage, then he escorted
the four of them to the guest suites.

Alaron introduced Corinea as Lily; they'd all agreed that publically
identifying Corinea should wait until it was absolutely necessary;
there would be shocks enough in their story without adding *that* to
the mix.

'Lily is an Ordo Costruo mage aiding our quest,' Alaron told the
Master, and if Puravai didn't seem to believe him, he didn't say so.

Before dining, and the stressful conversation that would follow,
came baths, and they all revelled in the sheer bliss of scrubbing away
the grime of the journey in copious quantities of warm, scented water.
That the Zains placed great store on cleanliness was a monumental positive in Alaron's view. He prepared himself for a barrage of
questions as he followed Yash to the communal baths, where several
dozen novices just happened to have decided they needed to wash
too. They all knew he'd gone to Teshwallabad, and he had to fend
off many questions in halting Rondian about what he'd seen and

88

done – Yash just ducked his head under the water and ignored his friends. Most of these young men were the very ones Alaron wished to offer the ambrosia. *I wonder how they'll react?* he thought. *Although that's assuming Master Puravai even allows them the choice.*

And what do I do if he doesn't?

With that worry added to the pile, he and Yash put on gloriously fresh clothing – crimson acolyte robes had been waiting on their pallets – then headed off for some much-needed food. Ramita and Corinea, also freshly washed and attired in the new clothes Ramita had bought in Baranasi – plain salwar kameez in similar blue-green hues – joined them for a plain but filling meal of curried vegetable and flatbread.

They ate largely in silence, not just because they were nervously awaiting Master Puravai's summons, but because there was little need to discuss what was to come: Huriya and Malevorn had vanished with the Scytale, inevitably they would use it, and the only chance they had to counter them was to create their own Ascendancy.

'I'll do the talking,' Alaron said as they stood, looking at Corinea. He didn't want her contempt for the Zains turning Master Puravai against them.

'I'll speak as and when I wish to,' Corinea retorted shortly.

'Do not undermine us,' Ramita told her.

'Don't tell me what to do.'

Ramita looked at Alaron. 'You are right. We should do this without her.'

Corinea scoffed. 'Go ahead, if you think you can brew the ambrosia without killing half of the monks and driving the rest insane. See if I care. I'll mind your baby.'

The next instant Ramita had whirled upon her, her hand extended with fingers splayed, and pale light flashed. Corinea was lifted from her feet and slammed to the rug. With gnostic sight instantly engaged, Alaron saw lines of force like an extension of Ramita's right arm wrapped around Corinea's throat. The old sorceress convulsed helplessly in her grip.

'Did you threaten my child?' Ramita demanded, bending over Corinea. Alaron was stunned by her sudden ferocity.

Corinea squeaked, 'You misunderstood—'

'Did I?' Ramita interrupted. 'I'm through being patient with you, you arrogant *kutiyaa*! You complain about this, you whine about that. We're all sorry for your sad story, but if you can't shut up and help us we're better off without you—'

Corinea's eyes bulged as she tried again to push herself from the floor. The veins in her neck went blue as she pushed, her own gnosis gathering behind her, and to Alaron it felt like the air was being sucked from the room. Yash, the only non-mage, was backing away, his face pale.

Then Corinea sagged. 'All right,' she choked out. 'You've made your point.'

'Which is?'

'That you're stronger than me.'

'No. Try again,' Ramita snapped.

'That I'm not behaving well,' Corinea muttered. 'I'm sorry.'

Ramita straightened and slowly withdrew the energy, all the while holding it ready.

Holy Kore, she just faced down the Queen of Hel . . .

But the old woman on the floor looked nothing like the demoness of legend right now; she was just Lillea, an aged Estellan widow with a bruised throat and aching body, her youth and vitality a distant memory.

'Get up,' Ramita told Corinea, not turning her back.

Corinea groaned and got her feet under her, but she had to accept a hand from Alaron to stand. She looked at him from under lowered brows as he did, humiliated. 'My thanks, *lordship*,' she said in a low, resentful voice. 'I'm *so* grateful.'

'Why are you like this?' he asked tiredly. 'What have we done to you? Anyone else would have run screaming when you said your name. I don't understand your attitude: you came to us, remember?'

'*Think*, trader's son,' she panted. 'Think what would have been, had Johan not forced my hand. I would have been *empress*! Johan's tragic death would have left me, the tragic heiress of his movement, as the first and only Empress of Rondelmar. *I should have had EVERYTHING!*

And now, after lifetimes of hiding, it's come to this: I'm trailing after a fool, a peasant and a eunuch, hoping a group of emasculated hermits will take up arms against men born to fight and kill. And you say I should be *rejoicing* to be part of your pitiful venture?'

They greeted her words with stony silence. He'd seen something like this coming, though he'd not really seen the depths of her bitterness until now.

If things had turned out as she'd hoped, she'd have been no different from Sertain and the rest.

'Well, why don't you just rukk off and join Malevorn?' he offered, in his most reasonable voice. 'He's everything you seem to admire: a ruthless villain with a mountainous ego. I'm sure you'd get on famously.'

'I'm with you because there's no other choice – none at all,' she spat. 'But that doesn't mean I think you'll triumph. You asked once whether I'd rather choose a random village? The answer is yes, only I'd select a legion camp: I'd rather kill nine in ten, knowing at least that the remaining survivors were trained to kill.'

All right, she really is the Queen of Evil . . . Or maybe she's just a desperate old woman in desperate times . . .

'That won't be happening,' he said calmly. 'Never suggest it again.'

'You're an idealistic fool.'

'No. I learned more about how to fight here in this monastery than in six years at the Arcanum, and the same with the gnosis. So why don't you show a little faith?'

She snorted. 'Don't you know one of my many titles is "The Faithless One"?' But she looked away, her face more thoughtful than angry.

'Doesn't mean you have to live up to it.' He looked at Ramita, who caught and squeezed his hand briefly. It calmed him like nothing else could have.

'All right,' he said. 'Let's go and see the Master.'

Explaining to Master Puravai what had happened in Teshwallabad took a long time, and Alaron's voice was hoarse by the time he'd told it all: Hanook's true lineage, Ramita's betrothal arrangement with the young Mughal Tariq, and then the horrors of that night when Huriya and Malevorn attacked. He left out nothing: the bloodbath in Hanook's manor, the underground flight to the Mughal's Dome, and the loss of Nasatya and the Scytale. When he paused to recover, Ramita filled in the details, telling him about Mughal Tariq, and the nature of the Dome.

Puravai took some time to grieve over Hanook: in their youth they had been the closest of friends; though they had not met in years, the loss clearly hurt deeply.

Then it was time to outline their plan and beg Puravai's permission to implement it. Alaron explained everything that he had discovered and worked out about the Scytale before losing it.

Finally, he said, 'I have the crucial details of almost forty of your monks here. Remember? I researched their details when I still had the Scytale, trying to formulate the recipe that would give them the gnosis. At the time it was just an exercise, to try and understand the process better. Now it is a lifeline!

'Master, it is the dream of every mage – probably of every person in Yuros – to be made an Ascendant. They have stronger gnosis than even the pure-bloods.' He paused, worried the Master would think that power was all he cared about. 'I wouldn't offer this to someone I didn't think would use it well. You and your monks are the best people I have met, in Yuros or Antiopia.' He looked at Ramita, who smiled her encouragement as the old man remained silent, and said beseechingly, 'I know this is in part selfish. We *must* regain the Scytale – and Nasatya – from Malevorn and Huriya, and we can't do it alone. But it's far more than that. Even without that, I would still wish you to accept this gift.'

The room fell silent. Alaron realised he was holding his breath and released it slowly. Yash was fidgeting, barely able to contain himself from falling to his knees and begging the Master to allow him at least to try. Corinea's face was unreadable, and her mere presence made Alaron increasingly uneasy. He dreaded her opening her mouth.

'We Zains are sworn to peace,' Puravai said finally, his voice pitched as if he were speaking to someone unseen. 'We are permitted to defend ourselves, and others also. We step away from the world to understand it better, but we remain a part of it. Yet the principles of moksha are clear: we can only detach ourselves from this world having made peace with it.'

He took a sip of water and fell silent, as if listening for a god to reply.

'Power ... *absolute* power ... is a venom that poisons the soul,' he said eventually. 'To hold life and death in one's hands, unconstrained ... Who can deal with that and still keep their soul intact?'

He closed his eyes, though his lips continued to move in silent debate.

Alaron looked at Ramita, his heart beginning to sink. *He's going to refuse?*

Then his heart went to his mouth as a cool female voice cut across the silence.

'I rather think you're overstating the matter, Master Zain,' Corinea said, her voice dry. 'Even an Ascendant mage doesn't have ultimate power. There are already dozens of other Ascendants, hundreds of pure-bloods, and tens of thousands of less powerful magi – and several thousand Souldrinkers too, so they say. And there are millions upon millions of ordinary people. Even an Ascendant is only one fish in a turbulent ocean. I should know: I am one. Do you think I could walk into a city and demand the throne? I'd end up dead, or ruling a cemetery. Dominion over others requires more than just personal might. The world is vast, and it will pull down any tyrant eventually.'

Puravai turned to face her while Alaron and Ramita held their breath.

'Yet your "Blessed Three Hundred" conquered an empire,' Puravai replied, his face intent.

'And now look at them,' Corinea replied. 'Divided, tearing themselves apart, their dissipated bloodlines spreading across the lands while their secrets fall into the hands of their enemies. Kingdoms rise and fall. Sometimes it's swift, other times it's with a slow toppling, but it all ends in dust.'

'So you say that I should let my charges lose their souls to power, for in the end it won't matter? I believe it will: it will matter very much. Our lives are a quest for oneness. By allowing this to happen, I will be allowing these young men who have put their souls in my charge to damn themselves.'

'Don't be so pompous! You're giving them a little gnosis, not the keys of Pallas! The gnosis is only one form of power in this world, and it ranks far below many: like legitimate kingship, or religious supremacy. Though by your terms maybe it is the ultimate test: can they stick to their vows in the face of real evil, not just the slow insanity of staring at brick walls until their eyesight goes? I've read your books, Zain: your guru talks about testing the soul, but you just hide away – that's not *overcoming* a test, that's *sidestepping* it. If you think your charges can handle some real tests, then you should be begging us for this opportunity, not whining about it.'

Alaron stared at her. *Well, that's rich, coming from you* . . . It was also most of the things he'd have said if he had the courage to do so. He turned back to look at Puravai, dreading what he might see.

The old Master chuckled wryly. 'Why, Mistress Lily, you're what we call an Early Rationalist. It is a view we respect. But even you must agree that there is an eternal aspect to who and what we are. Your gnosis is based upon it: *the soul*. Even you magi cannot say what occurs when soul and body finally part. Antonin Meiros himself has agreed that the teachings of Zain are as rational and lucid as any religion.'

'That's a low hurdle,' Corinea drawled.

Alaron's heart went to his mouth at the jest, but Puravai only chuckled. The old Master leaned forward, licking his lips, and when Corinea mirrored the monk's posture, Alaron realised that the argument had been effectively removed from his hands.

'Er . . . I think that the danger we face is rather more tangible than philosophical,' he pointed out.

Puravai was still looking at Corinea. 'All matters are governed by philosophy. The decision to kill one ant or ten thousand men is the same moral choice.'

'But the scale cannot be ignored,' Corinea scoffed. 'Otherwise we'd be hanging men for treading on beetles.'

'The teachings of Zain are clear on this point,' Puravai replied, and launched into a diatribe on ethics of the sort that Alaron had slumbered through many times at the Arcanum.

<What do I do?> Alaron asked Ramita silently.

<Let them talk. They seem to be enjoying it.>

<But—>

<Have you something further to contribute to this sort of conversation?>

<No. They're way past me already.>

<Well, then.> Ramita stood. 'I'm tired,' she said simply, as everyone turned to her. She bowed respectfully to Master Puravai. 'I do hope you enjoy your talking, and please don't overlook the fact that the life of my son hangs on the outcome of your debate, not just the fate of the world.' She held out a hand to Alaron. 'Will you show me the way back, bhaiya? I don't remember all the turns.'

Leaving the room felt like ceding power, but the debate had already left them both behind. Alaron looked at Yash, who shrugged, and indicated that he would come too. Corinea lifted her chin with the faintest air of dismissal. He bit his lip, then bowed also. 'I too will trust in your wisdom, Master Puravai.'

They walked in silence back to their quarters. He appreciated why Ramita had taken him out: anything he said would have sounded childish. *Better to be silent and thought a fool than to speak and remove all doubt*, his father liked to say.

They wished Yash goodnight, then paused in the lounge. Alone.

'What will be will be,' Ramita said quietly.

'I don't trust her,' Alaron said.

'Nor I, but in this she wants the same as us.' She squeezed his fingers in her small, tough hands. 'I've finished weaning Dasra,' she added, a little sadly.

'You need to thank the Omali Goddess of Weaning,' he replied cheekily. 'I presume there is one?'

'At least three.' Ramita plucked at the rakhi-string on his wrist. 'Thank you for standing by me, bhaiya. I don't know if I could do this alone.'

'I know I couldn't,' he replied, feeling his heart quicken. *Kore's Blood, I need to kiss her . . .*

She started to say something, but he didn't want to hear it, in case it was 'goodnight'. Two steps. That's all it would take. Before he could talk himself out of it he moved, bent, and kissed her small mouth. For a moment she was frozen, and he was scared that he'd made an awful mistake, then she seized him, went up on tiptoes and mashed her lips to his. Her small but full body pressed against his lean chest, the thin cotton they wore the merest of barriers. His mouth never leaving hers, he lifted her and seated her on the table, tasting her spice and salt, breathing her breath, while his heart hammered and his skin felt as if it was catching alight.

How long the kiss went on he couldn't tell, for he was living only from one slow moment to the next, his fingers stroking her neck and her bound-up hair, feeling the shape of her spine under the thin kameez, while his tongue tasted hers. He poured all his need for her, for her reassurance and comfort and affection and trust, into that kiss, even as he marvelled to be so close, to touch her skin, to breathe in her unique scents, to finally, openly, hold her as if he would never let her go.

'Bhaiya,' she whispered at last, 'it isn't good for brother and sister to be like this.'

He felt a sudden, crushing sense of loss. *She tied that rakhi string on me to prevent this very thing . . .* Was it even him she'd been kissing, in her mind, or someone else: her dead husband, perhaps, the mighty Antonin Meiros? Or the childhood sweetheart, Kazim? Who was he, a mere trader's son, and a ferang at that, compared to such memories?

He tried to swallow his disappointment, whispering, 'I'm sorry, I—'

She put a finger to his lips to silence him, then seized his right wrist and snapped the rakhi string.

'Now,' she whispered, 'I think we were kissing, yes?'

The door opened, and then the shutters, while Ramita struggled to work out where she was, tangled in blissfully clean, fresh-smelling sheets, naked and alone. She blinked at the sudden sunlight carving up the shadows as a female voice coughed and said in an arch voice, 'I'm rather surprised to find you on your own in here.'

Ramita pulled the sheets up and looked around, seeking the nightshirt she'd cast off in the night. Her blood had been pumping madly and she was too hot to sleep; she'd been tossing and turning for hours, too many thoughts galloping through her brain. 'What time is it?'

'Mid-morning,' Corinea replied, adding with a sniff, 'The young are so fragile. A little lost sleep and they can barely cope.'

Ramita forced herself to concentrate on the here and now. 'You are finished talking already?'

'It was an excellent debate,' Corinea said with some relish. 'It has been far too long since I've had the pleasure. I love a good argument. A shame it didn't lead to another type of bout, but he's taken one of those stupid chastity vows.'

Ramita pulled on her nightshirt, trying not to think about ancient monks and sorceresses lying together, though her heart was singing this morning and any kind of love felt like a good thing.

How she'd pulled herself away, she had no idea. She'd not had such an evening since she'd first fallen in love with Kazim on the rooftop of the family house, kissing passionately under the stars, and all the while dreading the sound of Father or Mother's footsteps. Somehow she'd remained a virgin despite the temptation – she'd been too scared of the consequences of weakness, and of the shame succumbing to the man she adored would bring. But last night, holding Al'Rhon – *my cuddly Goat* – had been a true torment, because nowadays she knew *exactly* what she was missing. Desire had almost overwhelmed her as she recalled how good lovemaking could be – as it had been with her husband, despite the age difference.

She had kept her senses enough to remind herself that a dutiful Lakh girl does not lay with a man outside of wedlock. That, and only that, held her back from the consummation she so badly wanted.

Alaron had not pressed the point, and she'd liked that, too. Her bhaiya . . . *no, no, not brother, not any more!* . . . had been a gentleman, in his foreign Rondian way. He'd kept his hands in seemly places and his private parts to himself, and that had felt right. The kiss had been enough, for now; there was no shame, nothing for either of them to be embarrassed of in the cold light of day – only a warm glow, and a longing to see him again.

Then she remembered why they'd been alone in the first place: others were deciding their fate – and the fate of her stolen son.

'So?' she asked Corinea in a hollow voice.

The old sorceress slowly smiled. 'The choice will be made by each potential candidate in turn.' She posed like a dancer taking applause. 'You may thank me as you see fit.'

6

The Valley of Tombs

Hunting for Ghosts

There is an intriguing thought that underpins the gnosis – that if everybody has a soul, and that soul dwells for a time in the aether before passing on to another place – then every person who ever lived, lives still! In particular, the quest to find and commune with the soul of Corineus has consumed many a life, and goes on even today in some religious orders.

BROTHER ZEBASTIEN, KORE SCHOLAR, 787

Valley of Tombs, Gatioch, on the continent of Antiopia
Shawwal (Octen) 929
16th month of the Moontide

Stark shafts of light cut the valley into geometric patterns of sand and shadow as the westering sun painted the cratered face of the moon in pale pinks and sullen crimson. Malevorn Andevarion climbed to the crest of a giant edifice in the Valley of Tombs, a memorial to a dead empire spread out at his feet.

Even he, a native of Pallas, couldn't help shivering in awe at the sight. He'd never thought to see anything to rival the famed Imperial Bastion in Pallas, but this place, even abandoned and falling into decay, took the breath away. Huriya, using Sabele's stolen memories, had told him the history of Gatioch, a kingdom to rival Kesh before the coming of the Amteh faith. The Valley of Tombs was where their kings and queens, princes and princesses and lords of high state had been buried. The gigantic monuments housed deeply buried tombs,

99

all richly adorned with the half-beast, half-man gods of the Gatti. Giant men with cobra heads, the details crumbling but still discernible, stood eternally on guard.

'Most were plundered long ago,' Huriya had told him. 'But there are still tombs to be found, supposedly crammed with grave goods.'

The Souldrinker pack that haunted these wastelands was smaller than Huriya's had been, but that still gave them an extra fifty much-needed fighters, mostly men of Gatioch, with tangled facial and body tattoos depicting the old gods. The Amteh might have thought they'd quashed the old religions, but such gods had only gone into hiding; they were still worshipped by many of the nomadic tribes of the deserts.

Distant movement drove the memories from his mind. Riders were filing into the valley a mile away.

Adamus has taken the bait ... He took a deep breath and kindled his wards, making sure there was nothing to show that he was anything other than alone. He hoped the arriving riders couldn't sense that the tombs below were crawling with Dokken.

He was standing beside an old altar on a dais some fifty feet above an open space in the heart of the valley, between two huge statues of alligator-headed men. He loosed his scimitar and sent his senses questing outwards.

If I were in charge, I'd have men in the air above, hidden by Illusion ...

Adamus Crozier had been deeply suspicious when Malevorn had finally managed to contact him, and reeling him in had been a delicate negotiation. He'd not at first been inclined to believe Malevorn's story, that he'd managed to escape from the Souldrinker pack he'd been captured by and hadn't been able to call for help until he'd created a relay-stave. It was only when he told Adamus that he had news of the Scytale that he'd managed to lure the clergyman here.

There were five riders approaching openly, riding khurnes, the new intelligent construct-beast: horned horses based on a mythic Lantric creature. His link to Huriya revealed four other Inquisitors on foot, two on either flank, creeping stealthily through the ruins. That left two unaccounted for, assuming Adamus had brought a full

Fist of ten Inquisitors. It was months since Malevorn had been taken, and they might have suffered further losses, but he couldn't afford to make such assumptions. *I know we've got the local Dokken onside now, but even with the whole pack, this could go badly wrong.* He straightened his back. *So I have to make sure it goes right.*

<*Acolyte Malevorn.*> Adamus Crozier's voice shimmered into his head and he squinted into the dying light, identifying the crozier as the middle of the five approaching down the central aisle, riding bareheaded, his bushy curls framing an olive-skinned face. The rest were armoured, sporting tabards of black and white. They'd be on high alert, gnostic senses no doubt fully extended. It was obvious to even an amateur just what a trap this warren of stone was, perfect for hiding and ambushing, while the rock hindered scrying. But none of them would be less than a half-blood and they'd all been trained to exacting standards of sword and gnosis.

Hopefully, they think I'm alone . . .

<*My Lord Crozier, welcome,*> he sent back. He glanced left and right, where he guessed other Inquisitors might be closing in, cloaked by Illusion. <*Tell those flanking me to pull back. They're making me nervous.*>

Adamus paused and looked up at him from the middle of the square below. Some kind of signal pulsed and he glimpsed a shimmer amongst the shadows to his right. His throat went just that bit drier. He kept his eyes on Adamus, calculating when the blow would fall.

Stepping to the edge of the tomb, he waited as the crozier urged his khurne forward, trailed by Commandant Fronck Quintius, the commander of the Fist. Malevorn raised a hand to stop the clergyman some forty yards from the foot of the tomb – too much closer and the taint in his aura might be discernible.

'Thank you for coming, Lord Crozier,' he called, making the Imperial salute. 'You have travelled a long way.'

'But to an impressive place,' Adamus replied. 'Quite the wonder, is it not?'

'Why did you not come to us?' Quintius called sourly, interrupting the niceties.

'I have also had to journey far to get here,' Malevorn lied. 'This was the easiest place to find that was equidistant. I have come from far east of here.'

Adamus and Quintius exchanged looks. The crozier cut to the chase. 'And you have news of the Scytale?'

Malevorn tapped the scroll-case hooked to his sword belt. 'I have more than just news of it.'

Surprise and greed flashed across both men's faces. Adamus leaned forward in the saddle. *'You have it?'*

Malevorn couldn't resist puffing out his chest. 'Not here. This is just the case it was found in.' He tossed it into the air and used his gnosis to drop it into the crozier's outstretched hand.

Adamus examined it carefully while Quintius watched, suspicion plain on his face. 'Well?' the commandant demanded.

'This is genuine,' Adamus admitted. 'I've held it before, in Pallas. Where did you get it, Brother Malevorn?'

So I'm your 'Brother' again, am I?

'The Dokken had indeed taken it,' Malevorn said, 'but they realised they couldn't decipher it. I tracked them all the way from southern Kesh to the mountains of Mirobez, as they sought knowledge, until I was able to steal it from them. Since then, I have been on the run . . .'

'Have they tracked you here, Brother Malevorn?'

'I lost them weeks ago.'

Quintius nudged his khurne closer. 'What is it you actually want, Andevarion? Your clear duty is to return this sacred artefact to the crozier and me. You will be amply rewarded.'

Sure I will. With a knife in the back.

'You must excuse my caution, Commandant, but when I and my colleagues were beset at the Dokken camp you abandoned us – so you will understand that I don't know if I can trust you.'

Quintius' rugged face hardened. 'You're in a military unit, Andevarion. We had other issues to deal with. We trusted you and your comrades to hold the Dokken outliers at bay – it was you who failed, not us.'

'I don't see it that way, Commandant.' Malevorn looked beyond the two leaders to the three riders behind them. He could see Artus

LeBlanc, his old rival, among them. 'The taunting from Brother Artus as my comrades fell around me, their bodies ripped apart, their souls eaten, still rings in my ears.'

Quintius threw an irritated glance over his shoulder. 'Brother Artus might have overstepped, Andevarion, but it's not his fault your comrades' blades were slow.'

Adamus Crozier hissed at him to shut up and raised a hand to command silence, clearly concerned that the commandant was antagonising the only person who knew where the Scytale was. 'Brother Malevorn, you have my personal guarantee of safety, and the right to the full rewards promised for the recovery this treasure. You will be publically acknowledged as a Hero of the Empire, and treated as such.'

Malevorn doubted his words meant a thing, but he bowed from the waist and let a look of relief cross his face. 'Then please come ahead, my Lord Crozier. I have something for you.'

The churchman's face lit up as he heard Malevorn's words. 'I'll handle this. You stay where you are,' he told Quintius. He dismounted, handed the commandant his reins, then walked confidently to the stairs leading to the dais Malevorn was standing on, his hands palm-side up, as if to demonstrate that he had no aggressive intent.

Malevorn wasn't fooled for an instant. The air around the crozier was positively crackling with energy.

As soon as he gets to the top of these stairs he's going to realise I'm a Dokken.

Malevorn had chosen the Valley of Tombs for this encounter for three reasons: first, because there was no one here to interrupt or report their preparations; second, because of the warren of tunnels and chambers beneath the sand and stone; no one could be scryed, but they could reach the surface in moments. And third, because it was a maze, strung-out groups could be split up and isolated.

But they were taking on eleven of the empire's best-trained warriors, in a confined area, where even the element of surprise would be short-lived. Any advantage would be lost if they didn't take down some of the Inquisitors in the first few seconds.

He stepped from the rim of the tomb, into the shadow of one of the giant alligator-men, putting himself out of Quintius' line of sight. He heard consternation in the voices below.

He'd specified sunset for very clear reasons: when the sun was gone, spirits were more easily summoned. *After all, what is this place but an enormous cemetery?*

While Huriya had started charming Xymoch, the Gatioch pack-leader, Malevorn had set to work on binding dead spirits to freshly culled bodies from the nearest villages. It had taken three weeks, but he had eighteen walking corpses – *draugs* – waiting in the tombs below. Now, as the last rays of the sun vanished from the west and the valley fell into shadow, just as Adamus Crozier stepped onto the platform, he released their bindings.

The crozier's soft-featured face stiffened in sudden alarm as he saw Malevorn, closer than expected and with a totally unexpected aura boiling with tentacle-like strands: *a Dokken!* His shields flared as he stared, and Malevorn realised he was trying to determine whether he faced the real Malevorn Andevarion.

Malevorn didn't give him time to work things out: vultures shrieked high overhead and dived through the purple hazy sky, beasts howled somewhere among the tombs, the ground churned as his draugs began to crawl from their tombs – and his scimitar leapt to his hand, igniting with gnosis-fire as he attacked the crozier.

Huriya Makani stepped from the subterranean passage into the twilight in the wake of a flood of shapechangers roiling into the open air in a variety of reptilian shapes. It was a real relief to be out at last; they'd been hiding underground for three days to avoid scrying, using the vast underground network the Gatioch kings had left behind.

Bringing the Gatti Souldrinkers onside had been a delicate matter: Xymoch their leader also carried the soul of an original Ascendant, borne through body after body for five centuries. He might have strangely lidded eyes, tattoos and twisted religious beliefs, but he was Huriya's equal in power, a man to be reckoned with who controlled his pack with vicious discipline. His people lived in terror of the brightly coloured snakes that were constantly slithering about his arms and torso.

As well as employing her own natural cunning, she had needed once more to draw on Sabele's knowledge, and she *hated* that. Every time she used Sabele's intellect, she could feel the old spider weaving more intricate webs around her brain. But it had been Sabele's wisdom that had made the difference in persuading Xymoch to aid them, instead of turning on them as he'd been inclined.

Now they had finally been unleashed, the Souldrinkers poured eagerly into the fray, bursting forth from the tombs in a dozen different places; most in reptilian forms that hissed and snapped as they stormed towards the Inquisitors.

Sixty-odd Dokken and eighteen of Malevorn's draugs against eleven Inquisitors . . . I hope it's enough.

The Rondians were split in four groups: five in the central plaza, two pairs skulking on the flanks and another pair circling overhead on winged constructs, concealed by gnostic illusions. The Souldrinkers were also divided. On all sides she heard shrieks and yowls as burly shapechangers in half-human forms stormed ahead of her towards the plaza. Her shields formed as she walked, flanked by men of her group: the boar-headed Sydian Tkwir and Toljin the Vereloni. Hessaz was somewhere on the far side, seeking a vantage point from where she could best employ her lethal bow. The rest of her pack were aloft, to deal with the venators and their riders.

Below the clamour was another sound: a faint hiss that rose as they walked. She heard shouting, felt staccato bursts of gnostic energy and light flashed through the gaps in the stone. Then flame washed overhead, torching the leading Dokken before dissipating on the shields of those behind. Xymoch's people screamed in fury and stormed along their designated approach routes. Huriya extended her own awareness as she followed Tkwir; her role was to cripple the minds of enemies from a distance, as she had done when they'd captured Malevorn. She had found to her shame that she did not deal well with direct threats.

She took up position in the mouth of a ruined stone crocodile overlooking the plaza. Toljin stood beside her, scimitar drawn and snorting like a bull. She watched as Dokken ran to engage the Inquisitors before they could reunite. In the sky above, the two venators were now clearly visible as they fought off a swarm of shape-changers. The venator riders were spraying bolts of mage-fire as they descended, and one bolt of lightning caught a winged reptilian Dokken and charred him to black ashes that drifted on the wind. She sought the lightning-wielder and saw a man on a rearing khurne in the plaza. She narrowed her eyes and reached . . .

. . . into the khurne.

Her intention had been to close down the beast's mind, a comparatively simple spell, for the minds of beasts were more vulnerable than human ones, but what she found was a landscape so strange it sucked her right in. This was a place where a beast's memories merged with those of a human in a bizarre swirl of thoughts: horse-headed women ploughed arid farms under searing suns; winged men galloped across the skies, wrapped in chains of throbbing sound and light. Commands from the voice of a god drove the khurne this way and that, bewildering Huriya until she realised in shock: *There's a person inside that creature!*

She reached again, differently this time, gripped and spoke her own command while sending a blaze of energy into the link that bound the creature to its master. The rider's wards weakened her spell, but it still took effect: the khurne reared up unexpectedly, hurling the Inquisitor from its back, and drove its horn into the unwarded back of the man in front, punching through the steel back-plate and straight into the man's flesh. The rider bellowed in agony, his sword slipping from his numbed grasp.

Blades plunged into the khurne's side from two directions, but Huriya had already let go. She reached for another, but this time her attack was slapped aside as the Inquisitors adapted to the new threat. Heads turned in her direction and she shivered in sudden fear as an armoured gauntlet rose: the lightning-wielder was now standing beside his fallen steed with blinding white light boiling in his fist.

He released it straight at her – just as Sabele, lurking like a viper, made a bid to seize control, leaving Huriya paralysed before the Inquisitor's bolt—

Malevorn's scimitar blazed against the crozier's shields while his left hand was hurling kinetic force into the churchman's flank. If Adamus hadn't been prepared, the sword would have skewered his thigh, then the kinesis would have battered him into the wall, but it didn't work out that way.

Using his crosier staff to deflect the scimitar, he stood his ground, his expression one of mild disappointment, as if a promising child had let him down. He twisted the shaft of the crosier and blades slid from either end as the shepherd's crook at the top became a sword-catcher. He flowed into a fluid, well-practised stance, his full lips baring his perfect teeth in a fixed smile.

'So, they've turned you against us,' he noted sadly. 'It can be undone, Brother.'

Malevorn hesitated, as he was no doubt supposed to. *Is it true?* If it was, it could change all he was about to do.

Or does it? They betrayed me before . . .

He closed down that line of thought and lashed out.

Andevarion has betrayed us – I knew he would! Artus LeBlanc yanked his blade from the flank of Brother Nayland's khurne, the rogue one that had spiked Brother Magrenius. He glanced up and saw Malevorn Andevarion fighting Adamus Crozier, but before he could react he found himsef shielding against a reaching mind of massive strength: someone was trying to snatch control of his khurne. He looked around, trying to spot the danger, and spotted a small Keshi woman standing in the mouth of a giant stone statue above. But before he could take her on, a crowd of snake-headed, tattooed men burst into the plaza, roaring their fury and hatred.

Nayland, now dismounted, loosed lightning at the Keshi woman, while LeBlanc widened his shields to protect the beast beneath him and edged sideways to allow Commandant Quintius to close up, forming a circle around the fallen Magrenius. Quintius was blasting away with mage-bolts while Margrenius used necromantic-gnosis to keep himself alive, then clambered to his feet with the broken horn still in his back. Nayland blazed more lightning, but a glance told Artus the space where that little Keshi bint had been was now empty.

Then the plaza turned into a vision of Hel.

As fire poured from Quintius' hands, painting the square a lurid orange, the flagstones at the sides rose and flipped over, and from beneath rose ragged bodies, long dead, but lit with a feral violet light. Snakes were coiled about their limbs, and more serpents boiled from the ground, moving in a wriggling wave towards the embattled Inquisitors.

LeBlanc roared in defiance, blazing mage-fire along his sword at the nearest walking corpse. Pure-blood force went searing through flesh to the trapped soul beneath and the draug shrieked, crisped and fell, toasted snakes dropping from it like blackened noodles. Quintius gushed fire too, torching a lizard-headed woman brandishing a spear and the three men behind her.

The four outriders who had been guarding the main party's flanks signalled that they were coming in.

<We'll link up and fight our way out of this!> Artus crowed. <We're invincible!>

He blasted another animated corpse, then set a wall of flame blazing across the path of the snakes, keeping them at bay. Brother Magrenius might have been half-dead, but he kept fighting; he and Brother Nayland duplicated Artus' wall, enclosing them in a circle of gnostic-fire. Outside it, the shadows had become black. His khurne, locked to his will in case that Keshi girl reappeared, stood steady as a rock, poised to fight if needed.

He took a moment to glance up: the two on the venators were beset by vultures and winged Dokken – then the beastmen on the ground hurled themselves at the fiery barriers, led by more of the walking corpses, and all his thoughts narrowed down to survival.

Lightning blazed from the hand of the Inquisitor, straight at Huriya – and just as she had in Teshwallabad, during the attack on Vizier

Hanook, she found herself immobile, paralysed by fear – of pain, of wounding, of disfigurement and death. And Sabele seized the moment—

—but Toljin, unaware of the battle within Huriya's mind for possession, saw only the Inquisitor's strike. He hurled himself at the Seeress, bearing her to ground, and the blazing light that would have cooked her in an eye-blink instead shattered stone above them, sending chips and fragments flying across the platform. Toljin's shields were shredded and he himself was grazed and battered, but he had saved her.

That jolt had another effect: it pulled Huriya's mind from its downward spiral, the pain of being slammed to the ground yanking her out of the web Sabele had woven for her. Suddenly aware again, she shredded the insidious attack, then pulled herself to her feet. She noted Tkwir had hurled himself sideways as the lightning blazed too – but away from it, not shielding her as Toljin had. *I'll deal with that one later.*

Those Dokken still able to fight jumped from the ledge into the plaza below, but the sound of hooves on stone made her turn: one of the Inquisitor's horned beasts was leaping with gnosis-assisted grace and power from the roof of one tomb to another, his rider cutting down Xymoch's archers as it headed straight for her. As it landed, the khurne's horn slammed through the side of a poorly shielded Dokken while the Inquisitor, a grey-haired, scar-faced man, swung his sword at Tkwir.

Again fear froze her in place as Tkwir, too slow to react, took the Inquisitor's longsword in his chest. The Sydian grunted and sagged, then toppled backwards from the platform.

The Inquisitor focused on her, an arrogant smile on his face as he sized her up.

Fury kicked in, overcoming her fear.

Her gnosis was primarily mind-magic, Clairvoyance and Divination, but she could also wield Mesmerism and Illusion. As the Inquisitor turned on them, she took all of Sabele's hatred from centuries of pogroms against her kind – the Souldrinkers, God's Rejects, the magi's oldest enemy – and sent it pounding into this devoted knight of the Church. For a few seconds his shields gave her no grip, but she was an Ascendant. The Illusion of darkness took: for a split-second, the Inquisitor couldn't see, and then his mind-shield cracked and she could sense his sudden terror, blinded in the face of his enemies. She melded that fear into an attack, feeding it while closing down his senses with more illusory darkness, grimacing in satisfaction as he shouted in horror, his eyes searching blankly. Then one of Xymoch's Dokken punched a spear into the Inquisitor's khurne and yanked and the barbed spearhead pulled out bloody coils of the beast's intestines. It shrilled horribly and collapsed, breaking the Inquisitor's leg as it fell, and before he'd even hit the ground Toljin had driven his scimitar through the knight's chest. He looked up despairingly, his vision clearing only to see his own death.

One down, she thought grimly, looking at the carnage about her. She had a method now, a way to attack. She stepped to the edge of the platform again and checked out the battle below: immediately beneath, four Inquisitors were penned in a circle of blue fire. To her right, Malevorn and the crozier were locked in combat. And above, the venators were circling closer, unhampered by the trailing vultures.

She began to fear that eighty against eleven might not be enough after all.

It has to be.

She selected her next target: the commandant.

Malevorn's scimitar struck sparks on Adamus' crozier as he ducked under a sweeping counterblow aiming to take off his arm and spun away. Another close-range mage-bolt flared off his shields, staggering him backwards towards an edge he'd momentarily lost track of. He hurled loose rubble at the churchman with a gesture, planted his feet again and piled forward.

When he'd planned this attack, his first priority had been to isolate Adamus and take him alive – he'd been certain that he was the man's better with both blade and the gnosis. He was beginning to revise that opinion now: the crozier's gnosis was rooted in Fire and

Air, but he was using other disciplines with flair to create a potent mix of mental and physical attacks, wielded with cunning and guile. And his crosier was a surprisingly effective weapon, one that could be switched from defence to attack in a heartbeat.

They circled again, both panting heavily, and Adamus puffed out, 'We can heal you, Brother. Nasette's fate is known to us – we've studied it. We can restore you to what you were, this I swear.'

The plaza below was a deadly maelstrom of flaming fire and clashing blades and ripping claws, and the flashes and blasts were coming ever closer. He couldn't tell what was happening except that shouts of triumph were few. Inquisitors habitually fought in near silence, but the Dokken were savages, and their silence was ominous.

Are we losing this?

'I wrote to your family when you fell,' Adamus added slyly. 'I told them you were dead. Can you imagine their despair? Think on their shame, if they could see what has really become of you . . .'

Before he'd even finished speaking he attacked, whirling into a spinning flurry, alternating between each end of the staff, then slashing low, an attack Malevorn barely managed to leap – but it was all a distraction, he realised too late: a shadow fell over him and his eyes went upwards just as a reptilian head with jaws wide enough to engulf a pig plunged towards him. Behind him, Adamus sprang into the air – and just kept going, elevated by swiftly deployed Air-gnosis.

There was no time to do anything but scream in dismay and fury as the giant beast ploughed into him and the open jaws fastened onto him with a metallic crunch. A dozen knife-long teeth slammed into his torso and thighs.

His cry was torn from his throat as he was snatched into the air.

Artus LeBlanc saw the moment the battle changed. They'd flung back the wave of Dokken and the walking dead, pouring mage-fire and lightning and flames into the mass as they came, incinerating them en masse as they crossed the gnostic barrier. Then they started targeting individuals, singling out the biggest and deadliest attackers, like the axe-wielding man with the garish tattoos and the screaming woman with snake-hair, roasting them alive, leaving Magrenius to use his own Necromancy to snuff out the violet light of the animated walking corpses. For a few moments, he really thought they would triumph.

That all changed in a blink of the eye.

He'd glanced upwards to determine how far they were from the stairs and reaching the crozier above, but that brief glimpse took in the Keshi girl, standing at the lip of the platform to his left, pointing at Quintius, then he saw one of the venators engulfed by Dokken, the beast and its rider thrashing about desperately in the air. The other venator was diving with jaws wide open towards Malevorn Andevarion's back.

Get him! Artus thought, his eyes glowing with elation – then an arrow with a glowing tip blasted through weak shielding and shot the venator in the eye.

Its jaws slackened even as it struck Andevarion, closing on him convulsively, but as the arrow entered its brain and the tip exploded, all its strength vanished as completely as a snuffed candle. The venator died instantly, its neck flailing convulsively as the left wing caught the leaping Adamus in mid-air and slammed him with massive force into one of the giant statues. The clergyman crumpled limply while the beast ploughed on, striking the platform with its hind legs and flipping, crushing its rider in a hideous crunch of metal and flesh before catapulting into another tomb, breaking the roof and crashing through.

For an instant all eyes followed it, then flew back to the crozier, lying twisted and still on the stairs. Artus felt stunned, disbelieving, and for an instant his brain couldn't grasp what he'd seen.

Then the Keshi girl shrieked in triumph and black unlight engulfed Quintius. It was as if night itself had become a living entity and snatched Quintius away. He heard the commandant roar in defiance, then bellow in horror; he tore the darkness away with a blazing counterblow of light, but it was too late; the Dokken were pouring in. Leblanc saw a man with snakes for arms and a cobra's head leap onto Nayland, and all three venomous jaws plunged into the Inquisitor's flesh, punching through armour as if it were cloth.

Artus LeBlanc cut another draug in half, kicking the still animated body away. A serpent bit his shin-guard and he stamped on its head, then drove his sword right through Cobrahead's left eye as something hit him from behind and latched on, gnawing at the back of his neck. He reversed his blade and stabbed blindly as a ropy coil of snake whipped about him. As his khurne toppled, its legs tangled in a seething mass of serpents, he caught a glimpse of Quintius, staring blindly upwards, then plunging his fingers into his own eye sockets. Magrenius, still with a khurne horn sticking out of his back, was felled by a draug: it took the Inquisitor's skull in both hands and twisted, and the snap of his neck echoed clear through the din.

Then Artus yowled in agony as a blade crunched through his left leg at knee-height and he lost his balance and fell. As he rolled on the ground, he gaped down at his body, past the snake coiling around his torso to the gushing stump where his left knee should have been. A python head reared in front of his face; he screamed, and after that the darkness came swiftly.

Huriya Makani turned from the blood and death below, panting like a dog. She was standing alone in the mouth of the giant crocodile-headed statue, amidst the wreckage of the Inquisitor and his steed and the Dokken dead. Below, the plaza was seething with serpents and the Dokken were backing away: the snakes, whipped to a frenzy by the Souldrinker Animagi, were beyond control; it would be hours before they slunk back to their holes and reverted to simple beasts again.

Her skin was slick with sweat, her bloodied clothes clinging closely to her as she trembled in the aftermath of the carnage. She recalled what it had been like to stare in helpless dread at the end of her life. *But I survived.* She felt stronger, somehow, for that brush with death.

She turned to Toljin, who was staring at her with rabid hunger and lust, pounding with blood and life, alive as only surviving such moments could make one; she recognised those feelings in herself. He wanted her, palpably, and for a moment she was tempted to give in, to let him do whatever he wanted.

No. If I want to rule these people, I have to master myself.

113

But that inner voice wasn't even her own, she realised. It was Sabele, thinking for her. She quelled the panic; Sabele and her skills had kept her alive today. She was beginning to doubt she could do this alone . . . and to realise that maybe she didn't need to.

I've been trying to rule my body alone. But this isn't a war . . . it's a merging.

Yes, girl, a dry inner voice responded, drawing near. *At last.*

Malevorn came to himself lying in semi-darkness soaked in fluids he couldn't identify, his body feeling like a giant ruptured boil. Anything that didn't sting ached. There was something or someone scrabbling in the rocks above. He blinked furiously, tried to will movement back into his limbs, deathly afraid that whoever was coming for him might be here to administer the *coup de grâce*. He sat up painfully, couldn't find his scimitar, but his knife was still in his sword belt. He drew it, trying to ignore his shaking hand, and kindled a gnosis-light.

For a moment he was stunned motionless. He was lying in a tomb chamber laid open to the night sky by a massive hole in the roof. There were no grave goods, so it was likely it had already been found and robbed, but the walls were covered with pictograms and depictions of Gatioch's old gods. In the midst of it all was the dead venator, an arrow jutting from its right eye: a miracle shot, to penetrate shields on a venator in full flight at just the right place to actually do real damage if it got through. *Incredible*, he thought. *Fluke or genius?* Right now he didn't really care.

The venator's rider was still strapped into his saddle, but his body was so badly contorted he couldn't possibly still be alive. His head hung at a sickening angle, and his limbs were all snapped or twisted.

The noise was someone who'd been climbing down into the chamber. Now she stepped into the light: Hessaz, an arrow nocked and trained on him. Her hard face showed no emotion as she recognised him.

Holy Kore, we must've won . . .

He could see the war in her eyes, but he had his faculties back now, enough to shield fully. Shields could hinder unseen blows a little, but against known attacks they were at their most effective.

Even though the Dokken were not well-trained in the gnosis, she'd know that.

Good to know where I stand with you, Hessaz, he thought, *though I think I knew anyway.*

'Is the crozier alive?' he asked, standing shakily, pretending he had no doubt she wouldn't shoot him.

Her face split into a rare smile. 'He is.'

Praise Kore . . . Then he smiled at himself. *I must learn some different oaths; the Kore ones are hardly appropriate any more.*

7

New Alliances

Daemons

The souls of the dead are not the only beings in the aether. There are many spirits native to that element. Most are insignificant and of little threat, though they can be useful tools. A Wizard can use them to perform simple tasks for him. But there are large aetheric entities too, beings that prey on the living and dead. Some believe there is no Paradise and no Hel – that all that awaits us are these daemons, waiting to harvest our souls as we pass from the world of the living to the long slow night of death.

ORDO COSTRUO COLLEGIATE, HEBUSALIM

Near Brochena, Javon, on the continent of Antiopia
Shawwal (Octen) 929
16th month of the Moontide

Gurvon Gyle, drably clad in browns and cowled against the sun, nudged his horse forward. Rutt Sordell, similarly attired, followed close behind as they made their way along the causeway through rice paddies southwest of Brochena. Canals carried all the fertile filth of the city to these growing fields, and the verdant lushness here was a stark contrast to the arid dust and rock that bordered the heavily irrigated paddies, making them look garish and overripe, almost diseased. Many were dried out though, through lack of manpower, as so many farmers had fled the area.

'Boss, here they come,' Rutt said, his voice tense.

Gurvon squinted against the glare of the sun at the two riders trotting toward them. As they drew near he could see both were richly attired in Imperial purple and sweating heavily in the Rondian clothes, woven for far colder climes than this. 'Perhaps if we keep them talking for long enough they'll faint from the heat,' he remarked.

As usual, Rutt took the jest seriously. 'I doubt it – they'll use gnosis to regulate their body-heat if it becomes—'

'I know that, Rutt,' Gurvon sighed. 'Never mind.' He looked the newcomers up and down, assessing their threat. Both wore their empty scabbards ostentatiously, but that meant little; there were plenty of places for hidden weapons, which was to be expected – he had one himself. And both were magi: weapons in human form. It just came down to caution: don't give the other party reason to think they could get away with treachery.

I really do just want to talk today.

'Magister Gyle,' rumbled Governor Tomas Betillon as he reined in forty yards away. He glanced at Rutt appraisingly, then introduced his companion, a grey-bearded Kirkegarde knight with the usual humourless face and steely eyes. 'This is Blan Remikson, Seer of the Fourth Kirkegarde Legion.'

Gyle vaguely knew the name; Remikson was a half-blood, which was what Betillon had promised, a balance for the mage's blood in this parley. They all assessed each other silently for a few moments, then he said, 'So, Tomas, I hear Kaltus Korion wouldn't send you any reinforcements.'

Betillon pulled a face. 'He's spread thin. No thanks to you stealing three of his legions.'

'And you "borrowing" another two. But that's old news.'

Betillon ran fingers through his curling grey mane. 'Indeed. Listen, Mater-Imperia is concerned that supplies aren't getting to Korion in the quantities required. We both know why. I've got Hytel and Brochena, so I've got the supplies, but you control the road south through the Krak. I can ship by air, but we both know windships can't carry near so much as a wagon, and windships ... well,' he added with a wry smile, 'they don't grow on trees.'

'That's also old news.'

'Gyle,' Betillon began, then he peered at Rutt. 'Does your man know about the plan?'

'He does.'

'Well then, perhaps he can give you better counsel! You know what's coming: when that Bridge comes down, there's going to be chaos. Lucia thinks it will all be clean-cut and surgical, but it won't. Earthquakes are unpredictable, and this will be the greatest ever known. It's going to be a *mess*. But if we work together, and keep Lucia off our backs until the hammer falls, we can carve up Javon between us afterwards like roast pork.'

'Lucia can't touch us,' Gurvon stated. 'She doesn't have the manpower to intervene, not without stripping the vassal-states of their garrisons.'

'Oh yes, she can,' Betillon scoffed. 'The empire has clandestine resources beyond even yours, Gurvon Gyle. How'd you like to have Volsai assassins on your tail, or a few Keepers? You know how the empire rewards the faithful: with the ambrosia. Those old bastards like to involve themselves if they feel the Crown is threatened.'

'She won't send Keepers: she's as scared of them as you or I.' Gurvon had a theory about Keepers: when they gained the Ascendancy, they faced a new test of loyalty: how many began to wonder why they weren't emperor themselves.

Betillon waved a hand dismissively. 'There are plenty of loyal Keepers, and she can unleash them any time.'

Perhaps he was right; only the most loyal magi were permitted the ambrosia and Ascension. *No emperor's going to be stupid enough to create his own usurper, not even Constant,* he thought. Keepers were usually only made once they could barely walk, giving them maybe an extra decade or two of life, in a decrepit body. It was really just a ceremony of recognition, the culmination of a glorious career in service of the emperor, not the creation of a new power in the realm.

'There have been no new Ascendants in decades,' Gurvon reminded Betillon. 'The Scytale hasn't been publically displayed in all that time.'

'But everyone knows it's there, waiting: House Sacrecour's ultimate reward for loyalty,' Betillon responded. 'And those who have been granted that reward are Lucia's most fanatical supporters.'

So no doubt there are a few strong enough to do as said Gurvon suggests. He waved the threat aside. 'Scaring me with legends isn't going to change anything, Tomas. I've got five legions, you've got three. You've got the supplies and I control the roads. And I really don't give a shit whether Kaltus Korion makes it out of this or not. I need a better reason to cooperate.'

'Then how about self-preservation?' Betillon growled. 'Gyle, listen: if we appear to be cooperating, Lucia's going to leave us be. Her only concern is that Kaltus is there in Kesh when the Bridge is destroyed, to hold the gains until he can be reinforced and the sultan brought to heel. With Echor of Argundy dead, her son has never been more secure. She doesn't care who's supplying Kaltus; she'll reward whoever it is – so let it be both of us, and afterwards, we'll both be in favour.'

Gurvon doubted it would be so simple, but even so, Betillon was making sense. Already his own mercenary legions were beginning to feel the pinch as they bled dry the regions they controlled, while the Jhafi migrated east to Forensa and the Nesti. *Who appear to have plenty of supplies.* The east of Javon was the food-bowl of the land: they would have to move against it soon – but that couldn't happen if he and Betillon were at loggerheads.

'All right, Tomas: suppose I take half of what you send south and pass the rest through?'

'Half? No way – you're feeding five legions; Korion has twenty or more.'

'He's got other sources.'

'You can keep a tenth,' Betillon offered brusquely.

'A quarter. I've got to keep my men strong, and I've a populace to pacify.'

'As have I. A fifth.'

He frowned, glanced at Rutt and then agreed, 'Very well, one fifth I keep, the rest passes through. Your men may escort the caravans all the way south to Kesh; I give them safe passage.'

Betillon laughed. 'No, they'll be handing over the caravans at the crossroads south of here. I'm not depleting my forces any more than they are. You'll provide the guards for the caravans into the Zhassi.'

'Half each,' Gurvon offered. 'No magi.'

'Done,' Betillon said. 'The first caravan will be here inside a week.'

They regarded each other distrustfully, then the governor nudged his horse closer, pulled out a metal hipflask and took a swig, wincing at the strength of the liquor. 'Local piss,' he grunted, tossing Gurvon the flask. 'Tastes like lamp-oil. Got a sting, though.'

Gurvon caught the flask, examined it briefly with the gnosis, then took a swallow. It was every bit as bad as he'd expected, but he'd live. He grimaced and tossed it back. 'Did you act on my tip?'

'The windship?' Betillon snorted. 'What do you think?'

Gurvon groaned inwardly. 'You'll regret letting them through. The Nesti have got their king back. I'd move on Forensa if I were you, as soon as the weather cools enough to permit a march.'

Betillon mopped his brow. 'When's that, eh? This Hel-hole never cools down!'

'Not so: the weather in Javon cools to bearable in Noveleve, and stays that way for three whole months. Noveleve is five weeks away.' He stopped the flask and threw it back to Betillon. 'I hear you killed Mustaq al'Madhi.'

'I hanged him and all his male kin, then fucked his women to death. You were too tolerant, Gyle. A ruler must be feared, and by Kore, the Noories fear me now.'

'And hate you too. Do you think Mustaq was the only man with a gang of thugs? There are dozens of gangs in Brochena who previously had no reason to care whether Dorobon or Javonesi ruled. They were pacified when I held Brochena, knowing that I turned a blind eye to their petty crimes as long as they stayed out of my way. You've united them now: against you.'

'Like I care. They're just mudskins. Do you know how many raids on Imperial possessions there have been in Brochena since I hung Mustaq? *None.* They're cowed, Gyle. Believe me, I know how to use fear. You should remember that.'

Oh, I remember, he thought. *I remember the Noros Revolt. I remember Knebb.*

His own sources said that the Brochena criminal fraternity had gone quiet since al'Madhi's death because they were reorganising, annulling feuds and agreeing a path forward. He had this from Harshal ali-Assam, whom he'd met just a few days ago. Harshal had told him something else too, about a certain maid and her daring escape. Should he? *Oh, what the Hel . . .*

'Tarita Alhani,' he said in a low voice, his eyes fixed on Betillon's face.

'You have good sources,' the governor replied stonily.

Gurvon smiled blandly. 'I take it she remains unfound?'

'What do you know of her?'

'She used to be Elena's maid, and then passed to Cera Nesti. She's an orphan, and during Cera Nesti's house arrest she was the queen's underworld contact. But she wasn't any threat; it was better I knew exactly who Cera's sources were than to break them and run the risk of not discovering who they were replaced by.'

'You do take an inordinate interest in these Noorie women,' Betillon said sourly. 'Were you rukking this maid?'

'I don't share your tastes, Tomas. She escaped your own chamber, I hear. A resourceful little bint; perhaps I'll recruit her.'

Betillon snorted with laughter. 'No Gyle, you'll not get a rise out of me. The little bitch got lucky, but no one escapes me in the long run. If you'd not been so soft, the Nesti children would be dead and so would Elena Anborn. You've had chances aplenty to kill them all and not taken them – too many complicated scams when you needed to keep it simple and ruthless.'

'You know it wasn't like that, Tomas. If I'd acted as you are now, we'd already be swimming in a sea of blood.'

'Noorie blood, Gyle, as we will be anyway in a few weeks.' Betillon straightened in the saddle. 'If you're so worried about Forensa, help me take it. I'll send a legion, you send a legion. We can divide up the spoils afterwards.'

Gurvon considered that. It might be a trap, but he knew he could outmanoeuvre Betillon, and he was a little more worried about Forensa than he wanted to admit.

I need to see Elena's head on a pole before I'll rest easy.

'If I were to agree to that, you'd let Lucia know that I'm cooperating?'

'I could do that. If I attack Forensa in late Noveleve, could you get a force there?'

I'll keep Staria at the Rift Forts, and send in Hans Frikter . . . 'Sure.'

Betillon considered him suspiciously, then grimaced. 'Very well. I'll report what we've agreed to Lucia. You'd better hold to it. I warn you: she's *this close* to unleashing the Volsai on you.'

She probably is. The last thing I need . . .

They each raised a hand in farewell, and trotted away. As soon as it was dignified to do so, Gurvon kicked his horse into a gallop and went thundering down the causeway – just in case the parley really was a trap and an attack was about to be unleashed. After a few minutes he began to feel foolish, and pulled up a little. Rutt slowed gratefully, wincing with each thud of his arse on the saddle. He'd never been much of a rider. After that they trotted on in silence while Gurvon replayed the whole conversation in his mind.

Yes, this is the right thing to do . . . Betillon doesn't acknowledge it, but with the Nesti children and Elena in Forensa, Javon is a lot more dangerous.

Forensa, Javon, on the continent of Antiopia
Shawwal (Octen) 929
16th month of the Moontide

Elena Anborn rode through the crowds trying to see every potential danger, but it was hopeless: the city folk had engulfed the procession as it wound into Forensa. The faces looking up at them were so joyous, so enraptured, that it scared her. Men and women, Jhafi mostly, but plenty of Rimoni too, were awed and exhilarated, weeping openly, chanting, hands reaching out to touch them. Their king had returned from captivity. Their queen-regent had risen from the dead. Amteh and Sollan alike, they all believed that their gods had spoken. Even she, a Rondian mage-woman, wasn't spared this excess of rapture. They clutched her hands and legs, kissed her feet and the hems of her clothes.

Since they reached the gates they'd been crawling through the streets at less than walking pace. Elena no longer had the reins of her mount in her hands; she had no control over where she was going or how fast. Her clothes, simple riding leathers, were dyed by the coloured powders being hurled everywhere in celebration. The whole crowd was stained red and pink and orange, the colours of joy. The sounds were deafening, drums and chanting and song filling the air. The air was so hot and close she was dripping in sweat and positively lightheaded. Behind her, Kazim was similarly bound, helplessly murmuring in her mind about just how badly he wanted to get out of this. But these people deserved the chance to finally celebrate *something*. This was part of binding their kingdom back together.

Some twenty paces ahead, engulfed in weeping women, Cera Nesti was being led through the press. Her white supplicant robes were now a rainbow of colour, her hair caked in the dyes, her face like a weeping jester. Every so often there was a ripple through the crowd like a wave on the ocean, mashing people together and sending dozens to their knees. There had been broken bones already, and Elena prayed there would be no deaths.

Timori was visibly overwhelmed, but somehow all the training of his childhood was keeping him upright, calm and smiling. If they didn't get a respite soon though, she was afraid he'd collapse. She sought among the soldiers for a face she knew, finding the young knight leading Cera's horse. She shouted aloud and into his mind, pitching her mental voice so that the man would think he'd simply heard her normally through the press. <*Seir Delfin, move us along – Timori is only a boy!*>

The knight gave an obedient nod and thankfully the pace picked up. It was still another half an hour before they finally got through the gates of the Nesti palace. It was here that Cera had first addressed the people, in the wake of the murder of her family: just over two years ago, Elena realised with a shock. Two tumultuous years. As she swung from her saddle and darted through the press to Cera's side she saw Nesti retainers she'd not set eyes on for a long time; noticing how they looked at her, uncertain but wanting to believe she could be trusted as before. That hurt, for it was not her loyalty that had ever wavered.

Nevertheless, when Pita Rosco was the first to embrace her in welcome, tears of relief stung her eyes.

'Donna Elena!' The portly Keeper of the Purse beamed, kissing her cheeks as if she were a badly missed daughter. 'Welcome! Welcome home!'

Her throat seized up as she let him crush her against him. *Home. Yes, this is home.*

He touched her wet cheeks. 'Si, si! It is good to cry.' He winked at her. 'Let them all see your tears. Let them all see how much you care.'

Then it was the turn of Luigi Ginovisi, the House Nesti Master of Revenues and Pita Rosco's dour shadow, less fulsome in his welcome, suspending judgement. So too Comte Piero Inveglio.

They were all cautiously fascinated by Kazim, though. All the Nesti knew that Elena had been enamoured of Lorenzo di Kestria; despite the stigma, a mage in the family would have been a potent addition to the Kestrian line. The Rimoni looked more than a little put out that she now had a Keshi lover, and what it said about her loyalties, even though Lorenzo was long-dead.

Apart from those three old friends, the rest of the noblemen were comparative strangers, newcomers to the Nesti ruling council, which hammered home to her that Luca Conte and Emir Ilan Tamadhi were dead. Paolo Castellini was a Gorgio captive, along with half the Nesti army. *So many to avenge.*

'Where is Harshal ali-Assam?' she asked Inveglio.

'Who knows?' he responded. 'He goes here and there, returns with information when it suits him. Some trust him, others . . .' He spread his hands doubtfully.

'Harshal may appear to play both sides, but he is Javonesi,' Elena replied confidently. 'He and I have been in contact and shared information. We can trust him.'

Comte Inveglio took that in without undue enthusiasm. He took Elena to meet some of the new men, including the Sollan drui and Amteh Scripturalist assigned to the royal family.

'Although their influence isn't what it was here,' he confided. 'The people know that both the Sollan and Amteh clergy condemned Cera to die; and that men who had shared table with us were part of that. They know that the clergy fought her will when she held her Beggars' Court.' He paused. 'They want a similar court here. Do you think that wise?'

Elena didn't, not right now. 'We've a war to fight, Piero. Let us tend to that first.'

The Comte's eyes warmed a little. 'It is good to have you back, Donna Elena.'

'So long as I agree with you on all matters?'

Inveglio laughed. 'Si, of course. But even so, for I don't trust that to last.'

Love: that was what Cera Nesti felt as she listened to the Jhafi prayer, the Mantra of Family, naming all present as family and therefore able to speak freely. Once it was completed, she and Elena, the only women present, were permitted to lower the hoods of their bekira-shrouds and debate freely with the men.

This is what I loved so much: not just being part of these meetings but making the decisions that guide this land.

For years she'd wondered if there was something wrong with her: women were supposed to think only of men and babies and jewellery and clothes and making a perfect home. Her mother had been like that, and so had her sister Solinde.

But I desire women, and I like to rule kingdoms.

She sometimes wondered if the two things were linked, but that didn't ring true to her: if men were supposed to be hunters, she knew herself to be different: she wanted to be hunted, couldn't imagine doing the hunting herself. And history did speak of women rulers, strong rulers, who were nevertheless wives and mothers of renown.

I'm different to them all. I'm unique.

'Welcome, dearest brothers and sisters,' she greeted her fellow council members. As head of the Nesti family, senior member of the family of the Crown Prince, she was entitled to lead this group, and these men had welcomed her back on that basis, which made her proud. 'Twice welcome and thrice welcome, my friends, to this first reconvening of the Regency Council of Javon. It is with great joy that I greet you.'

The men chorused greetings, she thanked them and they sat. She was immensely aware that Elena was back at her right hand, completing her dreams.

Please Ella, trust me as you used to – I swear I'll never let you down again!

There were a dozen men around the table, not all of them familiar, but Comte Inveglio was beside her, with Pita Rosco and Luigi Ginovisi, and Harshal ali-Assam had just returned from spying in Brochena itself. Beside him was the Keshi, Kazim Makani, whose slightly intimidating presence Elena had insisted upon. The young man was huge, and quietly sure of himself, even among the nobles of Javon.

She tapped the pile of papers before her. 'We've much to discuss, my friends. But first, I have some things to report.'

They all went still, and their eyes bored into her.

'As you know, I was condemned to death for the murder of King Francis Dorobon, and acts of immorality. I state here and now, categorically, that I was not guilty on either count. Another murdered Francis, and made it appear that it was me.' That caused a murmur, but she raised her hand for silence. 'Furthermore, nothing immoral has ever occurred between myself and any other woman.'

There was love, and pleasure, and I hold neither to be immoral, but natural and beautiful, and if it wasn't suicidal to do so, I'd say it aloud.

'I am a woman, like any other, desirous of marriage and children,' she said emphatically. 'Furthermore, I have heard rumours that I now have an overweening taste for power, that I am plotting to seize the throne in my own name and push my beloved brother aside! I hear that I am a new Mater-Imperia Lucia in the making! I refute this entirely, and you will see my words proven when, at the end of this war, I wed Sultan Salim and retire to his harem, as I have pledged.'

This reminder of her betrothal to Salim of Kesh, sealed before the Dorobon invasion and unpopular among her advisors, caused an unhappy mutter on all sides, but she didn't acknowledge it.

'Further, it is said by some that my marriage to Francis Dorobon was an act of betrayal. I accepted that marriage to protect my brother and enable me to work for Javon from within the Dorobon court. I give you the Beggars' Court as evidence of this.'

This was greeted with grimaces and small nods of approval. Her marriage had severely tested her friends, she knew; it might not have been as purely motivated as she pretended – fear had played a big part – but she'd survived.

'Finally, I have a confession. I fell into doubt, in the days prior to the Dorobon invasion, and I turned my back on that one person whom I should have trusted implicitly. I ignored the advice of Elena Anborn, and left us vulnerable.'

In fact I did far, far worse than that . . . But I pray that no one here will ever know the full extent of my betrayal.

Cera turned to Elena. 'I therefore beg her full forgiveness.' She fell to her knees on the cold marble before the Rondian mage, knowing that she was leaving Elena no dignified way of refusing her apology, but she could see no other way of lancing this boil, not when Elena continued to refuse to see her privately.

The silence in the room was total, and remained frozen for a long, awkward moment, while Elena whispered into her mind. *<Cera, you've a Hel of a lot more to beg my forgiveness for than just that.>*

Aloud, Elena said, in a voice that was pitched perfectly between relief and regret, 'That's gone, Princessa. There is nothing to forgive.' She reached down and pulled Cera to her feet. *<You manipulative little bitch.>*

The men looked on, excluded suddenly, wanting to react in appreciation but unsure why the tension remained. Cera bridged the moment by kissing Elena's cheeks. Elena's lips on her own cheek were cold, but she feigned a smile.

'Let us work together as we used to, dearest Ella,' Cera said solemnly.

'For Javon,' Elena replied, forcing warmth into her voice.

Someone clapped, and then all the men applauded, and the smell of relief was tangible. Cera carefully avoided looking at Elena again, peering down the table where Kazim was smiling fixedly, as if he'd sensed what passed and liked none of it.

'In token of Elena's service,' Cera announced, 'the king has given me leave to gift her a piece of land – a monastery on the slopes of Mount Tigrat where she made her home for a time.' The men frowned a little at this, but none raised any objection, probably because the land wasn't productive.

Then it was down to business.

They began with the status of the military. Seir Ionus Mardium, the new knight-commander, spoke first. 'We lost thousands when the Dorobon ambushed us at Fishil Wadi,' he reminded them. 'A thousand in battle, four thousand to the Gorgio slave-mines – that was half our strength, in terms of regular soldiers. But we've recruited heavily and replaced our losses with reserves. Also, sixteen thousand men of Loctis have marched south, mostly Jhafi, but many Kestrian Rimoni; and eighteen thousand men are under arms in Riban, also mostly Jhafi.'

'We have more men to send,' young Justiano di Kestria reported. He was representing his elder brother, the Lord of Loctis. 'But we must also ensure our home is safe.'

'So too with House Aranio,' Stefan di Aranio put in. 'Don't doubt our commitment, my Lady, but you must realise that it is Riban where the first blow will come.'

'Gurvon could just as easily approach Forensa from the south, leaving Riban untouched,' Elena noted, her voice brittle. 'They have two legions at the Rift Forts already.'

Piero Inveglio unrolled a large map. 'Where are the enemy?' he asked, looking at Harshal ali-Assam.

The shaven-skulled Jhafi lord stood, his silks rustling. 'I have just returned from Brochena and I have current word on all enemy deployments.' He placed a marker on the Rift Forts, to the south of Forensa. 'The Estellan legions, commanded by the woman Staria Canestos, are here.'

'The perverted ones,' Scriptualist Nehlan interrupted.

'Staria's men are capable soldiers, regardless of their other inclinations,' Elena pointed out.

'I'm told they fight like buggery,' Piero Inveglio joked, though no one laughed.

Cera guessed their hesitancy meant some still half-believed she was safian.

'Well, I thought it was funny,' Inveglio said diffidently.

Harshal put other markers on the map. 'In the Krak di Condotiori we have Adi Paavus' Rondian mercenaries. Near Riban, Argundians under Hans Frikter. In Baroz, the Hollenians of Endus Rykjard. Those are all loyal to Gurvon Gyle, of course.' Harshal chose different markers and placed two in Brochena. 'Two legions of Dorobon, at least, for they are recruiting among the settlers, and another of Kirkegarde loyal to Tomas Betillon. A total of eight legions – each with fifteen magi and five thousand men.'

'You can ignore Adi Paavus,' Elena said. 'He won't budge from the Krak di Condotiori unless it's an emergency. The real question is whether Gurvon and Betillon can work together.'

'Can they?' Pita Rosco asked.

'I'm damned if I know, Pita. The two have history: Gurvon fought for Noros in the Revolt, and Betillon was the commander of one of the Rondian armies. Betillon sent his men into the town of Knebb, which had already surrendered – he was new to the conflict, as was Kaltus Korion, after the previous Rondian generals were sacked for their failures. Betillon decided to make an example of Knebb, so he had every man, woman and child put to death. The women were raped first. We all swore we'd kill the bastard for that, but he won. That crime, and those he and his army of thugs committed afterwards, turned the war against us. He is still known as the Butcher of Knebb.'

'But both are pragmatists,' Pita noted.

'We were the first into Knebb afterwards, Gurvon and I. We were so angry . . .' Elena looked down at her clenched fists. 'But Gurvon's changed. I believe he would ally with Shaitan himself if it profited.'

'So the possibility of them acting in concert remains,' Cera concluded grimly. She placed a marker on Hytel. 'There are also the Gorgio.' *Portia, how do you fare?*

Harshal ali-Assam brightened. 'Let me tell you a tale of Hytel,' he drawled. 'You will recall that the lovely Portia Tolidi was also married to Francis Dorobon, only being a Gorgio, she threw herself into the rukking with enthusiasm.' The men snickered, and Cera had to control her irritation at this defamation of her former lover. 'Well, she got what she wanted – a child in her belly – and was sent north, where, surprise, surprise, she gained more than she had imagined. Donna Elena will tell us how a woman who becomes pregnant to a powerful mage can gain the gnosis herself.'

Everyone started, then looked at Cera, or more particularly, at her belly, a question in their eyes.

'No,' she said firmly. She bit her lip. 'I wasn't *enthusiastic* for Francis.'

'To your credit, Lady,' Pita Rosco put in.

Harshal resumed his narrative. 'Portia's been driving the Hytel court insane with her demands, and they're terrified of her. She has strange impulses, mostly concerning her dietary needs. She and Uncle Alfredo fell out in a big way. And now Alfredo is dead – he's killed himself.'

There was a collective intake of breath. 'Alfredo Gorgio's dead?' Comte Inveglio gasped. 'You're certain?'

'Absolutely. I have it from all sides. After Portia gained the gnosis, he went downhill in a big way. Some said she cursed him.'

Cera was torn between triumph and worry. *Oh Portia, what's become of you?*

'Curses aren't real,' Elena put in. 'They're superstition. But it is likely true that Portia Tolidi has gained the gnosis. Untaught, uncontrolled . . . she'd be a danger to everyone around her. I'm surprised Gurvon let her go.'

'I'm told it was written into the Dorobon-Gorgio alliance, and Francis was in control then,' Harshal said. 'But now Alfredo's bastards are vying for her hand, and they're beginning to knife each other in the back.'

The men looked pleased at this, but Cera could feel only dread, fearful that someone would take a blade to Portia. 'Then perhaps the Gorgio will not be a factor in the coming struggle,' she said, struggling to sound unemotional.

'Then these are the numbers,' Seir Ionus said, bringing them back to the main topic. 'Gyle has four legions, excluding the one at the Krak, and Betillon three: that's thirty-five thousand men, though many will be tied down on garrison and supply-route protection. But we have only twenty-one thousand men here, and eighteen thousand in Riban.'

'Where they must remain,' Stefan di Aranio said emphatically.

There was an uncomfortable silence.

To his credit, Seir Ionus didn't rise to this argument, at least not directly. The extent of the Aranio participation was an unspoken division in the room. Instead, he turned to Elena. 'Is it correct,' he asked, 'that armies without magi must outnumber a Rondian legion by five to one to prevail?'

'So they say,' Elena replied, 'although a single blade or arrow can kill a mage if he is taken unawares. A fully prepared and shielded mage cannot be surprised or wounded so easily, though. If they are protected by legionaries and are skilled, they can be nigh on untouchable, and devastating in the field. Five to one is accurate, I deem, and what is more, you must have men who are willing to sacrifice themselves in wearing down the magi so that others might triumph. That kind of fortitude is rare.'

'So we need a lot more men,' Harshal concluded for her. 'Probably every man able to bear arms.'

'Which is impossible,' Luigi Ginovisi said dourly. 'We'd never be able to feed or arm them, and if we gathered them all, our enemy would just laugh and harass us until we starved or fell apart.'

'That's about the sum of it,' Elena agreed. 'But we do have options; for one, we've some allies you don't know about.'

She told them about the lamiae, skimming through their history in the Rondian Animagery breeding facilities, and how they'd come to escape. Cera endorsed the tale, and as the counsellors were shaking their heads in disbelief, she added, 'Their windship is still moored north of here.'

Elena told them, 'I can take you there, if seeing is believing.'

'How many of these creatures are there?' Comte Inveglio asked.

'Most are still in the west, and some are helping Mekmud of Lybis. There are fifteen aboard the windship, all strong warriors with gnostic abilities.'

'Are they willing to fight for us?' Harshal asked.

'*With*, not for,' Elena replied coolly. 'With certain conditions.'

'What conditions?' Luigi Ginovisi asked warily.

'They want land, gifted to them in perpetuity.'

That made everyone pause: land was regarded as the key of wealth, and even barren deserts had a price.

Pita Rosco broke the silence. 'Where?'

'On the coast, northwest of Lybis. It is far away and completely uninhabited. The Emir of Lybis has agreed to give it to them, but that requires the endorsement of the King of Javon.'

'How long have they lived there?' asked Harshal, who hated not being first with any kind of news.

'Only since the beginning of the year,' Elena replied. 'But they claim a spiritual connection to the valley; they call it their Promised Land.'

There was some debate, but Elena was an eloquent advocate for the lamiae and Cera backed her and the condition was agreed in short order.

After that came boring but necessary discussion of revenues and treasury reports, and finally they got on to the well-being of the city. Forensa was not just heavily indebted, but struggling to support the tens of thousands of refugees from Brochena and the west who had fled the Dorobon. There were camps outside the city housing countless people in awful conditions, surviving only through the generosity of Forensa, Loctis and Riban. 'In normal conditions, Brochena buys all our produce, and houses these people,' Stefan di Aranio complained. 'I have another fifty thousand or more outside my city of Riban.'

'It is so,' Marid Tamadhi stated. He was now the prime Jhafi lord in Riban, following the death of his father Ilan, who'd been slain at Fishil Wadi. He looked much like his father, but seemed close to

Stefan di Aranio. 'The Dorobon have been moving their own settlers into Brochena and casting out Jhafi. Most came east.'

'Is there enough food?' Cera asked.

'Just – though only because the Loctis traders are accepting credit terms,' Justiano di Kestria replied.

'Your brother should be sending us supplies for free!' Pita Rosco snapped. 'He's letting these traders profiteer on the suffering of the people.'

'My people must also eat,' Justiano retorted. 'Food still costs money to produce, and we've no new gold flowing in to pay for it. My House is going broke as fast as yours, Nesti!'

'Peace,' Cera snapped. 'We're all being pinched. These aren't normal times. And yes, there are traders profiting from this. It is they who deserve our ire.'

'Then clamp down on them, Lady!' Luigi Ginovisi cried, slapping the table. 'Confiscate the stores of those who are stockpiling and distribute the food amongst the needy.'

'I can't just confiscate a merchant's stock,' Cera said, then paused. 'Or can I?'

Elena raised a hand. 'In Noros during the Revolt, we did this: all essentials were assigned a fixed price and distributed by rationing – everything: granaries, estates, mines, forests, private armouries, even the banks and money-lenders. It was a time of crisis, and it created fresh problems after the Revolt, but it got us through, and prevented certain men from profiting from the misery of others.'

Stefan di Aranio and Piero Inveglio shared a sick look. 'But the law protects—'

'So too in Noros, but the king overrode them,' Elena interrupted.

The men around the table, mostly noblemen of wealth, looked at each other with somewhat ashen faces.

Well, thought Cera. *That was very instructive.*

'Javon is fighting for her life, gentlemen,' she said gravely. 'The poor are losing everything; should a trader from Loctis or a banker of Brochena grow rich on their losses?' She left the question hanging, and no one grasped it. 'I want a report by the end of the week on the measures taken in Noros and how they might be implemented here. Elena, please talk to Pita and Luigi, and to my lords of Loctis and Riban, as this affects you closely too.'

'And me,' Piero Inveglio put in swiftly. 'Someone must represent the interests of the wealthy of Forensa.'

'I think you'll find that someone is me,' Cera told him firmly. She met his eyes, waited him out until he dropped his eyes and looked away sullenly. *So are you part of the problem, Comte? Interesting.* She looked around the table, wondering how many men would be rapidly reorganising their affairs to conceal their assets and hide them from confiscation.

'It is always stimulating having you at the table, Donna Elena,' Pita Rosco observed wryly.

They moved on to less pressing matters and as the day wore on, the meeting became more about detail. Finally, as they began to wind up, Elena raised a hand, addressing Cera. 'Princessa, there is one more thing. Returning to the subject of our need for magi, there is another option I'd like to pursue, although there is a risk.'

'What sort of risk?'

'The dying sort,' Elena replied drily. 'But the possible gains are huge.'

'What do you need of us?' Cera asked.

'Kazim and I need your leave to disappear for a while, no questions asked.'

This was greeted with stony silence, those not predisposed to trust a Rondian or Keshi mage showing their unhappiness.

'How long do you need?' she asked.

'A month,' Elena replied. 'Maybe more.'

The consternation of those present grew, but Cera spoke over it. 'You have our blessing,' she said in a firm voice. 'Just make sure that you brief me about the Noros Revolt arrangements before you go.'

Identity

The Gentler Sex

It is noticeable that most healers are girls, and most battle-magi are boys. We should seek to cultivate these natural predilections when helping our students towards their true callings. Women should be forbidden martial training and instructed to concentrate on areas where their nature will help them to excel.

SENATOR FARIUS TREY, SPEAKING AGAINST
ARCANUM REFORM, PALLAS, 917

*Near Vida, Southern Kesh, on the continent of Antiopia
Shawwal (Octen) 929
16th month of the Moontide*

Seth Korion spurred his horse into motion, for a moment missing the intuitive khurne he'd ridden before Shaliyah. He'd turned it loose once they'd left Ardijah, a little ashamed it had taken him so long to do so. The small army – the 'Lost Legions', as they liked to call themselves – were digging in twenty miles north of Vida on low heights overlooking the Tigrates River – although 'heights' rather oversold the position; in truth, they were glorified sand dunes, barely twenty yards high. The northern tip of them touched the riverbank, but there was a hundred-yard gap at the southern end where an attacker might outflank them without having to climb; that worried him most of all.

'Put my Bullheads there,' Fridryk Kippenegger was insisting. 'They won't take a backwards step.' He seemed to regard his entire maniple

– Rondians to a man – as honorary Schlessens, and oddly enough, his men did too.

'No, we need the most heavily armoured unit there,' Seth replied firmly. He'd read enough military manuals to know this much at least. 'I'm putting Jelaska's Argundians there. Your men can have the ridge on her left flank. Dig in! You need a spiked palisade running the entire length of this space – two hundred yards – anchored to Jelaska's men on your right and the Bricians to your left. Hold your line!'

'Yar, yar!' Kippenegger grinned. 'We'll hold. I promised Minaus Bullhead ten cows.'

Barbarian. But Kip was a solid presence and his men fought well. He threw the Schlessen a salute. 'Then get on with it.'

So it went down the line. He put the remains of his own legion, Pallacios XIII, in the centre. Estellan archers would be dotted throughout the lines, with orders to shoot carefully and not miss. They were low on arrows and every shot had to count. Massed archery could be deadly, but it was also incredibly wasteful. 'And remember,' he told the assembled magi, 'you're responsible for your maniple. Get them through alive and you'll make it too.'

There weren't many of them left. There were eight left from the Thirteenth: Seth himself, Sensini and Kippenegger, plus Baltus Prenton, Severine Tiseme – though she was still recovering from giving birth – the Andressans Hugh Gerant and Evan Hale, and the healer Lanna Jureigh.

He had only eleven from other legions: Lysart, from Noros, and the Bricians Sordan and Mylde, and three Argundians, the pure-blood Jelaska Lyndrethuse, Gerdhart the chaplain and another healer, Carmina Phyl. The rest were sole survivors from legions lost at Shaliyah: Runsald and Nacallas of Brevis, Hulbert from Hollenia, ven Lascyn and Barendyne of Bres; apart from Jelaska all low-bloods. So nineteen magi in all, three of whom were non-combatants. Nineteen might be more than the normal complement of a legion, but they had two and half legions'-worth of men to look after: more than twelve thousand rankers.

I wonder what gnostic strength Salim has? The Keshi army at

Shaliyah and Ardijah had been augmented by magi and Dokken, not so well-trained as the Rondian magi, but still dangerous. And even without them, Salim's men numbered close to one hundred thousand men.

Nearly ten to one . . . have you ever faced such odds, Father?

He left each mage marshalling their particular maniple, or in some cases, two maniples, using their gnosis to help fortify the ridge. They had a mile of elevated land to defend, some of it with a gentle sandy slope, other sections crowned in jagged spires. 'Keep the men digging,' he told them. 'We've probably got about two days before the Keshi arrive.'

Finally he and Ramon Sensini were alone on the northern corner, against the riverbank. Ramon's men, mostly engineers and clerks, were assigned this section, as well as organising the supply train. 'Well,' the Silacian said offhandedly, 'I'd better go and circle the wagons.'

'No, wait. I want a word.'

'Is there a problem?' Ramon asked, all innocence.

Seth took a deep breath. 'Have you ever heard of the poet Jolquar? No? "Spin me a tale of wonder", he once wrote, the opening lines to *Il Eroici dia Ryma*. It's about the founders of the Rimoni Empire. No? I thought not. Anyway,' he said, gathering his temper, 'I want you to spin me a tale of wonder. Tell me all about the thief Sensini, and why the whole of the Kore-bedamned Imperial Treasury wants his bloody head!' Seeing Ramon wince in discomfort brought a little satisfaction. Not much though.

'Well,' Ramon said evasively, 'there's not *really* that much to tell.'

'The Hel there isn't! Three days ago I had an Imperial Arch-Legate tell me all about you: you've been issuing promissory notes on behalf of the Imperial Treasury! You've been trading in opium! You've been using false identification documents to gain the trust of some shady investors, and started a flood of money that's destabilising the empire – not that I suppose you care.'

Ramon had the temerity to smirk. 'Should I?'

'When the whole Crusade could suddenly implode, leaving rankers in both armies stranded and starving because the Crown can't afford to send food? How'd you like that, Sensini? Would that make you laugh?'

The Silacian continued to play, if not innocent, at least not very guilty. 'As if . . .'

'You think not? When you convinced some of the most powerful criminals in Hebusalim that you could ship the entire opium stock of the whole Crusade, tons of the accursed stuff, stored ready for the Third Crusade to arrive, and underwrite the lot?' He jabbed a finger when Sensini looked startled. 'Yes, I know now! The Arch-Legate told me, in Vida! You encouraged those men to find more investors: they call it a "Prism" scheme in Pallas – and it's *illegal!* The Arch-Legate said that virtually all the gold coin in the army was diverted into your maniple's hands! You and Storn have stripped the noble Houses of Rondelmar and Bricia! You gulled them with false returns and issued counterfeit promissories! Need I go on?'

Ramon raised a placating hand. 'Can you keep your voice down,' he said irritably. 'There are men within earshot – at least, they are when you're shouting the rukking hills down.'

Seth glared around him, saw the men digging trenches nearby, and scowled. 'All right,' he said, more quietly, 'enough from me. Talk! You told us in Ardijah you had gold: is this how you got it? How much?'

Ramon frowned. 'All right, yes, there is gold. About two hundred thousand gilden. That's not so much. Your father spends that much in a year.'

'My father's the richest man in Bricia! And the gold price has soared! The Arch-Legate told me it's at least ten times more valuable now!'

Ramon gave a low whistle. '*Fantastico!* But still no more than small change to the Imperial Treasury.'

'The Treasury is indebted!'

'Then they can mint more coins! Stop giving me the Arch-Legate's arguments! To the empire these sums are a few percentage points, nothing more!'

'Ha! Heads will roll over this!'

'Then let them roll!'

Seth stared at him, then with an effort took another breath and calmed down. 'How did this happen? Was it as Arch-Legate Milius said?'

'That depends on what he told you,' Ramon replied, then he gave a sly shrug. '*Allora!* Very well, Lesser Son. I'll tell you, if you can listen without shouting. Yes, I solicited money from investors, to give us liquidity. Such things happen every campaign. And yes, I used a Treasury seal that I was perhaps not permitted to use to get more investment.'

'*Perhaps!*' Seth echoed scornfully. '*Perhaps?* For as long as I've known you you've pretended to be an unacknowledged bastard, but you're . . .' He lost his flow as he remembered the old question-mark about Ramon Sensini: how had a Silacian low-blood ever been able to afford Arcanum training. 'Who *are* you, Sensini? Who's your father?' Though he thought he knew now.

Ramon looked him in the eye. 'My mother was a twelve-year-old virgin who had to work in a tavern so her family could make ends meet. She was raped by a Rondian mage, a promising Treasury official. Pater-Retiari realised that the official couldn't afford the scandal and blackmailed him; he tightened the screws considerably when it became apparent that my mother was pregnant. Pater-Retiari demanded not just money, but guarantees of my acknowledgement, safety and continued education. He wanted an Arcanum-trained mage in his service, and my father wanted anonymity. So a deal was reached: I didn't get his name, but I was secretly acknowledged. By the time I attained the gnosis thirteen years later, the scandal no longer really mattered, but the name got me into Turm Zauberin. It was Pater-Retiari's money that funded my education.'

'So you're the tool of familioso scum, using the gnosis to help him steal?'

'I'm no one's tool,' Ramon replied fiercely. 'In addition to taking me under his wing, Pater-Retiari took my mother as his concubine, because she gained the gnosis while pregnant. No one ever taught her how to use it – not that it would have mattered, because he had her Chained. At least my father only raped her once. But Pater-Retiari, he's on my list too.'

His list. Something in the way he said the words called to mind tales of Silacian vendettas. *Holy Hel, he means it – and he's smart enough to do it, too. He pretended all through college to be a low-blood, but if I'm right he's a half-blood!* Seth recalled times when Malevorn Andevarion and Francis Dorobon had beaten Ramon Sensini and Alaron Mercer to a pulp. *He hid his true power the whole time.* He could barely comprehend the self-discipline that must have taken. Suddenly Ramon Sensini was a very frightening proposition indeed. 'And your father?'

'His name is Calan Dubrayle.'

The Imperial Treasurer . . . Guessing right didn't make Seth feel any better. *Holy Kore in the heavens* . . . He filled in the gaps himself. 'So when you gulled those crime-lords in Hebusalim, they thought that you were a cast-iron investment! The son of the Treasurer – under Rondian law the father guarantees the debts of his sons! You reeled them in using Dubrayle's name? You're incredible!'

Ramon sketched a mocking bow. 'I do try.'

'It's not a bloody compliment.' Seth scratched his scalp. 'Why? Was it just greed? Did you think you knew what you were doing and just lose control? If we could tell the Arch-Legate that you didn't realise, then maybe—'

'Rukk off, Lesser Son,' Ramon drawled. 'It's sweet that you want to protect me, but I knew exactly what I was doing. Pater-Retiari's money-man dreamed up the scheme with me about three years ago while I was visiting during a break from the Arcanum. His plan was to ruin the opium traders and bring them under our control. I'm aiming a little higher: I want to bankrupt the Imperial Treasury and destroy my father's career. If that hurts the empire too, well and good.'

Holy Kore, what do I do? He looked at the wagons. 'It's all down there, isn't it?'

Ramon grinned sideways. 'What we've got left after Ardijah, anyway. Getting out of there was expensive. There's about two hundred thousand gilden left.'

With a current market value in the millions . . . 'The Arch-Legate said he'd let us cross the river if I handed you over. Do you realise how tempted I am right now?'

'That bridge is already burned, Seth. We know about the khurnes and we know about Shaliyah: they'll lock us up and let our men be decimated for desertion.'

Damn, he's probably right. 'If you're planning to run away, I'll send Jelaska to hunt you down.'

Ramon winced. 'So little trust! No, Lesser Son: somewhere along the way, this Crusade became personal. I'm going to get Sevvie and our daughter home, and I'll smash Siburnius and whoever else gets in our way. I'm going to ruin my father and my familioso head, free my mother and leave every man in this column rich. So you're stuck with me until then.' He pulled an ironic face. 'It's good to have ambitions, si?'

The basic equipment of every legionary included a shovel. And while they spent plenty of time with the sword and spear, and learned to love and hate their heavy shields, it was the shovel that defined their lives. Every evening they dug: sanitary trenches, defensive ditches and palisades. Every camp had to be ready to be defended.

Right now, the entire line was digging in, and even Ramon's maniple were doing their bit. As most of his men were clerks and engineers, he had no choice but to anchor the northern end of the line in person, with his guard cohort. As the night fell on their third day there, he supervised their excavations with Pilus Lukaz.

'The lads want to know if you've any tricks to help 'em out, Magister?' Lukaz enquired, slyly wiggling his fingers in a magical way. The Vereloni pilus wasn't prone to humour but he had a dry touch that Ramon liked. 'They're thinking you don't like hard work.'

'I like hard work as well as the next man,' Ramon chuckled. 'That is to say, not at all. I can watch it for hours, though. Anyway, I wouldn't want to deprive them of the exercise.' He and Lukaz were atop a low ridge that ran right to the bank. The river lay about thirty feet below the top of the bank at the highest point, at high tide at least: it dropped another ten at low tide. Even so far from the seas, the pull of the moon could still lift river-levels appreciably.

'How long have we got before the Keshi arrive?' Lukaz asked.

'A good question.' Ramon replied. 'Apparently they're still messing about in a camp ten miles west of here.'

'I thought they'd come at us like an avalanche,' Lukaz remarked. 'They gave us until the end of Septinon and that was almost a week ago.'

'Perhaps they've got other problems.'

'We can but hope.' Lukaz stood and shouted down at the men, 'Manius, I want that damned hole another yard deeper! Yes, *a yard*! That's three feet! Or two of yours!'

Manius pulled a face. 'It's solid stone, Lukaz.' He flexed his shoulders ruefully. The front-rank men, including Ferdi and Dolman, the biggest in the cohort, had been doing the most work, though Ramon had seen no shirking.

'Then grab a pick! Dig, lads! The Noories could be here tomorrow.' Pilus Lukaz knew how to get his squad working, needling them with comments about how little they did until they set to proving him wrong, then encouraging them as if it was the first time they'd ever stepped up. It was an old routine by now, but it always worked.

'I reckon they found some drink and got lammy,' scrawny little Bowe suggested. His perpetual shadow, the tall, rangy and almost preternaturally stupid Trefeld, guffawed. The squad erupted with counter-proposals, and droll imitations of drunk Keshi.

'P'raps the Gen'ral made a deal wi' that Sultan fella?' the flaxen-haired swordsman Harmon put in perceptively. 'They got close, I heard.'

'Swappin' poetry an' all,' Vidran added wryly. 'Gen'ral was jus' leading him on, I reckon, knowing what them Noories is like.'

The cohort chuckled uneasily at that, glancing sideways at Ramon. He pretended he hadn't heard, because there really wasn't anything to say. He turned to Lukaz again as he rose. 'Make sure they get a swim afterwards, Pilus. They've earned it.'

This earned him a low cheer, and he acknowledged it with a small wave. These men would be closest to him when the fighting began. Their wellbeing and good spirits mattered. And he liked them, as a group. He wandered south along the river, which in contrast to the earthworks, looked like some kind of Noorie bathing festival. The off-duty rankers were swimming in the shallows, in little enclosures made by the Earth-magi to shield them from the fast-flowing current. The Tigrates had a vast catchment area; it was the liquid spine of Kesh.

Watching the thousands of men frolicking naked in the water like children reminded Ramon of summer by the lake in Norostein, only there the water had been frigid. Here it was bath-warm. There was a strange innocence to the scene, as if these were not trained fighting men come to pillage and destroy, but pilgrims joyously washing away their sins as the Lakh were said to do. And it reminded him of how sweaty and dirty he was himself after an afternoon amidst the digging.

I might have a dip myself later, when it's quieter.

'Magister Sensini,' a woman called.

He peered behind him and saw Lanna Jureigh sitting on a mound of earth. 'Not swimming, Lanna?' he asked as he joined her.

'Gracious Kore, no! There are catfish the size of horses in that muck. I'm amazed we've not lost anyone.' The healer looked like someone who would have been thought of as matronly from about six years old, but she was smiling gently as she spoke, with a hint of longing. 'Look at all these big strong men, playing like children. Even the greybeards are swimming. Don't men ever grow up?'

'I don't know,' Ramon chuckled. 'Ask me in fifty years.' He ran his eye over the acres of bare-skinned men and figured it was no wonder every woman in camp seemed to be here. There was even a cluster of Khotri women in the water, the new wives and camp followers who'd left Ardijah with the legions, gathered in a knot and covering themselves with their hands while peering shyly at the men who circled them like crocodiles. 'Now that's a sight for sore eyes.'

Lanna harrumphed. 'It's all right for these Khotri girls; they're all so young and beautiful. I rather suffer by comparison, I'm afraid.'

'No one would mind if you stripped off, Lanna. I'm sure the rankers would look away out of politeness.'

The healer-mage sniggered girlishly. She fought the illnesses and wounds of the army day in and day out, alongside the Brician, Carmina.

Somehow, despite being surrounded by men, she'd not just remained single, but managed to maintain an air of mystery. Ramon reckoned she was thirty years old or more; she could have passed as younger, but her eyes were tired, haunted by the blood and suffering they'd seen.

'I'll restrict myself to a rinse in my tub later on,' she said, 'or maybe a midnight swim on my own.' Her eyes went back to the Khotri women, basted golden by the sunset. 'Dark skin loves the sun, doesn't it? They never seem to burn, but we do.'

'Speak for yourself.' Ramon, swarthy as any Silacian, grinned.

'I do worry for those young girls, heading into the unknown.'

'I'm sure their new husbands will look after them.'

Lanna gave him a pitying look. 'Oh please! Most of these relationships won't last out the year. What feels like burning passion and eternal love in the midst of a war is an entirely different thing when you're home in the cold, trying to till frozen soil while your sun-dark woman struggles not to freeze to death. The brothels of Yuros do quite a trade in cast-off Noorie women in the years after a Crusade. It's terribly sad.'

Ramon's good mood slipped. Lanna was sweet, but she did exhale melancholy at times. 'Yuros seems a long way away, but we'll be home in nine months – provided we can get across this damned river.'

'As you say,' Lanna replied. 'How are Severine and little Julietta?'

He shrugged uncomfortably. Sevvie had been in a foul mood since they'd been denied crossing the Tigrates. She'd been threatening to take Julietta and cross by herself, and part of him thought it wasn't a bad idea, partly for her safety, but also – though he hated admitting it – because he was getting awfully sick of her tantrums. But Siburnius was across the river, and he knew their names and faces.

'An army isn't the place for a mother and a baby. I wanted Seth to ask for permission to have them both transferred across the river and sent home, but discussions broke down before he could ask.' This was true, but in his heart, he was beginning to wonder if he just didn't have the emotional stamina for any long-term relationship.

'Severine isn't made for this life,' Lanna observed sagely.

Too damned right. He looked at the healer thoughtfully. 'How long have you been in the legions, Lanna?'

'Twenty years, more or less.' She looked at him with an air of faint amusement. 'Yes, I'm twice your age.'

'But still a creature of light and music, undimmed by time,' he replied, quoting a well-known poem.

'Oh la! Harken to the bard! Has Seth converted you to the joys of balladry?'

'Rukk off! The only thing he's converted me to is Brician chardo.'

'You knew him at college, didn't you?' she asked, somewhat wistfully. She'd clearly not been impressed with Seth initially, but it sounded like she was coming round.

That didn't stop him speaking his mind. 'Yes. He was a nasty, shallow little arse-wipe who thought low-bloods like me didn't belong in his world.' *Though ironically, I had as much right to that world as him.*

'He's grown up a lot since then,' Lanna replied. 'I expect you have too. He says you're the last person he thought would have stuck around when things went bad.'

Well that's rich, coming from the boy who blubbed his way through his swordsmanship testing. 'Si, maybe.' He stared out across the river. 'But I've invested myself emotionally.' *As well as every other way.* 'We all thought this Crusade would be nothing, didn't we? Just marching and looting and trying to stave off boredom.'

'Then came Shaliyah.'

'Si.' He mused a moment. 'But this place will be worse. When the Keshi arrive here, we're in for Hel.'

'I know. Shaliyah . . . well, there was nothing we could do but get out, and Ardijah: you were clever there. Your plan saved a lot of lives. But this place could get really ugly. If they break into our defences, it will be slaughter.'

He acknowledged her words, then said, 'Lanna, if they break through, don't die with your charges, please. You and Carmina use your gnosis and cross. Siburnius isn't going to execute healers.'

'He's an Inquisitor; I'm quite sure he'd be happy to execute anyone

145

who knew too much.' Lanna looked into his eyes intently. 'These are all my boys, Ramon. I don't want to leave even one behind.'

She means it. And he felt the same, he realised. Somewhere along the road from Shaliyah to Ardijah these men had begun to matter to him too. Part of that was personal pride and competitiveness – he was damned if he was going to let Siburnius and his ilk beat him – but it was also something to do with shared dangers and hardship. They were his boys too.

'So, shall we have a swim, then?' he asked, pulling a leering face at her. 'I'll strip down if you do?'

'You think the sight of skinny little nethers like yours is going to impress me? Have you seen the men down there? They put you to shame!' She laughed. 'Piss off, Ramon. Have a cold soak, then go and make up to Sevvie.'

He ducked his head. 'I guess I should.'

Near Vida, Southern Kesh, on the continent of Antiopia
Shawwal (Octen) 929
16th month of the Moontide

While Cym and Zaqri tried to work out how to approach the Keshi army and speak to the Dokken war-leader, whoever that was, they found an old hermit's cave in a rocky outcrop about four miles from where Salim's army was camped. The previous inhabitant had died and his skeleton had been reduced to a pile of gnawed bones by jackals. No one appeared to have been here for a long time. Zaqri drove the jackals away, cleaned it, stockpiled dead wood and dried dung for fires and warded it. He made a larder and piled in dried meat and a bag of seeds, used Earth-gnosis to deepen the well until it was usable and even fashioned a bucket.

The rest would be up to Cym.

'It's better if I go into camp alone,' he told her. 'We know nothing about the dynamics of the army. We must be cautious who we approach, and how.'

'How will I know what is happening?'

'I'll send birds.' He put his hand on her arm in reassurance. 'Cym, this is the right thing to do. My brethren are part of this shihad, but the hatred of western magi runs deep. I can't take you into another camp of my people; I'd end up having to defend you all over again, just as I had to within my own pack. And then I was packleader.'

'I know.' She looked away, because looking at him was too hard. So much was unresolved between them.

They'd been trailing Salim's army west, the opposite direction to where they thought they should be going, though they had no idea where Alaron and the Scytale were; it was the only way they might find sympathetic Dokken prepared to leave the shihad to hunt for the artefact.

And as for what lay between them . . . her body was still recovering from purging her womb of his child, and that act had badly damaged the burgeoning trust that lay between them, but she could no longer see any future that wasn't with him.

Damn my vendetta pledge . . . I may never entirely forgive him for killing my mother, but there must be a better way. I want to be his. He's lost a child, and it's true that he killed Justina in battle, not cold blood. Surely he's been punished enough? Surely the gods will let us be now . . .

'Zaqri, must we do this?' She swallowed. 'Once we rejoin the hunt for the Scytale, there'll be no escape, no peace. It could destroy everything we have left.'

Zaqri looked at her curiously, rare indecision on his visage, he who had walked like a god into her life. 'Cymbellea, the Scytale means *everything* for my people. I cannot walk away from the chance of salvation for them.'

She bit her lower lip, then raised her eyes. 'Not even for me?'

He stared, surprised. Ever since they'd met, she'd been resisting him. The death of her mother, in combat, but at his hands, had lain like a shadow over them, though he wanted her and she him. She'd fought her instinctual need for him for so long, then succumbed anyway.

'Stay with me,' she said, suddenly tired of resisting her heart. She indicated the hearth of the hermit's cave, and the cot within. 'Forget the Scytale. Stay, and I'm yours.' A new future blossomed in her mind, of an impossible love between Souldrinker and mage, made possible because he was perfection, despite his condition.

'Cymbellea, I don't understand you. Everything you've done since we met has been to find your friends and the Scytale – and now you want to just forget it? I don't understand.'

She didn't fully understand herself just now, but she had a vision of another future, vivid as a gnostic Divination: it was full of betrayals and death if they continued to pursue the artefact. 'You must stay,' she begged. 'You must.' She leant in, inhaled his scent, whispered in his ear, 'I can feel it. They're out of our reach. If we go after it, we'll both die.' She was suddenly certain that this was so, and her vehemence gave him pause.

'It is said that the strongest foretelling comes spontaneously,' he breathed. Then his eyes narrowed. 'Cymbellea, I would be a traitor to my kind not to follow this through. And I do believe we can find them. Their lives may depend on us finding them first.'

She tried to believe he might be right, but the notion didn't take root. Instead she did something she'd never done before; she tried to use her body to get what her arguments couldn't. She seized his face, kissed him hard.

In the past she'd withheld her kiss even when letting him between her legs, but now she held nothing back. Her growing sense of foreboding – that if she let him go, they'd have no future at all – drove her to increasing desperation as she guided him into her, rode him and was ridden, all to try and persuade him to stay.

And still when she woke he was gone.

Zaqri saw the skiffs first, their triangular sails quite distinctive from Rondian windcraft as they fluttered lower and vanished with the light. Then he saw riders on pale horses, wrapped in flowing robes, pale against the brown lands. He skirted them in lion form, a dun ghost padding silently to an outcropping where he could overlook the sultan's army as it approached. After the cavalry came the infantry, who set up camp below him. Unlike the Rondian legionaries there was no fortifying the camp, and far less order. These men weren't professional soldiers but conscripts.

Their numbers were incredible, though: a sea of men flowing across the ground like a dirty stain, and as twilight fell, the camp-fires made a river of flame stretching out of sight down the valley. The soldiers looked poorly armed and fed, but there were so many, in dozens of different native attire from all over the continent of Ahmedhassa; it was bewildering.

As the night fell he engaged his senses, seeking the glimmer of gnostic wards that would mark out the Keshi magi and Souldrinkers. He marked out the command pavilions, which were pegged out near the windskiffs, row upon row of them. He shifted to human form, dressed from the satchel he'd carried strapped to his back, then walked into the vast camp. He found the magi first, the Ordo Costruo Bridge-sigils of Rashid Mubarak's renegades sitting uneasily alongside the Hadishah jackal-head. He skirted them warily, then found what he sought: rough-clad gnosis-users without heraldry, in a camp warded by lines of faint light, invisible to the naked eye. They were erecting a wooden palisade about their tents with sylvan-gnosis: driving staves into the ground then conjuring them to greater heights and shaping them together, sprouting thorns that dripped poison. Some were clearly adept at Animagery and morphic-gnosis too, like Zaqri's old pack, but the affinities in this group were more varied, and their clothing was of the towns, not the wilds. They were mostly Keshi, and the women wore bekira-shrouds. Many prayed openly to Ahm, on mats facing Hebusalim. Zaqri watched until he saw a familiar face: as a former packleader, he had at times met others of similar rank, to resolve disputes and forge tenuous links.

There were only a few thousand Souldrinkers in all of Ahmedhassa, almost all of them users of elemental or hermetic gnosis, the most tangible forms of magic. His own pack had been chiefly Hermetic and Fire or Air, making Animagery and Morphism their prime attributes: hence the facility for controlling and shifting into animal form. As shapeshifters they'd been drawn to the wilds, but Souldrinkers with more elemental skills were better able to hide in human society.

Dokken Earth-magi clans dwelt secretly in most Keshi cities, hiding behind a respectable façade as masons. Fire-, Water- and Air-wielders found similar ways to blend in.

Zaqri paused, recalling the previous night, the hours of increasingly desperate love-making by which Cym had sought to make him stay. She'd given up on the Scytale and saving her friends: her ambitions had collapsed; now it was all about trying to find any kind of life in peace . . . with him.

He couldn't deny he was tempted to turn around and return to her. No one had ever moved him the way she did, and to have her so passionate and yielding in his arms was a gift from the gods. But somehow, in trying to be everything to him last night, she'd ceased to be herself. The woman he'd fallen in love with didn't give herself easily; she gave grudgingly, and demanded a price. She made you earn her. This other Cym was a lesser being.

So he'd left her sleeping, to try and save his kindred.

I cannot let the Scytale vanish again. We must seize this chance for our salvation.

He couldn't put that aside for such a selfish thing as love.

So he stepped to the edge of the camp and called the clan-leader's name. 'Prandello!'

The Souldrinkers in this camp were Earth and sylvan gnostics. Prandello, their leader, was a builder from a village near Medishar, but he was of Silacian stock. His town was outside the territory of Zaqri's pack, but they'd met when moving fugitive Dokken. Prandello had lank grey hair; his olive skin was sun-darkened and his eyes so deepset they were black holes. He'd dwelled all his life in Medishar: his keffi headscarf was bound in the native way, and he embraced Zaqri as a Keshi, kissing both his cheeks and his lips.

'Sal'Ahm, my friend. How come you here?' he asked as he ushered him into his tent. Zaqri had been seen by Prandello's people of course, and some probably recognised him; that couldn't be helped. But Prandello had been honest in their past dealings. A woman worked within, preparing the bed – a human woman, Zaqri noted in surprise, no longer young, and clearly scared of Prandello as she scuttled away, leaving the two men alone.

'I had heard that your pack were sitting out the shihad.' Prandello remarked, without condemnation: many Dokken had regarded the alliance offered by Rashid of Hall'ikut as a trap.

Zaqri grimaced as his first lie approached. How much to reveal was difficult, but it sounded like Prandello didn't know about This pack's destruction. 'I've left them to Wornu while I undertake a quest of great importance to our people.'

'A quest? Quests are for ballads, my friend, not the real world.' But Prandello still sealed the tent flap closed with a gesture, then sat on a cushion, motioning Zaqri to another. He produced a metal flask and poured them both a thimble of the bittersweet lemon liquor of Silacia. They each took a sip while Zaqri marshalled his story. From outside came the crackle of a fire and someone struck up a traditional Rimoni song that set his heart-strings humming to the tune. He began to feel that he was among kin.

'I need your help, Prandello, and that of any you can trust to put their loyalty to their Brethren first, ahead of the shihad or any other allegiance.'

The Silacian glanced at his own hands, which were tattooed with lines from the Kalistham. 'That is most of us, brother. Tell me more: a packleader doesn't leave his charges lightly – your "quest" must be of grave import, yes?'

Here we go ... 'Brother, I have gained information about something of great moment to our people.' Zaqri proceeded to give an edited version of the truth: that the Seeress Sabele had sought his aid, guiding them to an island-refuge where they'd found magi concealing a famed artefact, one that could cure the Dokken of their need to consume souls.

'My pack tried to seize the artefact, but two magi escaped with it,' he said as Prandello listened intently. 'Sabele guided my pack in pursuit, but they've evaded us – I had to leave my people in Dhassa, and the Seeress is dead, but the hunt goes on.'

Prandello was intrigued. 'A cure for our condition? Is that possible?'

'I can scarcely believe it myself, but when you hear the name of this thing, you will be convinced.' Zaqri leaned forward and whispered, 'It is the Scytale of Corineus.'

Prandello was stunned. '*Sol et Lune!* But surely the Scytale of Corineus resides in the deepest vaults of Pallas? The pillar of Urte would crack before it left there.'

'Nevertheless, it is beyond all doubt. It's been stolen, and it's here in Ahmedhassa!'

'And Sabele is lost?' Prandello rubbed his brow. 'She's been with us for ever. The tales say it was she who discovered how to unlock our gnosis.'

'A Keshi girl named Huriya took her soul, then vanished, seeking the Scytale for herself.' Zaqri looked at Prandello enquiringly: it was quite possible that Huriya had also sought him out.

'Huriya? I don't recognise the name. Who else knows of your quest?'

'The Inquisition, or parts of it,' Zaqri admitted. 'They showed up during our attempt to seize the Scytale for ourselves and caused the confusion that enabled the two magi to escape. Presumably there are forces within the Rondian Imperial Court that are aware, but the emperor must fear revealing the loss, lest it trigger a revolt.'

'So Rashid doesn't know, nor the Hadishah?' Prandello mused.

'I presume not. I'd fear them knowing: they are magi, after all.'

'They have promised a new era between us.'

'And now they know your names and where you live. Will you be safe in Medishar after the war?'

'I acknowledge your point. But there were Rondian Inquisitors in Medishar during the Second Crusade. That was too close for us; we needed to make a stand. The shihad was our best option, but we aren't blind to the risks.'

'I'm not criticising,' Zaqri said mildly. 'I'm just glad you're here now.'

Prandello toasted him. 'What is it you want, amici?'

Zaqri exhaled slowly. 'I have a trail gone cold: I need hunters, loyal to the Brethren and willing to leave the shihad and accept my command. The future of our people is at stake, brother. Imagine a world in which our affliction is cured and we stand as the new power, a host of Ascendant magi united by our shared suffering and ready to right the wrongs of the past.'

'May it come to pass,' Prandello declared. 'I am with you.' He waved a hand to encompass the camp outside. 'Salim is close by, a lion attended by jackals. The sultan is a rare leader, a man to inspire anyone, but the alliances that bind this camp are weak. There are Ordo Costruo rebels here, and Hadishah, and all the sultan's human warlords. We Dokken know that our welcome here is tenuous at best, and that someday soon we will have to leave. Your coming is a sign that the time has come for us to disappear into the night.'

It became a pattern: a messenger bird, usually a sparrow, would arrive just before dawn as Cym sipped a weak tea made from dried astera leaves, boiled pre-dawn because she couldn't risk a fire during the day lest the smoke draw unwanted eyes. The bird would land beside her hand and wait, trembling and afraid, until she picked it up. Then the message implanted in its aura would flow into her and she would hear Zaqri's voice.

The news sounded good: a Dokken packleader named Prandello was sheltering him. The army was delaying to sort out some problems in the supply lines before they pushed on to the river. Prandello had agreed to help, but they were under constant surveillance by the sultan's magi, so they must prepare their move carefully. She should stay put, Zaqri told her, and await his instructions.

He missed her. He loved her.

It was strange how he could find the courage to say such things when he wasn't with her.

I love you too. She whispered it in her mind, but without the skill to implant a message in the bird's head as he had, she didn't know how to reply. It was too dangerous to move from her hideout in a faceless mass of rocks in the midst of nowhere. Whenever she went to the fringes to watch, she glimpsed riders passing in the distance. The sultan's army were near, and foraging – if they found her, a young woman alone, they would misuse her, so she stayed hidden, even when she was certain she was alone.

The rocks were snake-infested, but she had enough Animagery to drive them from the areas she frequented. The cave where she slept away most of each day and night wasn't big, and once she had rested and recovered, she was bored.

<I cannot come to you yet.> Zaqri's latest message said. <Prandello's Dokken are watched constantly by Hadishah. The factions within this army are many, and we've got to be careful. Be careful, stay safe. I will come for you soon.>

Then no bird came, and worry made her frantic. She prowled her little camp, fretting, convinced he was going to appear from any direction, right now. She sweated and prayed and cursed and couldn't sleep, no matter what she tried. Dawn found her covered in grime, rock dust sticking to her skin and her hair, itching and filthy. She hadn't washed in eight days, and her stores of food were running low.

Finally a wren swooped onto the rock above and bobbed to her hand. She almost crushed it in her desperation as she opened her mind and Zaqri's voice filled her head.

<I cannot come yet. Too many meetings, and the army is moving again. Your Rondian friends have failed to cross the river and are trapped. There will be battle soon. Stay where you are, lest my birds cannot find you. Be safe. I will come soon. All of my love.>

She found herself silently bawling, wracked with grief and utter frustration, so much that she could barely breathe. Eventually she calmed enough to wipe her swollen eyes and think.

How can you send me 'all of your love' when they are just words? All of your love means your face and your hands and your body and your smell and your taste and your heat!

Having broken through all of her self-punishing hate, and the cruel bonds of vendetta, she needed him all the more. Finding Alaron and the Scytale and freeing the Rimoni were like pallid shadows against the desire to see his face. And now Ramon was in danger too. The army is moving, he said. And she was running out of food.

That night she slipped from the cave and padded toward the sultan's camp.

My place is with him.

There was a spider in the corner of Alyssa Dulayne's pavilion, a big, sleek thing with purple swirls on its distended abdomen. Deadly poisonous, but she didn't mind. She understood spiders and their webs. You filled your world with strands, so thin and gauzy the creatures blundering past didn't notice. You wove patiently, repaired and tended constantly, then retreated to the shadows, always touching your web, waiting for it to tremble.

When Rashid Mubarak had gone north after Shaliyah, he'd left her behind in the sultan's court. Some fools wondered if Rashid was tiring of his white-skinned concubine, but she knew her value. She was his eyes and ears at the heart of the most vital web of all.

I'm the most powerful woman in Ahmedhassa. I'm the Lucia Sacrecour of the East.

If she'd been born in Pallas, she would have been spinning her webs at the centre of the empire. Instead she'd been born among the Ordo Costruo of Pontus, where intellect and seriousness were prized and beauty regarded as merely skin-deep. She'd shown them *skin-deep*: she'd gone deep under their skins, those pompous geniuses; they could be reduced to quivering jelly like any other man.

Magi like Rene Cardien had stormed about decrying her loose morality – so-called 'liberal' magi who hated that she lived with all the freedom they idealised yet feared. Antonin Meiros had called her 'that slattern', but all he'd done was drive his own daughter into her web.

Rashid had once asked her why she'd betrayed the Ordo Costruo, but the answer was simple: *Because I could.* The game meant so much more to her than the reasons why she played. Let others agonise over ideology and ethics. *All I want is the joy of victory – and the pleasures that come with it.*

She smiled to herself at the thought, and returned her attention to what she was doing: powdering her face ready for another night of intrigue. Her blonde hair was plaited into ornate patterns with pearls woven through the shining tresses. A ballgown of cloth-of-silver clung to her curvaceous body, even though she would have to endure a bekira-shroud over it while on public display. Tonight she planned to fascinate and entice, although hints were all anyone would be getting from her. That was the price for breathing these heady airs: the court of Salim was full of intrigue, but not hedonism, for Salim prized his own morality. Alyssa was accepted here as Rashid's woman, and because she was Ordo Costruo, but a scandal now would be harmful. She was already a ready target for the mealy-mouthed Godspeakers and jealous Hadishah.

Her maid tinkled the bell outside her tent. *Let tonight's games begin.* 'Yes, Lesharri?'

Lesharri scuttled inside and fell to her knees at Alyssa's feet. She was part-Hebb, and Alyssa's half-sister, her late father's bastard child. Alyssa had been bringing her under her control for years, reducing the girl's sense of self until she was merely an extension of her own will. Lesharri's only joy now was to do exactly as Alyssa bid. *Would that I had more like you, dear sister.* Of course, such mind-conditioning was illegal, and if the Ordo Costruo had ever realised, they both would have been executed.

How terribly short-sighted of them, she thought.

'Lady, the Dokken Lord's woman is here.'

'Prandello's whore?' That was a strand of her web that seldom quivered. Alyssa admired the glittering creature in her mirror, the goddess she became on nights like these. 'Bring her in.'

Lesharri bobbed her head eagerly and showed in the woman. She took her cloak, then settled in the corner, poised to act if there was any threat – for Lesharri was still a fully functioning mage.

The Dokken clan-leader's woman settled in the guest seat, clearly in awe.

Yes, I'm truly this beautiful. Alyssa cast about for her name . . . *Maddeoni: a Vereloni human, stolen by Prandello during the Second Crusade. More than a dozen years as Prandello's broodmare, and it shows. The mother of two boys she adores, but she longs to escape. Prandello is kind to her now, but she hates him still.*

A little sympathy had been all it took. While Prandello was away scouting during the siege of Ardijah, Alyssa had sought out his lonely concubine. *'Yes, it was awful what was done to you. If the chance comes, I may be able to help you, my dear.'*

Tonight, perhaps that time had come. Alyssa loathed the Dokken, and would welcome the chance to strike against them, even if it weakened the army. They were by far the older enemy, after all.

'Maddeoni, how are you this lovely evening?'

The woman tugged her bekira-hood down, her big eyes filling with tears. She was fading joylessly into middle-age, her face lined, her temples grey and the dark circles under her eyes turning to sagging pouches. Her voice was bitter as she announced, 'The clan is preparing to leave, Lady.'

Most of Alyssa's visitors told her snippets like this, things they thought important. Most were ill-informed or misinterpreted; she had learned to be patient, to encourage the giving, and examine each morsel thoroughly. 'The whole army is about to march, Maddeoni,' she said lightly.

'This is different. They're leaving the shihad.'

Opportunity chimed. 'Are they really? Tell me more.'

'They are going to forsake the shihad during the confusion of the march.' Maddeoni laughed drily. 'The fools thought me asleep as they discussed their plans, their routes. Prandello forgets I exist,' she added in a low, vindictive voice. 'They're taking us women and the children into the wilds to hide, and then the men are going off somewhere. He sits half the night drinking and planning with his closest people, and the stranger.'

Alyssa took the woman's hands in hers. 'They pledged to join the shihad, Maddy. To leave like this is wrong; it will make many people terribly angry. You've done well in telling me.'

Maddeoni's eyes narrowed. 'Will they be . . . chastised?'

'Quite possibly,' Alyssa said, affecting worry. 'Unless we can prevent them from doing anything foolish.'

'No, I want them to be foolish. I want them to be *punished*,' the Vereloni woman hissed. Then her face clouded. 'As long as my children are safe.'

Alyssa gripped the woman's hands, projecting fervent sincerity.

'Of *course* they will be safe, dearest. Children are so precious – even Dokken children. After all, if they never gain the gnosis, they are just like ordinary boys and girls, are they not?' She hugged Maddeoni to her gently. 'I'll see you safe, Maddy.' She kissed her cheek. 'Now, tell me about this stranger.'

'Tell me truly, brother, why can't your pack help us?' Prandello asked. 'I have only fifty Brethren after our losses at Ardijah. The rest of our kin went north to aid Rashid Mubarak – we need as many men as we can to search an area so vast.'

'I don't believe this thing will be able to be kept secret for long,' Zaqri replied, evading the question of his pack. 'It will come to light, I'm sure.'

'But who will hear of it first? Information wins wars: do you even know who we seek?'

'I do: a Rondian male and a Lakh female, both young. We'll find a way: they won't be able to stay hidden long.' He sighed. 'If only all of our Brethren could join the hunt! We all stand to gain from it. If we could work together, I'm sure we would find them first.'

'You are no intriguer, Zaqri. Whenever our people gather there is feuding, not unity. But if we do find this thing, they'll come at our call, I'm sure of it.' Prandello finished his liquor and called for another bottle. His human wife scuttled out, surprising Zaqri, who had forgotten she was there. She produced the required bottle then fled again into the shadows. Prandello poured him another and they shared it in silence.

There was another revelation Zaqri needed to make, and he judged this as good a time as any. 'Prandello, there is another thing. I have a woman, waiting near here for me.'

'Of course you do.' The clan-master chuckled.

'The thing about this girl . . . she is magi.'

Prandello's eyes bulged, and for a time he was speechless, then his expression became calculating. 'What is it you hope to achieve, Zaqri of Metia. Another Nasette? If so, then that isn't the way.'

'I know. But what does happen when one of them bears our seed?'

158

What nature will the child have? Do we know?' He shrugged, affecting callous disregard. 'I'm curious. There's been one miscarriage so far, but I plough her during her fertile period and hope for issue. Her time is approaching now.'

Prandello frowned, considering the presence of a mage-woman among his clan, then shrugged. 'As long as my clan can see that you rule her and not the other way around, there should not be problems.'

They parted soon after and Zaqri had just reached his tent when he was surprised to feel Cym's mental touch, seeking him. Despite the danger, his heart leapt and he slipped from camp to find her, then led her back through the sea of tents to his own. Inside they writhed together wordlessly, not speaking a word until they were done, they lay panting and sweating, inhaling each other's scent.

'I was about to summon you,' he whispered. 'The army is marching in the morning and we'll be splitting from them en route and going east. Prandello's been told about you; he says you'll have his protection.'

She laid her head on his chest, looked at him from inches away with big, nervous eyes. 'Can you trust him?'

'I believe so.'

'I almost didn't come,' she told him. 'My premonition is getting worse. I don't care about the Scytale any more – chasing it will kill us, my love. Please, let's just leave.' Her face was tired, her eyes red-rimmed, as if she'd not slept in his absence.

He stroked her hair. 'Cym, no one will harm you, I promise. But I must do this. It's for my people.'

'Please! I'll marry you and bear your children. Only let us leave, now!'

'I can't.'

For a moment he thought she would depart – he could see that she was contemplating it – and to forestall her he rolled onto her and took her again, as if he might nail her to the earth and prevent her going. It seemed to work, or maybe he'd just exhausted her, for afterwards she sighed as if contented, and closed her eyes.

She was deeply asleep within moments. He extricated himself

and went to empty his bladder, stumbling through the slumbering camp to the waste trenches, peeing into a foetid ditch, then turning to go back to his tent.

He froze.

There was a white woman standing some fifteen yards from him, her features lit by the moon. She wore a loose bekira-shroud, parted at the front to reveal a silver dress that barely contained her curvaceous form. Her blonde hair was caught up with pearls and her wide-lipped face had a sensuous, greedy look. There was a periapt of gleaming amethyst at her throat and a crystal-tipped wooden rod in her hand, the sort that amplified certain enchantments. She brandished it lazily. 'Zaqri of Metia, I believe?'

Behind her, dark shadows were stealing into the Dokken camp and lamps were winking out. The guards had vanished. He opened his mouth to bellow a warning when the crystal rod in her hand pulsed.

A hideous feeling gripped his insides, as if a demon with acid-tipped talons were ripping its way from his belly and he staggered, tried to fight it, but the blow was already struck. A bout of weakness rippled through him, sending him to his knees, and then his face hit the sand.

Dimly, he heard the screams begin, but they were drowned out by the crunch of her feet beside his ears. She said something, a deafening whisper that contained words he should know, but the agony inside him was too great. Even as men appeared behind her, shrouded in black and carrying blades, the next wave of pain swept him under and away.

'Lady Alyssa,' Lesharri simpered, 'the Dokken wakes.'

Alyssa was watching the Hadishah bind Zaqri of Metia. She'd Chained his gnosis herself as he lay unconscious in the mud that surrounded the waste ditches. The stench was rather nauseating, but the night had otherwise been perfect. 'Take him to my tent,' she directed the Hadishah men, then sent Lesharri to ensure they left him unharmed while she went to Prandello's tent.

The attack had been all she could have hoped. The Dokken had some powerful gnosis-wielders, but at this time of the night they were either drunk, asleep or both, and most died without ever waking. Those few that resisted had surrendered when their mates or children were threatened – and then they'd died anyway, because a monster will always be a monster.

Killing the women and children came next. They couldn't risk that the women might not be pregnant, nor that the children grow to become enemies. Maddeoni lay in a heap, stabbed to death while trying to protect her sons. They lay beneath her in a circle of churned and bloody sand. Alyssa barely glanced at the woman she had sworn to protect.

It is these unpleasant decisions that set leaders apart, she told herself, pleased at her own decisiveness.

She found Prandello lying on a carpet, clutching his right arm, which had been slashed to the bone. One of the Hadishah captains, Pashil, had Chain-runed him. Pashil was not someone she trusted, but he need not know that. As she greeted him, Salim entered – or maybe one of his impersonators; they all knew how to shield their minds, and she'd still not quite worked out who was who.

'Sal'Ahm, Great Sultan,' she breathed, prostrating herself. Beside her Pashil did the same.

'Have you achieved what was required?'

'We have, Great Sultan,' Pashil answered. He looked like a middle-aged scholar, mild of face, with grey peppering his hair. 'They are purged. Only this one lives.'

Then he doesn't know I have this Zaqri, Alyssa noted. *Nor Cymbellea di Regia.* 'Prandello must be questioned, Great Sultan,' she said. 'He was plotting against us.'

'Plotting what, Lady Alyssa?' the sultan asked.

'That is still to be learned,' she replied, internally quivering at the full import of what Maddeoni had overheard. 'But extricating his secrets will require great skill.'

'My torturers have great skill,' Salim noted. The sultan regarded himself a man of culture and honour and disliked torture, but he wasn't above using it when needed.

'These are matters of the gnosis,' she countered. 'I can extract his plots more humanely than a torturer.'

She watched the sultan's innate squeamishness settle the matter. 'Then you may question him, Lady.'

Pashil scowled. 'I will supervise personally, Great Sultan, and report the findings to you directly.'

Think you're clever, Pashil? Then perhaps I won't ask Prandello the right questions . . . I'll save those for Zaqri of Metia . . . For if Zaqri of Metia had information concerning the artefact Maddeoni had spoken of, then she and she alone had to extract it. *And if this is all true, then Rashid and I will be the heads of a new Ascendancy . . .*

Tremble, Urte . . .

'Wake up, girl!'

Cym had been drowsing, vaguely conscious that Zaqri had gone, but not far; she could still sense him. She had never sensed the attack, though, not until it was too late, when men had slashed their way into the tent and pinned her down and a sharp knife of pain that she couldn't fight stabbed through her mind. Her mental scream died stillborn, her last sight a blockish woman's face inches from hers, her eyes blasting through her. Then came the Chain-rune, the twisting agony of it binding her, like being wrapped in thorns, and she'd lost consciousness.

Now she was waking again, terrified for him, and for herself. She quivered in sudden fright as a woman spoke, right beside her. She went rigid, afraid to open her eyes.

'Oh, come now,' a woman purred. 'I'm not going to hurt you, Cymbellea.'

Hearing her name startled Cym's eyes into opening. A lush blonde woman with a seraphic face was sitting beside her pallet. She was dressed in a bekira-shroud, but it was carelessly worn, revealing her shimmering silver gown. 'Cymbellea Meiros, don't you remember me?'

Cym stared. 'No . . .' *She knows my mother's name?*

'Fie! I held you, newborn and screaming, you were. So angry to be born!' The woman sighed. 'I was upset when Justina gave you away.

I'd have kept you myself if I'd been allowed, but Justina was my best friend, so I had to support her. It was I who gave you to Mercellus when he reappeared.'

What? 'Who are you?'

'Has your mother never said?' The blonde woman looked hurt. 'I'm Alyssa Dulayne, of the Ordo Costruo: your mother's closest friend.'

Cym's throat went dry. 'My mother is . . .'

'I know, she's dead,' Alyssa interrupted. Her face hardened. 'And I know who killed her. I've been inside his head.'

Her words reopened old wounds in Cym's heart: the hatred she'd carried so long for Zaqri, the conflict that had poisoned their love. She'd resolved it, in her own mind, but what would this woman think?

'Do you have Zaqri?' she asked timorously.

Alyssa's eyes narrowed. 'I do.'

'Please, let him go.'

'I'm afraid not,' Alyssa replied. 'He's a Dokken. And he killed the best friend I ever had. And he has information about something I need. I'm sure you know what I'm talking about.'

Her hope began to wither. Zaqri had told her about the Scytale. They said every man broke under torture. It was just a case of how long it took. 'If you've . . .' she began, struggling to articulate her horror.

Alyssa's face was curious. 'Why would you care about him, Cymbellea?'

This woman is a reptile. She's lying. Mater Luna, save us . . .

'I'll tell you everything, voluntarily, if you just let him go.'

'But you intrigue me, dear girl. A Dokken and a mage together? You've fornicated with him, haven't you? Are you another Nasette in the making?' She leaned forward. 'I must keep you with me so I can unravel these mysteries. For your mother's sake . . .'

'The Scytale—'

'Yes, the Scytale . . . I'll return it to the Ordo Costruo, as I'm sure your mother would have wanted.' Alyssa stretched out her hand languidly and patted her. 'There is no reason you and I cannot work together . . .'

She stared mutely, wondering if she could somehow fool this Rondian bitch.

Alyssa Dulayne let loose a tinkling laugh. 'Oh my dear, you're so transparent. I've been a piece on the tabula board of power all my life. I've risen from pawn to queen and I know all the moves, darling girl. I'm not fooled by the likes of you. Caught up in the flush of first love, all you can think of is *him-him-him*. That won't do.' She stood. 'You will both accompany me. You will remain Chained. You will each cooperate, or the other will suffer.' She gestured, and the leather thongs binding Cym to the bed tightened.

'For now, you just rest, my dear,' Alyssa told her, her angelic smile not touching her frosty eyes.

Seth Korion was given time he never expected to prepare his defences on the banks of the Tigrates River. Baltus Prenton, observing the Keshi from the air, reported great disruptions in the sultan's army, with the result that they didn't advance on the Lost Legions' riverside position for another two weeks.

However, there was still no way for the Lost Legions to move out of the trap. Keshi cavalry hemmed them into their fortified position, which the men had started calling Riverdown. The river itself remained impassable, and there were Kirkegarde patrols on the far bank. They'd sent scouts north and south seeking a crossing place, to no avail, so all they could do was dig deeper, labouring night and day to prepare for the inevitable.

The Octen moon became a sliver and vanished, and the Keshi finally marched. As Noveleve dawned, Seth and his magi beheld a plain that was now thick with the enemy as far as the eye could see.

The men stayed calm, he noted with pride. All along the line, they watched the enemy force growing, marching out of the haze in bewildering numbers. But these were men who'd escaped Shaliyah and Ardijah, where they'd believed themselves doomed. There was fear, certainly, but there was faith too, that someone or something would get them out of this.

That someone being me, he reflected, troubled by their expectations.

If he strained his eyes, he could see the richly dressed cluster of Keshi nobility gathered about the throne of Salim, Sultan of Kesh. Perhaps Latif was among them, wondering what would happen here. He wondered too.

The one thing that won't happen is surrender.

9

Breaking the Code

Daemonic Armies

Summoning and controlling even one daemon can be deadly dangerous, yet there have been many attempts by ambitious Wizards to summons armies of them. All such attempts have been failures, for a variety of logistical reasons. For a start, unless the host-body is a mage, the daemon's powers are limited and the host is rapidly burned out. No mage would willingly allow a daemon possession of his body and mind. Secondly, some form of mass-control is required, and the power and intellect required exceeds the power of even an Ascendant. And, of course, the possession spell itself is banned under the Gnostic Accords, and rightly so.

BROTHER JACOBUS, SACRED HEART ARCANUM, 802

The Valley of Tombs, Gatioch, on the continent of Antiopia
Zulqeda (Noveleve) 929
17th month of the Moontide

'Adamus, your fortitude really is incredible.' Malevorn Andevarion was amazed that the broken wreck of a man on the wooden frame still breathed, let alone resisted. 'But it's useless, my Lord Crozier.'

He'd thought the clergyman would crumble inside an hour. He'd always despised him as an effeminate *frocio*, but Adamus had surprised him. Perhaps if it had been Raine Caladryn asking the questions, she might have carved his mind open in no time, but neither he nor Hessaz, who was helping him, were specialists in torture, and he was beginning to worry that the man would die unbroken.

166

'Look at you,' he whispered in what was left of Adamus' ear. 'Broken fingers and toes, broken face. Scalped. Shattered knees. Castrated. Branded. Blinded. What is the point any more? You will never have a life, if even by some miracle Kore Himself reached down and took you in his hands. Stop resisting, Adamus. Give up.'

The crozier didn't dignify that with any kind of reaction; for the past three weeks he'd somehow shut himself inside his own head and not come out. The physical tortures obviously reached him on one level, for he still screamed like a child, but his mind remained a tiny ball of shielded consciousness Malevorn couldn't worm a way inside, keeping his secrets inviolate, unreachable.

If Malevorn couldn't break Adamus, then his own fate would be like this: more Inquisitors would be sent, and eventually they would find him. He stared at the man, lashed to an X-shape of wooden beams, naked and ruined, and tried to think what else could be done that might reach him. *Perhaps . . .*

He turned to Hessaz. 'Cut his eyelids off.'

The Lokistani woman shuddered. 'Do it yourself, hero.' She backed away, her eyes full of loathing. 'I've had enough of you, Inquisitor. And enough of this.'

'Then go! And don't think to share in the rewards, Souldrinker. There'll be no "salvation" for you!'

She stopped and snarled, 'I like myself fine as I am.' She stalked out of the foetid chamber and Malevorn slumped into a chair and cradled his head in his hands. *Damn this all the way to Hel.*

This chamber, beneath one of the monuments in the Valley of Tombs, might have been made for the purpose, for it had manacles on the walls and this giant cross-beam had clearly been made to hold a man captive. Xymoch said that the God-Kings of Gatti used to wall up servants in their tombs with them. While the reptile-shifters feasted and debauched, and Huriya hunched over her divining bowls, it had been left to him and Hessaz to try and unlock Adamus' mind, but all he had learned was that he wasn't a torturer, for all his other sins.

He decided nothing further could be gained tonight, forced food and water down the crozier's throat, then sought a bottle of some liquor Xymoch's people brewed and his own quarters. He had taken a room far from the others, sick of the sight of these animals in human form. These days he drank himself into a stupor every night, to avoid dreaming of everything he'd done to Adamus. He'd stopped shaving, washing, caring; day and night meant nothing; he was lost in these lightless catacombs.

He was finishing the last swallow of a tasteless liquor that kicked like a mule when he realised that Huriya was leaning against the door frame. Unusually, she was clad in a bekira-shroud that kept her lush curves hidden.

'What do you want?' he slurred.

She sashayed into her room, sniffed the air and wrinkled her nose, but sat anyway. 'Hessaz says you've failed. And that she won't work with you again.'

'Cowardly bitch! She hasn't got the stomach for it.'

'She's no coward. Regardless, she wants no further part of the torture.'

'Then damn her. She misses out, if we get what we need.' Which was an increasingly forlorn hope. His bottle was somehow empty, so he hurled it into the shattered pile of empties in the corner.

Huriya stood. 'Come to me when you're sober: I'll show you how to break the good crozier.'

'You?' He scowled, knowing he sounded defeated. 'He's not going to break, Huriya. I don't have the skill. If I inflict any more damage on him he'll die and we'll have lost.'

'I know a way, "Heart of my Heart",' she told him. 'Tomorrow.'

Huriya stopped at the door of the crozier's cell. 'Wait here, and keep everyone else out,' she told Malevorn before entering and closed the door firmly behind her.

Of course he watched through the keyhole, but what he saw wasn't at all what he had expected. Huriya took the man down from the frame and laid him on a pallet. First she washed him, then she began to undo all that Hessaz and Malevorn had wrought upon him, repairing his hands and feet, working on those parts which hurt the most.

What he couldn't work out was what she thought to achieve: did she intend to betray him by allying herself with the crozier? It seemed inconceivable, but then, if she could enslave the man, where would that leave him? Several times he almost burst in, demanding answers, but he held back: the room was a dead end and there was no escape, except through him.

He pulled out the straightsword he'd taken from Artus LeBlanc's corpse and his whetstone and began to sharpen it, to while away the hours.

By the following dawn Huriya had used her Ascendant-strength gnosis to set regeneration in effect, re-growing the crozier's amputated fingers and toes, and even his genitals. She'd also begun to revive him. He was still clearly drained, but Malevorn could sense him regaining consciousness. When he opened his eyes to find himself clean and naked on freshly laundered sheets, whole, or nearly so, he clearly thought himself dreaming. He stared at his hands, then down his body, and began to weep, the most piteous sobbing Malevorn had ever heard in his life.

When at last he ceased to cry, his eyes filled with a dawning realisation that perhaps this nightmare ordeal might end in something other than total extinction. When he gazed at Huriya now he clearly saw someone sent from on high to save him.

Malevorn extended his senses to listen and her words, a constant flow of soothing and comfort, became discernible: <*Dear Adamus, soon you will be free. Soon the world will be yours and mine. Soon you will feel the joy of renewal and walk and ride as you used to. It will be as if the hurts of the past weeks never were. Even the scars of memory will fade and leave you innocent and pure in Kore's light.*> All the while that she salved him, Adamus' mind bled emotion: grief, rage, humiliation, all welling up, only to be soothed by her into something approaching peace.

Does she mean to betray us all? She and the crozier together . . . they wouldn't need the rest of us . . .

He loosened his sword and kindled his wards and as he did, Huriya's eyes flickered to the keyhole.

She's Ascendant, but she's not a fighter. She panics under direct attack . . . .

'Malevorn,' she called. She gestured, and the door swung open. He came to his feet in one flowing motion, baring his sword. She looked at it with some amusement, but Adamus didn't even notice; his tear-stained face saw only her.

'Malevorn, look: I have wiped the canvas clean.' She threw a look of pure cruelty at Adamus. 'I suppose you're just going to have to do it all again.'

Malevorn got it at last. *Sweet Kore, she's cruel as a Lantric nymph!* His eyes went to Adamus' face and he made himself smile with all the relish he could, to make Adamus believe that he was eager to go through the same ghastly ordeal again.

The clergyman broke, before his eyes. He didn't scream or beg, but something inside snapped: the thin thread that Huriya had given him, to which he'd clung and made into the central thread of his resistance. His face collapsed; he aged twenty years in a moment, his skin turned ashen and his eyes emptied.

She saw it too. She bent over him and did something with the gnosis that filled the crozier's eyes with grey light. She didn't even bother to bind Adamus again, simply turned her back and walked towards Malevorn. 'They do say that it's hope that kills you,' she murmured.

Sweet Kore! Her face mirrored his – a certain sickness at what had been done, but countered by the need that drove those acts. That surprised him, seeing vulnerability where he'd been accustomed to worldly callousness. She was obviously far more complex than he really understood. He'd heard that Souldrinkers only took power, not identities from their victims, but that wasn't what he sensed in Huriya. What eighteen-year-old girl behaved as she did? The Keshi girl's identity seemed to be morphing into someone else before his eyes.

How many ancient lives are inside her head? Who's in control? Whose idea was it that broke Adamus: Huriya's, or some other entity? Who is she now?

They stared at each other for a long time before he recalled their purpose here. 'Huriya, we've got a potion to brew, and we have to control Xymoch's clan while we do it. We still need each other, Heart of my Heart.'

'We do indeed, Malevorn Andevarion.'

For a while . . .

Very tentatively, he reached out a hand to her and she let him place it on her arm. 'There's a side-effect of that heart-spell,' he told her. 'Over time, our moods begin to align. You might have already noticed.'

She looked at him thoughtfully, searching his face. 'Only a mated pair may challenge for a position of rank in Dokken society. If we are to control Xymoch's pack, we must rule it.' She pushed her chest out. 'Are you prepared to dirty yourself with a mudskin, Inquisitor?'

'I would do anything for the power we will gain from the Scytale.'

'So would I,' she replied, looking at him appraisingly. 'So why don't you come to my chamber tonight?'

Malevorn was surprised to discover that mudskin girls weren't so different after all, at least, not when you pinned them down and filled them. There was the same sweet slickness and heat, the same excruciating pleasure when you came. It was far from love, or even liking, but the desire wasn't feigned.

The rest took time. They gleaned the ingredients and workings of the Scytale from the shattered thing that had once been Adamus Crozier, then challenged Xymoch and his savage wife. Naturally they triumphed: while Huriya gripped his brain, Malevorn gutted Xymoch; moments later they made an example of his mate. His people were quick to pledge allegiance after that.

Now they knew what they needed, they sent men out to the markets of the nearby towns to purchase the chemicals and herbs. Adamus even helped them brew the first batch.

Octen was gone and Noveleve begun. The desert was cooling at night, although the daytime heat was still suffocating. They dwelled in the cool rooms below the earth, sleeping through the day time and working at night. And as the Scytale revealed its secrets, Malevorn traced out the complicated formulae with growing excitement.

Finally, as the New Moon waxed and fattened, they were ready for the New Ascension.

10

Test of Faith

Pallas

Pallas was originally a village called Pilum, or Spear, where the Siber River met the mighty Bruin, in the Rimoni province of Turium. It was important only for the legion town on the north bank, that same legion destroyed by the Ascendants in 380. But after the destruction of Rym, Pilum became the new base for the Magi. It was renamed 'Pallas' after a Lantric deity of Learning and became the seat of a new empire. The city now covers more than one hundred square miles, has a population of two million, and is the richest city in Yuros, if not all of Urte. And this is just the beginning of what the Ascendancy set in motion.

ORDO COSTRUO COLLEGIATE, PONTUS

Mandira Khojana, Lokistan, on the continent of Antiopia
Zulqeda (Noveleve) 929
17th month of the Moontide

Alaron and Ramita sat side by side behind a desk, facing a shaven-headed acolyte in his crimson robes. The notes Alaron had taken five months earlier were spread across the table before him. The acolyte's name was Gateem, and he looked overwhelmed.

It had taken several goes, with added explanations from Master Puravai, but the young man finally understood what Alaron and Ramita were offering him: he could become a mage.

Gateem raised his troubled face and asked Puravai, 'Would I still be reborn to the Path of Light?'

This was proving a common question: Zain monks followed the

Lakh Path of Light, the cycle of life, death and rebirth; the goal in each life was to attain something they called 'moksha' – release from the cycle into a kind of paradise. Though the Zains did not believe in the Omali gods – to them, gods represented ideas and were not real beings – they shared belief in the Path towards wisdom and spiritual clarity.

Master Puravai answered thoughtfully and respectfully, 'Gateem, none who walk the Path of Light have ever been given such a choice. However, there have been times when a Zain monk has been put in a position of authority in society. The wisdom of the masters on that matter is that power amplifies the temptations we face, and that involvement in society complicates our choices, but neither of these things alters the nature of moksha.'

Gateem wrung his hands uncomfortably. 'Master, I don't understand.'

'These are indeed difficult concepts,' Puravai said sympathetically. 'Let me remind you of a tale of Zain. Long ago, when he was a lowly wanderer, there were many who mocked him. In one village there was a man called Mulat who struck the Master, leaving his nose broken, and drove him from his village. Some years later Master Zain returned to that village at the head of many disciples, and the village welcomed him and asked him to arbitrate on their disputes. One of the disputes involved Mulat, the man who had abused him. Do you recall what the Master did?'

Gateem nodded dutifully. 'He heard the case fairly and deemed that Mulat was in the right, ignoring his own previous encounter with the man.'

'And the lesson?'

'That power does not change the nature of what is right or wrong,' Gateem replied quickly, clearly a rote answer.

'Indeed. But consider also that the Master had been placed into a position of power: he was now judging right and wrong in others, and his decisions would be affecting the rest of their lives. Still he chose justice over personal satisfaction.'

'So if I do this, you are warning me that I will face harder choices that will place greater pressure upon me.'

174

'Yes: harder, more complex, and more ambiguous. The Path of Light remains, but it can be harder to see amidst the confusion and enormity of life. Power is a great responsibility that few have the strength to deal with.'

'Then I truly would be endangering my soul?'

'Gateem, it is written that to attain moksha, we must face our fears. One must look into the Darkness to understand the Light. A test not taken can never be overcome.'

Alaron looked sideways at Ramita and stifled a yawn. They'd been conducting these private interviews all day, giving each of those for whom they had an individual recipe for the ambrosia a chance to ask their questions, and express their doubts. Master Puravai had given no guidance to the candidates beyond helping them to look into their own hearts, and Alaron still couldn't tell if any or all of the novices were willing.

How can anyone raised in a monastery dedicated to nonviolence and self-realisation be ready for this? I was raised knowing one day I'd have the gnosis, and I barely knew how to cope.

Gateem had no more questions, and was eager to go, no doubt to seek out the other candidates, who had gathered in one of the upper courtyards. While each young man would make his own choice, peer pressure was obviously going to be a factor. The opinion-leaders would be influential. Gateem was one such, for he was popular. Yash too, for his skill with the staff and knowledge of the outside world. Well-educated Aprek, worldly Felakan and aggressive Kedak were the others: how they chose would be crucial.

As the young novice left, Ramita let out a tired sigh. 'Yes, it has been a long day,' Puravai agreed, getting to his feet and flowing into a few stretches, his joints popping a little. 'Gateem was the last candidate of thirty-eight. Four full monks and thirty-four novices: more than half of our trainees.' He looked intently at Alaron. 'You realise that you will cost this monastery many of its future brethren, should they all accept.'

'That's if they do. What if none want to?'

'That is also possible,' Puravai acknowledged. 'I do appreciate the restraint you are showing, Brother Longlegs. A lesser man would have been begging – or demanding.'

'Inside I'm doing both,' Alaron admitted. 'I want to shout at some of them! But where will that get us?'

'Recognising that fact is a sign of your growing maturity,' Puravai told him.

'Perhaps. But what if no one will help us stand up to Malevorn and Huriya?' Images of an Ascendant Malevorn Andevarion had been filling Alaron's nightmares for many weeks now.

'Only the willing will be of true value to your cause. Through your restraint, you show that you are a man worth following.' Puravai patted Alaron's arm. 'We've done what we can. The rest is up to them.'

Ramita fixed the old master with a frank look. 'What would *you* choose if Alaron had the recipe for you?'

Puravai smiled softly. 'The decision process isn't over, child. I'll not express any view, not even privately, until afterwards.' He bowed a little stiffly and hobbled away, leaving them alone.

Alaron looked at Ramita and yawned mightily. 'Well? What do you think?'

'I don't know. If you gave this question to any boy from Aruna Nagar he'd say yes so fast he'd bite your hand off. But these monks . . .' She pulled a sour face. 'Where I grew up, the Zains were considered weaklings who had run away from life.'

'We used to say that the only people who wanted to be Kore priests were milkbloods, fanatics and politicians – certainly no one you'd want beside you in a war. But these Zains are different: priests in Yuros don't learn weaponry. The martial training they do gives you a feeling of capability, that you have the capacity to do anything. They might *seem* passive, but if they're attacked, they are dangerous. They do know how to fight.'

Though not how to kill.

Ramita looked unconvinced. 'It must be almost dinner-time. I'm starving, and I haven't seen Dasra all day.' She took his hand and they walked together, dawdling, enjoying the contact. They paused at a bend of the stone staircase where a barred aperture opened over the valley and enjoyed the play of the sunset's warm glow on the snow-tipped peaks above. The chill of night was creeping through the building, and Alaron shivered. Ramita noticed and drew him against her, sharing warmth.

Since they'd finally acknowledged their attraction, spending time together alone had become more intimate – and more awkward. He was maddened by her closeness, wanted her with all his body, but she was holding back; she'd been raised to do what was right, which meant not making love to anyone but her husband. But the real reason for restraint was the ritual of Ascendancy. If he was going to risk his life in that way, was it right to put their hearts into something that could be brief and ill-fated? Half of those given the first batch of ambrosia had died. How could he honestly speak of commitment to her when he could be dead in a few days? So all he could do was hold her, and count down the days to that test.

'Are the potions ready?' she asked.

'Almost. We can't brew the final draughts until we know which candidates are going to accept, but Corinea is distilling the ingredients.' He glanced sideways at her. 'She says that we need to test it on someone.'

Ramita looked up at him, suddenly tense. 'Why?'

'Because she's not made it before. She knew a little of what Baramitius was doing, but she says there is still some guesswork involved.'

'But testing it on someone . . .'

'I know. It's not fair to use one of these poor novices as an experiment. So I'm going to take it myself.'

Ramita looked up at him with a horrified expression. 'No! You can't! You're too important.'

His heart chimed at her concern, but he'd thought this through carefully. 'I'm the only one who already has Arcanum training and knows what gaining the gnosis feels like. Those novices would be stumbling in the dark. It *has* to be me.' He hoped he sounded braver than he felt. 'Neither you or Corinea need it; you're both already an Ascendant or stronger. So it *has* to be me.'

'But . . .' Her mouth hung open as she sought the words, and he could feel her wrestling against his logic, trying to find an alternative. *Because she cares.* He was uplifted, but he really couldn't see another way. Someone had to ensure the potion worked, and be able to give the young novices a first-hand account of what they would experience. He really was the best equipped to do it. But he was still frightened.

The first Ascendancy killed four hundred of the thousand who drank the ambrosia, left one hundred irrevocably insane and another hundred as Souldrinkers. *More than half of them died or ruined. The odds are terrible.* He couldn't put aside his fear, but he had to do this anyway, if he wanted to be with her, if he wanted to get Nasatya back and if he wanted to stop Malevorn.

He watched her expression go from denial to pained acceptance. 'Corinea and I will be with you in case anything happens,' she promised. 'When will you do it?'

'Next week, once we know what the novices have decided.' When she opened her mouth to protest, he put a finger to her lips. 'I just want to get it over with. I feel like it's this huge hurdle standing between me and the rest of my life.'

And I want to leap that hurdle: so you'll know I'm here for the long haul. So that you can include me in your plans, and I can include you in mine – because they're all about you anyway.

Ramita held Dasra to her. Nine months old, and already learning to crawl. They had found a nurse for him, a village girl who adored children. *He's such a happy baby*, she thought, stroking his thick black hair. Though she was sure missing his twin brother was at the root of his occasional tears. *Of all the cruel things you've done, Huriya, that was the worst.* She stared gloomily into space, wondering where Nasatya was in all this wide world.

Alaron was sitting next to her on the stone bench overlooking a courtyard outside Master Puravai's rooms, fretting. He was such an open book, each mood written across his face with broad brushstrokes. Right now he was tension itself as they waited on the decisions of the Zains.

In the courtyard below them, Master Puravai and Corinea concluded a brief conversation, then the old sorceress slipped away, lest she intimidate the novices. They still didn't know who she was, but she was scary enough that Puravai was keeping her from interacting with them anyway.

We're asking so much of them: to put aside their safety and join a war against people they don't know, when they're committed to non-violence. To learn a magic they probably think is inherently evil, and risk their immortal souls.

She fully expected just one to agree: Yash, who didn't really fit here.

The first of the candidates entered the tiny garden below and bowed before the Master. His name was Felakan, one of the four full monks who'd allowed Alaron to interview him earlier that year: a worldly man, but completely committed to the Zain principles of life.

'Well, Brother Felakan, what is your decision?' Puravai asked.

'Master, I thank you, but I must respectfully decline this. To endanger my soul, when I feel so close to the Infinite here, would be wrong.'

Ramita's bubble of hope popped. *The arrogance*, she thought angrily. *You think yourself so close to perfection you can't risk getting your hands dirty in the real world?*

The next three, all graduated monks, gave the same reply, leaving her and Alaron feeling crushed. Perhaps she imagined it, but Master Puravai didn't appear to be entirely pleased with their answers. Perhaps he too saw pride, not piety. It was a worrying start, though.

Aprek, a scholar from a well-to-do family, was the first novice to enter the courtyard to announce his choice. She had no great hopes of him; he typified her view of Zains as young men scared of facing the responsibilities of being husbands and fathers and providers and citizens, preferring to lock themselves away and wibble about self-perfection.

'Master,' Aprek said meekly, 'respectfully I must ask to be released from my path, to test myself in the fires.'

She took a moment to decipher his reply, then looked at Alaron, who was waiting for her translation. <*I think he just said yes!*> she said, clutching Dasra in trembling hands.

Puravai inclined his head. 'Are you sure, Aprek?'

'Yes, Master. I have given it much thought, and I had meditated particularly on your words at our interview: that we must pass through darkness to attain light.'

<Yes!> she sent to Alaron, her heart thumping. <We have one!>

Soon they had many more than one; every remaining novice echoed Aprek's words in their own way. Some, like Yash and Kedak, spoke of fighting to overcome evil. Others were more philosophical, and in truth, many appeared to be following the example of their peers. But all of the novices Alaron had interviewed – all thirty-four – accepted. Only the four full monks had declined. She hugged Dasra and closed her eyes, whispered a prayer of thanks to Vishnarayan, Protector of Men.

Then, of course, a fresh round of worries began. She reflected on what the ambrosia had done in Yuros five hundred years ago: *The potion will kill some of them, and make Souldrinkers of others. How many of them have just volunteered to die?*

'This is it?' Alaron looked at the small vial of milky grey-green fluid and trembled. His throat was so tight he doubted he'd be able to swallow. He was clad in a white shift, propped up on pillows and sitting on a pallet in the sickbay, which had become their laboratory.

Corinea took the vial back. 'This is it, in exactly the proportions your notes say.' She tapped it thoughtfully. 'I hope you took good notes.'

He winced. 'I did my best. But I couldn't figure out about blood types, and though I wrote down all the variations, I'm still not sure—'

'Don't worry,' Corinea interrupted, 'that's what the test I did was for; I took samples of blood from all the candidates and mixed the blood with some powders.' She'd taken some of his too, pricking his thumb, then dripping the blood into a vial of clear fluid that turned green. They were increasingly in her hands. There was so much damage she could do if she chose, and they'd not find out until it was too late. He didn't know how to read her; he could only hope she would repay his own trust with honesty.

'So what am I consuming?'

'Your potion has twenty-six ingredients, with four functions. First is the brackroot, or khedichar, as they call it here. It's a slow poison which acts upon your heart over the space of a couple of hours. Then there are a number of ingredients designed to feed your nervous system and brain so that they don't succumb. Of course there's the stimulant: the senaphium or jolt-root. That's the hardest thing to judge: it has to take effect within five minutes of your heart stopping. The dose is determined by body mass, gender, blood-type, and other physical characteristics. Get the dose wrong and it either triggers too soon and dissipates before it's needed and you die anyway; or it triggers too late, and you're already dead beyond reviving.'

For the millionth time Alaron wondered if this was such a good idea after all. It was all very well to be brave when the act was theoretical, but right now it just felt stupid. But he'd come too far to back out – and he would never feel worthy of Ramita if he didn't do this.

'Finally, there are hallucinogenic drugs,' Corinea continued, 'to stimulate an emotional and sensual palate to make sense of the experience. Without them you would sink into darkness and never return, even if your heart does manage to restart. These drugs allow your imagination to guide you back to consciousness. For myself, I recall falling through clouds and then becoming a bird. It was a struggle, as I've always been afraid of heights. I've heard of others speak of overcoming similar fears to survive.'

Alaron tried to think of something he wasn't afraid of, on some level. 'Okay.'

'It is the hallucinogens that are specifically brewed for you: the sort of person you are means that different parts of the brain need to be stimulated to enable you to fight your way back.' Her voice was eager, as if she couldn't wait for him to drink. This was her re-admittance to the world's stage, Alaron realised. He tried not to resent her for it.

Puravai put a hand on his shoulder. 'Stay calm, Brother Longlegs. Be focused, as you were when you re-learned the gnosis. You succeeded then, and you will in this also.'

Alaron looked at Corinea worriedly. 'What are the odds? Fifty-fifty?'

'No, much better. When Baramitius made the first batch of ambrosia, he had four different doses, based on gender and eye colour. It was monstrously imprecise, and that's what killed so many. He refined it since then, and my understanding is that few have failed more recently.' He was about to sigh in relief when she added, 'But then, who really knows? The empire doesn't publicise its failures.'

Thanks for that.

'But you have Arcanum training, and a unique array of gnostic skills,' she concluded. 'I believe you will prevail.'

That helped. He took a deep breath and decided he was probably ready as he would ever be.

'Could Al'Rhon and I have a moment alone?' Ramita asked quietly.

Corinea looked at Puravai impatiently, but the old Zain master stood up and ushered her out. Ramita sat beside him. 'Al'Rhon, I won't say you don't have to do this, because you do. Even if it wasn't to help find Nasatya or stop that Inquisitor, you would do this: to prove yourself.'

'I don't know—' he began to deny, but she cut him off.

'You know you would. But Al'Rhon, you don't have to prove anything: you are already the truest man I know.'

'But I'm not *him* ... Antonin Meiros, I mean.'

'Al'Rhon, of course you are not! But I'm not comparing you. He occupies a different chamber in my heart.'

He coloured. 'But I'm not like your Kazim, either.'

'Thank all the gods!' She clasped his hand in both hers. 'You are utterly unalike. Where you are steadfast, he was flighty. Where you treat me as an equal, he treated me as a lesser: a valued lesser, but in his mind he was always master. He wanted to put me on a pedestal in a kitchen. You want me as I am.'

'You've told me how romantic and handsome he was ...'

'Oh, he certainly was. But those are the things that spark love, not what sustain it. The last time I saw him he had my husband's blood on his hands. Believe me, you don't suffer by comparison.'

'But—'

'If you think you aren't handsome enough: find a mirror. If you don't think you are worthy of Lady Meiros, forget her. She doesn't exist. My name is Ramita Ankesharan, market-girl of Baranasi, and I am in love with you.'

He caught his breath. 'I love you too.'

She kissed him slowly, until his mouth softened and the tension in him subsided. When he opened his eyes again, he was smiling, and ready to risk his life.

The Valley of Tombs, Gatioch, on the continent of Antiopia
Zulqeda (Noveleve) 929
17th month of the Moontide

Malevorn Andevarion stared at the wriggling beetle pinched between his fingers. It had an iridescent green-blue carapace with yellow-brown highlights and was almost two inches long: a Death Scarab, or *kheper* in the Gatti language, so Huriya told him.

He knew the theory: you formed a link to the creature and bonded with it, and it bonded with you as it nestled in the top of the mouth, adjacent to the brain-stem. In time it became symbiotic with you, and if your body happened to perish, you lived on through the beetle until you found a new host-body.

Revolting.

Yet he knew he faced dangers: among the pack, certainly. From Hessaz, definitely. And even from Huriya, despite their burgeoning physical desire. In their private chamber they performed as if there was an audience, seeking emotional weakness in the other even as they strove physically. Some nights he thought she might be succumbing to him emotionally, but he still feared treachery.

But to spend eternity contained by a dung beetle . . . No, that is beneath me.

He crushed the scarab beneath his foot.

The next morning, they began. He poured the first batch of ambrosia into a golden goblet they'd retrieved from a previously unplundered tomb and showed Huriya the dirty-looking fluid. She sniffed it dubiously. 'Is that it?'

'It is.' He looked her up and down. She was clad in embroidered evening robes that had once belonged to Xymoch's dead wife, dressed as if for a celebration.

If this is successful, then that is what there will be . . .

The other observer on this night of nights was bound to a pillar in the corner, too weak to stand. Adamus Crozier's body was restored but his spirit was entirely broken. Malevorn wanted him there, both for his experience, and to witness the consequences of any failure.

'Shall we begin?' he asked Huriya, as if her permission were needed.

'Why not?'

They turned to Toljin.

The Vereloni warrior was on the floor, chained to metal rings set in the floor. He lay within a summoning circle that crackled with force, all focused inwards. Malevorn had drawn them, and Huriya would empower them when the time came. The objective was to test the potion on Toljin . . . then kill him afterwards.

Malevorn raised the cup in his hands and bent over the Souldrinker, who struggled futilely against his bindings. He was the last male of Zaqri of Metia's old pack, and he wouldn't survive the night. *History won't remember him at all: only me.*

Malevorn had begun to envisage the path ahead: the ambrosia would remove the Souldrinker affliction and he'd leave the East, returning to Pallas to give the ambrosia to his family and kin, rekindle old alliances, make promises . . . then he'd smash the Sacrecours and everyone else who'd pulled down his father. *I will be Malevorn, first of the Andevarion Emperors . . .*

He stepped inside the circle, careful to leave one foot anchored outside, because he wouldn't have put it past Huriya to try and seal him inside too, then caught Toljin's chin in one fist. 'Keep still,' he snarled, letting his full menace show. He'd always known how to scare weaker men, and Toljin was certainly that. He quailed, and though he clearly wished to spit it out, he took the small mouthful of potion meekly and swallowed.

'It will begin to take effect inside two hours,' Malevorn reminded him. 'After that, it's up to you. You must stay conscious, no matter what. Fight to stay alive. This is your test, Toljin. Succeed, and you will be with us when we conquer the world. Fail, and, well . . .'

Toljin nodded mutely.

Malevorn stepped out of the circle and Huriya raised her hands. A web of light arose from the etched circle, becoming a hemisphere that quickly faded to invisibility. Within the circle Toljin groaned with fear, looking about him wildly as Malevorn and Huriya retreated to either side of the chamber. There was a flask of wine on a low table, but neither wanted to be impaired in any way when the moment came. They settled down to wait, and even Adamus Crozier's eyes grew attentive: this was something he'd surely longed to see – the actual transformation of a man to an Ascendant.

The first hour passed slowly, with only Toljin's increasing discomfort to mark it. He flushed a deep red as his blood began to race, his face turning almost purple, and his breathing became increasingly ragged. Then as the second hour began, he began to babble, first begging Huriya to free him, shrieking that he loved her, that only he loved her, that everyone else meant her ill. Huriya listened with blank contempt.

Then Toljin turned on Malevorn, spewing hatred. As his vitriol peaked, he thrashed violently, the poisons beginning to take effect. Then his breathing slowed, and this frenzied energy drained away. They saw the dregs of his gnosis engage – they'd deliberately not allowed him to replenish his powers, in case he might find ways to delay the onset of the potion. They saw him burn away his reserves in seconds, and still the potion gripped him and he went on dying.

Then it happened: he coughed violently, his chest thudded as if breaking open from inside, he thrashed for a few seconds . . . and then fell motionless.

Malevorn found he was holding his breath. The air was cloying, and he heard faint whispers with his gnostic senses, the voices of aetheric spirits, envious of life. He kindled Necromantic wards and drove them away. Seconds crawled past. Toljin needed to show signs of recovery within a couple of minutes or he was lost, but still he lay unmoving.

Then he coughed.

Huriya squealed delightedly, and Adamus swore. Malevorn clenched a fist triumphantly, and opened his inner eye wide. Toljin's head fell sideways, and his whole body jerked once, then again. His eyes flew open. Then he vented a scream that shook the dust from the stones.

Malevorn seized his periapt, because he could sense some kind of impending *arrival*, like giant wings beating and a shadow descending, while his gnostic senses cried a warning. He kindled fresh wards, specific ones he remembered from his Arcanum training, because he'd felt this sensation before. Toljin was breathing fast now, muttering incoherently. His eyes refocused and found Malevorn, and he looked at him with pleading in his eyes. Then something struck the penned man and he fell to the stone.

<*Toljin?*> Malevorn sent cautiously.

There was no response, but he caught the sense of a presence, powerful but disorientated. He quickly withdrew his mental probe.

'What happened?' Huriya asked sharply. 'I felt something.'

Gnosis use created a sensation, something like the feel of wind and the sound of distant thunder, that other magi could sense. If the spell was of a specific Study, it was easiest to discern by those who also used that Study.

We're all Wizards in this room . . .

He moved too late.

One moment, Toljin was lying contorted on the stone, still pinned in place by the chains.

The next he was upright, his chains broken and dangling from his wrist like flails. His eyes flashed indigo and his mouth opened, filled with darkness like a void as it stretched and stretched. He stepped through the protective circle and shattered it while Malevorn was still reacting, then the chains flashed and wrapped around the throat of the nearest person: Adamus Crozier.

He wrenched the clergyman to him and snapped his neck, almost pulling his head off as he kissed away his soul. Gnosis-energy kindled bright scarlet and coursed through Toljin's veins, then he threw the limp body away and stalked toward Malevorn, grinning fiendishly.

'Huriya, get out!' he shouted, terrified she'd be slain and trigger his own heart's demise. He conjured wizardry-gnosis, pulling a bolt of midnight-blue light into his hands and blasting it at Toljin. The Dokken staggered, shrieking in alarm, a sound amplified as if he had a hundred throats all howling in unison. He countered with a kinesis-infused mage bolt that threw Malevorn backwards into the wall.

Combat reflexes took over. Malevorn propelled himself upright as his blade leapt into his fist. Chains lashed; he swayed away from them and began to circle. From the corner of his eye he saw Huriya run for the door, but Toljin gestured and the door shimmered with light.

'You're not going anywhere,' Toljin rasped at her. 'I'm going to gut this pus-ball of an Inquisitor, then I'm going to finally do to you what you deserve.'

Huriya shrank against the wall, eyes huge and face pale. Malevorn tried to get between her and Toljin and nearly lost his legs as the chains flashed out. He danced out of reach and gathered himself for another try.

'I'm going to turn my cock into a serrated horn,' Toljin told Huriya while sending a torrent of sordid images at her to freeze her in her place. 'I'll tear you apart with it.'

Huriya resisted firmly, surprising Malevorn as he charged again, but Toljin's arm-chains flashed out, entangling his sword-arm. As Toljin closed in, Malevorn pulled his dagger and slashed – and the Dokken's left hand flopped wetly to the ground. He yowled as blood fountained from the stump, but it lasted only a second before a fresh hand, taloned and leathery, burst from the stump and raked at Malevorn. Beside the door, Huriya tried to blast through the seal, but Toljin reinforced it, making Huriya gasp and back away. Toljin had matched her strength.

Because he's now an Ascendant.

But he's not Toljin any more.

Mandira Khojana, Lokistan, on the continent of Antiopia
Zulqeda (Noveleve) 929
17th month of the Moontide

The ambrosia tasted bitter, and spread through Alaron like ice-water in his veins, slowing everything but his heart, which began to labour. Every sense was dimming, the concerned faces about the cot fading away. Corinea was twitchy and apprehensive; Master Puravai grave and analytical. But he really only saw Ramita, drinking in her face as if it was the last thing he would ever see. When she too faded into the throbbing silence he tried to tell her that he loved her one last time, but couldn't say if he'd managed to speak.

Then there was just himself, falling through space in slow circles as the darkness closed in. It might have been hours but maybe it was seconds. Corinea's warnings echoed in his head. *'First the poison slows your body, but your heart will try to keep pumping. It may hurt.'*

It did, and more with each passing moment. Each heartbeat was a blow striking his ribcage from within, while his sluggish blood seeped through him in weak pulses. He felt as if his heart were a child trying to be born. The pain peaked, but as it faded he could feel his consciousness slipping away, until there was just a small candle-flame of light and awareness before him, and voices speaking dimly.

Alaron? Alaron? Is that you? What's he doing?

Cym? Ramon? At first he was puzzled, because the cot was inside a circle, warded from the spirit-world. There shouldn't have been any way for ghosts to reach him, yet here they were, his two most beloved friends . . .

Who else would it be? Cym's acerbic voice cut through the fog, and suddenly he could see her face, just as she'd been when he last saw her. *We're with you, through thick and thin.*

Ramon smiled sardonically at him. *Hey, amici, what are you doing lying there?*

I just had a drink of—

A drink! Cym snorted. *Never could hold your drink, could you!* She and Ramon reached down and pulled him upright. Ramon was in his legion battle-mage robes, just as he had been on the day he flew out to join the army. Alaron's eyes stung to see them.

I love you guys! he told them fervently. *If I've never said it before, I'm saying it now. I love you both!*

Definitely been drinking, Ramon chuckled.

Alaron ploughed on, despite the dizziness that slurred his words and mashed his thoughts. *I've met this girl! She's so brave and steady, like a rock, but she's tiny as a mouse and . . .*

A stone mouse? Cym giggled. *You're hopeless, Al!*

How are you both? It's been so long. I thought you were dead, Cym . . .

His two closest friends looked at each other, then back at him, their expressions sad. *I am dead,* Cym told him. *I was killed at the Isle of Glass.*

I'm dead too, Ramon put in conversationally. *The Inquisition thought I knew where you were, so they tortured me to death. I screamed for a week.*

Alaron had just *known* this was what had happened. *I dragged my best friends into this and left them to die . . .*

He watched as they stopped moving and became desiccated skeletons that collapsed slowly into a pile of bones and were gone in the mists that closed in around him.

Then his father was there, in his old bedroom in Norostein. Vannaton Mercer looked exactly as he had on the day he'd left for the Moontide; hopeful, worried to be leaving his estranged wife and his son behind, but filled with purpose to do what was needed to keep the family fed and housed.

Da!

Hello, Son. Vann took his hand. *Easy there. Don't cry: everyone dies.*

But they were the best friends I've ever had . . . He looked up, heart in mouth. *Da, are you . . . are you also . . . ?*

Vann nodded gravely. *The Inquisition were looking for you, and they found me. They were asking about the Scytale of Corineus, of all things! You should have warned me, so I knew to take precautions.*

Tears stung Alaron's eyes. *I'm sorry! I know I should have told you, but we didn't think we'd ever truly find it . . . we didn't really believe in our hearts that it was all real.*

You always were a fool, Alaron. Vann's face hardened. *I'm disappointed in you. Leaving your mother to die alone. You've let everyone down. You failed us all.*

Sudden pain jabbed through Alaron, a knife that skewered his heart like meat on a spit, and he hung in the air, turning in agonised limbo while his father watched without sympathy.

Everyone dies, Son. Now it's your turn.

The Valley of Tombs, Gatioch, on the continent of Antiopia
Zulqeda (Noveleve) 929
17th month of the Moontide

Malevorn tried to intervene as Toljin launched himself at Huriya. He was sure she'd go down instantly, but somehow she held up, forcing the daemon – for Toljin was surely in the thrall of some kind of spirit – away with kinesis. Her shields held despite flashing deep red, buying them both time. She tried to attack it with her mind, but Malevorn knew mesmeric-gnosis wouldn't work. The strongest daemons, those the Wizards avoided, were a collective mind, dozens or even hundreds of souls bound together in the aether, too complex to duel mentally. But they were still vulnerable to Wizardry, the Study dedicated to binding and controlling them.

And it just so happened that he was well-honed in that particular Study, Turm Zauberin's star pupil. He lashed Toljin across the back with a spectral whip, designed to hurt the soul, not the body, and the daemon screamed, its back arching as it staggered, then it turned on him. Huriya scuttled along the wall like a rat seeking its hole. Toljin's shapechanger body grew scale and horns, the jaw elongated and nails sprouted as the daemon got a grip on the body's capacities. His knee-joints reversed with a sickening meaty crunch and fire kindled in his clawed hands as he stalked towards Malevorn . . .

. . . and stepped into the circle Malevorn had burned into the middle of the floor.

Malevorn shouted aloud and poured fresh energy into the circle, rekindling it with wizardry-gnosis, spells that were this time for confining a *daemon*, not a man. Then Huriya joined him, feeding the spell; Sabele had been a Wizard as well, and her aid tipped the scales. The circle lit up, and the daemon was confined.

Toljin hurled himself at the invisible boundaries, rebounding as if from a stone wall. He tried again and again, until he realised that he was truly penned there. Then he fell silent, and glowered at them both in turn. Malevorn could feel him mentally probing the circle.

Malevorn exhaled slowly while Huriya put her back against the far wall, panting and gasping, her eyes huge and frightened. 'What went wrong?' she asked. 'Was it the ambrosia? Did we get the dose wrong?'

'It's possible, but I don't think so.'

'You can't be sure!' she declared, her voice impassioned, and he knew why: if the ambrosia potion had been right, then it couldn't be blamed for this failure.

Which means that perhaps the ambrosia can't *cure Souldrinkers.*

Huriya looked shattered. 'This was our great hope . . .' she said in a broken whisper. 'How can it not work?'

Malevorn ignored her, his mind having gone beyond that particular question. *Never deal with what might have been*, his tutor once said. *Deal with what is.*

There might be no cure for what I've become. My family may never be restored. He almost screamed, but he made himself go on thinking. *So what have I created instead?*

A daemon had possessed Toljin during his transformation: he knew about daemons . . . They had secret names that could be used to bind them and enslave them. His eyes widened, and so did his horizons, until they were limitless. They'd hoped to create a *willing ally*, but instead had created a *slave*: an Ascendant Dokken daemon slave.

A slave is so much better than an ally . . .

And if he could duplicate this experiment, he had the means to make many, many more . . .

Huriya was sitting blankly on the floor, as shattered as her dreams. The Dokken would never be welcomed as equals by the magi. They would never be other than what they were, and the hopes of all her many lifetimes were ash before her eyes.

She never saw his blow coming: a kinetic fist that left her sense-less on the floor.

I know exactly what to do now, and I don't need her to do it.

This is . . . utterly . . . perfect.

Mandira Khojana, Lokistan, on the continent of Antiopia
Zulqeda (Noveleve) 929
17th month of the Moontide

'ALARON!' the voices chorused together, his name like a slap on his face, bringing him back from the very verge of oblivion.

His father's voice. Cym's and Ramon's. The earlier conversation melted from his mind as he realised that he'd not been talking to their ghosts, but their memories. *Alive or dead, I know they love me.* His mother's voice spoke a warning, Ramita's too, and he wrenched his awareness back from the brink: a dark shadow was diving at him, a venator, with Malevorn Andevarion on its back, a lance tipped with gnostic-fire gouging the air as it flashed towards him.

He rolled clear and came upright, saw a vast space open before him, teetered and regained balance. He was standing on the edge of a continent above a massive cliff. The sea was raging below. Beside him a waterfall flowed in a torrent, white water roaring into the void. Then he stared, for beneath the churning waves he could see the moon, its vast bulk sparkling copper and silver, close enough to touch, yet far beyond reach, warping his perspective. He stared at it as it rose through the water.

Then the shriek of the venator brought him back to the now as Malevorn hauled the winged reptile around in a spiralling arc, then dived towards him again, spears of light flashing through the air at him. He engaged shields and saw the light shatter against them, the blows shaking him, staggering him so that his heels hung over space, the emptiness behind him roaring, reaching—

He blasted back, but the venator came on and on, its jaws widen-ing, and he shouted in fear and alarm as the edge of the cliff gave way and he was falling, spinning towards the moon as it rose from the waves in a vast cascade of water and light and ...

... someone touched his hand: a small hand with tough skin and a strong grip, surer than the stones.

The moon burst like a bubble as he fell through it and then he was floating, soaring through the night sky, flying his *Seeker* beneath the stars towards the rising sun. Ramita was in the prow, her arms spread wide like the wings of a bird, and when she turned back to him she was laughing for joy.

Then she was gone, and there was someone else, larger, wrapped in a creamy-coloured robe, cowled and faceless. 'Who are you?' he shouted.

The man dropped his hood, revealing an ancient face, shaven-skulled, with an iron-grey goatee. 'Are you worthy of her?' the man asked in a penetrating voice that shivered through him.

It's him ... Meiros ... or how he imagined the man from Ramita's descriptions.

Alaron set his jaw. 'I'll try to be.'

Unexpectedly – or not if it was his own imagination – the old mage grinned. 'Fair enough. See that you are.'

Alaron's heart began to pound again. 'Sir! Is any of this real?'

Meiros snorted. 'Of course not. It's all in your head. But that doesn't mean you can't die here.' He looked at him intently. 'You'll never be more than my shadow, lad.'

Thanks for the vote of confidence, Subconscious. 'I'm still going to do my best!' he retorted.

'Good for you, son,' Meiros said. Or was it his father?

Then he was alone in the skiff, soaring at incredible speeds right into the heart of a rising sun. He had no control of *Seeker*, could only ride onwards as the heat kindled his clothes, wreathing him in smoke – and then the skiff caught fire. He yowled as the fire roared around him, caught in his hair, his clothes, his skin, as he soared on, a living comet that blasted into Sol's core and exploded in a storm of white light and fire.

And he woke.

They were all with him: Ramita, Puravai, Corinea, and faithful Yash, who must have inveigled his way in while he slept. His face whipped around the room, caught the after-images of Meiros and his father as they faded from view. Ramon and Cym, too. And his mother, whole and unburnt . . .

Ramita squeezed his hand. 'You made it,' she breathed.

'Welcome back, Brother Longlegs,' Puravai said with a smile. Corinea and Yash just looked at him, her with cool analysis, he with awe.

He took a deep breath, and kindled the core of his gnosis, the little flame inside him. Around it, his gnostic aura reformed, an image akin to Sivraman, four-armed and clothed in all aspects of the gnosis. It shone so brightly he could barely look.

I did it.

I'm an Ascendant.

11

Manoeuvre

The Katlakoz, or Javon Rift

The Katlakoz has played a vital part in the development of Javon. The desert below the Rift is the summer hunting ground of the nomadic Harkun, a northern Keshi people who dwell in the wilds east of Halli'kut throughout winter, the growing season, farming and raiding while the weather is cool. In the Keshi summer they retreat through the mountains and live off the massive horse and cattle herds of the lands below the Rift.

SISTER GULSEPPA, SOLLAN SCHOLAR, JAVON, 722

Brochena, Javon, on the continent of Antiopia
Zulqeda (Noveleve) 929
17ᵗʰ month of the Moontide

Governor Tomas Betillon stepped from the dark stateroom to the bright balcony overlooking the palace parade ground. Trumpets blared, then fell silent. The two legion commanders were with him; Kirkegarde Grandmaster Lann Wilfort was rubbing at his scarred face, while stolid Sir Roland Heale just stared at the massed ranks of the Dorobon legion he was leading east, to Forensa. Heale wasn't happy; he wanted to wait for reinforcements.

He'd be right if we were going to be reinforced, Betillon thought grimly, *but that's not going to happen. Korion's overstretched, and Lucia won't send more men here, not with the destruction of the Bridge still to come. We're on our own for now.*

The governor stepped to the edge of the balcony and saluted the ranks of Dorobon soldiers. They'd been promised wealth and land if they uprooted their lives and came to Javon, but now their ruling House had been obliterated, their loyalties played with and their commanders suborned. Only the fact that their families were here kept them loyal. Though they were fighting to protect those families, it was clear they'd all rather be shipped back to Rondelmar, and the tensions between them and Betillon's other soldiers were growing. At least getting them out of Brochena would remind them who their real enemies were.

Of course, he hadn't said that to Roland Heale. Instead he'd blathered words like Victory, Glory and Revenge. He doubted Heale was fooled. *If we can crush the Nesti rebellion the native resistance will die away, reinforcements will come, and we'll all be fine. Once I've dealt with Gyle, of course . . .*

He rattled off a prepared speech about the valour of House Dorobon and their proud history and other such turd-stained waffle; the men cheered and the drums rattled into a marching beat. He took the salutes of Heale and Wilfort and saw them off.

If they let me down I'll eviscerate the pair of them.

'The windskiff scouts say there are more than ten thousand Rimoni soldiers in Riban, and the same in Forensa, plus many more Jhafi,' Craith Margham commented as the Dorobon marched out the gates. He looked pleased to have his main rival for pre-eminence in House Dorobon marching away.

'It's two hundred miles to Forensa, through the desert,' Betillon mused aloud. 'Twenty days if they don't rest, but that would be foolish. When they get there, they must storm a walled city while possibly outnumbered. But if Gyle's people join them, they should prevail, especially given our superiority in the gnosis.'

'Yes, we've got the magi to do it,' Margham enthused, as if battles were won using textbooks. 'Thirty magi against what? Two?' He laughed derisively.

Betillon scowled. 'Yes. But one of those is Elena Anborn.'

The Katlakoz Rift, Javon, on the continent of Antiopia
Zulqeda (Noveleve) 929
17th month of the Moontide

'This place is said to be one of the marvels of Urte,' Rutt Sordell commented miserably. He'd been explaining that his eyesight was deteriorating to black and white, the latest in a series of complaints about his own well-being. Gurvon was past sympathy and just wished he'd shut up.

Gurvon had seen plenty of marvels, but he was still mightily impressed with the Great Rift. It was a giant cliff that ran roughly north–south for over one hundred and seventy miles, from the Tagraz Mountains near Forensa, all the way south to the Karebedi Mountains that separated Javon from northern Kesh. The Rift – called 'Katlakoz' in the Jhafi tongue – was a massive east-facing wall of stone reaching hundreds of yards above the desert floor. It reminded him of the sea-walls of Yuros and Antiopia, except that the ocean below the Rift was of sand, rippling in waves towards the horizon. All of that land belonged to the fierce Harkun tribes.

Only the Rift had prevented Javon being inundated by Harkun: there were just four places where a man could ascend the cliffs, and each was fortified. Currently, Staria Canestos' Sacro Arcoyris Estellan legions occupied three of those forts, including this one; the Red Fort, prosaically named for the colour of the sandstone from which it was hewn. The fourth such fort was near Forensa and Nesti-held.

'The Ordo Costruo believe this used to be the eastern coastline, thousands of years ago,' Sordell went on. 'Then something happened, maybe the same impact that destroyed the land-bridge between Dhassa and Pontus, and this was all lifted out of the sea.'

Gurvon tried to imagine that moment. *Will it reverse, when we destroy the Leviathan Bridge? Wouldn't that be a thing to see?* He pictured the entire Harkun nation drowning in a new flood. *Though of course, they'll be back in Kesh by then, so maybe not. A shame.* The Harkun weren't his favourite people just now; they were tying up Staria's legions at a time he badly needed them. That was why he was here.

He turned to Staria, who was peering out over the desert, her olive Estellan skin sun-bronzed, the hard planes of her face a mirror of the desert below. If she'd worn a bekira she'd have passed for a native, but she was in sweat-stained leather and chain-armour and looked entirely fed up.

'What's the latest from Hans Frikter?' he asked.

'Hansi's making decent time,' she replied in her dusky Estellan accent. 'He's in contact with the Dorobon man, Roland Heale, via relay-staves. They expect to reach Forensa by the end of this month. There's no sense in going faster, not in this heat.' It was still Noveleve, but summer was lingering, baking the ground hard and scorching any crops that weren't well-irrigated.

'And Endus Rykjard?'

'He's on a ridge over the Baroz Road, about forty miles south of Brochena. He's been passing the supply trains through and taking our share. No incidents so far.'

'Good.' Gurvon returned his eyes to the sea of sand below. Somewhere out of sight to the east was a large oasis with a Harkun camp of at least twenty-four thousand raiders kicking their heels. There were just six hundred men in the Red Fort, the smallest of the three, but the Rift itself was all the defence that was required. A child with a slingshot could have defended it.

Surely they wouldn't be stupid enough to try us?

Staria tutted softly. 'Do we really need these nomads?'

'In a word, yes. Basically, we're stuck in a three-way stalemate unless extra pieces are added to the tabula board. Betillon is begging Pallas for reinforcements, and he might even get them. We haven't the same option, which means dealing with these barbarians.'

'But aren't the Harkun going to just slaughter anyone they encounter?' Rutt asked. 'I've been stationed in Javon for six years now and it's the one thing everyone agrees on: only a lunatic would let the Harkun climb the Rift.'

'Well, I might be that lunatic. Is that damned go-between in sight yet?'

'You'll need to be nice to him,' Staria reminded him, peering into the distance.

'You know me, Staria. Charm itself.' He squinted as a cluster of small shapes appeared over a distant ridgeline. 'Here he comes.' The man they were here to meet was called Ghujad iz'Kho; he spoke Keshi, Rimoni and Rondian, and claimed to speak for fourteen different Harkun tribes. He was either a blatant liar or an immensely valuable ally. Time would tell which. 'Let's go down.'

The Red Fort guarded a slow and treacherous goat path up the Rift wall. An Earth-mage could easily have rendered it completely impassable, but Gurvon understood the mentality of keeping the path intact. If you didn't keep communication lines with your enemies open, they found other ways to sneak up on you. There had always been some trade between the Harkun and the Jhafi, strictly controlled but lucrative. He'd heard rumours that Cera Nesti had once been so desperate she'd tried to negotiate with the Harkun, but nothing had come of that in the end; the plan had been forestalled by his own subversion of the girl.

The three magi descended using Air-gnosis, reaching the bottom of the cliffs well before the Harkun, as he'd intended; frightening them with open use of their powers would be entirely counter-productive. The nomads arrived soon after, on comically lurching camels. Ghujad iz'Kho had brought six bodyguards; if one could judge from the patterns of their headscarves they were probably relatives. They made their camels kneel in a slow forward collapse that threatened to tip them all onto their faces in the sand, then slid gracefully down their flanks to the ground.

Ghujad iz'Kho greeted Gurvon like a long-lost son, embracing him and pounding his back. 'This is where the knife could have gone, but we're friends', the gesture implied, apparently. Gurvon suffered kisses to both cheeks then stepped back and introduced Rutt and Staria. Iz'Kho fawned over them while his guards set up a small pavilion, producing saddle-cushions to sit upon and even decanting some arak.

'So, my friend Gyle,' iz'Kho began as they sat, pronouncing his name 'Jill'. 'Please, tell me how may I be of service?'

'I have come to speak of the lands of your ancestors, which the Jhafi stole,' Gurvon replied, coming straight to the point. He didn't care whether the Harkun claims of being rightful rulers of Javon were true; what he needed was a horde of warriors prepared to fight where he told them to.

Iz'Kho smiled broadly. 'This is the chance all Harkun dream of. It is the destiny of my people, Ahm willing, to once more rule these ancestral lands.'

'I believe every nation has the right to dwell in their ancestral homeland,' said Gurvon, who believed no such thing.

Ghujad iz'Kho nodded agreeably. 'Our tales say that the Jhafi were once a Harkun tribe, one of many that roamed throughout Ja'afar, sharing it without conflict. A Golden Age. But the Jhafi betrayed the rest, seizing the highlands when the other tribes made the autumn trek back to Kesh. Now we are sundered by the Rift, and their intransigence. It is the will of Ahm that they be punished.'

'Then you're talking to the right person,' Gurvon told him. 'The Rondian Empire sympathises with your people.'

'Do they?' iz'Kho enquired. 'I understand your emperor claims "Javon", as you call it, as his own.'

'These are vast lands, Ghujad, with room for us all,' Gurvon replied smoothly. 'The plains north of Forensa, for example, are as large as the plains below the Rift, and offer far better grazing for your herds.'

'Those plains are only a fragment of our ancestral lands,' iz'Kho countered. 'Further, they are inaccessible except via the Rift fortresses, which you now hold.'

'Then let's get to the point,' Gurvon said. 'Last time we spoke, you said that fourteen tribes – almost thirty thousand warriors – had agreed to join this campaign?'

'This is so: we are eager to walk the cliffs above, my friend. We *burn* to do so.'

'I'm sure. Ghujad, if I allowed your people access to the highlands, you and I together could crush the Jhafi and their Rimoni allies, and I would happily give you all of the eastern plains from Forensa to

Loctis. But my emperor fears that you will not stop at that. He fears that we would be trading a weak enemy for a strong one.'

Iz'Kho rubbed his whiskery chin. 'Not an enemy, my good Gyle: a grateful friend.'

'Perhaps while you and I are involved, but what of the future? We both know that young men can be opportunistic and ambitious. Some might forget that Rondian magi can destroy swathes of men at will – we would be relying on you reminding them, lest we have to.'

'All know the might of the Rondian magi,' iz'Kho replied evenly.

I don't trust this villain as far as I could spit him . . . which wouldn't be far. But I need his men now.

Content to accept alliance in the short term, they haggled a little; Gurvon ceded Forensa and the eastern plains. 'But we keep Riban and Intemsa, and all lands west of Mount Tigrat.'

We . . . meaning me, once I've dealt with Betillon.

Ghujad iz'Kho declared himself entirely willing to take the proposal back to his tribal chiefs, and after more professions of undying friendship he and his bodyguards mounted up and lurched off across the flat land.

The three magi remained below the cliffs, now in shadow as the sun drifted west, while the camels plodded away into the haze.

'Well, "Jill"?' Staria asked. 'Are you content?' It didn't sound like she was.

'I think so. Here's the way it'll happen: Frikter's legion will join the Dorobon outside Forensa. That's enough to deal with the Nesti, or at least tie them down until we can bring the Harkun into play. The Dorobon either play along or not: in which case I set the Harkun onto them too. I don't think it'll come to that. Roland Heale will defect to our side, and together we'll crush the Nesti, then destroy Wilfort's Kirkegarde too if he doesn't see the light.'

'But how will we control the Harkun?' Rutt was always worrying.

'That's a problem for another day,' Gurvon declared. 'Like as not, give it a few years, they'll settle down. It's an old story: the barbarians sweeping down into the valley becomes the next generation of peasants defending it.'

'What about my people?' Staria asked. 'The Jhafi despise us, but they're *liberals* compared to the Harkun.'

You and your damned ladymen . . . Gurvon was envisaging a situation where Staria's legion was caught in the middle somehow and things just got out of hand. 'Don't worry,' he told her. 'We'll move you west after the fighting. You'll be safe, and able to live the lives you want.'

'I'll hold you to that.'

Sure, Staria. If you can . . .

They kindled Air-gnosis and, buoyed by the updrafts, flew back to Red Fort, high above the seas of sand.

'Well, my friend?' Ghujad iz'Kho turned to the smallest of the bodyguards once they were out of sight of the magi. 'What have you to say?'

Harshal ali-Assam lowered his keffi, glancing behind him at the stolid faces of iz'Kho's sons and cousins, framed by the massive walls of the Katlakoz beyond. He almost fancied he saw movement, three shapes rising into the skies, but in the heat and haze it was hard to be sure.

'I'd say that any man who believes Gurvon Gyle is a fool. And any Amteh man who takes up arms for the Rondian Emperor is a betrayer of his people and his faith.'

Iz'Kho chuckled at his defensive tones. 'Nevertheless, he offers a great bargain, does he not? From nomads to conquerors; a chance to right old wrongs.' He smiled wryly. 'You live in a marble palace, my friend. We live in tents. And yet we're of the same people. Why should you have so much and we so little?'

'Jhafi and Harkun are kin, of course,' Harshal acknowledged. 'But we've been sundered by the Rift for centuries – as you say, we've become a sedentary people. We grow crops and build permanent dwellings. We eat different foods, wear different clothes. But our languages remain similar, and so too our faiths. Our conflicts are resolvable without seeking accursed Rondian magi for aid.'

'But the Rondians offer us lands in the upper realm, something you've never given us. If that means some brief cooperation with the Rondians, what of it? In a few years they will tire of Ja'afar's heat and leave.'

Harshal wondered anxiously how much of this was real and how much was posturing, to wring some further concession. 'Consider the Nesti counter-proposal,' he said earnestly. 'The Regency Council have allowed me to offer your tribal clan favourable trading terms on all goods. We know that some seasons your people struggle. We know that you've little or no metal-working, such that most of your armour is boiled leather and a sword is worth more than ten camels. Imagine a future trading with the Nesti for *all* you need. You could dominate the Harkun plain yourselves, and keep the other tribal clans at bay.'

'Become clients of the Nesti, in other words.'

'Partners,' Harshal countered, 'working together. Ghujad, you don't even have *schools*. Imagine educating your children so that they can make better lives.'

'Civilising us?' iz'Kho scoffed.

Harshal took a deep breath. 'All right, yes, let's use that word: *civilising*. There are places on the Harkun plains where you could build, if you knew how. Places where you could create cities like we have. It is in our interest for your people to become more like us, and it's in your interests too.'

'Is it?' iz'Kho rumbled. He gestured back to the great Katlakoz, looming over the plains. 'You don't know what it's like to live in the shadow of that wall, my friend. You loom over us, like the gods of the ancients, judging and finding us wanting. "See the barbarous Harkun, illiterate and savage, wandering the desert like herds of wild kine. They can't build or grow, they can't write or count. Just primitives!"' He reined in his camel and suddenly Harshal was acutely aware of the men behind him.

Iz'Kho jabbed a finger at him. 'The thing about you *civilised* Jhafi is that you think we want to be like you. But that is not our dream!'

Harshal could sense the hands on the hilts behind him, and his mouth went dry. 'So what is your dream, iz'Kho?'

'To ride the highlands, free and proud as our fathers, and watch your cities burn.' He looked beyond Harshal at someone behind him and faintly shook his head.

Harshal exhaled softly.

Ghujad met his gaze, his eyes hooded and unreadable. 'I have a message for your queen and her counsellors.'

Harshal's heart sank. *I've failed.* 'What message shall I give?'

Ghujad's face emptied of emotion. 'A primitive one.'

Forensa, Javon, on the continent of Antiopia
Zulqeda (Noveleve) 929
17th month of the Moontide

Cera stared at the grisly trophy, felt her gorge rise and turned away. 'Sol et Lune, take it away,' she burst out, feeling her limbs turning to jelly and stumbling to a seat.

'A Rondian dropped it at the gates, then flew away.' Comte Piero Inveglio was ashen-faced, and so was the soldier who'd brought this horrible thing to her.

'Flew?' she said dazedly, her eyes going back to the bloody mess. A canvas bag, soaked scarlet. A severed head, the eyes wide and staring, the expression slack, all that wit and intelligence and charm gone, lost for ever.

Oh Harshal, I should never have let you go there.

'It was a mage,' the soldier said. 'A skiff-pilot.'

She strove for composure, looking away from what had once been her friend and trying to speak, though it took a couple of tries before she managed to thank the man and dismiss him. When Piero closed the door, she slumped over and wept. *Mater Lune, I sent him to die . . .*

'Take it away! Inter it respectfully. I can't bear to look at it.'

Inveglio closed the bag over its contents, gave it to a servant and sent him away. It left a hideous smear of gore on the table and she started rubbing at it furiously with her sleeve, sobbing as she worsened the mess.

'I've sent summons to the rest of the council,' Inveglio said grimly.

'We should never have sent him – you all warned me! They're *savages*, they always have been— It's my fault!'

'We might have warned you, but we all agreed, Cera,' Inveglio reminded her. 'He knew the risks; he'd been among them before.'

It was little comfort. Harshal ali-Assam had been one of those people she'd felt privileged to call a friend. He'd courted her sister Solinde, and was perhaps the only man she'd ever thought wistfully about. For him to be taken away from her – and like this, so *horribly* – was crippling, and she wanted desperately to strike back somehow.

If Elena were here, I'd send her after this Ghujad iz'Kho.

There was no doubt who had killed Harshal, for he'd carved his name into his face. And *Rondians* had delivered it, the blood barely dry.

'They're cooperating: the Harkun and the Rondians,' she noted.

'So it would appear, Princessa.' Inveglio looked as if he'd aged a decade.

One by one, her Regency Council arrived. She lifted the cowl of her bekira-shroud, which felt so appropriate on this day of death. Pita Rosco and Luigi Ginovisi looked sickened but unsurprised. The young Knight-Commander Seir Ionus Mardium looked mortified, as if he feared he might somehow be blamed. Justiano di Kestria had been a close friend of Harshal's; he was furious, and so too Camlad a'Luki, a Jhafi kinsman of the ali-Assam family who held personal grievances against the Harkun. Scriptualist Nehlan and Drui Tavis were last to arrive, clearly shaken by the news.

First they prayed, both Amteh and Sollan, for Harshal's soul, and speaking the ritual words helped to settle her, giving her the calmness she'd need to get through this meeting.

After the Rite of Family, she bared her face. 'Dear, dear friends, I cannot begin to express my sorrow and anger at what has happened, and I know you feel the same,' she started, her voice breaking despite herself.

They murmured agreement, some in sadness and some through gritted teeth.

'Harshal is irreplaceable to this gathering. His wit, wisdom and courage will be sadly missed. This is a grievous blow, the worst we've suffered since Fishil Wadi, and it is hard to know how we'll cope without him.'

'We will endure for him,' Justiano di Kestria vowed. 'We'll avenge him a hundredfold.'

All the men made noises of agreement, even the normally placid Pita Rosco. Cera, feeling the heat of their anger, reminded them of caution. 'We're all furious at this provocation, but we're not so foolish as they think. The Rondians are marching towards us, and they've obviously made alliance with the Harkun. If we march out to meet them, we'll be overwhelmed. We will await them here.'

The young ones didn't like it, but the more experienced heads nodded. 'Let them come to us,' Luigi Ginovisi said grimly. 'Home-cooked revenge tastes just as sweet.'

'How many Harkun will the Rondians commit to the battlefield?' Camlad a'Luki asked.

'Enough to sweep us away,' Piero replied. 'The magi will think they can control them afterwards.'

'Then Elena's mission is doubly vital,' Pita Rosco said. 'Our fate hangs on her.'

South Javon, on the continent of Antiopia
Zulqeda (Noveleve) 929
17th month of the Moontide

Elena nudged her horse through the tangled rocks while Kazim concentrated on using Animagery to dissuade a jackal pack that was tracking them. She could hear them as they yowled and whined a few hundred yards away. This cluster of broken hills south of Intemsa was some thirty miles from the Rift, a forbidding place scattered with sun-bleached bones; most of the birds above were vultures. It was three weeks since they'd left Forensa, unnoted riders leaving by the eastern gates, then looping southwest once out of sight. Evading patrols of Staria Canestos' Estellans, they'd skirted Intemsa, picking up supplies in small villages as they sought a place far enough from

Staria's magi to risk a calling spell. Reaching an unprepared recipient, undetected by others, took great delicacy. This particular call required them both: Kazim for his knowledge of the subject, and Elena for her skill in masking. They succeeded in making contact eventually, and she was fairly sure they'd not been overheard.

Whether the other party would honour their request to come alone was quite another thing. She'd never met the man, and had only Kazim's word that he could be trusted. But he was growing more worldly, her lover; she was learning to rely on his judgement.

The meeting place was a pool hidden within this maze of stone. It was muddied by all the animals that used it, but she purified it with Water-gnosis and refilled their bottles, then Kazim let the horses drink. Their mounts were Jhafi, feisty by nature but skittish from the pervasive stink of jackals in the air.

'If this goes well, we might have to abandon the horses,' she warned him.

'How about selling them in that village three miles north?' he replied, concerned for the creatures.

'It'll attract attention, my love. People don't sell horses out here. But I can set a compulsion on them to head towards Forensa. It's the best I can do.'

Kazim didn't look happy, but there really was no other choice. So they sat and idly talked through the gossip they'd picked up in the villages: the Rondians were closing in on Forensa, and the Aranio family were barely helping, just locking themselves in Riban to protect their own. She could feel the urgency of their mission mounting. 'My love, is your man going to agree to this? It's asking so much.'

'I don't know. I really don't.'

'If he doesn't agree, I'm going to have to ... *make* him agree.'

His face became troubled. 'I know.'

'I'm sorry.'

'It's war,' he said heavily.

Then she felt another presence and looked up. 'He's here.'

A triangular-sailed skiff appeared above, and circled until Kazim stepped into the open and waved. The pilot skilfully brought it to

DAVID HAIR

land beside the pool, then clambered out, eyeing Kazim and Elena warily. They kept their weapons in their scabbards and their hands raised, palms forward.

'Sal'Ahm, Molmar,' Kazim called. 'Peace of the Prophet be upon you.'

'And upon you,' the Hadishah pilot responded gravely. His grizzled features were taut with worry; his hand kept straying to his scimitar hilt. 'You've brought your woman.' He eyed her with hostility. Not only was she Rondian and a mage, but she was also the reason that many of his fellow Hadishah were dead.

'We're here in peace,' Elena called. 'Kazim speaks well of you.'

'He also speaks well of you,' Molmar replied. 'But he called Jamil and the others "brother", then killed them: for you.' His voice suspended judgement, for now.

'He had justifiable cause to do so.'

Molmar looked from her to Kazim and relented a little. 'What Gatoz sought to do to you was a crime, Lady. I wish only that it had not resulted in the loss of so many who did not share in that wrong.'

They stood aside, Elena thought coolly, but she kept her silence.

'We all do, brother,' Kazim said, stepping forward. The two men examined each other, then tentatively embraced. Elena knew they'd made peace to some extent earlier in the year, but she needed much more from Molmar than that.

Kore . . . Ahm . . . anyone: please let him agree to this.

Molmar, part of the small Hadishah group still operating in Javon, had been at a refuge in the south when Kazim's call came. He'd had to wait until he was sent out on patrol before he could slip away and meet with them. He'd promised not to tell his fellow assassins, and it appeared he hadn't, at least so far.

'Will you share water with us, brother?' Kazim offered. 'And listen to what we have to say?'

Molmar grunted his assent, still eyeing Elena warily, but he drank from his own waterskin, keeping his distance. The sun, dipping towards the horizon, cast his craggy features into sharp relief as he gestured for Kazim to speak.

'Molmar, the Rondians are marching on Forensa. I'm sure you

know this: two legions – ten thousand men – with a full complement of magi, loyal to Tomas Betillon and Gurvon Gyle. Our enemies
have united.'

'We Hadishah know this,' Molmar conceded. 'They have thirty
magi . . . and the only magi the Nesti have are you and your woman.
So why are you here?'

'Because we still have two weeks in which to do something to
even the odds.'

'If you are here to ask for Hadishah support, the answer is no. The
Brotherhood will never deal with you again, Kazim. You know this.'

'I do,' Kazim admitted. 'That isn't why we're here.' He took a deep
breath, then asked, 'Do you remember your mother, Molmar?'

The skiff-pilot froze at the unexpected question, then said slowly,
'My earliest memories are of a Hadishah orphanage. The mothers
were permitted to see us until the age of six, when we began our
education. She was a Dhassan prostitute who'd gained the gnosis
when she fell pregnant to a Rondian mage, a quarter-blood. My
father was an eighth-blood Dhassan, but I never met him – he died
in the Second Crusade. My mother is probably dead too. She would
be sixty if she lived, but women die young in the breeding-houses.'
His voice was filled with revulsion.

'Have you ever gone back?'

'To that *damned* place . . . ?' Molmar shook his head. 'Why would
I? There's nothing for me there, and I have never bred a child who
lived. My bloodline is not worth preserving, in the eyes of my superiors.' He looked at Kazim carefully. 'Why do you ask?'

'Because we wish to find a breeding-house and set the captive
magi free.'

Molmar's jaw dropped. 'But— No!' He took two steps backwards.
'Kazim, they are hateful places, but the strength of the Brotherhood
lies in them. If the East is to have magi, we *need* them!' He shook
his head emphatically. 'I will leave now.'

Elena calculated the distances and speeds required to take him
down.

'Please, wait!' Kazim said urgently. 'Hear me out, brother: Javon needs magi, and the remaining Ordo Costruo have been taken to the breeding facilities. Some would fight for Javon if freed.'

'No.'

'We Hadishah destroyed the Ordo Costruo,' Kazim reminded him. 'We killed or took captive the only magi who have ever helped Ahmedhassa. You were there: we stabbed them in the back, and now we've sent the survivors to a rape-prison. How could Ahm ever approve that?'

'I don't speak for Ahm,' Molmar shot back. 'Nor should you, who killed Jamil and Haroun. The Godspeakers have sanctioned the breeding-houses, and that is enough for me.' Another step back towards his skiff. 'I will pretend this meeting never happened. Do not contact me again.'

'Jamil's mother was born with no arms,' Kazim called. 'He told me that. But they still made her bear children – seventeen of them. *Seventeen!* What sort of man could sanction that?'

'*It's not my decision!*'

'I wonder how many times they had to rape her to get her pregnant?'

'*Stop!*'

'And who fathers these children? The high-bloods ... All those noble part-Rondian magi in Rashid's service, laying with drugged and unwilling prisoners to father the future!' Kazim took another step forward, his eyes locked on Molmar's. 'What *true man* could bring himself to do that? Or maybe they *enjoy* it?'

Molmar's eyes bled tears, but he didn't move as Kazim reached him and put his hands on the older man's shoulders. The Hadishah pilot began to sway as his head dropped and his chest swelled with sudden sobs.

'My friend, those places are monstrous crimes,' Kazim said.

Elena waited, unconvinced that this matter was decided yet.

Molmar rubbed roughly at his eyes. 'Brother, you ask too much. I know they are evil – yes, *evil!* But to betray my brothers in such a way? I cannot! Future generations of Keshi and Dhassans would curse me for ever! It is the Brotherhood that has given us the chance to resist the Crusade – I cannot jeopardise our future strength!'

'But the liberation of just one such breeding-house – the right one, the one housing the recent Ordo Costruo prisoners – could save all of Javon from Rondian rule. Yes, it would be a blow to the Hadishah, but not a fatal one. If the Rondians establish control of Javon, we will never remove them, no matter how many women we rape.'

Molmar swallowed. 'I hear you,' he admitted. 'But I cannot make such a decision. Let me take this argument to my superiors – please? If it convinces them, they could free those magi voluntarily. But do not ask me to betray my order.'

'Sorry, Molmar,' Elena put in, surprised to find herself feeling genuine sympathy for the man. 'You've already said it: your people will never work with us. Those Ordo Costruo are the only ones who might. You think a Crusade every dozen years is bad, but the Rondians in Javon are here to stay.'

The Hadishah man's face was a picture of indecision and misery.

'You know we're right,' Kazim said. 'Please, will you help?'

Elena added her silent prayers. The last thing she wanted was to have to betray this parley and put the Hadishah pilot to the question to find out where the Ordo Costruo were being housed. *Please, Molmar! Because otherwise I'm going to have to let the old Elena loose, and I really don't want to be her again.*

When Molmar broke down and gave his assent, she almost burst into tears herself.

12

Riverdown

The Cohort

*The base military unit of the legion is the cohort – twenty men who fight together
as a team. Each knows his part and trains to do it well, and in doing so makes
the cohort stronger than the sum of its parts. Each cohort is a mini-legion, whose
pride and spirit is the pillar upon which the maniple is built. Cohorts built the
Rimoni Empire, and cohorts are the foundation of the Rondian Empire.*

GENERAL GILLE DE BRES, BRICIA XVI LEGION, 874

*East of Vida, Southern Kesh, on the continent of Antiopia
Zulqeda (Noveleve) 929
17th month of the Moontide*

Holy Kore, there's so many of them! Seth felt his confidence fraying as
he surveyed a plain fill with enemies. At Shaliyah the sand-storm
had hidden the enemy strength to a large extent, and anyway, they
had nearly as many men themselves. At Ardijah, the riverbanks and
the terrain had obscured the bulk of Salim's forces. But here there
was nothing to conceal the sheer size of the army they faced. Seth,
standing at the highest point of his lines, was trying to ignore them
and concentrate on his own army, but it wasn't easy.

The Lost Legions could field 11,000 men, with another 1,000 ill or
long-term injured who were confined to the baggage train with the
camp followers, a couple of thousand Khotri women and children.
They were defending a mile-long curved front – almost two thousand yards of frontline, with only three hundred yards back to the

riverbank: there could be no fall-back position, no place to retreat to. One breakthrough was all it would take to destroy them. He was hanging his hopes on the fact that his legionaries had better armour than the Keshi and were trained in formation fighting. He had five rankers for every yard of front line: when the action started that would be enough men to rotate every three minutes, with twelve minutes off – plenty of recovery time.

If every one of ours kills ten of theirs, we'll wipe them out. He sighed. *Sure, that's going to happen . . .*

Conventional wisdom – *Rondian* wisdom – had it that a Rondian legion could defeat five times as many enemy . . . provided the enemy had no magi. *Ah yes, the magi . . .* His army had nineteen, and two of those, Lanna and Carmina, wouldn't be fighting. He wasn't sure Severine Tiseme *could* fight, so that left sixteen, less than one every two hundred yards, and that was if he himself fought, rather than observing the battlefield and coordinating the defence as he should.

No, fifteen: Baltus will have to be in the air . . . it just gets worse . . .

He wondered how many magi the enemy had. *Fifty? A hundred? Every one of us is going to have to take down somewhere between five and ten on our own . . . And if we don't, their magi will carve us all up . . .*

He couldn't see a way to win, no matter how optimistically he looked at it.

'You're looking a bit gloomy, lad,' Jelaska commented. Her face was utterly calm.

She's a Necromancer, Seth thought. *She's probably looking forward to death . . .*

'Yar, cheer up General,' Kip said brightly. 'It's going to be *vunderbar*.' He punched Seth's shoulder. 'Minaus Bullhead is watching. Embrace his rage.'

'He's actually right, Seth,' Ramon put in. 'I've noticed that you fight best when you're angry.' His voice was serious for once. 'So stop agonising over right and wrong: we're here, and the Keshi want to kill us just because we wandered through their desert on the way home. Your friend Salim could have let us push north to the upriver fords if he was really the sweetie he pretends to be.'

Travelling through three minor kingdoms and against the will of his entire army? I doubt that was ever an option. But he appreciated Ramon's words; there was going to be a battle, and he meant to win. He strained his eyes towards the Keshi army, watching it deploying with messy imprecision, all motley colours and haphazard lines. 'You'd think they could afford uniforms,' he commented. 'And they can't even march in a straight line.'

'That's the spirit,' Jelaska drawled. 'They're mostly conscripts: all they're given when they join up is a keffi in their lord's colours. Most aren't even armoured. The only standing army – the ones who are still soldiers in peace-time – are the archers. Oh, the cavalry too, I guess, but they're all nobles, not exactly soldiers either.'

'How do you know all that?' Kip asked.

'Seth wasn't the only one who wined and dined Latif when we had him in our nefarious clutches,' Jelaska chuckled. 'The Keshi cavalry are all young nobles, way down the pecking order for the family title. They're essentially mounted archers and swordsmen. If you spot a lancer, he's a servant.'

'Aren't you just a mine of information, my darling?' Baltus laughed. He'd just returned from an aerial patrol and as the skies were now dotted with Keshi windskiffs, he wasn't planning on going up again any time soon.

The five of them watched their rankers finish off their preparations by digging their heavy spears butt-first into the earth to deter cavalry. They'd effectively turned the ridgeline into a mile-long rampart, anchored by the river in the north and a three-hundred-foot-long wooden palisade made from wagon parts at the south end. The remaining wagons were circled inside the perimeter to make a sheltered camp for the invalids, women and children.

'How will they do this?' Seth asked.

'A parley first,' Ramon responded. 'They'll demand surrender. We'll refuse.'

'Then archery,' Jelaska said. 'Keshi archers like to fill the sky with arrows. They didn't do it at Shaliyah because of the storm. This time they'll go for broke: we'll have ten – maybe even twenty thousand

– archers, shooting six shafts a minute at least. They'll black out the sun.'

Seth tried to imagine the terror of cowering beneath a shield while the sky rained death. 'We magi can only shield so much,' he said anxiously. 'The men will be unprotected.'

'The men know what they're facing,' Ramon assured him. 'We've been reminding them for the past week. Notice the shape of the ditches and the walls? We've built the ditches high enough to shelter behind, with concave walls. It'll take a Hel of an arrow to hit anyone at all.'

'And the women have been told to shelter beneath the wagons,' Jelaska added, 'even if they think they're out of range. We've got more than two hundred wagons so that's ten women per cart; I know they've got the children too, but most are still babes in arms so they'll manage. It's their pilot-mages in the sky above that could be the main issue.' She put her hand on Baltus' shoulder. 'We've one skiff and they have Kore knows how many.'

'"Battles have been won and lost on command of the skies",' Seth said, quoting his father.

Baltus peered skywards. 'They've actually got only five skiffs in the sky today. They had more at Ardijah.' His eyes narrowed. 'And I've seen no shapeshifters here: there were dozens at Ardijah.'

'Maybe they've all flown off to somewhere important,' Ramon suggested.

'More likely they've got something planned,' Jelaska said dourly.

Seth grimaced and brought them back to the matter at hand. 'So, after the archery?'

'After the coward archers shoot from a safe distance, the spearmen will charge.' Kip sniffed contemptuously. In his view, real men fought toe to toe. 'They try to overrun us with untrained peasants. We smash them apart and they run. The Bullhead rejoices in the slaying, and his Bloodmaidens drink deep.'

'There'll be a lot of that,' Ramon agreed. 'They'll try to wear us down. The cavalry won't charge until it's a rout and they feel they can risk their precious necks in search of the glory: that's nobility for you.'

Seth looked about him. 'Well then: take up position and reassure your men. Be prepared for archery; they might skip the parley and go straight to the shooting. Ramon, stay with me: I'll take you if they want to talk.'

They all saluted him, and Seth was surprised by a genuine feeling of fondness. Friendship – real camaraderie – had been rare in his life. At the Arcanum, Malevorn Andevarion and Francis Dorobon might have befriended him, but they'd made it clear that they were superior to him. When he'd joined the Thirteenth, only Renn Bondeau and Severine Tiseme had been welcoming, and that was nothing to do with liking him and everything to do with his family name. His one true friend, Tyron Frand, was dead. But gradually, this motley, multi-racial, rough-spoken collection of magi had began to feel like, well ... *family*. They bickered and sniped and joked and undercut each other ... and then obeyed him, when he scarcely felt he deserved it, but which never failed to lift his spirits. They also exuded indomitable self-belief, as if they couldn't conceive of failure.

'We'll give these Keshi a shock,' Ramon said quietly when they were alone. 'Are you ready to write a new chapter in the Korion legend?'

Seth couldn't tell if he was being teased, but he decided it didn't matter. 'I'd love to, but we're going to need a miracle.'

'Then let's provide one. I've got some ideas, but there hasn't been time to flesh them out.'

Seth seized at the straw of hope. 'Really?'

Ramon chuckled. 'No, I've got nothing! But who knows? Ideas come.'

'You're a low-bred rat, Sensini.'

'High-bred, remember?'

'What: your father's in the Treasury? Your bloody mother was higher-bred than that prick!'

Ramon burst out laughing. 'Good point!' Then he squinted and pointed. 'There, see? They're marching the archers forward. It looks like there won't be a parley after all. I'd better go find my men.'

As Ramon turned to go, Seth reached out and caught his arm.

'Sensini . . . Ramon, I . . . um . . .' *I was wrong about you. I treated you abominably at the Arcanum, and Mercer too. I'm really sorry.* What he actually managed was, 'Good luck. May Kore protect you.'

'Si. Pater Sol guide you too.' Ramon winked. 'And the Bullhead too – Hel, let's invoke them all!' He smirked crookedly and turned away, leaving Seth grinning foolishly.

Are my best friends truly a Keshi impersonator and a Silacian familioso?

He looked around him to find the men of his personal cohort watching with stiff faces and amused eyes. He clapped his hands and shouted, 'Get your heads down, you lunkers! Here they come!'

Nothing moved in the cloudless powder-blue skies above the earthworks at the northern end of the perimeter. Ramon wondered whether three feet of dirt and rock stiffened with wards and Earth-gnosis was going to be enough, then his eyes went to the Keshi archers forming up beyond the ramparts, just two hundred yards away – in easy range. The Lost Legions had a few Estellan archers – and everyone knew they were the best – but they didn't deploy them en masse, for fear they would be swamped. Instead they were dotted here and there with orders to snipe at the enemy and make every arrow count.

By now, every man was in place and Ramon took up his own position among Pilus Lukaz's cohort, wedged between the two serjants, Vidran and Manius, whose solidity always steadied him. The cohort were standing, watching the enemy, waiting for the signal to take cover. The air reeked as eleven thousand men sweated and farted and sucked down air. It was the hottest part of the day, no doubt chosen by the Keshi especially to weaken their cold-climate enemies. Behind them the baggage train had gone silent. The women and children were cowering beneath the wagons, knowing they would be shown no mercy if the men protecting them fell. Severine was with them, still too weak to fight, or so she said. *Too scared* was Lanna Jureigh's sneering assessment. Ramon sent up a prayer for her anyway, and little Julietta.

He distracted himself by wondering where the enemy magi were.

217

There were only five skiffs in the skies above, and none of the flying Dokken. Was Baltus right? Were the rest up to something sneaky?

What if they've got Water-magi in the river?

He peered at the shimmering strip of water flooding past. 'Tell the men on the left to watch the river,' he told Lukaz.

'You reckon they'll come in from there, boss?' Vidran chuckled. 'They do that, they'll drown in shit.'

Manius snickered. 'We all left a big dump in there 'specially, Magister. Raised the river level three feet.'

Ramon laughed, slapped Manius on the shoulder and returned his attention to the enemy. The cohort would be keeping their heads down, but someone needed to watch in case the Keshi attempted a rush under the cover of the arrows. That was his job.

'Be ready!' he called. Keshi archers had a rhythm, a routine to planting their feet, nocking and drawing their bows. 'They'll fire in twenty seconds!'

All down the line the more nervous rankers hunkered down immediately, while the rest altered their stance, ready to drop into cover, but unwilling to miss seeing the final few seconds before that moment. Through the haze they all saw Keshi officers walk to the front of the serried ranks of archers then, like a breaking wave, the men bent, straightened, drew their bows and pointed them skywards.

They all heard the thunderous commands – '*BIR! ICHI! USH!*' – and then, '*SUR!*'

Thousands of bows *thrummmmed*, and discharged their arrows into the air, rank after rank of them. Ramon gulped down air, swallowed bile and prepared to drop.

'DOWN! DOWN!' the cohort commanders screamed, taking cover themselves as the air filled with shafts, flooding across the sky in a dark wave. Ramon was awestruck at the sheer volume of wood and steel in the air, reducing the sun to a blurred after-image. The day darkened momentarily as he dropped behind the earthworks along with the rest, pressing against the forward wall of the ditch. Everyone held their shields over their heads as they tried to melt into the earth, their defiant cries merging with the hiss of falling missiles.

Then the arrows came.

They fell as one, lancing into the earth, each impact blending into one massive *crack* as they struck the earthworks. Many dropped behind their position, slamming into the earth and sticking there, a forest that grew and thickened as the seconds crawled past.

'Fuckers know how to shoot!' Vidran shouted in his ear. 'Right on target, first volley!' Even he looked a little tense. All around them were shafts impaling the earth or breaking on stone and pinging in every direction.

Ramon forced a grin. 'Nice bit of shade though, si?'

Vidran snorted, then an arrow glanced off his shield and slashed past Ramon's face. They both flinched.

The volleys blurred into one until not a moment didn't contain arrows slicing through their world. Finally Ramon plucked up his courage, strengthened his gnostic shields and put his eye to the viewing slot he'd left in the wall. The Keshi archers were still at it: one rank firing while the next was reloading in a magnificently precise motion: aim and loose; bend and nock; aim and lose, rhythmic and practised, drilled to perfection.

Through the hiss and crack came other sounds: a wailing shriek as a lucky shaft struck flesh; the cry of someone teetering at the edge of panic; the stentorian bellow of an officer offering reassurance. Women beneath the wagons called fearfully to their men, separated from them by a curtain of death. A howl of terror caught his ears and off to his right a panicked ranker broke cover and ran for the wagons. The first arrow took him in the back, the second in the thigh as he fell, and inside a minute four more had pierced him. Another ten paces and he might have broken through, but the air was so thick with these deadly shafts that making that dash was inconceivable. Gradually the man's body became a hedgehog, then a scrap of debris.

For unending minutes, each one lasting longer than the last, the volleys went on, and had Ramon not been watching, he'd never have spotted the enemy movements – but he'd expected something like this. More men were trotting through the lines of Keshi archers: ragged Lakh spearmen with no armour at all, wearing only cotton tunics and brightly coloured turbans. They were pouring to the front while the archers fired over their heads.

'Spearmen! Two hundred yards!' Ramon called, then broadcast to the other magi, <Enemy spears, left flank!>

<Here too!> Gerdhart sent from the centre, confirming Ramon's suspicion: it was happening all along the front, a massed assault to try and break them quickly. The rankers grasped their javelins and snarled encouragement at each other.

'Stay down 'til the last!' Ramon shouted to his cohort. 'They'll try and go right over us while we're hiding.' He peered through his viewing hole. 'One hundred yards . . . Seventy . . . Fifty! They're running! They're at the base!'

The arrows never stopped and the Lakh spearmen didn't flinch as they came storming up the small slope, screaming their battle-cries. Perhaps they'd been told the barrage would cease when they reached the enemy, but it didn't. Dozens and dozens went down, shot in the back by their own archers.

Then Ramon shouted: 'UP! NOW!!!' and moving as one, the men of his cohort and the rest of his line leaped up and hurled their javelins over the lip of their earthworks into the faces of the Lakh attackers. Ramon fired mage-bolts as fast as he dared and on either side of him the Lakh went down in swathes, clutching the javelin shafts that spitted their chests, bellies and thighs. And still the Keshi arrows rained down, punching through their backs and erupting from their chests. The charge disintegrated and those behind wavered until Keshi officers with whips roared them on again.

The rain of arrows was starting to take a toll on the Rondians as well. One of Lukaz's flankmen, Neubeau, sprawled on his back with an arrow through his right eye. To his left, Ilwyn was clutching a broken shaft in his left shoulder, and Gannoval, the stolid Hollenian, was sitting in the sand contemplating the thick Lakh spear that went in his stomach and came out his back, before toppling sideways.

The Lakh gathered at the foot of the mound, then flooded forward again, ignoring the incessant arrows to leap at the barricades. Thrown spears hammered into Rondian shields, and then the attackers were on them, trying to pull the shields aside so others could thrust spears through the gaps, while the rankers met them with straight-arm sword-thrusts. Ramon's sight was filled with the wide-open eyes and mouths of the Lakh trying to reach him, as he shielded blows and blasted with mage-fire, or shoved with kinesis, dispersing a dozen men at once, until finally the charge was broken – and he suddenly realised that the arrows had stopped, though he couldn't have said when. One Lakh tried to leap past Vidran, who took the man's left leg off with a roundhouse slash, and the rest of the man hit the barrier and slid down it.

Lukaz darted in to stab a Lakh spearman in the throat as he bore Trefeld over backwards, then pushed the young ranker back into line. The Vereloni officer was calmness itself as he told Ramon, 'We're holding, sir. Go and check on the Nambies next door.'

Ramon ran to join the Nambies, a Rondian cohort from the Nam-borne district, and found them embroiled in hand-to-hand fighting along the earthworks. As he arrived a cluster of Lakh punched through, so he slammed mage-bolts into them until they wilted and were driven back. Then suddenly the attack was over and the Lakh pulled back, like an ebbing tide.

All along the line, the Estellan archers Seth had stationed at inter-vals broke cover to shoot at the retreating men. Someone whooped, and then there was a thunderous cacophony as every unit shouted in defiance and relief.

'See to the hurt!' he heard Lukaz shout. 'See to the fallen! Then take cover!'

Good idea, Ramon thought, dashing back to his place. He made it just before the cries came up from the enemy lines again: '*BIR! ICHI! USH! SUR!*'

Sultan Salim Kabarakhi I of Kesh walked to the edge of the carpet that had been laid for him at the highest point in the centre of his lines so that his slippers wouldn't get dusty as he surveyed the battle three hundred yards away. Around him his Hadishah magi kept watch, lest the Rondian magi try something. Behind him, in the huge royal pavilion, three of his impersonators were playing dice. His Godspeakers trailed behind him, denouncing the lack of faith among the Lakh and Gatioch conscripts they'd thrown at the enemy lines that afternoon and blaming that for their failure.

They didn't lack faith . . . just armour, weapons and training.

'Leave me,' he interrupted curtly, then gestured Pashil, the Hadishah captain, forward. He was a half-blood mage, and Salim considered him his most reliably honest courtier. Right now he needed to hear some truths. 'Your assessment, Pashil?'

'It went as expected,' Pashil replied flatly. 'They are dug in, and well-drilled.'

'What were our losses?'

'Final tallies are not complete, but I estimate five thousand dead or wounded.'

So many? Dear Ahm! 'And the enemy?'

'At best a few hundred.'

Salim winced. 'Then what have we gained?'

'Today? Nothing. Unless you count reducing pressure on our food stores.' Pashil glared towards the Rondian lines. 'The disappointment was our southern flank, where there is no natural defence, but they've stationed the Argundians there, and the Necromancer-woman.'

'Jelaska Lyndrethuse,' Salim said. 'How are our men?'

'The Lakh and Gatti are dispirited. They claim you give them the impossible tasks and protect your Keshi.' Their eyes met; both knew the accusation to be true.

What ruler does not protect his own?

'And my Keshi?'

'Our morale remains high. The archers have plenty of arrows, the lancers are chaffing to ride out, and the young lords are clamouring for their chance.' Pashil lifted an eyebrow. 'Not that any of them want to go in first tomorrow.'

Salim half-smiled. 'And what of tomorrow?'

'The same, over and over. It is tiredness that will break the Rondians, exhaustion from constant alertness, constant combat, constantly being under fire. In the meantime, we have plenty of conscripts, and plenty of whips to drive them on.'

They shared a long minute of silence, watching the sun set and picturing the slaughter tomorrow would bring.

'What can your magi do to help us?' Salim asked finally.

'Not so much, without exposing ourselves.' His eyes were disapproving.

Yes, I know. I let Alyssa Dulayne butcher the Dokken, then leave with most of our magi.

'We both know the why, Pashil. If what she learned is true, then the opportunity could not be passed up. I only wish I could have given her more men.'

In that one bloody night he'd had more than eighty Dokken warriors, women and children slain, then released the best of the Hadishah, twenty-seven of Pashil's finest warrior-magi, to follow Alyssa on this almost unbelievable mission to claim the Scytale of Corineus. That left Pashil with only thirty mostly young Hadishah. The decision had crippled his own army and the required reorganisation had cost them two whole weeks: time that Seth Korion had used well in digging in. Thousands had died for that choice already, and thousands more would follow.

But surely we have enough men to win here?

'Attrition will win the day,' Pashil reassured him. 'It is inevitable. Keep a few archers firing right through the night, so that the Rondians cannot rest. Keep them on edge and they will break sooner.'

'A good suggestion. Let it be so.'

'Attrition,' Jelaska said, as Seth's magi gathered to review the second day of battle. 'That's their strategy.'

Seth yawned, wondering how many of them had managed any sleep since the attack began; he certainly hadn't. There had been five major assaults through the day, and sporadic arrow-fire all night. But the attacks today had been half-hearted, just ill-armed rabble who had broken quickly. 'We're already exhausted.'

'Not us, General.' Jelaska gestured towards her grim Argundians. 'My lads are happy as larks.'

Argundians: how do you tell?

'Have you seen any magi on your flank?' he asked. Jelaska's Argundians were holding the weakest part of the line and they had half the reserves waiting behind her in case of a breakthrough, but there had been none yet.

'Only a few skiffs above, and they've not come near me, sadly,' she grumbled.

'Why would they hold them back?'

'Same reason we're only getting conscripts thrown at us: the magi and the nobles want the glory without the danger. Often in one-sided battles, the best men hold back. Everyone wants someone else to do the dirty work.'

'So it'll be more of the same tomorrow?'

'Probably. I'll try and make sure the lads get some sleep tonight, General. The whole army doesn't have to be awake.' She yawned too. 'I'm getting too old for this *vulnessia*.' When he cocked an eyebrow she translated. 'Garbage.'

'Vulnessia . . . Sounds like the name of one of my father's consorts,' Seth remarked.

'Ha! You're starting to get the spirit of this lark, lad.'

'I think I've been spending too much time with Sensini.'

Jelaska scowled. 'That little rat . . . I heard he's plugging Lanna Jureigh behind Severine's back.'

Seth wrinkled his nose in distaste. First Severine, which had been unbelievable enough, and then there were those rumours about Calipha Amiza in Ardijah. But Lanna as well? He *liked* Lanna. She'd once hinted that if he wanted, she was willing. But it hadn't felt right. It never seemed to, with any woman he met. 'Should I speak to him?'

'No!' Jelaska snorted. 'There's no law against it out here.'

'How does the scrawny little rat do it?'

'Women like men who know what they're doing – or who *look* as if they know what they're doing. *Meesterhaften* – masterly men, as we say in Argundy – they project confidence and purpose: an attractive quality that comes in all shapes and sizes.' She looked at him critically. 'In case you're wondering, you don't have it, but it's coming.'

'Then there's hope for me yet?'

'Yes, General, there is.' Jelaska chuckled sympathetically, then she went back to yelling at her Argundians.

Ramon slipped into the space beneath the wagon where Severine Tiseme was sleeping in a blanket with Julietta tucked against her. He must have triggered wards as he entered because Sevvie's eyes flashed open, her body tensing until she recognised him. 'Wha' you wan'?' she mumbled.

'To see my daughter. And her mother, of course.'

'Piss off. I'm tired,' she said. 'What's happening?'

'Nothing much. The Keshi are still firing their rukking arrows into the camp, but only a few, to keep us on our toes. As long as you keep a good shield above your head, you're mostly all right. We've got sensing-wards in front of the lines to warn of any raids, and we're rotating the cohorts. Most of the camp's asleep.' He pulled Julietta into his arms. '*Buona sera*, little one: it's Papa.' The infant wriggled into a fresh position without waking. Her tiny round face made him feel soft as wool inside. 'She knows me,' he said proudly.

'She loves her mother best,' Sevvie replied. 'Because I have tits full of milk. I should have been born a cow.'

'Who says you weren't?' He rocked Julietta in his arms, marvelling at the delicate detail of her face. 'How are you feeling, Sevvie? Any stronger?'

She looked away. 'I'm so tired. Being Julietta's milkmaid isn't easy. All my energy goes into her.'

'We need you out there, even if it's just to set wards and scry the enemy lines for movement.'

'No – stop asking! Your daughter needs me!'

'So do our soldiers! We have wet-nurses by the dozen – let someone else feed her.'

Severine looked appalled. 'I'm not letting some dirty Noorie woman breastfeed my baby! How could you even suggest such a thing?' She snatched Julietta away, making her wake and start crying. 'Now look what you've done! Go away and leave us alone!'

They exchanged hot glares, then he swore and rolled from beneath the wagon. He unloosed a salvo of words behind him. 'You're letting us all down with your ... *hiding*. You could get up if you wanted. You know you could.'

She burst into tears and from left and right he saw Khotri women glaring at him. A few shouted abuse in their own tongue; he didn't need to know the words to get the gist. He stumbled away and took up their suggestion, heading to the ditches and pissing away his anger and disappointment.

With no welcome in his own bed, Ramon drifted towards the healers' tents, close to the river and as far from the firing zone as possible. Lanna and Carmina were assisted by two dozen nurses and around forty Khotri women who'd volunteered. The grey-haired senior nurse, a Pallacian man named Rousham, saw every man brought in and assessed his needs, freeing the two mage-healers to tend the worst cases. Ramon passed down the lines of men lying in blood-stained blankets, some asleep, most awake and in pain. Lanna was bent over a man with two arrows imbedded in his ribcage. His breath was coming in agonised wheezing, sucking gusts. Pale light seeped from her hands into the wound, while a bubble of light pulsed in his open mouth, Air-gnosis pumping clean air into his lungs.

He died as Ramon arrived, giving up as if all this effort was just not worth it.

Lanna sagged as well, her compassionate face first going sickly, then resigned. She looked up at Ramon blankly. 'What?'

'I'm just doing the rounds.' He put a hand on her shoulder, wanting to comfort her.

'Don't touch me,' she snapped, shrugging his hand away. Then she sighed. 'Sorry. Carmina heard a rumour that you're screwing me, which is ripe because I've not noticed.'

'Nor I. You know the way this army gossips.'

'I surely do. Look, I've got another four serious cases before I can sleep. So unless you're here to help, piss off.' She gestured to the far end of the tent. 'Seth's helping Carmina. He's a good healer; he missed his calling.'

Ramon conjured light in his hand. 'What do you need? I've enough of an affinity to cleanse a wound.'

She looked up and her face softened a little. She pointed to a row of prostrate men. 'Those men need their dressings changed and any infection cleansed. Get to it.'

Fridryk Kippenegger stalked along the rows of sweating, nervous men lining the barricades. It was afternoon on the fourth day of battle, though the first three barely counted in his mind. The incessant arrows were just annoying, and the attacks by the enemy spearmen had been dismal. Minaus Bullhead, looking down from his throne of skulls, would have seen little to rouse him. The Schlessen war-god admired mighty hand-to-hand clashes, not cowardly skulking and the hurling of missiles.

But *this* looked more promising.

The enemy archers were back, but this time they were bearing wicker shields and scimitars, not bows. They were far better armed than the conscripts, and they could at least march in straight lines, not a thing Kip really valued, but it did imply some measure of competence. They were massed in ranks twenty- or thirty-deep, ready to attack. The drums began to pound and his heart took up the rhythm.

'Look at them!' he called to his men. 'Plenty for us all!' He pointed skywards, 'And for you, Minaus!'

His men held the south end of the natural ridge, buttressing onto Jelaska's narrow, flat section. The Argundians had worked hard to strengthen the line, digging a ditch across their front, raising earthworks and wooden palisades. And of course, Jelaska herself was there. Kip could see the Argundian standing alongside Baltus Prenton's skiff, which was ready to take to the air: a little surprise for the enemy. Then his eyes were drawn to his own front as the drums rolled then fell silent.

'Minaus is watching, my Bullheads!' Kip shouted. 'He drinks to your courage!'

'*MINAUS!*' his men shouted, Pallacians all. They'd cheerily adopted the Schlessen war-god as their patron following Shaliyah, where Kip had kept them alive through the disaster.

'Kore be my shield!' one man added nervously.

'Kore is a weakling!' Kip roared at the man. 'Only the Bullhead gives strength in battle! Minaus is your strong arm! Minaus is your blade!' He slapped the man on the shoulder. 'Rejoice! The test is now! We are strong and the enemy is puny!'

His diatribe was interrupted by another massive drum-roll that became a steady beat and then the Keshi were marching forward, their footfalls shaking the earth. Estellan archers began to shoot, each arrow dropping a marching man in his tracks, but they were few, and the Keshi just strode over the bodies.

'Why are we here?' Kip shouted.

'TO KILL!'

'Who will we kill?'

'THOSE CUNNIS!' And his men grabbed at imaginary cocks and waggled them contemptuously at the Keshi. As the Keshi came closer and their faces became clearer, Kip could feel their anger: they knew what the gesture meant.

With a wild cry, the attackers suddenly burst into a run, and the Rondians readied their javelins. Kip let the Keshi get close, sprinting through a withering storm of Estellan arrows and reaching the base of the mound some thirty yards below. As they bunched and slowed, he bellowed, 'THROW!'

The javelins, a wall of them, were hurled with brutal force into the faces of the climbing Keshi. Their wicker shields failed to protect them; the javelins burst through and transfixed the men behind. The entire front rank of the enemy went down as Kip brandished his massive zweihandle. The next rank of Keshi hurdled the bodies of their comrades, eyes bulging and mouths screaming as they threw themselves up the slope.

They were met by barricades topped with interlocked shields, and the legionaries slamming their shortswords through the gaps into faces and chests. The first Keshi were trapped by the wall before them and the mass of men behind and had nowhere to go; they couldn't even drop and crawl away as they were slowly hacked apart, dying on their feet, and impeding the men behind them. Those following could barely keep their feet, let alone fight, but the wall began to waver from the pressure of those pushing on it.

'SWITCH!' Kip ordered the first rotation, pouring kinesis into the mass in front of him and buying a second for the switch of ranks, then following up with mage-bolts. But his whole section was wobbling from the sheer weight of numbers: momentum was shifting against his men. He recognised it instinctively and knew he had to act.

Leaping to the top of the barricade he swung the zweihandle without finesse, just brute strength and heavy steel, shattering the first Keshi's scimitar and his helm beneath, then wrenching the blade free and plunging it into a second man, straight through his shield and breastplate. Scimitars and spears scoured his gnostic shields, ripping through in showers of sparks as steel bit into his shins and thighs, though not deeply. He hacked about him ferociously, carving a space. Javelins flew all around him as his reserves followed him, bigger men than their foes and more heavily armed. Keshi blades snapped, caught in shields, or glanced off armour, the wounds they inflicted superficial, but the Pallacian shortsword thrusts were practised and deadly.

'VORWAERTS! VORWAERTS!' Kip bellowed, carrying his men with him as he stormed down the slope, sending a shockwave through the mass before him.

'THIRD RANK!' his officers bellowed, and the next rotation of men pushed through: flankmen, the best swordsmen and most suited to a broken mêlée. They dashed into the Keshi, and individual duels broke out, one-sided and brief. Kip went with them, hacking down men who barely saw him coming as they turned to flee.

Blue fire flashed into his shields and through, searing his left forearm and as he bellowed in rage he saw a black-robed figure darting through the press. *Hadishah!*

He went for the assassin, ploughing through the mêlée. The Hadishah saw him coming and fired again but Kip's shields were ready. The Keshi were scattering, opening the space between him and the assassin. More mage-fire struck and he staggered on, then he was swinging his blade as fire burst around him. The world became a red-orange tunnel with a black shape at the end of it. His zweihandle swept through the Hadishah's shields, smashed ribs and embedded itself in the assassin's spine. The Keshi went down in a heap as he spun and hacked and spun and hacked, over and again, because some magi just didn't know how to die.

Verdamnt Shizen!

Some brave soul grabbed his right arm. 'Sir! Hold, sir! She's dead, she's dead!'

She?

His vision cleared. The Hadishah lay hacked in half a few yards away, and her head was another foot from the stump of her neck. She'd been maybe twenty, with big soft eyes and perfect skin. Kip spat the sudden ill taste from his mouth, then looked around.

'You weren't to know, sir.'

'Bloodmaidens,' he snarled. 'My people have woman warriors also, sworn to the Bullhead. When they die they join his Stormriders. I've sent dozens to his ranks!' It was bravado, but he needed it: his clothes were still smouldering and his gnosis was strained. The Keshi were falling back to their lines, but their cavalry were circling, hoping to catch the Rondian footmen in the open. It was time to pull back.

They hurried back to the barricades, his officer shouting out orders: 'Clear the dead! Wounded to the rear! Recover your javelins! Fix those barricades!'

Kip sucked air into his big chest, then lifted his head. 'The Bullhead is speaking to me, bruden!' he shouted. 'He is *pleased*! His goblet is full of Keshi blood!'

They cheered his savagery, cheered themselves. He was proud of them, and though he'd not show it now, he was grudgingly respectful of their enemy too. Minaus was known to accept brave heathens into his Stormriders.

We sent you many Keshi today, Bullhead, and a new Bloodmaiden for your guard.

Away to his right, the fighting wore on. Like the Pallacians, the

Argundians were bigger and stronger, man for man, than their foes. They bore huge ash spears which could be wielded by men two and three ranks back, presenting a forest of spearheads. Jelaska wasn't even needed; her lines held by sheer brute strength.

Then Kip sensed a rush of power in the skies above and lifted his eyes to see Baltus Prenton's skiff sweeping over the enemy assailing Jelaska's position. Hugh Gerant was in the bow, hurling a bundle of the enemy's own arrows, recovered from the incessant barrage. With an explosion of kinetic force, he sent them into the horde below, streaking downwards with deadly force. Kip's eyes widened as he saw the impact, a circle of some ten yards of close-packed men collapsing en masse, and those around them recoiling. Baltus swept on, Hugh already preparing another bundle, while two enemy skiffs converged on their position.

Then the Keshi drums rolled again before his position and he turned away from the distant struggle to prepare for the next assault. 'Here they come again!'

Baltus tacked away from the battle, soaring over the river. The far bank was just a dark line in the hazy west, like a mythic island that could only be seen on certain days. Brevian myth was full of such islands, places of sunshine and warmth. *Probably because Brevis is such a mucky hole.*

'Bring it round!' Hugh shouted; the Andressan mage-archer had been shaken out of his habitual reserve by the taste of battle. 'I'm ready for the next run!' They'd made seven passes now and had one bundle of arrows left. Below them the battle had been raging for over an hour. The Argundians had not ceded an inch, and the fighting around Kippenegger's section of the line had stabilised, despite a palisade collapsing and the Keshi almost spilling into the perimeter. He turned his craft for the next sweep across the enemy when Hugh pointed southwards, shouting, 'Ware! Enemy skiff!'

The Keshi skiff's triangular sail billowed as it caught the wind, half a mile south and to windward. They generally worked in pairs, so Baltus scanned the sky until he found the other, lurking to the

DAVID HAIR

east. Their next run would take him between the two of them, leaving them vulnerable. But Jelaska was counting on them ... He thought for a moment, then turned the rudder, gracefully ducked the boom as the sail swept from left to right, and swept back towards the fight.

From up here, the Riverdown camp was tiny and the enemy forces vast, but the desert was even greater, sweeping on beyond them and far into the shifting mirages, as if to say that all men were insignificant, just fleeting stains on the land. Every time he took to the air there was an almost overwhelming temptation to simply fly away. Up here, everything was softened by distance into perfection; the earthbound world only ever let him down.

Take Jelaska, for example: from his vantage in the sky her grey hair shone like a banner, and her lean and stately form could have been that of a young beauty. But up close she was wrinkled and acerbic, so enamoured of her gnosis and her legion that there was no room in her life for anything more than a casual coming together of bodies. Her emotions were so numb from loss that she was just a mask of irony and cutting words. The half-serious joke about being cursed irritated him. *I'm not cursed. I'm going to live through this, like I always do.* And she *smelled* old, and her flesh sagged. She wasn't *perfect*.

Baltus had never met the *perfect* woman, the one who would change *everything*. Young women were so naïve; older ones so jaded. The magi-women all played games and the non-magi were either awestruck or sly. No one truly moved him, and relationships were so fleeting he sometimes wondered why he bothered at all. But they were also addictive, and he was never quite settled in his own skin unless there was a woman in his bed, even one he fancied only in passing, like Jelaska.

'Baltus—?' Hugh snapped. 'Angle right!'

He waved a hand in apology and corrected, with one eye on the Keshi craft angling into an intercept course. The triangular Keshi sail interested him; it was smaller, but it made the craft more nimble; the Keshi skiffs were all faster than Rondian ones, all else being equal,

232

which wasn't right. *We've been doing this for* centuries – *we should be better at it than them.*

He set his prow towards Jelaska's position, where the Keshi were pressing again, trying to break the lines by sheer weight of bodies. But the Argundian legion was a mincing machine, unrelentingly hacking the Ahmedhassans apart. All along the southern front the attack was building though, and he could see it would take only one breakthrough – and these were Keshi regulars, trained soldiers, not the conscripted battle fodder they'd been using until now. They were proving tenacious.

They went in, the Keshi skiff ahead correcting to intercept, the southern one sweeping in from high above. There were two black-robed bowmen in the fore-deck of each craft, and he could see gnosis-fire on their arrow tips. 'Ware the archers, Hugh,' he sang out, adding, 'They're magi!'

Hugh nodded to show he'd heard, but his focus was the bundle of arrows, which he'd split into two. <*Can you get above one of them?*> he called silently, kindling gnosis-fire.

Baltus read his intention and focused on the oncoming Keshi skiff. The roar of the battlefield grew as the sea of Keshi beneath them started hurling spears that fell pitifully short; the odd arrow whistled past in their wake. The enemy skiff ahead sheared elegantly through the air, apparently on a collision course, and the archers bent their bows.

He pushed a little more Air-gnosis into the keel, then with a cry he engaged it, sending his craft on a rapid spiralling climb, cutting across the tip of their foe's mast. Hugh stood and, shouting trium-phantly, hurling the arrow bundle downwards with a kinetic blast, even as two shafts slammed into his shields. The impact almost threw him overboard, but he held on. Baltus glanced back and saw the Keshi craft stall in the air, its sail shredded. The pilot and two archers were each nailed to the hull by arrows, the rest having shat-tered on their shields and left them open. The pilotless skiff slewed sideways and began to drop, slowly, then faster as the gnosis in the keel, now undirected, leaked out uselessly. It fell into a crowd of

Keshi, crushing them, and Hugh, normally the most imperturbable of men, whooped aloud.

Baltus poured more into the keel and lifted even higher as the second skiff came at them. In the past few months he had practically rewritten the rules of skiff-to-skiff fighting. He was usually the only Rondian windcraft in the skies, and having to evade an enemy who was usually more numerous, usually faster and generally had more crew. But he was a half-blood mage, while most of these Keshi were low-bloods who preferred archery to gnostic duels. He'd had to adjust the normal rules – a Rondian might even say cheat– but it was all rather fun.

Lift was vital for getting above the enemy unexpectedly, so he poured his energies into climbing above the trajectory of the incoming second skiff. They were adjusting too, coming at him hard, their archers predictably aiming at his sails, trying to disable him, but he and Hugh swatted the projectiles away and he swept past as they turned in his wake. Both craft were now travelling south, away from the battle, cutting across the westerly wind; his craft higher, but theirs was gaining.

<Spin-turn!> he called to Hugh, then executed the manoeuvre, trusting the Andressan to react in time, and he did, dropping and throwing his weight into the turn, as Baltus released the boom and hauled the tiller sideways. The skiff jerked as if an invisible giant had grabbed the bow and spun the little craft in the air. They came about with nothing in the sails, but facing their enemy head-on.

<Now!> Baltus shouted, calling the wind to his sails while Gerant poured raw gnosis energy into the keel. The craft bucked, the sails cracked and the mast groaned, the canvas bulging, and they regained their speed in a few seconds and were now speeding back towards the unprepared Keshi. The enemy skiff tried to veer away, the archers' eyes widening in alarm.

Sorry, no way. Baltus leaned right, hauling the tiller with him, and the skiff swung, keeping the Keshi craft lined up: his bowsprit was reinforced shaped steel formed with Earth- and sylvan-gnosis to grip the hull and strengthen it. It made the craft slower and heavier, but made up for that in other ways.

They struck the Keshi craft just above the hull, ripping off their sail and breaking the mast, sending the craft rolling in the air, and Baltus heard at least two wails of terror as they ploughed through the enemy rigging, tearing it apart. His craft lost some momentum, but he kept filling the sails, looking behind to see the enemy skiff dropping and the furious Keshi soldiers below staring open-mouthed and pointing. His prow was draped in torn sail and tangled ropes and they were slewing wildly, but they were whole.

Cop that, lads! He grinned fiercely, revelling in the moment. *This, he thought, is why I'm alive!*

'Clear that wreckage,' he called to Hugh. 'Let's get her home!'

Hugh slashed at the tangle of rope from the broken Keshi skiff and the last of the wreck fell away, but to Baltus' surprise, the performance of the craft didn't change much – it still felt heavy.

'Something's snagged below!' he shouted.

Hugh gave him another laconic thumbs-up and leaned over the edge of the hull.

An arm came out of nowhere and buried a dagger in his left eye, right to the hilt; barely a second later the Andressan was flipped from the craft and fell away as a black-robed shape swarmed aboard with frightening agility.

Though shocked at the unexpected loss of his comrade, Baltus reacted just in time to shield as blue fire blazed from the man's right hand. The Hadishah had a mild face and grey-flecked hair, but he moved like a trained fighting man.

The bastard must've grabbed on as we hit them.

Now Baltus was the vulnerable one. He tried to counter with mage-fire, but the Hadishah shielded well. Baltus set the craft's trajectory for his own lines, guessing the perimeter was around a minute away . . . if only this bastard let him sail.

He won't, of course; he'll—

He'd not even finished shaping the thought before the Keshi mage did just as he'd feared, plunging his blade, that same knife that had

235

taken out Hugh Gerant and was still slimy with his blood, into the canvas sail and ripping; the cut instantly billowing top to bottom from the force of the wind, and the skiff bucked as it lost speed. Baltus groaned and drew his shortsword.

I can fix that . . . but only when he's dead.

He stood, placed a hand on a keel-sprite so he could manipulate the stored gnosis, and lunged at the Keshi. Steel clattered weakly, their blows hindered by lost balance and uncertain footing as the craft wobbled onwards, but still they thrust at each other through the hole in the torn sail and around the mast as the skiff continued to follow the trajectory he'd set, slowly drifting north towards his lines, but now losing altitude.

This is going to be touch and go, Baltus thought as he thrust at the man's arm; their blades clashed, the curved and the straight, then disengaged. He threw a mage-bolt and followed up with a blow, but the Keshi parried both and fired back. To his chagrin, he had no discernible advantage over the other man.

I hate fair fights.

Jelaska lifted her eyes from the clamour below her, unconsciously deflecting a spear thrown her way from some optimist among the Keshi, and fixed her gaze on the windskiff that was slewing drunkenly towards her lines. There were two men in it, fighting, and the craft was beginning to stall and drop.

It's not going to make it.

She cursed her Earth-bound gnosis, but there was no point wishing for what wasn't. If Baltus couldn't reach the lines, then the lines had to reach him. She turned to Gylf, her legion's tribune, the senior non-mage officer. 'Bring up the reserves, and form a wedge! We punch through, there!' She jabbed her finger to where Baltus' skiff looked like it would be landing.

There were no questions, no hesitation; after all, she'd been with these men most of her life. Jelaska, a pure-blood female mage, had fallen in love with army life and death during the incessant Argundian border wars, and now obedience was instant. Gylf raised a blade, trumpets blared and they surged forward, enveloping her as they formed up. She reached for her Death-light, the necromantic-gnosis that was her most deadly affinity. Shadows formed, her eyes turned violet and her skin grey and she strode through the press, her men opening a sudden path to the front line for her. The Keshi staggered and fell forward as the men they were shoving gave way, the first few dead on their feet – literally, having died minutes ago but unable to fall through the sheer press of bodies. Now they collapsed to the ground and those behind poured towards the Argundians, trying to swamp the breach. The barricade came down with a crack and they spilled into the perimeter – and into her path.

The death-light bloomed about her.

Purple lightning jagged from her hands, gripped the Keshi soldiers and leeched them, turning them to desiccated corpses before they hit the ground. The men around her thrust two-handed with their war-spears and the Keshi assault died stillborn. Then her wedge slammed into them, pouring through the broken barricade and beyond, scattering the Keshi with cold ferocity. The rest of her legion bellowed their battle-cries and followed.

Then the shadow of the skiff fell over the press and it ploughed into their midst, cutting down the Keshi before her and crashing to earth amidst the front line, splintering spears and breaking bones of men on both sides.

A man rose from the wreckage, bloodied and staggering.

Baltus Prenton jabbed again, keeping up the attack, forcing the Keshi mage back. The man was a fine fighter, better than he was, in truth, but Baltus had one advantage: he controlled the tiller. With each thrust he nudged it with kinesis, making the craft pitch in his chosen direction, throwing the other man off-balance, until the Hadishah snagged his heel on a brace and fell sprawling to the deck. Baltus stabbed at the man's exposed left thigh; the shortsword went into the man's leg and hit bone.

The Keshi gasped and his grip loosened on his scimitar, which spun away.

Gotcha!

Then the Hadishah grabbed Baltus' sword-arm. Their eyes locked; the look of agonised concentration on the assassin's face was terrifying. He pulled at Baltus' wrist, almost breaking it, not allowing him to withdraw the blade, while with his right hand he fished inside his robes until he came up with a curved dagger which he thrust at Baltus' chest.

He caught the man's arm in his left hand, planted his feet and tried to wrench his sword-arm free – then the ground came up and they struck, pancaking into the ground and slewing prow-first through the packed Keshi, crushing them. The jolt made the blade in the Hadishah's leg wrench to one side, causing fresh agony to bloom and breaking his strength. At last Baltus' blade came free; he staggered as he lost hold of the man's right arm but he concentrated on his quarry and rammed the shortsword into the man's chest, piercing his chainmail into flesh, even as something punched into his belly. He gasped, panting, as the light went out of his enemy's eyes.

Holy Kore! Thank you thank you thank you . . . He thought wryly of Kippenegger, who promised animal sacrifices to his war-god. *Perhaps I should send Kore a bull . . .*

Then he looked down and saw the dagger in his stomach, and the damage that the gnosis-fire on its blade had wrought. Numbness spread, and his legs started to feel like they belonged to someone else. He looked about dazedly, saw Jelaska, only some twenty yards away in the press, and tried to tell her that—

The Keshi around the skiff reacted before she could as Baltus fell on his face. They swarmed in, blades rising, and her lover was buried beneath a dozen or more. She blasted at them with mage-fire and terror and the closest to her died of fear while others burned and broke. But the Keshi counter-attack was coming in from all sides.

She screamed Baltus' name as her commanders bellowed orders, demanding another surge from her exhausted men, and they swept forward, launching themselves at the skiff and those around it, and she was borne along by the throng. The Keshi fought tooth and nail, but the Argundian war-spears chewed them up, stabbing from out of reach then trampling the fallen as they continued their advance until the enemy broke and fled, leaving her men in control of the field.

Jelaska didn't need to shove through her men, for they parted silently, respectfully, before her. Their eyes told her all she needed to know.

Baltus' torso lay amidst a pile of severed limbs. His head was gone, a trophy for some bloody-handed Keshi, and his intestines had been blasted to charred meat. He was lying on top of a dead Hadishah in the bottom of the hull.

Life is a dark joke, love is a lie and curses are real. She spat a bitter curse on all Keshi, *knowing* such magic to be real now.

I am cursed, and Baltus paid the price.

Sultan Salim sat on his throne in his pavilion, the front wall opened so that he could watch the sun fall amidst the smoke and ruin of the day.

Pashil was dead, slain while killing the enemy skiff-pilot, and eight other Hadishah had also fallen. Thousands of their best footmen had been slaughtered too, the losses horrific, and for no reward. The Rondians still held.

Another day like today and the men will begin to doubt . . . if they do not already.

He glowered at the Godspeakers, who earned their reputation for wisdom by staying well away. There was no one he wished to speak to; no one whose words could bring comfort, except perhaps his impersonators, whose role it was to share his burdens and his pain.

Great Ahm, is this truly what you wish of us? When we die for you, do you truly rejoice at our devotion? When we offer you our suffering, do you even want it? What possible good can you derive from so much loss?

There were no answers to such prayers.

Finally, Dashimel, Emir of Baraka, made his way up and prostrated himself – with some difficulty; he had become paunchy of late – before the throne. Dashimel was a gentle man, a poet, but he was also a soldier of long experience.

'Dash, my friend, tell me what we should do,' Salim said.

Dashimel glanced over his shoulder at the Godspeakers and at the Hadishah Qanaroz, Pashil's second; they'd been posturing for the last hour, making loud speeches to each other about avenging all this tomorrow. 'The battle remains to be won, Lord,' he started. 'The enemy must surely be weakened—'

'In all honesty? Please! Don't give me the same words as them, Dash. It's a strip of land where nothing grows and no one lives! Remind me why we should die over it.

Dashimel bowed his head, then spoke quietly. 'Great Sultan, it is true that we could break this camp open, but it will come only at even greater cost. Our losses will mount, because the Rondians are masters of close-packed combat. They have the armour, the weaponry – and the discipline. Their men are not conscripts but highly trained soldiers. And their magi know how to fight in such formations.' He scowled, but he went on. 'Our strength is in archery and numbers. Moreover, we have open supply lines and they do not. Let time do what assault cannot: pen them here and starve them out. Let disease take hold in their camp. And when they break cover, rain all the arrows in Kesh upon them. But save your men, Majesty, for there are other, far more vital battles to fight elsewhere.'

At last, Salim thought, *some advice that rings true!*

'Well spoken, my friend. They cannot attack for fear of our archers so we will starve them out, until their magi slip away across the river and they capitulate. We're needed elsewhere.' He made some calculations. 'I will keep thirty thousand here to hold them – I will leave an impersonator here, and General Darhus. Then we will march the bulk of our army north and cross the river.'

'As you command, Great Sultan.' Dashimel touched his fist to his heart.

Salim looked again at the Rondian camp, shrouded in cooking-fire smoke, legion banners flying defiantly overhead. *Seth Korion and I could solve this over a glass of wine . . . but that is not the way of the world. Instead, men must die.*

13

Persuasion

Lanti a'Khomi

The greatest beauty of all time was Lanti a'Khomi, a daughter of the Mirobez royal family. It is said that her smile could stop a man's heart. Her beauty brought her no happiness, however. When she refused to marry the man he had chosen for her, the Sultan of Mirobez had his daughter suffocated and embalmed in crystal to preserve her beauty for ever. It is said that she lies perfectly preserved in a shrine within the Royal Catacombs in Mirobez.

ORDO COSTRUO, HEBUSALIM, 794

Southern Kesh, on the continent of Antiopia
Zulqeda (Noveleve) 929
17th month of the Moontide

Alyssa Dulayne stretched luxuriantly across the divan, cascading her blonde hair over her shoulder as she savoured the wine sliding down her throat. *War is so stressful,* she thought. *It's good to get away from it.* She offered her empty cup to the young Hadishah girl serving her tonight, and she refilled it silently. Sadly, the girl was a blockhead with no conversation, so this would be just another boring evening in the middle of nowhere.

For three weeks her party of twenty-seven Hadishah mage-assassins had journeyed hundreds of miles on an eastward trajectory, spread over eight windcraft, one a large dhou carrying a dozen passengers, and the other seven bearing three warriors in each.

241

Though her own people were poor company, the two prisoners had intriguing stories.

Zaqri of Metia hadn't told his tale willingly, of course. But Alyssa could get the most unwilling man to talk without so much as touching him. She was skilled enough at Mesmerism and Illusion to leave someone so confused that they leaked their secrets without realising. Zaqri was like a pomegranate, with so many glorious seeds of truth inside him.

The Scytale of Corineus is loose in the world. The Inquisition know, and are hunting it. The Dokken know, and are just as desperate to find it, for they see it as their salvation!

The people involved intrigued her: Ramita Ankesharan, who'd been snatched from her by Justina in the first months of the Moontide. She remembered the girl, a stubborn but naïve bint – no threat then, though she'd have the gnosis now. And this Zaqri, the handsome Souldrinker with a foolish heart who was in love with Cymbellea, Justina's daughter – there was a ballad to wring tears from the stoniest eyes! And Alaron Mercer . . . who was he – and more importantly, *where*?

Without firm news to guide her, Alyssa's search had been slow. They'd been taking their time and stopping often to question locals and scry for their quarry. She'd heard little that was pertinent to her quest, but she could be patient, and she was certain that the Scytale would reveal itself.

Everything bends to my will eventually.

They'd commandeered a rural mansion in southern Kesh for this evening, comfortable enough by local standards. She planned to spend the time drowning a very specific regret in whatever wine was to hand.

She'd felt genuine sadness when she'd learned of the death of Antonin Meiros' daughter Justina. *We shared so much.* They'd become the closest possible friends, two secret rebels in the close confines of the Ordo Costruo and all their sanctimonious moralising. They'd delighted in breaking taboos and offending those prissy scholars – disrupting classes, sneaking out at night to steal, trying alcohol, and learning all about what boys really wanted. No one hurt them because they were magi and could do much worse than any thug who might try to take them on. And over the years they'd laughed and cried together, shared lovers and beds – in fact, they shared everything but ambition. She could picture Justina effortlessly: the cold, brittle face she showed the world, and the softer, vulnerable woman beneath.

I miss you, my dear friend.

It saddened her that they'd parted in anger – she'd been transporting Ramita Ankesharan to confinement in Halli'kut when Justina had appeared and taken the girl. *She could have killed me, but I meant too much to her. And now she's dead.* Alyssa wiped her eyes and took another swallow of wine.

Zaqri of Metia killed her. Once she was sure she'd gleaned every last morsel of information from him, she was going to punish that crime.

Thinking of Justina led naturally to the other prisoner: Cymbellea di Regia, Justina's errant daughter. She was not yet an ally, but she was softening; of that Alyssa was sure. A patient, subtle Mesmerist could turn most heads eventually; it just took time, and a starting point: something upon which to build trust. Most magi thought only in terms of battering minds into submission, but the best Mesmerists *persuaded.* They *seduced.*

Though Cym wasn't quite ripe for seduction yet.

Rashid would make putty of her, but she's not ready for more exotic pleasures . . . A pity . . .

Alyssa looked speculatively at the Hadishah girl serving her but immediately dismissed her as beneath notice; Tegeda was not just drab, with her dull skin and great heavy eyebrows, but she was too muscular to be feminine. She was one of the newest generation of Hadishah from the breeding-houses; her body had been shaped by a daily regime of strength-building exercises, her mind moulded into an aggressive, fanatical mentality. *Ugly ugly ugly. Girls should be pretty and feminine.* The breeding-houses were hideous places, though she conceded that Rashid was right: they needed them.

If I asked Tegeda what the best thing in life is, she'd say 'Slaying Enemies of the Faith' or 'Praying' or something equally dismal. Alyssa shuddered. *What kind of life is that?*

She drained her goblet again, wishing that Rashid was here to distract her mind and transport her body, but he was far away. Then someone knocked at the door and pulled her mind back to the present. Tegeda admitted Satravim, a young pilot-mage, one of those Alyssa had sent ahead hunting for news of their quarry. She sat up and flicked a finger to dismiss Tegeda as Satravim fell to his knees before her.

He was interesting, this one, though low-blooded; he was permanently angry at life for the hideous wounds that had ruined his face, a rage he channelled into his gnosis and his faith. She'd shown him a little kindness, enough to turn his contempt of her skin colour to something more worshipful.

'You may rise, Satravim,' she said, holding out a hand to him and putting on her 'elder sister' face. She poured him some water, he mumbled his gratitude and fell a little more in love with her. 'You went to Ullakesh, yes?' she said. 'So, what did you learn?'

Moments later she was storming through the palace, rousing the sleepers and sending them into a frenzy of preparation for flight as she cried, 'We're going to Teshwallabad! *Ramita is in Teshwallabad!*'

'Get up, Slugskin!'

A boot-toe slammed into his stomach and Zaqri was torn from a nightmare of fire and blank faces into harrowing reality – or so it seemed; since the blonde woman had begun questioning him, there was little he could trust. The most ghastly tortures could be revealed as tricks, blending with dreams of rescue, or making love to Cym – and all lies. Whole lucid conversations that felt so real he became immersed in them . . . only to discover not a word had been said. No one could be trusted; nothing could be relied upon.

The cloaked figure standing over him kicked again, harder. 'Get up!'

It felt real – but then, everything did, every delusional moment . . . In his delirium he had told Alyssa Dulayne everything – of that he was almost certain. She'd unpicked him so deftly and easily it was humiliating. Every weakness had been turned on him, all his illusions of courage stripped away.

He expected to die now, for what further use could they have for him? But he didn't want to, not without seeing Cym again. He knew she was also aboard this craft, shut up in the hold; he could sense her, even through the Chain-rune; he would be able to find her anywhere. For her to be so close, but out of reach, was maddening beyond endurance.

Likely Alyssa was merely kindling hope in him for the pleasure of snuffing it out, but he couldn't help dreaming that the two of them might somehow break free.

Alyssa Dulayne. The golden-haired witch. He was going to rip her throat out; he just needed to live long enough to get the chance.

'Get up!' the Hadishah snapped, hoisting him with kinesis. 'We're moving.'

He caught his balance, his ankle chains clanking. His hands were free, but his feet were manacled so closely together so that he could only shuffle. The assassin shoved him to the latrine and stood over him while he peed, then escorted him outside. It was still early evening, but they were on the move again, only a few hours since they'd arrived here – wherever *here* was; he had no idea, but the architecture suggested southern Kesh or the eastern part of Khotri. He staggered up the gang-plank and was locked to the railing in his usual place while the Hadishah settled around him. The craft rose, the large triangular sails unfurling about the two masts. The dhou was smaller than the Rondian warbird he'd seen, but much larger than the two skiffs that rose alongside them; the three craft swung southeast together, the wind rose at the pilot's call and the wind-dhou surged away, bathed in moonlight. He could feel the renewed energy among the Hadishah and his heart sank as he guessed why.

They've got news of the Scytale.

Teshwallabad, Lakh, on the continent of Antiopia
Zulqeda (Noveleve) 929
17th month of the Moontide

Alyssa stared down at the blood-spattered, alien face and caught the monk's final thoughts as he faded, his body shuddering into stillness.

Zains, she thought. *Impotent, pathetic Zains . . .*

If there was one thing she despised more than scholars, it was clergy: men who couldn't deal with the real world disappearing into a fantasy one, preaching love of imaginary beings to hide their inability to love real ones, all the while telling their congregations to give freely, to *them*. Kore priests, Amteh Scriptualists, Lakh pandits, Zain monks and all the myriad fringe sects . . . what was the point of any of them? Nothing more than balm for the emotionally needy. If she had her way they'd be eradicated like the parasites they were.

So this afternoon had been a rare treat.

Lesharri stood behind her, distressed. She didn't like blood, but there were buckets of it here, staining the steps and draining into the river. They'd arrived at night, trapping seventeen Zain monks, forty-two acolytes and twenty-six beggars they were feeding in a badly timed act of charity. Only the dead man at her feet had known anything useful, but the rest had to die for the crime of seeing her face and hearing her questions. She didn't want the word 'Scytale' being bandied about, not even here in Lakh.

The Hadishah agents at court had met her on her arrival in Teshwallabad, but they knew little of what had happened in Septinon, *three* whole months ago. They were unaware Ramita Ankesharan had been here – with a Rondian mage! All they knew was that there had been an attempt on the life of Tariq-Srinarayan Kishan-ji, his Sacred Majesty the Mughal of Lakh, and that Vizier Hanook and his son were dead.

Three months ago – what incompetent *fools!*

Ramita was long gone, though she'd stayed at this monastery for several nights after the mysterious tunnel collapse and the death of the vizier. They'd departed for a monastery in Lokistan and now she knew its name. *I'm closing in on you, Ramita.*

She could guess at the purpose Ramita had in coming here: she was Lakh, and a mage in her own right; the mughal would surely crave a mage-bride, to bring the gnosis into the Lakh royal family. *Intolerable.*

There's much more to learn here, but I don't have time to get to the mughal, spoiled little brat that he is. I need to find Ramita, before she moves again. She sighed at the thought of another long and arduous trip, to Lokistan this time.

Am I fated to traverse the whole of Ahmedhassa looking for this damned artefact?

She looked about her, spotted Satravim hovering in the hope of being of value and rewarded him with a smile. 'Dear Satravim, my sister Lesharri is feeling unwell. Please, take her back to the dhou and see to her comfort.'

The young Hadishah almost swooned in delight as he led Lesharri off.

Next she sought Megradh, the Hadishah captain. He was quite the ugliest, most brutal-looking man she'd met, with a blockish skull and the heavy jowls of a savage, barely covered by a patchy and unkempt beard. He quite clearly loathed her, but still couldn't keep his eyes off her body.

'Take the maps, burn the bodies and prepare to leave,' she ordered. 'We have far to go.' She indicated a pair of his warriors, unconscious on the ground. 'What happened to them?'

Megradh scowled. 'These monks and their staves ... We've not fought such a weapon before.'

'It's a stick,' she sneered. *I sometimes think Rashid places too much confidence in these people.* 'I've half a mind to leave them behind, but perhaps they'll have learned from the experience.'

'What of the prisoner Zaqri?' Megradh asked. 'He weighs down the ship and he stinks. Fucking beast-man. What use is he any more?'

The captain has a point ... but there was much about the Dokken that intrigued her. There was something in his memories relating to the old fairytale about Nasette – if there was any truth to that legend, it might be something worth knowing. And while he was alive, she could use his safety to control Cymbellea. But he had slain Justina, and for that he deserved to die.

Let's see how the mood takes me . . .

'We keep him for now.' She clapped her hands briskly. 'Enough – we go!'

Cymbellea groaned, and blinked her way back to consciousness. *They put poppy in my food again . . .*

'I know you're awake,' Alyssa Dulayne drawled. 'How are you, darling girl?'

Cym tried to sit up, groaning at the deep ache inside her skull, until Alyssa put her fingers to her temple and the pain eased enough for her to open her eyes. They were in a broken-down chamber, looking at the desert wilderness outside through the hole left by a missing wall. A large triangular-sailed windship rested on its landing struts on the flat space outside.

She was lying on a rough pallet, dressed only in a thin cotton nightgown. There was no sign of her few personal effects. The only other person present was a dumpling of a woman with the placid composure of a nun. She resembled a softer Alyssa, so it was no surprise when she said, 'You remember my half-sister, Lesharri?'

'You're among friends, dearie,' Lesharri burbled brightly. She was dowdily dressed, and her face was oddly vacant. But it was Alyssa who filled Cym's sight. The blonde Rondian was studying her carefully.

A friend wouldn't imprison me, or drug me . . .

'Where's Zaqri?' she managed to ask at last, her throat rusty with lack of use.

'Not far away,' Alyssa said. 'We've travelled a long way, my dear, and you've been a handful, so we've had to sedate you, entirely for your own good, of course.'

Cym tried to reach her gnosis, but she found nothing. 'What—?'

'Just a Chain-rune,' Alyssa replied airily, 'only to prevent you from doing something foolish.' Her face was all concern, but her eyes were predatory. 'My dear girl, you are so like my poor Justina, aren't you? Your mouth, your eyes . . . so beautiful.'

It's like having a lioness describe how succulent you smell. Cym fought to hide her revulsion, but Alyssa saw it and gave a heavy sigh. She turned to her sister. 'Lesharri, help Cymbellea sit up, would you.'

Cym brushed Lesharri's hand aside and pulled herself upright. *I'd like to rip your face off . . .*

The blonde woman tutted sadly. 'So much anger and resentment. It's what happens when mothers abandon their children: you see it in the streets of Hebusalim all the time, the damage of broken families. You're a lost soul, aren't you?'

'A lost soul,' Lesharri agreed.

'Worse than that, really,' Alyssa went on. 'A *damned* soul. Zaqri's told me *everything* about you and him.' She turned to Lesharri. 'Leave us, sister, for I fear this may become unpleasant. Send Megradh in.'

The dumpy little woman looked pained, but she scampered away, leaving Cym alone and afraid. Alyssa leaned towards her and her voice dropped to a hiss. 'You've been rukking that Souldrinker animal, you dirty little slut. *And he killed your poor mother!* Justina was my dearest friend . . . and you've *made love* to her murderer. Sweet Kore, child! Have you no morals?'

'You don't understand. It wasn't like that!' Her drug-addled mind swirled.

'Of course I don't understand! I find your behaviour utterly incomprehensible!'

'Who are you to judge me? You're rukking that emir who murdered my grandfather!'

'Ignorant girl! Rashid Mubarak represents the ideals of the Ordo Costruo more truly than Antonin Meiros did in the end! Meiros chose to stand aside from a war he helped create, not just once, but thrice! It split the Order, and I have to tell you that Rashid was right to take a stand. He had the courage to face that old despot when no others would, and I'm proud to be his concubine and share in his glory!'

Silence fell between them. Alyssa sat back, waiting, until they were joined by a burly, hairy Keshi man with a leering face. He stank of sweat.

They both stared at her until Cym had to speak or scream.

'Zaqri isn't evil – he *hates* what he is!' she burst out. 'The Scytale can cure them – his whole people!'

'Nonsense, child,' Alyssa said dismissively. 'The first Dokken became what they are *because* they were evil already. So says the *Book of Kore*. Their descendants inherited that nature.' Her face took on the patient irritation of a disappointed mother. 'You've been raised by gypsies, dear. You don't know how to judge good and evil.'

You rukking bitch . . .

'Tell me about the Scytale, Cymbellea dear. And Alaron Mercer. Who is he? How did he gain this artefact, and where is he going with it?'

'Go to Hel!'

'I'm sure I shall,' Alyssa replied lightly. 'But not for a long, long time. And you've got to deal with the here and now, so let me make it simple for you: you'll tell me everything I want to know, or I will have your Dokken lover executed. "Thou shall not allow the Soul-drinker to live". So says the *Book of Kore*. But cooperate, and I'll grant you both mercy.'

We should have stayed in the wild! Cym thought bitterly. *I told him, over and again . . .*

But she was Rimoni: the magi had destroyed her ancestors' empire, taken their lands and driven them to the margins of society. She'd been sheltered by her father and his caravan, but always aware that safety was an illusion; you made the best of what fortune gave and you *survived*. That had always been her people's way. You found reasons to go on. You salvaged scraps from the ruins. You saved what you could and went on.

Alaron's not helpless, but Zaqri is, right now . . .

'All right,' she said, hanging her head. 'I'll tell you what I can. But you have to promise, on your soul, that you will let Zaqri and me leave afterwards.'

'My dear child . . . Your mother must be weeping in Paradise.'

Alyssa paused cruelly. 'No, wait: your mother's soul never made it to Paradise, because your lover *consumed* it.'

Cym looked up at her. 'I hate you.'

Megradh snorted, but Alyssa just sighed. 'Child, tell me everything: how did you gain the Scytale?'

Everything came out, as if Cym were vomiting and couldn't make it stop, all about Alaron and Ramon and the secret gnosis lessons, about finding General Langstrit, and Watch Captain Muhren helping them to hunt for the Scytale. She hung her head when she got to the bit where she'd stolen the artefact from her two best friends, taking it from the dead hands of Alaron's mother. She left out nothing, not her trek across the continent, seeking her mother and her grandfather, the lamiae, the Isle of Glass, and especially the joy and pain of finding and losing Justina. Meeting Zaqri, and Huriya. Fighting with Zaqri in the Noose for control of the Dokken pack, and then the dreadful attack by the Inquisitors . . . and she spoke of lust, or love, or maybe something of both . . . and finally, she whispered about her aborted child as tears fell silently down her cheeks. She thought she had no more tears left in her, but that clearly wasn't so.

I killed my own child.

After that came the questions: how could she bear Zaqri's child but not become a Dokken, like Nasette? She didn't know. Where was Alaron now? Was Ramita Ankesharan still with him? She didn't know those either. There were other questions as Alyssa sought to fill in the details, each one draining her until finally there was nothing left to tell, and her voice was a gravelly whisper.

'I think we have everything.' Alyssa turned to Megradh. 'Bring in the Dokken. He can die in front of her.'

The Hadishah captain grinned savagely, leered at Cym and swaggered away.

Cym came upright, screaming, '*NO! YOU CAN'T— YOU PROMISED!*' She tried to launch herself at Alyssa—

—and the world flipped as she was slammed into the wooden floor and was held there, winded and gasping for air. Alyssa rose, icily regal, her gnosis holding Cym immobile.

'Cymbellea, do you honestly believe you can steal from your friends, fuck your mother's killer, murder his child and then walk away guilt-free?'

That everything she said was so horribly true when held up to the cold light of logic was as crushing as the power that held her pinned to the floor.

But there were reasons . . .

'I'm going to teach you a valuable lesson, child. It is this: true strength lies in unity. It's in your *friends*. Look at me: I have Rashid Mubarak in my bed and the sultan's court feeding from my hand. They're *my* friends. But where are *your* protectors? I'll tell you: you don't have any. You're alone.' Her eyes bored into Cym's mercilessly. 'This won't feel like it, but I'm doing you a favour: I'm going to sever your ties with these animals you've been dirtying yourself with and give you the chance of a fresh start in my service. Lesharri is delicate, and sometimes her duties overwhelm her. If you swear to serve me, I'll let you live: because your mother was my dearest friend.'

Cym tried to plead mercy for Zaqri, but Alyssa shut her mouth with a gesture. 'No, girl. I'm offering this in memory of my dear Justina. I see something of her in you, the way she was when she and I were young. We were rebels against the Ordo Costruo and their sanctimony: I see that spirit in you. You could – you should – be one of us.'

'Kill Zaqri and you'll never know,' she snarled, playing the only card she still held.

'That's a chance I'll take,' Alyssa replied. 'Ah, and here he is!'

Cym's heart leaped to her mouth as the Hadishah captain dragged Zaqri into the chamber, then levitated him and held him effortlessly against the wall. Cym stared at him, her heart in her eyes, as Megradh drew his gleaming scimitar with his right hand.

Zaqri gazed fiercely at her, his dread for her clear on his face. She kept remembering how she'd pleaded with him to walk away from this bitter quest . . .

Alyssa gave her just enough freedom to grovel before her and beg, 'I'll do *anything* – just let him live!'

'Dear girl, you're just proving my point,' the blonde woman told

her, her eyes glinting. 'While your Dokken is alive, your first loyalty will always be to him, and if that's the case, what's the point
in letting you live at all?'

'No! I'll serve only you – make me like your sister if that's what
you want—'

Alyssa's lips curled upwards. 'And what use would you be then?'

'But—'

'Cym.' Zaqri's voice cut across her rising hysteria. 'Cym, enough.
You won't change her mind.'

Alyssa pouted a little, then she smiled down at Cym. 'He's right,
of course. I never thought him stupid.' She waved airily at Megradh.

Cym screamed as the Hadishah's blade lifted. Zaqri's eyes locked
onto hers, trying to drink her into his soul with his eyes. She tried
to launch herself at Alyssa, and was brutally slapped down, then
Megradh's blue-black scimitar blade, honed to razor-sharpness, slashed
through precious flesh and sinew and bone. She howled at the slow-mo-
tion parting of head and body, at the great gout of blood as the man
she loved collapsed like an axe-hewn tree.

She wanted her heart to stop then. But the damned thing just
went on beating.

14

A New Ascendancy

The Bond Among Souldrinkers

*It has been noted among those who hunt the Souldrinkers that they appear
to share a bond akin to a mysticism-link, but permanent, and open to any
others of their kind within reach. It is unclear whether this came with their
curse or has been developed by them, but it helps to explain how elusive they
remain.*

GRANDMASTER CENTURIUS, PALLAS, 852

Gatioch, on the continent of Antiopia
Zulhijja (Decore) 929
18th month of the Moontide

Malevorn Andevarion looked up from the mortar and pestle with
which he was grinding a wad of pungent leaves, more ingredients
for the next batch of the ambrosia. He and Hessaz were working
alone, day and night, using the gnosis to keep their energy levels
up. He'd commandeered a ruined palace next to the Valley of Tombs,
and though Xymoch's old pack was growing restless, none of them
knew what their new packleader was doing, or that Huriya was now
chained up in a dungeon.

'A few more days, and we'll have enough,' he told the Lokistani,
who looked at him out of the corner of her eye, her face unreadable as ever. She seemed to have only two facial expressions: sullen
resentment and burning hate.

'Another clan arrived today,' she told him. 'Water-magi from

Mirobez. They want to see you and Huriya and hear what you plan first-hand.'

'You talk to them, Hessaz,' he told her. 'I can't spare the time. Tell them that in three days' time, I'm going to change their lives for ever.'

No one else yet knew about the Scytale; all Xymoch's pack knew was that if they were patient, Malevorn would reveal the cure for their condition.

He'd told Hessaz that Huriya had tried to run away with the Scytale, not sure she'd believe him. But she'd offered to cut Huriya's throat herself and take her place as his mate, which was a little surprising, considering how much she hated the Inquisition, the Kore, and all Rondians. It told him how utterly committed Hessaz was to seeing her people healed.

But much as he would like to see the end of Huriya, until he could find a way to break his heart-bond spell, the Keshi girl had to remain among the living, and therefore, locked away safely.

'The crueller punishment is to let her rot,' he'd said.

Hessaz hadn't looked pleased, but she'd let the matter drop.

He smiled to himself. *Poor Huriya . . . destined for oblivion . . .*

Huriya Makani sat in the darkness, powerless and terrified. Food and water was brought and the slop-bucket changed once a day. Malevorn had done it himself at first, then Hessaz took over – but she obviously believed her a traitor, and refused to speak to her. She herself couldn't speak at all: Malevorn had bound her tongue with a spell. Her gnosis was Chained, and hope was extinguished.

All Huriya's life, Sabele had promised that she would sit on thrones; that wealth, power and pleasure beyond her wildest dreams would be hers. At least once a year the old fortune-teller had visited Aruna Nagar Market and whispered in her ear. Some nights the old crone would send her visions, showing her the palaces of the world. She'd had to promise to tell no one, not her foolish brother Kazim, or even her dearest blood-sister Ramita, which had been a torment. But the sense of destiny sustained her through childhood disappointments because she'd always known that better things awaited her.

Now look at me. All he needs is to keep me alive and imprisoned until he finds a way to unbind the heart-link. After that, I'm dead ... or worse ...

The coming centuries unfolded for her, clear as a Divination vision: Chained alone in the darkness as the years passed, sustained by the gnosis, never ageing, never dying, but growing weaker, going blind and deaf as her senses withered without stimulus.

Ahm! Someone! Please free me!

She groped about with her fingers until finally she found a small chip of stone. She considered trying to choke herself with it, but doubted she could. So instead, she scratched with the fragment on the wall behind her head, until it crumbled to dust.

'There there, *accha bacca*,' Hessaz cooed. 'Don't be afraid. I'll be with you.' She bared her teeth at the little man whose hand she held, smiling, an expression that sat oddly on her hard face.

He was golden-skinned, black-haired and perfect, tottering along beside her and babbling incomprehensibly. The one being she'd truly loved had been her daughter, Pernara, but she'd been killed by the Inquisition almost a year ago; now Hessaz lavished all that love on ten-month-old Nasatya Meiros.

Whenever Malevorn could spare her from the holy task they shared, brewing the sacred ambrosia, she spent it with the little boy. He lived in a chamber next to Huriya's, but his was more comfortable, and she was allowed to take him out for walks twice a day. They'd just spent an hour together, helping him learn to walk among the stone tombs, spotting geckos and watching the distant tents of the Souldrinkers camped at the edge of the valley. It was time to take him back, then to feed the captive Huriya.

They went to the kitchens and gathered food; warm bread and wrapped sweets for him, and a pot of curried daal for Huriya. Then they went down into the makeshift dungeon, a converted crypt. Nasatya was tearful at having to go back below ground, but he quietened for her. *He's a good child ... just like my Pernara was.*

Guarding the passage to the crypt was the only other person allowed in this part of the Valley of Tombs: Toljin.

Something about Toljin had changed so that she scarcely knew him. He'd always been a crass buffoon, the sort of man she despised, but of late, he'd been cold, watchful, and strangely . . . *simple* – it was almost as if someone had taken his personality away and replaced it with a studied fixation on whatever task he'd been set. As she passed him, he looked her over, but there were none of the leering comments and crude offers she'd have expected, and nor was there even any simple small talk to relieve the boredom.

What's happened to him? she wondered for the hundredth time.

He was all but mute, as if his words had been stolen, but he would grow animated and upset if she didn't surrender her weapons, so she always put her bow and dagger against the wall. 'Having a good day?' she asked Toljin, but as usual he didn't even acknowledge that she'd spoken. Looking at him with her inner eye revealed a strength to his aura that had never been there before, but there was something else too, a shadow presence that was like an oil-smear slithering across his aura. He followed her to the cells, his mere presence chilling, and it was a relief to leave him outside the door to Nasatya's cell.

She produced a little carved toy she'd got from one of the Dokken children in the camp and used it to settle Nasatya down, then she sang lullabies until he slept.

Only once she was sure he was asleep did she go back outside. Toljin unlocked Huriya's cell and lit the room with the lamp.

'Don't use the gnosis in here,' Malevorn had told her. 'Toljin's under orders to stop anyone who does.'

Maybe he thinks I'll take revenge on Huriya for betraying the cause. Although she'd sworn not to, maybe he needed to be sure. But she'd begun to wonder if there were other reasons.

Huriya was pressed against the wall she was chained to, looking up at her with frightened eyes. She gurgled, but Malevorn had taken away her speech. The Seeress looked dreadful, her skin and rags filthy, her elbows and knees scabbed and one side of her face bruised. Her hair was matted and she stank of fear.

This isn't right, Hessaz thought. *She was our Seeress, once.*

But she tried to steal the Scytale and go over to the Rondians . . . or so

Malevorn said. Can I can trust that? Sabele's spirit is inside the girl, and she would never have acted as Malevorn says . . .

She dropped to one knee, dipped the ladle into the daal then thrust it at Huriya. The Seeress looked up at her, accepted one mouthful, then very obviously looked at Toljin before letting her head drop forward, twisting to reveal the portion of the wall behind her head, while ensuring Toljin was not paying any attention. There were scratch-marks on the stone, a dozen characters that petered out into a dusty smear. They were Rondian symbols, but Hessaz could read them easily; her pack spoke as much Rondian as Dhassan.

SKTL
FAIL
AFRE
KILM

She stared, then gagged to prevent herself gasping out loud. Huriya's eyes were pleading with her, but what they were saying, she couldn't tell. Hessaz stared at her while trying to interpret the marks.

Sk'thali fail . . . ?

She went on feeding the girl, mechanically shovelling in food, waiting for her to chew and swallow, while her mind swirled. Did this mean that the Sk'thali *would* fail? Or that it had *already* failed? And failed to do *what? And what is 'AFRE—'?* Her eyes flickered sideways and met Toljin's, cold and fixed.

Afreet . . .

Hessaz began to tremble, and when she looked at Huriya, the bleak despair took her breath away. KILM. She let forward, whispered, '*Sk'thali fail?*' Huriya nodded, tears dripping from both eyes.

'*Afreet?*'

Another nod.

She paused, swallowed. '*Kill me?*'

Huriya sobbed voicelessly, and her head jerked down.

Behind her Hessaz heard his grunt and step closer, sniffing at her as if she was food. Toljin's eyes bored into her, then he stepped away.

'No speaking, Hezzaz,' he said in a voice that was flat and dispassionate and slurred, and utterly unlike his normal intonation. It was as if something else was using him as a puppet, and it chilled her to the bone. Especially as the way he pronounced her name – *Hezzaz* – was exactly the way Malevorn *mis*-pronounced it.

Afreet.

It took all Hessaz's years of personal discipline as huntress and warrior not to bolt. She finished her task and made herself walk calmly from the crypt, feeling Toljin's eyes on her back the whole time. When she got out into the night air she bent over and vomited, then she closed her eyes and prayed for guidance.

From the stone platform, Malevorn Andevarion could see the whole of the Dokken packs and clans who'd gathered, waiting for him to perform his miracle. It reminded him of the *Book of Kore*, and the crowds who'd gathered to hear Corineus preach.

He took a deep breath, then projected his voice across the crowd. 'Let the Second Ascendancy begin!'

Amidst a massive cheer, he dipped a ladle and poured a measure of ambrosia into the open mouth of the first Souldrinker lined up in formation. At his side, Hessaz did the same, blessing the recipient with some Amteh sign. He would have felt a fraud uttering such words, and doubted that a Kore sign would have been welcomed, so he just muttered, 'Good luck.'

Not that luck will avail you.

The massive batch of ambrosia was an approximation, probably much like Baramitius had brewed first time round; he had neither the time nor the inclination to brew exact doses tailored to each recipient. There were six hundred Souldrinkers in the Valley of Tombs, so if history ran true, they'd lose a third, stone-dead. But the rest would be Ascendant Souldrinkers: two hundred, give or take a few. And then . . .

. . . Guard your throne, Constant Sacrecour!

He could feel the presence in the aether of the daemon who controlled Toljin. He'd spoken to it, told it what he wanted, and they'd reached a bargain. *Bahil-Abliz*, its name was; it wanted to extend itself into this world, and his Ascendancy Ritual would allow that to happen. It had pledged to serve him, and his wizardry-gnosis would ensure it did.

He fancied he could feel the physical effects of its proximity: colder nights and the withering of the sparse vegetation, and bad dreams. The air was oppressive, doom-laden, but still the Dokken came, from small, half-wild packs of animagi barely a dozen strong, to clans of almost a hundred, born and bred in the towns, all drawn to the Valley of Tombs by the rumour of a cure. Xymoch's pack had spread the word discreetly, jealous of rivals gaining 'their' prize, and they were impatient, wanting to know why they weren't permitted to go first – but Malevorn knew he had only one shot at this.

They were all were about to become his slaves, the young, the few old, men and women, even unblooded children. Or they would die.

Ablizians. That's what I will call them: for the daemon I'm planting in their souls.

He looked sideways at Hessaz, wondering what was going through her mind. The gaunt Lokistani had been subdued in the last couple of days, even more taciturn than usual, and with none of the zeal she'd shown earlier in the process. When challenged she'd claimed that she was just awed by what they were about to do, but something in her manner didn't convince him. *She suspects something*, his instincts whispered. But she'd performed her duties without fuss, no sign of fight or flight. And there had been no opportunity for her to sabotage this moment.

After tonight, she'll be just like the rest . . .

It took almost half an hour until the last of the Dokken had swallowed their measure. The final one was a young mother from Mirobez, where the people were tall and lean, their skin jet-black and their hair close-cropped. She had a three-year-old child cradled in her arms. As she took the poison and fed it to her son, she said something grateful to Malevorn, something worshipful. He looked sideways at Hessaz for a translation.

'She gives you thanks and blessing,' the Lokistani woman told him. 'She says that you are a messiah, a new prophet.' She sounded faintly disgusted.

'That's what I am,' he replied, amused. 'I'm another Corineus.'
Only I won't end up dead.

The Mirobezi woman rejoined the rest of her family and Malevorn surveyed his new brood, now all gathered in the middle of the central plaza inside a giant circle carved into the stone. One by one they lay down in preparation, as he'd told them, and the poison was already taking effect in those who'd been first in line. That left about forty minutes to prepare for the first of them to start dying: plenty of time.

Hessaz turned to him. 'What now?'

'Now? Your own reward, my dear Hessaz,' he replied mockingly. The dying sun glinted off the jewels in the gem-studded collar he had started wearing around his throat as he held out a spoonful of the ambrosia to her. She met his eye and a tremor ran through her, but she opened her mouth and took her measure calmly. 'Go and join your people, Hessaz.' She bowed and walked away towards the massed Souldrinkers in the plaza, her step unsteady, as if the potion had already begun to take effect.

And as easily as that, the Hessaz problem is solved.

He settled down to watch the show.

Hessaz made her way to the plaza, trying to hide her terror, stepping over the etched lines and symbols that Malevorn Andevarion had carved with Fire- and Earth-gnosis into the flagstones at the edge of the open space. They meant little to her, but she could guess what they were: Wizardry sigils.

She'd never had an Arcanum education, and whole swathes of the gnosis were a complete mystery to her, but she was a hunter, filled with practical intelligence and cunning. Over the past two days, working alongside Malevorn, doing his bidding without any sign of her thoughts, she'd begun to piece together her theory of what was *really* going on here.

He's fallen out with Huriya. That's a fact.
Toljin is not himself. That too is a fact.
This plaza has been prepared for a large-scale spell.
SK'THALI FAIL. AFREET.

She couldn't work it all out: she didn't have the knowledge and couldn't make the connections, and she knew she never would. Elaborate schemes weren't her way; she had always seen the world in black and white, straight lines. But as the day that should be the greatest in the history of her kind progressed, she began to feel trapped, dread rising within her, and all the instincts she trusted were urging her to run.

But she couldn't; she was constantly under Malevorn's eye, and the fervour of the Souldrinkers gathered below was such that no one could have deflected them: this was their day of days. So she was left muttering benefices and doling out poison, and no closer to working it all out.

Sabele will know what to do.

She had to get to Huriya somehow, actually talk to her – but as she swirled the ambrosia in her mouth, she was terrified that she had missed the chance. She quickly found the place behind the rocks she'd already scouted, and making sure no one was looking at her, she spat it all out and surreptitiously rinsed her mouth from her waterskin.

She was careful to feign the same symptoms as the rest, conscious that Malevorn was only a hundred yards away, sitting on an old stone throne and observing them all. Her weapons were stowed in her tiny room in the ruined palace, her pack prepared.

When night falls and he is tending to the first drinkers . . . that's when I'll run . . .

In the meantime all she could do was lie on her side, and watch her happy, exhilarated, guileless brethren die, certain that they were about to be born again.

SK'THALI FAIL.

AFREET.

KILL ME.

To the east, the waning moon was a sliver carved into the pale blue sky. Opposite, the sun fell towards the horizon in a scarlet blaze. There was a cold hum in the air, and Malevorn could feel the multi-faceted mind of the daemon waiting in the aether for each of these little gateways to reality to fall open.

Some had panicked as the throes of death began and were trying to crawl out of the plaza, but gradually each succumbed. He kept a special eye on Hessaz, but she'd gone still from the moment she'd lain down, as many others had, surrendering themselves to the ambrosia. The woman from Mirobez went last, her son already corpselike in her arms – the ambrosia had been brewed for bigger bodies than his. She was screaming at him, hers the only voice left as the plaza fell silent, tearing at her hair, shrieking prayers that slurred into mumbles until she rolled over and went still.

And now it begins . . .

He rose, walked to the edge of the platform and raised his hands. Calling wizardry-gnosis to his hands, he triggered the protective circle – a rectangle, in fact, for the shape didn't really matter so long as it was regular. He shouted aloud in the Runic speech – not magic-words, but a verbalising of his intent to aid focus, and a warning to the daemon waiting to enter these dying Souldrinkers that the moment was nigh, though he doubted it needed telling. Indigo rays of light shot from his fingers and suddenly the whole plaza lit up, then it faded again, leaving the wards in place.

Those inside could still leave, though they'd feel some resistance in crossing the boundaries he'd etched: but anyone possessed by Bahil-Abliz would suffer excruciating pain and be unable to cross. That was the purpose of the circle: to keep the summoned daemon from its summoner, giving the Wizard time to take control.

How many will survive? He licked his lips in anticipation, calculating how many he might need to conquer Pallas. After he'd been broken, Adamus had admitted that there were no more than a dozen Keepers still alive, and they were mostly decrepit. *I think a hundred new Ascendants will be enough, but the more the merrier . . .*

A few minutes after the Mirobez woman collapsed, the first of the bodies began to twitch and stir back to life, their jerky movements spreading like a virus. From his vantage atop one of the tombs they looked like maggots exposed when rotting timber is pulled aside,

DAVID HAIR

ugly, clumsy wrigglers. He fingered the jewelled collar he'd found in the unplundered tomb, getting used to the unfamiliar weight, for after today he'd seldom be without it.

Then the first of his brood sat up, kindling gnostic-fire, then ramming head-first into the protective circle, making the invisible web of light suddenly flash a very visible scarlet. It laid both hands on the barrier and began to rip.

This is it!

There were risks to a mass conversion, but it was the only way: had anyone seen what happened to those that went before, they would have resisted. This was the trade-off: putting himself in mortal danger.

He conjured the name of the daemon – *BAHIL-ABLIZ!* – then hurled it like a javelin into the skull of the Dokken trying to destroy the circle. The daemon clutched its skull, trying to reject the binding as it came steaming towards him, out of control and changing shape, growing horns and teeth, humanity falling away as the aether-beast took over its host. Hate blazed from it, and fear rippled like a shockwave as the rest of the dying Dokken stirred. But he fed the hook he'd planted, shouted the command – *SUBMIT!* – and left the mental link open. It locked wills with him instantly, tried to blind and stun him, to overwhelm him.

All he had to do was speak three words, and make the daemon believe them.

You. Are. Mine.

It wasn't so hard, not with the daemon's name to anchor his will and the gnostic power at his disposal. The demon caved in, fell to its knees and put its forehead to the ground in worship. He swallowed and stared down at it while panting from the exertion of his gnosis.

One down. Six hundred or so to go, with luck . . .

It wasn't so many, of course. Almost half died while he lost himself in the job of subduing the rest, presumably Hessaz among them, for he never saw her as he fought to subdue those who survived. Sometimes singly, at other times four or five at a time, he pacified them before locking in his control of each individual using a gem in the jewelled collar around his neck. Each gem turned scarlet as

264

it took on the binding of an individual Ablizian, and with each one he added, the necklace's own aura of power grew and began to fuse with the rest, until he was wearing a collar of red diamonds, glittering with energy.

After an hour, with his gnosis running low, he cut the throat of a newly-made slave – a young man with fanatical eyes – and inhaled his soul to replenish himself. He took care not to let the daemon inside him. A brief vision filled his consciousness – the young man's life – then power blazed through him: of Ascendant's might.

More than renewed, and carried along on a wave of exultation, he laboured on, until far into the night, the last of the newly possessed Dokken fell to its knees before him. Two hundred and ninety-three of them, all possessed by Bahil-Abliz and his multi-faceted mind, which was enslaved to him. Two hundred and ninety-three . . .

Hel, let's call it Three Hundred . . . of the 'Blessed'.

I'm going to crush the sultan and the Sacrecours and rule the whole of the known world. My reign will last for ever.

He assembled his possessed Dokken – his *Ablizians* – and accepted their worship.

Malevorn never saw Hessaz slip away, so caught up was he in his great task.

I'm just another body, one of those who didn't get up again . . . She slithered around the edge of the plaza and darted down an alley as behind her the Souldrinker Brethren rose and began to chant Malevorn's name. She could scarcely move for trembling, could barely see through her tears.

Dear Ahm, what has he done to us?

But there was no time for that. She had to get out.

She raced for her room, threw on her pack and armed herself with feverish speed, straining her ears all the while for footfalls or nearby expenditure of the gnosis. But the reverberations of power from the plaza was echoing over her awareness, deafening her to all other powers.

Then she dashed towards the crypt and Huriya's cell. She didn't know how much time she might have, but she assumed it wouldn't be long. Malevorn had chosen his prison cleverly: there was only one way in or out, and the cells were underground, so even a powerful Earth-mage couldn't dig fast enough to reach them without Malevorn sensing it. She had to get in and out before Malevorn realised what she was doing.

I have to kill Toljin and get Nasatya out. Huriya too . . . Toljin was the first problem; she had a disturbing certainty that Malevorn was somehow linked to him.

But she was a shapechanger, and a hunter.

Around the corner from Toljin's post, out of sight, she shed her pack and weapons again, and then her clothes. Relying on the gnostic echoes from the plaza above to mask her efforts, she drew on her strongest affinities: Morphism and Animagery. Like most of her kind, she knew four or five animals well; the one she chose now wasn't one she took often, for it disturbed her. But tonight it was her best choice: so she pressed arms and legs together and let the gnosis-energy shiver down her spine, changing in a flood of sensations, an agonised ecstasy that hurled her to the stones and made her twist and bend and flow.

Twelve seconds later, a cobra the size of a full-grown python slithered its way along the passage, then using kinesis she flowed to the roof and began to coil her way forward.

She took the final bend and saw Toljin, standing to attention like a statue. His eyes were unfocused, and there was a strange emptiness to him.

She reached a point above him, opened her mouth—

—as he suddenly became aware and shields began to flare. She lunged, burst through the unformed wards and six-inch fangs clamped onto his left shoulder and flooded the wound with venom. She wrenched, pulled him upwards and hammered him against the ceiling beams, then the wall. He tried to reach his sword, but she tossed a coil around him, pinned the arm and bit again, constricting all the while.

He burst into flame, and as her scales seared, the sudden pain sent her squealing and writhing away. Her convulsions threw him from her, momentarily out of reach, and she slithered backwards, beginning to lose control of the shape-change in the pain. As they both rolled apart, a new agony gripped her as the spell reversed and suddenly her tail was splitting and shortening to legs, her burned skin screaming in protest. A few yards down the corridor Toljin was trying to rise, but his shoulder was mottled black and yellow and he was choking and struggling to breathe, asphyxiating before her eyes. They stared at each other in the full throes of agony, each unable to move, each in a race to recover first. Hessaz screamed at herself to *change-change-change*, plucked arms from her side, snatched up his scimitar then hacked down with all her strength.

His head rolled from his body and the blade snapped on the flagstones beneath his neck. She fell over him, clinging to the hilt with six inches of broken blade remaining, gibbering prayers.

Nasatya wailed from behind his cell-door, and she thought that maybe Huriya gurgled something; those sounds gave her something to cling to, forcing her to go on. Shaking like a newborn colt, she pulled the keys from Toljin's belt and scrambled to Nasatya's door.

As she flung it open the little boy squealed at the sight of her, standing there bloody and naked and terrified, and hid his face. That left her at a loss for a moment; somehow she'd thought he'd be silent and compliant, even eager to see her. 'Stay there!' she told him, praying he would obey her.

After a moment she turned to Huriya's cell door, and as she did, the eyes in Toljin's severed head opened.

'Hezzaz, Hezzaz,' it slurred, 'what are you doing, Hezzaz? I'm coming for you.'

She'd never fainted in her life, but she almost did then; everything lurched as she clung to the doorframe and fought off a wave of dizziness. She steadied herself as the head fell silent, jammed the key in the lock, twisted and threw the door open.

Huriya looked up at her, eyes bulging in hope and dread as Hessaz ran to her, wrenching at the chains; she tried to smash them, but her blade was already broken, and the gnostic bindings threaded through them were well beyond her ability.

Lord Ahm, please help us!

Huriya looked at her with desparing, pleading eyes.

Hessaz understood immediately: there was no way to get Huriya out, not in time. She had to get Nasatya out before they were trapped here. But it still brought a lump to her throat as she stared down at the tiny Keshi girl.

I despised you. I resented that you took Sabele, who was our guide, then toyed with our pack for your own purposes. If it wasn't that you are also Sabele now, I'd leave you to your fate.

She placed the broken blade over Huriya's heart and looked her in the eyes; she saw only calm acceptance now. 'This is for Sabele,' she said softly.

She drove the blade in, and kissed the girl on her lips.

'Get to her! Now—! Kill anyone who comes between you and her!' Malevorn strode through his Ablizians, shouting orders, the scarlet diamond necklace glowing in his hand, his senses extended to instruct his charges. But the command he wielded felt sluggish, for the lines of control were still taking shape. He'd lost Toljin a few seconds after seeing the face of the bitch who'd killed him.

I should have killed the fucking Noorie cunni.

The danger he was in was all too apparent; he hadn't yet managed to undo the heart-binding that linked his own life to Huriya's.

How the Hel did she slip past me? He gripped his sword tighter and sent the guards sprinting to the cell to protect the one thing that made him vulnerable. 'Hurry! Bring—'

He staggered as something burst in his ribcage, a feeling like being torn apart by giant invisible talons. Strength drained from his limbs; he stumbled and fell to his knees, and the Ablizians all turned their faces towards him, their eyes filling with curiosity at this newly unveiled weakness.

'Get me . . . *out* . . .' he gasped at the nearest. 'Hide me . . . protect me . . . Bahil-Abliz, I *command* you to protect me!'

The Ablizians cocked their heads as if listening to other voices while Malevorn slid down the wall.

'I am . . .'

The Lokistani woman stared at her hands . . . if they were still hers. 'I am . . .'

Huriya hung like a broken doll in her manacles, limp as a puppet with snapped strings. She was as dead as it was possible to be . . . and yet she lived on.

In me . . . She lives on in me . . .

There had been sounds in the passage outside but they'd receded and gone silent a few moments after she'd taken the other woman's soul. It had been unlike any other taking: somehow more solid, more tangible, and the burst of memories had been so vivid she'd lost all grip of reality, on identity and purpose; she had floated in a sea of voices until she woke to this.

I was a huntress . . . I was an archer . . . And for a brief time, I was a mother . . . I was Hessaz . . .

'I am . . .'

I am Sabele.

She rose and cautiously opened the door, finding the corridor empty of all but Toljin's corpse. She retrieved her gear and dressed with calm haste before going to the other cell. She went down on her haunches in the doorway, and called in her kindest voice, 'Nasatya . . . come here, my dear. Come to Mami.'

15

Moksha

Religion: Omali

There are many lives that the soul may be clothed in during samsara, the endless wheel of life. Did I say endless? Then I misspoke, for it isn't endless: but only those who have attained perfect harmony may leave the wheel for the state of moksha, that blissful freedom enjoyed by the gods, from which no mortal returns.

THE SAMADHI-SUTRA (THREAD OF ENLIGHTENMENT),
HOLY BOOK OF THE OMALI

Mandira Khojana, Lokistan, on the continent of Antiopia
Zulhijja (Decore) 929 to Moharram (Janune) 930
18th and 19th months of the Moontide

'Are you sure?' Alaron asked, looking hard at Yash.

Two weeks earlier it had been Ramita, Puravai, Corinea and Yash sitting around *his* bed in the sickbay. But this time it was Yash on the bed and Alaron beside it, looking on anxiously as his friend prepared to take the ambrosia.

With fragile calm the novice said, 'Yes, Al'Rhon, I'm sure.' He waggled his head in the Lakh way, which was enough to make Alaron smile through his fears.

He and Corinea had talked Yash through the experience, explaining exactly what they'd gone through and how they'd survived, and Puravai gave Yash assurances of his own skills and discipline. But the young man was putting his life on the line, and he was the only one who would be able to pull himself through.

'Remember,' said Corinea, 'that everything you go through is just a dream. Any dangers you face will be of your own making, and the only thing you need to do to overcome them is wake up.'

Yash threw Puravai a sly look. 'You know me, Master. I'm a very bad monk, but I'm a very good fighter. And a bad sleeper.' He raised the thimble as if toasting the old monk, then drained it in one swallow.

Alaron gripped Ramita's hand and they settled down to wait for their friend to die and live again. Her strong little fingers entwined with his and their eyes strayed from the young man as he fell into slumber, to each other.

The past two weeks had been full, working with Corinea to brew the individual vials for each of the thirty-four candidates, ensuring that each ingredient was at its optimal potency, each measure precisely measured. Alaron had been an indifferent student of potions: like the other boys, he'd preferred blasting things. But under Corinea's tutelage, he was gaining an appreciation of the niceties of the art. They had scheduled one transformation a day for the whole of Octen and into Noveleve. They would all be devastated if a mistake led to a death, though they were steeling themselves for the possibility. But losing Yash would be a crushing blow.

Working with Corinea hadn't been easy. She was irritable, sharp-tongued and waspish, and remained entirely sceptical of the Zains' ability to deal with power or the real world. She was also scathing of his burgeoning relationship with Ramita.

In her usual hectoring tone she'd said, 'East and West are incompatible, and lasting love is impossible, so you are doubly doomed.'

And as proof, she'd cited all her failed relationships as evidence, until he'd snapped, *'Perhaps it was you!'*

That hadn't helped their own relationship, but it had shut her up for an hour.

Despite this, Corinea was invaluable, and he doubted they'd have managed without her. Alaron had even mixed potions for Cym and Ramon – because you just never knew. He'd calculated their individual ambrosia recipes on a whim one night, when they still had the Scytale, and he couldn't stop himself daydreaming of being able to hand them both their vials, imagining the looks they'd have on their faces ... but in his heart he feared them dead.

As Yash's breathing slowed until it was barely perceptible, Ramita said quietly, 'Al'Rhon, please remember that he must get through this himself. It's not your fault if he doesn't come through.'

'It is if the mix is wrong,' he replied tersely.

'We've been careful,' Corinea said, 'but Ramita is right: we can't do it for him.'

'He has much determination,' Puravai noted.

'What will we do if he becomes one of *them* ... a Souldrinker?' Corinea asked. It wasn't the first time the question had been raised, but they hadn't come up with an answer.

'No one who must kill to gain the gnosis will be permitted to do so,' Puravai said. 'We're Zains. We don't kill, except at the utmost need.'

Corinea scowled but said nothing; she'd been arguing over the morality of war with the Zain master for weeks now. Alaron could see both sides: the need for every novice they could get, and the invidious nature of the Souldrinkers poisoning all they were trying to achieve.

'If any become Souldrinkers, they will accept being kept in isolation,' Puravai said firmly. 'Each has agreed this, should the worst occur. That is my decision.'

'What causes it?' Alaron wondered.

'I don't know,' Corinea said, 'and to the best of my knowledge Baramitius never worked it out. Something lacking in the potion? Something chemical in their body reacting with the ambrosia? Or maybe even something in their personality? I've heard one theory that something in the aether may have been involved – some kind of daemon who was present at the first Ascendancy – but no Soul-drinker I've encountered was possessed. The reality is we don't know.'

Unexpectedly, Puravai spoke up. 'Antonin Meiros spoke with me once about this. He said those afflicted had been of all types, some virtuous, some immoral, so he ruled out personality or "spiritual" reasons. He too had examined Souldrinkers and found no trace of possession, though he said that there was a level of psychic linkage he couldn't trace or explain. So he believes it is an unknown physiological reaction to the ambrosia.'

'Johan Corin realised what he was, during our shared vision,' Corinea mused. 'Of course, I say "shared", but at that point, I was the only one with the gnosis: he only experienced it because I was subconsciously sharing it with him. I foresaw what he would become; he tried to make that happen.' She sighed. 'It's so tangled.'

'That implies that some part of you recognised what he was,' Puravai commented.

Corinea's eyes went wide. 'It does, doesn't it?' She looked around the circle with uncharacteristic openness. 'I've not thought of that before, but it makes sense. Somehow I knew – but how?'

They had no answers to that, and gradually the silence deepened as they waited. It was hard to watch; Alaron found it more distressing than going through the change himself. He was profoundly glad Ramita did not need to take the potion.

When the crisis came, they watched and waited with bated breath, until Yash suddenly coughed and shuddered and his eyes snapped open. Ramita gave a small cry and Puravai sat forward, his white knuckles the only indication of his anxiety. Then the young man sat up, looking dazed, and for a moment struggled to speak. Finally he said weakly, 'So what happens next?'

Alaron frowned, then realised and silently spoke to Ramita and Corinea, <*Of course, Yash has never had the gnosis – but neither had the first magi . . .*> He looked at Corinea questioningly and she winked at him, then bent over the pallet and studied the young Zain.

'Yash, look at me,' she ordered, then turned, picked up her wine goblet and suddenly dashed the contents into his face. Half of it spattered over his face as he flinched and threw up an arm – but the rest of the fluid was swept sideways, a fan-shaped cascade of droplets pushed aside by an invisible force that knocked Corinea backwards off her stool and sent Master Puravai spinning into the corner.

'Master!' Yash cried out, but the old monk sat up, beaming as he rubbed his skull.

With a rueful smile he said, 'Don't worry about me, young Yash.

273

I'm quite well.' He came to his feet nimbly, his face shining, proud. 'And so, it appears, are you.'

Yash stared at his hands. 'I am! I truly am!'

Ramita shuddered at the sound of the wind howling against the iced-up shutters. A storm had blown up the valley that afternoon in the midst of the eighth acolyte's transformation, which had been successful – they all had, so far, and she was so thankful. It was going better than they'd ever dared hope – luck, perhaps, but she didn't believe that; she put it down to their thorough preparations. Now she and Master Puravai were instructing the new magi, while Alaron and Corinea worked on the ambrosia.

This storm was the worst yet. She'd experienced downpours in Baranasi that turned the sky liquid, and sand-storms that stripped stone, but snow was something else entirely. The peaks had turned white, and even the river that normally thrashed through the valley had frozen. Ice hung from balconies, turned into frozen waterfalls larger than a man. Translucent spears hung from the rims of the walkway covers. The air inside, though heated by the fires that burned in every room, was still cold enough to frost her breath.

She'd never seen snow up close, and now she had, she never wanted to again. The bitter, numbing chill made her feel like her toes and fingers were going to snap off. Leaving the guest suite meant braving frigid galleries where the cold was a solid thing. Even the blankets weren't enough, but using the gnosis to stay warm was tiring and wasteful.

Ramita had always been a pragmatist. She slipped out of bed, ensured Dasra was warm enough in his cradle, then went seeking body-heat in Alaron's room.

Alaron was sprawled across his bed, still clothed and half-covered by a great pile of blankets, sound asleep. The fire was unbanked, dying in the hearth, and his meal was unfinished; it looked as if he'd succumbed to exhaustion halfway through dinner. She put more logs onto the glowing embers and puffed until they caught, then went to his bedside. His face, earnest at the best of times, looked positively naked when he slept. She smiled fondly as she pulled up his blankets and tucked them in around him properly, then settled more blankets over the top, making a cozy nest. Then she crawled under his left arm and nestled against his side. Alaron groaned dozily as she nuzzled against his chest and put her arm over him. She murmured, 'Sleep, my Goat,' appreciating his warmth, and closed her eyes.

When she woke, he was already awake; she could hear it in his breathing, no longer slow and regular. She wriggled against him, feeling tentative, but happy too. 'Namaste,' she whispered.

'Hey.' He twisted slightly, self-consciously turning his hips slightly away. She could guess why. *An excitable body*, she and Huriya had used to joke about certain of the young men when they were growing up. But he had a good body, athletic and lean, and pleasing to the eye, for all it was so pale. She put her hand on his chest to keep him close and strained her neck to kiss his cheek, but he was turning to face her and she got his mouth instead. He tasted of spiced meat, strong but good.

She and Alaron had shared a blanket many times while travelling in the windskiff, but that was before they had started kissing. Since then there had been a new awkwardness; the agreement that they would do nothing more intimate than kissing had created tension, it was an almost tangible barrier between them – but to some extent, she knew, that barrier had always been there: she'd been pregnant, or wrapped up in motherhood, or they were somewhere uncomfortable and dangerous, or she was promised to another. It had never just been them, together and free.

She was tired of all that, tired of tiptoeing around each other – and she was tired of waking up cold.

'Al'Rhon, what are the marital customs of Noros concerning widows?' she asked.

He blinked at the unexpected question and thought for a moment. 'Well, widows can marry, same as anyone, I guess. It's like any other marriage – you have a priest of Kore leading the ceremony, of course – but it's usually much quicker than first marriages. I think that's because usually the widow marries another man from the same family

275

as her first husband, so you don't need to celebrate the merger of two families. We're big on that sort of thing in the West.'

'In Lakh most widows don't ever remarry,' Ramita said, a little sadly. 'If they are lucky they will have their dowry to support them – but most never have new suitors, because men want virgin brides with many years of fertility ahead of them. Most widows stay in their husband's family, but as servants. If they are not allowed to stay, or if there's a problem, they end up in widow-houses – I think that would be like your Kore convents. They aren't happy places. Widows are not valued in our land.'

Alaron murmured, 'You're valued.'

'I know.' She wriggled up to nuzzle his face while surreptitiously pulling the bow fastening her leggings undone. She edged them down, baring a strip of flesh around her belly, then took his hand. 'Could you do something for me?'

He sensed the change in mood and went very still. 'Sure . . .'

She kissed him again, while placing his palm against her bared midriff, then pushing it down until his fingers were resting in the thatch of hair beneath. He froze, holding his breath as if trying not to scare this moment away, then moved his fingers over her mound. She sighed happily and guided him to her cleft. His fingers brushed the wetness there and he hesitated, then slid one finger inside her, making her shudder at his touch. 'Mmm, just there . . .' she whispered. 'Small movements, just there.'

He leaned over her and kissed her open mouth while his fingers explored, his member hard against her thigh, until she turned her face away because what he was doing was beginning to make it hard to breathe slowly and instead she pulled her nightshirt up over her breasts and gave him something else to do with his mouth. Dasra was weaned, and they'd receded to their normal size: ornamental again, finally. She cradled his head, enjoyed being suckled, but her awareness was continually drawn lower, to her little pleasure nub, and what he was drawing from it.

It was alarming to be so forward, so wanton, but she'd been so lonely, and wanting him for such a long time. She knew what she was missing – the wonder of having someone trusted and desired in her bed. And she was discovering just how powerful it was to be the experienced one, to know what she wanted and how to get it.

All at once, touching wasn't enough; she pulled him onto her, opened herself and drew him in.

Alaron lay on his side in a state of stunned bliss, cradling Ramita to him, her back against his chest. It was close to dawn, the fire burning low, but his skin gleamed like snow against her darkness. He liked the way they looked together, and how they fit together, far better than he had feared, given the mismatch in height. But it had felt so natural and perfect. Already, she was all he could ever imagine wanting.

> *A golden thread my love has tied*
> *round her heart-strings and mine*
> *Betimes it chafes, betimes it cuts*
> *Betimes it feels like chains*
> *But most oft it is a sunbeam,*
> *My lover's golden thread.*

The old Rimoni love song was playing over and over in his head. In that tongue it rhymed. Cym had taught it to him after a gnosis lesson – just to tease him, he could see now, but at the time he'd thought it was all about him and her. It was a little painful to think of Cym now, surely dead, but it was only a passing thought, because all he had to do was look at the girl in his arms and all other thoughts were gone.

Most of the blankets had been cast aside, unneeded after all their exertions. The air in the room was steamy and close. He'd tried to go slowly like she wanted, and sometimes he'd even managed it, but it didn't really matter. He'd recovered quickly each time, and then the dance started again. He loved the sounds she made, the way she moved when she lost control, the sheer joy of being so close to her. It wasn't like he'd imagined; it was better – far more earthy and sweaty and human. But most of all it was *her*.

'Are you awake?' he whispered.

'You know I am.'

'Was it okay?'

'What do you want, more praise? It was *everything*.'

Everything. It had been tumultuous, primal – and all his notions of needing to be gentle, to treat her like a fragile flower, had been quickly discarded as he'd found his need had overcome him, and even more importantly, it'd been Ramita demanding *more, harder, faster*, until they'd been wrestling fiercely.

He'd felt a little ashamed after that first time, afraid he'd been too rough and uncaring in his urgency, until she'd chuckled earthily, 'Mmm, *so* good.'

'It didn't hurt?'

'Ha! That little thing?'

'Hey!'

She'd giggled. 'Don't worry, Goat, you are perfectly perfect.'

They'd occasionally dozed, but never for long, not with their blood racing and their heads and hearts pounding. He moved the curtain of long black hair from her neck and kissed it. She felt so small and precious in his arms that he wanted to hold her there for ever. But thinking of for ever brought other thoughts. 'Why did you ask about widows?'

'You know why,' she purred. 'It will be expected that we marry, if we wish to keep doing this.' She looked up at him. 'I presume you wish to, my Goat?'

He kissed her. 'I do.'

'Then we must marry.'

So they did, three days later on the next Holy Day. Master Puravai presided over a simple Zain ceremony in which they exchanged pledges of love. The whole monastery came to watch, including the eleven acolytes who'd so far taken the ambrosia. Corinea brought Dasra forward and Alaron pledged to be a father to him, an honour he was determined to live up to. He made the same promise to Nasatya too, although they still didn't know where he was.

Touchingly, the Zains brought gifts for the newlyweds; Master

Puravai gave a leather-bound book that made Ramita very excited. Alaron leafed through the first few pages, but it was all in Lakh and the occasional wood-cuts appeared to picture Omali gods, so he put it to one side for later study. The wedding feast was modest, just a little meat, and sweet-cakes for dessert, with an extra glass of wine for everyone.

They took two nights and one day to cement their new marriage, to just be themselves, Alaron and Ramita, alone together. Around midday they broke the ice around the shutters and stared out at the mountains for a while, but mostly they just lay together, alternately sleeping and coupling. It was the most blissful day of Alaron's life, the closest thing to the Zains' *moksha* that he could conceive: too perfect to last, and all the more precious for being fleeting.

16

Rifts

The Jhafi

The Jhafi were once a Harkun tribe, who escaped the cycle of migration between northern Kesh and southwest Javon to found their own kingdom, Ja'afar. They built towns and started farming crops, giving up the nomadic life to become settled, and they fortified the Rift to prevent their Harkun kin from following and destroying everything they had built. But it was not until the Rimoni came that their nation achieved real prosperity.

SISTER GULSEPPA, SOLLAN SCHOLAR, JAVON, 722

The Jhafi were great before the coming of the Rimoni, and we will be great when they have gone to dust.

GODSPEAKER URKUL, INTEMSA, 807

The Katlakoz Rift, Javon, on the continent of Antiopia
Zulhijja (Decore) 929
18th month of the Moontide

Another trembling Harkun walked his mount over the brow of the Katlakoz, dropped to his knees and kissed the ground. He removed the blindfold from his horse, swung into his saddle and trotted down to join his fellows, puffing out his chest and feigning nonchalance, as if scaling the barrier that had haunted his people's nightmares for hundreds of years were no great thing to a man such as he. A minute later another followed.

'Are we almost done?' Gurvon asked Rutt, who had a better view.

'A dozen to go,' Rutt reported. They'd been watching most of the day from a tower on the Red Fort, the northernmost of the Rift Forts. They were there ostensibly to greet Ghujad iz'Kho, but they were also using the occasion for a show of strength, to deter the Harkun from trying anything stupid with their Western allies, like trying to seize the fort. Staria Canestos' magi were not just visible, but making occasional flamboyant use of the gnosis to awe the nomads. So far it looked to be working.

'They hate us,' Staria noted.

That hadn't been lost on Gurvon. 'How many today?'

'Another three thousand,' Staria replied, 'as many as they're permitted. But there are hordes below still.'

'Those are just the woman and children, and the old men,' Rutt replied loftily. He and Staria had an entirely mutual dislike, which was growing now that Rutt was reduced to an insect inside another man's skull. 'They'll be there waiting until their men return victorious: that's the deal.'

'I *know* that,' Staria snapped back.

Gurvon forestalled further acrimony by raising his hand and pointing to the vast camp outside the Fort. 'That's the lot: thirty thousand mounted men, pledged to fight for us in Forensa, after which they'll move on to Loctis while we deal with Stefan di Aranio in Riban.'

'If they keep their word,' Staria said.

'Which is why I've got your full two legions here,' he reminded her patiently. 'You've got to be the gatekeeper, or we'll be flooded with these savages and lose control of them. Can you handle it?'

'Of course. But that doesn't mean they won't try.'

True enough. 'Look, this isn't a last-minute deal thrown together in desperation. I've been wooing Ghujad iz'Kho for a year or more. He'll keep his word.'

'I'm so glad you've finally found true love,' Staria replied snarkily, 'but when will we be relieved from this dump? My lads are going half-crazy in this rukking wilderness. We've been here for months with *nothing* to do – except jump. That rukking drop mesmerises you ... we've lost three already. Not to mention that the supplies are always late, and too little—'

'I'll look into it,' Gurvon replied, not really interested. 'Look, you're here until the end of the Moontide, so I suggest you keep your men busy. That's the best remedy for boredom.'

'I know how to run a legion, Gurv! But this place saps the soul. We really need to rotate—'

'They can rotate on each other's fingers,' Rutt jeered.

'Why don't you go find some dung to feast on, scarab-head?' Staria shot back.

'Shut it, you two,' Gurvon sighed. 'Staria, you'll be relieved when it's convenient.'

'For who? You think you can string my people along for ever? We want what we were promised; we're not patsies to your ambition!'

Yes, you are. But he put on his most placatory voice. 'Staria, I promise you, your wellbeing is as important to me as that of Hansi and Endus and everyone else. But we need you here, where you can control the most vital line of communication we have, barring the Krak. You're absolutely necessary, and that will be recognised. I've told you: you'll have Intemsa after this, a whole city to make into whatever you want. Your own kingdom, effectively. Where else would you get that?'

She lowered her eyes, then said slowly, 'You're right.'

'Thank you,' he said tersely, impatient now to be gone. 'In the meantime, stay alert.' He threw her a salute and walked away, Rutt trailing after him.

'Staria's lot are going to be a real problem,' the Argundian muttered. 'Once this war's done, they'll be a liability.'

'Yes, maybe, but for now, we need her,' Gurvon agreed. 'Someone's got to control the Rift for us, or we'll be swamped by screaming fanatical nomads. So this is the best place for her and her froci. If we're lucky, they'll all fucking jump!'

Staria tapped her fingers on the old stone bulwark, watching one of their windskiffs as it zipped over the Harkun horde, sending panicked riders scattering in all directions. Leopollo, her adopted son, laughed, but she wasn't in the mood to enjoy the moment.

The young man stretched sensuously. The desert sun, the bane of everyone else, had merely bronzed his cheeks into something even more godlike. He was in his mid-twenties, and beautiful enough that he could make even battered armour look fashionable. 'Look at all these Noories,' he grinned. 'Imagine the mess they'll make of Forensa.'

Ah, my Leopollo: conscienceless and amoral.

'Imagine them battering down our walls,' Kordea replied darkly, which was more along the lines that Staria had been thinking. Lately she and her adopted daughter had more often been of similar mind.

'They're primitives,' Leopollo yawned, 'no threat, not to *us*.' He peered towards Gurvon Gyle. 'Are they going already? I thought they were staying the night?' Leopollo was fascinated by Gurvon, and couldn't imagine the spymaster wouldn't be equally entranced by him in return.

'Mama mentioned that you fancied him and he ran away,' Kordea snickered. They both laughed and mock-sparred with each other while Staria watched with worried fondness. They were her chosen successors when the time came – and if her senior men were willing to allow it. But they were both problem children. Leopollo was like his father: charming, arrogant and so vain he'd erected statues of himself all over Estellayne. And Kordea's defensive belligerence got on even Staria's nerves at times. Neither was ready, not yet. But they had time to mature, she hoped.

'Listen, you two,' she said at last, stopping the fight, 'Gyle is sidelining us. The rest are being given plum cities and the chance to really establish themselves: Paavus at the Krak, Rykjard in Baroz, Frikter . . . maybe Hytel. We're *here*.'

'Let's seize Intemsa now,' Kordea suggested. 'Why wait for Gyle's permission?'

'We can't just abandon the Rift,' Leopollo countered, 'not during this season, and not with the Harkun here. We need to wait for them to go south for the summer, so Martrois at the earliest.'

Kordea scowled, knowing he was right. 'What then?'

'If we do nothing, we'll get nothing,' Staria told them. 'Leo, go and fetch Capolio and a bottle or two of the scarlo. I think we need to have a long talk about all this.'

Kordea and Leopollo exchanged a look. Capolio was Staria's spymaster and closest advisor.

'What are you thinking, Mama dearest?' Leopollo drawled.

She tapped the side of her nose. 'You'll have to see.'

Forensa, Javon, on the continent of Antiopia
Zulhijja (Decore) 929
18th month of the Moontide

Sir Roland Heale reined in and peered at the approaching riders: an Argundian and a Harkun, with a guard each. The Argundian was Hans Frikter, commander of Argundia XX, a royal legion that went rogue after the messy end to a recent invasion of Estellayne; it now operated as a mercenary unit. Frikter was a big, dour man riding a giant Argundian warhorse. Heale wrinkled his nose; he disliked Argundians for any number of reasons, and having met Frikter in Brochena and shared a few pints of ale, he'd concluded that the man was a buffoon.

But at least they're real men, not like Staria Canestos and her froci.

The nomad was the first Harkun that Heale had seen. He was heavily wrapped in robes, his face only clear when they got close enough to speak. Scars disfigured Ghujad iz'Kho's already shifty visage, and Heale felt his inclination to dislike him solidify; partly due to the rumour that iz'Kho had beheaded a Nesti envoy. Heale had little time for men who flouted laws of parley. Such laws had to be obeyed or all would revert to chaos.

'Greetings, Sir Roland!' Frikter boomed as he dismounted and they went through the usual 'hail-fellow-well-met' backslapping before turning to the Harkun. Heale had to endure having his cheeks kissed and his back patted by the sinister Noorie.

I'll have to wash after this, he found himself thinking. 'How many of your people have come, Lord iz'Kho?' He had no idea if that title was the correct term of address, and didn't care. He thought it higher than the dirty nomad deserved.

'Thirty thousand, as agreed,' iz'Kho replied, his Rondian awkward. 'We have many more. Our riders long for Jhafi blood.' He didn't appear to be speaking metaphorically.

'Let me show you the city,' Heale offered, and led them up a slope to a vantage point overlooking Forensa. The Nesti capital shimmered in the heat-haze. Like many cities in Javon, Forensa had spread beyond its walls and before them was a ramshackle maze of abandoned Jhafi huts of mudbrick that had been burned out by Heale's men as the army advanced. There was a clear space before the walls, which were of a pale brown sandstone that glinted as if powdered in gold; the battlements were festooned with violet Nesti banners, and red ones too, for the Kestrians from Loctis.

'What are we facing?' Frikter asked.

'We estimate no more than twenty thousand Rimoni soldiers inside,' Heale replied. 'The Rimoni are experienced in close-formation fighting, like we are. They also have Jhafi archers, akin to your own people, Lord iz'Kho.'

'Only akin as the donkey is to the horse,' iz'Kho sniffed. 'They are weaklings, city-bred beggars who have lost their pride.' He was chewing a wad of brown-orange betel-leaf that turned his spittle a dirty colour. He hawked and spat messily.

Disgusting peasant. Heale looked away and pointed towards the city again. 'Within the walls, the buildings are generally several storeys high, the streets are narrow and there are many canals. Once we get inside, it'll be messy. And then there's the Krak al-Farada, the Nesti castle. We've been constructing siege-engines – towers and catapults – to get us inside that.'

'Who for, yourselves, or to share?' Frikter grunted.

Heale frowned. 'For us Dorobon, of course. You should have thought of that before you marched. We'll breach the walls, then we all go in together.'

'We will not be able to take horses in there,' Ghujad iz'Kho commented.

'None of us will. It'll be street-fighting, hand to hand.' Heale doubted the Harkun would relish that. 'We Dorobon will take the north flank. Hans, your men will launch from here, the western side. Lord iz'Kho, deploy between us and assail the northwest.'

Frikter pointed. 'What are those peaks east of the city? Can we get men up there?'

'Not without a major engineering project,' Heale replied. 'The cliffs are sheer and treacherous. Essentially, it's impassable.'

'There's a road through them leading to the fourth Rift Fort,' iz'Kho said. 'With magi aid, my people could seize it and assail Forensa from the rear.'

Meaning you'd be able to slip tens of thousands more of your men into the upper plateau. I don't think so.

'No. We will take Forensa with what we have,' Heale replied stiffly. 'Lord iz'Kho, your tribesmen's role will be as archers, until the walls are breached. Thereafter, what you do in the city is your business. But the Nesti palace is for the Dorobon to plunder, and the Nesti family are to be our prisoners, as agreed.'

'Of course. Though in the midst of battle, there is always confusion.'

Heale looked at Frikter for support, but the Argundian looked away. *Because he knows what the real fight is here.*

It was a sobering thought: Frikter might have white skin and speak with a familiar accent, but in truth, *he* was the real enemy here. The Nesti held the walls, but they were chaff; iz'Kho might be unsettling, but he and his savages were no real threat. It would be Frikter's Argundians the Dorobon really had to worry about.

'Let this battle be a model of future cooperation,' Heale proposed. 'Then we can all have a drink and go home.'

Frikter laughed, but iz'Kho murmured, 'You are both a long, long way from home.'

Next morning, the catapults were rolled forward and the assault began.

The Krak al-Farada had been built on a spur of the mountains behind the city, about half a mile from Forensa's outer walls. It was the best vantage for Cera to witness the destruction of her city. The seige had been underway for more than a week now. Sometimes Timori and a flock of counsellors joined her; other times it was just Tarita and her, watching the Rondian catapults destroy everything she loved. The crunch of every hurled boulder on the distant city walls seemed to ripple through her tower, until she was convinced it too would collapse.

Today, it was just she, Tarita and her confessors watching.

Despite the distance, all of her senses were assailed: the stench of fire mixed with nauseating wafts of burnt flesh and the roiling miasma of wrecked sewers. She could taste the smoke from the burning buildings in the back of her throat – the Rondian catapult loads had some gnostic-power built into them that made them explode in bursts of flame or ghastly clouds of noxious gases, and every explosion shook the ground, reverberating through the city. Then came the dreaded sound of massed clarions, signalling another frontal assault on the battered walls. There had been three, each one coming closer to breaking the defences open.

'Dear Gods, how can we stop them?' she whispered.

Tarita squeezed her hand. It wasn't seemly for queen and maid to do such a thing, but right now she was so scared she couldn't let go. She didn't think Tarita was any more composed.

Behind her, Scriptualist Nehlan and Drui Tavis ignored each other, each chanting ostentatious prayers to their gods. Pita Rosco and Luigi Ginovisi had been coming and going throughout the morning, in between coordinating the logistics of war. There was much more to it than placing soldiers on walls: setting up feeding stations, getting newly made arrows to the archers, sending runners to keep the commanders informed, overseeing the dousing of fires and bolstering of weak points, and much else.

She was proud of her people: every citizen was playing their part, be that on the walls, hurling javelins and firing arrows, or dousing flames, bearing supplies, or tending the wounded, and so much else. What they lacked in training and equipment they made up for in courage and numbers. Conventional wisdom might say that only one in ten of a city's populace could fight effectively; the rest, the women and children, the aged, the infirm and the crippled, and those unsuited in other ways, being nothing but a nuisance. But when faced with extinction – which they all knew was what they were threatened with – even those who thought war beyond them had come forward. The Rondians might just be here to conquer, but the Harkun tribesmen were here to exterminate every single Jhafi. That left no room for shirking; it was fight, or die.

The losses were *atrocious*. With so many working in the space behind the walls, the Rondian catapults and Harkun archers couldn't help but kill every time they loosed their weapons. But they were taking their own toll as well: every man or woman who could draw a bow was firing back – poorly, no doubt, but the enemy were so numerous and tightly packed that even the meanest shot hit often enough.

Thus far they were managing to keep the enemy magi at a distance, but no one was fooled; the magi weren't leading the assault because they didn't have to. The catapults and the archers were doing enough. It had been eight days now and the dead were stacked two- and three-deep in the mass graves, and every day they were digging more. The outer walls were teetering, and unless something changed, the enemy would be through the breaches within a day or two.

Seir Ionus Mardium was dead, his whole command group torn apart by exploding catapult stones. Camlad a'Luki was gone too, blasted by a precise mage-bolt from a skiff that swooped unexpectedly overhead: young Saarif Jelmud, a kinsman of Camlad, was now coordinating the Jhafi fighting men. Justiano di Kestria was commanding the western walls now, against the mercenaries and the bulk of the Harkun. Piero Inveglio was directing the northern defences against the Dorobon and more Harkun. They'd given up any hope of reinforcements from Riban – the last missives from Stefan di Aranio made it clear that the defence of his own city was paramount to him, despite the fact there was no Rondian army within fifty miles of his walls.

Cera was wondering if it were time for her next Regency Council meeting when Tarita glanced up and gasped a warning. Cera saw a shadow flit across the rooftops and looked up to see a square-sailed skiff. For a moment her heart sang, that it might be Elena and Kazim returned to her, then blue fire seared towards her.

She couldn't stop herself opening her mouth to shriek, but a web of light blossomed around the entire cupola and the mage-bolt frayed into jagged skeins of light. Someone had warded the tower, she realised dimly as she grabbed Tarita and pulled her towards the stairs, where the two clergymen were standing like startled statues. Someone shouted in Rondian and a young man leapt from the skiff, sword drawn. He pushed through the wards, his face alive with adrenalin and adventure.

'Cera Nesti, I deem,' he greeted her in Rimoni, smiling rakishly. His blade extended towards her and light flashed from his hands, sealing the doors. The skiff circled the tower and she could see the pilot grinning excitedly. 'You're coming with me, Lady.'

'No!' Drui Tavis shouted, launching himself into the space between them and immediately staggering backwards as the mage's sword blurred into and out of his chest. The young Sollan priest toppled backwards and rolled onto his side. 'My Lady,' he croaked, then his face emptied as Cera stared in shock.

Tarita pulled a knife from inside her robes and put herself between the young mage and her queen as Scriptualist Nehlan shouted for aid, hammering on the doors, but they crackled with light and didn't budge an inch. The mage stepped closer.

With a dignified lift of the head, Nehlan also interposed himself between the Rondian and his queen. 'Then you must kill me also.'

'If you insist,' the Rondian said offhandedly, and blasted another mage-bolt, this one into Nehlan's chest. The Scriptualist reeled, hit the ledge and slid to the ground. Cera fought a wave of faintness, choked a sob and straightened her back as Tarita brandished her knife fearfully.

The mage looked at Tarita with an amused face and raised his hand again. 'Don't waste your life, girl.'

Tarita lifted her knife defiantly, but Cera shouted, 'No! Please – I will come—!'

Then a fork of pale light blasted off the Rondian's shields and he staggered backwards, turning as a muscular arm reached over the top of the battlements and a face out of nightmares snarled at him: a serpentine visage, crested and cowled by folds of scaly green skin. The lamia slithered over the wall of the tower and onto the platform, brandishing an enormous sword.

The Rondian sent blue fire at the creature and the lamia shielded, then lashed out with his tail and flashed forward, smashing his giant blade at the Rondian. Steel belled and sparks flew in a flurry of blows and the two young women backed as far out of reach as they could. Then the Rondian threw himself into the air as the skiff came about again and was snatched away. The craft circled the tower once more and the pilot – his eyes agog at the mythic beasts who were now climbing over the walls – sent his windskiff soaring away, leaving Cera and Tarita shaking with relief.

'My Lady,' the serpent-man said in his dry voice, bowing from the waist, but before he could say anything more the wards on the door gave way and the guards burst in. Seeing the lamiae and the two dead clergymen, they raised their weapons and started to rush towards the monsters, but Cera threw herself in front of the lamia.

'STOP!' she cried. 'They saved us!' Tarita joined her and they held out their arms to protect the serpent-men. 'These are our allies,' Cera said firmly, adding, 'They saved my life. It was not they who killed Tavis and Nehlan . . .' When she was sure that violence was averted, she fell to her knees over the two holy men, fighting not to wail in grief, and very conscious of the alien eyes of the snake-men watching her.

After a minute, Tarita lifted her to her feet and led her down the steps as a sense of impending doom enveloped her.

She remembered something her father had once told her: that when city walls fall and soldiers pour into the streets, it is as if Hel has come to Urte. He'd seen it from both sides, and it was the look on his face as much as his words that convinced her. The thought of such scenes happening here in Forensa was dreadful, and reasons to hope were becoming fewer and fewer.

She had only one such hope now. *Oh Ella, Ella, where are you?*

Northern Kesh, on the continent of Antiopia
Zulhijja (Decore) 929
18th month of the Moontide

'Where are we?' Elena demanded as the wind swirled tendrils of mist about them and peaks and cliffs flashed by alarmingly close. The air was frigid, visibility almost gone.

Molmar raised a placating hand. 'Hush; we're close now.'

She threw Kazim an anxious look, then relayed their position to the windship somewhere in the clouds above. Ice glittered on the ropes and timbers of the skiff and she was frozen despite her gnosis, and terrified they were going to plough into a mountain peak any second. The journey had been like this for days, wearing her nerves to a frazzle, but Molmar claimed he knew this route well.

He'd better be right.

They'd travelled more than a thousand miles – normally just a few days in a windcraft, but these mountains made the journey so much more difficult. Most of the peaks were over nine thousand feet high, higher than it was safe to fly, forcing Molmar to weave a complicated route through a maze of valleys and ravines against a prevailing wind that could swat them like a giant fist at any minute. The thin, freezing air caused altitude sickness – without Molmar, they would never have managed to get this far.

She'd scryed the start of the assault on Forensa before they entered the mountains and lost touch. If their plan went as she hoped, they might be back inside three days – if they flew without rest. She prayed the city would hold out that long.

Her senses penetrated the space ahead of them, feeling out the shape of the air currents and what they implied about the terrain, but as they crossed another ridgeline fresh winds struck their sails, sending them lurching sideways. As Molmar fought the tiller, they dropped through cloud and into a small valley, grey slopes streaked with snow. Molmar put his thumb in the air. 'This is our landing place!' he said, with a hint of satisfaction. 'The breeding-house is in the next valley.'

They landed, and while the two men dragged the skiff into the lee of a stand of boulders, Elena reached out with her mind to the windship above, and a few minutes later it dropped through the cloud and into view. The crew, human and lamiae, were working feverishly together, lowering and tying off the sails, as the craft fell slowly to the earth. The buffeting winds made the landing rough, and they had to lash the craft down quickly.

Elena hurried to greet Kekropius. 'The breeding-house is in the next valley and we've an hour of daylight left to find it,' she called to the Elder as he dropped from the hull and slithered towards her. 'Come – we need to hurry.'

Leaving enough men to secure the windcraft, Elena followed Molmar up the far slope with Kekropius' war-party at her heels. The lamia windship had more than a dozen Air-magi to keep the keel powered, enabling them to carry more than the usual two dozen passengers, and helping it stay aloft for longer, but they were all exhausted, and worried to be so far from home. It showed in Kekropius' face as he put a hand on Elena's shoulder. 'Elena, our stores are almost gone, and my people don't cope well in these cold places.'

'We'll not stay long,' she promised. 'We must return to Forensa as soon as possible.'

Please Kore, may we not already be too late!

From the ridge, they surveyed the breeding-house: a large compound set in a square almost three hundred yards across, divided into two clear areas with a central yard. The smaller area contained a blockhouse with tiny slit windows three storeys in height; it had a landing area for windcraft on the roof. The other area had what looked like barracks, exercise areas and stables, all centred around a small Dom-al'Ahm. They could see there were soldiers stationed in the corner towers, but there was an air of complacency that suggested the guards had little to do.

Molmar moved to her side and she turned and smiled at him. 'Thanks for guiding us here, Molmar.'

'Lady, I only pray that this is the right thing I am doing.' He still didn't sound convinced.

'Your heart is telling you it is,' she replied, hoping that really was the case.

'Perhaps.' His eyes softened a little. 'Lady, behold: the blockhouse is where prisoners are confined. The men and women are chained to their beds; they are forced to comply with those arranging the breeding. At any time there are up to sixty magi-prisoners.' He pointed to the second set of buildings. 'The other area is for the infants and children. They are cared for here until they are old enough to be sent to the Hadishah training facilities. There are usually at least a hundred children aged up to six, and they are tended by those mothers who are willing breeders.'

'How many Hadishah are here?' Kazim asked.

'It varies,' Molmar answered. 'Normally the strongest Hadishah magi come here to mate with the high-blooded prisoners, but this is war-time and right now those Hadishah cannot be spared. It is possible that the fertile women are being transported with the armies, so only the pregnant will be here. Or it may be that the high-blooded come here between battles? I fear I am not privy to that information.'

'Well, all we can do is go in and hope for the best.' Elena winced, hating having to act without solid information. 'Are you sure the Ordo Costruo were brought here?'

'I transported many myself,' Molmar replied, stony-faced.

This isn't easy for him, Elena reminded herself. *The breeding programme is for a cause he clearly believes in – and he himself was born in such a place. But he clearly loathes the suffering that is endured here.*

'Where will the strongest Hadishah be?' she asked, keeping her voice neutral.

'The top floor of the breeding-houses has a number of luxurious rooms for their comfort,' Molmar replied. 'The high-bloods will be there.'

'Reserved for Rashid and friends, like a high-class whorehouse?'

Molmar looked away again.

She turned to Kekropius. 'I think we should stick to our original plan, don't you?'

'I'm in reluctant agreement,' the lamia Elder replied. 'I don't like the chance you are taking,' he added, giving Molmar a meaningful look, 'but we do need to get people inside before the fighting starts if we're to succeed.' He gazed at the compound. 'My ancestors were bred by the Pallas Animagi in places similar to this.'

'Then it is right you are here to end this one,' Elena told him. She glanced at Molmar. 'You'll play your part?'

The Keshi mage gave an unhappy nod.

The skiff came in low, hugging the slope as the winds yowled through the taut rigging like mating cats. They were below the snowline, just, but it was the bleakest place Kazim had ever seen.

He glanced at Elena, her gnostic aura bound up by his own Chain-rune. He'd ached to cast it, for the pain it had caused her, and worse, because it had severed their gnostic bond, leaving the place she normally occupied in his heart and soul empty. It was like a foretaste of her death, and that was hideous. Worse, his own power was also Chain-runed, by Molmar.

But it was the only logical way to get in: Elena was Rondian and if she was to seem to be a prisoner, she had to be Chained. And as a Souldrinker, his own aura would have been unexplainable. But it made them vulnerable, especially as their hands were bound as well.

I can break Molmar's Chain-rune, he told himself. *I'm stronger than he is. But what if he turns against us and enlists aid to prevent me breaking free?*

Trust: that's what it came down to.

They skidded over the walls and slewed towards the blockhouse before skidding into a rough landing on the blockhouse roof. They slid to a halt and looked warily at each other. Molmar busied himself securing the sails while he and Elena sat and waited, playing the part of defeated prisoners.

The doors to the floor below flew open and three robed figures emerged, two men and a woman, clad in black with only their faces bare. They were pale-skinned, but all had a distinctly Keshi caste to their faces.

'Molmar?' the leading man called. 'I've not been told of any deliveries—!'

'Special prisoners, Sadikh!' Molmar called. 'The emir wanted it kept quiet.'

'We should still have been forewarned,' Sadikh complained. 'Who are they?'

Molmar smiled darkly. 'These are Elena Anborn and Kazim Makani.'

The three Hadishah faces went from suspicion to vindictive triumph. 'They've been captured? Ahm be praised!' Sadikh exclaimed. Kazim and Elena's killing of Gatoz and his men had clearly reverberated through the Hadishah ranks.

He strode forward, kindling the gnosis in his hands. 'Well, well, well,' he murmured, almost salivating. His face had turned so violently ugly that Kazim wondered whether they might not have miscalculated. *What if he just kills us?*

The other Hadishah man cupped Elena's chin and spat in her face. 'I want first use of this one,' he growled. Then he turned to Kazim. 'As for you . . .' His hand went to his dagger.

'No, Yimat!' The woman behind him caught his arm. 'We've been wanting more like him,' she said in a low voice that was no less hate-filled.

It was plain they knew that he was a Souldrinker. Kazim held his breath as Yimat toyed with his dagger.

'As you wish, Gulbahar,' Yimat said resentfully at last, then abruptly he backhanded Kazim across the face. The blow was gnosis-enhanced and Kazim's head rocked sideways, his mouth filling up with blood. 'A Rondian screwing a Souldrinker?' he snarled. 'Ahm only knows which is the more degenerate.'

The woman Gulbahar went to Elena, grabbed her hair and yanked it brutally. 'Hello, Bitch. We've been *longing* to get hold of you.'

'Have a care,' Molmar put in. 'She is with child.'

Elena flinched and looked away, so convincingly that Kazim found his heart leaping. *What if she is——?* But he knew it was a lie; they'd already agreed to say this, to make it less likely they'd abuse Elena on arrival.

Gulbahar added her spittle to Elena's face. 'She's an obscenity,' she hissed. 'Pregnant by choice to one of these Souldrinker monsters!'

Soldiers were summoned to manhandle them below while Molmar drew Sadikh aside. Kazim watched worriedly: if Molmar was going to betray them, it would be in the next couple of minutes – it wouldn't take much, after all, not with them both properly restrained. The pilot's expression was unreadable, and Kazim found himself increasingly nervous.

The soldiers took them down one level, to the top floor of the blockhouse. A pair of stony-faced guards in armour stared at them, their eyes going round in astonishment, their normal rigid discipline overcome by their fascination with the identity of the new prisoners. Someone called aloud for Scriptualist Tahir; the name rang dim bells in Kazim's memory, but he couldn't take the time to work out where he'd heard it before, not while Sadikh was whispering to Molmar.

Molmar's eyes met his, and then he whispered something else in Sadikh's ear.

Something unseen passed between them, and the grip on Kazim's arms tightened.

Then a blade was pressed to his throat.

17

Breeding-House

Hadishah

The advent of the Leviathan Bridge had another effect, Majesty – the inciting
of many of the heathen Amteh towards a more violent and fanatical expression
of their religion. The Hadishah are the most dangerous of these sects, and have
committed many atrocities even against their own people. I urge you to send
further resources so that we might stamp them out once and for all.

GOVERNOR TOMAS BETILLON, HEBUSALIM, 918

The Jackals of Ahm are as feared by their own people as by the Rondians.

ORDO COSTRUO COLLEGIATE, PONTUS, 917

Northern Kesh, on the continent of Antiopia
Zulhijja (Decore) 929
18th month of the Moontide

Elena staggered as the two guardsman wrenched her along the corridor towards a door at the end. As she glanced back at Kazim she saw
a hidden web of meaningful glances: Molmar whispering in Sadikh's
ear, the guardsmen looking about with sudden tension on their faces,
and blades coming out. Then the men holding her tripped her and
shoved her to her knees.

She struggled, trying to twist and catch Kazim's eyes.

If Molmar doesn't release him in a moment we're going to have do this
alone.

The doors at the end of the corridor flew open and a tall man dressed in heavy black velvet ceremonial robes emerged. He had a hawkish face and wore a big emerald periapt on his forehead. 'What is this?' he demanded. 'New prisoners? Why wasn't I told?'

'Secrecy was required,' Molmar replied, stepping forward and bowing. 'This is Elena Anborn.'

Damn it, Molmar, free us!

The newcomer's eyes widened. He yanked on her hair to force her to look at him. 'I am Scriptualist Tahir,' he said in stilted Rondian. 'So, you are the famous Elena Anborn?'

She averted her eyes and the man, still gripping her hair, slapped her hard, making her eyes water and her scalp burn. 'Speak when you are spoken to, whore!'

Molmar . . . I trusted you . . . Please . . . do it!

'My Lord Tahir, have a care,' Molmar reminded them all. 'She is with child: it is a unique situation!'

'How so?'

'It is the child of a Souldrinker.'

Elena exhaled in relief. Molmar was sticking to the story. *But if he's really with us, why isn't Kaz free already?* She winced as Tahir pulled her hair again; she could feel his eyes boring into her.

'Whose Chain-rune is on her?' the Scriptualist asked. 'I don't rec-ognise the touch.'

You wouldn't . . . it's Kazim's . . .

Tahir released her hair and tried again to break the spell, then pulled back, puzzled. 'It is damnably strong. Whose Chain is it?'

'Rashid himself,' Molmar lied. He stepped away and bowed again, casually laying a hand on Kazim's arm.

He really is with us . . . Elena braced herself to move.

Molmar waited until Tahir looked back at Elena, then a gentle glow suffused Kazim's aura – dissipating one's own spell took none of the time and energy needed to dispel something done by another mage. As the three Hadishah magi stared, puzzled by the light, the Chain-rune vanished. The moment Molmar freed him, Kazim was in motion, rising in one flowing moment and grabbing the wrist of one of the soldiers, spinning him with brutal force to smash into the other. There was a sickening crunch as he burned his bonds away and slammed kinetic force at Tahir.

The Scriptualist flew backwards through his own double doors while Kazim roared his war cry and splayed his hands, smashing the two men holding Elena off their feet. Then his counter-spell knifed through her chest, breaking his own Chain-rune – it was a lost second, a necessary one, but it meant Molmar had to face Sadikh, Yimat and Gulbahar on his own.

Molmar spun, his shields kindling, then he was hammered by three instantaneous flashes of blue light; the first was deflected, but the second two, from Sadikh and Gulbahar, blazed into him at once. His shield coalesced against Sadikh's bolt, but Gulbahar's struck his chest and smashed him over backwards. The smell of charred meat filled the air.

Even before the Chain binding her vanished, Elena was in motion; breaking her bonds as she evaded a mage-bolt from Gulbahar and as her own gnosis re-engaged she hurled mage-fire back, then launched herself forward, using kinesis to pull her own blade from the scabbard at Molmar's waist, dodging a bolt from Sadikh before ramming her shortsword at his chest. He was shielding, but blocking a handheld weapon with just shields was hard; he managed to cover his chest, but her other blow, a brutal kick to his right ankle, passed through effortlessly. She heard the crack of breaking bones and he collapsed to the tiled floor.

She barrelled straight on, knocking Yimat's arm sideways with her forearm as she passed him, and drove her shortsword straight into Gulbahar's breast. The Keshi woman gaped down at the steel, then fell backwards, the blade sliding free with a sucking sound. Yimat threw a kinetic shove at Elena, but her shields absorbed it and she spun, catlike, as he drew his scimitar.

Sadikh was sitting up, kindling fire in his hands, and other doors were opening along the corridor. Kazim had followed Tahir back into the room at the end of the corridor and Molmar was down.

Elena didn't have time to wonder whether they'd gotten in over their heads this time.

Kekropius felt rather than saw his people slithering into place. The slopes above the compound were rough, studded with boulders and rockfalls, clear signs of neglectful security. Finding and moving under cover was easy for the lamiae, practised hunters, and they got to within sixty yards of the walls undetected, and settled in to wait. As the twilight deepened and Molmar's skiff landed, they began to fret, anxious to be on the move.

His people were uniformly young: even he, an Elder, was barely twenty; most of the young warriors, with the exception of a pair of nineteen-year-old females who were too old to breed, were in their mid-teens and unused to patience. The Animagi who had made the lamiae had created them to die young, to avoid them ever becoming a problem.

But we became a problem anyway. You wanted warriors, Emperor Constant, and that is what we are.

<*They've landed and been taken inside,*> Simou, the other Elder on this mission, added. <*Let's go.*>

The war-party broke cover, slithering faster than a running man towards the walls. Someone must have been paying attention, for the alarm went up almost immediately, with panicked shouts and ringing bells. Arrows flew, but the lamiae were moving fast and erratically, and none were hit. They reached the walls and began targeting defenders with their own gnosis, sending boulders smashing through the battlements and bringing down whole sections. Then mage-fire flashed and they started swatting aside the guards with kinesis.

Kekropius went through the breach he'd smashed with a gigantic boulder, moving at a sprinter's pace. His spear caught the first guard he saw and skewered him. Arrows bounced off his shields – and then the defenders saw their enemy: not men but monsters. The resistance wavered, then those who could, ran.

<*To the breeding-house!*> Kekropius shouted, to keep his kin, so young and easily distracted, focused on their mission. He swerved

that way himself, cutting down another soldier as he passed, then racing unopposed between the small huts. His kindred swarmed behind him.

He almost didn't see the vivid blast of blue light from above; it slammed into his shields and hurled him backwards, tearing the breath from his lungs. He was semi-stunned and still gasping for air when someone grabbed him from behind and pulled him backwards into cover. *Simou.* As he recovered he glimpsed a man on a balcony above. His head filled with the cries of alarm from his kin, then someone shouted <ATTACK!> with all the exuberant foolishness of youth, and they all surged on again, into the fire.

It took him a few seconds to realise that the one who'd shouted was him.

Kazim realised he was in trouble half a second after he burst through the doors and into the most opulent room he had ever seen. It was positively *dripping* with luxury, from the smallest trinket on the elaborate marquetry table to the largest marble statue, a representation of a naked woman preening at her own magnificence. *Not a traditional Amteh work*, he thought, shielding as the current of energy between him and Elena flowed again, full of power and information. She was fighting in the corridor, outnumbered and under pressure.

I have to finish this, fast.

Tahir had taken up position to the left of the statue; he had dropped to one knee, with his scimitar drawn. As the Scriptualist blazed at Kazim with gnostic-fire, his shields went critical and Kazim realised, *He's a pure-blood!* He concentrated on his shielding, and pretended to falter. *Come and get me, Scriptualist.* But Tahir was no fool; Kazim could hear him calling silently for help.

I've got to stop him warning the rest . . . He jumped towards Tahir with a kinetic-empowered leap, his blade sweeping towards the man's neck – but the Hadishah wasn't there; he'd whisked himself backwards and sideways, putting the marble statue between them, then he hurled it at Kazim with a kinetic push. Kazim caught the statue and sent it back, three times as hard, and the Scriptualist bellowed in alarm, barely wrenching himself aside in time to avoid the massive marble figure, which went through the wall with a crash, bricks tumbling after. The ceiling in that corner, no longer supported, wobbled, and began to come down.

Kazim didn't let up; he kept attacking with blade and gnosis. Steel belled on steel, and then Tahir was gone again, leaping to the far side of the bed. Kazim jumped over it too and their blades locked. They shoved each other, momentarily matched, until Tahir gave ground, panting.

'You are Kazim Makani?' he gasped. 'Why do you fight us?'

Kazim ignored his question, driving him back with another flurry of blows, scouring his shields and almost breaking through. Tahir defended well, with scimitar and gnosis, but he was being beaten and he knew it. He shouted for help again, and this time Kazim heard responses. Then Elena cried out, and his heart almost froze.

Kazim could see Tahir take heart as someone burst into the room behind him; he counter-attacked, trying to drive Kazim back onto the newcomer's blade.

Elena drove Yimat backwards, feinted high and went low, driving her shortsword into his groin and pulling it out in a great spray of blood. The mage folded over and slumped to his knees, but as she jumped free she moved into the lee of a door that was flying open. A black-clad young man came out and saw Sadikh writhing in agony on the floor, not just because of a badly broken ankle, but the dagger buried to the hilt in his back. Molmar's dagger. The skiff-pilot was back on his feet, burned and moving too slow; he looked up at the young newcomer and saw death coming.

But the young man hadn't seen Elena. She darted in, ramming her sword into his side and kindling enough energy to blast through shields – but he wasn't a mage and instead that energy exploded in his torso. The wound was lit from within, charring the inside of his ribcage and breaking his spine; his consciousness extinguished as he fell.

She was long past recoiling in horror at such things. She dashed into the room he'd emerged from, lifted a hand and blazed away at the first thing that moved: a Keshi girl cowering beside a large bed where a plump white man was chained, naked and faintly ridiculous. Her mage-bolt hit the girl in the face, blasting it to unrecognisable blackened bone – she hadn't been a mage either. But the man on the bed most certainly was: he was Lord Rene Cardien, of the Ordo Costruo.

There was no time to free him; a pure-blood would have Chained him and she'd take far too long breaking it. 'Don't go away,' she shouted and returned to the corridor in time to see Molmar cornered by two Hadishah. She blasted a mage-bolt into the back of the nearest, encountering shields, but at least it made the man spin round to face her, leaving Molmar fighting painfully against the other. Her link to Kazim told her that he too was hard-pressed, pulling at her gnostic resources.

She sent three blasts, almost too fast to separate, at her target, and the third breached his shield, leaving him unconscious on the ground.

'Hey, you—' she rasped, breaking her shape with Illusion as she flowed forward to help Molmar. The pilot-mage's foe was momentarily bewildered to see two Rondian women coming at him – then his gnostic sight engaged and he saw her truly, just as she struck out with blade and gnosis. He managed to anchor his feet with Earth-gnosis and countered, parrying her blows desperately, while behind him Molmar slid ungracefully to the ground.

She pretended to give ground, drawing him away from the prostrate pilot-mage, until the Hadishah man bellowed triumphantly and lunged.

Kids! Do they teach them nothing? She dropped under his blow and hacked through the frayed edge of his shielding at his knee, feeling her blade bite into the joint. The young man cried out in pain and couldn't stop himself lurching sideways; as she realigned her weapon. She lunged, straight-armed, the sword pierced his belly and she wrenched it sideways viciously. He collapsed forward with a wailing shriek and fell next to his fellow mage.

A swish of silk caught her attention as the door opened between her and the room where Tahir and Kazim were still fighting. A majestic woman of mixed race emerged; she was dressed in a shimmering ivory gown, her hands cradling her swollen belly protectively. Her skin was almost black, but her hair was blonde and piled up on her head. She was festooned with jewellery, looking as if she was just going to a ball, but her expression was filled with hope.

For a moment Elena froze at the sight, until the pregnant woman was suddenly wrenched back into the room from which she'd come and a man with a crossbow emerged, firing at Molmar. He was barely six feet away – but the woman grabbed the crossbowman's arm and the bolt punctured the opposite wall instead of Molmar. Before he could react, Elena launched herself at him, shoving the woman aside with kinesis and hurling a mage-bolt at the Hadishah. He shielded, dropping the crossbow and drawing his scimitar in one fluid motion; he caught Elena's blow with a smooth parry then slapped at her with powerful kinesis, battering her backwards. His scimitar crackling with energy, his style all power and ferocity, he came after her and now it was Elena parrying frantically, forced to give ground and finding herself being driven back step by step until she was trapped against a wall.

She didn't dare take her eyes from his darting blade. *Rukka, he's good!*

Then the Keshi coughed, his whole body convulsing as the head of a crossbow bolt burst from the middle of his chest. He staggered towards her, then fell onto his face.

Behind him the pregnant woman – possibly the most beautiful woman Elena had ever seen, and that was even before she'd saved her life – was holding the emptied crossbow with a satisfied smirk on her face.

'Darling,' she said to Elena in Rondian, 'if you're here to rescue us, I am your blood-sister for ever.'

In the half-second Kazim calculated he had, he twisted and saw three identical young women coming at him, their blades virtually invisible. Gnostic sight showed the true image and he ignored the rest, catching her up in a kinetic hold and throwing her at Tahir, who was midway through some kind of Fire-spell involving the braziers.

The girl fell into the middle of it and was immolated, screaming in agony and terror as she was torched. To his credit, Tahir went pale and immediately tried to douse the flames, but the girl had stopped screaming already ...

Enough of this. Throwing all his strength into the blow, Kazim unleashed a kinetic push of barbaric simplicity and monumental strength: *Ascendant's* strength. Tahir's attention was far less on his shields than it had been, for his mouth was shaping the word 'daughter' ...

A moment later he was a boneless pile of flesh and blood sliding down the cracked and broken wall. The concussion from the spell recoiled, and Kazim wobbled like a newborn colt, then fell to his knees. He crawled to the fallen Hadishah girl, but she was beyond help: her blackened skin was blistering and peeling before his eyes and her hair and her clothing were crumbling into ash. Her eyes were pools of yellow fluid. He could hear her mind screaming, a silent howl of agony that wouldn't stop.

Killing her was a kindness.

He was pulling his dagger from her chest when Elena lurched in. 'Kaz?'

He waved a hand in reassurance and clambered slowly to his feet. Then Kekropius slithered through the hole in the wall the statue had made, followed by his kin.

'Kekro!' Kazim gripped his hand in relief. 'Glad you made it.' He took a deep breath and looked back at Elena. His strength was regained, and his blood was up. 'All right, who else do we need to kill around here?'

The pregnant beauty in the ivory-coloured gown named herself as Odessa D'Ark, a pure-blood mage from an original Ordo Costruo family, and the man she'd killed was Narukhan Mubarak, the younger brother of Rashid Mubarak al-Halli'kut, the Emir of Halli'kut. Narukhan was also the father of her unborn child. She was utterly unremorseful about his death.

'They *bid* for me,' she told Elena in her deep, fluid voice. Her dark eyes were examining both Elena and Kazim analytically. 'What strange auras you have ... ?' Then she saw the lamia and her eyes bulged. 'What in Hel—?'

'Later,' Elena said. 'Right now we've much to do. But you'll have the story ...'

It took an hour to mop up the rest, and the lamiae did most of the fighting. All the senior Hadishah – Narukhan, Tahir, Sadikh and the others on this floor – were already dead, and without them the rest, low-blooded and demoralised, either fled or surrendered. Kazim freed Rene Cardien from the Chain-rune – set by Narukhan himself, Odessa said – then the four of them went from room to room, freeing the rest of the prisoners.

After penning the remaining guards in the dungeons below – and remarkably clean and civilised dungeons they were, compared to Rondian ones, Elena thought – they turned their attention to the children's compound. They weren't greeted as liberators however, and the children clung to their Keshi mothers in terror, clearly convinced they'd be slaughtered. And even the Rondians were aghast at the snakemen.

Finally Elena, Kazim, Kekropius, Rene Cardien and Odessa D'Ark, with some of the released prisoners, convened in the central records office, on the ground floor, to take stock. Elena had already checked on Molmar, and set one of the Ordo Costruo women to look after him; he was in pain, but awake. They'd lost only two lamiae – the element of surprise combined with terror at the sight of the snakemen had been decisive and once the resistance broke, there had been little more fighting.

'How many are you?' Elena asked the freed Ordo Costruo, translating the Rondian to Kazim through their link.

Rene Cardien's dignity and natural pomposity had flooded back now he was fully dressed. 'We've freed fifty-three of our Order, Lady Anborn, as well as another fourteen magi.'

'What are your loyalties?' she asked, and he looked at her strangely.

'To our Order,' he declared, as if her question was ridiculous.

'Though a few of us are rethinking our principles of neutrality,' Odessa D'Ark glowered.

'Some of us weren't given silk and jewellery,' growled one of her colleagues, a middle-aged grey-haired women also sporting a bulging stomach.

'Narukhan dressed me this way, Clematia,' Odessa snapped back. 'He liked to fuck well-dressed women. Perhaps you'd prefer I was beaten instead?'

'We were,' a young blonde girl with a black eye scowled, then silently mouthed the word 'slut'.

'Enough,' Elena said tersely. 'What of the fourteen non-Ordo Costruo?'

'Crusaders, like me,' replied a young man with pale skin and lank black hair. 'I'm Valdyr of Mollachia. My brother and I were captured during the Second Crusade.'

'How old were you then?' Elena asked – Valdyr looked no more than twenty, the same age as her nephew. They'd found him naked and tied to a bed, a Keshi girl hiding beneath it, trembling in terror. She didn't know much about Mollachia; it was a mountain kingdom bordering Midrea and Schlessen, wild lands with strange customs and a bloody history.

'I was ten. I was my brother's bannerman,' Valdyr replied. 'We were ambushed, and I've been here ever since.' His eyes bored into Elena, then trailed sideways and focused on Kazim. 'I'm going to make these Noorie scum pay.' A few of the others, men and women both, growled approval.

Of course he feels that way . . . most will. But it means he's useless to our mission.

'Where's your brother?'

The boy's face fell. 'He went with the Godspeakers.' The betrayal in his voice was painful to hear. His brother had clearly been his hero.

Lock a man in a room with no one but a priest to listen to and that'll happen sometimes, Elena reflected. She'd seen it on both continents. She gave Valdyr a sympathetic look, then turned back to Rene. 'How many children did we recover from the other compound?'

'One hundred and eight under six. Nearly thirty women are still wet-nursing – I would guess half of those mothers have gained permanent gnosis through pregnancy manifestation.' He shuffled uncomfortably. 'Three more Keshi women are pregnant and also likely to gain the gnosis; they are bearing my children.' His voice had a hollow tone.

<He's a pure-blood: those children will be half-bloods, and so will the women he impregnated,> she told Kazim.

'We've recovered five windskiffs,' Kazim put in, 'but even with our own craft, that's not enough to transport everyone.'

Odessa fixed Elena with a hard look. 'Then the path is clear: those who are loyal to us, or aligned to the West, we take away. Those who aren't must die.' The controlled hatred in her voice spoke eloquently of what she, and the rest, had gone through.

Elena returned her gaze levelly. 'I'm sorry, but you're misunderstanding the situation, Magister D'Ark. We're not here on behalf of the Crusade, and we don't murder children.'

'If you knew what we'd gone through, blood-sister, you'd feel less inclined towards mercy. I've been *longing* for the chance to strike back at these bastards.'

The other freed prisoners stirred uncomfortably.

'Who are you, then?' the matronly woman, Clematia, demanded of Elena. 'And *what* are you? Your aura is very strange.'

'And what of these snake-creatures?' asked a grizzled Pallacian mage-knight called Beglyn, the oldest of the crusader captives. 'What in Hel are they?'

Elena looked sideways at Kazim. *Well, here goes . . .*

'They call themselves lamiae; they were originally constructs made by the Pallas Animagi,' she said, starting with the simpler issue.

'That's illegal,' young Valdyr said indignantly.

'That's never been a problem to the Sacrecours,' Odessa replied disdainfully.

'They're abominations, nevertheless,' Beglyn growled.

'We didn't ask to be made, but we were,' Kekropius said. 'We have children, we have lives and dreams. And we have the strength to deal with anyone who wishes us ill.' His eyes trailed over the old knight, challenging.

'Laws are made for reasons,' Beglyn countered, not quite meeting his eye.

'Are you always this grateful to those who save your life?' Elena asked. She looked at Rene. 'Can we agree that whatever the crimes of the Pallas Animagi, Kekropius' people are alive and as sentient beings have the right to remain so? I believe that the Ordo Costruo have taken that view in the past, in similar matters?'

The Ordo Costruo magi looked at each other uncomfortably, then they all nodded agreement. The Crusaders were slower to do so.

'What the empire sows, the world reaps,' Rene said resignedly. 'What troubles me more, Lady Elena, is the nature of your . . . erm . . . Kazim Makani. I've seen his kindred before . . .'

'What are you saying, Rene?' Odessa asked. 'What is he? Another construct?'

This time the explanation took longer – the first mention of the word *Souldrinker* sent hands to periapts and wards tingling; the tension rose as Elena showed them the way her aura and Kazim's were entwined. The abhorrence on the faces of all but a few was clear and she could see their attitudes were shifting from gratitude to fear that their rescuers were worse than their gaolers.

'This is not what you think,' she said forcefully. 'Since Kazim and I fell in love, he has not needed to renew his gnosis as other Dokken do. He draws from me.'

The Crusaders looked sickened – no doubt as much from the fact that her lover was a Noorie as that he was a Souldrinker; she expected that and she didn't care.

But Rene and Odessa, the opinion leaders of the Ordo Costruo, were intrigued: they were clearly still scholars at heart.

'So this link . . . you feed each other gnosis-energy . . . and Elena replenishes as normal . . . and it's enough for both of you . . . ?' Rene's eyes grew round. 'That's incredible!'

'No,' Elena told him, 'it is *credible*. It's *real*.'

'And you . . . ?' Odessa put in. 'You've not become as Nasette? You're not a Dokken yourself now?'

'No – although we've been careful to avoid pregnancy.'

Odessa cast an ambiguous look at her own midriff. 'Lucky you.'

'So if he doesn't need to kill . . . then you're saying he's effectively like any other mage?' Beglyn eyed them both with a troubled expression. 'This is a hard matter, Lady Anborn.'

'I know,' Elena replied. 'Believe me, I've had all my own preconceptions overturned in the last few years. I scarcely know my life any more. I'm a Noroman mage, yet here I am in Ahmedhassa, sharing my life with a Dokken. Kazim's journey has been just as strange.'

'He has evidently taken at least one life, to gain the gnosis,' Rene noted. 'Tell us of yourself, Kazim Makani.'

All the eyes in the room went to Kazim: the man who'd killed the head of the Ordo Costruo and taken his soul.

Elena and Kazim had already debated what they would say at this juncture; every instinct, drilled into Elena during her years with the Grey Foxes, was to conceal the truth, especially one so inflammatory. But Kazim thought the opposite. *Lies rebound on the liar*, he had repeated during the debate: it was a quote from the *Kalistham*. She took some convincing, but she herself could cite recent events where secrets had indeed been corrosive and deadly. Lies had a way of outing at the worst time, and destroying everything in their path.

She gritted her teeth while Kazim told the truth.

'My father was a Souldrinker, but I never knew that,' Kazim began. 'He lived in Lakh, and I was born there. He never used his gnosis in all the time I knew him – I never even knew he had it – though he had burn wounds that gave him constant pain. I believe that he must have renounced his powers, perhaps without ever kindling them. Either way, I was ignorant of that part of my heritage, until I joined the shihad, and was seduced into joining the Hadishah.'

That revelation caused a stir among the listeners, and Elena braced herself for the worse that was to come, sure that the room was about to explode.

'In the Hadishah I was taught to hate all white people, and to give total obedience to my masters, so I didn't question – indeed, I was proud to be given a great task.'

He paused, and all present held their breath, caught up in his story.

'I was ordered to slay Antonin Meiros.'

Strangled cries came from everyone in the room, but most especially those of the Ordo Costruo. Odessa's face was bewildered, Rene's flummoxed; all of them looked appalled, looking at each other for guidance.

Then one of the young women, the blonde girl, screamed and threw herself at Kazim.

Elena grabbed her; the girl was too enraged to stop so she flipped her and slammed her on her back. 'HOLD!' she shouted. The room reverberated to her cry as shields kindled on all sides. She glared at Rene. 'Open-minds, Magister! It's a core tenet of your order!'

The Ordo Costruo Magister's eyes narrowed, but he raised his hands and the rest of his people, while not exactly relaxing, settled to await developments. But the girl Elena was holding wasn't the only one with hatred in her eyes.

'Afterwards, I was stationed at the Krak di Condotiori,' Kazim went on. 'I killed one of your number, and I aided in your capture – I am sorry for that, now.'

'You're *sorry*?' Clematia wailed. 'You murdered our Lord and helped destroy us and you're *sorry*—'

'I was raised to view you and your kind as enemies ... afreet, even,' Kazim replied evenly. 'I believed the shihad to be a glorious thing.'

'Like a *Crusade*,' Elena put in, as they all opened their mouths to protest. That shut a number of them up. She looked down at the winded girl on the floor. 'Are you going to play nicely now?'

'Fuck you,' the girl wheezed.

'Lunetta,' Clematia said warningly. 'We're Ordo Costruo.'

'I'm not,' Valdyr said, coming to his feet. 'We've been rescued by monsters. That's not a rescue at all.'

'Then perhaps I'll lock you back up and leave you here,' Kazim snapped. 'Perhaps you'd prefer that, *chotia*? On your back with a girl on top: better than fighting, yes?'

'I'll kill you for that, mudskin,' Valdyr snarled at him, his pale, haughty face looking almost bestial. But he didn't move, not yet.

There was a ghost of fear at the back of his eyes, a haunted quality Elena had seen on the faces of many young women but seldom a man . . .

Rape victim . . . Even if it's by a girl, and you're chained to a bed, you're still the victim. The Mollachian was just a boy; he had been humiliated, made to perform, over and over again. He'd doubtless been mocked and teased, beaten, maybe other things. His self-respect had been crushed.

'Valdyr,' she said sympathetically, 'we're not your enemies.'

The young man didn't take his eyes from Kazim, his aggression wavered, as if he'd just recalled everything that he'd been told of Kazim's gnostic strength. Crusader honour commanded him to attack anyway, but each passing second visibly leeched at his resolve. Elena waited him out, and when he wilted, the tension in the room eased noticeably.

They were all waiting for guidance, she realised, confused by the weight of everything that had been revealed. She couldn't blame them, but she focused on Rene Cardien, spoke silently into his mind.

<Sorry Lord Cardien, we're not exactly shining knights riding to the rescue. But we have rescued you. Let's not lose sight of that, shall we? I'll take over our story.>

At his faint nod she went on aloud: 'Kazim and I were thrown together in Javon. He forsook the shihad and joined the struggle of the Javonesi against the Dorobon invaders. I was the protector of the Javon queen – we have killed many Dorobon, in the name of freedom for Javon.'

'What care we for Javon—?' Sir Beglyn began, but Cardien cut him off.

'Your name is known to us, Elena Anborn,' Cardien said. He looked at Kazim with heavy reproach. 'I weep at the damage you caused our Order, young man. Antonin Meiros was a great man.'

'Blame Rashid Mubarak,' Kazim told him calmly. 'He pulled my strings and I danced.' He lowered his gaze. 'When I slew Antonin Meiros, I gained an insight into his nature. I had believed him to be Shaitan himself . . . but he wasn't. From that moment, I doubted everything I'd ever been told. And then I met Alhana . . .' He stretched out his left hand and touched her. 'Everything changed for me then.'

The rescued magi looked at each other, bewildered, but at least they were now seeing that there was another side to this issue. Elena allowed Clematia to help Lunetta to a seat and Valdyr shuffled backwards, his shoulders crumpling. Silence fell again, though Elena could sense debate between them.

At last Cardien turned back to her. 'Lady Elena, what is it you are here to achieve?'

More explanation: the situation in Javon, her certainty that it was to be the new permanent base for the Rondians in Antiopia, and the battle raging even now in Forensa – if it wasn't already over – that would most likely see the end of Javon's self-rule. 'I am Javonesi now,' she said. 'I'm here for them.'

'We're the Ordo Costruo,' Clematia sniffed. 'We don't take sides in wars.'

Elena focused on Rene. 'My Lord, the Javonesi Regency Council have authorised me to offer you the following terms for your aid: the eternal bequeathing of the Krak di Condotiori to your Order as your new base. The protection of the Javon Crown. And a permanent seat upon the ruling council of Javon.'

Cardien didn't reject the offer out of hand, which she took as a good sign. 'In return for what?'

'Aid against Tomas Betillon and the Dorobon, and Gurvon Gyle's mercenaries.'

'To fight *against the empire* in Javon?' Sir Beglyn asked derisively. 'You must be insane, woman! Look what the Kore-bedamned shihad has done to us!'

'Look what your Crusades did to Dhassa and Kesh!' she snapped back. She turned back to Rene. 'Javon is an independent kingdom, Magister. They're offering you sanctuary in your time of need. Their cause is just. Who else is going to take you in? The empire hates you and so do the Keshi!'

'And if we refuse?' Beglyn demanded. 'I'm not Ordo Costruo myself.'

'No, you're not,' Odessa snapped at him. 'You're a Crusader, who thinks it's your right to march into Dhassa and take whatever isn't nailed down. I don't care what you do – you can go to Hel for all I care.'

'*HOLD!*' Elena was forced to shout again. She turned to Beglyn. 'You are free to go where you will. We'll even give you a skiff. Javon doesn't want people who think that the right to freedom doesn't extend beyond Yurosians.'

'I didn't say that,' Beglyn snarled, but Valdyr shouted, 'I'll never take a damned Noorie's side! *Never!*'

Rene Cardien stood, and the weight of his authority as presumptive leader of the Ordo Costruo – everyone knew he'd been Antonin Meiros' heir – meant they all fell silent again. 'Lady Elena, these are hard matters: your nature, your history – yes, I know about you and Gurvon Gyle, Lady – and there are Master Makani's deeds . . . all these things colour what would be a difficult and complex choice in any event. We need to talk openly among ourselves. Will you give us leave to do so?'

She sighed. 'Of course. We want your *willing* aid, Magister Cardien. Nothing else has value. But we cannot give you long: those Hadishah who escaped will be informing their superiors. This place won't be safe for long.'

While the rescued magi talked amongst themselves, Kekropius went outside to ensure that his people had set a watch, and to oversee the arrival of the windship. Kazim retrieved Molmar's skiff from the rooftop, while Elena saw to the Keshi pilot himself. She found him on a bed which had broken chains at each corner, staring into space. Someone had dressed his burns and given him a sedative. She checked the wounds and found them well-cared for.

Molmar watched her distantly, then reached out and put a hand on hers. 'I have done as you asked, Lady: I have betrayed my oaths, for you.'

'Believe me, Molmar, I know how that feels,' she said. 'I don't ask you to take pride in it. I think you've done the right thing, but right and wrong are not easy to measure in such choices.'

'I know. I was born in a place like this, Lady, thirty-five years ago, after the First Crusade. I grew up like those children out there, believing everything that I was told of the evil of the magi, yet knowing that I was one myself. I've been dealing with that contradiction all my life. It strains my faith on days like this.'

Elena realised he needed a listener, so remained silent.

'It's hard to believe one is a good person when the Godspeakers preach each and every day that your blood is evil,' Molmar continued. 'So I ask myself continually: can a person be *born* evil? I cannot allow myself to believe it is so. I want to believe that I am a good man.'

'I believe evil is a choice,' Elena said carefully. 'But some take to it easier than others.'

'Truly,' Molmar agreed. 'I have met people whose future evil is apparent from a young age. Some are so predisposed to harm others that it is impossible to see them and not believe in inherent evil. Gatoz was such a one: causing hurt gave him pleasure from the time he could crawl.'

'Nurture or nature, we call this quandary. No one knows the true answer.'

'That is understandable, but I believe I know now what the answer is *not*,' Molmar replied. 'We should never condemn an entire race – or a religion – as evil. Such generalisations are clearly wrong. It is individual deeds that we must judge, in the context they are made. It is a harder path, stripped of the simplicity that princes and priests love.' He gestured to indicate the compound. 'I have no issue with Rashid wanting magi of his own, to aid the shihad against the unjust Crusade. He can screw as many willing girls as will have him for all I care. But to condone rape and forced begetting: that is a line we should never have crossed.'

'Desperate times make desperate men,' Elena replied. 'If the Rondian Empire had not invaded the East . . .'

'Rashid Mubarak instituted the breeding-houses well before your Crusades, Lady Alhana,' Molmar replied in a low voice. 'He always planned to move against his own Order.' He pulled a copper brooch from his pocket: a jackal head. He looked at it sadly, then threw it into the corner of the room. 'I'm with you now, Lady. There is no going back.'

An hour later Rene Cardien and Odessa D'Ark found her sitting beside the compound gate. She was watching the remaining soldiers herding the pregnant women and the young children away into the night, towards the nearest village. Their torches were receding down the valley. *We don't murder children.*

'Well?' she asked coolly, though her heart was pounding.

Rene puffed himself up a little, and said, 'Lady Elena, we of the Ordo Costruo agree to the terms offered by the Regent of Javon.'

'We'll fight for our right to exist,' Odessa put in darkly. 'Even alongside the likes of you and your Dokken.'

I guess we're not going to be blood-sisters after all, Elena reflected.

'The former Crusaders will not be joining us,' Cardien went on. 'Sir Beglyn, Valdyr and the rest wish to seek the Rondian Army. But we Ordo Costruo will accompany you to Javon.'

Elena closed her eyes and thanked whoever was listening.

Hold on, Cera. We're coming as fast as we can.

18

Crocodiles

Rivers of Urte

Like the oceans, the rivers of Urte are subject to tidal change, but the effects are far less dramatic, as the moon's influence is not so marked on smaller bodies of water. It is upon rivers and lakes that man has learned to float and to sail, and indeed, riverboats have provided the model for windships. Rivers have been the arteries of trade on Urte for centuries, and more goods are shipped on any major river than all of the windfleets together.

ORDO COSTRUO COLLEGIATE, PONTUS, 896

Riverdown, near Vida, southern Kesh, on the continent of Antiopia
Zulhijja (Decore) 929
18th month of the Moontide

Ramon stared blearily across the Tigrates River. Half the army was in the water swimming, and he was on crocodile-watch. The giant reptiles, realising there was meat in the water all the time here now, were hovering on the fringes. Anyone with a touch of Animagery had to take their turn on duty, day and night, to keep them at bay. They'd lost three men before realising the danger; since then they'd killed about two dozen of the beasts, enough to deter most of them ... but sometimes one got desperate.

Crocodile meat fell somewhere between fish and chicken, with – in Ramon's opinion – the better points of neither. But fresh meat was hard to come by at the moment so no one was complaining.

He yawned, wondering how long until he'd be relieved. He'd been up most of the last few nights, using Baltus' repaired windskiff to scout upriver, seeking some way out of this trap, but the problem with night-flights was that one really couldn't see very much. He yawned again, and rubbed his eyes.

'Buongiorno,' Lanna drawled in a really bad Rimoni accent, settling beside him.

'Shh,' he replied, touching his temple to show he was concentrating. 'They like to sneak in underwater. They're tricky bastards, crocodiles.'

'Really? Are they Silacian crocodiles?'

He laughed and threw up his hands. '*Rukka mio*! How can I concentrate?' They shared a look. He'd been helping in the infirmary a lot recently, in exchange for a cot in the corner, as Severine had made it plain she didn't want him around. It was awkward and embarrassing, and none of the other magi knew how to talk about it. He and Lanna weren't precisely friends yet, but he'd proven himself willing and able to help out when he could, and she seemed to be thawing a little.

'How was last night?' he asked. The flow of wounded had slowed to a trickle, but the long-term cases and the usual mishaps of army life kept Lanna and Carmina busy.

'Dull. Seven more dysentry cases, and a dozen afflicitons I can't even name. And an Estellan archer was brought in at midnight, too far gone to save. A scorpion bite, we think. We need to warn the men about checking their boots again.'

'It never ends, does it?'

'That's the lot of the healer-mage: on duty all the time, performing miracles as a matter of course, and given the blame if the soldier dies, even if it wasn't our fault. Oh, and we get half the pay of a battle-mage.'

'Not in this army.'

'Really? Who put you in charge of pay?'

'I mean it: you'll get the same, or more. I'm going to make sure of that.'

'Mmm. I'm told you've got all sorts of gold and treasure secreted away somewhere?'

He tapped his nose. 'Don't tell the rankers. They'll be paid too, but I don't want a riot before then.'

'Your secret's safe with me.' She studied him, frowning. 'You know, this is the first Crusade where I've actually felt valued by the battle-magi. Duprey took me completely for granted, right down to the usual sordid approaches.'

Ramon wrinkled his nose. 'I'm sorry to hear that. I kind of liked Duprey.'

'He was an arsehole. Most people are.' She looked away gloomily. The Keshi attacks might have ended three weeks ago, but they were still pinned in Riverdown, supplies were beginning to run low and the far bank was still patrolled by Kirkegarde. The Keshi were dug in around them, having erected their own earthworks and fences to keep them penned inside. Morale was holding up though, buoyed by their successful defence.

'How's Jelaska?' Ramon asked, dropping his voice.

'She's not taking it well.'

Jelaska had been in decline since Baltus Prenton's death; she'd been sleeping badly and was oozing gnostic power in her sleep, calling ghosts from the aether while unconscious. They'd had to start sedating her, but Lanna's stores of those particular herbs were running low.

'She's a tough old bird,' Ramon replied, 'and I'm sure she doesn't believe in curses any more than we do.'

'Perhaps. I know she's tired of losing people. She just wants to go home, like the rest of us. Except me, of course. I like it here. I'm thinking of staying: I'd put my villa on this rise, and the dock for my luxury barge just here.'

'You wouldn't want to go downstream any further. This army has poisoned the river for decades to come.' He grinned. 'So, you're going to capitalise on our popularity in these parts, are you?'

'Mmm. The Keshi love us so much they won't let us leave,' she said drily.

Suddenly Lanna was hurled twenty yards into the river, landing with a violent splash. The roar of kinetic gnosis slammed Ramon sideways and he rolled to his feet, utterly bewildered, as Lanna came up out of the water, spluttering with outrage.

Severine Tiseme was stamping towards him, her little round face livid. *'I'm sick of seeing you and that raddled harlot together!'* she shrieked, storming to the water's edge and slamming more kinetic energy at Lanna. This time Lanna shielded, but Sevvie's blood was far stronger and she slammed the healer over backwards and under again. *'Keep away from my man, you ancient whore!'*

All along the foreshore the rankers had stopped swimming and were staring, caught between amusement and fear of being caught in the middle of a mage-duel. Severine was fully shielding as Lanna came up again, her thin smock clinging to her in a way that had the men whistling. Her normally placid face was set with anger. She stalked out of the river, holding her head up. 'I will not make a spectacle of myself with the likes of you,' she said to Severine.

'That's because you only know how to go behind people's backs,' Severine declared loudly.

Lanna's face went red and she poked a finger at Severine. 'Don't make an enemy of me, princess.'

'You don't frighten me. You've got wrinkly old-woman hands,' she added spitefully.

Lanna's face burned a deeper scarlet, but she had little skill in offensive gnosis, and weaker blood than Severine. She backed a step, looked at Ramon with a withering look that said *Thanks for your help*, and walked away, her back straight.

Ramon saw Severine contemplate shoving the healer in the back and intervened with a touch of the gnosis that disrupted her control. She whirled on him, her eyes blazing. 'As for you, you slimy rodent – I know all about you!'

'What? I haven't—'

'Lying rat!' She stomped away, leaving him with about a thousand gawking soldiers grinning from ear to ear.

For a minute he just stood there, torn between trying to fix his reputation with either woman, and staying put to look out for crocodiles . . . and to wait for one particular contact.

In the end he just sat down, ignored the smirking soldiers and sulked, the pleasure gone from the day.

The contact he'd been expecting didn't come for another hour, but at last there was a gentle touch in his mind. He responded immediately. *<About time,>* he sent in Rimoni.

<You think this is easy? There are Quizzies all over this bank.> The sender, a mage-agent named Silvio Anturo, sounded uncharacteristically edgy for a familioso enforcer, but then, he wasn't usually enforcing Inquisitors. He wasn't a Retiari man, but an agent of the Petrossi, a rival gang the Retiari were currently cooperating with. He and Ramon had been in contact sporadically for several days now, and Ramon was a little surprised it had taken the man this long to find him.

<We need to meet,> Anturo sent. *<My patrona, Isabella Petrossi, is growing impatient. You claim the promissory note game has been lucrative, but then you vanished for a year. That nearly precipitated a war between you Retiari and we Petrossi. Isabella wants to know: where is the damned gold?>*

<Let me reassure you: the gold is safe.>

The relief that exploded through Anturo's brain was palpable. *<Where is it? In your camp?>*

<Some, but not all,> Ramon lied. *<But we're in a bit of a hole right now.>*

<The legion is.> Anturo sniffed. *<I can get you out, no problem.>*

<Of course – I could leave whenever I like . . . but not with twenty wagons of gold!> Though when it came down to it, Ramon didn't want to leave the legion behind. They were his boys, and the other magi were friends now. His daughter was here. And Sevvie, for what that was worth at the moment.

<I have more than enough men here to drive twenty wagons,> Anturo replied. *<Come on, Sensini, the Retiari must have a plan for extracting you! It was your own people's idea: lure the Rondian pompinari in with promises and fleece them. You must have an extraction plan!>*

Ramon baited his hook. *<Si, si. Of course we do. But listen, Anturo, are you happy with your cut?>*

The link went silent. Ramon could almost hear the other man's brain cranking through the possibilities until he whispered, a little unnecessarily, <*Are you serious, Sensini? You really want to rukk over both familioso?*>

<*Who's taken all the risks? You and I, Anturo. We're in the desert swallowing flies while Pater-Retiari and Mater-Petrossi are at home drinking vino. Who's earned this?*>

<*But . . . The whole of two familioso would come after us . . .* >

<*Would they? If the word went out that you and I had screwed them over brazenly and had all the money? I rather think we'd be flooded with men joining us. We could set up our own familioso, you and me. We're* magi, *Anturo! We're scarier than anyone they could send against us.*>

Another pause then, as Anturo struggled to take this in. His loyalties clearly went deeper than Ramon's, but then, Isabella Petrossi was his aunt. She'd purchased a week with a Rondian half-blood for her sister, and Anturo was the progeny of that union. But for many familioso agents, time in service bred cynicism.

<*Even were I to agree . . . Pater-Retiari has your mother and sister!*>

Ramon affected a sneer. <*My mother is a tavern-girl and my half-sister is Pater-Retiari's. What of them?*>

<*I didn't think you to be so cold, Sensini.*>

<*Try being stuck behind enemy lines in this damned desert and see how loving you feel to those who sent you! I want out, with the rewards I deserve. But those pezzi di merda in Retia don't understand. They think hardship is having to pour their own drinks, my rukking mother included!*> He winced at his own words, but the conviction in his voice never wavered as he reeled Silvio in. <*Silvio: you don't need to decide now; just think about it.*>

Silvio Anturo was silent for a long time, then spoke in just the way Ramon had wanted; with indecision, heavily tinged with greed. <*You're a sly culo, Sensini, but I like the way you think.*>

If he'd leaped at the offer, Ramon would have smelled a rat. Dio mio, I'm plausible sometimes . . . <*Then do we have a deal, Silvio?*>

<*Maybe.*> Anturo fell silent again. <*Oh, and I may know a way to get your legion out of that camp.*>

Other people weren't so keen on the way Ramon thought. He went looking for Severine as night fell, finding her as usual in the women's camp, cooking while watching over a sleeping Julietta. She looked wretched, her face tear-stained and grimy, her ringlets limp and dull. She smelled like she hadn't washed in weeks. There were moths swirling in clouds about the lamps and flies crawling over the uncooked food, but she wasn't even mustering the gnostic energy to drive them away.

There was no welcome in her eyes when he hunkered down beside her. And he was still angry at her for that scene beside the river, angry enough not to care if this was it between them. 'What was all that about?' he demanded. 'Lanna and I have done *nothing*.'

'Oh please! You're sleeping in the healers' tent! The whole damned legion knows it! It's *humiliating*!'

'I'm *helping out*, Sevvie! And I have to sleep somewhere!' He gestured futilely. 'I'm not sleeping with her, I swear it – although why you care, I don't know. You don't want me – you never have. All you wanted was a child, and now you've got one.'

'She's yours too,' she snapped. 'Not that you care.'

'Of course I care! I see her every moment I can!'

Severine snorted, looked away. 'Why the healer? She's thirty! She's *plain*.' They glared at each other, then her face softened. 'Don't you abandon me, Ramon Sensini. I'm a *Tiseme*: no one leaves me!'

'Then why don't you do the leaving,' he snapped. 'Go ahead, if your pride is all you care about! Go ahead!' He spun and stamped away.

The parley flag came as a surprise, after weeks in which the enemy did no more than pen them in; they'd stopped bothering with even sporadic archery. But one afternoon a white flag was waved by a skinny Keshi boy trotting towards their lines: a well-dressed lad in embroidered silks and wearing a dapper red turban – a sheik's son, maybe. He brought a message for Seth, written on white scented parchment, requesting an audience. It bore the insignia of Salim I of Kesh.

Seth found he couldn't think straight after reading it.

General Seth Korion,

I send my greetings, and request a parley, between our lines, tomorrow.

I wish to discuss the situation of your army, and seek a resolution to this impasse.

Salim of Kesh

'It's not him,' Ramon maintained. The Silacian had been very subdued for the past few days; there'd been some massive argument with Severine about Lanna Jureigh. Seth had considered weighing in, then decided not to get caught in the middle; he was disappointed in all of them.

Most of the Keshi had left the enemy camp and marched north, taking most of the royal banners with them. But there was still one large pavilion across the way, and the sultan's personal flag flew over it. They'd decided it was worth hearing what the sultan, or more likely one of his impersonators, wanted.

The meeting was arranged for the middle ground between the armies, in a pavilion the Keshi built then abandoned so that the Rondians could inspect it before agreeing the meeting. The tent was a big, airy affair in white and gold. The Keshi had set up two low divans with a table between, laid with platters of fruit and set with wine goblets. Chaplain Gerdhart had checked earlier for poisons and hidden dangers and found all in order.

Seth Korion walked into the pavilion in trepidation. He sat, helped himself to a grape, then stood up again and paced until the flap on the opposite side of the pavilion opened and a man in his late twenties stepped through.

Seth caught his breath. '*Latif?*'

He had to look closer to ensure it was indeed the man they'd held prisoner in Ardijah for two months, during which time he'd become someone Seth considered a friend: someone with whom he could talk poetry and music, someone who shared his sense of humour, and who was blessed with a bewitchingly exotic face.

'Are you sure?' Latif smiled, embracing him, kissing his lips briefly in the Keshi way, patting the small of his back. As ever, his Rondian was perfect. 'I have many impersonators, after all.' He winked drolly.

Seth held him at arm's length, drank in every detail. 'Of course I'm sure. Though it must be confusing for your people to have Salim apparently here and also away in the north?'

Latif's eyes twinkled. 'News crawls here, my friend. You magi speak across the miles, but most news takes months to travel a few miles, during which time it is garbled beyond comprehension. "Salim is here, Salim is there": this is normal. All of the impersonators speak with one voice. To all intents and purposes, we're all Salim.'

'I can't imagine Emperor Constant ruling that way.' Seth laughed. 'Well, "Salim", to what do I owe this pleasure?'

'Affairs of state, I'm afraid.' Latif waved a genial hand about the pavilion. 'I'm sorry I cannot welcome you to my court and show you how a true ruler hosts a guest.' He raised his eyebrows ironically, in clear reference to his own incarceration in Ardijah at Seth's hands.

'We were trapped in a little town – come to Bricia and I'll show you how a Rondian noble lives!'

'Would that I could.' Latif shrugged eloquently. 'But we must make do, must we not? Look, here there is good wine – from Bricia! Plunder from your army at Shaliyah. It's a vernierre, and cooled in the river upstream: you're favourite, is it not?'

They poured goblets, clinked them together and took seats opposite each other, still exchanging small talk, with the slightest tension that came of having to leave much unsaid. The impersonator looked rested and full of energy. Seth knew that he himself didn't: he felt ground down by the tension and cares of command.

If I were alone, I'd just lie down on this divan and close my eyes . . .

'So, what's this matter of state?' he asked, sipping the cool, cleansing wine, a treat for his parched senses.

'Well, my friend, I regret that I must request your surrender.'

'After the battering we inflicted last time you attacked?'

'But still you are trapped. Your food supplies are running very low, yes? And though your miraculous healers toil, disease must be a growing threat.'

All of which was very true. Seth looked away.

Latif went on in a regretful voice, 'Very soon, in desperation, you will be forced to try and break out: ten thousand men, with attendant baggage train and camp followers, trying to break across open ground into archers who outnumber you three to one. It will be a slaughter, my friend.'

Yes, it would be, if that were our intention.

'Seth,' Latif went on, 'if you surrender, we will be merciful. You and your magi will be taken as Salim's personal prisoners: Chainrunes, of course, but not handed over to the Hadishah and their breeding-camps. Your rankers will be disarmed and imprisoned, but only until the end of the Moontide, after which they will be released into Rondian hands.'

'And the camp followers?'

'You must know that any woman who has sullied herself with a Rondian is not welcome anywhere. They will be sold as slaves. Such a life is not so bad, for a woman.'

Dear Kore, does he really think that? 'That's out of the question. Those women are wives now, and entitled to the protection of their husbands.'

'Don't pretend these women will be welcomed in Yuros,' Latif retorted.

'They won't be enslaved.'

'No? What is a wife but an unpaid domestic slave? What is a warwife but a trophy? Do not try to tell me there is any true feeling between your soldiers and the women they've taken.'

'You'd be surprised,' Seth replied. 'I was. Once I thought as you did, that between East and West there could be no love. But now I see things differently. These women had no kind of life in Ardijah: they were the downtrodden – widows, slaves, outcasts, beggars, for whom there were no better options than a foreign soldier. This isn't unique to Khotri: there are many like them in Antiopia, and in Yuros also. Why shouldn't they risk marrying a foreign soldier in the hope of a better life?'

Latif frowned, settled back on his divan and considered. 'Your point is fair,' he admitted eventually. 'All right, what if I also guaranteed the lives and safety of those women who wish to remain with their "husbands"?'

Ah, so that threat was just leverage ... I wish you and I didn't have to play these games, Latif ...

Seth sat up. 'I'm sorry, but we're *not* going to surrender. We've marched from Shaliyah through Khotri to reach our lines. We'll not let this predicament deter us. We'll find a way.'

'We understand that your own army have blocked you from crossing the Tigrates?'

'Then you heard wrong.'

They fell silent, looking at each other.

Damn this war, Seth found himself thinking.

Latif sighed, affecting nonchalance. 'Then if you will not see sense, at least find some relaxation for a moment. You look tired, my friend: so drink, eat! This fruit is fresh. It is the best to be had this side of the river, and you might not taste its like again for some time.'

'I've lost my appetite. Though if I could take some back for my men?'

Latif gestured his assent affably. 'Of course.' He clapped his hands with forced cheer. 'Well, how are you keeping? Do you still have time to read?'

'No – well, not poetry or literature, anyway. Despatches, supply-lists, hospital reports, scouting reports. I've had to put pleasure aside for a while. We're at war, after all.' Seth thought about the stack of parchment on his desk. *I could get through some of that pile, if I return early*. Abruptly, he stood. 'I must go.'

Latif looked taken aback. 'My friend? Our aides have agreed a meeting of four hours at the least. What is the hurry? Let us relax and enjoy some time together. I can even send for my jitar?'

It was tempting. *I could just put all this damned stress behind me, forget about where I'm stuck and how much shit I'm in* ... But he shook his head. 'No. I have work to do. I'm sorry, I truly am.'

Latif began to reach out, then stopped and withdrew his hand. 'Undoubtedly you are right.'

What's changed? Seth wondered. *Is it because there was no need or point in talking about the war when we were in Ardijah? Or is it because I'm not the one in control any more? Am I that shallow?*

Or is it just this Kore-bedamned war?

Their farewell was perfunctory, and he walked away without looking back.

'So,' Ramon Sensini greeted him when he returned, 'how is your friend the Fake?'

'Very well. He thinks we're helpless and doomed unless we beg for mercy.'

The Silacian smiled for the first time in several days. 'Now, about that . . .'

Southern Kesh, on the continent of Antiopia
Moharram (Janune) 930
19th month of the Moontide

Ramon took the windskiff in low, skimming the water. The craft was handling sluggishly due to the outriggers and empty kegs they'd fixed to the hull to make the craft riverworthy. They'd blackened the sails and the hull with ash, renaming her *Blackbird* as they did. Baltus Prenton wouldn't have recognised her.

The dead Brevian was very much on Ramon's mind, not only as this was his old craft, but because his last lover was in the prow. Jelaska Lyndrethuse had roused from her listless mourning with a new grimness, her long, morose face expressionless, her eyes remote. She was ready for action, she claimed.

Ready to kill someone, more likely.

'Brace yourself,' he called. 'I'm bringing her in to land.'

He took the craft lower, dissipating Air-gnosis until the keel caught in the water, the new outriggers splashing down and carving furrows until momentum was lost. They held their breath, but the craft settled. They'd tested it, of course, but this was the real thing and they were far from Riverdown.

When it became clear the skiff wasn't about to capsize and sink, Jelaska said, 'Well done, Magister Sensini. What now?'

'We visit some shady characters.'

'I'm sure you'll feel right at home,' she observed.

Ramon had been hesitant about taking anyone else on this negotiation, but Seth had insisted. It meant opening up to the Argundian woman a little about the gold hidden in the legion's baggage carts, though he'd kept the details light. He wasn't sure how much she believed him.

Their destination was downstream a little, and though he was unused to sailing on water, the dull gleam of the town's lamps soon appeared. Yazqheed was a small river-port between Vida and Peroz that hadn't been on any of their maps. And they hadn't known about the Keshi river-traders, either – apparently even the Sultan of Kesh was unaware of this enterprising group of men. Ramon had found both a week ago, thanks to Silvio Anturo's guidance.

In both Yuros and Antiopia, the rivers, unlike the oceans, played a vital role in travel and commerce, both goods and people. The tidal movements were nowhere near as extreme and deadly as the ocean's, so the rivers and canals were both much safer and more predictable. Riverboat fleets in the West probably transported more in a month in Yuros than the windfleets did in a year. In Antiopia, which had no real windfleet, the waterways were even more important.

When Duke Echor's southern army marched into southern Kesh, they'd seized and garrisoned the major river-ports like Vida, but the Keshi rivermen, anticipating this move, had gone to earth in the smaller ports to wait out the Crusade. It kept their ships safe, though it meant two years without proper income.

So I'm sure there'll be a few who'd like a little side-job . . .

He sent a gnostic pulse ahead to alert Silvio. Involving the Petrossi mage had helped cement the trust between them; they were now actively collaborating.

Sailing on water was quite different to flying, but Ramon got them to the edge of the massive flotilla on the east bank of the Tigrates. Most of the riverboats were bobbing at anchor, for the docks were too small to cope with this many vessels. The bigger ships were wedged together so closely you could walk from one to the next with little difficulty. There were hundreds of small tiller-craft at the fringes, for running errands up and down the river. His own vessel was one of many sailing after dark. The sultan's soldiers might hold the township, but the port of Yazqheed was ruled by the rivermen.

<Sensini?> Silvio called. *<Make for the blue lantern at the north end.>*

<I see it.> Ramon steered for the bobbing lantern while Jelaska scanned for trouble, listening in on the surface thoughts of any minds that focused on them. Her eyes were glinting with pale light, but she didn't look overly perturbed.

He took the skiff into the shadow of the lantern-boat and looked up.

'Sensini?' The mage appeared at the rails above. Ramon recognised him from their scrying: a narrow, well-formed face framed by long curling hair. His mother, Isabella Petrossi's sister, had been a famed beauty. 'Who's with you?' Silvio demanded. 'You're supposed to be alone.'

'Buona notte, Silvio. Relax! This is Jelaska Lyndrethuse.'

Anturo looked taken aback, but recovered well. 'An honour, Lady.'

Jelaska smiled as sweetly as her face allowed. 'The pleasure is mine, Master Anturo. Or it will be, if you can give me a way to disembark from this damned tub.'

'Please, call me Silvio. Come, climb aboard. Your skiff will be safe here, I promise you. The captains await us.'

A rope ladder rolled down the flank of the ship and Jelaska led the way. Ramon tied up the *Blackbird* and set wards before joining her.

He shook hands with Silvio Anturo, every bit the confident, impatient man he'd expected, then followed him through a maze of decks and ladders and masts and ropes, committing their route to memory. Eventually they came to a large fore-deck, where a dozen Keshi men in well-worn robes were gathered. All were bearded and sun-darkened, with grey in their hair. They eyed the Yurosian magi with undisguised worry, but the scent of gold was in the air too, and they had the sniff of it.

Silvio addressed the group in Keshi; Ramon knew enough of the local tongue to get the gist: introductions, and the promise of an opportunity, and the men all looked interested. It had been a lean season.

The Petrossi agent introduced Ramon and Jelaska as *guklu jadugari*, which were formidable things, judging by the captains' nervous reactions. Then he handed over to Ramon and turned translator.

'It's a simple enough job,' Ramon told them. 'Yazqheed is four days upstream of my soldiers. We're low on provisions, but we have much gold. Sail down, ship my men and baggage train across the Tigrates in a single night, and you'll be paid – and well paid, too.'

The captains proved to have little loyalty to their sultan. After some private discussion, they had but one question: 'How much?'

He offered them each the value of their craft and what Silvio had assured him would be three months' income, and bargained hard, lest they begin to think they could get too greedy, allowing himself to be pushed to six months' income. It was an insane amount of money for them, but it would barely dent his funds.

I want to make sure every single ranker gets paid when we get home, he reminded himself. The deal left enough, though Jelaska, was worried.

<Have you really got this much?> she enquired silently.

<Just about.>

<'Just'?> She fixed him with a chilly stare.

'What of the sultan?' one captain asked. 'If he learns who helped you to escape, we'll all be dead men.'

'That's why I'm offering you the value of your craft as well,' Ramon replied, 'in case you have to abandon them and go into hiding. If I were you I'd sail south until you're well out of his reach – but the truth is, he's got bigger problems than you.'

After the logistical discussion, and the all-important agreement on payment – one third upfront, the rest on completion – Ramon then had a few questions of his own, about how many ships it would take to move fifteen thousand souls and their stores in one night, and whether they could also purchase more food and supplies once they were on the west bank of the Tigrates. Then they were asked to wait patiently at the other end of the deck while the captains conferred amongst themselves.

'They'll go for it,' Ramon told Jelaska and Silvio confidently as the men huddled together to decide. 'I'll bet they've been squabbling over bit-jobs and smuggling runs for at least a year. They've clearly got no loyalty to Salim, and by the look of them their boats are in need of attention after being tied up so long. They're in.'

'Then all of the money really is in your camp?' Silvio asked.

'No,' Ramon lied, 'this will take all that I have to hand: I've been caching it in the desert, all the way along our route – both before and after Shaliyah,' he added. 'I had to do so, otherwise my logisti-calus tribune would have noticed something.'

Well, Storn would have, if he hadn't been in it up to his eyeballs anyway!

'I still don't see why you insist on bringing the legions across,' Silvio complained.

Ramon saw Jelaska's face harden and answered quickly, 'Because I'm thinking ahead, *partner*. We're going to want loyal men after the Crusade, aren't we? Who could be more loyal than men who owe us their lives? There are always a few in any army who can't settle back into civilian life after a war. They'll think of us first.'

Silvio smiled appreciatively. 'You always play the longer game, don't you Sensini?' He looked at Jelaska. 'And Lady Lyndrethuse is part of your arrangement?'

'Clearly.'

Jelaska proved she too could play the game, giving Silvio a hard, knowing smile.

'Small groups need a threat that others respect,' Ramon said. 'I think a pure-blood sorceress of Lady Jelaska's reputation provides that, don't you?'

'Is she a full partner?'

'Oh, Ramon's the boss,' Jelaska said airily. 'He and I have our own arrangement.' She fluttered her eyelids coyly, making Silvio's eyebrows shoot up.

<Thanks for that,> Ramon sent sarcastically. Jelaska smirked and looked away.

Ramon was right; the captains agreed to take part, so they settled down over some food for several hours of serious planning, sorting out which vessels would go, the timing, number of men and wagons per craft, and most importantly as far as the rivermen were concerned, how the bullion would be exchanged. The fleet would sail south laden with food and drop that at the chosen spot on the western shore before going on to pick up the legionaries. The next Darkmoon, two weeks away, at the end of Janune, was chosen, so that Mater Luna wouldn't reveal all to watching eyes.

'We need a signal in case there are Inquisitors or Kirkgarde on the western shore that night,' Ramon added. 'That'll be down to you, Silvio. I don't want those bastards wandering in while we're scattered between two camps and a mile of water.'

'I'll take care of it. I have contacts in Vida; a few fires inside the city walls in the days leading up to the move should keep them busy elsewhere.'

The meeting broke up soon afterwards and Silvio led them back to their skiff. The *Blackbird* still bobbed in the river, her wards undisturbed. The Petrossi mage turned to Ramon and they clasped hands. 'It's late for you to be returning to your camp, amici. I have a safe house outside Yazqheed where you and Lady Jelaska may rest.'

Ramon glanced sideways at Jelaska. They were supposed to be back by dawn, but Silvio was right; that wasn't very likely, not given the distances and the hour. He decided Silvio had no reason to betray them, not yet. 'Thank you, we accept gladly.'

<*Do we?*> Jelaska asked with an arch look.

He ignored that, and in a few minutes they were following Silvio Anturo's skiff in a southeasterly direction.

The safe house, an abandoned farmstead, had been quietly seized by Silvio Anturo and a small gang of his associates – a mix of Silacian and Dhassan men – and the locals left them alone, or so Anturo said. He gave Ramon and Jelaska adjoining chambers on the top floor, just along from his own. They declined the offer of supper and went to their separate, sparsely furnished rooms.

Ramon warded the doors and shutters, then, just to be sure, he did the walls, ceiling and floor too, though he doubted Anturo would try anything until after the gold was delivered. The adjoining door opened just as he went to snuff the lamp.

'I'm just checking that you're safe,' Jelaska said, brandishing a bottle of brandy and two pottery mugs.

'There's safety in numbers,' he agreed.

They pulled up chairs, toasted silently and drank. Ramon refilled the mugs as Jelaska reached inside her cloak and with ironic ceremony brandished a piece of paper; one of his own illegal promissory notes. 'That's Storn's handwriting, isn't it? With an Imperial Treasury Seal, a forged signature which looks rather like that of Calan Dubrayle, the Lord Treasurer – and it's dated Junesse 929. That's last year, when we were marching east to Shaliyah.' She looked at him wryly. 'So what's going on?'

He told her virtually the whole tale – he only left out the Scytale, and his true parentage; bad enough that Seth Korion knew. It took some time and several refills, and the eastern sky was pale by the time he'd explained it all.

'So apparently, the amount of investment from the old Imperial families has been ridiculous and now many face destitution,' he added with a smirk. 'So sad.'

'And you're doing all this just to free your mother and half-sister?' Jelaska asked, her voice sceptical.

'Si. And because I can,' he admitted. 'You must admit, it's more fun than just marching around a desert.'

'Why not just kidnap your mother and half-sister and run?'

'Because that wouldn't really damage the familioso. This hurts all manner of deserving people – or at least, it does provided I can keep the gold out of their hands.'

'Burying it would do that.'

'Si. The original plan was just to run away and live like a king somewhere. But even before Shaliyah, I began to feel responsible for the men. Then after Shaliyah – well, what can I say? They *are* my family. *My* familioso. And I want to see them get the rewards promised them. I want to see the demi-gods of Pallas sweat. I want to see these familioso thugs who prey on their own people *broken*. I can do that: I've been given that opportunity.'

'Good grief! Ramon Sensini is an idealist! Who'd ever have thought?'

'Oh, I'm full of surprises.'

She yawned. 'Well, young Ramon, that's a lot to absorb and no mistake.' She stood and ruffled his hair with a fond smile. 'I need some sleep, and I'm not going to do it in the same room as you: bad for both of our reputations, I don't doubt.' She jabbed a finger at him. 'I'll play along with being part of your conspiracy, but if you betray our boys back at the camp, I'll pursue you to the grave and beyond.'

He nodded meekly.

She snorted. 'I'm not fooled by you, Ramon Sensini. I know what manner of man you are.'

That worried him more than any threat.

Riverdown, near Vida, Southern Kesh, on the continent of Antiopia
Moharram (Janune) 929
19th month of the Moontide

The transfer of the Lost Legions to the western shore of the Tigrates took place on a still night, the stars giving just enough light for the men and women to safely embark from the makeshift docks the legion magi had thrown together. Seth and Ramon watched over them, standing with the last cohorts manning the walls, maintaining the illusion that this was just another quiet night in Riverdown.

'Once again you've got us out of a tight spot,' Seth said in a subdued voice as they joined the last men slipping away.

Ramon tried to appreciate the attempt to cheer him up, but he really didn't give a shit whether they all lived or died right now. 'This was baby stuff,' he said morosely. 'Even you could have done it.'

He was dimly aware of Seth clenching a fist then exhaling forcibly, but he was too far down misery creek to wonder why. 'We'll find Severine and your baby,' Seth said after a few moments.

'She can't have gone far,' Ramon muttered, although the truth was, he had a very real idea where Severine might have gone, and was scared he'd never see her or Julietta again.

He'd been exhausted when he and Jelaska got back to Riverdown. He knew they were late, but he hadn't expected to walk straight into another tirade from an overwrought Severine: a screeching, embarrassing and humiliating dress-down in front of half the army. But next morning the *Blackbird* was gone, and so were Severine and Julietta. No one had foreseen that, so there had been no one guarding the skiff. No one saw them leave, and no amount of scrying or gnostic calls was eliciting a response. He felt crushed and empty as a broken eggshell.

But there was more to be done. He looked up at Seth and felt for the minds of the magi on the boats, awaiting the signal. He'd planned one last surprise for the Keshi, a warning to them not to follow, and to ensure his men didn't have to suffer yet another archery barrage as they left.

'Do we proceed?' he asked quietly.

Seth looked chilled at the thought of what they had prepared. They'd initially conceived this as an emergency plan – something to throw at the Keshi if they were discovered mid-evacuation – but from there it had evolved into something more. 'It's not necessary,' he said. 'We're clean away.'

'It's a war, Seth,' Ramon said. 'If we kick them here, they'll not try so hard to follow us.'

They both looked down at the surface of the river, the gentle starlight illuminating the backs of the crocodiles, so many you could have crossed the Tigrates on their backs. Their eyes were gleaming, their tails steadily churning the water as they waited; there were occasional harrowing glimpses of teeth flashing. And that was just a part of what they'd planned.

Ramon waited. *Come on, Lesser Son*, he thought, *I want this. I want to know someone else is suffering too.*

Seth could doubtless feel the eagerness of his magi, poised to strike back at the enemy who had pinned them in the camp for so long. They all wanted to show what they could do – and perhaps he felt a little that way too. His own role in this wasn't small, after all. 'Very well, let's do it.'

'Great Sultan—! Please, waken!'

Latif stirred groggily, the insistent hammering on the gong and his aide's call dragging him back into the waking world, which was filled with noise: shouting and screaming, blaring trumpets and the hammering of spears on shields.

Are we under attack?

Rubbing at his eyes and shivering at the chill air, he desperately tried to focus. It was still dark, the lamps glowering like the eyes of jackals. 'What is happening?'

'The enemy—! They're *escaping*!'

'Where? *How?*'

'Ships, Great Sultan!' the aide babbled, handing him his robe.

'Windships?'

'No, Great Sultan, *riverboats*!' The aide sounded furious. '*Our own riverboats!* General Darhus is leading the attack – we can still catch most of them!'

Darhus was a veteran of two Crusades, with the scars of failure to prove it. He'd been descending into a morass of drink and bitterness until Shaliyah had rejuvenated him. He had been appointed to the command here when Salim went north.

Latif sat up. 'I need to see him – there will be a trap. I know these people.' He thought of the cunning one, Sensini, with a chill. 'We can't just rush in. Where is the general now?' He pulled the under-robe over his head as a dozen more aides flooded in to start the well-practised drill of dressing him fit to meet a visiting ambassador or king in a matter of minutes. But it felt like it was taking for ever, while all around him the clamour of men spoiling for a fight grew louder. Their fury was boiling over.

Finally he was ready, surging from the pavilion in a cloud of guardsmen out into the confusion of a waking camp. The cry went up: 'The Sultan comes! Salim is here!' Men crowded closer, trying to look purposeful and fierce.

He gestured to a senior aide, Barzin, a Mirobezan eunuch, a clever slave who had risen high in his service. 'Tell me what has happened – and what General Darhus is doing.'

'Great Sultan, our sentries saw torches in the enemy camp and we sent scouts closer; we found the enemy mustering, and boats on the river – a great flotilla, loading the *ferang* soldiers onboard.'

'Whose ships are they?'

'The rivermen, Great Sultan,' Barzin said, wincing.

We should have burned them out. 'Where is General Darhus?'

'He's leading the attack, Great Sultan.' The aide pointed towards the front lines, a seething mass of men, dimly lit by the torchlight, some hundred yards away. Beyond them a thin line of enemy torches lined the barricade. Just then trumpets blared again, sounding the charge, and the whole mass of men lurched forwards, shouting their war cries.

A frontal attack in the dark? It felt foolhardy . . . but if the Rondians were embarking, they'd be unable to man their walls and would finally be swept away. His fears hovered, though. *What might a Rondian mage achieve in such a situation?*

'Get me a horse,' he snapped at Barzin. 'I must be able to see.'

By the time his white mount had been saddled and brought over, the attack was underway, with a great deal of shouting and gesticulating as more and more men flooded forward, ignoring their officers in their eagerness to overrun and plunder the enemy camp. The assault was beyond recall; it was just a mob, the noblemen as out of control as the conscripts. He could see little from the ground, but once he had swung into the ornate, jewel-encrusted saddle on his mount's back, he was above the masses. He held the reins lightly and steadied his white gelding while trying to make sense of the ocean of movement around him. He felt like a twig in a whirlpool, swirling helplessly towards some dark end.

'Get us closer!' he shouted, and Barzin whipped his guards into movement, spearheading a way through the press, approaching the

Rondian barricades in fits and starts as the oblivious conscripts kept impeding his progress. The gelding, a riding horse not bred for war, was unhappy with the great mass of people, so Latif kept him to a walk to avoid crushing some poor soul. 'Faster! Clear a path! I want General Darhus!' he shouted to the oblivious soldiers.

The mob had reached the top of the Rondian barricades, waving their weapons triumphantly before being swept over the top and out of sight by the mass of men coming up behind. Everyone was jubilant and excited, and desperate for loot.

Then the earth *shook*, an alarming great rumble, so intense the gelding staggered, and all around him men grabbed at each other, many falling, all yelling in fear.

The ground shook again, harder this time.

Then the screaming started.

An hour later, Latif sat on his throne and awaited his commanding officers. A gong boomed and an aide stepped inside the pavilion, and dropped to his knees. 'Great Sultan, General Darhus awaits your pleasure.'

'Send him in. And the Hadishah captain – what was his name?'

'Selmir, Great Sultan,' Barzin said, walking down the long intricately patterned carpet to ensure the general and the Hadishah had been disarmed before escorting them to the throne. As the men prostrated themselves in front of their sultan, he withdrew to the desk to await further orders. A dozen guardsmen stood with bared blades as the general and the Hadishah knelt with their foreheads on the mat, as if they were slaves. Both were pale and shaken, fearing the consequences of failure – for they had most definitely failed.

Latif turned to Darhus, a man in his fifties with greying hair and beard, first. 'General, what are our losses?'

Darhus kept his face lowered. 'More than three thousand men, Great Sultan.'

Three thousand . . . Ahm forgive us!

'Great Sultan, the enemy were further advanced in their evacuation than we had thought,' he began in a plaintive voice. 'By the time we broke into their camp, they were already boarded on the river-boats and were standing off the shore – and then the earth shook, firepits opened, the land subsided and the river rushed in, full of crocodiles . . . thousands of them. My lord, you saw . . .'

'Yes, Darhus, I saw.' He had indeed seen: a vision of Shaitan's lair, enough to convince everyone that these magi truly were the afreet of legend. *And to think I believed Seth Korion to be almost human . . .*

'Captain Selmir, explain what was done.'

The Hadishah captain, a handsome, almost pretty man, raised his head, daring to meet his gaze. He had taken the time to shave and oil his jet-black hair; with his aloof air one might almost have thought he was the man in charge. 'It was a trap, and this fool fell into it like a child.' He threw a contemptuous sideways glance at Darhus. 'When the alarm was raised, General Darhus ordered the advance blindly, and his men rushed straight in. Earth-gnosis shook the ground – of such intensity that it suggests the spells were long-prepared. This caused the encampment area to collapse, letting the river and the crocodiles in. There were thousands of the beasts, and they had been whipped into a blood-frenzy.' For a moment his composure dropped and he faltered, shuddering at the memory. 'It was a slaughter . . .'

He recollected himself and straightened his shoulders. 'Meanwhile, many firepits had been prepared and they started exploding, triggered by the approaching men. There were other things too: bound spirits of the dead, water-spirits, snakes.' He looked down. 'Some of these things we have never encountered before.'

Behold, Rashid's feared Hadishah, who tyrannise the courts and villages of Kesh and Dhassa, but cannot stand against half or a third as many Rondians. 'Should you not have detected their activity?' Latif enquired.

Selmir was smart enough to see the trap in the question. If he claimed they had been alert and on watch, as they should, then why did they fail? If they had not been vigilant, then why not? 'Their training is so much superior to ours,' he muttered.

The usual excuse. At what point does it stop being inferior training and become a betrayal? 'Selmir, you were charged with monitoring their activities,' he said, his voice quiet. 'You boasted that we would know what they were doing as soon as they did it. Perhaps you will explain how you missed this?'

'Great Sultan, they are more skilled – their Arcanum, their systems – we are still learning! It is not the fault of my people! My Lord Rashid would say this!'

Yes, hide behind Rashid's omnipresent cloak, as always.

The galling thing was that not even Salim could punish this arrogant man the way he deserved for his negligence and incompetence. Magi were too precious, and of course they all knew it.

He gritted his teeth. 'Leave us, Selmir.'

The Hadishah captain bowed, his certainty restored; sure now that he was escaping punishment. 'Thank you, Great Sultan.'

'Selmir, you misunderstand: you will leave the camp and report to Lord Rashid in Halli'kut, so you can explain your failures to him in full, and in person.'

Selmir went pale. He might be precious, but he could still be punished by the Hadishah commander, Rashid himself. He opened his mouth, then closed it again. 'Great Sultan, please—'

'Perhaps you will be chained to a bed in a breeding-house for your failings, Selmir – tell me, is that punishment or reward in your eyes?' The mage bowed his head, mortified, his cocksure demeanour entirely vanished.

For the first time, Latif raised his voice. 'Get out of my camp!'

When the Hadishah had gone, he stood. 'Darhus, my friend, get up.' He signalled for wine, poured two cups and handed one to the general. 'Drink. Tell me, how long have we known each other?'

The general stood shakily, sipped a mouthful of the wine, then another. He was sweating profusely, not just because of the morning heat. 'Great Sultan, I was present when you were first presented to the people by your father.'

Has it truly been so long? It probably has. 'What were your mistakes last night, General?'

Darhus dropped his eyes. 'I did not control the advance until the facts could be verified. I allowed a mob mentality to overtake us, resulting in our men rushing in headlong in the dark. Even when the trap was sprung, those behind thought battle joined and continued to pour in.' He raised his head again. 'I am sorry, Great Sultan. I will not let you down again.'

Because you will not be given the chance.

'Thank you, General Darhus. You know what is expected. Your descendants will praise your name for a thousand years.' Ritual words, to strengthen him through the ritual he would soon be facing alone. To be stripped of command was to face eternal disgrace, but to die in service preserved status and face.

By midday, the general was dead by his own sword and the Hadishah man departed. The riverboats were long gone, leaving behind a wrecked camp so dangerous that no-one had even ventured inside again to take down the remaining Rondian banners. They fluttered on the breeze like a taunt.

Seth Korion's army had escaped again.

19

The Battle for Forensa

Krak di Condotiori

The Krak di Condotiori, or 'Fortress of Mercenaries', acquired its name after Rimoni mercenaries, settling in Javon after the opening of the Leviathan Bridge, seized it to defend and control the southern passes into Zhassi Valley. To prevent the incessant border warfare between the Zhassi Keshi and the Javonesi, the fortress was strengthened by the Ordo Costruo; it became the most impregnable castle in northern Antiopia.

It is also an object lesson on the folly of trusting mercenaries.

ORDO COSTRUO COLLEGIATE, PONTUS, 881

Forensa, Javon, on the continent of Antiopia
Moharram (Janune) 930
19th month of the Moontide

Sir Roland Heale nudged his horse through the broken gates of Forensa and surveyed the sea of destruction beyond. Every building within two hundred yards of the inside of the city walls had been pounded to rubble by the explosive catapults. His legionaries were filing into the wreckage, a maze of shattered buildings, seeking an approach to the main citadel where the Nesti flag still hung limply in the ash-laden breeze. The air was so thick with ground-mist and smoke that he could barely make out which way to go.

Someone shouted, and a volley of arrows fell among his officers. None struck flesh, shielded away in flashes of light, but the men shouted indignantly and counter-shots flew to where they thought

343

the volley had come from, somewhere beside a smashed Dom-al'Ahm. 'There are still pockets of enemy in the rubble,' an aide shouted.

'Well, that's bleeding obvious, isn't it?' Heale snapped, making the man cringe.

'They're still thick as bugs south and east of here,' a rival aide said. 'After the breach they fell back to a canal that flows through the city. The Harkun have pushed right up to it, but they've not been able to cross yet.' The aide pulled a face. 'Even the Nesti women and children are fighting. These Noories surely hate each other, sir.'

'They certainly do,' Heale agreed. He'd not realised before how people of the same breed could loathe each other so much, but it was proving very useful. Betillon had under-estimated the resistance of the Nesti; they really did need the Harkun hordes.

'They're barbarians, sir,' another aide chimed in. 'Even the Rimoni have been fighting like savages.'

It's this stinking hot land, Heale decided. *It degenerates even civilised people*. Fury had been rising inside him at the slow pace of the siege and the mounting casualties. When the gate crashed down, he'd thought it would be all over quickly, but if anything, the defence had intensified. He wanted to get in, now. *Badly*. Victory could not come soon enough.

'Force a way over the canal and they'll crumble,' he replied. 'Forward!'

Ghujad iz'Kho smelled victory amidst the stench of smoke and death. He slithered down a broken wall and ran to a window of a miraculously still-intact house overlooking the choked canal. He cautiously put an eye around the corner and looked out; an arrow flashed by and smashed on the wall behind him. He withdrew, laughing at the near miss. 'Our Jhafi kin can still shoot, eh?'

His nephew Cabruhil drew his own bow and stepped to the window. 'Not so well as we can,' he replied brashly. He was only seventeen and thought himself invincible.

Ghujad caught his shoulder. 'No, nephew. Never appear at the same place twice.'

Cabruhil coloured and slithered to the next window, scanning

344

for targets. 'We should rush them,' he said. 'There is hardly anyone over there.'

'They're there,' Ghujad told him. 'The myrkas' – *the mercenaries* – 'tried to cross fifty yards downstream, over a footbridge. Thirty got over, then it collapsed and hundreds of the Jhafi scum emerged from every rat-hole and cut them to pieces.' He smiled cheerily: he viewed Rondian casualties as a bonus.

The third member of their scouting party, Lekutto iz'Fal, a squint-eyed man with a swift blade, asked, 'What have we found, cousin?'

'Rats,' Ghujad replied. 'A nest full of them.' The Jhafi had been known among the Harkun as 'The Rat People' for generations. 'Across the canal it's thick with them.'

'Is this a good place to force a crossing?' Lekutto asked.

'As good as any.' They all winced as a catapult launched from somewhere to the rear and a few seconds later, a rock whistled overhead and smashed into the far bank, exploding in shards and a burst of flame. Fifty yards away across the filthy waterway one of the defenders laughed derisively.

We'll teach you how to laugh, Ratman.

'This place will do,' Ghujad told Lekutto. 'That building, there: see how it's fallen into the canal? It'll be easiest to cross there. Bring timber to lay across the gap and set archers to provide covering shot from the roofs.'

'Half the defenders over there are women,' Cabruhil sneered.

'Handy,' Lekutto quipped. 'We won't have to go looking for them after their men are dead.' They all chuckled, then Lekutto added, 'I've heard that the Nesti queen is a tribaddi.'

'So it is said.' Ghujad wrinkled his nose. 'When we find her, you can fuck her back to righteousness. But first we must cross this canal: we punch through, then push on to the castle. We'll take Nesti keep, not the Rondians.'

Ancestors, behold! We're going to crush the Rats in their holes once and for all. 'This is the beginning, kinsmen,' he told Lekutto and Cabruhil. 'Inside a year, all of Ja'afar will be ours.'

•

'Lady, I wish you wouldn't—'

Cera put her finger to her lips and cut off Justiano di Kestria's latest plea. 'Seir Justiano, I *have* to do this. I must be seen by my people; I must share their struggle.' She ignored Justiano's worried expression and with Tarita in her wake – the maid had refused to go back to the palace – she shuffled along the crowded alleyway that ran behind the canal-front houses, her escort of Rimoni legionaries trailing behind.

The alley was filled with armed men and women, and children too. All were battle-stained and exhausted, but they moved with quiet purpose, handing bundles of arrows along their lines, or packages of food. When they saw her they all looked twice, the first time blankly, without recognition, then the second time with widening eyes. Some tried to acclaim her, but she put her finger to her lips lest the noise draw enemy bombardment, then seized their hands and pressed her lips to their cheeks. She had no idea how many of her people she'd kissed in the past two days, but it felt like thousands.

There had been absolute tumult when the outer gates had broken, and for a terrifying two hours there'd been no certainty that they could hold against the Harkun and Rondians, but Justiano had led his heavily armoured Kestrian knights in on foot, buying time for the bulk of the defenders to retreat across the canals to their new defensive line, as they'd planned. Too many had died – both Jhafi and Rimoni – trapped in the wreckage on the far side of the canals as the defences crumbled. But Justiano had prevented a rout.

Since then, Cera and Tarita had been going amongst the defenders, without fanfare, to encourage whoever they could, and show her people she loved them. This was no ordinary battle, fought between trained soldiers; this was the whole community, working together to prevent annihilation. Sharing the ordeal was the least she could do.

Timori had begged to be allowed to do the same thing. 'Father would allow me,' he'd said brightly, bringing tears to her eyes. So he was off with a strong guard, somewhere south of her, facing the Argundian mercenaries.

But her sector was where the major breakthrough had come, on the north flank where the Dorobon were deployed, aided by thousands of Harkun. The opposite side of the canal was filled with nomads, hovering just out of sight in the ruins. Arrows had flown incessantly for two days and nights, and there had been dozens of attempts to force a crossing, turning the canal into a slaughterhouse. So far they were holding: the townsfolk standing firm against the nomad warriors, for all they were losing three to one in casualties. They were giving all the strength they had, but only the canal and bloody-minded willpower were preserving them now.

'If we stop believing, we'll be destroyed,' Cera muttered to herself, but she pasted a smile on her face and on she went, moving from one person to the next: a young man, wounded; a young woman, his wife, maybe, asleep beside him, a spear clutched in her lap. An old man with one eye holding a bow. Cooks. Washerwomen. Smiths. Message-runners, young children. She blessed them all, kissed them, let them hold her hands, even kiss her feet, an honour she felt unworthy of. It was painfully awkward, and yet they rose from their knees stronger than when they knelt.

Then the dreaded cry went up again. 'They come! Harkun!'

Someone screamed a warning as a rock plummeted into the building two doors down, smashing through the roof. Everyone roused and surged towards the canal. Cera grabbed Tarita, or perhaps it was the other way round, as men burst from the houses behind, wiping their faces and spilling food bowls, as they dashed to the front line. Justiano tried to reach her, then the building between them shuddered and a wooden support beam crashed through the brickwork, crushing the people beneath. From over the canal came the wailing ululation of Harkun warcries.

As the wall above them teetered, Tarita pulled Cera into the nearest doorway, which faced onto the canal. The building had been gutted and was now packed with two dozen of her people, of all ages and genders. Most were holding crude spears, and some at the front were shooting bows through holes in the walls. Through those portals, Cera caught glimpses of Harkun tribesmen only thirty yards away across the canal, bursting from cover. They were carrying planks looted from destroyed houses. Three men dropped instantly, pierced by arrows, but more came, and retaliatory fire sent arrows back this way too, hurtling through the windows and thudding into the packed defenders. Choked cries were torn from the lips of those they struck. A man in front of Tarita went down, a shaft transfixing his throat.

'Cera! Be careful!' Tarita cried, pulling her back towards the door, as a wall of Harkun stormed over the planks and launched themselves at the building. Wild-eyed nomads shrieked as they plunged their spears and scimitars through the windows. The Jhafi defenders fought back, fighting furiously, but they weren't real soldiers and it quickly showed. In these close quarters, the strength and the honed savagery of the warrior took over and she saw defender after defender beaten down – and then the Harkun were pouring in. A young woman she'd blessed just a few moments before the attack was brutally gutted as she tried to protect her fallen husband. Her killer stepped over her, his eyes fixed on Cera. He lunged.

Tarita leapt forward, her dagger in hand, and batted away his thrust, but the man just bellowed angrily and smashed the tiny maid in the face with his left fist, sending her flying limply to crunch into the wall. Then he turned on Cera again.

For a helpless second, she froze—

—as a straight sword swept over her shoulder from behind and into the attacker's chest. Justiano di Kestria shouldered her aside, kicked the corpse off his blade and parried another blow from the next attacker.

'Please, my lady, you must *get out*!' he bellowed as three more of his knights barged into the room. One grabbed Cera and threw her behind them and she stumbled, cracking her knee and cried out in pain. Then she crawled to Tarita, who was unconscious, but at least she was breathing. She threw her arms around her and hauled, dragging her out into the alley as more men poured in from the rear: Nesti legionaries, moving with calm urgency. A pilus saw her and called, 'Get to the rear, you stupid bitch! Get out of the rukking way!'

She grabbed the man by the arm. 'Please, my maid—! She's hurt—! Help me!'

The pilus bent over Tarita. 'She's dead,' he said, wrinkling his nose and pulling away as if death were infectious. He clearly had no idea who either girl was.

'No, she's breathing,' Cera said, in her most imperious voice. 'She's not dead – I need you to help me!'

The cohort commander scowled impatiently, but he looked around and snapped an order and a young legionary pulled Tarita from her arms. 'There are healers at the rear,' the pilus said. 'Genas will see her to them.' He bent over and dropped his voice, spoke in Cera's ear. 'It's a broken neck, girl. She's better off dead.'

Cera clutched the wall, her throat seizing up as she stared at the man, but he'd already stepped away and was ordering his men forward. The man he'd assigned – Genas – threw a resentful look back over his shoulder, then hauled Tarita away from the front line and laid her down in a line of wounded and dead men at the next plaza before running back towards the canal. He clearly hadn't recognised his queen either.

Cera pulled out her family brooch to identify herself, then shrieked until she got help: a Sollan priest of the healing order, who dripped water into Tarita's unresponsive mouth until she swallowed convulsively. Cera squealed with relief and tried to speak to the maid, but she'd slipped back into unconsciousness. A few minutes later a stretcher-bearer took the girl away, leaving Cera feeling horribly lost and alone, just another terrified and bewildered young woman in a falling city.

So she went back to the front line.

My people must keep believing . . . even if I don't.

The attack lasted all day and well past dusk. Three more times the Harkun forced their way over the canal, forcing their way two or three streets further in, before being hurled back by swarms of desperate defenders. The last counterattack was led by the lami-ae-magi, though the mere presence of the snakemen terrified the defenders just as much as the attackers. But as darkness closed in, the Jhafi regained the canal by dint of pushing men into the area in such great numbers that the Harkun had no choice but to give back the ground, foot by bloody foot.

Cera found her way back to the citadel in the dark, to be met by near hysteria when she was recognised. Apparently the rumour had gone round that the queen-regent was dead, or a prisoner. Timori, who'd been waiting anxiously, rushed to her arms. He was white with exhaustion and beside himself, his whole body shaking uncontrollably. Others crowded in, Pita Rosco, Comte Inveglio, the house servants, all crowding about her and weeping in relief.

Pita grabbed her and almost squeezed the air from her lungs. 'Where in Hel have you been, girl?'

'Trying to help,' she panted. She pushed free, grateful but anxious to appear womanly and calm, not some teary-eyed ragazza. 'Are we holding?'

Piero Inveglio bowed. 'My Lady, we're holding. They tried to punch through in four places along the canal, and they breached us in two, but we've held them off.'

The court – Mater Lune knew who all these people were – cheered, while a burst of pride surged through her, filling her eyes and threatening to reduce her to a sobbing mess again. 'Thank you, all of you,' she choked out.

She gave orders for them to find Tarita and bring her back to the Krak al-Farada, then at last she corralled Pita Rosco, Piero Inveglio, Justiano di Kestria and Saarif Jelmud in a private chamber for a meeting.

'How long can we hold?' she asked them.

Inveglio exhaled heavily. 'Against another attack like today? Dusk tomorrow, perhaps? We almost lost everything today, my Queen.'

'It is as Piero says,' Justiano added. 'The mercenaries attacked on the southwest flank with mage-support and we were broken. But those lamiae: they took down a mage-knight and that stiffened us.'

'Rondian battle-magi don't like to fight toe-to-toe, and they don't like arrows,' added Saarif in a low voice. 'They like to kill from safety; but my archers made sure the skies weren't safe, and so took away their vantage points. Then we just threw bodies into the gaps, all day long. Only the darkness saved us, really,' he concluded grimly.

That summation chilled them all. Then Pita raised a hand and reported, 'On our right, the northern flank, the Dorobon broke us quickly, using their windskiffs above, and Fire-gnosis below. But we were lucky: there is a secondary canal behind the first at that point, much wider, and we fell back to that and they couldn't cross, not with so many archers protecting us. I think we wounded one of their magi.'

She listened with an ashen face. 'Can we do the same tomorrow?'

None of the men responded with conviction. 'If we're fortunate, then maybe,' Inveglio replied at last, for them all.

'But we'll not surrender,' Saarif glowered.

'Cera, in some ways the presence of the Harkun is helping us,' Pita said. 'Though I'd prefer a lot fewer of them! But their presence is removing all doubt from our minds. Even the smallest child knows that this is a fight for survival.'

'It is so,' Piero agreed. 'The people know that the Rondians come to conquer, not slaughter. But the Harkun are here to kill us all. Their presence unifies us.'

'We must send Gurvon Gyle our thanks,' Cera said drily. 'But can we win?'

'If Riban were to send aid, perhaps,' Justiano said in a low voice, but they all knew by now that Aranio wasn't coming.

Pita Rosco put his hand on hers. 'Lady, we must think beyond this battle. We've been moving the apparatus of governance out by the mountain road for a week or more now; not just the vital documents and holy relics, but pregnant mothers, newborns and the like. The Viola Rift Fort can only house a few hundred, but it's something.' He looked at her apologetically. 'My Queen, you and Timori should join them. It would give us hope, knowing that you're safe.'

'No,' Cera said flatly. 'I'll not hide while my people fight.'

The men looked at each other. To her relief, they didn't ask again.

'Then that just leaves prayer,' Justiano di Kestria said. 'We can always pray.'

Hans Frikter had beer froth in his moustache when Gurvon Gyle stepped unheralded into his tent. Gurvon had flown all night to get there, reaching Forensa mid-morning, as the camp was preparing for battle. He was tired, and the sight of his legion commander sitting around swilling ale did nothing for his mood.

I never lose my temper – I know exactly where it is. 'What in Hel are you doing, Hansi?' he barked. He flashed a blazing look around the command tent at the Argundian magi with their thick beards and complacent faces. 'Drunk before a fight!'

'Nay, Gurv,' Frikter laughed, 'we're not drunk.'

'Takes more'n a couple of beers to knock us over,' one of the battle-magi drawled.

'Just settles the gut,' another guffawed, slapping his own ample girth. 'From las' night!'

'Shut up and get out,' Gurvon snapped and the tent fell silent, the Argundians glancing at their commander for guidance. Gurvon realised he'd overstepped and raised a hand. 'All right, lads. That came out harder than it was meant. But I just want to know why this assault has taken almost two weeks, and it'd better not be because of the drink!'

They all glared at him, not in the least bit placated. 'It's 'cause them fuckin' Noories can't fight,' one grumbled.

'They're holding you off,' Gurvon retorted.

'He means the Harkun,' Frikter added, hooking a finger through his belt. 'All right lads, off you go. I need a word with the paymaster.'

The battle-magi left, still sourfaced. Frikter looked at Gurvon crossly. 'All right, we all know you're the boss, Gurv, but you don't come into my command tent and throw your weight around. My lads don't like Noromen, and they don't like big-headed boss-men coming in all high and mighty.'

'Sorry—! I know, you're right.'

'I'll do what I like in my own bloody command tent.' Frikter belched. 'And for the record, my boys could down a keg each and still beat any Noorie in a scrap.'

'Of course, of course.' Gurvon exhaled impatiently. *Damned chest-beating Argies: they're all the rukking same.* 'Listen, Hansi, seriously: what in Hel is going on? Why do the Nesti still exist?'

Frikter pulled a sour face. 'Gurv, it's just not so easy as we thought it'd be. These Jhafi, they're fighting like cornered nyxen. You know the nyxen, the Argundian wildcat? You say "Boo" and it'll run, but you corner one and it'll come for you, claws and teeth flying. These Jhafi are like that. The whole populace is fighting – shooting bows and throwing spears and rocks and whatever. We're not fighting an army: we're fighting a *city*.'

'Give them a whiff of mage-fire! That's usually enough.'

'We have, Gurv, but they just keep hanging on. We must've killed five of theirs for every one of ours, but they keep on fighting.' Frikter shook his head. 'It's these fuckin' nomads you brought in. The Jhafi hate 'em – they hate 'em worse'n the Estellans hate my people. An' I don' trust 'em neither, an' nor should you.

'I don't, Hansi, not for a moment. But two legions weren't going to be enough for this job.'

'Sure it was, providing we was all on the same side. But I'm jus' waiting for Heale to fuck me over and he's coverin' his pucker-hole jus' the same, an' meanwhile these Jhafi and Harkun are going at it tooth and nail.'

Perhaps he's right. Without going right into the front line, Gurvon couldn't judge for himself, but Frikter's words were ringing true. *Did I really misjudge this so badly?* 'I'm told you almost broke them yesterday.'

'Sure, we did. But even a pure-blood can't shield a dozen arrows a second for long, and I swear that's what we're facin'. My lads want to see this dump razed, Gurv, same as you. But let the Harkun take the blooding, I say.'

Gurvon scowled. It was well-known that mercenaries could be notoriously tentative when faced with determined opposition. 'But we're winning, yes?'

'Sure.' Frikter picked up a roughly hewn lump of garlic sausage and gnawed on it. 'We'll break 'em today, luck holding. Or tomorrow. They can't have much left to throw at us, an' sooner or later even fanatics despair. It's only a matter of time.'

'All right, Hansi, I believe you. But we need to finish this. Attack again today, in force. The longer this goes on, the more the other Javonesi lords will be encouraged. And I want you into the citadel first: *we* need to capture the Nesti children, not Heale.'

'He tried,' Frikter commented. 'Sent a skiff right to the top of the tower, but they were beaten away. Some wild tale of snakemen,' he added with a chuckle. 'Stupidest excuse I've ever heard.'

Snakemen? Gurvon blinked. *Are the lamiae here?* Memories of his captivity reared up and he shuddered. If Elena had brought that infernal tribe of constructs here, then no wonder this fight was going slower than expected. *Should I warn Hansi . . . ?*

He opened his mouth, then the humiliation came roaring back to him. He pictured himself trying to explain gnosis-wielding serpent-men to the stolid Argundian and still managing to keep his respect and couldn't.

Bugger it, let him find out for himself.

He went with Frikter to the muster, then followed the mercenary commander through the smashed outer walls of Forensa and into the rubble within. Morning mist and smoke fouled the air, so badly that the rankers had rags tied over their mouths and noses. Flights of arrows came and went in flurries, emanating from away to the left, where their Harkun allies were massed. Frikter estimated the nomads had lost six thousand, with many more wounded, but they'd slain three times that number of defenders. Right now they were burning naked Jhafi and Rimoni corpses, looted and stripped, in pits outside the walls. All genders, all ages. It reminded Gurvon of the Noros Revolt.

War always smells the same: like shit and scorched meat.

By now Roland Heale knew he was there; he sent an invitation to dine at midday, but Gurvon politely declined. *I want to be supping from Cera Nesti's goblet by then.* He made his way towards the front and watched Frikter's men forming up in tortoise formations. Their warspears were jutting in all directions like porcupine spines.

'That should be unstoppable,' he remarked to Frikter.

'Not over broken terrain, Gurv. That's the problem. We can't hold together over the rubble, an' we can't cross the canal in formation.'

'You're turning into an old woman.'

'You'll fuckin' see,' Frikter said grimly.

The drums rolled and the legion marched forward. Visibility was poor, but the Jhafi were obviously watching because as the Argundian phalanx shuffle-stepped out of the smashed buildings and approached the canal, arrows began to sleet down. Initially the shafts were ineffectual, for the tortoise formations protected the rankers head-to-toe. The men bellowed Argundian drinking hymns and slammed their spear-butts into the ground in rhythm as they advanced. It was stirring, in its way. Alcohol fumes clogged the air, overlaying the stench of death. The wailing of the Harkun away to the left was an eerie counterpoint.

They were checked at the canal though, where the arrows came thicker. Voices bellowed orders or shrieked in pain and terror, the cacophony punctuated by the recoil of the catapults and the crunch of falling boulders: the unforgettable, horrific sounds of war. Gurvon edged closer, well-shielded behind the tortoise formation as it clambered forward and waded into the canal, now fordable thanks to the weight of the rubble and dead bodies choking it. He began to hope they might cross safely.

But it turned out Frikter hadn't been exaggerating.

The Jhafi shrieked orders and suddenly the broken buildings on the far side were alive with archers and people hurling rocks, and before he knew what had happened, the sheer weight of fire had shattered the tortoise, the rocks battering the shields aside an instant before a wall of arrows shredded the air, deadly as the Bullhead's axe. He saw the phalanx stagger and break, and then half of them were dead, their boiled leather armour punctured in a dozen places. The rest died a few seconds later, shrieking at each other even as they tried to surge forward.

'Fuckin' told yer,' Frikter snarled as he broke cover and hurled fire at the archers, incinerating half a dozen before a hail of arrow-fire forced him to dive behind a wall, his shields flashing from pale pink to scarlet as the projectiles ripped them apart. Gurvon, beside him, was truly awed at the ferocity of the defence. The Jhafi cheered as the assault faltered and the Argundians who could slunk back into cover.

It's like the walls at Norostein. The Pallacians didn't think a mere militia could fight trained soldiers, but we did. I should have remembered that.

'Well?' Frikter snapped. 'How many more o' my lads d'you want to see die?'

'None.' He slapped Frikter's massive shoulder. 'Listen, we can do better than this. I've got an idea.'

The second assault began soon after, driving forward behind gnosis-propelled wagons he'd ordered up from the rear. He sent them ploughing over the rubble and straight into the canal, choking it entirely, while impotent arrows flew all around. He followed that up with another wave of wagons, seeking to choke the canal and render it a non-factor. The Jhafi tried to burn them with hurled oil-lamps, but the Argundian magi, roused by his presence, wanted to prove themselves and they doused the flames as swiftly as they began, or hurled them back through the windows into the enemy. They could see the Jhafi clearly now, and the exchange of javelin and arrow fire intensified. It was a war of attrition, of who could kill whom faster.

'Just about . . .' Gurvon called, then as a large rock flew and splashed into the deepest hole, he stood and pointed forward. 'Now!'

With a roar, the Argundian mercenaries charged, this time over ground that was more or less flat and dry.

Gurvon followed, blasting archers on the roofs with mage-bolts, directing his attackers to the weak points, while ten yards to his right, Frikter did the same. The magi fanned out to support the attack, fighting in unison for once, and sheer momentum carried them forward across the water-course and into the rubble. In amongst the houses it was brutal, a kill-or-be-killed mêlée, but the heavily armed and experienced Argundians were finally making headway. They broke into an alley behind the canal houses packed with Jhafi, Gurvon right behind the fighting men, although he dared not intervene for fear of blasting his own men.

But they were winning now, driving forward step by step.

Then the Jhafi line broke.

He'd seen it before, the way the will of even the most desperate, dedicated men could fail when faced with an inexorable advance, especially when they had space to retreat into. The Jhafi began to turn and look for ways out; the panic now clear in their voices and faces. He began to select targets, anyone who was standing his ground, lancing mage-bolts at them, until with a wailing cry the Rimoni and Jhafi defenders began to stampede backwards. The Argundians roared lustily and began to trot forward, their weapons raised. Anyone who tripped and fell in their path were stabbed or hacked apart before they could rise. One woman was dragged aside screaming by two burly rankers who were tearing her robes; a Jhafi man turned to help her but before he could even raise his scimitar, he was gutted by a warspear.

The rout was on.

Then the mist overhead parted at a sudden gust of wind and someone shouted in alarm. Gurvon looked up, and stopped dead.

Sweet Kore . . . But how—?

A windship hung over them – no, not just any old windship but an Inquisition warbird: a giant of the skies with ballistae fore and aft, and specially elevated archery decks. Then he looked closer and swore: the warbird was packed to the rigging with bodies, most of them snake-tailed, and gnosis energy twinkled in every hand. Three skiffs plied the air at its sides, darting lower, and bolts flashed from magi riding in the prows, straight into the front ranks of the Argundians, who were gaping upwards in horror. The Yurosian rankers scattered for cover as the windship came lower and giant balls of fire came whooshing towards them. Gurvon cried aloud in fury and shock, darting for shelter as the flames seared around him, engulfing whole cohorts trapped in the packed, narrow alleys.

In the distance, Nesti horns brayed and arrows began to fly again. He looked up in time to see men and women with impossibly bright auras dropping from the side of the ship and floating down on a wave of destruction.

There was a woman standing at the prow, shortsword drawn and grey cloak fluttering.

Elena.

He ducked into the shadows and began to slink away.

Elena had seen warbirds in action over a battlefield before. She herself had faced military windships during the Noros Revolt and felt lucky to have survived, fortunate not to have been singled out, nothing more than one face among many on a crowded battlefield that day. But this was her first time on board one during battle. She'd been vaguely aware that the keel of a well-made windcraft not only stored Air-gnosis for flying, but also pure energy, which could be siphoned off by the magi on board. This was the first time she'd benefited. Her sister had flown an Imperial skiff in the First Crusade, and had used its power to level buildings in Hebusalim – just flimsy hovels, Tesla told her later, but nevertheless. In the hands of strong magi, a warbird could be a thing of majestic destruction.

Catapults couldn't target something that moved so fast. An archer couldn't penetrate the shielding on something so high up. And from such a vantage, no one could hide. The only things she'd ever seen bring one down were gnosis-powered ballistae or other warbirds – but nothing else.

Now she directed the craft over the battlefield, raining fire and missiles onto the mercenaries below, targeting the mage-knights for special treatment. Some of the Ordo Costruo, those who considered themselves best equipped for fighting, had descended to the field, but she remained aboard. It felt good to be the one holding the whip-hand for a change.

She identified the enemy below: Hans Frikter's Argundians. They were fighting desperately now, not just against the warbird, but against the returning Jhafi archers, who'd taken heart at the sudden arrival of such powerful allies; the battle had turned into a storm of crossbow bolts and arrows and javelins and spears, as the defenders flooded back. For once the mercenaries were disadvantaged: they might be well-armoured, but they were not archers by nature, and were unable to engage at close quarters. Instead they gave ground, retreating beyond a rubble-choked canal where it looked like most of the fighting had been taking place.

'Take her round to the north,' she called to the pilot, one of the humans captured with the ship who had elected to join the lamia community. 'Get above those Harkun in the centre!' She glanced at Odessa D'Ark, who was revealing herself to be the scariest pregnant woman on Urte, a tempestuous Fire- and Air-witch. They shared a look of immense satisfaction – *blood-sisters again!* – then she sought Kazim. All he'd been allowed so far were a few fire-blasts, and he was visibly chafing.

She judged that the time had come for them to join the fray below. *<Come on, my love, let's go!>*

Together they threw themselves over the side and swooped towards the ground, accompanied by a dozen more Ordo Costruo magi.

Hans Frikter bellowed in fury as another pile of debris came to life, rocks and rubble flowing together and forming into a twelve-foot approximately human shape: an improvised *galmi*. The Brician-discovered art of animating the inanimate could be terrifying, and it was too far off for him to be able to stop it, or affect it in any way; he could only watch as it waded towards a line of his lads, rankers from the third maniple. They were good men, but those who weren't immediately crushed ran like panicked sheep.

'Fall back!' he shouted, turning to Ogdi, his aide and nephew. 'Get Hullyn here! He can use Wizardry: we've got to neutralise that blasted galmi!'

'Hullyn's dead,' Ogdi replied, his normally placid face completely bewildered. 'Some Keshi bastard cut him in half, down by the canals!'

Merda! Hans gripped his axe as he looked at the circle of men around him: his personal cohort, men of his own village, who'd been at his side most of his life. Seeing them anchored him. *We've got out of worse.* There were days you fought and days you ran, and this had suddenly become one of the latter. 'Get everyone out – head for the staging point beyond the walls.'

Ogdi saluted, visibly trying to contain his own panic. He was a better soldier than mage, but he gripped his periapt, closing his eyes and straining. 'I can't find Eafyd,' he groaned, then suddenly he gasped, clutching his skull. 'My head!'

Frikter swore, gripped his nephew's shoulder and felt the whine of some kind of psychic attack on him. 'Hold to your wards,' he encouraged, as his cohort shuffled anxiously, worried by the uncertainty on his face. Then a crowd of Jhafi broke from the rubble and spewed towards them.

'Form up!' he bellowed, though his lads didn't need telling; they were already slamming their shields together and brandishing their axes as they shouted to Taurhan, the Argundian war-god, the *true* Bullhead. *Good lads!* Frikter raised his hand to blaze fire into the enemy charge.

But before he could strike, a torrent of rock rose like a wave and slammed into the shield-wall, smashing his men backwards like toys, wrecking armour, breaking bone and cracking skulls. Frikter shouted furiously, seeking a target, but the air was filling up with dust and the screaming of the injured. He loosed fire blindly into the space in front of his men and was rewarded by shrieks of agony and the sight of two shadowy figures going up like torches. Then blue fire slammed into his shields from two flanks, staggering him with the strength of the bolts.

That's it, we've got to get out.

But the Jhafi were already on them; turning their backs would mean death. Hans looked around desperately, seeking a way to buy his lads the space to run. He blasted the nearest Jhafi off his feet, then two more of those overpowering mage-bolts hammered his shields again, one high and one low, perfectly synchronised. His shields blocked the high one, but his left leg crumpled beneath him, with searing pain following a moment later as he tasted the dust. He crawled upright and hurled a spear-waving Jhafi woman away with a gesture.

Ogdi screamed, 'My head! My eyes!'

Frikter blanked the pain from his blackened leg and rallied, threw kinesis behind his battle-axe and hacked through a circle of Jhafi.

Some of his lads were still up, but few, too few. The Jhafi swordsmen backed off, but they were replaced with archers, who were pushing their way to the front. He heard his lads furiously praying, while behind him Ogdi rolled over and fell on his face in the mud and blood.

Where the fuck is Gyle?

<Don't know, Hansi,> a woman's voice scratched inside his head. *<I was hoping you did.>*

<Elena, you shizen hexen,> he sent. The old jest-name "Shit Witch", but he meant it now. He cast about, raised his left hand and kindled fire but couldn't see her in the dust. The Jhafi were obviously awaiting an order; they were poised ready to shoot, then charge.

One fire-blast and I'd kill half these fuckers . . .

'Boss?' one of his lads muttered as they edged towards him.

'*Kill 'em all!*' He raised his fist to pour fire on the Noories when two more mage-bolts struck him with that same deadly synchronisation: one took him square in the midriff, in the centre of his wards—

—as the other took his left hand off, in the instant before he let loose his own lethal fires. His spell fell apart as his hand became a smouldering stump. He howled as his legs went out from under him and he pitched forward, not even seeing the arrow-storm that was carving into what remained of his cohort.

The dark earth swallowed him up.

Kazim Makani strode through the Jhafi, who parted fearfully, clearing a path for him. He tried reassuring them, praising them, patting men on the back, but they fell over themselves to get out of reach. He wondered if he'd ever again feel the camaraderie of being one of the gang. Back in Aruna Nagar, when only kalikti games mattered, he'd been part of a close-knit group of young men who crowed and joked and laughed at the epic feats and ridiculous failures, the mighty hits and the dropped catches.

He felt so isolated now.

And I am sick of war . . .

<I am too, amori,> Elena sent. She was bent over the fallen mercenary

commander, the Argundian – another of her old comrades, no doubt. She seemed to know everyone they were killing.

The fighting was done here. With their magi either dead or fled, the Argundians were running, chased by the victorious Jhafi, who were butchering the wounded and anyone stupid enough to surrender.

'Is he dead?' he asked, peering over Elena's shoulder. The soot on her face and the ash in her hair made her look older than her years.

'He's alive. I've Chained him, and Cardien is sending someone to pick him up. I want him kept safe.'

'Who is he to you?' It came out tense and jealous.

'Hansi?' Elena shrugged. 'No one much. We've shared a few pints. What's wrong, Kaz?'

'Nothing!' He stamped away, and she didn't follow.

It was hard to explain his feelings, even to himself. Right now, all he was thinking was what a *disappointment* war had turned out to be. All his life, he'd dreamed of battle, as all young men did: war was how the great won eternal fame; it was the pinnacle, the ultimate test of manhood, for which even his beloved kalikiti was a poor substitute. He and his friends had *longed* for war, seeing themselves striding across the battlefield seeking out the enemy heroes and slaying them in epic hand-to-hand combat, demonstrating their superior prowess and worth, creating legends . . .

But from the moment of his first kill – the execution of a helpless old man – he'd tasted nothing but sourness. He'd come to loathe the whole thing, the driving of steel into flesh, cutting sinews and carving muscles, slicing veins, and the myriad ways that wounding could lead to death: the ruination of bodies and the emptying of eyes, it all haunted him. The sickening stench of blood and the reek of voided bowels and bladders wouldn't leave his nostrils. All he kept thinking was, *So much waste*.

His wandering took him to the old outer wall, which had been breached and broken down in half a dozen places. He climbed a battered turret and gazed blankly towards the Argundians' rearguard, protecting their wagons as they rolled away. The Jhafi, realising they'd gone past their own mage-support, were content to pepper them with arrows and abuse.

I could go down there, he thought. *I could break that shield-wall, let them through so they could slaughter the women and children in the mercenary camp. That's what a hero would do.*

The idea sickened him.

To his right, the Harkun were pouring out of the city too, driven by a moving wave of fire and archery. He listened in with his gnostic senses and heard the Ordo Costruo coordinating their attack, moving the Jhafi archers into positions on either side so they could trap the nomads and unleash Justiano di Kestria's mounted knights on flat and open ground. He could taste the hatred in the air between the Jhafi and the Harkun. It was nothing to do with him, he decided, so he sat and stared with empty eyes.

He wasn't sure how long he sat there before that familiar linkage tightened. Elena was coming, climbing the turret. The boy in him wanted to keep on sulking on his own, but the man lifted his head.

'Hello love,' she said, topping the stairs and joining him, climbing up behind him on his perch and wrapping her arms about him from behind. He laid his head back against her shoulder and blanked all else out.

At last he sighed deeply, and admitted quietly, 'I'm sick of killing.'

'I know. So am I, and I've been doing it a lot longer than you.'

'But it's all we're good at, isn't it?'

She flinched. 'No! No, we could do so many things. Anything we want. And we will, once this is all done.'

'Anything?'

She hesitated, clearly unsure what he was thinking, then said, 'Anything.'

He looked up at her as the quite unexpected answer fell into his mouth. 'I want us to have a baby.'

Cera Nesti watched proudly as her little brother walked onto the royal balcony of the Krak al-Farada, the place from where for centuries the Nesti kings had addressed their people. He looked scared, clutching the sheath of papers in his hand too tightly. The crown on his head was still too big, despite all the padding they'd used. She was standing with the rest of the Regency Council: an honour-guard for the young king-in-waiting as he delivered his first proper speech. She blinked back tears, feeling the unseen eyes of her father and mother, her elder brother and her sister, all casualties of this war: ghosts now, but never forgotten.

She looked down the line to her left, where Elena was watching, her tanned face grim and distant. Her lover Kazim was nowhere to be seen. Beyond her were a group of Ordo Costruo, the legendary Builder-Mages. In the flesh they were strangely ordinary, though their eyes looked haunted – but then, they too had seen their world torn apart. Each of the women was with child, raped and impregnated by Hadishah. The few surviving men looked brittle, their habitual pride obliterated by all they'd been through; everything they'd failed to do. They had been made to serve as well. In a different way, they too had been violated.

These wars must stop. They're destroying us all.

The young heir stepped onto his stool, and the hordes below erupted with cries of victory and welcome.

The plaza was packed with people, like straws in a haystack, barely able to move or breathe. Tears stung every eye. Those who fainted were passed back on a sea of hands. Bells rang, and songs to Ahm and Pater Sol and Mater Lune rolled through the heavy air. But as Timori raised his hand, a hush fell across the masses.

'My people . . .' Timi began in Jhafi, his high-pitched, boyish voice ringing out as he cried, 'We have been victorious! People of Forensa – and our brothers of Loctis, who came to our aid! *Beloved* people—!'

The surge in sound washed his voice away as the entire populace shouted their lungs out in sheer relief and triumph. This was *their* victory, each and every one of them had taken part, not just the soldiers, but every single person had given their courage and endurance, their muscle and their skill, and their blood and their lives, to the defence of the city.

It took several minutes before Timori could resume, but now he was bouncing with excitement, caught up in the energy of the crowd. 'We give thanks! We give thanks to Ahm. Praise to Him on high! Ahm has seen our suffering and given us succour! Ahm saw our need and sent us allies! Ahm saw the destruction, and sent us Builders!'

He switched to Rimoni and repeated the first few lines, then said, 'We give thanks to Pater Sol and Mater Lune, for through the light of their wisdom we have found allies to bring us succour, and Builders to alleviate the destruction that has been visited upon our land!'

Those clad in violet in the crowds below – scarcely a tenth, but equally loud – waved their pennants and cheered, as he added, 'Through the chaos, Pater Sol and Mater Lune have shone above, lighting our path to freedom.'

Cera and the council had worked hard on this speech, up half the night finding ways to give thanks to all the diverse factions who'd come together to save the city, and to bind them closer. She bit her lip, waiting to see how the Jhafi and Rimoni would respond.

The people could not help seeing the Ordo Costruo arrayed about the king, clad in their pale blue robes, but their mood was all jubilation – whatever their fears about magi, they all knew what the Ordo Costruo had done, how the warbird had brought the Builder-Magi who had turned defeat to victory.

Then Timori reverted to Jhafi and shouted, 'Most of all, we give praise to *ourselves*! It is written that the gods help those who help themselves: this we have done! You have all put their shoulder to the wheel! Whether you fought, or laboured, or treated the wounded, or cooked, or ran messages, you are each and every one a part of this victory! You *are* this victory!'

He said it all again, in Rimoni, and everyone cheered again. Cera was almost overcome with pride. It was asking a lot of a nine-year-old boy to make any kind of speech, but it was important that he was seen. The people had to be reminded that he was their king; in anticipation of the day his regents stepped aside. *Including me.*

Timori walked to her side, struggling to maintain a dignified gait. She bent and kissed his cheek, whispered, 'Well done, little button.' He jiggled, throbbing with energy.

'Cera!' A cluster of Jhafi women began chanting, 'Cera! Cera!' They were fervent, holding out hands to her. 'Ja'afar-mata! Ja'afar-mata!'

Mother of Javon? No! It's too much . . .

But they kept chanting.

Ever since she'd come back from 'death' there had been this undercurrent, first in Lybis, and now here. There was too much reverence – and now silly stories were spreading, like the one that she'd driven back the Harkun merely by standing before them and raising her hands, forbidding their advance. And everyone wanted something of her: a blessing, threads of her clothing, just to touch her hand or foot. It was embarrassing, and frightening.

'They love you,' Timori said, looking up at her with shining eyes.

One day he might fear me, for that very reason.

She glanced at Elena – who knew *everything* – then raised a hand to try and make them stop, but they didn't; the gathering had become a chaotic festival of celebration.

She couldn't even escape the unwanted rapture inside the palace, where the Nesti court had gathered to sip arak or wine and share the moment. People kept approaching her with flattery and little requests: Comte Inveglio was still trying to wriggle his way onto the emergency confiscations committee; Justiano di Kestria wanted to be made permanent Commander of the Nesti Army, despite being a Kestrian. They both knew the only way that might happen was if he married her – and he'd started dropping hints that he was open to negotiations.

I'll bet he is, Cera thought cynically.

Elena appeared at her side. 'Cera, with your permission, I'd like to leave the celebrations. You don't need my protection tonight.'

'Actually, I'm sick of it. Let's both go.' She licked her lips nervously as she said the words; being alone with Elena still wasn't comfortable. But they left together and headed towards the living quarters. 'Are the prisoners secure?' she asked.

'The captured magi – five Argundians and three Dorobon – are in the dungeons; we've used a Rune of the Chain on them all, so you'll be quite safe. Justiano's got around four thousand prisoners in a camp north of here. Most of them are Dorobon; there's only eight hundred or so Argundians – the rest got away.' Elena frowned. 'There are no Harkun prisoners.'

'They didn't take prisoners either,' Cera retorted stonily. She struggled to feel any sympathy after what they'd done to poor Harshal. *A better person would feel more for an enemy*, she supposed. They walked on in silence to the place where they would normally part.

'Will Tarita ever recover?' Cera asked. Her guilt tore at her as she thought of that clever, vibrant, *loyal* girl. 'Is there any hope?'

Elena gave her a hard look. 'She shouldn't have been there, and nor should you.'

'I tried to make her stay behind – I swear I did—'

'She saw her duty to be with you.'

'And I had to be at the front! I had to *see* . . . It's all right for you, you can fight – I had to be there, to show them I cared!'

'Feeding the legend, were you?' Elena's eyes burned into her. 'Cera, you need to find a new champion, because I don't want the job any more. I'll fight for you until Gurvon's beaten, but not beyond. I'm sick of all this.'

Cera nodded mutely; it was obvious protesting wouldn't change her mind.

Elena gave a sarcastic bow. 'Goodnight, "Mother of Javon".' She stalked away, leaving Cera alone in the back corridors of the palace.

She wiped her eyes on her sleeve as loneliness swept in. *I just want someone to talk to – just a friend, that's all. But there's no one now.*

Portia didn't write any more, so neither did she. The young ladies-in-waiting were awestruck by her, rendered almost incapable of speech by her mere presence – and even if they could talk, it would only be about which knight or nobleman they fancied that day or what dress they'd be wearing to the next court event. And all the other courtiers wanted something; a decision or a favour or a problem to be solved, or just to be seen with her. So she drifted along the corridor, subconsciously making her way towards the only real friend she still had.

The infirmary was a small wing of the palace set aside for the well-connected casualties. The Kestrian and Nesti knights here were mostly unconscious. They'd had their wounds cleaned and bandaged, but that didn't conceal the hideous, crippling injuries most had sustained. It was a relief to pass onwards, into the smaller room set aside for female patients.

Tarita was lying on her bed, bandaged across the nose, her lips swollen and eyes blackened. Clematia was with her, a matronly Ordo Costruo healer in the late stages of pregnancy.

'Is she awake?' Cera asked.

Clematia looked at Tarita pityingly. 'She is.'

The maid flicked her eyes sideways at the sound of Cera's voice. She was deathly pale, and so skinny her bones could be seen through her skin. They'd been feeding her through straws, but her appetite was non-existent.

'I'm sorry,' Tarita whispered, 'I can't . . .'

'Hush, hush,' Cera murmured. 'We'll have you up in no time.' The words of the cohort commander came back to her: *broken neck, she's better off dead.* She sat in the chair beside the cot and took her hand. 'I'm here . . .'

She didn't think Tarita heard; she just gazed at Cera and wept until she fell asleep.

'Will she ever recover?' Cera whispered, fighting back tears.

Clematia shook her head. 'I'm afraid not. The spinal cord has failed to re-bond with the nerve-endings. She's paralysed for the rest of her life, from the neck down.'

'Oh dear gods – that's hideous!'

'I know. We've tried everything we can, believe me. But our gnosis cannot be fine-tuned enough to repair the nerve connections. If she was a mage herself, she could rekindle the connections using the gnosis: such self-healing cases have been documented, but of course, she's not a mage.'

More tears stung Cera's eyes. 'What can we do for her?'

'Make her comfortable, and wait and see. Sometimes, after a few years, these things can begin to fix themselves.' Clematia smoothed Tarita's hair. 'I'm not sure you know that Elena Anborn has offered to adopt Tarita and tend for the girl herself. I'm told she already calls herself "Tarita Alhani" anyway.'

Cera swallowed an enormous lump in her throat. 'Elena is her hero,' she managed to choke out, then turned away as more tears convulsed through her.

Outside, the victory celebrations raged on.

20

Imperfect

The Reputed Power of Anger

There is a celebrated incident in southern Argundy where a half-blood, filled with righteous rage at a crime committed by a pure-blood against his family, slew that pure-blood in a duel. Some say this proves that anger enhances power in combat. Others claim the revenge was taken in cold blood, and the lesson is in fact that a cool head is more effective in battle. But we've found no true proof of either theory. Like many things of this nature, there is no universal rule; different things work for different people. Simple 'universal truths' are usually untrue.

ORDO COSTRUO ARCANUM, HEBUSALIM, 774

Mandira Khojana, Lokistan, on the continent of Antiopia
Safar (Febreux) 930
20th month of the Moontide,
4 months until the end of the Moontide

Ramita stared at the young Lokistani acolyte lying prone on the bed, his lips blue and his skin pale beneath his native colour. His eyes were closed, thankfully, because she couldn't bear to see them staring emptily into nothing.

It was the second death in their Ascendancy programme. The first had come when the fifteenth young man, a Lakh, had gone into panicked convulsions as he failed to deal with the fears his subconscious was conjuring, instead falling into a death-spasm. That had been horrible. This second death, four days later, had been very different – unexpectedly peaceful. The novice had just gone to sleep and never awakened.

'What happened?' Alaron asked, sounding raw, wounded.

Corinea replied in a distant voice, as if she was disassociating herself, 'The sephanium didn't restart his heart. That means the potion was wrong. He might have given you a wrong answer when you questioned him. Perhaps he had a heart weakness . . .'

'Or we might have measured it wrong!' Alaron snapped. Ramita gripped his arm, restraining him.

Corinea looked irritated, but restrained herself. 'We did our best, Alaron.'

'It's a bloody waste!'

'Two from nineteen,' Corinea retorted. 'Better than Baramitius.'

Alaron drew from Ramita's calmness. 'Sure. You're right, I know.' He exhaled heavily. 'But he was as healthy as the others. And he was a good person.'

Ramita stroked his back, trying to comfort him. 'It was always likely we would lose some,' she said sadly. She stood on tiptoe and kissed his neck. 'Tomorrow's candidate will be a success.'

'I hope so.' He bowed his head while Corinea draped a blanket over the dead novice. 'How is the training going?'

'Well enough.' Ramita glanced at Master Puravai. For the past week she'd been leading the instruction of those novices who'd gained the gnosis, teaching them the basics of shielding. 'But it could be better.'

Puravai chuckled. 'They are Zain, and obedient. But some are struggling to adapt.'

Ramita snorted. 'That's a polite way of saying that nothing a *mere woman* says is worth listening to, as far as they are concerned. I tell them a thing, they look to Master Puravai to ensure it is true.'

Puravai looked a little hurt. 'They are making progress. Some have managed to create this "mage-fire" already.'

'How's Yash doing?' Alaron asked, yawning widely; he'd mostly been cooped up brewing potions with Corinea.

'He's better at burning things than shielding,' Ramita said with a laugh. 'Today he broke Haddo's leg. He is very aggressive.' In truth

Yash was one of the few whose progress encouraged her. 'The rest – well, they're very timid,' she added. That was frustrating when they needed warriors for the days to come.

'Gateem set Haddo's bones,' Puravai put in. 'He's a skilled healer.' He frowned thoughtfully. 'It is interesting: most of them are displaying "affinities", just like you did when I met you, being naturally drawn to certain gnosis and unable to reach others. Only a couple are so far showing the balance of mind to achieve what you and Ramita have in attaining all of the gnosis. But it's early days.'

'We've got fifteen more to give the ambrosia to, then Corinea and I can help with the training.' Alaron looked properly exhausted, not just a little bleary-eyed from a late night or two.

Perhaps I should just let him sleep tonight, Ramita reflected, then her own greedy needs replied, *He sleeps better after we have made love.*

As usual, that voice won out.

'Now!'

Alaron surveyed the training yard, as lines of young Zain novices kindled blue mage-fire in their hands. 'Hold it! Don't lose it!' he encouraged, Master Puravai translating his words.

He walked down the rows, trying to impart what he knew. 'Nurture that spark, feed it – and if you lose it, try again!' He passed Yash, who was struggling to contain the conflagration in his hands. 'Not too much! Control!'

Corinea was helping him, speaking in terse Keshi and Lakh. He could only hope she was reinforcing his words, not contradicting them. Ramita was in the other courtyard, helping the last novices to Ascend to catch up with the rest.

Thirty new magi: they'd lost four. One more to panic and heart failure, and the last one ... he'd come round all right, but when he'd tried to draw on the gnosis, his aura had been all wrong ... the Souldrinker curse. He'd been overcome by what he described as a ghastly hunger that felt like claws ripping out his insides. It had only subsided when Corinea bound him with a Chain-rune. But he'd been the only one.

Corinea appeared to be glad of the anomaly, as if the information they might glean from that case was of more interest than the young man's life. He was now in solitary confinement, but when Alaron confronted her about it, she just looked at him blankly and said, 'He's a monk: they enjoy being alone.'

Not slapping her had been hard that day.

From now on, the focus was on training the new Ascendants, and in the evenings, scrying for Malevorn, Huriya and Nasatya. He didn't know how long it might take to find them – indeed, with the monastery surrounded by the Lokistan Mountains they might not even manage. He figured they would have no choice but to leave in the end, and take their search into the warzone – but before that, these peaceable young men, reared to be monks, had to learn to defend themselves from other magi.

Which brought him back to this moment. He raised a hand: 'Now, kinesis!' The novices slammed their fists towards a target before them, a clay disc on a string. Some of the discs were swatted into motion, most weren't.

'Again!'

Teaching the gnosis wasn't a new thing for him: he and Ramon had secretly taught Cym in Norostein, and he'd instructed the lamiae on their journey across Yuros, pursuing the Scytale. This was only a little different. He and Puravai agreed that learning needed to be engaging, and certainly in his Arcanum days the fun lessons had also been the most productive. So he tried to turn the lessons into games: using kinesis to juggle small objects, or throwing snow at each other – trying to protect oneself from snowballs needed shielding, which required kinetic-gnosis and aura-awareness. He made a game of firing mage-bolts at targets, and challenged them to use wards to lock doors, then have their fellows try to unlock them. 'Practise all the time, in every available moment,' he told them repeatedly.

'Except during prayer,' Puravai would add, making them all laugh. Puravai had told him he was a natural teacher, which the best praise he'd ever had.

But time was marching on. Dasra, a year old, was walking now, a tiny, upright and infinitely curious child. A girl from the nearest village had been hired to be his nanny while Ramita was busy: Juppi had no toes, the legacy of frostbite as a child, but she was gentle, and fascinated by the monastery, a legendary place in her mind. Most importantly, Ramita trusted her.

Alaron also did a lot of one-on-one work, trying to overcome specific problems – like Yash who, predictably enough, had developed Fire-gnosis first; he'd been a menace until he'd learned to control it – the courtyards and walkways were liberally adorned with charred streaks. Kedak had started inadvertently taking to the air. Gateem had been deliberately cutting himself to practise healing and almost bled to death one night. Aprek was developing an alarming affinity in Spiritualism and couldn't keep inside his own skin, slipping out while his body fainted, at table or in mid-stride.

And then there was Felakan.

'Excuse me, Master Al'Rhon,' Felakan said one evening, surprising Alaron in the corridor leading back to his and Ramita's rooms. Alaron turned in surprise. Felakan wasn't a novice but a full monk, clad in saffron. He'd seldom deigned to speak with Alaron, apart from when he'd shared his details for Alaron's research. *He turned down the ambrosia because he's too close to perfection, or some such rubbish*, Alaron recalled as they faced each other.

The young monk had a troubled look on his face and Alaron sighed, expecting another string of complaints . . . Some of the older monks had been protesting that Puravai had deliberately invited sin into the monastery, and from time to time Alaron had been stopped and berated by the old men; he might not understand the words but he certainly got the gist of their feelings. He really wasn't in the mood for that tonight.

'I'm not your Master, Felakan' he said shortly. 'What is it?'

Felakan collapsed to his knees, dropping his face to the floor so fast Alaron was afraid he'd slam it into the stone. 'Master, I was prideful! I was wrong! I thought I had attained Holy Serenity – the precursor to moksha! I thought myself Chosen! How wrong I was!'

'You should be talking to Master Puravai, not me,' Alaron said awkwardly. 'Please, get up—'

'I'm too ashamed – he was right about me. I see it now. I'm not worthy.' Felakan's voice became plaintive. 'Master Al'Rhon, I want what you offered – *please!*'

You want what the Ascendant acolytes now have. You've been watching them and envy is burning you up.

'I will ask Master Puravai to see you.' He doubted that the Master would agree. Felakan had been so arrogant, and this new desire smacked of self-regard and jealousy. *But maybe I'm reading him wrong; after all, I don't know the man.* 'I'll talk to Master Puravai for you,' he said, more kindly this time.

The next day, Puravai asked Corinea to prepare another potion. The day after that, Felakan died while screaming in his trance-dream about a spider creeping up on them all. The incident left Alaron with a nasty sense of self-doubt. *I was certain he would fail, but I passed the decision to Puravai. I should have spoken up.* Perhaps he was being unfair on himself, but Felakan haunted his dreams for nights afterward.

Alyssa Dulayne's skin quivered as the wind-dhou swept through the glittering white mountain peaks, piercing the wispy clouds. Falling sun and rising moon combined to light the twilight eerily. Febreux was always a windy month, and traversing these maze-like mountains had been an exercise in navigation she wasn't keen to repeat. Time and again they found themselves lost, and the shepherds captured to guide them became panicky and disoriented when taken into the air. What should have been a week's journey had taken almost a month, and she was fretting now. Would Ramita Ankesharan and Alaron Mercer have moved on? Did they even still have the Scytale? Rashid's army was taking dreadful casualties as he assailed Kaltus Korion's crusaders near Halli'kut. He urgently needed the artefact.

Then at last she saw what she sought: straight lines and architectural curves amidst the jagged rock formations, and the dim gleam of night-lights. *This is it: Mandira Khojana.*

She glanced at Megradh, who was grinning savagely at the prospect

DAVID HAIR

of the bloodletting to come. The Hadishah captain still worried her. He was nothing but a lecherous brute, having bullied the girl Tegeda into submitting to him, and was now demanding access to Cymbellea di Regia as well. Alyssa had denied him that, of course; Cymbellea's bloodline was far too important to be wasted on the likes of him. Right now the Rimoni girl was tied up and stowed in the hold to keep her from trying to jump overboard again. Since they'd executed the Dokken, Cymbellea had completely collapsed, both physically and spiritually. It didn't look like she'd be joining Alyssa's coterie willingly. That was both a shame and a vexation.

But perhaps she'll be useful in extracting the Scytale from this Alaron Mercer, if I need some leverage . . .

She engaged her Inner Eye and one wing of the monastery came alive to her gnostic sight, revealing a faint mesh of wards, invisible to normal sight. Wards could be concealed from mage-sight, but it took extra effort and energy: whoever had set these clearly thought that unnecessary, here in the wilds where no magi came. *But you're wrong, Ramita. I'm here . . . and you've got no one but a clutch of pitiful Zains to defend you.*

Caution would advocate waiting until the middle of the night, but the winds were rising and looking at the heavy clouds, more snowfall was threatening.

To Hel with caution!

'Find a place to land out of their sight,' she told Megradh. 'We'll go in on foot.'

Ramita tucked Dasra into bed and kissed his forehead while extricating her hair from his fingers. Her eyes beamed with love for the little boy. She couldn't really see anything of Antonin Meiros in him, except perhaps for the grey eyes, and maybe the shape of the skull. It was her own face she saw for the most part, in his composed, serious expressions – but when he smiled, he was her generous, gentle brother Jai.

'I adore you, my little man,' she whispered, 'I love you so much . . . and your brother Nas too. And one day we will find him, I promise . . .'

376

Suddenly shaking, she kissed her son again, and reluctantly left the room. She locked and warded the door behind her, because Alaron insisted she should, even here, so far away from the rest of the world. *It's a good habit*, he kept telling her, and of course he was right; she knew that . . .

Alaron was with the novices, playing another game to help make using the gnosis second nature. It involved lots of shouting and laughter, and the ancient monastery's thick stone walls reverberated to the sound. She wondered what the older monks were thinking. *Are they irritated, or envious?*

She was passing Corinea's chambers when she saw her door was open and on a whim, she knocked, then entered. The room was almost empty, unlike her own, which had accumulated all manner of clutter. 'Shaitan's Whore' was sitting on a stool and combing her long silver hair while staring into a mirror that didn't reflect her but instead showed a moonlit desert. She was scrying.

The old jadugara had linked minds with Alaron and Ramita a few weeks ago in an attempt to boost her scrying range, but Ramita had found it too frightening to continue. The mental linkage had brought back too many unpleasant memories of Alyssa Dulayne, Justina Meiros' so-called best friend; in her first few months in Hebusalim, Alyssa had taught Ramita the Rondian tongue, mind-to-mind – but the Ordo Costruo traitor had also used that link to steal her most secret thoughts. Opening up to Corinea after that had been hard, even though she now knew how to protect her mind.

'Where is that?' Ramita asked, setting her discomfort aside and peering at the desert scene in the mirror.

'I'm riding the mind of a vulture and projecting what it sees into the mirror,' Corinea explained. 'What you are looking at is part of the Sithardha Desert, southwest of Ullakesh – right now. I'm trying to use your memories of Huriya Makani to find her.' She conjured an image of Huriya in the mirror, plucked from memories of Ramita's last sight of her, beneath the dome of the Mughal's Palace in Teshwallabad. Then she brought another image to the mirror: the Inquisitor Malevorn Andevarion.

Corinea exhaled a little. 'He's handsome, yes?'

'I don't find killers good-looking. Have you found them?'

'I've found traces: places where they've been. I've been working outwards from where you last saw them, in Teshwallabad. They went north, that much is clear, but the trail is cold and they're shielding. But I'll find them, you'll see.'

'Is there any sign of my son?'

Corinea shook her head. 'Nothing.'

'Do you have any children?' Ramita asked boldly.

Corinea considered, then said, 'He's probably dead.'

'He?'

'We called him Hiram. He went East more than a hundred years ago, chasing a legend. I expect he's dead now, like his father.' She changed the subject firmly and asked, with a little leer, 'How's married life?'

Ramita let the matter of Hiram go. 'It's very good.'

'It is, for a time – I've had eight husbands, and many lovers besides, and I left them all behind. Romance is all very well, but it grows stale.'

'Al'Rhon has stood by me through many dangers,' Ramita replied confidently. 'Our love is for ever.'

'The number of times I've thought the same . . .' Corinea sighed melodramatically. 'No love is for ever, girl. Time has taught me that, at least. It's not all kisses and bed-play, you know.'

'I know this.' *I, who was married to Antonin Meiros and made to watch him die. I, whose lover killed him.* 'I have experienced much. I know what to expect. And I have a father and a mother who are my models in this: they've shown me that love and marriage aren't all joy. There are seasons of sadness and suffering, there are trials, there are temptations. Sometimes marriage is a duty and a burden; this is known. But they also showed me, every day, that making the sacrifices that love requires is always worthwhile.'

'Well, aren't you just a perfect little Lakh wife?' Corinea remarked sarcastically. 'Have you ever had a thought of your own? Or do you just spout the words your parents and gurus put in your mouth?'

I don't need her jealous bitterness. 'Goodnight, Lillea. Sleep well.'

She turned and started to walk away, but not before she'd seen Corinea's face drop, her misery clear for once. Her voice sounded morose and sour. 'I did believe in love,' she called after Ramita, 'but my lover – the man I loved more than life – tried to murder me. Every love ends like that.'

Ramita pulled the door shut behind her, because she didn't need to hear such things. *I will not let her failures curdle my joy . . .*

She walked down the corridor to the room she and Alaron now shared wondering briefly if they would ever find her lost son, then turning to the more practical question of when Alaron's game would be finished below . . . She was well inside the room before she realised that she wasn't alone.

Beside the window was a tall figure in a dark bekira-shroud, and two figures were standing guard, knives in either hand and masks over their faces. Their stance and attire recalled that night in Hebusalim, two years ago and more, when her new life had been torn apart. By Hadishah . . .

The tall woman in the bekira pulled down her hood, and a voice she'd hoped never to hear again floated across the room. 'Hello, Ramita. How lovely to see you again.'

21

Blood on the Snow

Theurgy: Mysticism

I commend to you the subtlest of Studies, the art of the Mystic. With it you can obtain the deepest communion of minds and thus share knowledge, thought and even gnostic strength. But beware: what is shared can also be taken. How well do you know the person to whom you've entrusted the keys to your mind?

ORDO COSTRUO COLLEGIATE, PONTUS

Mandira Khojana, Lokistan, on the continent of Antiopia
Moharram (Janune) 930
19th month of the Moontide

Alaron, standing at the edge of the mêlée of young novices, shared a boyish grin with Puravai: the game of 'Hoop' had come to Lokistan, direct from the streets of Norostein.

The courtyard where Alaron had convened his latest teaching game had a high wooden roof to keep out rain and snow. There were seats around all four sides, sheltered by the wooden walkways above that were currently off limits now that ice made them too treacherous. Normally the courtyard was a quiet place, used for exercise or meditation, but not this evening.

Alaron was pleased at how well the novices had picked up the game – in fact some, like Yash, were already becoming passionate about it. In Yuros non-magi played Hoop in the streets using any part of their body except their arms to move the ball, no hands, but at the Arcanum the students had adapted it for their own needs. There weren't many rules in either version. Two hoops were hung at either end of the courtyard, out of reach above their heads, and each team of five had to guard 'their' hoop and score through the opponent's one. Non-magi mostly kicked the leather ball, but the magi had added rules for shielding and kinesis. Both variants were a contest of agility and teamwork; for the magi it was also about the gnosis.

Alaron had enough novices for exactly six teams, and they had been playing a round robin to find a champion team. It was hilarious entertainment, but the novices were also becoming increasingly keen on winning.

'Good,' Alaron remarked quietly to Puravai. 'They need a little competitive spirit.' Then he turned back to the game. 'Come on!' he shouted at Aprek, 'you're two to one down – get working!'

Aprek waggled his head and pulled a determined face, but then Yash robbed him of the ball, stealing control while bumping Aprek aside. The air sparked as their shields collided, but Aprek went down passively. *Some of them still just don't get it*, Alaron thought. Then Sindar slammed into Yash hard and they both fell over, and came up with balled fists.

'Hey!' Yash shouted. 'You played me, not the ball – you *cheat!*'

'I didn't!' Sindar – usually a mild young man – protested.

'Calm yourself, Yash!' Aprek called from the ground. 'You're the cheat!'

'Yeah?' Yash strode towards Aprek, bent down and grabbed at his collar, and suddenly they were in the early motions of unarmed combat.

'Oi!' Alaron leaped from his seat and ran into the middle, where Yash and Aprek both turned to him and began making their cases at the tops of their voices.

He almost missed it, but in the growing silence that fell as everyone strained to hear what was going on, there was a faint crackling sound all the way around the courtyard. Looking up, he frowned. On the wooden walkway, the ice had broken from the shutters, as if they'd all moved at once . . .

Sal'Ahm on High. I place my life in your hands. Megradh only ever prayed on the verge of battle, and the rote words spilled automatically through his mind, though he had no intention of relinquishing his life into anyone's hands tonight. He glanced sideways as his men worked their way through the dimly lit stone-walled corridors.

Their wind-dhou and skiffs were out of sight of the monastery, just half a mile down the valley. The dhou-pilot had been put to work replenishing the keels, and they'd left Tegeda to guard the gypsy girl. *My current amusement, and my future one . . .* He couldn't keep the smile from his face.

After leaving their windcraft, his Hadishah had found an ill-defined path which climbed through the ice and snow to the monks' refuge. The air was bitter, and in seconds they were all calling upon the gnosis to supplement their body-heat as they soldiered on through knee-deep snow. The monastery itself looked hewn from the bones of the mountains, a forbidding place – had it been fortified and guarded. But the main gate was neither locked nor attended and they flitted without pause into the yard beyond. At his gesture his men fanned out, while Alyssa waved Megradh closer. Her peremptory airs were getting more and more irritating, but he listened dutifully as she pointed to a high bank of closed shutters accessed by partly covered stairs: the guest rooms, maybe. They were warded, in a place where no magi should have been.

'I'll take half a dozen and go up there,' she'd said. 'You find the monks, and ten minutes from now, you can start killing them.'

He approved of the plan: Zains were weaklings, and anyway, these two mystery fugitives weren't expected to present any risk. He was more concerned about the aftermath. Alyssa had been reluctant to divulge – even to the Sultan – that the Scytale of Corineus was at stake; he intended to gain the artefact first.

Counting out the seconds, he sent his jackals prowling into the Zains' inner sanctum. They didn't meet a single monk, but the shouting and laughter coming from deeper in might explain that. Whatever was going on sounded distinctly un-monastic to his ears. *Puzzling,* he thought, *but convenient.* He raised a hand and moved his fingers, sending his warriors to right and left, down the wooden galleries that overlooked a courtyard. Peering through an iced-over shutter, he saw a throng of monks arguing vociferously just twenty feet below him.

And standing in the middle, towering over them all: one Rondian, wearing the same monastic garb.

Ahhh . . . Alyssa thought the Rondians would be in the wing she went to, but here's one of them. Even as he sent silent instructions to his jackals, he was wondering how he could turn that to his advantage. <*Surround the courtyard, pick your targets . . . but the Rondian is mine.*>

Then he crept into position, muttered his prayer and took aim at the Rondian's back, aiming low to disable rather than kill outright. Alyssa had been very plain: she wanted the fugitives alive.

Ahm Most Holy, may my aim be true.

Cym lay with her cheek pressed against the cold wood of the hull. Her hands had been bound behind her back then knotted about a stanchion. Everything had gone quiet, she dimly realised, but was too tired to think beyond that. The boot-steps on the deck above had just stopped and now the only sound was the wind's distant moan. Even the hull was no longer vibrating, as it did when they flew.

We've landed . . . Is this the place Alaron ran to? Her brain told her body to get up and *do* something, but even if she had the strength, she was too well bound. The air was so cold that her breath came in foggy clouds, but the keel was radiating heat from the gnosis it channelled, so she wasn't in any immediate danger of freezing. Not that she would have minded; she'd heard it was a gentle death.

Death wasn't what she'd get, though. Alyssa might have made all kinds of offers to her, but she was in Hadishah hands and for a mage-woman, that meant the breeding-houses.

I don't care, she told herself.

When Zaqri died, all else had died as well . . . except she hadn't. Not yet.

Mostly she was just tired of the struggle to go on. Lying here alone and helpless, locked away from the gnosis . . . that was *perfect*. That was *deserved*. Alyssa was right: she'd selfishly run her own course, and it had led her nowhere.

If I'd not stolen the Scytale, Alaron, Jeris Muhren and I would have set out together. My father's caravan would never have been destroyed and Muhren would still be alive. We'd have saved my mother, and we'd have ... Her imagination stalled after that; everything that had actually happened crushed her fantasies, crushed them into meaninglessness. Alyssa was right: individuals didn't matter. The Great Causes – like the Crusade and the shihad – rolled by like avalanches, while little lives like hers were swept along or buried beneath.

Boots suddenly thudded above her head, making her flinch violently. The hatch rattled, ice cracking as it was wrenched open, and someone wrapped in layers of black dropped down and walked towards her: a homely Keshi girl with thick eyebrows and big, sad eyes, offering a small bowl of something steaming.

Cym stared at the bowl, her stomach growling and her mouth salivating. She hated herself suddenly, for wanting to go on, for her need to *live*.

The past two weeks, since that awful moment when Megradh had slaughtered Zaqri like an animal, had been one long waking nightmare. She couldn't remember having slept, though she must have. The image never left her, the sight of that horrible *thing* – the headless trunk – that her lover had been reduced to. Now he felt infinitely precious to her, and the resistance she'd put up against his love stupid beyond recall.

'Here, eat!' the girl said brusquely, in Rondian.

'I'm not hungry.'

'Yes. You hungry.' The Keshi yanked her upright, putting her back against a post. 'Eat.' She shoved a spoon of lumpy mush to Cym's lips, prodding them with the spoon to get her to open her mouth.

She couldn't refuse. The mush was bitter, over-spiced and already only warm, but it consumed her, not the other way round: the tastes burst through her mouth as the warmth burned through her body, and before she'd realised what she was doing, she was eating greedily, desperately. The Hadishah girl's lugubrious eyes regarded her with apparent compassion. When she had finished, the girl gave her water from her own flask.

'Where are we?' Cym asked.

The girl's response was hesitant. 'Monastery,' she offered. 'I . . . me . . . Tegeda.'

'Cym.' She looked about her, feeling the brief energy of the meal coursing into her blood, pulling her momentarily out of the void, though the slide back into entropy beckoned even now. To fight it off, she asked, 'Men gone?'

'Yes, to monastery,' Tegeda replied. 'Find enemy.' Her eyes narrowed a little. 'Your friend.'

Alaron . . . This is where he's been hiding, and now Alyssa has found him. And Megradh will cut off his head.

A sob burst from her lips unbidden.

Tegeda flinched. 'Megradh is bad man,' she said, as if she knew exactly what Cym had been thinking. She lifted a finger skywards. 'Ahm is Good. Ahm is Light. But not Megradh.'

Cym shuddered. Two nights ago, Megradh had come with the meal, and he had told her in broken Rondian that she was his, as soon as Alaron was found. 'You've no value after that, except in breeding.' Then he'd rammed his finger into her, in token of everything else he intended, sniffing it like a dog, and she'd vomited up everything she'd just eaten. Just the memory had her throat tightening painfully.

'He's an *animal*,' she rasped. *Pater Sol, Mater Lune, help me!*

'He does . . . things . . . also to me,' Tegeda said, those few words conveying her bitter sense of betrayal with overpowering intensity. 'My brothers . . . They know . . . no protect me. They are like Megradh. *Laugh.*'

'Evil,' Cym growled.

Tegeda nodded fiercely. Then she looked her full in the face and pulled out her curved dagger. Cym looked at it longingly. The girl shuffled forward and lifted Cym's chin with her left hand. For a moment Cym thought Tegeda was going to cut her throat, but instead she kissed her cheeks, as if acknowledging a kindred soul, and severed Cym's bonds.

Cym's hands came free and they stared at each other. Her whole body was at first too numb to move.

'Somehow, Cym now free,' Tegeda whispered. 'Outside, snow . . . big fall, right side.' She cupped Cym's face. 'Go . . . find good death, not bad death. Seek Light.' She backed away, her gentle face shining, then flowed up the hatch, closing but not locking it.

Cym stared after her, scarcely believing, but when she tried the hatch, it opened freely. She raised it cautiously and looked about. For a moment she froze: Lesharri was standing on the deck, looking up the slope. But Alyssa's sister didn't react, apparently unable to function without Alyssa's guidance. When she was sure Lesharri really wouldn't move, Cym jumped over the side of the dhou, her fall cushioned by the deep snow below. The mountains reared all about her, the peaks lost in the fluttering snowflakes that danced like thistle-fairies in the failing light. They had landed on a narrow flat plain barely a hundred yards across. Tegeda was huddled beside a fire with another person, who had their back to her. They were sipping from mugs, and Tegeda was pointedly looking away.

Cym got to her feet and tottered onwards, quickly losing the wind-craft in the flurrying snow behind her. A few steps later she found herself teetering on the edge of a crevase, only the fierce updraft saving her from plummeting into the void. She wavered, looking down into nothingness.

A good death.

Then a light, shining high above and to her left, pierced the darkness.

A monastery, Tegeda had said, and now she could see a trail of trampled snow, gradually being covered by new flurries, heading towards that light. Megradh and Alyssa and all their killers, they'd left – what . . . no more than five minutes ago? Gone to find *Alaron*.

She looked back at the void and then stumbled towards the path, staggering until her blood began to pump, and then she began to run.

She'd thought of a better way to die.

•

Alyssa Dulayne felt the pieces on the board settling into their places. Down below, Megradh's Hadishah were surrounding the monks, preparing to slaughter them; the captain's sporadic mental updates had revealed that they'd found most of the Zains gathered in one courtyard, which made life easier.

And here's little Ramita.

It was a year or more since she'd last seen the Lakh bint and she had no idea what affinities she'd developed. *She'd be the equivalent of a half-blood,* Alyssa guessed, from what she knew of pregnancy manifestation. And she was sharing this room with the Rondian, Mercer, judging by the clothing and gear scattered about, and the one unmade bed. *Meiros must have left her with a taste for white skin.* You could judge a lot about a woman from the men she clung to. *This Mercer dresses in poor cloth ... So she's still a peasant, when all's said and done.*

But there was an unexpected stillness to the girl before her, and Alyssa was a little puzzled by her composed reaction; surely this must have been a huge shock? She probed a little and found Ramita's gnostic aura to be curiously strong. Alyssa had cloaked the room to prevent any mental communication except her own, but Ramita hadn't tried anything yet.

'Don't do anything foolish, Ramita,' she purred, gliding towards the girl. Satravim was behind the Lakh, poised to lunge at her signal, and she was quite certain Ramita hadn't noticed him. The two Hadishah at her back shadowed her attentively, awaiting her signal. 'Let's keep this quiet, shall we?'

The little Lakh girl lifted her chin defiantly, but though she said nothing, her aura changed subtly, and strangely – it had too many colours, hinted at too many possibilities. A little uneasy, Alyssa paused and asked. 'Where's the Scytale of Corineus, Ramita?'

'The what?'

'Don't play games! I know you and the Mercer boy have it. Tell me where it is, or I'll make you.' She prepared her attack. *Illusion spells firstly, blended with Mesmerism, then I'll go inside with mystic-gnosis and pick her soul apart.*

'We don't have it any more,' Ramita said calmly.

Alyssa flicked a glance at Satravim, about to command him to move in, when Ramita suddenly stepped to one side and raised a hand towards the young assassin. 'You! Don't come any closer!' she ordered.

Everyone went still, then Alyssa kindled blue fire in her right hand. 'Satravim, go to the nursery and bring back Ramita's baby – I heard a child as we came in.'

Ramita flinched. 'No—!'

'It doesn't work that way, dearie,' Alyssa told her. 'Attachments are weaknesses; surely you have learned that by now?' She waited until Satravim had slipped out the door, then focused anew on the girl. 'I take it you bore twins, as you expected?'

The Lakh girl's face became stony and realcitrant.

'Don't try and lie to me, girl! Alyssa warned, not liking this flash of stubborness. 'I'll ask you once more, did you bear twins, as you believed you would?'

Ramita's face closed up, completely unreadable. 'There's only one,' she said. 'I warn you, don't you touch him.'

As the two Hadishah came up on either side of Alyssa, she pondered her strategy: *If we attack her now, she might just manage to raise the alarm before Megradh is ready . . . We just need to keep her silent a few more moments.* So she continued speaking. 'I have thirty Hadishah here, Ramita, and though I'm prepared to do this without blood, violence is very much an option. So answer truthfully: where's the Scytale?'

Before the girl could reply, the door opened and Satravim poked his head through. 'I can't open the nursery door,' he whispered.

'Why not? Are the wards unusual in some way?' *Can't these low-blood cretins do anything right?*

'No, Lady. It's just too strong for me.'

Too strong? Alyssa looked at Ramita. 'Who set those wards?'

Ramita lifted her chin, but she said nothing. Alyssa scowled: she knew the inside of Ramita's mind well, having taught the girl Rondian mind-to-mind when she first came to Hebusalim. The market-girl had a certain street cunning. 'Come Ramita, you can unlock it. Then we'll see how brave you are with your son's life at stake.'

She signalled to Satravim to fall in behind the girl again, but was shocked when the young man had the temerity to question her. 'Lady Alyssa . . . a child?'

Good grief! Scruples from a Hadishah? 'Satravim, the thing we seek could save the entire East from conquest,' she said patiently, 'and this little bint – this traitor to her own kind – is concealing it. Do you understand?'

His burn-marred face twisted uncomfortably, but she sensed the scales falling from his eyes. She smiled reassuringly. 'She's no innocent, Satravim.' She gestured to the bed. 'She sleeps with the enemy.'

Satravim stiffened, then nodded obediently and she gave him an approving look which appeared to settle him. *He's still mine . . .*

Ramita's defiance must have been ebbing already, because she allowed herself to be ushered out into the corridor, where two more Hadishah were waiting, one stationed beside each unopened door. *<Well?>* she sent silently to the assassin at the far end. *<Is there anyone in that room?>*

<It's locked,> the Hadishah replied, an older man with a calm demeanour. *<A very strong spell. There is a woman inside; I have heard singing.>*

Another mage? Alyssa looked at Ramita. *<Who?>*

The Lakh girl smiled as if she wasn't surrounded by blades. 'Knock and find out.'

I've just about had enough of your cheek, mudskin. She looked at Satravim, about to order him to batter the girl into unconsciousness, but she stopped. For some reason she felt exposed here. Megradh's men were probably only seconds away from attacking and that would likely alert whoever was within that chamber to the danger. And she still didn't know where Alaron Mercer was.

She stepped to the nursery door, set her hand to the lock and scanned it for a locking ward, then flinched. *Holy Kore on High! That's damnably strong – simple, but the raw power . . .*

She turned back to Ramita. 'Did you set this?' The touch of the spell wasn't familiar, but when she'd plundered Ramita's mind two years ago, she hadn't developed the gnosis.

Ramita just smiled again.

Alyssa stared indignantly. *Was it possible? Did Meiros do something to make his Lakh human wife as powerful as a pure-blood? If that's the case, she'll be priceless to Rashid's breeding programme.*

'If it's yours, unlock it, or Satravim will carve out your eyeballs. You won't need them in the breeding-house.'

A mental call forced her to pause. *<Lady,>* Megradh whispered into her skull, *<I'm looking at the Rondian along a crossbow bolt. Shall I loose?>*

She glared at Ramita, considering her options. After a moment, she sent, *<We don't need Mercer. The girl will suffice. Kill them all.>*

Megradh grunted agreement and broke the connection. He altered his aim to the Rondian youth's chest, while sending a silent order around his men. There were twenty-one bolts aimed and ready. Below them, the monks, totally oblivious to the danger, were still arguing about their game. Those seated at the sides had staves at their feet, their own, and those belonging to the participants in the game. Otherwise, they were defenceless.

<Two volleys and they'll be a pile of meat,> he sent to his men. *<Await my signal.>*

He engaged gnostic sight to ensure that Mercer wasn't shielding, but that gave him sudden pause: there were clear signs of gnosis-use below – and not just from Mercer. Several of the monks had vestigial shields in place, and as he widened his gnostic field of vision, he saw one of the players on the fringe of the argument was juggling a ball using kinesis. And there was a faint buzz, as if a current of mental communication was running beneath the audible words.

These are magi ... some of them anyway ... maybe all of them. He felt a flicker of misgiving. The Zains in Teshwallabad had barely resisted, apart from the younger ones with their fancy staff-tricks, but this place felt different. He almost contacted Alyssa, then decided that would be perceived as a show of weakness. A captain had to be decisive at all times.

<Some of these monks can shield,> he warned his crossbowmen. *<Be aware.>*

His jackals responded with little surprise; no doubt some had also begun to notice the shielding. But a crossbow bolt could penetrate steel plates. At this range, even a fully aware mage would struggle to repel a volley, and these targets were unaware. But a second volley might not be possible, not when crossbows took the best part of half a minute to reload – that would be too long if any of these Zains did turn out to be halfway competent magi.

<A change of plan> he sent. *<One volley and then we'll drop on them and cut them to pieces.>*

His finger tightened and he took a deep breath, beginning his inner mantra for an accurate shot: *Exhale, await that perfect moment of stillness . . . then—*

Suddenly a woman's voice rang out: '*ALARON! BEWARE! WATCH OUT—!*'

Megradh cursed, his aim wavering as a newcomer burst into the courtyard. As heads turned towards her he recognised her instantly: *the gypsy kutti!*

Someone shouted '*SHIELDS!*' and gnosis light flared below.

Megradh's aim settled on the gypsy as she ran towards Mercer and he bellowed, *<SHOOT!>* both out loud and through the gnosis, even as he loosed his own bolt. It slammed straight into the gypsy's chest and pinned her to a pillar.

A second later the air was filled with bolts and the gnosis.

CYM! Alaron recognised Cym's voice the instant it rang out and her warning crystallised his anxiety about the ice breaking above. He shielded himself as he shouted a warning. Part of his training had included throwing in surprise commands, to test the novices' reflexes and get them used to reacting instantly, so most of them did just that – but it was mostly luck who survived the next two seconds.

As blue light flared and clashed across the courtyard, the shutters on the walkway above crashed open and a hail of crossbow bolts lanced into the crowd of novices. Those at the sides took the brunt of the attack; one young man was struck in the back by two bolts and driven to his knees; beside him another was pierced through his neck, breaking it and killing him at once; he was dead before he fell. More bolts tipped in gnosis-light burst through the shields; though some were deflected, too many were deadly, and all around him Alaron saw limbs and torsos being impaled, while the young men howled in pain and shock.

He whirled back to where Cym's voice had come from, his heart in his mouth as the scattering monks revealed her impaled on a pillar by a crossbow bolt. She was white as a sheet, but she was alive, just; he could see her trying desperately to breathe. He screamed her name and ran to her, calling his staff to his hands.

'*STAVES!*' he shouted, and the Zains went for their weapons as the shutters above crashed open and twenty or more black-clad shapes dropped from the gangways above, blades in hand.

'Hadishah!' someone shouted, sounding panic-stricken, and the air filled with cries of fear and fury.

'Master!' Sindar shouted, and Alaron turned to see the young man, staff in hand, looking bewildered, his training failing in the face of genuine combat. A black-clad figure landed behind him, his sword raised.

'Watch out!' Alaron cried, but it was already too late; even as Sindar turned the Hadishah drove his scimitar down, straight through Sindar's weak shield and into his back. The young man fell forward, his face still uncomprehending.

Aprek shrieked and launched himself at the Hadishah. His normally placid face had gone white and he was frothing with rage. He began to rain blows down on the startled assassin, but even as he gave ground, another was darting in on his flank. Then Yash flew in, making a gesture that flung the Hadishah away and into the walls with backbreaking force.

Alaron darted through a gap, still making for Cym, when a black-clad attacker came at him. For a second he confronted a pair of dark eyes that flashed with mesmeric-gnosis, trying for a spell to fog his parry, but it was weak. *Mesmerist, huh? Try this!* Alaron spun his staff and lunged, blasting Ascendant-strength kinesis into the Hadishah's shield, fusing and shattering it. The follow-up blow, a continuation of his original movement, saw him slamming the iron heel of his staff into the assassin's temple, so hard his skull cracked. He went down, as Alaron flowed onwards.

All round him, the fight was taking shape. Many – too many – of the Zains were already down, and those still standing were trying to encircle the wounded and protect them, all the while fighting desperately to survive themselves. Master Puravai, the only non-mage, was in the middle of the press, protected by his novices while he bent over one of the wounded. But the Hadishah, trained to kill and with the advantage of surprise, were carving into them.

Even as he tried to reach Cym, Alaron could see the invaders were beginning to meet stronger resistance. At first most of the Zains had thought only of defence, with only a few, like Yash and Kedak, fighting aggressively. But that was changing: as the young men shielded themselves and the wounded from a storm of blades, mage-bolts and fire-bursts, Alaron sensed the realisation growing among them that they were holding their own; that their gnostic training really worked – and that their kon-staffs could be as damaging as a blade.

He reached Cym, to find Gateem – apparently oblivious to the mêlée around them – already had his hand on her chest, white healing-gnosis blooming in his hands.

<*Please, please live!*> Alaron begged her, but she didn't respond.

Just in time, he sensed a blow coming and set his shields blazing as a mage-bolt struck. He darted into a gap between two of his trainees and blazed gnosis-fire at his attacker, which overwhelmed the Hadishah; as the assassin's shields turned scarlet, he drove his staff into the man's chest, using kinesis to cave in the ribcage. The nearest Zains, seeing what he'd done, followed his lead, and started bludgeoning their attackers backwards.

Then the fight changed again: someone – a Hadishah commander, Alaron assumed – shouted aloud and with his mind and the Hadishah darted backwards. As one, they raised their hands.

'WARE!' Alaron shouted, in unison with several others as a storm of flames and blue mage-bolts slammed into their shields.

But despite the number of attackers and their undoubted strength, they scarcely penetrated, and Alaron felt the confidence surge among his young charges, a new self-belief fusing with anger. *Right you bastards, now it's our turn!* He waved an arm and shouted, 'KHOJANI, ATTACK!'

He went straight for the Hadishah commander while his novices went for their nearest foe.

Ramita sensed a sudden eruption of the gnosis below, coming from the direction of the courtyard. She stiffened, dreadfully aware of Satravim's knife resting beside her eye. But she couldn't drag her gaze from Alyssa Dulayne, whose beautiful, sultry face was taut with tension.

'Open the lock, Ramita!' she snapped. 'Last warning.'

Then at the far end of the corridor, Corinea's door swung open and the old sorceress stepped out. 'What's—?'

The older Hadishah man stationed before her door didn't hesitate. He'd positioned himself a few paces away so that he'd be behind whoever emerged, and even as Corinea spoke, he drove his dagger into the old woman's back.

The blade broke.

Corinea didn't gesture, or even glance in the man's direction, but he shrieked and fell to one side, where he collapsed in a concussion of unseen gnosis. Ramita recalled the awe she'd first felt when the old woman had appeared before her in Teshwallabad, in the guise of Makheera-ji: a goddess come to life.

'Who the Hel are you?' Alyssa demanded hoarsely. Satravim, his breath suddenly shallow and hot, pulled Ramita against him. His knife-point, shaking alarmingly, filled her gaze.

'I am Lillea Sorades, if that name means anything to you,' Corinea replied mockingly. She twisted her fingers, her eyes flashed violet, and the next Hadishah, the one standing beside the nursery door, screamed and collapsed. The remaining two assassins standing behind Alyssa and Satravim squeaked with fright and backed away.

Alyssa was still reacting to the name. '*Lillea Sorades*? That's impossible!' She looked frantically at Satravim, then back at Corinea. '*Stop there! Or the girl dies!*'

It was time to act.

From the moment that Satravim had put his dagger against her face, part of Ramita had been trying to follow her training: to find the right spells for the situation. And now everyone was looking at Corinea . . .

With her left hand she *shoved*, using kinetic-gnosis to thrust the dagger violently up and away. Satravim gasped as the bones in his wrist snapped, but that wasn't her *real* blow; that came from her right elbow, which she drove backwards into the assassin's midriff. She was already inside his shields so he couldn't do anything to weaken the blow – but even if he had, it would have done no good, for her elbow wasn't just an elbow any more. In the instant between preparing the blow and striking, a nine-inch spur of bone had erupted from the joint; it was that which speared into Satravim's stomach.

Satravim gagged as hot blood erupted over her, and for a moment Ramita was aghast at herself – but that lasted less than a moment. *They threatened my son!* The assassin staggered, his eyes bulging, his scarred face stretched into the beginnings of a scream, but she caught his knife with her gnosis and stabbed it into his chest, pouring energy along the blade as it went into his heart and he collapsed, his mouth gaping silently. In the brief moment as their eyes connected, the image was burned onto her brain. She'd never deliberately killed before.

But why stop now?

She whirled and found Alyssa Dulayne staring at her as if she'd never seen her before. *Well, she hasn't* . . .

Then gnosis flared behind her: Alyssa too had been preparing her spells, but hers were to find a way out, and that went through the walls: into the nursery . . .

It's impossible! I refuse to be gulled, Alyssa told herself, but her mind was fixed on that dreadful name: *Lillea Sorades? Corinea? No – it's just a lie to scare me!* But when Alyssa saw the look on Ramita's face as she turned from Satravim, drenched in blood, fear took over.

She'd once been told that in peril, there were two gut responses: to fight, or to run. She'd always been one of the latter – in fact, she accounted it a virtue. Heroes fought and died; smart people ran, and lived to run again.

All the while she'd been threatening Ramita, she'd been working at that overpowered lock; it was strong, certainly, but also simple, and that meant a skilled counter-blow would break it. She thrust and the locking-spell came apart, the door swung open and she dashed through, feeling Ramita's dagger scouring her shields as she sought an escape – a window to the outside. Someone moved in the dimly lit room and she loosed a mage-bolt, blasting the face off a young Lokistani woman. In the corner a baby boy sat up in bed, blearily opening his mouth—

A hostage! That's what I need! She reached out with kinesis to draw him to her—

—when something picked her up and hurled her towards the far wall. She spun in the air, trying to protect herself, and saw Ramita Ankesharan in the doorway, shining like a small sun – then she struck the wooden shutters and smashed through, keeping her shields tight around her as the timber splintered – and then she was falling through darkness, plummeting into the ravine amidst wooden splinters and shards of ice . . .

'NO—!' Ramita roared. She ran to Dasra, to make sure he was unharmed, then glimpsed Corinea even as the ancient sorceress flashed past the door. Two Keshi voices cried out in terror, then there was silence and her eyes went back to the broken shutters, and the wind howling through. She'd not meant to throw Alyssa out; she'd wanted to keep her right here. The smell of blood was in her nostrils, as well as warm and sticky on her skin, and she wanted *more*; she wanted that Rondian *kutti* to *suffer* for threatening her son.

She ran to the window, rage coursing through her.

The goddess Parvasi, Sivraman's wife, the mother, was Ramita's patron – but Parvasi-ji had a wilder aspect: Darikha, the warrior-woman who rides the tiger, and it was Darikha-Ji who was in her mind as she roared in fury, flashing to the window in time to see the comet-trail of Alyssa's aura as she fell away into the darkness.

She's a pure-blood – that fall won't kill her . . .

She threw herself out the window.

The novices fanned out in all directions, only a dozen or so still upright, but no one hesitated. Even thoughtful souls like Aprek tore into their foes. Yash was blazing with aggression, Fire-spells pouring from him with increasing intensity as his inhibitions fell away. They were all growing into the fight, taking confidence in their skills.

They were still outnumbered. Alaron found himself facing two of half-blood strength, judging by their spells, and though his power dwarfed theirs, facing two foes was always a deadly game. Then his fighting instincts rose.

Twice before in his life, in deadly situations, he'd reached the mental state that magi called 'trance', when instinct took over and utilising two or even three gnostic skills at once became possible. Though he'd tried to achieve it in training, he'd never managed to – but now, in the heat of the fight, it began to happen again.

He engaged *divination*, to see his enemies' blows even as the intention formed; and with *illusion* he blurred his form to conceal his footwork, which any trained fighter could use to anticipate the next blow. And with *kinesis*, he locked and layered his shields to parry more than one blow. Raw energy blazed at both tips of his kon-staff and he glided between his foes, parrying two thrusts in successive moments before flowing into a flying kick aimed at one while simultaneously slashing the staff at the other, drawing them into his wake as he spiralled by and slammed his staff at the left-hand assassin's skull. The concussion of his blow pierced the assassin's shield and sent him staggering straight into Yash's reach. Yash shoved his own assailant back, then smashed his staff on the off-balance Hadishah. Gnosis-fire exploded and the assassin flopped bonelessly, the back of his head blasted open and smouldering.

The second Hadishah spun and slashed back at Alaron, who parried effortlessly and launched a rapid-fire attack, striking in a succession of blows that a single blade could never hope to follow – but a knife appeared in the Hadishah's left hand and he blocked deftly, kindling energy on the blade as he riposted. Alaron parried again as power throbbed through the dagger, scouring his staff – then the Hadishah's dagger snapped.

The assassin staggered backwards and Alaron followed, divining a sweeping scimitar cut at his head and ducking under it, then hurled a burst of illusory darkness at the Hadishah's eyes. The assassin bellowed in alarm, suddenly blind, and began flailing about desperately and seeking to flee – the wrong way. Alaron drove his staff into his chest, gnosis-energy concussed through his foe and he flew backwards, landing in a broken limp-limbed heap.

Alaron had already moved on. Now the Hadishah captain was before him: a burly, brutal man who very obviously knew his business. He attacked with ferocity and skill, his scimitar and dagger flowing in perfect unison, scouring Alaron's shields and almost taking his fingers off when the scimitar scraped down the shaft of his kon-staff. The next instant he lashed out with his boots and drove his blade at Alaron's face, an attack designed to skewer his skull while his shields were fused elsewhere.

But it didn't happen; Alaron's shields were too strong. Instead, he hurled the man away and threw mage-fire at him, then battered at him with kinesis before wading towards him again.

All round the courtyard, the Hadishah were beginning to die. Like young lions realising hitherto unknown strengths, the novices were flexing their muscles now. Some remembered their first lessons as a Zain, fighting with restraint yet still battering the weakest Hadishah into submission. But the young monks also made mistakes. Though the assassins were far weaker than them, half-bloods and quarter-bloods against Ascendants, they'd been trained since childhood not just to fight, but to survive. Rather than kill his foe, one young Zain tried to take a wounded Hadishah prisoner, only to suddenly stagger away with a knife in his chest. The assassin ran for the doors – and was immolated from three sides. Mercy was forgotten.

The fight had clearly turned, but Alaron knew he had to finish it quickly. Ramita was upstairs, and he'd heard nothing from her. Cym was now lying motionless on the ground. Others were wounded, needing attention before they died.

The captain saw him glance at the Rimoni girl and spat out words in broken Rondian, clearly trying to goad Alaron into a false step. 'Your woman? I fuck her! I shoot her!' He grinned evilly.

It worked: Alaron saw red, all finesse vanished and he launched himself at the man, gripping the staff with both hands at one end and wielding it as if it were a broadsword, trying to belabour the Hadishah to death.

I'll kill you I'll kill you I'll kill you—

The man parried, again then again, and though his gnosis was less, his power wasn't being wastefully squandered. He blocked Alaron's staff, hacked it in half, then riposted with a straight-armed drive that pierced Alaron's shields. Suddenly Alaron was gasping at a foot of steel plunging through his right shoulder, straight into the joint and out the back. He staggered, his shields dissipating.

An old Arcanum lesson echoed in his brain: *A good fighter remains calm . . .*

Then someone rose behind the Hadishah captain and buried a dagger in his back amidst a scarlet starburst of shattered shields. The man's brutish face went slack, his mouth fell open, then he collapsed, his scimitar torn from Alaron's wound in an agonising wrench and clattering to the ground.

Behind him, Gateem stood staring aghast at his bloody knife. He dropped the weapon and stepped away as if trying to disassociate himself from it entirely.

Alaron gave him a grateful look, then the pain hit him. He shielded hard, lest he leave himself vulnerable, but those few Hadishah still standing, realising they were trapped, were dropping their weapons and holding up their hands in surrender. For a moment, carnage beckoned, then Mercy regained her grip on the minds of the young novices and they withheld their weapons.

Alaron's eyes went back to Cym.

DAVID HAIR

Oh no . . . He staggered to her, dropped to his knees. 'Cym?' <Cym!>

She opened one eye. Her lips tried to move, but nothing came out. His mind caught the word. <Al?>

<Cym! You're going to be okay! We can help you—!>

Her mental voice sounded resigned, and horribly faint. <Not this time, Al . . . >

He looked about wildly. 'GATEEM! GATEEM!'

The novice looked at him helplessly. 'Already done all I can, Al'Rhon-sahib.>

'No! No you haven't! We've got to do more—!' He gripped Cym's arm, shouting at her as he flooded the wound with all the healing-gnosis he could, skills he'd not learned until recently, from Corinea's sporadic tutelage.

Stop the blood-loss, reconnect the veins, bind the flesh, seal the wound, cauterise!

All the while he was shouting into her brain, <Cym? Listen to me! You're going to make it – just keep listening to me. Keep talking – you can't die if you're awake! You can't die if you're awake! You can't die—!>

<I don't want to stay, Al . . . >

<NO!>

<He's waiting . . . Zaqri's waiting . . . Zaqri . . . >

Her eyelids fell, her head flopped sideways and her gaze emptied. Alaron stared, disbelieving, as something broke inside him. <Cym?> He turned to Gateem. 'You're our best healer! Do something!'

Gateem's face was awash with tears of futility. 'I can't do anything more . . .'

'Then get Lily!' Alaron cast his eyes upward. <CORINEA! CORINEA!>

The sorceress arrived a minute later, tight-lipped and angry, Dasra cradled in her arms. She looked at Alaron's face and her expression softened, and she bent over Cym dutifully, but by now even Alaron could see she'd already gone. And then he realised, when he thought nothing could be worse than what had already happened, that Ramita hadn't appeared . . .

As the ravine opened beneath her, the air ripping past as she plummeted towards the icy rocks and frigid water, it occurred to Ramita that she had never really learned how to fly.

She'd principally been an Earth-mage, until Master Puravai's teaching had opened her up to the other Studies, and though she'd been broadening her skills in what little spare time she had, flying was one of the more challenging aspects of Air-gnosis.

Below her, Alyssa Dulayne's aura flashed blue, and suddenly the Ordo Costruo traitor was no longer falling but gliding, heading down the valley. Ramita screamed in fury. She tried to gather the air and control her fall, but nothing made any impression.

'Then forget flying,' she muttered. 'I'll do it my way.'

She let the Air-gnosis go and called kinesis instead, caught the walls flashing by and used them to push off. The concussion of force against the rock face broke part of it away, starting a small avalanche. Her bones jarred, but now she was hurtling in Alyssa's wake, swooping down the main path towards an outcropping. She landed on the path some hundred yards behind her quarry and began to run along it in ever-greater bounds, growling in fury.

There was another, darker aspect of the Goddess, beyond even the controlled ferocity of Darikha-ji: Dar-Kana, the embodiment of female rage.

Ramita let the darkest aspect of the Queen of Heaven engulf her from within. She roared in wordless ferocity, and her aura took flesh about her as she grew and changed, pulling weapons out of the air, with extra arms grown to wield them. The transformation was agonising but perversely fulfilling, as she strode on with the thought of that *kutti* Alyssa getting away fanning the flames of her rage. She rounded a bend in the path with orange flames blazing in one left hand and blue mage-fire in another, while her right hands held ready shards of ice and stone. Her cloak rippled with Air-gnosis and she began to attune to it, leaping a gully and closing the distance to her prey.

'*I'M COMING, ALYSSA!*' she screamed. '*I AM COMING FOR YOU!*'

The cry echoing down the valley after her chilled Alyssa Dulayne's soul. It was a roar of rage, and so enflamed she could feel the heat of it. The words were Lakh, but needed no translation.

I'm coming for you.

She called more Air-gnosis to her, frantically trying to escape.

Ramita Ankesharan isn't a mage – she's possessed! Corinea did it – surely that had to be it? Shaitan's Whore has erased the girl's humanity and made her into something out of Hel.

Alyssa was certain she was right, but she wasn't going to stick around to work out the details. She took to the air again, though her exposed skin was frozen from the air streaming over her. Her robes, torn to shreds by her fall, offered no protection. All her ambitions – of bringing Rashid this great prize – were coming apart too.

But we'll come back, in force and prepared. Then we'll see . . .

So she ran, swooping over ice and snow toward the skiffs, screaming for help. She'd left a pair of Hadishah to keep the windcraft ready, and Lesharri was here too. Names sprang to mind: *Tegeda, good, faithful Tegeda . . . and that pilot . . . Neridho?* She couldn't see him anywhere. 'Lesharri! Sister!' she screeched, casting a panicky look about, then seeing her, slumbering on a seat beside the cabin door, 'Sister! We must flee!'

Lesharri didn't stir, even though the valley was magnifying a high-pitched scream of rage, like a demoness from Hel, or one of the Bullhead's Bloodmaidens. Alyssa suddenly felt herself trapped in a nightmare, helpless to affect the outcome.

'Lesharri?' Alyssa tugged her sister's shoulder fearfully, then whimpered as the blanketed figure rolled off the seat and flopped to the icy deck, her throat cut open in a bloody arc, the scarlet fluids frozen over the wound. Alyssa staggered backwards, then looked in utter incomprehension at Tegeda.

Tegeda produced a bloody dagger from behind her back and said, 'You let Megradh use me.' Her voice was emotionless, hollow. 'Ever since I gained the gnosis, I've kept myself innocent, and let no man touch me. But *you* . . . you let him do to me whatever he wanted.' Her eyes focused beyond Alyssa on a monstrous shape that had appeared at the head of the plateau. 'The Great Goddess is coming, jadugara: she is going to rip you limb from limb. And even that is not punishment enough.'

Alyssa stared at her, uncomprehending. *How can she turn on me?* she thought, bemused. *Everyone loves me!*

Then a roar of triumph came, alarmingly close, and she turned to face Ramita – but whatever was rampaging through the snow towards them was no longer the girl she'd known. It was something from the Lakh pantheon: a twelve-foot-tall four-armed black-skinned giantess. Alyssa snatched at Air-gnosis and threw herself sideways just as the Ramita-thing hurled a spear of ice, carving through her shields as if they were gauze and slashing an inch-deep gouge in her hip. She landed near one of the skiffs and darted away again, terror lending her the wings to fly as the Ramita-monster shot fire at her. The skiff was engulfed in flames but Alyssa evaded the centre of the blast by an instant. She cartwheeled across the snowy plateau, shrieking in terror as a crossbow bolt shattered against her shields – not Ramita, this time, but Tegeda, and she was already cranking the weapon for the next shot.

I don't understand . . . Tegeda never said—

Then a gigantic leap brought Ramita to her, and though Alyssa leaped skywards, a huge taloned hand shot out and raked her back. Pain lanced through her as flesh and muscle was shredded. Then a colossal weight landed on her – a massive foot, smashing into her back – and she *heard* her spine crack.

Alyssa blacked out on a numbing wave of emptiness.

The goddess screamed in triumph and slashed her prey's back, the razor-sharp claws shredding cloth and flesh. Her mouth slavered as she gripped the fallen witch's face, ripping at skin then gripping her blonde hair and *wrenching*. The scalp came away and her talons tore through right to the skull.

Then she realised that her prey was unconscious and paused, disappointed; there was no joy to be had from her in that state. She moaned, and cast about angrily. But her fury faded, until Ramita regained some degree of self-awareness. Then memory of the carnage she'd left behind in the monastery overcame her, and she heard a silent wail of desolation from her new husband, a cry of loss that penetrated her inner raging storm. The moment for rage had passed – the intensity was unsustainable.

Dasra needs me. Alaron needs me.

As the goddess' power ebbed away, so did her shape and Ramita shrank back to her own form. Her own clothes had been ripped to pieces and the icy winds began to bite. She dropped the bloody blonde scalp in disgust and wrapped her arms about her, panting heavily.

'Lady?' said a timorous voice in Lakh.

She turned, startled and frighted, to see another Hadishah, just twenty feet away, a crossbow in her hands. But before she could gather her gnosis, the serious-faced young woman fell to her knees in the snow and began babbling, 'I am no enemy of yours, Lady Dar-Kana! My name is Tegeda: I was Omali before the Amteh took me! Please let me serve you!'

The Vexations of Emperor Constant
(Part 5)

On Monarchy

What is a king? Someone not just bred and raised to reign over others, but divinely ordained to do so? Or is he a despot clinging grimly to power, hammering down those who threaten him? Or is he just a figurehead, someone the truly powerful can agree upon for stability's sake, so that they can get on with their own agendas?

ORDO COSTRUO COLLEGIATE, HEBUSALIM, 884

Pallas, Rondelmar, on the continent of Yuros
Summer 927
1 Year until the Moontide

The room fell silent, and for a few seconds, everyone looked reflective, their gaze turned inwards. The Plan had been laid out: the cards were on the table and they were more or less in agreement. This was the culmination of months of preparation, secret meetings between individuals, and no little wining and dining. Gurvon Gyle picked up his goblet, noticed with considerable disappointment that it was empty and put it back down again. He needed something considerably stronger than watered wine.

If there really were gods, any now listening to us would be appalled, he thought as he silently reviewed the meeting.

I'm going to seize Javon, then hand it over to the Dorobon. He smiled privately at that. *Well, maybe.* He could sense opportunities there.

The Rondian Empire underestimates Javon; they think that just because the Dorobon seized it once, it'll be easy. They forget that the Dorobon also lost Javon. Perhaps we can capitalise on that. Elena will have a view. He shied away from thinking about Elena. Their relationship wasn't what it once was.

After Javon, we send the Duke of Argundy into a trap. He wondered if they could rely on Rashid Mubarak to fulfil his side of the bargain; he suspected more likely Echor would just be weakened. There was no way the Keshi would be able to defeat a trained Rondian army.

It's Naxius and his soul-stealing that worries me. What a Hel of a thing! Naxius is dangerous . . .

And then this final act: the destruction of the Leviathan Bridge. Even though he and Belonius Vult had conceived the whole plan, he was still stunned at the immensity of it. To destroy the Ordo Costruo's great construction was one thing, but to also lift the ocean floor and restore the isthmus? That would be truly astounding. The world would be so profoundly changed he could scarcely encompass it.

His eyes roved the room, assessing what each stood to gain.

Belonius Vult, his friend – well, so-called. Bel was an adept courtier, and was no doubt already angling for a bigger role. After all, the emperor would be requiring some special envoys and legates as the Crusade began.

For Tomas Betillon and Kaltus Korion it was another chance to plunder the East and fatten already bulging treasuries. *But will Korion be content to remain subservient to a young – and immature – emperor?* he wondered.

Calan Dubrayle played his hand close to his chest, but the treasurer had revealed hitherto unsuspected links to Belonius too. Wars were notorious for bankrupting the state while enriching well-placed individuals, and Dubrayle's allegiances were distinctly murky.

Grand Prelate Dominius Wurther had been withdrawn, only becoming passionate about distracting things, playing the clergyman role even when it made the others impatient. It was tempting to write him off as a buffoon, but fools didn't rise so high in the Church. *He'll have some angle too, I'm sure of it.*

He turned next, unwillingly, to Erwyn Naxius. The old Ordo Costruo traitor was nodding his way like a senile dodderer, but when their eyes met, Gurvon saw reptilian cunning. *How much of Vult's contributions to the plan can be attributed to Naxius?* he wondered, keeping his lips fixed in a light smile.

Finally, he studied Emperor Constant and his mother Lucia, because really they needed to be considered together. Constant couldn't rule without his mother's guidance, and Lucia would have no role without her son on the throne. If this plan went as planned, they would become unstoppable: masters of both Yuros and Antiopia. The thought gave Gurvon no pleasure, but the rewards that were promised did: a lifetime's worth of gold. Yes, crime did pay, if you did it properly. But what really excited him were the two things one couldn't buy – well, not exactly: immunity from prosecution, and a hereditary title, finally allowing him to join the aristocracy. At a stroke, he would become one of the great of the empire, with the seniority to force the old pure-blood families to give him at least the semblance of respect. And if Elena wasn't with him in that lakeside manor they'd always dreamed of . . . well, she wasn't the only woman in the world.

Betillon's rough voice broke the silence. 'I have a question,' he said, looking at Lucia. 'We all understand that the emperor will be unrivalled after this plan is brought to fruition, and we all rejoice in that. But what reward do we personally derive? We in this room, that is.'

Gurvon was a little surprised: Betillon prided himself on being a man who told things as they were, but this was pushy, even for him. Lucia looked at the Governor of Hebusalim with an amused surprise on her face, which Gurvon instantly distrusted. Lucia was seldom genuinely surprised or amused. 'Ah, Tomas! We can always trust you to bring venal self-interest to the table.'

'Spare me, Lucia! Look around the room: we're the kings of venality, all of us! We all want to better ourselves; we want to rise when you rise! That's why we're here, working for you! We all know it, even if I'm the only one with the balls to say it!'

'If it takes *balls* to speak like a Tockburn thug, then I'm glad I don't have any,' Lucia retorted. 'What further reward do you imagine you deserve, friend Tomas? You've already been promised yet another king's ransom.'

'The Ascendancy,' Betillon replied, and the room fell silent – a different sort of silence than before. Everyone was shocked ... and more than a little curious.

The Ascendancy! Hel's Belles ... Gurvon realised he was sitting there open-mouthed, and he closed it at once. *Yes, please!*

'All of our lives,' Betillon continued, 'we've had the Scytale of Corineus dangled above our heads like a carrot on a stick. "Be a good, loyal subject and the emperor will reward you!" Well, here we are, handing you the world on a platter. Who could be more worthy of Ascendancy than we in this room?'

Kaltus Korion was now nodding along to Betillon's words, and the rest, whilst loathe to risk siding with such a confrontational approach, were most certainly *intensely* interested.

'My dear Tomas, even I have not been permitted to Ascend,' Lucia replied slowly.

'And why is that?' Betillon affected confusion, perhaps genuinely. 'You're a Living Saint, Mater-Imperia. If anyone deserves the honour, surely you do?'

It's a damned good question, Gyle thought, *although I'm not sure I'd ask it myself.*

'The Keepers decide on whom the Ascendancy is bestowed, not I,' Lucia replied, clearly wanting the subject closed. The Keepers – the mysterious group of surviving Ascendants – answered to no one, not even the emperor. They had no other role in society except to guard and preserve the Scytale.

'Don't give us that shit,' Betillon snapped. 'If we're going to conquer all of Urte for my Lord Emperor, the Ascendancy is the least we deserve!' He looked around the table, but only Korion was showing open support. His face changed as it finally dawned on him that he might have overstepped.

Gurvon glanced at Belonius Vult, who had a strange look on his face, as if he knew something pertinent.

I must ask him what he knows later.

Lucia's voice was brittle. 'I'm sure that if we're successful, the Keepers will consider us all closely.'

'I want to hear that from one of them,' Betillon declared, but Korion touched his arm warningly.

Lucia eyeballed Betillon unflinchingly. 'Enough, Tomas. The Keepers stand apart. It's not my decision.'

The tension remained for a few moments, then Betillon sat back, grumbling under his breath. Gurvon was watching Lucia's eyes. *There's something she's concealing about this matter*, he thought, *and I think Betillon just earned himself a knife in the back when the time is right.*

'Mother, we're due in chapel soon,' Constant interjected. 'Are we finished here?'

'Yes, we are,' Lucia replied firmly, as the men facing her gave up the matter of the Ascendancy and relaxed. 'Gentlemen, thank you for your time. In particular I wish to thank Governor Vult and Magister Gyle. We now have a stratagem: no victory can be won without one. Let the thanks of the emperor be recorded.'

Betillon, Korion, and Dubrayle made perfunctory murmurs while Naxius smiled benevolently. Constant just looked like he badly needed to pee.

Everyone stood as servants entered with fresh wine. Betillon and Korion were locked in immediate conversation. Wurther hobbled off in the opposite direction to Naxius and Dubrayle, while Constant scuttled out. Lucia glided over to join the two Noromen. Vult bent over her hand reverently, and Gurvon made his best courtier's bow.

'Gentlemen, we are all very impressed,' Lucia told them. 'Kaltus, Tomas and the others may not act like it, but if they weren't in full support, your plan would have been ripped up. You men are so competitive,' she scolded, as if all of womankind were a sisterhood of mutual support.

'We're proud to serve the House of Sacrecour,' Vult smarmed.

'And we're very grateful to you both. So is my son.'

'He's fortunate to have your guidance,' Gurvon said tactfully, not adding, *Without you he'd last about three minutes.*

Lucia smiled gracefully, with just the hint of knowingness. 'The Rimoni Emperors used to have a slave whose role was to murmur "hominem te memento" in their ears once an hour: *Remember that you are only a man.* The first mage-Emperor abolished the custom, of course, because we are now more than men. I sometimes think that we should reinstate it.'

'Needless, when our emperor has you, Gracious Lady,' Vult replied, which was undoubtedly meant as a compliment, but Gurvon found other meanings in his words. Lucia caught his eye; so had she. It was strangely chilling, to share a moment of understanding and intimacy with the most frightening woman on Urte.

I think Corinea herself would run if she saw Lucia Sacrecour coming, he thought, followed immediately and inexplicably by the thought, *I wonder what it would be like to bed her.*

She looked at him sideways, the faintest hint of a knowing glance, then a dismissive smile.

I guess I'll never know.

'So, gentlemen,' she said, disengaging from them coolly. 'You know I'm something of a Diviner, and it came to me unbidden during the meeting today that in three years time, when the Moontide is over, those of us who see this through will be enshrined as leaders of a New Era. One empire, spanning the whole of Urte.'

Gurvon accepted a goblet from a servant with a tray. 'I'll drink to that, Holiness.' He did, savouring the taste and the soothing jolt of the alcohol. *I needed that.*

'Look around you,' Lucia said. 'Those you see in this room are the men you will rule Urte with ... and my son, of course,' she added as if in afterthought. 'Cultivate them, for they will be your peers.' She nodded farewell, her eyes locking with Gurvon's one last time. *<Magister Gyle, Betillon will suffer for his impertinence. Mark the moment when it comes, and learn.>*

He bowed wordlessly.

When she was gone, he and Belonius exhaled wordlessly, then clinked goblets.

Belonius raised the toast. 'Gurvon, we Diviners believe that the unbidden vision is more trustworthy than a planned seeing. I believe she's right: in three years time, we will all be immortal.'

22

A Minor Setback

Sorcery: Divination

Can I see the future? Of course: I can see thousands of futures! It's trying to pick the right one that drives you to drink!

CYRILLA SETTERBERG,
ARGUNDIAN DIVINER AND BREWER, 866

Near Forensa, Javon, on the continent of Antiopia
Safar (Febreux) 930
20th month of the Moontide

Gurvon Gyle was in a reflective mood, thinking about Belonius Vult and his parting toast that day in Pallas, almost three years ago, when they'd presented their plan. *So you thought you'd be immortal, Belonius . . .*

Vult had been hated by many and loved by none. Though his plan really was coming to fruition, he himself was gone, beyond praise or blame – Gurvon had learned of his death some time ago, with little sadness.

Of more moment now were Mater-Imperia Lucia's final, silent words that evening: *Magister Gyle, Betillon will suffer for his impertinence. Mark the moment when it comes and learn.* It made him wonder just how powerful a Diviner Lucia was, because here they were, he and Betillon, three days after the battle for Forensa, and Betillon's pleas for reinforcements were falling on fallow ground. Lucia's revenge had begun.

Gurvon's camp was six miles east of Riban. He was with the

remnants of Hans Frikter's Argundians, but there was no word of Hans himself, and only six of his eighteen battle-magi had got out alive after Elena's allies had turned up and focused on the mercenary magi with deadly precision. According to his spies, the Dorobon legion, now stationed somewhere to the north of Riban, was in even worse shape. Sir Roland Heale still led them, but they'd left half their number behind, dead or captured. The Harkun who'd taken part in the attack on Forensa had retreated with them, professing loyalty, but they'd been raiding Jhafi villages for food, leaving slaughter in their wake.

What a rukking mess.

To salvage the situation, he'd burned out a dozen relay-staves calling in favours all over the kingdom. So it was no surprise when the alarm sounded and a Rondian warbird appeared low in the west. He'd known it was coming for hours, but as it settled in the air above, furling sails and dropping anchor, an Argundian muttered aloud, 'If that had been here four days ago, maybe we wouldn't've been nailed.'

'Betillon didn't think we'd need it here,' Gurvon told the man, so that at least some of the blame for Forensa would be cast Betillon's way.

Though I know they're all blaming me.

He could scarcely deny that it was he who'd convinced Hans that there'd be easy pickings. But somehow Elena had engineered their defeat, and the Argundian commander was missing.

I wouldn't trust me either. But setbacks happen; it's how you recover that marks you out as a winner or a loser . . .

He closed his ears to their grumbling and went to greet the warbird as it landed, sagging onto the landing stanchions which extended like a spider's legs beneath the hull. A pair of escorting Kirkegarde knights mounted on venators landed alongside, the giant reptiles hissing and snapping at the watching men.

Tomas Betillon's grizzled face appeared above the hull of the windship, his eyes narrowing to slits. It was their first meeting since the débâcle: Gurvon had run out of relay-staves and Betillon had made no effort to contact him. The Butcher of Knebb levitated from the windship's decks to the ground and strode towards Gurvon, his fingers curled into fists.

'Well met, my Lord Governor!' Gurvon called heartily, silently adding, <*Tomas, these men are frightened. Be calm.*>

<*Calm? Fuck you, Gyle! What the Hel happened?*> Betillon did make an effort though, waving a casual salute towards the Argundians before grudgingly shaking Gurvon's hand. He dropped his voice. 'How did you lose this, Gyle?'

'Please, come to the pavilion for refreshment, my Lord. The officers are waiting,' Gurvon replied aloud, then adding softly, 'We'll talk frankly away from the rankers.'

'You bet we fucking will,' Betillon whispered, allowing himself to be drawn to the command pavilion. Frikter's magi were inside, along with Gurvon's own people – Rutt Sordell of course, and now also Sylas, Brossian, Drexel and Veritia, all newly arrived, plus seven apprentices waiting out the back. They were all who were left of his senior Grey Foxes, recalled from missions in Yuros to shore up things here. Staria Canestos was with him too, and Leopollo, her adopted son and presumptive heir.

Betillon had brought his own seconds; Grandmaster Lann Wilfort of the Kirkegarde, with six of his knights, and a brutal-looking Pallacian called Kinnaught who was his spymaster. The introductions were terse, they swilled some ale – there was no wine – and then the servants were sent away.

Betillon cut loose. 'You failed us, Gyle – this is all your fault! You're the so-called mastermind, so how in Hel did they blindside you?'

'Because the inexplicable happened,' Gurvon retorted, matching Betillon's tones. 'Ordo Costruo who were supposedly dead or prisoners of the Hadishah turned up to fight in Javon! Who could predict that?' He jabbed a finger at Kinnaught. '*Your* man didn't fucking know either! Kore Himself couldn't have known!'

'So you say,' Betillon shouted, 'but Elena Anborn bloody well did!'

'And I don't know how!'

'Do you not?'

'*No!* She's my *enemy*! To say otherwise – *when she is ruining me* – is ridiculous!'

'Is it?' Betillon drew a piece of parchment from his coat. 'I have an Imperial Warrant for your arrest, Gyle, authorised by Emperor Constant himself.' He gestured, and the blades came out on his side of the pavilion. 'The emperor thinks you've become superfluous to this war.'

Gurvon's people also drew steel, but no one was advancing on either side. He took heart from that. 'You know I'm not superfluous here, Tomas,' he replied. 'If we don't work together, we'll fall separately. Forensa has shown that! I presume that warrant is Constant's idea, because Lucia wouldn't do something so stupid.'

Betillon put the warrant down and picked up a cup of ale. 'Yes, it's Constant's order. He's the emperor and it's my duty to carry it out.' He shrugged. 'For the record: I'd have done it months ago.'

'If we fight, the only people who win are Elena and the Nesti.'

'Who said anything about a fight? I'm going to *execute* you, and any who try to protect you.'

Gurvon cast a glance either side of him. He didn't know the seven Kirkegarde, apart from Wilfort, but it was a fair bet their Grandmaster owned their souls. At his back, he could trust Sylas, Drexel, Veritia, Sordell and Brossian, but he had considerable doubts about Staria and Leopollo – and who knew whether Frikter's men would stand with him? Twelve against eight, ostensibly, but the better fighters were undoubtedly on Betillon's side of the tent.

If anyone's double-dealing me here, this is going to be a mess, and I'll be in the middle of it . . .

'You should rip up that warrant, Tomas. We can't afford this disunity.'

'I wholly agree,' Betillon drawled. 'Look at us: two Yurosian armies divided by *your* ambitions. Remove you and the whole situation becomes crystal-clear: we become a united Imperial army with a Noorie revolt to crush.'

Gurvon took a deep breath. 'Last chance to back down, Tomas,' he said firmly, but when the other man made no reply, he went on. 'I

415

am sure you're familiar with Mystic Writing, Tomas – the opening up of one's mind so that another may write through you? An hour ago I had Veritia link minds with Mater-Imperia Lucia herself.' He took a rolled-up piece of paper from his sleeve. 'Here's what the Living Saint wrote. It's a warrant for *your* arrest, authorised by Mater-Imperia herself.' He unrolled the warrant and laid it over Betillon's. 'I believe this trumps yours.'

Betillon's eyes bulged as he looked down. 'A trick! This is a forgery – there's no seal! Prove it's real!'

'That's been done already. Those who needed to know have already been contacted by Lucia herself.' He gave a small nod to the man behind Betillon's shoulder and Grandmaster Wilfort plunged his blade into the back of Betillon's left thigh, where the shielding was weak.

The Governor of Hebusalim bellowed in shock as he staggered and clutched at the table. Another Kirkegarde man, to show his enthusiasm, hacked at Betillon's arm, cleaving through the shielding wards and breaking it at the elbow. The Butcher of Knebb fell onto his side, curling up like a child, trying to cover his vital organs as blood splattered the carpets.

Gurvon bent over him. <*Remember that meeting, back in Pallas?*> he asked. <*Remember how you tried to dictate to Lucia at the end? She marked your piece that very moment. That's the kind of goddess we all pray to.*>

Betillon gasped for air, cradling his left arm and fighting the pain, gathering his gnostic energy to do something. Before he became a threat, Gurvon lifted his foot, then slammed it down on the broken arm. Betillon screamed and his spell-energies dissipated.

'Have you anything to say, Butcher?'

'I've done nothing I wasn't ordered to do,' Betillon gasped.

'Exactly, Tomas: too little initiative, and too much ambition. That's never going to be enough to satisfy the throne.' <*And you're a depraved mass-murderer.*> Gurvon pulled out his dagger and gouged it under Betillon's chin. <*What you did at Knebb made me what I am, Tomas. I've never been able to get the blood out of my eyes.*>

The Butcher of Knebb's wide-eyed stare said he didn't understand, so Gurvon took it upon himself to clarify. <*The thing is, Tomas, no one* likes *you*. *You're just a bully whose only skill is making others afraid. But making people feel threatened takes you only so far before they begin to align against you.*> He waggled a finger in Betillon's face. <*Lucia suspects that you and Kaltus are plotting against her son. Whereas with me, you always know what you get: I'm just a self-serving, greedy little prick who wants a nicer house to live in. And you know what, I think Lucia rather likes me.*> He grinned triumphantly. <*She must do, to allow me this.*>

He drove the dagger into Betillon's skull and the most hated man in Noros and Hebusalim fell sideways with a soft deflation, his eyes rolled backward and the tent filled with the sudden stench of voided bowels.

You always were full of shit, Betillon. Gurvon wiped his blade on the governor's velvet doublet, then looked around, nodding thanks to his people, then proffered a hand to Grandmaster Wilfort. 'Thank you, Lann. A pleasure to meet you.'

The scar-faced knight clasped hands slowly, measuring him. They'd not known they were to align with each other until an hour before, when Lucia and Wurther had contacted them both, personally. 'You appear to be in high favour, Gurvon,' Wilfort commented. 'I have no idea how, or why.'

'Don't fret, Grandmaster, it's not so mysterious. After Forensa, it was clear that we had to pull together. The problem is, my people were not about to rally behind Betillon at any price, whereas you and the Dorobon are happy to do as Lucia wishes. So there was only one real candidate.'

He'd also had to waive the last part of his fee, but that was going to be paid in Treasury promissory notes anyway, and he doubted they'd be worth the paper they were written on.

'You're aware that my first loyalty is to the Holy Church?' Wilfort asked coolly.

'Of course.' Gurvon smiled. 'I go to church on Holy Days myself, when I can. I understand you're to be inducted as Prelate of Javon? I look forward to a long association between us.'

They shared a brief moment reflecting on their newfound destiny while studying Tomas Betillon's corpse.

Ah well, another 'immortal' gone . . . Gurvon turned to the rest of the gathering. 'Shall we thrash out the details, yes? Oh, and can someone get rid of this damned carcase littering the place?'

A low chuckle lifted the tension a little, and minutes later they were all focused on the tasks at hand, like the well-seasoned conspirators they were.

There were sticking points, of course, because Wilfort and his Kirkegarde could barely conceal their disgust of Staria's people. Gurvon compromised by agreeing that Staria's legions would be stationed at the Rift for another two years, which angered Staria, but she wasn't in any position to refuse. And he had to request an amnesty for Drexel, who'd once assassinated an Inquisitor. Then the rest of the Argundian battle-magi were brought in. They'd already been shown Betillon's corpse and there was no dissent amongst them; the rest of the meeting was purposeful and united.

'The next time we take on the Javonesi, it'll be different,' he declared. 'We'll have one command tent, not two. It'll be on ground of our choosing, and we'll be the ones throwing the surprise punches. Forensa was a minor setback. We're going to win, I promise you.'

'You *promise*, Gurvon?' Staria Canestos raised her eyebrows. 'That's uncharacteristically bold of you.'

'But I do promise,' he told the room, 'because we're going to abandon the Rift. I'm going to bring the whole Harkun nation up here. We'll let the nomads loose on their own kind.'

He saw Staria stifle a shocked gasp, and watched her carefully as she shared a look with Leopollo.

'Much good they did us in Forensa,' Wilfort commented.

'On the contrary, they gave us the men we needed to run a battle of attrition. We almost won, because of the Harkun. We lost because of the Ordo Costruo.'

Staria spoke up. 'Gurvon, these Harkun are *savages* – they'll be a bigger problem than the Jhafi.'

'Then we'll deal with them in their turn.' He met her eyes, forestalled her retort. <*Enough, Staria!*>

<*Gurvon, they hate us all—*>

418

<They might hate your kind, but they hate the Jhafi more. I don't want to hear your misgivings! You agreed to come here on my terms and you know full well we stand or fall together, so you need to get into line on this!>

<Yes, my Lord,> she sent back, with stiff sarcasm.

He stared at her coolly, then turned back to the room. 'All right, let's get down to business. We've got an army to pull together, and a war to win.'

Forensa, Javon, on the continent of Antiopia
Safar (Febreux) to Awwal (Martrois) 930
20th and 21st months of the Moontide

Kazim wants us to have a child. Elena hadn't known what to reply. His desire enfolded her – the need to have something other than death in his life. And when he said the words out loud, a part of her that had never before spoken suddenly sang, a ringing tone of pure love that brought tears to her eyes. It felt right, when it never had with any other man.

But then the doubts began. She wasn't even sure that she could bear children any more: some months she barely bled, and a mage-woman struggled to conceive at all times, but especially out of her twenties. And he was a Dokken; she had no idea what kind of child a mage and Dokken would create – or what it would do to her. Would she suddenly become like him? Would their unique Mage-and-Dokken bond disintegrate? And could he even father children himself? Perhaps he was almost sterile, the way high-blooded magi were? They'd been consciously avoiding conception thus far, so none of this had been put to the test.

What if I did conceive, tonight? The Moontide still had more than four months to run, during which time she'd be suffering morning sickness, and then she'd begin to bulge . . . She tried to picture the remainder of the Crusade spent in the background, unable to fully contribute. Perhaps it would be more prudent to wait until the Moontide was over?

DAVID HAIR

Except the Moontide might not be the end of this fight. The Rondians were in Javon to stay this time; the war didn't have an end date. *And what if I lose him?* That was the thought that froze her mind. She couldn't imagine separation, or how she'd endure it. *It'd be like an amputation.*

She sighed and sipped her wine, waiting for the sounds that would tell her that he was back from the baths below the palace, freshly washed and ready to hear her answer. The sun was creeping towards the horizon, a big pink-orange disc shimmering in the haze of the cooking smoke. The Godsingers began to wail, calling the people to the sunset prayers, and the Ringers in the Sollan Churches joined in, tolling their bells. The warm fug of an eastern city enveloped her, made her feel sleepy and peaceful, despite all her worries. When she heard Kazim enter the chamber behind her, she felt languid and willing.

Willing to make love, of course ... but to try and conceive?

She adored that he was willing for it to be her choice – throughout Yuros and Antiopia alike, the unspoken rule was that it was the man who decided if and when a woman should conceive, and Kazim had been raised with the same expectation. Instead, he was deferring to her.

She finished her wine and drifted through the gauzy curtains, drinking in the sight of him, waiting on the bed like a Lantric god descended from the Holy Mountain to seduce a mortal.

She shed her clothes while he watched, feeling as desirable as a nymph, then crawled across the sheets and kissed him, drank his mouth, stroked his chest and belly, let him know he was wanted, let him suckle her and stroke her, tease out her juices. Then she reached out and grasped him, and guided him to her.

'You do wish this, love?' he whispered, his eyes bright.

'Yes,' she said, firmly, 'I do want your child, Kazim.'

When he pushed into her, she felt an almost suffocating kind of joy, her breath shortening and her heart so filled with liquid warmth she thought she would dissolve into him. Then her body responded to his movements, and the spirituality of her feelings blended and blurred with the animal lust now surging through her, until wanting became needing.

Later, she lay on her side, still glowing inside, while he slumbered beside her. She should have been sleeping too, but her mind wouldn't rest. Part of that was because of the gnosis; there was a prickling feeling nagging at her awareness, the sensation of being stalked. Someone was trying to find her using spiritual-gnosis. They were skilled, narrowing down on where she lay despite her wards. She could shield herself and prevent any contact, but she wasn't sure if she should, even though the touch was unfamiliar.

She edged from the bed, wincing at the deep ache in her loins from being ridden so hard – her consent had enflamed him, driving him to fill her, over and over. No wonder he slept so deeply now. She smiled to herself, feeling fecund as a drui priestess who'd been ploughed at the Sollan rite to renew the sun. She stood, wrapped their discarded blanket around her and went to the balcony doors. They were shut and warded. Cautiously, she extended her awareness.

Something surged at the edge of her senses and began to form outside her wards, on the balcony. A ball of silver became a man-shaped being, a sleek cat-headed man with shifting grey fur, holding up his right hand in both greeting and placation. It was a spiratus, a projected soul – it could be any shape the mage willed. It was a skill she had, but not one she'd used a lot of late; leaving one's body in war-time wasn't something one did lightly.

She kindled a spiratus-sword in her hand, unseen to the naked eye but deadly effective against such a spirit, then spoke. <Who are you?>

<Magister Elena, I presume,> the cat-man purred in Rondian, with a heavy Estellan accent. His voice suggested that he was habitually very pleased with himself. <Lady, I'm here to parley on behalf of my commander. My name is Capolio.>

Staria's spymaster . . . A quiver of excitement run through her. <What does Staria want?>

<She wants to talk, Lady. What shall I tell her?>

Elena restrained the urge to punch the air. *<Tell her I'd love to see her again.>*

A week later they met in person, at a small Dom-al'Ahm above the Rift abandoned to the elements decades ago. Vultures now roosted in the broken dome, and the interior stank of bird-shit, but from the takiya – the raised open-air prayer hall for the worshippers – the views over the desert below the Rift were spectacular. Amteh worshippers prayed facing Hebusalim, and the platform of this Dom-al'Ahm extended northeast, towards the cliffs.

Elena and Capolio agreed to four in each party. Elena brought Kazim – together, they could deal with any treachery – and Cera Nesti and Piero Inveglio to do the talking. She knew Staria's party would all be magi, which was worrying Kazim.

'I doubt there'll be any tricks; Staria has always been a straight arrow in the past,' she told Kazim. 'Well, unless crossed.'

'And have you?' Kazim asked as they waited. 'Betrayed her, that is?'

'Not really.' Elena cast her mind back. 'A woman of her legion tried to seduce me once, and I broke her jaw – but I don't think that counts.'

Kazim wrinkled his nose, clearly uncomfortable at the thought. *But he'll follow my lead; I can trust him on that.*

'This could change everything,' she reminded them all. 'In my experience, her people are like anyone else, with the same human wants and needs. And we *need* them.'

'That's good enough for me,' Cera said, but Piero Inveglio was less comfortable. He was a very traditional Sollan, and profoundly concerned about the idea of two legions of openly frocio men and safian women. On the other hand, he didn't want to lose the war.

'Here they come,' Kazim called, pointing to a skiff approaching from over the desert. It came in below the line of the Rift and landed south of the ruined dome.

Four figures disembarked, and Elena called, 'Shoes off, please. This is still a holy place.' All her party were already barefoot, at her insistence. 'And no weapons or periapts either.'

The newcomers made show of disarming, taking off their gem-stone necklaces and their boots before climbing onto the takiya. Elena hadn't seen Staria for a long time, but the crook-nosed woman hadn't changed much; she might look stringy, but she had strong shoulders, and her long black hair was thick and glossy. She was a three-quarter-blood mage, no one to take lightly. Her skin was tanned, but her feet were almost white.

'You need to go barefoot more often, Staria,' she called teasingly; her own feet were deeply tanned.

'I don't go barefoot outside for just anyone, Elena,' Staria replied with crotchety amusement.

'Oh, I do it all the time,' she replied. 'I'll always be a country girl.'

Staria raised an eyebrow at that, then introduced her party: Leo-pollo, an impossibly gorgeous young man wearing a waistcoat over a bare upper torso and Keshi pantaloons, as if this was a Pallacian pantomime. The other man had a shaven skull and a black goatee: Capolio, her spiritus contact. The young woman with the burly frame and pugnacious face was Kordea, Staria's adopted daughter; she was the only one exuding any hostility.

Elena began her introductions. 'Staria, this is Cera Nesti, the Queen-Regent of Javon.'

Cera was clad in violet beneath a black bekira-shroud. 'We met in Brochena,' she said to Staria; 'at the Beggars' Court.' Her eyes trailed coldly over Leopollo.

Elena recalled belatedly that there had been bad blood over an incident in Cera's 'Beggars' Court'; while she empathised with Cera's point of view, this meeting couldn't be allowed to descend into wran-gling over the past. 'This is Comte Piero Inveglio,' she said quickly. 'He is also a regent, and represents the interests of many nobles, as well as having decades of experience in public affairs.'

'Please, I feel old just hearing about me,' Inveglio said modestly.

'And this is Kazim Makani. He's mine,' Elena added drily.

Leopollo purred appreciatively, but Staria's eyes narrowed and she went still. 'He's a Souldrinker!'

'El es un *Diablo*?' Leopollo gave a startled yelp.

'Yes. And still mine,' Elena replied. 'Is that a problem?'

Staria looked genuinely shocked, but after a moment she said, 'Clearly it isn't to you, Elena.'

'No, it's not. You're seeing his aura. Now look at mine.'

Staria's group engaged gnostic sight and peered at her intently, then as one they gasped. She knew what they were seeing: tendrils of gnostic light joining the two of them, so many it was as if they were almost the same being.

'Yes,' Elena confirmed, 'you are seeing right: to put it simply, we share my gnostic energies. Kazim hasn't needed to kill to replenish his powers since first we found love.' She let them digest that revelation, then said, 'Shall we continue?' She pointed to blankets that had been spread across the ground. 'I'm sorry, but we'll have to sit cross-legged. Our skiff wasn't big enough to bring chairs and tables.'

'It'll help keep the negotiations brief,' Inveglio remarked with a grimace.

'Si,' Staria chuckled, 'I have no more padding on my arse than you do, Comte Inveglio.'

They sat, all of them looking wary, then Elena and Staria quietly set wards down the middle, enough to weaken any surprise attack and alert all present of any gnostic movements; a sensible precaution for both sides, although she didn't detect any ill-will here.

'So,' Staria Canestos began, 'let me state my interest in talking to you plainly, so there are no misunderstandings. Likely Elena will have told you all about my legion, but if not . . .' She looked at Cera Nesti frankly. 'You know, but perhaps the Comte doesn't: many of my legion are frocio: homosexuals. My father recognised during a recruitment crisis that there are many of them, but they were being driven out of other legions. He let it tacitly be known that any such men wouldn't be punished in his legion, that their desires would be treated as normal. The response was overwhelming: he was flooded with recruits seeking to escape persecution, men and women both, enough that he soon commanded two legions, not one. It was a condition of inheriting his legion that I continue that legacy.' She looked

424

at each of Elena's party. 'I see you all know this already? Good. It will make our discussions more straightforward.'

'Knowing is not approving,' Piero Inveglio replied. If the deeply conservative Sollan couldn't be persuaded to hear Staria out, there was no sense in taking the idea back to the full Regency Council. That was why Elena wanted him here.

'Of course,' Capolio put in, 'but something disapproved of can still be tolerated, under law and in the breach.'

'Our laws are a blend of Amteh and Sollan, and statutes devised by our Rimoni ancestors,' Cera said. 'Of course, I was recently stoned to death for contravening those very laws,' she added drily. 'Miraculously, I survived.'

Staria chuckled. 'A miracle indeed. But my people live every day with that threat. They all know that capture in battle will bring them a fate worse than death.'

'Why are you in Javon, Staria?' Elena broke in.

'Because Gurvon Gyle promised us a place where we could live free,' Leopollo blurted. '*These* lands.'

'Our lands,' Cera and Piero said in unison.

'We're not welcome anywhere,' Kordea said in a surly voice. 'Wherever we go, someone will try and "cleanse" us. Javon seems as good a place as any.' She set her jaw defiantly.

Staria raised her hand placatingly. 'As my children say, we wanted a place where we could be ourselves. Javon sounded good, at least the way Gurvon described it. But it doesn't look so good now.'

'There's a lot of empty land in this world,' Piero Inveglio noted. 'Even in Estellayne, I warrant.'

'That's true in principle, but oddly enough, any viable bit of soil is immediately claimed by someone with an army and a holy book,' Staria replied. 'Anyway, we're soldiers, not farmers – we can protect land, but we wouldn't have a clue how to till it.'

'Javon belongs to the Javonesi,' Cera said carefully. 'Like any people, it is down to us to decide who dwells in our lands.' She raised her hand. 'And before you protest that Piero and I are Rimoni and therefore also settlers, yes, of course that is so, but we were both born in

Javon, and most Rimoni alive today in Javon were as well. Many, like myself, are of mixed blood: we *belong* here. My point is,' she went on, jabbing her finger fearlessly at the magi facing her, 'that we claim the right to approve settlers. For now, you don't have that approval.'

'We're not easy to chase away,' Leopollo boasted. Kordea nodded in agreement.

'Neither are we,' Cera replied steadily. 'Hans Frikter would attest to that.'

'You talk big, for someone with no gnosis,' Kordea sniffed.

'And you talk too much for someone with nothing to say,' Cera flashed back.

'Peace!' Staria snapped at Kordea. 'The Queen-Regent is right: don't speak unless you've something constructive to say.' The young woman lowered her eyes sulkily, glowering at Cera.

Elena suppressed a smile, remembering when she'd been much the same.

'How is Hansi?' Staria asked Elena.

'He's alive – Chained, but well enough treated. His wounds are healing, but he's lost a hand.'

'The sword hand or the drinking hand?'

'Drinking.'

'Oh dear – that's serious.' She winked at Elena, visibly seeking to reduce the growing tension.

Elena played along. 'Ah, don't worry about Hansi; he's become ambidextrous – he's drinking us out of beer with his sword hand alone.'

Staria smiled, then turned back to Cera. 'May I go on? I was speaking of why I requested this meeting. Three things have happened recently that have caused me grave disquiet. The first was your stoning, Queen-Regent. Though we now know it was a ruse, I didn't like that Gurvon Gyle had the leading clergy eating out of his hand enough for them to assemble a vicious and bloodthirsty mob with the intention of stoning to death a woman most of the people of this country clearly revere – and for the very crime my people commit every night they can manage. That disturbs me greatly.'

Elena could only agree. Cera, sitting beside her, flinched visibly at the memory, and Piero Inveglio looked distinctly uncomfortable. 'The Sollan faith doesn't condemn people to death for such crimes,' Piero replied defensively.

Staria gave him a withering look. 'The Sollan are no less cruel to frocio, Comte: solitary imprisonment in a convent or a monastery for the rest of one's life is death of a different kind, would you not agree? Which is better, a quick death or a slow one? We don't differentiate between religions: all the gods condemn my children.'

'It breaks our hearts,' Capolio added. 'I'm a devout worshipper of Kore, like most Estellani, but because of our ... *difference* ... we're forbidden to worship.'

'But you choose to do these things,' Piero argued. 'You could choose not to.'

Elena saw Cera frown, but Staria's party all curled their lips.

'"Choose"?' Capolio shook his head. 'With respect, Comte, I tell you this: we would love to be "normal", but our minds and bodies are not, and it was Kore himself who made me this way! In the same way you are stirred by a pretty woman, I'm stirred by a handsome man – it's been that way all my life. I can't change. I don't know how to.'

Inveglio still looked sceptical. 'I've heard the arguments, Magister, but I'm not convinced. Both Kore and Sollan teachngs say the pleasures of lovemaking are the reward for accepting the responsibility of bringing new life into the world. To take that pleasure without even the intention of accepting the divine task it entails? That is wrong. It is like theft.'

Capolio's face darkened. 'I have heard those bigoted arguments, Comte! I say—'

'Enough, Capolio,' Staria interjected. 'We're not here to debate these matters. Hearts aren't changed by words.' She looked intently at Cera. 'I spoke of three things that have disturbed me: the stoning was one. The second was, of course, the battle last week at Forensa. Gurvon brought us here with the promise of easy victories, but your people have shown their teeth. I have heard the reports: a whole city fighting as one, and magi of the Ordo Costruo aiding them. Mine is a mercenary company. We fight for winners, because only winners can pay us. Despise that if you will, but the defeated make poor debtors.'

'The Nesti have never hired mercenaries,' Piero told her in a disdainful voice. 'We've always known your worth on the battlefield.'

'You fight us, you'll learn our worth,' Kordea growled back.

Staria's eyes flashed impatiently. 'Kordea, *contribute*, or remain silent.'

'But—'

'Or go and sit in the skiff.'

The young woman pressed her lips firmly together, glaring.

Elena met Staria's eyes. *<She reminds me of me, before the Arcanum knocked some sense into me.>*

<I doubt you were ever quite so headstrong,> Staria replied, then the wards flared at their gnosis use and as one they both cried, 'Sorry!'

'Don't do that,' Kazim grumbled. 'I thought I needed to kill someone.'

'Think you're good enough, Diablo?' Leopollo enquired.

'Easily,' Kazim replied, his weight shifting subtly.

Why do young men always do this? Elena shifted her gaze to Kordea. *And certain young women.* 'I wish we hadn't brought the children,' she said to Staria. 'They're spoiling our picnic.'

Kazim threw her a wounded look, and she winked.

Staria grinned crookedly. 'I rather think yours is more than a child, hmm?'

Elena brought them back to the question at hand. 'So, Forensa made you think twice. Good! But what's your third concern about Gurvon? I can think of *thousands*.'

'The Harkun. My children have been stationed at the Rift Forts for months now. We've seen the Harkun up close, and whatever the rights and wrongs of their plight, letting them onto the upper plateau is sheer folly. But Gyle now wants me to abandon the Rift Forts and march to join his army.'

Inveglio looked sick. 'But the Harkun will run amok – we'd have to send men . . .' His voiced tailed off.

'Which is exactly what he wants,' Cera concluded. 'He knows that we'd either have to abandon the Forts and let the Harkun come, or divide our forces to man them, and either move would be disastrous for us.' She gazed steadily at Staria. 'Gyle is stringing you along, Senora Canestos. You know this, otherwise you wouldn't be here. You're reconsidering your loyalties, but you want to know two things: *can* the Nesti win, and will we *tolerate* your differences afterwards? Those are the essential questions, are they not?'

Staria glanced at Elena. 'Maybe I should have adopted this one.'

Leopollo and Kordea pulled identical pouts.

'The answer to the first question is: yes, we can win, with or without you.' Cera's voice was firm and assured, which impressed Elena. You had to make statements like that with complete certainty.

She's so good at this now. Urte really is her stage.

'As for the second point,' Cera said, 'I remember a case in the Beggars' Court of Brochena, last year.' She jabbed a finger at Leopollo. 'I remember *you*. A young woman allowed her family to sacrifice her to protect her brother, whom *you* had seduced. There was nothing I could do about it, and you did nothing to prevent it.'

The young man hung his head. 'That was . . . unfortunate. It wasn't meant to happen that way.' He looked to his mother for support. 'What could I do? It shouldn't even be a crime!'

'But it is,' Cera said tersely. 'You used your protected status to prey on him, then he blamed the girl. You destroyed that family thoughtlessly with your lustful whim, and yet you demand the right to be protected.' She glared at Leopollo until he squirmed and looked away. She turned back to Staria. 'There's a middle ground, Senora Canestos. If we're to work together, we need to find it.'

'Fair enough – but I swear, for every one case like that you trot out, I'll throw ten straight back at you!'

'Then we'll both deal with it, when we can. If we're to tolerate your people, be tolerable! I'm not saying I don't sympathise, but most of my subjects are uneducated and conservative, and I must heed them. The equality you seek isn't possible here, but something approaching it might be.'

Comte Inveglio looked increasingly uncomfortable. 'This matter has not been discussed in Council,' he reminded Cera.

'I know, Piero. All I'm saying to Senora Canestos is that I'm willing to contemplate matters that others might not, such as the thought that frocio are born, not made. I'm also willing to contemplate that perhaps love between two of the same gender, provided they are old enough to understand what they are doing, isn't wrong. But I'm fully aware that neither civil nor religious laws agree.'

'We must step carefully.'

'I agree. I will not sacrifice the laws of Javon for expedient allies. But there is an opportunity here for us all.'

Inveglio said in a cautious voice, 'I am not opposed to the discussion taking place.'

'Thank you, my friend,' Cera said, relief evident in her voice.

Staria rubbed her chin. 'We can talk some more, certainly. But Gyle undoubtedly has his spies in both our camps.' She glanced at Capolio, who nodded. 'We can talk, but if we're seen to be delaying our withdrawal from the Rift, we'll draw suspicion.'

'So what?' Kordea growled. 'What's Gyle going to do about it?'

Staria threw her adopted daughter an impatient look. 'I'm not going to make any open moves just yet.' She looked at Elena. 'You understand that, don't you, Ella?'

'Of course,' Elena replied, a little disappointed, but Staria was only being realistic. 'You'll likely need both legions if you're to hold the Forts anyway. Delay, procrastinate, just don't show up in his army, and we'll be grateful.'

Piero and Cera were frowning, and so was Kazim, but she sensed that this was as good as they'd get.

As both parties drifted back to their respective skiffs, the tension between Leopollo and Kazim especially was still conspicuous. Then Kordea said something insulting in Leopollo's ear, judging by his reaction, and the low words in Estellan they exchanged quickly turned into a fiery screaming match.

As the pair threw their hands in the air and stomped off in opposite directions, still hurling insults, Elena said, 'And *they're* going to inherit your legion, Staria?'

'If they earn it, they'll get it. What more can I do?' Staria looked at Elena slyly. 'I offered Kordea to Cera as a bodyguard, back in Brochena when you were missing. She turned her down.'

'She chose rightly, then,' Elena sniffed. 'Kordea has a fair bit of growing up to do.'

'True. But they're both lonely, in their own ways, and it might have done them good. She's not a bad girl.' Staria looked at her. 'You've never had children, have you Ella?'

'No, no children. Not yet.' Elena replied, unable not to glance at Kazim.

Staria wasn't blind. 'Perhaps I'll ask again in a few months, hmm?' She smirked knowingly, then opened her arms up, offering a hug. Elena hesitated momentarily, then decided that a show of trust was required. They embraced, kissed both cheeks. 'There, not so bad,' Staria whispered. 'No need to break my jaw this time.'

'I think we were both a little different back then,' Elena acknowledged. 'Friends?'

'Of course! It's a man's world, Ella. We girls have to work together.' Staria looked at Cera. 'All of us.'

23

Vulnerability

Thaumaturgic: Earth

Most magi see the powers of the gnosis only in terms of its destructive potential. This is especially true of our young men, who want to destroy, to break, to kill, as if true honour can only be demonstrated by such acts.

We must impress upon these young magi, especially our Earth-magi, that there is also honour in making, in constructing things that last, things that will still be used and enjoyed by our children's children's children.

ORDO COSTRUO COLLEGIATE, PONTUS

Forensa, Javon, on the continent of Antiopia
Safar (Febreux) to Awwal (Martrois) 930
20th and 21st months of the Moontide

The weeks after the Battle of Forensa were marked by the sounds and smells of funerals. The city was steeped in the smoke of the pyres, and the wailing of tens of thousands at the huge ceremonies to mark the passing of the fallen. Soldiers mourned lost comrades, and girded themselves for battles to come. Bereft families echoed the wails of the Godsingers and the dirges of the Rimoni drui in the streets. The grief was all-pervasive, seeping through the stone and into Cera's bones. There was a music to the sadness that fed Cera's own distress.

She and Elena spent long hours sitting with Tarita, though seldom together. The little maid was still in a state of numbed shock, her lively personality drowned by the shock of paralysis. Timori sat with her too, and he was probably better for her than either woman, because after his initial shyness he babbled away about all that was happening, just as if Tarita was exactly the same as before.

When Cera wasn't beside her maid, or visiting other crippled survivors, she toured the city, wanting to see and be seen as the people tried to clean up and regain some kind of normality. What she saw was a slowly unfolding miracle.

Like most of her countrymen, she'd never seen the good things that magi could do. She knew little of the rebuilding of Hebusalim by the Ordo Costruo after the Leviathan Bridge opened, or all the aqueducts and civic works. The only magi they had seen in Javon were battle-magi, waging war; this was the other side of the gnosis, with the Ordo Costruo labouring in the service of the city.

Earth-magi did as the trembling human officials directed as if they were humble servants, clearing the major roads and the canals, which the Water-magi quickly purified so there was drinking water everywhere again. Temporary bridges were thrown up and rubble cleared; work that would have taken weeks for hundreds of labourers was done in days. Fire-magi took care of cremating the piles of bodies in pyres, saving their precious fuel; Animagi summoned wild kine herds to the slaughter to feed everyone. They healed the injured and scouted the enemy retreat, each day achieving huge feats – and yet the tasks multiplied: there were so many homeless, so many who'd lost their families, so many missing, and so many to feed.

Cera moved cautiously regarding the delicate matter of cooperation with Staria Canestos. Though the understanding they'd reached didn't require joint actions, it did imply a softening of attitudes towards froci and safian. This was no time to try and change civil laws, not with so much else to do, and anyway, alliance with known social aberrants was technically illegal.

Her compromise position, which would require no new laws and was therefore eminently practical, was to make the mercenaries legally responsible for their own people – for which there was precedent. This relied on Staria being willing to prosecute her own people if they committed crimes, but allowed her to also turn a blind eye on other matters. Relying on Staria to punish her own if they committed crimes other than being homosexual might not be ideal, but it was expedient.

But first Cera had to clear that with her own counsellors, and to her relief, that was not quite as hard as she'd feared: Piero Inveglio's vocal support from the beginning was invaluable. Pita Rosco and Luigi Ginovisi had enough to worry about just coordinating the city's repairs. Warriors like Justiano di Kestria were only concerned about the battle to come; and happy to make any deal that secured the Rift Forts and prevented the Harkun from being reinforced. The Jhafi captains were more difficult. At last they agreed to be bound by the decision of the senior Godspeakers.

Cera summoned the clergymen last. The Sollan drui rolled over easily enough once she pointed out that the Rimoni Empire was known to have tolerated all manner of behaviours seen elsewhere as vices, provided they were kept from the public domain – and anyway, the Sollan Church typically deferred to civil law.

The Godspeakers were harder work, but after an hour of batting aside arguments, the most senior of them, Luqeef, steepled his fingers and said, 'With respect, Queen-Regent, might we change the nature of this conversation from these "frocio" and their perversions?'

Cera glanced at Elena. 'What is it you wish to talk of, Godspeaker?'

'I wish to speak of Victory, Queen-Regent.'

Cera's heart pounded a little faster. Not all Godspeakers were so obsessed with their god that they barely saw the real world. Godspeaker Luqeef did have a well-deserved reputation for iron-willed faith, though. 'Victory is our goal,' she replied, wondering where he would go with this.

The cleric looked at Cera intently. 'Many forget that the Prophet Aluq-Ahmed, Blessings upon his Name, was a warrior before and *after* Ahm came to Him. The Second Book of the *Kalistham* is a war chronicle, and it tells us very clearly that alliances of *convenience* were made, with Ahm's blessing.'

'I've never read the Second Book,' Cera confessed. It was considered more of a chronicle than a religious text, and believed to be notoriously unreliable at that.

'It is often overlooked,' Luqeef said mildly, 'but it has much to teach us, especially about the concept of holy war. The First Shihad, declared by Aluq-Ahmed against the Kings of Gatioch, was joined by men of Mirobez. The Prophet courted them even though he had targeted the heathens in the Mirobez Mountains for conquest. He knew he could not succeed in Gatioch without these allies, even though they were heathens.'

Elena frowned. 'Godspeaker, Staria Canestos is no fool. If she perceives that our alliance is one of pure expedience, she will break it off, and at the most disastrous juncture she can conceive.'

'Eventually, all alliances are a matter of expediency, Lady Jadugara. If you'd read Book Two, you'd know that.'

Cera saw Elena recoil irritably and put a hand on her arm. *We've got what we need.* 'Then do we have your support to take this to the full Regency Council, Godspeaker? We propose a formal alliance with the Sacro Arcoyris Estellan, granting them immunity from civil law, provided they enforce military law.'

Godspeaker Luqeef gave a slow nod of assent. 'You do.'

When the clerics had all gone, Elena barked out a harsh laugh. 'Well, that was an eye-opener!'

'Yurosians are not the only practical people, Elena. Luqeef knows that a defeat in war to Rondian invaders will harm the Amteh faith worse than some dubious allies.'

'He'll expect you to turn on Staria afterwards,' Elena said in a low voice.

'I won't let that happen.'

'You might not be the one in control then,' Elena reminded her.

'I know,' Cera admitted. During the most desperate moments of the period when she'd assumed the Regency, she'd felt compelled to accept a marital alliance with Sultan Salim I of Kesh. It had seemed like a good idea – well, maybe not a *good* idea, but the *only* move she could make at the time. Now it felt like a death sentence. 'At the end of the Moontide, the Sultan's ambassadors will come and collect me,' she said glumly, adding, 'that's if he still wants me.'

'You're no longer a virgin, you're a widow, you don't bring the throne of Javon with you and you've been condemned as a safian,' Elena pointed out. 'You're not quite the catch you once were.'

Cera smiled faintly at Elena's dry tones. 'I suppose not. Let's hope Salim sees it that way . . . but either way, I'll need to make sure that Timori completely understands our arrangement with Staria. And I'll need Piero to hold to it as well – he'll be taking over my role as senior Nesti representative until Timori comes of age.'

Elena bit her lip. 'I'll still be in Javon; I'll remind him of what's been agreed.'

Cera was grateful for that, but her own plight was weighing heavily on her mind now. 'I'll be no one again,' she said gloomily.

'If Salim doesn't want you, one of the Javon nobility will be more than happy to marry a Nesti.'

'Either way, I'll just be a broodmare and a token of alliance,' Cera said bitterly.

'Don't underestimate the power the woman of a great House can have,' Elena replied. 'My mother was a mage-noble and she was far from no one.'

'I don't *want* to marry,' Cera declared. 'I don't even care about love – well, all right, a little, obviously . . . but if I had to choose between love and the power to control Javon's destiny, the choice is easy. I would rule! I want to pass laws and judgements to make Javon a better place!'

'I know that, Cera. I've always known your priorities. But love teaches compassion and tolerance. A ruler without love is a tyrant.'

'I'll find love, one day,' Cera replied, hoping that would be so. 'But it won't be easy to find, the love I want.' It was as frank an admission of who she was as she was prepared to make, even to Elena.

'I hope you do,' Elena replied. 'It's a man's world, truly, but there are other women who have ruled successfully.'

'Staria once told me that a woman can't have both leadership and love. She said it's one or the other.'

'Staria's an old sourpuss. Queen Faltinia of Argundy was renowned for having three or four lovers a night, and yet she ruled alone for decades. It's all in the way you project authority.' Elena drummed her fingers on the table. 'If you defeat Gurvon and retake Brochena, you'll be in a strong enough position to break the engagement.'

'Perhaps. But Kesh is Javon's largest trading partner, so upsetting them wouldn't be smart.'

'You're right, of course.' Elena shrugged. 'I don't have a solution for you, I'm sorry.' She yawned. There were dark circles under her eyes, and the hint of uncharacteristic vulnerability. It was Darkmoon, the last week of the month, when Mater Luna hid her face. Which reminded Cera of something.

'How is the baby-making going?' she asked, the sort of comment that would have made Elena laugh when they were proper friends.

But Elena didn't laugh. Cera knew she'd bled in the last week of Janune, but Febreux was another opportunity, and if the rings under her eyes were any judge, she and Kazim were seizing it.

'We'll see, won't we?'

This decision was a big thing for Elena. She'd been with Gurvon Gyle for nearly twenty years and never had children. And Kazim was a Souldrinker – not that Cera fully understood the concept, but she knew such a union was unprecedented. There were obviously risks to Elena's well-being, and it was clear many of the Ordo Costruo didn't approve of the relationship, let alone taking it further – although the rest of the mage-scholars were treating it as an interesting experiment.

'Good luck,' she offered.

'Thank you.' Elena stood and bowed stiffly, clearly wanting to bring this discussion to an end. 'Good night, Cera.'

After she was gone, Cera sat alone a while, then went to change for the evening's court. She stayed with Timori through the evening meal; he needed the experience of speaking with older, more experienced men. After she'd put him to bed, she visited Tarita again, reading a tale from *The Book of Before*, a collection of folktales from northern Ahmedhassa, filled with afreet and djinn and princesses with magical powers. The girl listened with big moist eyes, and fell asleep halfway through, but Cera kept reading anyway, finding some kind of release from the day's stresses in the familiar words.

Poor Tarita slept three-quarters of the day, the healer-nurses said. *Perhaps death would have been kinder . . .*

The fourth night-bell had rung by the time she got back to her rooms and changed into her nightdress, but instead of getting into bed, she lit the lamp on her desk and went back to the ever-present paperwork that was her burden and her release.

Brochena, Javon, on the continent of Antiopia
Awwal (Martrois) 930
21st month of the Moontide

Gurvon Gyle prowled the upper storey of Brochena Palace, the only person on the whole floor. He'd taken the royal suite, the very bed where Francis Dorobon had been murdered. He'd publically blamed that murder on Cera Nesti, which was feeling like an error now: the credit for that death far outweighed the truth of her sexual deviancy. The Jhafi of Forensa had greeted her return with reverence, and during the defence of her city she'd been an inspirational figure, by all reports. Increasingly, she was beginning to feel like his most dangerous enemy.

And my most vulnerable one.

He wandered into the guest suite where he'd installed a map-table and examined the tabula pieces he'd placed there: a visual reminder of how things stood. In western Javon there were six legions of Rondian rankers, fully supported by their battle-magi, with four warbirds and a dozen skiffs – thirty thousand men. Plus he had at least ten thousand surviving Harkun. His forces were the white pieces, of course.

A cluster of black tabula pieces were gathered on the right-hand side of the map: the Javonesi armies. An estimated twenty thousand Rimoni and twice that of Jhafi, feudal soldiery of their nobility. Sixty thousand men, perhaps – but the truth was, he had no real idea. In

Forensa the ordinary citizens had fought like lions, but he doubted they would be a factor away from their home city.

He stroked the white pieces, calculating. The situation wasn't as rosy as these pieces inferred either: Hans Frikter's Argundian legion was wrecked, less than a third-strength, with broken morale, barely a fighting force at all. The Dorobon were not quite so badly damaged, but they were certainly weakened. The Kirkegarde were in fair shape, but only Endus Rykjard and Staria Canestos had intact legions.

He moved Rykjard's piece closer to Brochena, then fingered the two pieces representing Staria and her people stationed at the Rift: the ten thousand under her command. *What's she up to?* he wondered. For three weeks all he'd had were delays and excuses. The paths beneath the Forts had been sabotaged by Elena, apparently, so they could not reinforce the Harkun as required. He'd talked to Staria through the relay-staves and she'd played it down. *She's stalling; I can feel it. But she's over there and I'm here and the Nesti forces lie between us.*

He clenched his fists, staring at the map.

I lost her when I brought in the Harkun. She's trying to stay neutral now, and side with the winner, whoever that will be – she'll probably have made overtures to Elena as well . . . The galling thing was, there was damn all he could do about it from here. He'd happily have sent the Harkun to assail the forts, but he doubted they'd succeed, and anyway, he needed them to protect Brochena.

I need to change the game, before it turns against me even more . . .

It had occurred to him that he'd not been playing to his strengths of late. Open warfare was all very well, but his specialty had always been in more shadowy manoeuvres. Rutt had been reminding him of that; he'd even proposed a plan . . . one he'd been reluctant to initiate, but this news of Staria was tipping his hand. And as Rutt had pointed out, his plan had only a short window of opportunity.

Before I lose Rutt too . . . for other reasons.

He closed his eyes and sent a call. *<Rutt! Drexel! Attend upon me at once.>*

Inside a minute the men he'd summoned had ghosted into his map-room, carefully avoiding getting too close to each other.

'Boss?' Rutt Sordell asked deferentially, eyeing Mayten Drexel coldly. The younger man had been Elena's apprentice for a year and had habitually taken her side during her frequent clashes with Rutt.

'Sit, both you.' He indicated the decanter of Jhafi arak. Rutt shook his head – he didn't like Antiopian liquor – but Gurvon knew Drexel had acquired a taste for it.

Mayten Drexel moved like what he was: an assassin – Elena's understudy once, but he'd been operating independently in Yuros ever since Elena had been assigned to Javon in 924. He was barely memorable, with thinning red hair, a patchy beard and pockmarked cheeks, a man of slight build, and easily ignored – no bad thing for a killer. His affinities were ideal for his role: Animagery and Morphism, Fire- and Air-gnosis, perfect for disguise and vicious strikes. So far he'd not failed on a mission, and in the short time he'd been in Javon, he'd adapted quickly. Gurvon had introduced him to his own underground contacts, bequeathing him most of his spies – he'd realised he couldn't be his own spymaster and still rule effectively. He needed to delegate, and for now, Drexel appeared to be both competent and trustworthy.

For now. *They all betray me in the end, except Rutt, who hasn't the imagination.*

'Mayten, do you think you could get into Forensa and reach the Nesti children?'

'Of course – but there will be guards crawling all over the Nesti palace, and Elena will be right beside them.' Drexel's voice hinted at uncertainty over taking on his former mentor – but it also betrayed his eagerness to try.

'Perhaps, but you've gone into tighter holes, and got out again too. We've been focusing too much on the strategic situation, and losing touch with what got us here in the first place: good old-fashioned political murder. Before the Dorobon came, the Rimoni here were rivals – they might have had a democratic kingship, but they never had any deep love for one another. Remove their rallying points – Timori and Cera Nesti – and their alliance will fracture. When men like Stefan di Aranio realise that we can reach out and kill anyone

440

we like, he'll distance himself, and the rest will seek to make peace. We don't have to rely on actual battle to achieve our aims.'

Gurvon saw Drexel smile grimly; this was why he'd joined the Grey Foxes in the first place: for the chance to indulge his addiction to killing. He was competent enough in open battle, but that was a waste of his real value.

'When do I leave?'

'Get some sleep first. Leave tomorrow. I want Timori dead before the Nesti march. Then we'll see how firm their alliance holds.'

Drexel stroked the old silver Kore medallion he wore about his neck. 'I have a skiff: I'll be ready at sunrise. Who else would you like me to kill while I'm there?'

'Anyone of value,' Gurvon said, 'but don't jeopardise the chance to strike at the Nesti children by getting too ambitious.' *He wants to kill Elena . . . he's always wanted to, just to show her who's best.*

'I won't let you down.'

Of course you won't . . . not after tonight . . . 'By the way,' he said, as if in afterthought, 'I've had Rutt here working on a special weapon which will be of some help to you. Ready your skiff, then report to Rutt's laboratory in two hours' time.'

'Of course.' Drexel looked sceptical; he clearly didn't feel Rutt could add anything of value, but accepted the order stiffly. He half-bowed in thanks to Gurvon, then hurried out, closing the door behind him.

Gurvon turned to Rutt. 'Are you sure he can't do this on his own?'

The Argundian shook his head. 'His chances are very low. He'd get close, but Elena knows his gnostic touch, and mine too. Something different is required; and my plan provides that. And we both know he's ambitious; his instincts for self-preservation will tell him he can't get out alive, which means he'll under-commit to going in. He can't do it otherwise; I'm certain.'

'Then you still mean to go through with your plan?'

Rutt nodded gravely. 'Gurvon, you know what I am now: a Death Scarab – a beetle living inside another man's brain. Even using a pure-blood's body isn't sustainable for long – the scarab's very presence rots the brain. I can't survive indefinitely. But it's more than

DAVID HAIR

that ... I'm *sick* of this existence – my perceptions are dimmed, taste and sound and all other sensations. I'm *diminished* ... and I hate it.'

Gurvon scowled. He had always relied heavily on Rutt, even if the Argundian was devoid of personality. Planning for a future without him was disorienting. 'I really wish you didn't feel this way,' he said, completely honestly.

'It is what it is. Most men would have died when Elena collapsed that tower with me in it. I'm grateful to have been able to aid you despite that, but my time is nearly over. If I can take down Elena, and the Nesti too, then it will be a worthy sacrifice.'

A sacrifice ... How on Urte did I engender this much loyalty in him? Gurvon wondered. *Though I suppose he is a born Number Two; he would have always latched onto someone more decisive than himself.*

'Then do what must be done, and good luck.'

Rutt Sordell was already waiting in his laboratory when Mayten Drexel walked in. Rutt poured a brandy each, and they toasted each other watchfully, though Drexel was careful to make sure Rutt drank first before he gulped down his own shot greedily; brandy had always been his favourite tipple.

'So,' he asked, 'what's the plan? Where's this secret weapon? What is it?'

Rutt tapped his own chest. 'It's me.'

Drexel looked puzzled. 'What do you mean.'

Rutt didn't reply, just held the other man's eye, keeping his face expressionless despite what was happening inside his body.

The poison struck them both at the same time.

It was a venom, a fast-acting one, the strong taste disguised by the brandy that contained a pain-agent that would scramble all thought but leave no lasting damage. It wasn't fatal, but would paralyse for about an hour.

They both clutched their throats, but for Rutt the feeling was muted by the distance between this body and his intellect housed in the scarab. For Drexel there was no such buffer; he went down in

442

agony. They staggered apart, then collapsed. Drexel tried to scream, tried to fight the venom, but he hadn't the affinities.

Nor did Rutt, but then, he didn't need to fight; he had prepared another option.

They were both on the floor when he detached his awareness from the mind of his host body; through the eyes of the scarab he saw Drexel's own eyes grow huge in horror as he saw what emerged from Rutt's mouth, drop from his face to the floor . . .

. . . and crawl across the stone towards him.

An hour later, the venom quite dissipated, Rutt sat up and began to explore his new body and the mind it housed and engage with all the fresh options it gave him.

One final mission for Gurvon, inside the body of Mayten Drexel: a sacrifice to ensure that his mentor, his master – his friend – would be victorious.

He didn't spare even a glance for the other body on the floor . . . it had never been his own anyway.

The next evening, Gurvon raised a hand in farewell as he watched the skiff rise into the dusk from the battlements and peel away towards the east, towards Forensa. Rutt Sordell had been his most loyal and reliable colleague for more than two decades – he'd saved his life more than once – and yet he was almost instantly forgettable. And in a different body . . . well, it was difficult to think of the man who'd just left as Rutt at all.

Nevertheless, Rutt-in-Drexel had almost wept as he hugged Gurvon goodbye, possibly the first time in his life he'd ever done such a thing. It had been oddly touching.

As the skiff passed out of sight, a frightened young Dorobon page approached. 'My lord,' he squeaked.

'What is it?'

'My Lord, a man from Hytel has arrived – he says he is a son of Alfredo Gorgio.'

The late Alfredo . . . one of his bastards, no doubt. 'Ah. Bring him to me here.'

Gurvon had decided to abandon the Gorgio stronghold in the north to his allies: the Kirkegarde garrison was largely wasted there, and the Gorgio could be counted upon to support his rule, for they had tied their star to Rondelmar decades ago. He'd been keeping one eye on the power struggle that'd been going on among the Gorgio at Hytel for the past few months as Alfredo Gorgio's bastards fought for pre-eminence. One of Alfredo Gorgio's several illegitimate sons had seized Portia Tolidi and her Dorobon son and was claiming to be acting as the child's regent until he was old enough to claim his throne: as king of all Javon.

Like Hel that's going to happen.

Gurvon pictured Portia Tolidi, a vision of feminine perfection, her slender and exquisitely proportioned body and porcelain-skinned face framed by a curtain of radiant golden-red curls. Francis Dorobon had been besotted with her, never knowing that Portia had been bedding her sister-wife behind the young king's back. Gurvon presumed that only he and Cera and Portia now knew that. And her child was indeed the Dorobon heir, by Imperial calculations.

But not my calculations.

A young man in Gorgio red and black quarters climbed to the battlements and joined him. He was lean, with a lady-lure face.

'Who are you?' Gurvon demanded.

'Ricardo Gorgio-Sintro,' the young man replied, with a bow. 'I'm the younger brother of Gabrien Gorgio-Sintro, rightful heir to Alfredo.'

'A bastard line?'

The young man shrugged. 'Si; Alfredo had no legitimate sons – but my brother is reducing that number every day. He has secured the safety of Portia Tolidi and her son and pledged to marry her and adopt the Dorobon heir – for their protection.'

'And to bring the gnosis into his line,' Gurvon observed. 'Your brother has acted swiftly.'

'He's a man of action,' young Ricardo replied smugly. 'But there are rebels – other bastards, mostly. Alfredo, my father, was prolific.' He smirked in a way that suggested he had inherited the characteristic.

'What brings you to Brochena?'

'I come to ask your aid. You have Kirkegarde stationed in the north who could render us great help. But now I hear they are to withdraw.'

'You've heard correctly.'

'But it is in your interest to support us. The other bastard lines have their own adherents. My father even has a part-Jhafi son gaining some support among the Noorie peasantry.'

Gurvon raised his eyebrows. The Gorgio disgust for dark skin was well-known. That Alfredo had screwed some Jhafi whore was in itself somewhat surprising. 'Is there some danger of a Jhafi coup?'

'Of course not – his Noorie bastard was by a maid, and even Jhafi will not follow one of servant stock. Emilio, his name is; he calls himself Gorgio but he is just a Noorie stronzo.' Ricardo smirked again. 'We've all been curious about Noorie purses at times, si?'

Gurvon shrugged noncommittally. 'Why should my men back your brother?'

'Because we're going to win. We control the Gorgio knights and the mines; the others have the dregs.'

'But you need our help?'

'To speed our victory, and yours,' Ricardo smarmed. 'My brother will aid you against the Nesti queen, si?'

Gurvon considered, then nodded. 'Very well, I will instruct the Kirkegarde in Hytel to provide support to your brother – but I warn you, the situation here in the south will take priority. They will be marching south in three weeks' time, and I will expect your brother to follow them.'

Ricardo's smile faltered. 'But, my lord – only three weeks to secure Hytel is not enough time, and it is two hundred miles away.'

'You rode, yes?'

'In four days, using relay horses. But men cannot march at such a rate!'

'It's ten days for cavalry, twenty for footmen: that's just over three weeks. I can relay an order instantly with the gnosis, telling my Kirkegarde to give you two weeks to force battle, but then they will march south.'

'But that would leave us only a few to hold the north—'

DAVID HAIR

'If we fail here, Ricardo, you'll be facing all of Javon on your own. We must unite to succeed. So you must send your men here. You can retake Hytel afterwards. There is no other option!'

Ricardo bowed, his face now sorely troubled. He began to clasp his hands together in supplication, then realised he was wasting his time. 'Si, we will come to your aid when we can.'

Gurvon waved him away, thinking, *I'll believe that when I see it.*

24

Assassin's Reach

Boundaries

The Gnostic Codes were written by certain mage-bureaucrats to create boundaries and curb the powers of those with more initiative and courage in the pursuit of knowledge. I contend that such boundaries are needless fetters which do not make the Empire stronger, but weaker. How many opportunities to advance the might of Rondelmar have been lost because our brightest minds are constrained by the Gnostic Codes?

ERVYN NAXIUS, PAMPHLET, 884

Forensa, Javon, on the continent of Antiopia
Awwal (Martrois) 930
21st month of the Moontide

If you listen, Kore will speak to you. Rutt Sordell had always known this. Few thought of him as religious, and he seldom spoke of his beliefs, for they might be considered heretical by some. He'd come to his particular faith after studying the universe.

The Kore that Rutt Sordell worshipped was not a rule-maker or a judge. He was a force of nature, without judgement or morality. Kore simply *was*. All souls were part of His soul, and at death all returned to Him. Kore did not care for virtue or sin; He was simply aware. If you meditated on Him, you also became aware.

This revelation had come to him over years of killing, and using his affinity for Necromancy to blur the barriers between life and death. Men died, men lived; their deeds mattered little in isolation, and few

447

were truly remembered. Seeking the immortality that monuments or tales brought was wasted effort; neither availed you anything in the afterlife. Success was the only true legacy: imposing your shape on the world so that your deeds changed it in the way that you desired.

His desire was for Gurvon to rule Javon: *that* would be his legacy.

His melding with Drexel's body was almost complete; his experience in subduing previous bodies was accelerating the process. And Drexel's skills were well worth mastering – martial and gnostic skills Rutt had never used before, plus a body that knew how to fight. He'd never quite managed to break Elena's mental resistance when he'd inhabited her body, but he'd had a lot more experience since then so he broke Drexel's easily, quickly opening up his neural paths. He could function as Drexel and as himself, for a time at least. Best of all, he was seeing in colour and could taste again, as Drexel's senses had not yet begun to atrophy. He'd have a little time to enjoy a fuller sensory palate, for a while.

Long enough to complete this mission . . .

And right below him was Elena Anborn, just fifty yards away, and completely oblivious . . .

Elena was practising in the training yards with her Noorie lover. Rutt watched her surreptitiously as he laboured among a group of Rimoni and Jhafi. He was plastering a wall, just another anonymous worker, but his attention was on Drexel's former mentor . . . and thanks to Drexel's martial skills, he could see the way she was favouring her left leg . . .

He was careful not to focus on her too hard, though. Elena had always had a sensitive mind. And the Noorie with her . . . Rutt had to force himself not to stare as gnostic sight revealed a tangled blur of shifting colours about the pair of them, as if they were one creature. *Mage and Souldrinker . . . an interesting abomination . . .*

Rutt had arrived in Forensa four days ago, during the week of the waning moon, and set about blending in, which wasn't difficult in the aftermath of battle. He'd barely had to use the gnosis at all – every willing labourer was welcomed. Simple disguise techniques, learned by drawing on Drexel's memories, had darkened his skin and hair, leaving him looking native enough to pass muster. His story was of a Rimoni widower, a refugee from Brochena who'd stumbled into one of the refugee camps and was helping to rebuild the shattered city for three meals a day. At night he crept about, learning the shape of the Krak al-Farada, the Nesti stronghold. Elena's wards – he recognised her touch – served to identify where his targets were. He was certain his and Drexel's combined skills would suffice. Nowhere large was entirely secure against a skilled assassin, but confined spaces were another matter: a careful protector like Elena would be ensuring that the royal children went only to a small number of rooms that would be well-warded and guarded. He wouldn't have long, once inside, so his strike needed to be as simple and sudden as he could contrive – the more intricate the plan, the greater the chance of failure.

It didn't trouble him, knowing that he would not even try to escape. If he was to die, why not do it with the blood of the Nesti on his hands, knowing he had advanced Gurvon's cause?

After Elena finished her bout and *limped* away, he returned all his attention to the task at hand and finished the plastering, then left with the Jhafi labourers, silent among the chattering men. No one took much interest in him – subtle use of the gnosis ensured that. He detached himself from the group and went into the less destroyed areas, seeking the Rimoni taverns where the guardsmen drank. All evening he watched them until he'd settled on a loner of his own, and he followed him to a brothel and waited outside until he'd finished. Then he trapped the man with mesmeric-gnosis and led him, as if supporting a drunk friend, into a ruined house near the canals.

He used Drexel's Mesmerism to gain access to the man's memories, and when he was certain he'd learned all he could, including the man's distinctive mannerisms, he cut his throat. He used Drexel's other prime affinity, morphic-gnosis, to change his own appearance; when he stood up ten minutes later, he had become Benirio, a Rimoni guard. He dressed in Benirio's uniform, weighed down the body with stones and threw it into a blocked drain, then walked back to the palace.

Getting into the barracks was easy: men came and went constantly, coming on and off duty all the time in a haze of tiredness, drunkenness and boredom. 'Benirio' was off-duty until dawn, but he knew men who were routinely assigned to the royal suite. He'd pillaged Benirio's dying mind so he knew the names of those who might speak to him; he could improvise the rest. Some luck was always required, but Rutt had the gnosis, the ultimate luck-maker.

Morphic-gnosis was hard to sustain, but he made sure they all got a good look at him as he entered, then wrapped himself quickly in a blanket, yawning ostentatiously, fielded some ribald comments about where he'd been, then pretended to sleep. It didn't take him long to scan the minds of everyone else in the room, until he'd discovered who was part of the royal guard, and who was on duty the following night. He targeted one guard in particular, a rough-spoken man called Tello.

Rutt waited until most were asleep, then crept through the darkness and laid a hand on the man's forehead, implanting the notion that they'd swapped duties, then crept back to his cot.

See, Elena? It's that easy . . .

There would be additional layers of security to penetrate, of course. But they didn't overly concern him – they would be less effective against a killer who didn't care if he got out alive.

Which one do I target . . . Timori or Cera . . . ?

He closed his eyes to meditate on that, to listen to Kore.

Her name was Drus, and she hated working alone. Yes, it was an honour to be selected as poor Tarita's replacement as Queen Cera's maid – and yes, Queen Cera was touched by Ahm, blessed above ordinary women – but Drus loved company. A friendly ear to chatter into wasn't so much to ask for, was it?

She'd had to be examined by Alhana, Cera's terrifying protector, before she was permitted to enter the royal suite for the first time. That had been a strange sensation, her memories shuffling past her inner eye like a hundred dreams replaying in rapid succession, after which the blonde Rondian women had said 'She's harmless' to Cera, and it was decided.

Harmless! Drus wasn't sure how she felt about that. Her young husband, who'd once slapped her and been struck back twice as hard, wouldn't have agreed. They'd reached agreement after that: he could pretend he was boss and she would pretend it wasn't otherwise. *I am not harmless . . .*

She'd just finished making the queen's bed when there was a click at the doorway and a pair of guards peered inside. One was the regular, Jerid – a creep in her view. The other she didn't really know, a rough fellow with thin hair and a slightly brutish face. 'Who's he?' she demanded of Jerid. 'Where's Tello?'

'He's Benirio,' Jerid replied. He looked a little hazy, as if he'd been drinking.

'Tello swapped with me,' Benirio said. 'Everything all right in here?'

'Why wasn't I told?' Drus demanded. 'I'm supposed to know whoever is on duty outside the Queen's door.' She peered past them to the open door opposite, the entrance to the king's room, and glimpsed his nurse, Borsa, readying the boy's bed for him. The second nightbell had sounded and Timori would be finishing his meal soon. The Queen would be later; she always had meetings in the evening, readying for the march west.

'The serjant was supposed to tell someone,' Benirio said with a shrug.

Useless men! 'Guards aren't allowed inside the rooms,' she reminded them. 'And remember, I'm supposed to be told in advance if the roster changes, got it?' She waggled her finger at them. 'Now, get outside.'

'Sure, you're the boss,' Benirio sniffed. They closed the door again, leaving her alone.

Drus clicked her tongue angrily. The usual routines were all messed up since the battle. She could understand it: everything had been on the verge of collapse, and sometimes when so much was happening the little details got lost, but she believed in details. You had to, as a maid. It was the small slips that got you dismissed.

She fussed about the room until she was happy that all was spotless, then slipped outside. That damned guard – Benirio, yes? – had vanished again, and she was alone on the top-floor landing. Then she heard movement in her own room, to her right. She stiffened, then heard a grunt and her temper flashed.

If that Benirio is in my room, I'll give him what for!

She flung open the door, and froze.

Jerid was slumped on the bed with a red flower of blood blooming at his throat, and a strange man in Benirio's uniform was standing over him, bloodied knife in hand. Her mind refused to engage as the stranger turned and his eyes locked on hers. She tried to fight the feeling that she was being engulfed in darkness, but swiftly the only light she could see was his eyes.

'Little girl,' the man whispered, 'harmless little girl . . .'

Cera Nesti caught Timori yawning out of the corner of her eye, and in the contagious way of yawns, she was soon doing the same, trying to hide it so the guests wouldn't think her bored. It was yet another evening of trying to smooth ruffled feathers over her plans to confiscate produce that did not come to market at a preset price. Piero Inveglio had been flooding her evenings with rural nobles, mostly Rimoni, who owned olive orchards and vineyards and vast wheatfields and were in a tither over what it would mean for them. It was all she could do not to slap them.

I should be confiscating their damned estates!

But progress was being made: the mere threat of fixed-price markets had seen them frantically donating and distributing produce in an effort to be seen visibly helping the cause, to stave off public opprobrium. Every concession helped, whether willingly given or not.

'Timi,' she said softly, 'I think it's time for you to go upstairs.' She raised a hand in apology to the nobles who were trying to charm her into easing her war-time economy measures, then linked her fingers with her little brother's and squeezed. She turned to Elena. 'Timi wants to go up. Can you take him?'

'I want Kaz to take me!' Timori exclaimed, his face coming alive. Elena smiled at Kazim; the giant Keshi had become Timori's personal favourite of late. The young king was desperate to emulate Kazim's energetic, masculine enthusiasm for riding, running, fighting and all the things that young boys dream of. Timi would be ten soon, and his training in martial skills was about to accelerate.

Cera found herself sharing that smile with Elena, and that made her heart just a little lighter. Things were still awkward between them, but the growing friendship between Timori and Kazim was helping to bring them closer together again.

'In a few months, you'll be old enough to stay for the council meetings,' she reminded him.

Timori pulled a face. 'Boring.'

'I know. But Father would want you to stay and listen and learn.'

The little boy pulled a dutiful face. 'Yes, Cera,' he intoned, yawning again. It wasn't really fair to invoke their dead parents, but it usually worked. 'Can I go now?'

She looked at him fondly. 'Sometimes I don't think you want to grow up at all.'

'Yes I do! I'm going to be a giant warrior like Kazim, and chase the Crusaders back to Yuros!'

I don't think you'll ever be a giant, little brother. He'd always been small for his age: a narrow-shouldered, bony child with an angelic face. *But everyone will love you.* 'You'll be king, darling, and you'll have whole armies to fight for you.'

Timori grinned, then paused. 'What will you do when I'm king, Cera?'

'I'll be living in Kesh, having babies, I imagine,' she told him, her light-heartedness evaporating at the thought.

Timi's eyes narrowed. 'You don't want to, do you?'

Her smile froze, more at his perceptiveness than anything else. 'I'll do my duty, as a woman must.'

'When I'm king, I'll summon you home, and you can do all my council meetings for me, so I can do fun things,' he told her magnanimously. 'Kings should only have fun, and you enjoy boring things.'

She raised her eyebrows showily. 'Do I just?'

'Yes! You think dull things are interesting and fun things are dull!'

He gave her a hug. 'What will happen if I fall in battle?' he asked solemnly. He knew they were about to march, and in his imagination, he was going to fight in the front line beside Kazim. Comte Inveglio gifting him a suit of armour and a new sword hadn't helped her moderate that fantasy.

She didn't tell him that he wouldn't get within a mile of the fighting unless things were going disastrously. Instead she went down on her haunches and looked him in the eye. 'Nothing will ever happen to you, my darling. Kazim and Elena would never allow it, and nor would I.'

'You'd be the last Nesti,' he noted, determined to see this morbid line of thought through.

'Yes, I would, but I'm only a girl, so when I marry, the family's wealth and titles would revert to the Vernio-Nesti, our cousins at the Northern Rift Fort.'

'I don't like them,' Timori said. 'They sweat a lot and don't wash.'

Which was about what Cera thought too. 'So you see, you can't die, Timi! Think how smelly Forensa would be if they were in charge!'

He wrinkled his nose and giggled. 'Then I won't die in battle. I promise I'll be very careful and use my shield a lot.'

'You do that, little man.' She stood and nodded to Kazim, who lunged in playfully, grabbed Timori and lifted him onto his shoulders, which was not at all seemly for a king-in-waiting, but Timori still had a few weeks left of being able to be treated as a child, so Cera let him enjoy it. As they swept out of the room, she stared after them.

Everything I'm doing, I'm doing for you, darling boy. You're the last male of our line, the last chance of the Nesti name passing unbroken into the future. Don't you dare die. She glanced upwards, invoking the gods. *Pater Sol, watch over him. He is everything.*

She put to one side the nagging thought that she wanted to be exactly where she was, at the hub of the decision-making, for the rest of her life.

Then Pita Rosco said something about tariff rates that just *would not do*, so she had to rejoin the conversation and correct her garrulous treasurer without undermining him, and the evening's duel of wits began anew.

Rutt Sordell wiped the blood from his dagger with one of the little maid's rags, then sheathed it and dumped her limp body beside Jerid's. He'd have loved to have reanimated them, but that took time and created gnostic echoes that would alert any mage within the castle, so he reluctantly let them lie. He did seal them in a protective circle to contain the stench of death. Then he went outside and shut the door.

Now comes the real test . . .

He carefully rebuilt Benirio's face over his own, and replaced the mask of the guardsman's surface thoughts as he resumed his position at the top of the stairs.

For a few minutes he was carried back, through old memories of childhood in Argundy, of the Noros Revolt, and discoveries in the fields of Necromancy and Divination, the solitary triumphs of his lonely life. There had never been love, not from his cold magi parents consumed with social elevation in Argundy, and women had always been sinister, secretive creatures to him, witches who latched onto the weak. Sex had proved joyless and disappointing; he had never understood why people craved it. Only wine had truly stimulated his senses, but even that pleasure had been stripped from him when Elena collapsed his tower and destroyed his body. Since then, everything had been a slow descent into sensory deprivation: a fall that would end tonight.

Then sounds came from the foot of the stairwell: a boy's happy crowing, and a deep masculine laugh. He banished the memories and focused his mind as the sound of boots on marble echoed, getting louder and louder. Then the big Keshi, Kazim Makani, appeared, carrying a tired but exuberant Timori Nesti on his shoulders. The Keshi glanced at him, and paused.

'Who are you? Where are Jerid and Tello?'

'I'm Benirio – I'm standing in for Tello tonight – and Jerid's off having a piss. He won't be long.'

Kazim frowned. Clearly two guards were expected to be on duty at all times, and familiar faces at that. But Timori was bouncing on his shoulders and then the nursery door opened and a plump Jhafi woman waddled out.

Timori greeted her cheerily, 'Borsa!'

The nurse exchanged a torrent of Noorie speech with Kazim as they all entered Timori's suite and closed the door behind them, amidst much shouting and laughter from the boy-king.

Rutt watched them, his eyes narrowed in thought as he made some hurried recalculations. He'd been expecting Elena, but it wasn't altogether surprising – she must be guarding Cera while Kazim took responsibility for Timori. If he waited until Cera arrived, he risked facing both magi, and Elena would probably be more wary than Kazim Makani; she would certainly demand sight of two guards, not one. In theory, if he was still unmasked by then, he'd have all night; but he doubted it would be that easy. His mind teetered one way, then the other, in an agony of indecision. How could he lure in and kill all four of his quarry?

I must listen to Kore . . .

As he thought, the path became clearer: killing both Nesti children together was highly unlikely tonight, not with both doors warded. And Gurvon had said that Kazim Makani's gnosis was very, very strong, in which case his wards would likely be beyond him to penetrate, at least in the time-frame available. And though the rapport between Elena and Kazim was their great apparent strength, Rutt could see a way of turning it into their greatest weakness. With one down, how would the other fare?

And what would be more likely to bring Cera Nesti to me, than the screams of her little brother?

The decision taken, he gripped Benirio's spear and walked towards the nursery door.

'I don't think you quite understand our position,' Piero Inveglio was saying, resuming the discussion interrupted when Timori left. The little coterie of rural Rimoni nobility had left their seats and were filing into a lounge where drinks would be served. 'We have no desire to profiteer from the warfare ravaging Javon. But we are custodians of a legacy. Our Houses trace their lineage to senatorial families of old Rimoni, transplanted in foreign soils to preserve them. We live and breathe the history of an empire! We all have treasures of that ancient time in our custody, in safekeeping for future generations. Our estates are museums, gateways to the past! That is surely worth treasuring!'

'So you are overcharging for your grain to preserve marble statues from Rym and Becchio?' Cera asked coolly.

The whole room winced, and everyone began to protest.

Except for Elena, who gave a sudden weak gasp and clutched her belly.

Cera stared, suddenly deaf to every other voice, as her protector began to double over, all colour draining from her face as she began to wobble. Her mouth worked soundlessly, while someone made a thoughtless remark about women and their inability to deal with alcohol, then someone else squeaked, 'Is she ... *poisoned* ... ?'

All of a sudden everyone in the room was clutching at their own throats, turning pale and breathing heavily, but Cera felt no affliction at all, just the tightening of her breath in sympathy for Elena as she clutched her hand.

The Noros woman's eyes locked on hers in dread. '*Kaz* ...' she choked out, then fell to her knees, her whole form becoming softly luminous, white light coalescing about her and then streaming upwards through the ceiling as the guests backed away from them.

Cera dropped Elena's hand, frozen and terrified as the image of the giant Keshi filled her mind ... *with Timori on his shoulders.*

She screamed her brother's name and pelted towards the stairs to the royal suite.

Kazim Makani was still laughing at a teasing jest from the nurse. 'Borsa, too much!' he cried at another outrageous comment about him and Elena. He was seeking a riposte as he opened the nursery door, about to exit the room, and his eyes didn't even register the deeper patch of shadow to his right, where Borsa's door was partly open.

Then a spear thrust from the darkness and the leaf-bladed head plunged into his side, smashing into his lower ribcage, breaking bones and ripping through muscle and flesh, straight into his right lung. A man emerged behind it, smaller than him, but with considerable gnosis augmenting his strength. The blow was a brutal shock and he gasped, strangely numbed to the impact, though he could feel every inch of that spearhead as it tore him inside. He staggered, thrown against the doorframe, and then slid down it.

The man holding the spear wore the uniform of a Nesti guard – perhaps that of the strange guard he'd spoken to – but the face was different now: a straggling red beard and thinning hair, his nondescript, unknown face gleeful as he bore down and shoved Kazim to the floor.

Then purple gnostic-light coalesced in the spearman's hands, flowed down the shaft of the spear and into Kazim. He fought it, but the sheer agony of the steel embedded in his flesh destroyed his resistance, and his limbs went numb. He crashed over on his back, his skull bouncing, dimly hearing Timori and Borsa cry out in terror.

With a hideous leer the spearman locked gazes with him and for a moment, Mesmeric energies coursed through his skull, freezing his brain as his intellect locked with his assailant's. For just a moment, alien thoughts tore through his mind—

—and he *became* the other: a pale misanthrope, conjuring in darkness, stealing bodies from graves and brewing poisons and scratching at the future ... uncertain and afraid, hating people, but craving them ... seeking the approval of others and never getting it, until his god – *Gurvon Gyle* – took him in ... Then a torrent of information filled his skull as conversations with Gyle, treasured like diamonds, blurred past him—

—and then the link closed down, its purpose served, for now the assassin knew *him*. The killer gripped the spear anew and twisted it in his wound, tearing sideways, then ramming the spearhead all the way through his body until it emerged from his back and crunched into the tiles, pinning him to the ground. Purple light – necroman-cy-gnosis – gripped him, and leeched at his very being.

Kazim's senses began to fail – then white light burst through him from below and he almost blanked out.

Rutt Sordell released the spear, content with where it was right now. He wasn't alarmed about the pale healing-gnosis that had manifested about the Keshi; that stank of Elena Anborn. He'd expected it from the moment he'd plunged the spear into the Keshi's side. He under-stood their link better now that he'd raped the Keshi's mind as he held him immobile and helpless. Killing her lover would be a blow for Elena – but forcing her to try and save him would utterly neu-tralise her. The life-drain spell he'd imbedded into the spear would continue to suck the Keshi's life-force, forcing Elena to give more and more . . .

She's got about a minute before she either lets him die, or passes out herself, he estimated. And there were no other guards up here, so he now had a free hand . . . and Cera Nesti was on her way.

With a snarl, he turned on the others in the nursery. Before he could focus his power, the nurse screamed and threw herself at him, but he flicked his left hand, catching her in a kinetic grip, and slammed her backwards, headfirst into a pillar. Her neck snapped audibly and she thumped bonelessly to the tiles and went still. He barely broke stride.

But somehow, in the space of that blink of an eye, the boy-king had disappeared. He snarled in baffled fury as he stormed into the centre of the room, widening his senses, seeking where he could have gone.

Elena found herself on the floor, vomit in her throat and the most incredible agony she'd ever endured spiking her through the right side of her chest. She spat a thick red stream of phlegm and wine and half-digested food, but she barely noticed, for all of her awareness was spiralling upwards, following the stream of light that led to her stricken lover. She fed that link with everything she could muster,

459

gave all that she had to keep him alive, but it was like pouring water down a drain – it was taking more and more, and having no effect whatsoever. *What's happened . . . ?*

Her eyes fluttered open and she saw a circle of terrified Rimoni, Inveglio's dinner guests, staring down at her. They had realised that they weren't poisoned at all, but that something else was happening. Then Pita Rosco dropped to his knees beside her and pulled her hand from her throat, trying to clear her windpipe so she could breathe. Behind him, Piero Inveglio was shouting orders and running for the stairs, from where Cera's panicky cries were echoing.

Timori . . . Kazim . . . something's happened to them. She clutched Pita's arm desperately and choked out, '*Pita! We have to save Timi!*' Her vision blurred as a fresh spasm of light burst from her, pulled from her body by Kazim's frantic efforts to stay alive. Her whole grip on what was around her wavered, almost tearing her awareness from her body and sending it spinning upwards, but she anchored herself, spat her mouth clear and grabbed Pita harder. '*Get me up there!*'

She dimly felt the treasurer's big arms enfold her, then she was hoisted upright and managed somehow to get feet beneath herself. They staggered towards the stairwell, then she managed to separate just enough energy from the flow pouring into Kazim to pull clear of Pita's grasp, draw on Air-gnosis and take flight, soaring past the guardsmen who were flooding the stairs to the third floor and the royal suite.

'Where in Hel . . . ?' Rutt stared about him, initially mystified, until the simple solution became clear: Timori Nesti had simply dropped and scrambled under his bed. He bent down and peered into the darkness until he saw the frightened face and big, glistening eyes. 'Now, now, my king,' he sneered, raising a finger and letting mage-fire kindle and grow.

The nurse Borsa was motionless; if she was still alive – which he doubted – she wouldn't be for long. Her neck was broken, and her soul would soon disconnect from her body. In the doorway, Kazim Makani had perhaps another half a minute, and though killing him would be simplicity itself, it would also free Elena; right now Rutt could see that Kazim was draining her, like a millstone around the neck of a drowning woman, dragging her to her death.

By the time I'm done here, she'll not be a factor any more. I'll be able to run amok, until the Ordo Costruo can rouse some kind of defence. If they even can . . .

For the first time in years he felt truly alive. Death stalked the room: the colour of the blood pooling beneath Kazim Makani was vivid scarlet; the reek of sweet iron and voided bowels was glorious in his nostrils, and the Death Scarab inside his skull felt like it was swelling up fit to burst his head.

'Goodbye, little king,' he smirked, and blasted.

He never saw the wards at all: the crystalline shields that reflected his mage-bolt back at him like a mirror, striking his own shields and hurling him across the floor in a dizzying spin. He hit the wall beside the dying nurse and rebounded off it.

He lay there panting, bewildered, then he realised what had happened: Elena had made a haven there under the bed, the place any child would flee to . . .

He snarled in fury, picked himself up and turned to where Kazim Makani, ashen-faced, was choking out his final breaths. The spear-shaft was jutting from him.

Then a girl in a violet dress appeared in the doorway, her long black hair coming loose from some elaborate hairstyle and her face filled with horror. *The Nesti really are queuing up to deliver themselves to me . . .* he thought with a grin, and he re-gathered his energies. His left hand stretched towards Timori beneath the bed and his right to Cera as she saw him and froze.

Then he blasted mage-fire from either hand, engulfing the royal bed with the left – *survive that, you little pipsqueak!* – while his right sent it straight towards the defenceless queen-regent—

—just as the door flew closed . . .

It wasn't a plan for survival, just sheer reflex as Kazim registered that Cera had appeared; he saw her eyes swell in sudden terror and with the last of his strength, he kicked out at the door, smashing it closed just as a bolt of energy struck it with a roar, splintering and charring the timbers – but the bolt didn't get through.

That movement cost him dearly: a tearing sensation inside his chest almost struck him down, and the pain he'd somehow blocked from his mind hit him like a wave, sending him into shock. He clutched the spear-shaft, trying to expel it from himself, as the room around him ignited and Timori cried out in terror.

It was the boy's voice that galvanised him, keeping him conscious. Ignoring the indescribable pain, he rolled himself sideways, wrenching the spear-head from the broken floor. In the extremity of pain, the room flashed pure white, and for several seconds he couldn't see, couldn't breathe . . .

But his hands gripped the shaft anew, and this time he *pulled* . . .

Elena slammed Cera aside as she reeled before the burning nursery door, then hurled herself at it, the portal flying apart as she blazed through – then something like a giant fist hammered her shields and threw her sideways and she hit the wall hard, her shields flaring scarlet. She smacked into the floor, her leg twisting beneath her, and she yowled as her left knee ligaments tore in half. Her eyes were wide open but she barely registered the burning bed, and Timori's fearful cries were almost lost in the roar of the flames; all she could focus on was the dreadful sight of Kazim, hauling a spear with purple runes pulsing on its shaft from his own body.

Mayten Drexel was in the centre of the room, twisting his head to follow her impact, bloodlust and hatred all over his face, but his aura was wrong, it wasn't Drexel at all, or not entirely.

'Farsheyd, Elena,' the man rasped – *farewell* – and that single Argundian word told the whole tale.

'*Sordell*,' she gasped, then Kazim blacked out and the link sucked almost all her energy into him, stripping her shields, and the kinetic blow designed only to keep her off-balance instead hurled her like a toy across the smoke-wreathed room. She struck a pillar legs-first and her link with Kazim all but snapped as something shattered in her ruined left knee. Her entire grip on the world almost winked out; all she could do was howl as she landed onto a soft lump that expelled air. Her eyes found Borsa's face beneath hers, her eyes emptying, her mouth falling slack.

She didn't quite black out, but as she lay there, helpless, she glimpsed Timori under the bed, still inside her wards – but they were no protection from the smoke, and he couldn't get out. Then Cera appeared at the doorway and Rutt shouted 'Ha!' with chilling satisfaction. Lightning coalesced again in his right fist.

Pale light like mist was forming in Borsa's mouth.

Elena didn't stop to think . . . she just clamped her mouth over the dying nurse's and inhaled.

Energy blazed around her and was ripped away whole, then darkness swallowed her in one gulp.

Rutt Sordell stopped and stared, momentarily stunned, as Elena quite clearly soul-drank the nurse. *Since when—?*

Then he realised the danger, but it was a moment too late, for the link between Elena and the Keshi flashed back into life and an intense light flew from Elena in front of him to her fallen lover behind him, burning itself on his retinas. For a moment the life-drain spell embedded in the spear fed him anew—

—then it shut off abruptly as he turned to face what he now realised must be his main threat—

—but that was all the time it took for Kazim Makani to raise the bloodied spear, its death-runes glowing, and hurl it with brutal strength the six yards between them. It took a tenth of a second for it to leave the Keshi's hand and pierce Rutt's body, ripping through him and knocking him from his feet and onto the burning bed. His shields already shredded, he tried to reset his wards, lost in the impact, but there wasn't time and he had nothing to protect him when the flames roared and seized hungrily upon his stolen uniform. Pain engulfed him and he went rigid – and then instinct took over as inside his head, something as big as a clenched fist wrenched itself free of all the tendrils of sensory links and nerves and scrabbled towards the light ...

Cera was too aghast to scream as Kazim collapsed onto his front. She staggered forward, stumbling over his leg and almost falling, dimly conscious of boots pounding in the landing outside and people calling for her to *stop*, to *beware*.

She saw Elena motionless in the corner beside Borsa. Beyond Kazim, the impaled attacker was hurled onto the bed and quickly engulfed in flames. Timori's voice was faltering, and the radiating heat was a physical blow, making her stagger backwards. Dimly in the smoke and shimmering air she saw something black and gleaming push itself from the attacker's mouth.

Then Timi choked and coughed weakly from beneath the bed.

'TIMI!'

She forced her body towards the bed, ignoring the roiling heat and calling at the top of her voice, '*Yagna! Yagna!*' – the word Elena had implanted in her bed-wards so Cera or Timori could neutralise them. She blindly thrust her hand beneath the bed, tried to grab him—

—when something huge and black, big as a rat but shiny like a giant flea, launched itself from the burning bed and gripped her face.

She screamed and convulsed, then started gagging as legs with hooked claws latched on to her, ripping her skin, and something slick and bulbous rammed itself, pulsing, into her mouth. It got halfway, then she fell and struck her head as she flailed about, seizing the huge beetle-thing and trying to jam her fingers into the edges of its carapace, seeking to prise it from her face.

The creature squirmed and rammed its abdomen all the way into her mouth and she started choking on it, retching, losing her breath and almost blacking out. Something gushed out of it and her mouth was flooded with some sort of liquid – then her fingers found enough purchase and she ripped the scarab from her face, her skin tearing and blood filling her eyes as she gripped it around the thorax in her right hand, then rolled on her side, spewing a white mucus that was filled with inch-long larvae that writhed and snapped their tiny mandibles. But her eyes were on the thing in her right hand: she thrust it into the flames, careless of her own flesh, vomited again and again, then spitting furiously, trying to get every last bit of it *out* of her, oblivious as her hand turned red then black, and started to blister—

—and the insect in her hand screamed, shrivelled and burst into flame—

—then the pain hit her.

Booted feet slammed into the tiles beside her head and suddenly there were people everywhere, men in armour covered with violet tabards, bellowing panicky orders, wrenching her from the flames. She saw a man lift the burning bed, frantically reaching, and saw a small body that was blackened and still, then the red-searing agony struck her again, and she fell away from it all, into nothingness.

25

Funeral and March

Oil and Wine

The Rimoni brought two things to Javon, or Ja'afar, as the local Jhafi name it: olive trees and grapevines. Finding their stock well-suited to the climate of certain areas, they produced olive oil and wines of an intensity not known in Yuros, products that have since become justifiably famous.

ORDO COSTRUO COLLEGIATE, HEBUSALIM, 874

These are hard lands, and they are not home. We are in exile, and our oldest songs speak of our return. But that dream does not grow closer with the passing of time; it recedes, like a tide that never turns. Instead we seek to make our exile as homely as we may, to ease our souls.

ANONYMOUS RIMONI TRADER, JAVON, 869

Forensa, Javon, on the continent of Antiopia
Awwal (Martrois) 930
21st month of the Moontide

The customs for burying a King of Javon were many, filled with symbolism and meaning to both Amteh and Sollan. The preparation of the body had taken three days, while the sarcophagus and the tomb were readied. There were honour guards, purifying rites, vigils, prayers, and many, many tears to cry.

'Fuel for the pyre,' the drui chanted, the traditional funerary call of the Sollans, inviting donated fuel, but also reminding all that the ultimate fuel for the pyre would be the bodies they were here to burn.

Cera had always thought cremation to be heartless, but it felt sacred today. The small Sollan chapel within Krak al-Farada was packed so tight, and so heavy with incense and sweat, that it was hard to find air that didn't taste as if it'd been inhaled already.

Shears reaped the fuel: hair from the heads of the chief mourners. Cera had been shorn first; her hair, which had reached to the small of her back, was now reduced to a black tangle of tresses on the ground, crudely hacked with seven cuts, the traditional number. It was now only a finger's-length, and she felt like a stranger to herself. One of the younger drui gathered the clumped hair from all down the line and threw it into the fires. Every woman she saw in the crowd had cut her hair, as if their own son had died, and she felt a surge of kinship to them, like being held in giant hands. It gave her the strength to keep breathing. Her already dark skin was smeared in ash, and blood was dripping from the ritual cut above her left breast. Her eyes stung from crying so much. She hadn't slept; she couldn't be alone.

'Hear us, Pater Sol!' the drui cried. 'We bring you our king!'

The bier was draped in purple cloth and festooned with strings of flowers and Jhafi prayer beads, burying the body lying upon it until he could barely be seen. Both the funerary bed and the knights who had borne it were coated in the brightly coloured powders that the Amteh worshippers had thrown into the air as it passed, light to drive away darkness, a garish and defiant blaze of colour railing against the gloom and sorrow. But nothing could dispel the anger that was seething through the masses. 'Death to the Invader!' they had been calling, in Jhafi and in Rimoni. 'Death to the Infidel!'

The Amteh rites had been performed at midday under the burning sun, where dark forces would not tread and afreet could not find a way into the bodies of the dead. That had been a turmoil for Cera, to see them all laid out so. Then came the burning of the Jhafi dead; dear Borsa, her nurse, slaughtered by the assassin when she tried to protect her youngest and dearest charge. Her hugs and kisses had accompanied the Nesti children through all their lives, and Cera couldn't imagine life without her. And Drus, that poor maid, ripped from life before she'd really begun to live it.

The sun kissed the rooftops. It was time to burn and bury her little brother.

'Hear us, Mater Lune!' the drui called. 'We bring you our king!'

The knights lifted the bier once more. They had born it through the streets of Forensa all day, timing their arrival at the Nesti tombs for an hour before sunset. The king would go into the earth as the sun left the sky.

'Receive your son, Timori Rex!'

Someone tugged on her sleeve: Pita Rosco, his chubby, normally cheerful face ash-stained and solemn, offered his arm. She stood shakily and clung to him as she followed the bier down the aisle towards the gaping mouth of the crypt. Each step was harder than the last as faces loomed out of the crowd; it felt like a nightmare procession, as if she had crossed from the land of the living, and only the dead were here in the chapel to welcome Timori to the grave.

The sun vanished and while the knights carried Timori into the earth, the Godspeakers lit the pyre, burning the king in effigy so he would have both Amteh cremation and Sollan burial.

Ritual demanded that she drop to her knees and scream in grief and loss, but she found she had already done so. Her right hand, poulticed and wrapped in bandages so thick it looked like she had no hand at all, pounded the earth and she came to herself at last in the echo of that scream, staring about at the sea of awestruck, silent faces.

She came to her feet, as for once in her life, her emotions snapped the control of her rational mind. Her voice cracked as she cried to the skies, '*Gurvon Gyle – I know your agents are listening! So hear this! I am the last of the Nesti, the family you have destroyed for your own pleasure! I am coming to destroy you! Hear me! I am coming to kill you!*'

Elena didn't go to the funerals – she told herself the living needed her too much. Though others among the Ordo Costruo could have tended Kazim during the ceremony, she couldn't bear to see all that grief. She had enough of her own.

The sounds were inescapable, pouring through the windows from the courtyards and plazas, vibrating up through the timbers and stones permeating the smoke-reek from the scorched rooms on the upper storey. The wailing of tens of thousands of Jhafi women and their menfolk's angry shouting, accompanied by the rattling of spears on shields, imploring Ahm to strike down the Rondian invaders; the low funerary chants of the Rimoni and the wailing of the Godsingers in the towers of the Doms-al'Ahm, and the indignant shrieking of the crows, driven from their roosts by the clamour. None of it could drown out the voice of guilt inside her, though.

My negligence killed them.

It didn't matter that she'd known the risks, or that her task was all but impossible anyway. It wasn't hard to infiltrate a large group of people, not for someone as talented as Rutt Sordell or Mayten Drexel – and especially combined. The part of her that had once been just like them understood the nuances of the attack: the infiltration that had been required, the delicate balance between preparation and improvisation, the identification of weaknesses and the deadly ruthlessness of exploiting them. She doubted Sordell had ever intended to escape; there had been no obvious contingency plans. He was there to kill until he was stopped.

A hideaway like that little warding circle under the bed could only hold so long at any rate, especially against so powerful a mage, but I'd never thought of smoke . . . Poor little Timori must have forgotten the escape-word in his panic . . .

She clutched at the chair-arm and tried to shift her left leg, which had been fixed straight; she couldn't bend it. The convalescence would be months, Clematia had said, and unless she could free up her own gnosis to guide the internal workings of her body, she'd likely never be able to do more than limp again.

But that wasn't even registering as one of her worst fears at the moment.

It was Kazim's plight that was destroying her. He was barely alive. The Ordo Costruo magi had saved one lung and were using a bellows powered by captured kinetic-gnosis to keep his body oxygenated, but his brain had been shutting down when they got to him and he still hadn't awakened. Their link had been broken, and she hadn't been able to re-establish it. Her own gnosis was a powder-puff as a consequence, her former powers reduced to almost nothing; she could barely shield a thrown stone.

And Kazim wasn't her only problem: without Timori, Cera's reign as regent was over. Theo Vernio-Nesti was now head-of-family, and custom demanded that he be called to court from his home in the northernmost Rift Fort, which was many days' travel away. Moreover, Theo's family were ignorant, provincial fools, banished by Olfuss Nesti because they couldn't be trusted.

Even so, messengers were riding to summon them to the court.

Worse, Stefan di Aranio had sent a messenger – with suspicious alacrity – demanding the election of a new king immediately; the Lord of Riban had a large body of support and obviously fancied his chances. She suspected that Stefan had lost his nerve for dealing with Gurvon; he would surely want them to sue for peace.

Well done, Gurvon. You hit us right where it hurts.

She closed her eyes, took Kazim's cool, limp hand and squeezed. It had taken all Clematia's skill to keep him from the grave, and even now there was no certainty he would even wake, let alone recover. Healing-gnosis was far from perfect, and the internal workings of the body were still largely a mystery, even to the magi.

In the neighbouring bed, Tarita slept on. She too was still paralysed, her numbed suffering as terrible in its way as Kazim's.

I've failed them all . . .

The duty healer, a gloomy young Ordo Costruo mage called Perdionus touched her shoulder. He was not yet thirty, but his lank hair was already greying. 'Magister Anborn,' he said respectfully, 'you should be resting.

She knew what he was inferring – it was difficult to keep medical secrets from healer-magi. It was her bleeding week, and there had been nothing. She was scared that her body was now failing to ovulate, that she'd lost any chance for a child, waited too long. But perhaps, *perhaps* . . .

'We will have revenge for this,' he added fervently.

Vengeance. Hatred. Retribution. Yes, oh yes! She stroked her stomach and whispered, 'I pray so.'

The Godspeaker concluded the Rite of Family and the women lowered their keffis. Cera saw the men wince at their faces; she knew what they were seeing, for she'd been staring into her own mirror as she rehearsed all the things she needed to say today.

She'd washed the ritual ash away that morning in the chapel below, three days after the funeral, as custom required. Her eyes were lined with thick kohl, black lines that made her look ghoulish. Her eyes were vividly bloodshot, like bleeding sores. Her hair was still a close-cropped mess – she'd refused to have it tidied since the funerals; such trivialities could wait – and anyway, her mother's crowning circlet tamed the worst of it. Her right hand was still wrapped up and she couldn't use it.

Beside her, Elena looked just as bad. Her blonde hair had also been hacked short, and she could barely walk, even with a stick and her kinetic-gnosis. Whenever she forgot herself, her eyes were murderous. She looked about as far from a mother-to-be as conceivable.

Around the table the Regency Council were gathered. The official mourning period was over and the men were arraigned in their usual garb, but Cera knew she'd be mourning for the rest of her life.

Pita Rosco was moist-eyed, visibly worried for her. Luigi Ginovisi looked downcast and bitter. Piero Inveglio was dignified and caring. Justiano di Kestria had his jaw set grimly. And there was a scattering of other nobles surrounding Stefan di Aranio who had arrived the previous day like a prince come to claim the throne, and he'd brought Marid Tamadhi with him. As the most senior Riban Jhafi, Marid was entitled to vote on matters of succession, and he seemed friendly to Aranio.

Also present were Rene Cardien and Odessa D'Ark, representing the Ordo Costruo. They were a comforting presence, but they had no legal status here.

'I am the last of the Nesti,' Cera said at last, breaking the silence. 'My father Olfuss was murdered by Gurvon Gyle. My mother Fadah was murdered by Samir, an agent of Gurvon Gyle. My elder brother Gremio died in what I must now believe was an accident contrived by Gurvon Gyle. My sister Solinde was murdered by an agent of Gurvon Gyle. And now my brother, Timori, is dead' – she grabbed the table for support and forced herself to go on – 'murdered by an agent of Gurvon Gyle.'

Snarls rippled around the room.

'There is a plague on my House and its name is Gurvon Gyle.' She balled her left fist. 'I wish to cure this plague. He must *cease to be*! He must *suffer*, and *he must die*!'

She realised she was shouting and clamped her jaw shut, but that didn't stop the room from echoing to her anguish. *Breathe. Just breathe.*

She put her hand on Elena's and gripped it, made sure they saw. *They need to understand that I don't blame Ella.*

She knew what the other woman was going through, the recriminations and self-flagellation, and she wasn't having it. *It's not your fault, Elena, and I refuse to let you believe it is. Our enemies move like ghosts and you can't be everywhere. We cannot live in prison cells. The fault lies with our enemies. We need you.* She hoped that maybe, *maybe*, on some level, Elena understood that.

'We will march on Brochena,' she said firmly. 'We will meet this enemy in battle and overcome: this I believe with all my heart. And I believe in you people gathered here: you are the people who will make it happen.'

Then the moment she'd feared happened. Stefan di Aranio raised a hand. 'We all sympathise with Signora Nesti's loss, obviously – we all have hearts. We all have families of our own. But we cannot blind ourselves to the facts.' He looked around the room, then fixed Cera with his narrowed eyes. 'We have no legitimate ruler.'

'This is no place for ambition,' Pita Rosco snapped, while Piero Inveglio made a Rimoni gesture of insult in the Lord of Riban's face.

'This is not ambition! You demand that we march to war for you! Who are you any more? The widow of our dead enemy, that's who! You don't outrank us any more, Cera Nesti! You don't even belong in this room, a fact I'm sure you'd be swift to point out were it someone else!'

Cera swallowed her anger. This was all so distressingly predictable – and yet, technically, Aranio was right. Her mother's sister's son, Theo Vernio-Nesti, was now the senior family member of her House – even though he'd been more or less banished by her father, he was now riding from the Rift Fort to take her position. And Timori was dead: Aranio was within his rights to demand the election of a new king.

But it couldn't happen now.

'My Lord of Riban, the *lex regalus*, the laws for the election of a new king when the ruling line fails, states that *all* of the Ruling House must be represented for a vote to be taken. I see only Riban here, and Forensa, and the lesser heirs of Loctis' – she nodded to Justiano – 'so you cannot call for a vote on the kingship now.'

Stefan di Aranio clearly knew this; he waved a hand dismissively. 'Under the *lex regalus*, there are also laws permitting the election of an Autarch, a dictator who rules in emergency until royal elections can be held. This role can be anyone chosen by a majority vote of any Ruling Houses present.'

'I know that too,' Cera replied, 'and I am more than happy for you to take that vote.' She reached down and plucked a copy of the *lex regalus* from the table, opened it to the marked point and read, '"Let the electors settle upon a single Autarch, with full kingly authority, for the period of ninety days. His eligibility is not limited by birth or any other quality, as the nature of the emergency which led to the loss of the king cannot be anticipated."' She tapped the key phrase and repeated, 'Not limited by birth or any other quality.'

Stefan stared at her as he realised what she was saying. 'The Autarch can only be a man, Lady. It says "He", as you've just read.'

'The term "He" in this context is genderless: I have the required legal opinion on that point from the Grey Crows.' She gestured to the bureaucrats waiting beside the walls.

'One of your paid toadies,' Aranio sneered.

'A man loyal to Don Perdonello in Brochena,' Cera countered, while the official went puce. Insulting the integrity of any Grey Crow was never a good idea – every ruler inevitably leaned on them for support at times.

Aranio scowled, realising his misstep, then spun back to the table. 'An Autarch must be able to deal with the emergency at hand! We face battle! Can you lead an army, girl? Can you swing a sword?'

'I think none will deny that I have the loyalty of our fighting men,' she countered, earning nods from Justiano di Kestria, Saarif Jelmud and others who'd fought at Brochena. 'And I was in the front lines beside the canals of my city as the Harkun poured through the breach, while you cowered in Riban, my Lord!'

Aranio turned white. 'I'd challenge you for that calumny, were you not a weakling girl!'

'Then try me,' Elena rasped. 'I'm still her champion.'

He started to retort, then closed his mouth, not looking at the Noros woman. His entourage also found other things to gaze at as silence fell on the room. Then he barked, 'I nominate myself as Autarch.'

The rest of the room looked at each other while Cera calculated the odds. Each city had a Ruling House – one Rimoni and one Jhafi – who functioned as electors for the kingship, or in this case, for the role of Autarch. Only the Ruling Houses of Riban, Loctis and Forensa were represented here today, and as Theo Vernio-Nesti was still en route and not formally appointed, she retained the Forensa vote. Aranio's Jhafi counterpart, Marid Tamadhi, could vote here, but the late Harshal ali-Assam's family, who would likely have supported her as the Ruling Jhafi House in Forensa, had been coordinating the transfer of the government records into the hinterlands and so weren't present. *Only four of us here can vote, and two of those are likely to support Stefan . . .*

'I nominate Justiano di Kestria,' one of Justiano's own knights said.

Cera glanced at Justiano, who wouldn't quite meet her gaze.

His elder brother Lorenzo died protecting me and he's never been satisfied with the explanation. She glanced at Elena. *Especially not Elena's role in his loss . . .*

Pita Rosco responded, 'I nominate Cera Nesti.'

Stefan di Aranio grunted sourly, but the Grey Crows had given their opinion and the nomination stood. 'Anyone else?' he asked coldly. No other hands were raised. 'Then shall we?'

There was a delay while the Crows produced the four voting tokens and the voting plates, silver platters for receiving the tokens, with the emblems of each house beaten into the metal. The voting tokens were numbered; they were handed out randomly, with the numbers hidden. As soon as they were issued to those four eligible to vote, Stefan Aranio grunted in satisfaction; he held token Number One, and voting first had advantages. He tossed his token into the Aranio platter, then glared around the table.

Cera's heart sank as Marid Tamadhi produced the second token; he too voted for Aranio. Already, Stefan could not lose the vote.

It also meant that whoever had the third token – whether it was she or Justiano – would effectively eliminate the other. Heart beating, she opened her hand as he did.

She held token three.

She exhaled, and placed it in her own platter. Justiano's head dropped – he couldn't vote for himself without conceding the victory to Aranio – then placed his token reluctantly in Cera's platter.

Two each.

'What is the tie-breaker?' Aranio asked rhetorically; he clearly knew already.

'Combat,' one of the Grey Crows announced, and Aranio smiled, then his face stiffened as the man continued, 'However, a champion can be nominated.'

'You mean her?' Aranio spat, eyeing Elena. 'She is magi.'

Elena just stared at him. Her leg might be useless, but both knew there would be only one outcome to such a fight.

The Crow coughed. 'If combat is not selected, then the selection is by ordeal.'

'What?' Aranio grabbed the *lex regalus* notes that Cera had brought. 'Where does it say that?'

'Clause thirty-three,' Cera replied. 'The candidates must hold burning coals until one concedes.'

Aranio's eyes bulged, then he turned pale as Cera started to unwrap her bandaged right hand. It was a ghastly mess of wet tissue and white new skin, and incredibly painful to move. They all knew how she'd got it: holding Rutt Sordell's scarab in the flames until it perished.

Stefan di Aranio looked at his own hands and shuddered.

'I would have gnostic healing afterwards?' he asked, his voice now uncertain.

'Of course,' Rene Cardien said. 'I'll have Clematia do it. Your hand will be ready to hold a sword again in . . . oh, about four to six weeks, I'd guess.'

Aranio swallowed, and looked at Cera's right hand again. In some places, the bone was still visible though the translucent flesh. They all knew the scarring would be permanent, that she would have to learn to write left-handed.

Cera met his eyes. *Well, my lord. How badly do you want this? What's ninety days in charge worth to you? Especially if you believe you'll be king eventually anyway?*

Aranio looked away. 'Anyone determined enough to go through that deserves their moment,' he said grudgingly. 'Let the Nesti be named Autarch.' He glanced at Tamadhi, then leaned away from the table, disengaging from the group. 'I will of course provide men for the struggle.'

No doubt, but fewer than we need, and with orders to preserve themselves, Cera thought, watching his face. But now wasn't the moment to call him out; there were oaths and ceremonies, and this was in itself a historic moment: the first woman ever to be voted into such a role in Javon. She could see pride in the eyes of Pita Rosco, Piero Inveglio, and others too, as she met their gaze. Even in Elena's eyes, perhaps.

'Then let us do what is necessary, then reconvene,' she told them all. 'We have much to do.'

Riban, Javon, on the continent of Antiopia
Awwal (Martrois) 930
21st month of the Moontide

Gurvon Gyle had to wait until almost midnight for his quarry to
be finally alone. Night in the unlovely trading-post city of Riban
was never quiet; the streets were filled with the homeless, refugees
and indigents, seeking one last drink or morsel of food before they
wrapped themselves in their threadbare cloaks and huddled in a
doorway to try and sleep. Since the Dorobon invasion, the city had
been filled with refugees from Brochena, all fleeing east. Public order
was breaking down, the Rimoni and Jhafi soldiery maintaining the
peace were at each other's throats more often than not, and feeding the masses was becoming impossible as stores were exhausted.

Occupying Riban would have been more trouble than it was worth,
so for now at least, it remained the seat of Stefan di Aranio, a Rimoni
of senatorial stock from the old empire whose forebears had grudgingly married into Jhafi nobility to ensure candidacy for the Javon
throne. Stefan barely acknowledged his Jhafi blood, saw himself as the
natural alternative to the Nesti, had a flock of heirs already and was
a staunchly conservative Sollan. But Aranio's attempt to be elected
Autarch had failed, ending any hopes for a negotiated settlement.

Aranio had just returned to his home city, ostensibly to prepare his
forces to support the Nesti in their march west, unaware that Gurvon
was waiting in his office – not in person, but as a spiratus; his body
was in his own bed in Brochena, a hundred miles away. Traversing
the distance in spirit-form was quick, but it wasn't instantaneous;
he'd arrived two hours ago after an hour's travel, using kinesis to
move the doors to allow himself ingress. Then he'd settled down to
wait, conserving his energies.

Now he stepped forth and allowed himself to be seen. 'Greetings,
Lord Aranio.'

Stefan di Aranio choked, sprayed wine over his desk and clutched
at his chest. For a few seconds Gurvon was worried the man was
actually having a heart attack, which would have been an unfortunate

complication. Aranio was a stolid, almost plump, man, with brownish hair from his northern Rimoni blood and a drinker's mottled complexion. Now his florid face was distinctly pale as he gazed at Gurvon in some consternation.

'If you call for your guards I'll be forced to act,' Gurvon warned, before holding his hand in front of a flame, making it obvious that he was not physically present.

Aranio sagged into his chair. 'What do you want?'

This wasn't Gurvon's first visit; he'd started by terrorising Stefan's youngest son, just to make a point – Aranio had many flaws, including overweening ambition, greed and bigotry, but his biggest weakness was his love of his family. Gurvon had spent quite some time working on the man's fears – he'd been far easier than Cera Nesti to twist and break.

The thing with Aranio, Gurvon had found, was that you could only push him to a certain point: he wouldn't do *anything* to protect his line, but he would do a lot. Coercion made him antagonistic, but bending his loyalty, that was another thing. He was ambitious, and he'd disliked the Nestis for a very long time, which gave Gurvon plenty of hooks for the man to swallow.

You should be king, not some mere boy. These times are too dangerous for boy-kings.

Cera Nesti . . . you should believe those whispers about her: look at her new friends, Staria Canestos and her degenerates . . .

Elena Anborn is in the thrall of a Keshi Souldrinker . . . Do you know what they are? The whisper is that she's turned into one herself.

You can't be expected to defend Riban and send all your soldiers to aid the Nesti.

What if the Nesti lose? Where are you left, then? Surely adults like you and I can find common ground? We're not idealistic girls, are we?

Many a general has been tardy in battle, haven't they? Late to advance, early to withdraw . . . and who will be left to blame you if you 'misjudge the situation' by a few crucial minutes?

He bent over the shaken Rimoni lord and used kinesis to force his chin up until he met his eye.

'She's going to lose anyway, Stefan: why should she drag you down with her? And your cooperation will ensure that your line continues afterwards. I'll need men like you to pacify the natives. Someone strong.'

The 'strong' man nodded in mute and frightened acquiescence.

Forensa, Javon, on the continent of Antiopia
Awwal (Martrois) 930
21st month of the Moontide

The Nesti army was ready to march at Darkmoon, the last week of Martrois. Cera had to fight for the right to accompany it: her counsellors wanted her to stay 'safe' in Forensa. But she knew she had to be there, though explaining her reasons to her allies was a little awkward: this had to be a Nesti victory, not a Kestrian or Aranio victory that might give someone too many ideas. Allies could become enemies all too quickly: history was very clear on that lesson.

Before her were ranks of bright-eyed men filled with frightened bravado, waiting to take their first steps on the road to Brochena and battle.

There'll be no fortress to retreat to; no walls and canals to shelter behind, nowhere to take cover. There will be nothing between us and our enemy except for our shields and our courage.

The past weeks had been a blur of activity. Justiano di Kestria was coordinating the Rimoni, two legions of men supported by a dozen Ordo Costruo acting as battle-magi. Saarif Jelmud would coordinate the Jhafi contingent, supported by the rest of the Ordo Costruo. And Stefan di Aranio's men – if he actually sent them – would join them west of Riban.

Word had come that Staria Canestos had been assailed by the Harkun survivors of the Battle of Forensa, who were trying to take the Rift Forts so they could bring their kin up from below; as yet, that battle was still in the balance. The thought that at any moment thousands more Harkun could join the fray was almost paralysing

Cera's counsellors – but at least it meant that the alliance with Staria's Sacro Arcoyris Estellan was now out in the open, and her people were learning to appreciate the fact that Staria's people were both on their side, and invaluable.

Elena arrived on horseback, her movement strained and awkward. She'd had to tease her leg into a bent position to ride at all, and from the look on her face she was in constant pain. Cera couldn't begin to know what being apart from Kazim was doing to her. Elena clutched at Cera's reins, then had the gall to try and warn her against going to war, when she looked equally useless. 'You don't need to march with the army, Cera. No one would think the less of you.'

'I'd be no safer here.'

Their eyes met, and Cera saw Elena's face alter, ever so subtly – not a sudden change of heart, but the realisation of one that had already happened. 'I forgive you for what you did,' Elena whispered.

Cera swallowed. Tears stung her eyes, but she was already cried-out from saying goodbye to Tarita in the infirmary. She waved to the trumpeter, then turned back to Elena and said, 'Well, let's go.'

The trumpeter blasted out a lively call to arms, then she shouted into the resounding silence that followed, 'Free People of Ja'afar! Today we march into history! Today we go to reclaim what is ours: our own land! Today we take up arms against the invader! All the gods are watching, and all smile upon us, for our cause is just! Our cause is freedom! *Freedom!*'

Simple and easy shouty words always work best, her father used to joke. She could picture him now, his shaggy face alight with determination, as the people's response set the ground shaking.

'Freedom for Ja'afar! Freedom for Javon!'

The drums thundered and the first ranks stepped off on the road leading west.

26

Family

The Mage Houses

The Pallas Magi are obsessive about family, being the guardians of magical blood-lines. They will marry only among themselves, and any barren marriage is the source of severe opprobrium. Quite simply, the mage-blood is the foundation of the empire, and real power is procreated through the loins of the pure-blood families.

ORDO COSTRUO ARCANUM, PONTUS, 807

Southern Kesh, on the continent of Antiopia
Awwal (Martrois) 930
21ˢᵗ month of the Moontide

Ramon Sensini nudged Lu, his mare, down the slope to where Silvio Anturo was waiting. Above and behind him, a shadow on the gloomy ridge, Jelaska waited. Silvio spurred forward to meet him.

Anturo had his own bodyguards, a squad of a dozen men, Silacian and Dhassan toughs who eyed the figure on the ridge above uneasily. All were big, muscular men, but they knew who Jelaska was, and none wished to make a false move.

One of Anturo's party, waiting a little aside from the rest, trotted forward and lowered his hood: an older man with silvery hair and a cheerful face that could go stony as a grave-marker. Ramon knew him well: Tomasi Fuldo, Pater-Retiari's right-hand man. 'Buona sera, Ramon,' Fuldo called in musical Rimoni. 'Come sta, amici?'

<Trouble?> Jelaska sent. She was loosely linked to his mind, her touch watchful.

<Could be. Shield yourself. There will be archers – Tomasi always brings a few.>

Ramon reined in, reassessing. 'Capo Tomasi, to what do I owe this pleasure?'

Tomasi Fuldo had been Ramon's mentor in the world of the familioso. To say he was the brains of the organisation was to exaggerate: Pater-Retiari was highly intelligent himself, and no one's pawn. But Tomasi was the smartest man Ramon knew. He had once been a treasury official for the Imperial Governor of Silacia, but always in the pay of Pater-Retiari; up until the day he was exposed and had to flee, he'd robbed the governor blind. Now he applied his expertise to aiding the familioso finances; it was he who had suggested the misuse of the Imperial promissory system that Ramon had been carrying out.

They dismounted, embraced and kissed each other's cheeks, and Ramon noticed Tomasi's smile was getting nowhere near his eyes. 'You've been a worry to us all, *giovanotto*.'

'Things haven't exactly gone to plan,' Ramon told him.

The Retiari capo nodded as if approving, but Ramon sensed unease. He would already be noticing changes in his pupil: maturity, perhaps even hints of disaffection. 'The Petrossi familioso are also anxious, Ramon – it had been so long since we lost touch with you, while investment has continued to flood in – far more than you and I even dreamed.'

'How so?'

'These Rondian nobles think the world owes them money,' Tomasi replied. 'We've made full use of all the excesses of the Imperial system – the greed of the magi, who believe that no one would dare to defraud them; the corruption in the legions, and the flimsy controls around the whole promissory note system itself. But now we have to close the deal.'

'We can do that,' Ramon assured him.

'But where have you been? Sol et Lune, I've had to work hard covering for you! We even maintained interest payments after the Second Army left Peroz, to quiet the rumours. We've had to use our own reserves, gambling that you would reappear with the bullion.'

Tomasi's face tightened. 'I was confident – others less so. Where is the gold, Ramon?'

Silvio Anturo edged closer. 'My patrona, Isabella Petrossi, also wishes very much to know this.'

The Crusades were a financial wilderness, ripe for exploitation, but if Tomasi was right, their ruse had been almost too successful. No one involved had known what was coming: Shaliyah. That catastrophe had left the familioso as exposed to the promissory notes as anyone else – and now it was beginning to look like Tomasi had gambled the wealth of the Retiari on finding Ramon with the gold.

Which is exactly what I wanted, Ramon thought, *but I have to keep this illusion going, or all Hel will break free.*

'I have some of it, and I know where the rest is,' he told them. 'There are caches on our route, all the way from here to Khotri.' He'd already told Silvio Anturo this: it was good for lies to be consistent.

Tomasi scowled. 'It's inconvenient that you've buried it, but understandable. I expect I would have done the same. But the Treasury also knows you're here: your arrest, and the recovery of that gold, has become an unspoken objective of this phase of the Crusade. I am told the Church and the Crown have joined forces to that end.'

Nice to feel important, Ramon mused as he studied Tomasi. Confronting his Capo at some point had always been an inevitability. What he would do next he still wasn't sure; whatever it was, he would have to step carefully. *If I can't get my mother and sister out of Retiari's hands, it's all been for nothing . . .*

That meant keeping the gold out of everyone's clutches but his own. Though he was also going to pay the Lost Legions soldiers what they'd earned. They were his kin now, that much he knew, far more so than the familioso had ever been.

'We had some losses, and some of the recoveries will be difficult,' he said.

'Then we need to get what we can,' Tomasi said. 'You must leave the army and bring your wagons with you – that ruse is over.'

'That's twenty-five wagons,' Ramon replied, 'all with false bottoms and cargo. How're we going to conceal so many? Especially with the Inquisition trailing me.'

'The Quizzies are after you?' Tomasi looked at him anxiously.

Silvio Anturo frowned. 'You've not mentioned this before, Sensini.'

'I didn't think it was related – we discovered secret Inquisition death-camps on the far side of the Tigrates, and the Inquisition has been plaguing us since. They arranged the destruction of the bridges at Vida to cut us off. But now it appears they're working hand-in-glove with the Treasury people in Vida.'

Tomasi grimaced. 'It makes your escape even more urgent. What are your movements from here?'

'Seth Korion has sent messages to his father, apprising him of our situation as we rest and prepare for the retreat north. We're still six hundred miles from Southpoint, and then it's another three hundred across the Bridge. It's early Martrois: we've got four months to walk a thousand miles. Seth wants us on the road inside the week.'

'There will be opportunities to escape on the north road.'

'No doubt, but the wagons are well-guarded – by my own men, for sure, but it's not a simple thing.'

'We have the manpower to snatch the wagons,' Tomasi assured him – which was alarming – but then he added, 'I don't think we'll be ready to make that move for several weeks.'

That bought Ramon time. The meeting broke up cordially, with perhaps a little more trust than it had started. As he rode Lu back towards the legion camp, Ramon rejoined Jelaska. She clearly wanted to talk, but refrained from speaking until she was sure the last tracker had turned away.

'What are you going to do?' the Argundian woman asked. 'You've got the Inquisition, the Imperial Treasury and now *two* familioso after you. I imagine the Hebusalim underworld are going to want a word too.'

'I'll hide behind your skirts,' he said with a grin.

She wasn't in the mood to laugh. 'The Hel you will. If you're going to get that money back to Pontus and keep all your promises, you're going to need a few more fox-tricks.'

'Fox-tricks are my specialty. My children – I mean my *child* – needs me.'

'Children?' Jelaska pounced. 'You've more than one child? Who else . . . ? Calipha Amiza in Ardijah, right? Tell me I'm right!'

'Si,' he admitted. 'And my maid in Silacia was pregnant before I left for the Crusade, so that one will be a year old – no, more by now.' He thought of another encounter. 'And then there was a girl in Pontus – but she was also a mage, so the odds of her conceiving were low.'

'Oh la! Anyone else? How's Lanna?'

'She says she's barren.' Since Severine left, Lanna had taken to sliding into his bed after dark – he'd thought no one knew, but Jelaska had always had a nose for what went on in camp.

They reached the Lost Legions' perimeter and parted before re-entering. He headed for his tent, the one Severine had cast him out of. It felt empty, the absence of Julietta a painful void, the silence a reproach. So after lying alone fidgeting for a while, he got restless and went wandering.

The night was hot and sultry and the men were lively. They had plenty of water from the river, and their escape from Riverdown had lifted them immensely. Once again their commanders had delivered, keeping them safe and one step ahead. The suffering of that confined camp was forgotten, and the men who noticed him called his name, offering drink from dozens of illicit stills.

The rankers were in good spirits, despite the army having lost more than a thousand men at Riverdown. They now numbered around eleven thousand. He eventually found his own guard cohort: down to sixteen having lost Neubeau, Hedman and Briggan at Riverdown. Most were wounded, but they were in better shape than many units.

'When do we march, sir?' Pilus Lukaz asked after Ramon had accepted a thimble of the liquor that Ilwyn brewed, which travelled down his throat like a liquid fireball.

'In about a week. We're trying to talk to Papa Kaltus by relay-stave to clarify orders, but even Seth has to go through the protocols, apparently.' He raised his voice to encompass the whole cohort. 'Don't you lads worry about food: we'll be back in the Imperial supply network soon. Standard issue: beans and hardtack. I bet you've missed that, si?'

The men laughed. 'Don't think I c'n stand food that en't cooked in Noorie spices any more,' Vidran remarked. 'Gonna get me a Dhassan wife, one that can cook eastern grub.'

This elicited a chorus of comments about the relative merits of Yurosian and Antiopian food; soldiers could be relied upon to go on for ever about food. Then, as men will, they turned to the merits of Dhassan woman – soft bodies, good cooks, compared to Keshi women – slim, passionate, but devoutly Amteh; and Khotri women, who were earthy, bony creatures who offered few creature comforts but were fiercely loyal. Ramon shook a few hands and drifted on, leaving them to it.

He found his maniple's tribune, Storn, sitting inside one of the wagons containing the gold, ticking off supply-rosters and shaking his head. He looked up in alarm when he heard movement, then relaxed when he identified Ramon. 'Evening, sir.'

'Evening, Storn. Any problems?'

Storn could have given him an hour-long recital of problems, but they both knew what he meant. 'No one knows but me and the other logisticali. That's two dozen, who've proved they know how to stay mum,' he assured Ramon.

The twenty-five bullion wagons all had false floors, beneath which they were lined with one-pound ingots of pure gold, melted down en route from all the coin they'd accumulated. If Tomasi Fuldo was right, the latest spike in the gold price meant that it was now worth close to two million auros, a mind-boggling sum. A pound-ingot was the size of his hand and half as thick, and they had six thousand of them, about eighty thousand auros per wagon. It didn't look like a lot, but each ingot represented approximately the lifetime earnings of an ordinary farmer in Yuros. With gold now so rare, they were potentially carrying enough to mint about a fifth of the coins in circulation in the empire.

'The horses must be struggling with the weight?'

'No more than the other wagons – gold is heavy, obviously, but we've balanced the bullion loads with lightweight material to fill the wagons,' Storn answered. 'The water wagons are actually far heavier when full. But I've been wondering what's next, sir? When do we *divest* of this weight?'

Ramon leaned in close. 'For now, we stay silent. And I want you to find some smelting equipment. First place we stop, start minting coins – take a mould from a Rondian auros, use tin and copper to make the coins, then dip them in liquid gold. Make sure it's the requisite amount: I want our boys to be able to use these coins in the West, si?'

'I'll be happier when we've distributed the bulk to the boys, sir,' Storn confessed.

'That can't happen until we're safe,' Ramon replied. He patted Storn's shoulder. 'You're doing well, Tribune. We'll be home soon, and you'll be a rich man.' He saluted, and moved on.

Seth Korion stared around his tent at those of his magi who'd joined him. The appointed hour was almost here, and he found his hands were beginning to shake. *Tonight I'm going to talk with Father . . .* He didn't feel at all ready.

Beside him Jelaska was chatting with Evan Hale about the merits of Keshi versus Yurosian bows. Hale, like all Brevians, used a long-bow, but the Keshi used recurved shortbows. Hale was a taciturn man who seldom spoke, but he played the lute and sang sad Andressan laments beautifully.

Chaplain Gerdhart was also present, because Seth wanted a priest at hand – not for any logical reason, but Father might expect it. And Fridryk Kippenegger was here when he'd not been invited, having wandered in and poured himself a drink and now Seth didn't know how to ask him to leave. Kip was muttering about something to Ramon, who was still subdued after Severine Tisseme's desertion.

I wonder where she went? I hope she's safe – and little Julietta too.

On the table before him was a metal platter of water and various powders heating over some candle-stumps, slowly steaming to create a billowing cloud in which the scrying image would emerge. As the hour-bells rang, they all lapsed into silence, and their eyes drifted back to Seth.

'General, surely you would prefer to speak with your father alone?' Chaplain Gerdhart asked.

Heavens, no. Seth wanted the conversation to be civil, businesslike, and as formal as possible. *If I talk to Father in private it'll be hideous.* 'This is a conference between ranking generals of the Rondian Army,' he said, 'not father and son.'

They all exchanged looks, not fooled at all.

He'd made contact using the army's open network of gnostic communication and had his request passed north to his father, together with a few details of how many units he had brought across the river. He could have gone direct, using the relay-stave that Jelaska had painstakingly crafted, but he didn't want to waste it – and anyway, he knew his father: proper protocol would have to be followed.

The contact arrived, the steam above the dish flashing with colour then forming a foggy image of Kaltus Korion. The hawk-faced visage of his father was somewhat distorted, but his voice came through clearly. 'This is Korion.'

'Father . . . er . . . *Sir*: this is Seth Korion, Commander of the Second Army, reporting from north of Vida.'

'I know who you are, Seth,' Kaltus replied with bored irony. 'Are you alone?'

'No sir, I'm with my command group. I've linked them to this contact so that you can hear their voices and—'

'That won't be necessary,' Kaltus interrupted. 'I don't wish to talk to them. I wish to talk to you, alone.'

'Sir, perhaps after we've reported our posi—'

'Now. I have a million things to do and no time to waste on a ragtag of low-bloods.'

Seth shuddered. The tone of voice, the manner . . . childhood and all its misery came flooding back. It was worse than charging towards the ballistae at Ardijah . . .

No it isn't! I could have died then; this is just a bloody chat!

Anger fuelled his reply. 'My magi are the men and women who have guided the survivors out of Shaliyah and back to Rondian lines. They are heroes, and entitled to hear what is happening in the wider Crusade, so that we can formulate our strategies.'

The hazy image in the steam was clear enough to see Kaltus Korion's expression: dismissive and irritated. 'All right, let's have this conversation in front of your *juniors*. Firstly, you've taken the title "Commander of the Second Army". You don't have the right. You are a battle-mage of Pallacios Thirteen. There is no "Second Army", since that débâcle at Shaliyah.'

Seth's mouth went dry while his brow dripped perspiration. He glanced around the tent; Evan Hale was making an obscene gesture at the image, Jelaska and Gerdhart were exchanging looks, Kippenegger was rolling his eyes, and Ramon was tapping his fingers idly as if bored.

'Sir, I have eleven thousand survivors of the Second Army and we are very much intact! Furthermore, when the commander falls in the field, the ranking officers must choose from among the survivors a new commander: that's what the manual says. That's what we did. I can give account for our—'

'I'm not interested in your account, boy. The Courts Martial will hear it.'

The Courts Martial?

'What am I charged with?' he asked incredulously.

'Desertion. I've read and heard the reports from Shaliyah. Those who fought, died. Those who escaped, ran: they are deserters, and will be treated as such.'

Seth looked wide-eyed around the pavilion at the fury of the other magi. They all went to speak – to yell, shriek, bellow – at once, and he raised his hand.

'We held the line until the very end, Father!' Seth protested indignantly. 'We fought until it was hopeless! Since then, my men have marched and fought for every step home.' When his father barely reacted, his anger rose another notch. 'You don't know what we've been through! We've stormed castles, held barricades against over-whelming odds, and regained the safety of our lines intact!'

'Don't call me Father, Seth. I'm not your father.'

Seth felt a wrenching in his stomach. *'What?'*

'For some time it has been apparent to me that you are not my natural son. The failures at college – your weakness and lack of spirit. I confronted your mother, and she confessed to an extramarital affair just prior to your conception. I have had the marriage annulled and you are disinherited.' Kaltus leaned forward, eyes fixed. 'You are no longer my son. You never were.'

If the ground had been sucked into a sudden vortex, swallowing everything around him, Seth couldn't have been more stunned. *It's not true. I'm a Korion. It's not true. I'm a Korion.*

'You are ordered to hold your position,' Kaltus went on. 'In three days' time, a detachment from Peroz will reach your camp. They will include Kirkegarde and Inquisitors from Vida, who will accept your surrender. You and your magi will submit to the justice of the Courts Martial, or face the disgrace of all of your Houses.' Kaltus looked away, as if someone had just addressed him, waved a hand dismissively at Seth. 'This interview is over.'

His image vanished.

For a moment everything was utterly silent as they all stared at Seth, trying to think what to say. Then everyone spoke at once. Evan Hale was inchoate with rage, hurling abuse at the brazier as if Korion could somehow still hear him. Jelaska was seething, snarling that they could *just try* to arrest her and see where it got them. Gerdhart was beseeching Kore, Kippenegger was shouting in guttural Schlessen, while Ramon Sensini was laughing as if this were just a joke.

Seth couldn't even cling to that illusion: his father had never made a joke within his hearing. Perhaps he was hilarious among his friends, who knew?

'I really am his son,' he said, aware it sounded like bleating.

'Of course you are,' Ramon snickered, still treating this as a huge joke. 'The man couldn't be that much of an arsehole without being related to you somehow.'

Seth glared at him. 'This is no jesting matter!'

'Who's joking?' Ramon winked and Seth stood, ready to punch him.

Gerdhart interposed, saying, 'Please, sirs! We need to talk civilly about this! The Courts Martial—'

'—can go fuck themselves,' Jelaska snapped. 'I'm not to be judged by a bunch of inbred Pallacians. I'm going back to Argundy and they can come and fetch me if they can.' She cracked her knuckles and glowered about her.

'The Argundian maniples must stick together,' Gerdhart declared. 'We'll fight our way across the Bridge if necessary—'

'I'm going to make a run for it,' Evan Hale declared. 'We all should – if we fan out, they won't catch us all – I'm not dying on a rope!'

'Yar, nor me,' Kippenegger muttered. '*Verdamnt* Rondian *shizen*.'

'We're not guilty – there's no evidence,' Seth found himself babbling.

'A Court Martial can prove whatever it bloody wants,' Hale replied. 'Ask my people! Andressea has been made scapegoat for every military disaster since—'

'Wait!' Ramon Sensini said, standing up. 'This is ridiculous. We've got eleven thousand men. The safest place we can be is right where we are.'

'Right where the Inquisition can find us,' Gerdhart moaned.

'And with enough men to tell them to piss off,' Ramon countered. 'Listen, we got out of Shaliyah and Ardijah and Riverdown. We can get out of this.'

'We can't ask the men to protect us,' Seth protested. 'They don't share our crimes – they'll be allowed home!'

'Crimes? What fucking crimes? We're *not* deserters!' Hale railed.

'Tell that to the Quizzies,' Jelaska sneered. 'The bastards will brand the whole army.'

'They wouldn't dare,' Gerdhart retorted. 'It's just us they want.'

'Yar, the ones who know what really happened at Shaliyah,' Kip said.

'Exactly!' Jelaska jabbed a finger at the big Schlessen. 'Kippenegger's right, for once: they sent the Second Army in to die and now they're cleaning up afterwards.'

'I agree,' Ramon said. 'You heard what Papa Korion said: those who escaped Shaliyah were executed. Any who weren't his spies, I warrant.'

Seth felt ill. *Everyone here, and everyone in the camp outside, has given everything for this army, and now they're considered traitors? And my father – he is my father, damn him – is pretending I'm not his. I have his blood!* He was trembling with rage. *What are we going to do?*

His eyes went to Ramon Sensini. The little Silacian had fallen silent while the rest continued to rant, his gaze faraway. As the talk petered out, he looked up, blinked and said, 'If you think I have a plan, I don't. Not yet. But I do have some thoughts.' He raised a finger. 'First thing: we have roughly two legions. Korion has roughly twenty legions, but they're spread all over Kesh and Dhassa – about half must be on garrison duty or protecting the supply-lines; the rest will be with him in the north. All he's got near here is the garrison at Vida, and they're pulling out.

'Two: our men aren't going to submit to being branded as deserters – *physically* branded, remember – after what they've been through. And I'm not either.

'Three: what happened at Shaliyah is – if those in Yuros can come to believe it – enough to incite widespread rebellion. Not in Rondelmar maybe, but in Argundy and Estellayne and Noros and elsewhere. Remember that Constant didn't just betray an army, but the magi in that army, and that's what the magi of those vassal-states will see. So we need to tell them.' He stood. 'So here's what I think. We don't ask Kaltus Korion's permission any more. We make our own plans.'

'But that's desertion,' Gerdhart said.

'We're being treated that way anyway,' Ramon replied. 'To get home, we've to cross Dhassa and the Leviathan Bridge by the end of Junesse. The empire will try and stop us. Are we prepared to let them?'

'No,' Seth blurted, although he was frightened the others wouldn't back him.

Kippenegger growled his agreement, and so did the two Argundians, who if nothing else were pledged to see their own countrymen home. Evan Hale, the Andressan, seemed to be teetering, but when he saw the others resolve to stay, he amended his thinking. 'All right. But you heard Kaltus Korion: the Inquisition are on their way.'

'Indeed,' Ramon said confidently. He pointed to the map. 'We're upriver from Vida and downriver from Peroz. The Inquisition are supposed to be here in three days, right? And we can't outrun them. So I think we owe them a very special reception.'

They looked at each other as the enormity of it all sunk in. Seth found himself wondering if it wasn't better to surrender after all. At least then the men would only be decimated, not wiped out.

But he doubted anyone here would accept that.

Sweet Kore, we're going to war against our own people.

27

Speaking with God

The Argundian Grand Prelate

Only one non-Pallacian has been elected as Grand Prelate of the Church of Kore: Goetfreyd of Delph, a compromise candidate elected during peace talks between Rondelmar and Argundy in 722. His reign was short-lived; he appeared for morning service a few months later, drooling and babbling of having spoken to Corineus himself. It was found that he'd fallen prey to a daemon and become possessed, barely surviving the experience. The daemon was exorcised, but he was now tainted and had to be formally deposed. He lived out his remaining months in solitary confinement before taking his own life.

PALLAS ARCANUM, 839

'Bahil! I give you all I am! Bahil, Father of All!'
THE FINAL WORDS OF GOETFREYD OF DELPH,
GRAND PRELATE OF THE KORE, 723

Mandira Khojana, Lokistan, on the continent of Antiopia
Safar (Febreux) to Awwal (Martrois) 930
20th and 21st months of the Moontide

Alaron Mercer watched the sunset in the Garden of Bones, as had become his habit of late. Sometimes others joined him, but mostly he came alone.

'The thaw's coming, Cym,' he whispered to the carved stone in one corner of the garden. It was newly hewn, only a month old. *Cymbellea di Regia-Meiros*, it read, *Beloved daughter of Mercellus and Justina. Janune*

Y930. It was a Yurosian conceit, to have a grave-marker. None of the Zain monks already buried here had them, not even the masters, but he *needed* to have his friend's passing marked, and Master Puravai had given his consent.

'The clouds are higher today, and the river below is finally melting – just a trickle, so far. The frozen river is amazing, like a mad sculpture by the Queen of Winter.' It had frozen entirely for two weeks at the end of Janune. 'Just like in Noros.' He wiped at the tears that always came when he talked to her. 'I wish we'd all stayed at home.'

The silence was her reply.

Four weeks had passed, twenty-four days, since the Hadishah attack. The funerals were all done, the pyres lit and the ashes interred. There were nine prisoners, all Chain-runed; Alyssa Dulayne was still unconscious most of the time, her healing far from complete. Ramita had torn up her back, face and scalp so badly it was doubtful she'd ever move properly again, nor regain her looks. They had recovered four small windskiffs and a larger warbird, and now that the midwinter storms were beginning to pass they could begin learning to use them. The outward damage of the attack was repaired, but the inner hurts were still raw and bleeding.

Eleven of the thirty novices had died, and seven more had been invalided, recovering from wounds that would most likely have been fatal without the healing-gnosis – three were still bedridden, which meant only sixteen of the new Zain Ascendants were currently training.

Alaron felt each loss like a separate weight in the pit of his stomach.

He heard the slap of leather soles on the steps and sighed. He didn't want company. Even when he saw it was Ramita, he had to force a smile onto his face.

'Namaste, husband,' she said softly.

He mumbled a reply, and held her hand when she sat beside him, but he didn't look at her. He was aware that he'd gone into a shell since the attack. He'd thrown himself into the repairs and done everything he could to speed the healing, but when he'd resumed lessons, the joy was gone. He and Ramita had found peace and sanctuary here at Mandira Khojana, and they'd repaid that gift by bringing death in their wake. The guilt piled up on his shoulders and bowed him down: if only he'd taught them faster. If only they'd set a watch. If only he'd reacted sooner . . .

'Al'Rhon, Das is asking to play with you.'

Dasra liked to play loud and boisterous games with Alaron before dinner; they'd been fun . . . until the attack. Now he felt so exhausted and depressed by the end of the day he struggled to rouse himself. 'I'm too tired,' he murmured.

'Come anyway. He wants to play Hoop.'

No – not that. No.

'Come,' she said, wagging her head expectantly, 'your son needs you.'

'He's not my son.'

'Yes, he is: a boy that pig-headed, he must be yours.' She stood, pulling at him until he faced her. 'Come!'

'Mita, what happened to you that night?' He'd asked before and she'd not answered, but he *needed* to know. *This for that.* If she wanted him to come and play with Das, she could answer his question: they were both traders' children, after all.

'I don't really know,' she admitted. 'I have told you of Darikha-ji, the Warrior-Queen. It is said that when the battle against the rakas-demons went badly, a great rage rose inside her and she became the ogress Dar-Kana. She is a monster who rips the heads from her victims and drinks from the fountain of their blood.'

Alaron raised his eyebrows. 'Bloodthirsty.'

'Very. Dar-Kana is the most terrifying being in the heavens. When she becomes enraged, the foundations of the world are shaken – if she cannot be appeased, Urte will shake itself apart and time will end.' She looked up at him, completely serious. 'When Alyssa Dulayne threatened my son, I became Dar-Kana. I was filled with power and rage, out of control, and all I wanted was to kill and kill and kill.'

She sounded so afraid of herself that Alaron forgot his own problems, and put his arm around her. 'But you did stop,' he reminded her. 'You're still *you*.'

'For now. When Alyssa fell, the rage left me.' Ramita shuddered. 'But only just.'

He reached out and pulled her against him, for the first time in a month holding her openly, fully. They'd hardly touched each other in weeks; their loving had become furtive since the attack, shy groping in the dark, fulfilling a physical need but no longer revelling in it. He'd thought it was just him, but for the first time Alaron realised how deeply upset Ramita was too. He took her head in his hands, tilted it up and kissed her, pressed his mouth to hers until she responded, until it felt natural, then he whispered, 'I'm glad to have a fierce Lakh wife to protect us.'

'But you don't understand. It was like insanity—'

'I *do* understand: you fight to protect those you love, and so do I. Both you and Das, and Nasatya too. I love you all, and I always will.'

Her eyes were gazing into his as if to see through him until she glimpsed the truth, and at last he saw them lighten, the weight of mourning lifting. It was right to grieve, but life continued. He turned his eyes to the marker-stone. *Goodbye, Cymbellea. I never knew you as well as I thought. I never understood you, but I loved you anyway. I'll miss you always.*

Then he turned back to his living, breathing, loving wife. 'So let's go and find our son.'

When they got to the courtyard, Dasra was playing catch with Yash, giggling every time he missed. When Yash saw their interlocked fingers he grinned. There were others lingering in the courtyard, haunting it like the ghosts of their friends who'd died here. A few looked up, but most looked away. In the corner sat Tegeda, the Hadishah woman. She alone was unChained and permitted to walk freely, on Ramita's word.

Dasra beamed. 'Dada!' He threw Alaron the ball clumsily; he might still be too small to catch it and throw it, but he was desperate to try. Alaron drew the ball to himself with gnosis, then tossed it back. Dasra reached, missed, chortled and tottered after it as it bounced away. Then Ramita reached out with kinesis and grabbed the child and they played, passing Das about them as if he were a ball as well, while the boy giggled and shrieked happily.

'He'll be too excited to eat,' Ramita said at last, bundling him into her arms. 'I'll go and feed him, put him to bed.' She threw Alaron a meaningful glance. 'I'll see you later,' she called, and sashayed away.

Yash punched his arm mischievously. 'Hey,' he called out, 'anyone feel like a game of Hoop?'

For a moment everyone in the courtyard was silent, and Alaron wondered if this was a step too far, too soon, then Aprek stood up. 'I'm in.' Alaron smiled at him gratefully. Then others rose, one by one: Gateem. Fenan, who'd almost died. Bhati, Joa, Vekati.

Yash let out a stream of words in Keshi, and the monks nodded slowly. He turned back to Alaron. 'Boss, let's play for Sindar and Kohli and the rest, yes? All who died.'

'That sounds right.'

Eschewing the gnosis, playing as children in the streets of Yuros did, they barged and hollered as they scrapped over the ball until they were laughing again, and more and more joined in until, to a loud cheer, Master Puravai himself entered the courtyard and threw himself into the game like a young man, and then Tegeda was in there too. For a moment her presence made the young men a little wary, but none demurred, and before it was as if she had always been one of them. As they played, a feeling of togetherness grew, and the laughter never dimmed.

Finally it was too dark to play and they all collapsed in the middle of the courtyard, arms draped round each other's shoulders, sweating and joking in a motley mix of Keshi and Rondian.

Aprek grinned at Alaron. 'Boss, you better wash if you want a friendly wife tonight – you sweat like a hog!'

'She likes me this way,' Alaron chuckled, knowing the opposite to be true. He fielded more teasing comments and gave a few back, basking in the camaraderie.

'Hey, sister,' Yash said to Tegeda, in Rondian, 'where are you from?'

The young woman, sitting apart with her back against a pillar, hesitated then replied, 'Near Gujati.'

'Ahhh,' Yash said, and his face brightened. He spoke to her more fully in Lakh, and when Tegeda answered in kind they smiled shyly at each other, making the other novices chorus, 'Ooooh,' and look at Master Puravai meaningfully.

'I only said that I have been to her city,' Yash explained, a little defensively. 'You idiots want to make a thing of it?'

'Idiots,' Tegeda echoed, and when they smiled at each other again the rest of the novices nudged each other.

Master Puravai stood. 'To the bath! And then you may eat – Evening Prayer can be late tonight!' He clapped his hands, then looked at Alaron and winked. 'You go and see your wife.'

Alaron sat back in the half-barrel, luxuriating in the hot water. Ramita was on the couch, leafing through the religious text or whatever it was that Master Puravai had gifted them at their wedding.

'You should have stayed and played Hoop,' he told her, still exhilarated by the togetherness he'd felt with the surviving novices. 'You don't have to do . . . you know, women's things . . . all the time.'

Ramita looked up, cocked her head seriously. 'I do the things that give me pleasure, the same as you.'

'But you missed out – it felt really special.'

'That's nice. But I don't wish to be bowled over by rowdy boys chasing a ball.'

'But you could've practised using the gnosis.'

'I did: while cooking: I can now chop onions without touching the knife and keep the hot-plate at the right temperature using just Fire-gnosis. Can you?'

'No, but—'

'Then don't tell me what I should be doing.'

'Sorry. I just mean that I think you missed out.'

She waggled her head and peered intently into her book.

'I mean, you're capable of so much. Things your mother never dreamed of—!'

'But I esteem my mother.' She put the book down. 'I know what you are saying, Al'Rhon. You think I should concentrate on these new things life has given me – and I do: I learn your magic and I *read* – you have no idea what that would mean in my family! And I live in an all-male monastery where I am given respect as a woman; I'm proud of that too. But the things that give me most pleasure are the things my mother raised me to do. When I cook, especially, in the ways she taught me, I feel her alongside me, and her mother too, my grandmother. It is like I'm speaking with them, and that makes me happy because I miss them very much. Do you understand?'

He bowed his head, feeling stupid. 'I'm sorry. I didn't mean to criticise.'

'I know. You just speak without thinking sometimes. I can live with that. Now get dry! Dinner is almost ready.'

He clambered out and grabbed a towel. 'What are you reading, anyway?'

Her face lit up. 'This is a very famous book from southern Lakh. It is so wonderful, to be able to read! Antonin taught me: no one teaches a woman such things in Lakh, but I think it is quite as magical as the gnosis!'

'No one teaches a poor girl in Yuros either,' he told her. 'You're certainly luckier than most.' He began rubbing himself down, peering at the tome in her hands. 'So, what's this famous book?'

'It is called the *Pamca Sutra*: this means The Five Threads. It was written by the gods, to teach men and women how to live their lives.'

'Actually written by the gods?' He pulled a dubious face. *It's just a religious text.*

'Of course! The gods created writing, and this was the first book ever written,' she went on, in that endearingly certain way she had whenever she spoke about her beliefs. The more preposterous a notion seemed to him, the more absolute she was. 'The *Pamca Sutra* was written by Vishnarayan, the Protector, and his wife Laksimi.'

'I can't read Omali writing,' he admitted, 'but the pictures looked religious.'

'That's just the first thread: the sutra called "Sarvajanika-Adami". It means "Public Man". In this thread, Vishnarayan tells how a man must be in public life: honest, virtuous, courageous and devout, and many other virtues too. Then there is the "Adami-niji", the "Private Man", which tells a man how to act with his family. You should read it: it reminds men not to dictate to their wives how to live, for example.'

Alaron felt suitably abashed. He finished drying and looked about for his clothes.

'You have a good physique,' Ramita told him.

He looked down, surprised. 'I suppose I do, now.' There were a lot of new muscles, the fruit of hours of exercise here at Madira Khojana. 'So this book is just advice for men?'

'Oh no, the other three books are written by Vishnarayan's wives.'

'Wives?'

'He has three, although they are in fact the same being. Just like Parvasi-ji, Laksimi is one being and also three beings. The first aspect is Laksimi herself, who is the model of all wives. She wrote the "Patni" sutra, the "Wife" thread. This teaches a woman how to be a good wife, to be dutiful, to be loving, and to cook well. It has many recipes.'

'A holy cookbook?'

'All things are holy, Al'Rhon. Including cooking. This is why my cooking is divine,' she added, waggling her head. 'This is an old Lakh joke.'

'I do love your cooking,' he conceded, pulling on his nightshirt.

'The second of the wives' threads is written by Padma-ji,' Ramita continued. 'She is the Mother aspect. Her thread is the "Matritva" sutra and it teaches a woman about bearing and raising children. This is what I am currently reading.'

'Okay. What's the fifth thread about?' he asked, because he was clearly going to be told anyway.

'It is called the "Khusi" sutra, and it is written by the aspect of Laksimi-ji named Kamini, Goddess of Beauty.' She glanced up with a teasing look in her eyes. 'It is about how to make love.'

That stopped him. 'Really? It's a holy love manual too?'

'I thought that would get your attention.' She smiled pertly. 'What is more holy than the making of babies, hmm? So, are you ready for dinner now?'

'No, I'm ready to look at your book!'

'Ha! You are indeed a male. Well, I'm thinking tonight that I'd like to try *this*.' She flipped to a page near the back with a large coloured woodcut on it. He looked, then looked again and his face began to radiate heat. The picture showed a man and a woman, lying entwined about each other. It looked ... *possible* ... if one had very few inhibitions. 'What does that say underneath?'

'It says "let love engulf you, and hasten the coming rains".' She giggled. 'The "coming rains" means—'

'I get it.' He reached for her and she darted away.

'After dinner. Not before!'

As they ate, everything became right between them again. The gloom at the loss of Cym had been lifted by the friendship of the novices, and the love of his wife, and with that, desire had also returned.

I won't forget you, Cym, but I can't grieve for ever.

Somewhere out in the world, Malevorn Andevarion held the Scytale of Corineus; and Huriya Makani had his other adopted son captive. Outside, Cym's grave-marker was vanishing beneath the snows again. But the snows would lift, and he was ready to live again, and do what must be done.

Ramita considered the proposition, while those around the table waited expectantly: Master Puravai, patient, neutral; Corinea, who'd already made her feelings known, full of disapproving, warning looks; Alaron trusting in her.

'I believe it is worth the risk,' she said at last. 'If Tegeda is willing, I believe she has the right to try. I also believe that she is sincere.'

Corinea let out her breath with a hiss. 'Oh for goodness sake,' she began, then stopped when Puravai raised a hand. She gave the old monk an impatient look. 'Tegeda thinks Ramita's an Omali goddess! It's ridiculous—!'

It was embarrassing, because it was true. Though Tegeda, born a by-blow of a Hadishah mage, had been raised with knowledge of both Omali and Amteh faiths, as a Hadishah she'd renounced the Oma as false gods – until she saw Ramita defeat Alyssa Dulayne.

Now she claimed to wish to serve only Ramita.

'She seems genuine,' Alaron said cautiously.

'She's a trained assassin who came here to kill us,' Corinea snapped. 'Her group couldn't do it by force, so now she's infiltrating us – you damned children are so trusting it makes me want to slap you! Open your eyes!'

'I too believe Tegeda is genuine,' Puravai put in.

Corinea threw up her hands in disgust. 'Are all Zains this naïve?'

'I am a market-girl from Aruna Nagar,' Ramita replied. 'I am not easy to fool.'

'We're not so gullible as all that, Lillea – have you even spoken to her?' Puravai asked. 'She's no fanatic. In fact, she's an interesting case: she had no idea she was a mage until she manifested, and then she barely escaped stoning as a witch.'

'Because the Hadishah rescued her! She owes them her life,' Corinea countered sharply. 'She should be locked up with the rest of the prisoners.'

'She's caused no trouble at all,' Puravai noted.

'So far. And that's apart from the fights between the novices trying to impress her,' Corinea added acerbically.

'That's not her fault.'

'Isn't it? I thought you lot were sworn to celibacy, but she leads them on—'

'She does not!' Ramita countered. 'The young men just don't know how to deal with her.'

'Exactly!' Corinea exclaimed, dripping sarcasm. 'They're all carrying on like love-struck boys . . . Oh, wait, that's what they are!'

Puravai rapped his fingers tetchily, the closest anyone ever got to seeing him angry. 'They have been spoken to about that. You must remember that most of them haven't even *seen* a women for much of their lives – and they are young, regardless of their vows. And they are as yet only novices; they have not yet taken their full vows. They may choose never to do so.'

'What do you mean?' Alaron broke in, looking at Puravai.

'Well, Brother Longlegs: they are hardly Zain novices any more, are they? Mandira Khojana teaches the creed of Attiya Zai, the path to attain moksha. But we have given these young men the gnosis and a new purpose: defeating evil. You have been training them for this task and you wish them to leave very soon, to seek your son and the Scytale. So who are they now? They are a group, but they have no identity, no structure, no rules, no formal goals or creed. They are confused, my friends, and this matter of Tegeda is part of that.'

Ramita hadn't been thinking of anything beyond the recovery of Nasatya, but the Master was right. They had taken from these boys their futures – at least, the futures they had expected and believed in – but in so doing, they had created something that would, if the Gods were kind, endure beyond their immediate goals.

Alaron looked thoughtful. 'Actually,' he started, 'I have thought about this. Two years ago, when Cym and Ramon and I were hunting the Scytale, we talked about just what we'd do with the artefact if we ever found it. Of course, we never really believed we'd find it ... then Jeris Muhren and the General joined us, and it started to become a bit more possible. Anyway, we agreed that we'd use the Scytale to create a force for good; that was the whole point of all this.' He looked a bit embarrassed as he said, 'We decided we'd call ourselves the *Ordo Pacifica*: the Order of Peace, but I'm not so sure any more. I'm the only one of the original group ... *left*.' The pain in his voice reminded Ramita that he didn't know the fate of his friend Ramon, but he feared the worst.

Ramita liked the name: it echoed what her late husband had told her of the Ordo Costruo. 'Antonin would have approved,' she said firmly.

Corinea made sarcastic noises. 'These are Lakh, Dhassan and Keshi boys, and anything with "Ordo" in it won't feel right to them,' she sniffed. 'Anyway, your late husband could be damned ruthless when he wanted to be. He certainly wasn't all peace and forgiveness.'

'You didn't know him as I did,' Ramita retorted.

'I knew him in all ways, and for longer, girl.'

Ramita glared at her and Corinea glared back.

Alaron and Puravai exchanged glances and the Master said, 'Putting the name aside, is your idea not the Ordo Costruo again?'

'Well, yes – but we don't know if they even still exist. Anyway, they don't have exclusive rights to sensible ideas.' Alaron looked at Ramita. 'What do you think?'

'I agree with my husband,' she replied, looking up at him fondly.

Corinea looked skywards. 'I despise newly-weds.'

Puravai gave her a stern look. 'This is important: we need to consider what exactly your new "order" might be. For example, do you wish to start with novices or trainees who graduate to being a full member of the order? Do you wish to acknowledge different levels of expertise? What moral constraints do you wish to impose? What educational qualifications? What level of expertise in martial training? Do you wish the novices to maintain their Zain vows? Obviously I would prefer they do, but I recognise that pacifism is not so easy when one is confronted with deadly force.'

'Clearly,' Corinea said in an ironic voice.

'Nevertheless, restraint seems to me to be important,' Puravai went on, unperturbed. 'And do you wish to allow them to put aside their vows of celibacy, to have children or to wed? And what if their offspring do not wish to be in the order – or what if they themselves wish to leave the order, having their heads turned by the world?' He smiled apologetically. 'I could go on . . . but you begin to see the complexities.'

Ramita slipped her hand into Alaron's under the table. 'We need to include people, not shut them out.'

'I've no quarrel with that,' Corinea agreed. 'There aren't a lot of us to start with.'

Alaron frowned. 'My father used to say, "If you want a broad church, build a big roof and lots of doors."'

'My father would say that if you want to sell things, ask what the buyers want,' Ramita put in.

Everyone looked at her. Alaron squeezed her hand. 'Actually, I think my father would probably agree with that.'

'We're both children of traders,' she reminded the others proudly.

Corinea rolled her eyes again, but she turned to Master Puravai. 'It's actually sensible. We need to find out what the novices want.'

As the young men honed their skills in the gnosis, use of the kon-staff and the mental disciplines of the Zains, each was taken aside and asked, 'You agreed to learn this gnosis to fight a very specific evil. But if this evil is overcome, how do you wish to live afterwards, now that you have the gift of this power?'

It was soon apparent that only two – Gateem, the most pacifist, and Yash, the most worldly – had given the matter any thought. Oddly, for all they were opposites in many ways, their ideas were quite similar.

'We cannot go back to being Zain monks,' Gateem said in his serious, impassioned manner. 'If we're to engage with the world, we must do so completely. Gifts such as these are for using.' Under Corinea's tutelage, he was becoming a very skilled healer. His face lit up as he added, 'Imagine the work we could do among the poor!'

'We cannot go back to being Zain monks afterwards,' Yash echoed in his own interview. 'If we're to fight evil, we can never stop – evil goes on, and so must we. We must be a new thing to do this – new vows. New ranks.'

Both young men must have started bending the ears of their comrades, because after that everyone else started suggesting much the same things – and so the new order began to take shape, a process which culminated one evening when they all remained in the foodhall after the meal.

Somewhat to Alaron's surprise, it was Aprek who stood and took the lead, but he quickly realised that while Gateem and Yash were opinion-leaders, Aprek, the most thoughtful and well-read, was the more comfortable speaker.

'Master Puravai, Magister Alaron, Lady Meiros, Lady Lillea,' he began, hands clasped and bowing, 'we have given this matter much thought. Not all have agreed – in fact we have argued long and hard into many nights.' He eyed Yash, Kedak and Gateem especially. 'I feel those discussions have brought us closer together. Perhaps my fellows even agree with that ... ?'

There was a murmur, and a smile passed from face to face.

Aprek bowed again and continued, 'So after many tangents and wild ideas, we returned to the core tenets of who we are: Zain novices. Master Puravai will know this, but you' – he looked at Alaron, Ramita and Corinea – 'might not; Attiya Zai taught that the soul – the *fravarshi* – is eternal, and that it creates the *urfan* – the body – when it enters the world, and thus we are born again and again, the same soul in renewed bodies. Those who are in touch with their spirit are in touch with their fravarshi, which we see as our guardian spirit, protecting us from evil and harm. It is said that Attiya Zai performed miracles through his fravarshi. Your ambrosia, Magister Alaron, has given us the ability to reach our fravarshi, so we must use this ability to be the guardian spirits of *our* world. That will be our role, both in aiding the pursuit of your enemies, but also afterwards. Our purpose shall be to find, to understand and to resolve conflict.' He paused, looking especially at Master Puravai for approval.

The Master gave a slight hand gesture, one used only when a pupil had done exceptionally well; that tiny sign was an indication of *great* praise. Aprek struggled to remain impassive while around him his fellow Zains looked at each other in mutual congratulation.

Aprek swallowed and went on, 'We considered our nature as a group. We are already brothers in belief, backing each other, protecting each other, caring for each other. So we wish to be known collectively as Brothers, or "Bhaicara", which is the Lakh word for brotherhood.'

'What if a woman wishes to join?' Ramita interrupted. She exchanged a look with Tegeda, whose position was still nebulous.

Aprek admitted, 'This was a point of great debate, but with you as our shining example, Lady, we will welcome any woman who joins. But unless we recover the Scytale, we don't know where any future recruits will come from.' He bowed to Tegeda. 'Our one female novice is welcome here, and we pray that if we are successful, she and future female trainees will be able to drink the ambrosia.'

Tegeda ducked her head shyly, but looked very pleased.

Puravai raised a hand. 'There have been many requests through the years for women to form Zain hermitages, though the heads of our order – men far holier than I – have thus far declined those requests. But there are sisterhoods dedicated to the Omali gods with not-dissimilar ideals. I would be happy to approach them: if we can recover the Scytale.'

The young Zains looked at each other, faintly surprised, but Aprek was already bowing again and continuing, 'Our trainees will be drawn from the Zain monasteries and other approved orders, including those female hermitages of which Master Puravai speaks. They will be "Aspirants", to be inculcated with our purpose and ideals and trained in how to survive the ambrosia. Those who gain the gnosis will be "Brothers" or "Sisters" – Bhaiya and Bahana. And those who master all sixteen aspects of the gnosis will be "Savants" – this word was taught to us by Lady Lillea; it means gifted. We create this rank because it is good to have a higher standing to aspire to, as seeking to better oneself sharpens one's skills and understanding. But above the Savants are the Masters, who need not be magi at all, and are appointed by consensus. We wish to name them "Pahali" for a male and "Pahala" for a woman: the word signifies both authority and mastery of a discipline, so is very appropriate.'

He paused, and again Puravai gave his small gesture of approval.

Aprek beamed. 'Thank you, Pahali Puravai,' he said, bowing very low. 'And finally, the name and badge of our order: first and foremost, we are Zains, and we continue to seek a path to moksha. That has not changed. But the path we walk is new, and our guides are magi: both the fabled Antonin Meiros and the one who through his wisdom and courage has brought us to this path: Pahali Alaron.' He ignored Alaron's blush and demurring gesture. 'We therefore wish to be known as "Merozain", to honour our three progenitors. We wish our badge to be the fravahar – the winged man symbol that Attiya Zai used to depict the soul. Do we have your approval?'

The hall fell silent, and filled with nervous expectation.

Puravai, Corinea, Alaron and Ramita looked at each other. Corinea was the first to speak. 'Well, I've heard worse,' she drawled. 'Once a group of mage-knights decided they wanted to be "The Glorious Knights of the Temple of Golden Redemption" and call each other "Exalted Paladin". I had to kill them.'

Everyone stared at her, a few mouths dropping open.

She rolled her eyes. 'They'd trapped me; I had no choice.'

Ramita harumphed, and then beamed at the novices. 'Well, I entirely agree.'

Alaron nodded his own agreement and they all turned to Puravai.

The old Zain had a slightly sad smile on his face. 'Behold my young charges, going off on a different path, when I had other hopes for them . . . but I did help persuade them to take that path. And yes, I think they have done well.'

He stood and bowed low to Aprek and the circle of waiting novices.

'Let the documents be written, founding Brothers and Sister of the Merozain Bhaicara. May you prosper, and attain your goals!'

A cheer rang out through the hall.

The newly named and constituted Brothers of the Merozain Bhaicara went back to work, and weeks flew by as the experienced magi tried to impart all they knew to their eager young protégés. Progress was mixed, predictably, but they concentrated on the basics of mental and physical defence and from those building blocks, the Brothers improved rapidly.

When they weren't teaching, Alaron and Ramita worked on their own wider skills, concentrating on spiritualism, clairvoyance and divination, the Studies they'd need for their search, with Corinea as their guide. They started using their dreams to explore both the future and the present. With Corinea in attendance and wards carefully set, one would watch while the other began searching Ahmedhassa from the comfort of their sleeping pallet.

Nasatya's name was on Ramita's lips as she fell into the trance and invoked spirit-gnosis. She floated above her body and saw Corinea and Alaron watching over her: Alaron appeared oblivious to her otherworldly presence, but Corinea looked up, her eyes piercingly bright and focused, as if to say: *Yes, I see you*. Then Ramita whispered her son's name, picturing his tiny face, and she *shimmered* and flashed outwards in a blur of darkness and light—

—and into Dasra's nursery, the next storey up. She hissed in annoyance and quested outwards. The world blurred, then she cried out when she saw a child held by a woman in a tiny, smoky hut in the mountains. But it wasn't Nasatya at all, and the woman cradling the boy wasn't Huriya. The vision frayed and she flashed on to another and then another, until her conscious mind reminded her subconscious that it had been six months since Nas was torn from her hands and she found herself back in the nursery, gazing down at little Dasra, lying on his back, sleeping.

He opened his eyes . . . except he didn't – but he saw her in his own dream and smiled, and she blinked back to her body, trembling as she woke.

'You're back already?' Corinea enquired. 'It's only been twenty minutes!'

'I was trying to find Nasatya but that led me back to Dasra in the nursery,' she mumbled apologetically.

'Then try again, and stay focused.' Corinea clicked her fingers and a wave of tiredness rolled over Ramita, instantly carrying her back down into the dream-state.

Over the next few weeks, Ramita and Alaron grew progressively more tired. Sleep yielded no rest, for their dream-searches were draining them of gnosis – and their spiratus had a range of only a few hundred miles. Once they learned to use the eyes of other spirits – the Web of Souls – they could go further afield, although this too had its problems: the desert had few beings whose eyes they could borrow, while the cities had far too many – and on top of that, they could be more easily deflected by gnostic wards.

The search became increasingly distressing for Ramita as Nasatya remained unfound, and she began to doubt that she would ever find him.

The Valley of Tombs, Gatioch, on the continent of Antiopia
Safar (Febreux) to Awwal (Martrois) 930
20ᵗʰ and 21ˢᵗ months of the Moontide

It was somehow appropriate to awaken in a tomb.

I've come back from the dead.

Malevorn had no memory of how he'd come here – in fact, he had no memories at all after that sharp moment of painful awareness that his heart was stopping.

Six pairs of eyes gazed at him as he sat up on the stone slab. Something shifted on his chest and he clutched it to him: the necklace anchoring the possessing spirits of each Ablizian. Moving was horribly painful: his whole body was stiff, his joints were locked, and almost worst of all: he stank. He'd evidently soiled himself repeatedly.

But I'm still here . . .

A Necromantic scarab was one way to save yourself from death, but the arts of Wizardry provided another: you could house your spiratus in an artefact, preferably a gem like a periapt, instead. While a necromantic scarab dwelt in the skull; a spirit-gem remained separate from the body it protected. Rather than becoming a death-magic parasite, one becomes one's own possessing daemon.

This was the preferred means of cheating death among Wizards, but it wasn't as reliable as the Necromancer's scarab – and it came with other limitations, chief of which was that the wearer was vulnerable to Wizardry himself. But that was still preferable to dying – and in Malavorn's view, much better than being reduced to a Death Scarab. And right now he felt utterly vindicated: he'd survived the heart-link with Huriya being snapped – for the necklace of gems that contained the souls of the Ablizians had also contained his own.

Hessaz, you treacherous bitch . . .

As his awareness extended, he let his gnostic sight drift, reacquainting himself with the Valley of Tombs. Huriya's dead, rotting body still hung from the manacles, but the Lokistani woman was gone and so was the Meiros boy. The Ablizians were still here, though there were far fewer – he probed deeper and found that in his absence, they'd been eating each other for want of other food, the weakest voluntarily baring their throats to the strongest.

He counted the gems on the necklace; as well as his own, there were just seventy-eight Ablizians left – he'd lost *hundreds* of them. Still, it wasn't as bad as it might have been. He looked at the nearest Ablizian, a male, who'd been regarding him with narrow, focused eyes. These creatures had kept him alive when he was utterly helpless, and that told him much about what he'd achieved: multiple possessed daemons devoted to him alone.

Then it spoke. '*Master, welcome.*'

He caught his breath as the six slaves went down on their knees.

'A bath is prepared, and a meal awaits,' the Ablizian said as he extended a hand to help Malevorn rise.

As he clasped the proffered hand, something utterly unexpected shocked through him, and changed *everything*.

Malevorn examined his diamond-studded spear: each stone, pulsing like hundreds of heartbeats and glowing with a peculiar inner light, was the anchor-spell for an Ascendant slave. He'd taken his necklace and fused it to a spearhead; the spear was much more warrior-like – and in this configuration, it had produced an interesting effect: it worked just like an unusually powerful periapt, which was something he'd not been able to use since becoming a Souldrinker.

But he had discovered there was an unexpected price, though he hadn't at first noticed it: he hadn't slept in the past month. He'd been working day and night, sustained by greedy use of the gnosis. His slaves had to remind him to eat and drink, for he had lost any cravings at all, except to hold the spear and commune with the inner landscape he'd found there – and his new Master. This was an endlessly fascinating world, far more interesting than the drabness around him. The Valley of Tombs was just ancient statuary, a reminder that all things failed in time. Only the spirit was eternal.

Like an addict reaching again for the mouthpiece of his hookah pipe, he clutched the spear tighter and plunged back into its eternal and ever-changing vista. Choosing a diamond at random, he threw his awareness into it, his senses separated into two. The core of him remained inside his own body while a shadow-self plunged through the gem and along the link to the daemon it anchored, an Ablizian presently stalking the perimeter of the Valley of Tombs. It flinched when it sensed his presence, but he caressed its sensory nodes to reassure it, then sent his awareness delving into its soul like a worm through layers of soil, pushing aside the detritus of memory and sensation until he burst through into an entirely different place: into the mind of Corineus Himself.

His Saviour became aware of him and turned his way, like a galaxy forming a visage from the stars. A massive voice sang inside his mind, *<Friend Malevorn, welcome back!>*

<My Lord.> He fell to his knees as an image of his own body formed around him, a perfect version of himself, clad in silks that felt rich and soft. Gold rings adorned his fingers. He felt impossibly strong and alive, as he no longer did inside his own body.

<Your friend, not your lord,> his Saviour said, pulling him effortlessly to his feet.

Johan Corin was astonishing to behold: outwardly just a man, perhaps, but if you looked closer, you saw that His strong, gentle face held the wisdom of ages. His warm visage was framed by blond hair, and His brilliant blue eyes were both penetrating and joyous. When He was impassioned, His voice could crack like thunder and shatter the sky like eggshells, but when He spoke, Malevorn heard music and laughter, and most of all, an all-embracing love.

Today Corineus was robed like a simple peasant, a wanderer, a preacher in the wilds of Yuros, proclaiming His own godhood, and he, Malevorn, was His most fervent and loyal follower.

Until he found Corineus inside his Ablizians' souls, Malevorn had not realised what a desperate state he'd fallen into. He was filled with fear and hatred, detesting himself for becoming a Souldrinker, a Reject of Kore. He had been cast out by the Inquisition, cast adrift among heathens, his moral compass lost.

Johan Corin had given back his pride, spoken the words he needed to hear: *<Be not ashamed, my Son. You are not one of Kore's Rejects – you*

are one of Kore's Chosen. You are a superior being, Malevorn Andevarion: a true predator. You are My Sword and I am your Armour. Open yourself to Me and together, we will bring about the Paradise on Urte that was snatched from Our grasp by Corinea's Dagger.>

The world made sense now. The magi were not the ordained of Kore; they were usurpers. Corineus had not been the Prophet of the Magi but of the Souldrinkers: the first of that kind. The First Ascension should have meant an Empire of Souldrinkers, given a whole world to feed upon – but that beautiful vision, of Lions shepherding the Lambs to the slaughter, had been snatched away by a single dagger-stroke.

Malevorn had wept for what should have been when Corineus revealed the truth, but his Saviour had pulled him erect and told him what could be done to bring about that world. He *understood* now.

As the first Souldrinker to die, Johan Corin's soul had been cast into the aether, but when His Souldrinker brethren also began to die, He was there to greet them, to take them into Himself. Corineus was now a being comprised of thousands of dead souls: His Brethren, his legion. In the absence of real gods, He had become one. Already He had worshippers on both continents – and now Malevorn had brought Him more. Together they would restore Urte to what it should have been: His.

<You are to be My hand upon Urte, Malevorn Andevarion. You will be My Prophet. I am the fulfilment of every creed's wish for divinity. I am the Bahil of the early Lakh, and the Abliz of the ancient Keshi. I am Minaus and Zanux, Ahm and Oma. I am Kore. You will conquer and rule for Me, and your reign will be eternal.>

In their first mental communion He had clothed Malevorn in silk and gold, raised him up and fed him wines with tastes hitherto undreamed-of, liquors of a sweetness beyond description, and He had shown him the past and postulated the future. From a dream-like Lantric palace of columned marble lavishly embellished with gleaming gilt high on a mountain peak He showed Malevorn the world in incredible detail – the most perfect scrying imaginable – including the positions of the armies of Kaltus Korion and Salim of Kesh, laid out like pieces on a war-map, with so much detail he could pick out the faces of men and women walking through market-squares or tilling fields. Only the magi were hidden. It was incredible – and it was just one facet of Corineus' power.

As a reward for the enslavement of so many minds to His, Corineus opened up the full range of the gnosis to Malevorn, allowing him to channel every affinity without having to learn it. He perfected his body and mind without exercise or study – it was all so easy now that he began to forget how hard his life had been before. He was ready to take on the world again.

Corineus was attuned to his mood. *<You are ready to conquer,>* He noted. They were seated on an illusory islet in a beautiful lake, a place that though wholly conjured in Corineus's mind, seemed utterly real – and yet it obeyed His every whim. They were reclining on divans, eating grapes while observing the court of Salim of Kesh in the real world, and though Malevorn spoke not a word of Keshi, every word was clear and understood.

<Upon whom will your wrath first fall?> Corineus asked.

My wrath. Malevorn tasted the words pleasurably. He was to be the blade of Corineus' conquest of Urte. 'Wherever my Lord commands.'

Corineus waved a hand and the surface of the lake transformed into a map of Gatioch and eastern Kesh, detailed right down to the tiny buildings and herds of beasts. His command of the Web of Souls beggared that of mere magi. He pointed to a small Gatti town built around a fortress northwest of the Valley of Tombs. *<This is Vaqo, a minor kingdom on the borders of Gatioch and Kesh. The inhabitants are ungodly. It would please Me to see them punished.>*

Malevorn promised, *<My Ablizians will annihilate them.>*

<That sounds like an adequate punishment,' His Lord replied. *'Do as you will, in My name.>*

Malevorn floated high above the keep, surrounded by his Ablizian slaves. Vaqo, the Keshi desert town on the edge of Gatioch, was built around a dirty little lake. Tonight it slumbered, oblivious to the Judgement about to be cast upon it.

He still hadn't slept since awakening from near-death, but he felt perfect. His dreams had grown as his favour with Corineus grew; he was no longer content just to restore his family name, and even titles like 'emperor' sounded a little pallid when one could be God of all Urte. Information kept on flooding his brain, gifted by Corineus, stoking his ambitions higher. But this would be his first great test: to control his Ablizians in battle.

He looked up to see all but three of his creatures hovering; those he'd left to guard the Valley of Tombs. The seventy-five Ablizians floating in the skies above the sleeping village had all altered to take the shapes of Kore's angels – which were more or less identical to the apsaras of Ahmedhassan myth – to awe any who caught sight of them. They had huge wings and shone like fallen stars.

<Shields,> he told them, and their wards flared. <Attack!>

The Ablizians dropped from the skies in a loose ring about the town, while he gripped his bejewelled spear and floated in their wake. His senses expanded and divided so that he could be with each Ablizian: he could see what they saw, smell what they smelled, hear what they heard, overloading him with stimuli as eye-blink decisions flashed across his mind. He was expanding, his brain filling like a god's, one who was aware of every worshipper's prayer. *Yes, go there – yes, destroy that – kill him – burn her – rip them apart.*

It was intoxicating, overpowering, all-consuming. It was *divine*.

Using Earth-gnosis, the seventy-five Ablizians brought each house crashing down, burning any survivors to cinders or cutting them down. Every scream was cut short in a torrent of flame or a flashing blade, and the terror of the inhabitants was reflected back into their brains so that many died simply of fright.

Malevorn gave free reign to his own expanded gnosis, experimenting with killing in ways he had never before been able to even contemplate: rending souls and bodies with esoteric spells, feeling Corineus as a companion inside his mind, guiding him as he controlled the Ablizians. He followed the carnage down the central road into the town, saw the slaughter redouble as a knot of survivors tried to fight, though half-dressed and poorly armed, desperate to shield their women and children.

Combat images almost overwhelmed him as the fighting became more intense. Searing pain struck his chest as one of his Ablizians took a blow from behind – a spear to the heart – and the connection winked out. He found another Ablizian and guided it as it incinerated the spearman. *<Shield!>* he shouted, *<Kill!>*

As resistance increased he lost more of his creatures, half a dozen, but lessons were learned. He had not before thought to shield them from each other's awareness a little, so they saw only what was before them, allowing them to fight independently. And he tempered their attacks, making them fight cautiously, blasting from a safe distance while flying above the reach of the peasants' feeble weapons. Here it hardly mattered: their shielding was strong enough to render any archery harmless and they could char a man in seconds, but against magi it would be harder, so it was good to practise. He concentrated on keeping them together, keeping their guard up, ensuring they protected themselves.

The Ablizians slaughtered the remaining men, all except the local ruler and his sons and daughters, then herded them, together with the women and children, into the central square. Then he let his Ablizans loose, because they were still mortal men as well as servants of Corineus. He rode their perceptions as they butchered the ruler and his offspring and disembowelled the Godspeakers who tried to dispel them with amulets and prayers. He rode their minds as they rode each woman, and each orgasm his slaves experienced felt as if it were his own: a rapture that almost paralysed him.

Afterwards, they burned what was left of the corpses in one giant conflagration and were gone by dawn, taking their fallen fellows away so none would know that they could be slain. The echoes of the power they'd unleashed resounded through the aether – had probably been sensed all over Ahmedhassa – but that didn't concern him. He was elated.

The assault had been imperfect, but the potential was clear. There were improvements to be made, but this trial had shown him what had to done. Next time would be better. A garrison town in daylight, perhaps . . . with some Rondian magi inside to spar with. He had to hone this weapon he'd built, but it wouldn't take long.

Tremble, Urte. He smiled wryly to himself as he stroked the diamond-encrusted spear. *I am the Spear of Corineus Himself, and I am feeling wrathful.*

In a town three hundred miles northeast of Vaqo, a tall, lean woman huddled inside her bekira-shroud, listening to the trembling of the aether. It was like an unseen wind that only she felt. All round her, refugees huddled over bowls of rice, wolfing down pitifully small mouthfuls while resting their legs. They were sun-blackened and travel-worn, clinging to the vestiges of their human dignity as they fled the wars. None sensed what she felt: the hidden wind that presaged a storm to come.

He survived. After all I did, Malevorn Andevarion survived . . .

She bowed her head, cursing the Gods for betraying her. Her dark, austere face was closed-in; only her left arm moved as she stroked the shoulder of the sleeping child at her side. The echo she sensed only confirmed her decision to leave Ahmedhassa. It held nothing now but sadness and loss, and the memories of suffering. There was only disaster to come.

In the Uttermost East, the legends of the Brethren said, was a paradise where there were no magi, and Souldrinker rule was unchecked: where they were as as princes, and the common herd was theirs to cull. It rained there often, and the lands were lush, the sun warm, the flowers and birds brilliantly coloured. Happiness reigned. Hessaz didn't believe any of that to be true, and nor did Sabele. But what that legend hinted was that somewhere, perhaps, she might find a place where Malevorn Andevarion couldn't find her.

She looked down at the small boy sleeping in her lap and her heart warmed. She pulled him to her nipple. He was drowsy, but aware enough to suckle – she had enough morphic-gnosis to cause her breasts to fill, as they had for Pernara, her lamented daughter. It helped anchor her, to keep the Hessaz part of her involved, though in truth she didn't know any more who she really was: she had Sabele's lives, and Huriya's too now: she was all of them, but also herself: she was a new being.

'Drink, child,' she whispered, and as he fed, she could sense him changing, becoming Brethren. It was a sign that one day all of the world would be as she was.

Then the first bell of morning rang and the leaders of this group of refugees clambered to their feet, calling on their flock to rise. Wearily, every joint protesting and every bone aching, Hessaz took her sleeping child and joined them on the road leading east into the mountains.

28

Hammer and Anvil

The Siege of Perane

Perane was a Rimoni fortress, notable for the fact that the Ascendant Mage Rostrea the Red captured it during the Liberation of Yuros. It remains the only instance of a legion surrendering entirely to a single person: Rostrea, an Air- and Fire-mage, had already destroyed most of the fortress when it capitulated. She remains an icon for young mage-women to this day.

THE ANNALS OF PALLAS, 890

Kesh, on the continent of Antiopia
Awwal (Martrois) 930
21st month of the Moontide

The alarm bells rang, just before midday, but none of the battle-magi in Seth Korion's tent spoke. There was nothing to say; in truth, they'd made their plans, even if hasty and perhaps utterly ill-conceived. The board was set and they were the pieces. It was time to play.

As Ramon left, he glanced back and saw Seth's pale face, and felt a flash of pity. Disinherited and falsely accused in the same moment? That had to be hard.

The gnostic-contact with Kaltus Korion had happened three days ago; those alarm bells meant that the Inquisition was here. On the ridge-line to the west, Ramon could see horsemen strung out in a line, but just ten of them: an Inquisition Fist. Many would be pure-bloods and all would be superbly armed and trained. Then more men appeared: lines of red-clad Rondian legionaries cresting the rise, marching into position with shields abutted and spears held high.

Here they come. Ramon swallowed, but part of him thrilled also: danger and opportunity walked hand in hand, as Pater-Retiari had always said.

Fridryk Kippenegger whooped excitedly, shouting, 'This is the day, yar?'

'Si, amici. Let's teach the Inquisition a lesson!' Ramon responded, trying to sound just as enthusiastic. 'Ready your men.'

'My Bullheads are always ready!' Kip slapped him on the shoulder, almost knocking Ramon off his feet, then strode off towards his maniple. His soldiers now resembled a barbarian horde, having adopted Schlessen dress, behaviours and ferocity through the sheer force of example of their young battle-mage.

War is madness, and we're the proof.

The camp was on full alert; they'd been drilled to receive a possibly hostile parley, which was as much as the rankers knew. At a meeting of all the legion's magi and officers, Seth had explained the situation in full, and they had taken the decision – after much discussion – not to tell the rankers, partly for fear of spies in the ranks, although that was unlikely. It was more because Ramon had persuaded them that the rankers needed to react spontaneously; given time to think, he'd argued, there would be wavering in the face of the enormity of what they were accused of. He wanted red-hot anger, followed by irrevocable action, and he'd won the argument.

Over the past three days, they'd gone among the men, reminding them of the death-camps and the Inquisitors' other crimes back at home. Even the chaplains, whose loyalty to the Kore forbade any criticism of the Inquisition, had needed little persuasion to spread the word: the Inquisition wasn't loved by the ordinary clergy.

As the camp came alive and the men first looked up and saw the Inquisitors, Kirkegarde and regular army banners on the ridge above, an audible hiss ran through the ranks. Then the officers and battle-magi started bellowing orders and the chaos gradually became orderly as the camp armed itself swiftly and formed up on one side of the parade ground, ready to face the newcomers. Their own pennants were hung at half-point, as if in mourning for what was to come.

'Magister Sensini!' Tribune Storn hurried out of the hurly-burly. 'Is this it?'

'It is. Battle-stations, Storn.'

'Are the scouts in?'

'We never deployed them, in case they were captured. The look-outs on the ridge rang the bells. They should be back by now.' Ramon gripped Storn's shoulders. 'If this goes wrong, get the wagons out – distribute what you salvage among those who escape.' He put his mouth to the tribune's ear and said forcibly, 'Don't die for nothing. It's only money.'

Storn looked at him like he'd just blasphemed.

Ramon left him and started hurrying through the ranks. 'A lot of shit will be spoken in a few moments, lads,' he told the men as he passed them. 'Remember, all Quizzies are liars. If you want truth, listen only to General Korion.'

'Not you then, sir?' someone quipped and he whirled, finding his own guard cohort hurrying into position around him. 'Thought you reckoned we could trust you too?'

'That goes without saying,' Ramon said, peering for the speaker. 'Was that you, Vidran?'

'Me, sir? Nah, I think it was Bowe.'

'Weren't me! I fink it was Ilwyn!'

'Enough,' Ramon told them, looking for Pilus Lukaz. His cohort were among the few outside the magi and officers who knew what was planned. 'Pilus, when the signal comes, you know what to do?'

'We do, sir,' the pilus replied calmly. 'Some of us have been waiting for a chance like this for a long time.'

'They're mostly pure-bloods, Lukaz. They won't go down easy.'

'Then we hit 'em twice as hard, sir. It was Quizzies what did for my father in Verelon, just at random, to make an example of some-one. Another Fist performed the decimation of the Thirteenth after the Second Crusade. We had to watch 'em garrotte one man in ten for that riot. That was five hundred of our lads.'

Serjant Manius leaned in, his normally mild face taut. 'The fuckers enjoyed it too. Not saying we weren't wrong to riot, Magister, but them Quizzies joked 'bout it, even took bets on the lots they drew on who to choke.'

'How many men here went through that, Serjant?'

'I reckon 'alf of us, sir. All the older lads.'

Ramon could feel their anger as they moved them into their assigned position, arrayed before a pair of canvas-covered shapes which they blocked from view. Each man had javelins to hand, and plenty of spares.

'Remember lads,' he said firmly, 'no matter how much you're provoked, hold your position, and be ready for my signal. I'll be with the General, but I'll get back to you as soon as I can.'

he looked up as the Inquisitors cantered down the slope and into the parade ground. All down the lines on either side, the force from Vida formed up a few hundred yards away, providing a reminder of what legions were supposed to look like: all regulation uniforms and red cloaks. The sun-darkened Lost Legions men in their cobbled-to-gether gear and Keshi cloth eyed them grimly.

Ramon leaned toward Lukaz and whispered, 'I bet these Vida lads haven't even drawn their swords this Crusade.' Then he slapped the man on the shoulder and went off to join the other battle-magi.

He reached Seth Korion and his fellow magi just as Seth exchanged salutes with the Rondian commander, who was wearing the plumes and braids of a General of the Northern Army and the crest of House Jongebeau, rural Rondian nobility. Behind him were a line of armoured Inquisitors and a dozen battle-magi. Perfunctory greetings were exchanged as the ranks of men on either side started edging closer, straining their ears despite the growling of the officers to stand still. Ramon could feel the tension, the fizzing charge of impending violence, hanging in the air between the front ranks on either side, only some fifty yards apart – close enough to eyeball opposites. He slithered through the group to a spot behind Seth, then looked up as General Jongebeau turned and brought forth the Inquisition commandant.

Ramon swore softly. It was Ullyn Siburnius.

The commandant stepped to the fore, his iron face composed, over-laid with a hint of triumph: this was his revenge for being forced to shut down his death-camps. He signalled to his trumpeter, who blew the call to attention. Then Siburnius stood up in his stirrups and his voice rang out, gnostically enhanced and dauntingly authoritative.

'Men of the so-called "Second Army": I am Commandant Ullyn Siburnius of the Holy Inquisition and I am here to discharge the will of General Kaltus Korion, Commander of the Third Crusade!'

Not a sound greeted his voice as it echoed through the ranks like a slap to the tanned, rough faces that stared back at him.

Undaunted, he went on, 'General Kaltus Korion wishes the fol-lowing to be known: firstly, that all men who fled the battlefield of Shaliyah face charges of desertion. I have been given commission of a Court-Martial to ascertain the rectitude of the charges. Those found guilty of cowardice and abandonment of post will face the lottery of decimation: one in ten will die by the garrotte, in front of the rest.'

There were disbelieving gasps from the ranks, but his stentorian voice rose above the dissent. 'Secondly, any who have taken to wife an Antiopian will be executed with that wife. Such unions are forbidden by Imperial decree!' He paused, looked down his noses at the men of the Thirteenth and called, 'The executions will begin this afternoon.'

The massed rankers shouted angrily or gaped. Those of Pallacios Thirteen, decimated for rioting twelve years ago, were the loudest. All along the lines, the Lost Legions' rankers began hurling abuse and defiance at the stone-faced Inquisitors.

'Furthermore,' Siburnius called, 'I am here to arrest the imposter, your false commander! He claims to be a Korion, but he is the prog-eny of Laetitia Fetallink's adultery, legally disavowed wife of Kaltus Korion. He is charged with desertion, collusion with the enemy, falsely claiming kinship of a peer, falsely claiming the right to command, and unnatural relations with the enemy commander. The penalty for each and every charge is *death*!'

A hush fell over the camp, a collective sucking-in of breath.

Ramon saw Seth swallow, saw him trying to speak and failing, caught up in the bombardment of emotions at the charges.

Siburnius went on relentlessly, 'Furthermore, Ramon Sensini, the imposter's partner-in-crime, is hereby charged with conspiracy against the Holy Inquisition, conspiracy to defraud the Imperial Treasury, false issuance of Imperial Treasury notes, theft of Imperial funds, speaking calumny against Emperor Constant and his Mother, the Living Saint Lucia Sacrecour, collusion and fornication with the enemy, the purchase and trafficking of opium, and desertion on the field of battle.'

Well, he's done his research, Ramon acknowledged. *But who told him all that?*

'All other Second-Army magi are charged with conspiracy against Emperor Constant, collusion with the enemy and desertion. All must surrender their periapts and submit to the Rune of the Chain.'

He paused, then added, 'Any man who comes forward with evidence against these accused will be given immunity from retribution.'

So: sell out your commanders and you'll walk free.

The lines fell silent as the rankers looked at each other, and then at Seth. General Jongebeau's men were deployed on the high ground above, less than half their own numbers, but with legal authority on their side. It was one thing to propose it, but men did not fight against their own easily, especially when it would condemn them for the rest of their lives. Their faces were pale and sickly as they contemplated the choices before them.

Either we capitulate to this travesty and lose every married man and his wife, and a tenth of the remainder . . . or we resist, and condemn every single one of us.

The rankers were staring up at Seth, awaiting some kind of response. But he looked stunned by the sheer effrontery of the commandant and his vicious accusations, clearly calculated by Siburnius to overwhelm the rankers, and break their trust in their commander. His fragile confidence was visibly collapsing.

Our plans are set, Ramon thought, *but will Seth go through with them?*

A mental contact drew his eyes to one of the Inquisitors, standing fearlessly before them: the grey-haired woman Alis Nytrasia, with her young scar-faced shadow, whose name he'd never learned.

Nytrasia met his eyes coolly and her voice crackled into his skull: *<Better come quietly, Sensini, or it'll go ill for Severine.>* She waited until his heart froze, then added, *<and your baby daughter.>*

His insides churned and all his stratagems collapsed into terror for his precious little girl.

<Sang like a little canary, your woman did,> Nytrasia smirked. *<Told us all about what you've done.>*

Severine had known everything: the promissory notes; the death-camps; Ardijah . . . everything. But the loudest sound in his head was a high-pitched wail: *Julietta!*

Nytrasia's face was pitiless. *<Submit, Sensini, or we'll kill them both.>*

Seth's world was collapsing in slow motion around him. He looked sideways, saw at a glance that Ramon was no better, his normally assured face ashen and wavering, and that shook him more than his own fears. He *needed* Sensini, and without his visible assurance, the plans they'd laid seemed to fold into nothing. There was no ground beneath his feet any more, and the cliff-edge was out of reach.

An act of war against our own people? Treason and inevitable death, or exile? Or submission, to save as many as I can?

But a glance to his right showed him Fridryk Kippenegger. The young Schlessen giant wasn't speaking aloud, but Seth could hear his mind, sending a rant of defiance to his own cohorts arrayed behind him. *<We are the Bullheads! We submit to no one! Minaus is watching us!>*

His men were boiling up towards violence. Seth felt like he had no control any more, over any of this. His eyes went back to Siburnius. The man's arrogance made his blood simmer, but his flesh was trembling. *I'm a Korion*, he told himself, but even that felt like a lie now. *Am I really not his? Is that why I'm so scared?*

Siburnius read surrender in his face and turned to the rankers with all the unthinking arrogance of his rank and order. 'You will commence disarming! I want your officers to—'

'Hey, big man!' someone with a rough Tockburn accent shouted from amidst the press of the Pallacios Thirteen rankers, 'shut yer flappin' arsehole! Y'en't in charge o' nuffink out 'ere!' Seth thought he recognised the foul mouth of one of Ramon's guard cohort: Bowe, was it? A chorus of abuse rose in support of the ranker. 'Y'en't our general! Our general's *Seth bloody Korion*, so ye can jus' fuck off back to where ye came from!'

Siburnius frowned quizzically and then lifted a hand, gnosis-light shimmering. 'The next man to voice dissent will have his lungs pulled out through his mouth,' he bellowed.

A deafening crescendo rose as if the cork had popped on a fermenting bottle of abuse: fury and defiance exploded among the men who had marched across half a continent and weren't about to be told that they'd deserted and consorted and betrayed. They'd seen their commanders' mettle and believed in them: they weren't going to submit meekly to decimation, or bare the necks of their Khotri wives to the knife before going quietly themselves. They were fighting men, willing to die rather than submit, even when faced with the most feared warriors in the empire.

And now they were spoiling for that fight.

'Hey, Fisters! Get the Hel outta here!'

'You wanna taste o' this? You wan' some steel, Quizzy man? Come'n get it!'

'We'll fuckin' dec'mate you, ye cunni!'

The air fizzed and crackled about Seth as wards and shields burgeoned, and he realised he'd lost control of this – and so had Siburnius. The commandant had come to cow mere mortals, like a barking dog snapping at the heels of a herd of kine, only to find that these cattle had sharp horns and hooves.

But to Siburnius they were still just cattle. Inflexibility had been ingrained into him every day of his life as an Inquisitor – and had probably been part of his make-up from birth anyway. Perhaps if he had hesitated, the moment might have been defused, but that wasn't in his nature: as he went for his sword, all down the row of Inquisitors shields flared and newly drawn steel glinted in the sun.

Ramon Sensini stared at Alis Nytrasia. *<Please – she's a newborn—! I'll come, I swear!>* he begged, while he mentally readjusted his plan, seeking a way out of this that might see his daughter live, and her mother too.

The cold-faced Inquisitor glanced at the scar-faced young man beside her and said, *<Hear that, Perle? He's folding. Make sure he comes to us.>*

<When you're called forward, make for me,> Perle told Ramon. *<We'll take you to your wife and child.>*

Ramon nodded stiffly. His mind was swirling at the building violence. There was no stopping it now, and no way he could guarantee anyone's safety. *They've got Julietta and Severine . . . where? Where would they hold her? In the main camp, or away from it?* If he were in Nytrasia's boots, he'd have had some mechanism to ensure that the prisoners died if she did – but would that even occur to an invincible Inquisitor?

Probably not. He raised his hands, as if about to yield.

He'd forgoten that was also the signal to get ready to fight.

Nytrasia smirked in triumph. *<Surrender now, traitor. Set the example.>*

Ramon was as stunned as anyone by what happened next.

'Take this ya fuckers!' screamed a familiar voice, and a javelin flew. As it shattered on the Inquisitor's shields, all the fury and pent-up violence broke forth. Siburnius' eyes blazed as gnosis-light coruscated on both sides: first defensive spells only, then mage-bolts flashed, mostly around Seth, whose shields flashed with fire. Ramon redoubled his own wards as he tried to melt through the press, and with a cry of rage, Siburnius raised his hands and launched a gout of blue fire.

The Fist, moving as one, blasted at Seth's magi, Ramon included; the world ignited, brilliant and deadly, and their shields went scarlet and were torn apart. The rankers shouted in terror, but all round the square they surged forward, the air full of sweat and dread and clamour. Ramon shielded again desperately as he hauled his little mare sideways, Lu somehow keeping her footing as three of his fellow magi went down, the Brevians Sordan and Mylde scythed in half, the Brician Runsald screaming as he fell to some unseen blow. The gaps they left were filled with blazing gnosis-bolts that struck the rankers behind them.

Ramon saw Nytrasia take aim at him, fended her first attack with difficulty, then ducked in behind Seth. *He's a rukking pure-blood, let him shield!*

From the corner of his eye he saw General Jongebeau haul his khurne around on a tight rein, backing away from the line of Inquisitors towards his battle-magi.

Trumpets sounded and someone screamed, '*CHARGE!*' and the legionaries on the slope began to pour down the hill.

Siburnius's Inquisition Fist were gathered in a group to share their shielding. Javelins and crossbow bolts shattered around them as they used blasts of mage-fire and kinesis with fatal effect, driving back the rankers trying to reach them, or leaving them charred and dead.

The small knot of Lost Legions magi still standing were gathered around Seth and Jelaska. Pinned back by the overwhelming power of the Inquisitors, all they could do was defend. Ramon saw Hulbert, the Hollenian Water-mage whose skills had been vital in getting Jelaska's sortie into Ardijah, crumple under a mental attack and topple, then Lysart, beside him, who'd been relying on Hulbert to cover his flank, took a blast of fire, shrieked and fell. The shields around Seth were turning scarlet again, on the verge of breaking, and even Jelaska looked desperate.

Ramon couldn't see Kip anywhere; he prayed he'd stayed with his maniple.

Then someone shouted and as the men of his own cohort dropped to the ground, Ramon realised that he'd forgotten to give the next signal, but reliable Lukaz had ordered the second volley anyway.

As the cohort cleared the line of sight, the two ballistae they'd hidden under canvas were given their chance. The serjants shouted the order and two six-foot-long shafts were hurled at the Inquisitors from mere yards away.

A God of War couldn't have aimed them better.

One shaft blasted straight through their interlocked shielding, plucked Ullyn Siburnius from his horse and slammed him into the man behind, an Acolyte who found himself with the honour of dying impaled on the same shaft as his commander. The other ripped through the body of one man and then the hip of another, snapping their spines and all but tearing them in half.

Four of the Fist were gone in an eye-blink, and their linked shields were wrecked.

An instant later, before they had a chance to rebuild their defences, the tripod crossbows started firing into the press.

A heavy crossbow could punch through steel – Ramon had seen it at Shaliyah. He saw it again here as the withering hail of bolts flashed into the massed Church knights and tore them apart. Many missed or were deflected by the fraying shields, but enough went through to cause havoc. Two punctured the breastplate of Siburnius's second-in-command and dropped him beneath the rearing khurnes; if he wasn't dead already, the scything hooves of the terrified constructs would do the rest. One Inquisitor had his shoulder pierced, while his khurne was shot from beneath him. And two bolts hammered straight into Perle's belly. He coughed blood and slumped, then fell to the ground as his khurne went mad with terror.

So did Alis Nytrasia. She howled like a bereft orphan and then, her gaze locked on Ramon, erupted in fire – then a javelin glanced off her shoulder, spinning her around. Ramon conjured mage-fire, but someone grabbed him and pulled him back as his cohort plunged into the mass of dead and dying Inquisitors, yelling triumphantly.

It was big, dumb Trefeld. 'Stay safe, sir!' the young ranker said. 'They're ours!' Then he was gone too.

The cohort waded in, stabbing and hacking at the surviving Inquisitors, while beyond them, Jongebeau's magi fled under scarlet and torn shielding. Nytrasia was still reeling in the saddle, but she steadied herself and started firing mage-bolts furiously at whoever came closest. Holdyne and Ferdi were blasted and dropped. Trefeld, screaming with battle-rage, flew backwards as a mage-bolt took him in the chest. Ramon lost sight of Nytrasia, then he saw her again on the far side of the mêlée, Perle's body in her arms. Her eyes were wild.

She spurred her khurne and fled off to his left, heading south. A fresh wave of Vida men flooded into the space between them, pounding towards Lukaz's cohort: a Kirkegarde unit, here to serve the Inquisitors. They were beautifully armoured, impeccably trained, from the highest echelons of Pallas society. Before the battle-hardened rankers of the Southern Army, veterans of three major battles, they crumbled in a bloody half-minute.

Manius and his front-rankers, augmented by Vidran's second rank, stormed over the top of the Churchmen with brutal, businesslike butchery: hurling javelins, then drawing shortswords and punching them between gaps in their shield-wall, *thrust-step-thrust* and then breaking through so Harmon's flankers could dart in, their longer blades dipping and darting faster than the eye could follow, stabbing necks and armpits and eyes. The first rank of Kirkegarde folded and the second tried to turn, but the third locked shields and finally held as a line of crossbowmen joined them.

Ramon flinched as he saw more of his men go down: little Ollyd, scythed by a javelin, the two Herde brothers shot by crossbows, side by side. Then a flood of Kip's Bullheads hit the Kirkegarde from the side and carved a bloody path straight through them, wielding axes like maniacs.

The Fist was gone. The Kirkegarde went under, and then a gap opened between the two armies as Jongebeau's few surviving battle-magi, their maniples battered, started pulling back, cowering behind shields and seeking only to protect themselves. As their bloodlust and rage subsided, Seth's men let them go.

A riderless khurne careered by and Ramon went for it, reaching out with Animagery to grip its mind. He had some difficulty, for it was alien and slippery and unnaturally intelligent, but he managed, holding it in place as he propelled himself into the saddle. Nytrasia was a black blur in a cloud of dust as she fled south with Perle slung over the front of her saddle. He threw a look back, seeking Seth, and found him beside Evan Hale, who was on his knees, staring at the stump of his left arm. Gerdhart was bellowing for Lanna Jureigh or Carmina Phyl. Beyond, on the slope above, the Vida men were reforming, but it was clear that with the Fist destroyed, Jongebeau didn't have the will to push this confrontation into full-scale battle. There were a lot of officers on both sides yelling, 'Hold! Hold!'

But Alis Nytrasia was getting away.

Without further thought, Ramon kicked the khurne into motion and gave chase.

29

Delta

Men and Beasts

The mythology of Lantris is filled with men and women who are part-animal. These hybrid beings – lamiae, satyrs, centaurs and the like – speak to the fascination that the animal kingdom has for us, who feel at once part of it and at the same time above it: kings of all we survey. It is our ambivalent relationship with beasts – predator, companion and prey – that lies behind such famous tales as 'Hektus Lionhead' and 'Derra and the Cygnus King'.

PALLAS ARCANUM, 703

Kesh, on the continent of Antiopia
Awwal (Martrois) 930
21st month of the Moontide

Ramon kept his khurne moving. It was tireless, and in some ways magnificent, but it was also appalling, knowing a human soul was trapped inside this beast. Right now though, he needed every advantage and was prepared to use any tool that came to hand. As they rode he linked his mind to it, gaining sharper control, and learned a little of what it could do.

Nytrasia's khurne would have left him well behind normally, but the Inquisitor was hampered by the weight of the wounded Perle and it soon became clear she wouldn't risk wounding him further by travelling too fast. Ramon was catching up.

The battleground was miles behind him now, and he was moving cautiously again, not wanting to blunder into an ambush – Nytrasia was dangerous enough without ceding the advantage of surprise. He didn't need to be in sight to follow her anyway – he'd slid a mental probe past her wards during the chase: she was heavily distracted and it hadn't been hard. Now he scryed her gently, just enough to pick out distance and direction. As long as he kept his touch light, she'd remain unaware of his pursuit. She'd stabilised Perle's bleeding, but he was still doubled over in front of her in the saddle. It would be dark soon, but she was barely a mile ahead, hidden by the undulating ground.

Where's she going? Ramon wondered as he put on an extra spurt. The khurne seemed inexhaustible, but he was struggling himself. Desperation drove him on: Nytrasia's aura had the same deathly reek as Jelaska's and he was pretty sure she was a Necromancer. If that was the case, the hours of darkness would be her sanctuary and strength.

He'd tried scrying for Sevvie or Julietta but found nothing. They were warded, or perhaps stashed somewhere beneath the earth. He could only hope that he'd be able to deal with whatever he found when he caught up.

Pater Sol, protect my daughter.

Severine Tiseme rolled herself into a bundle on the sweat-reeking cot, dabbing at her eyes and trying not to let her daughter see that she was scared to the edge of reason. The little hut had no windows, just a low door that even she needed to hunch over to go through – not that she could, for it was locked and bolted. Her gnosis was Chained, completely out of reach, and she couldn't stop shaking. There was a Dokken with the Inquisitors, and his very presence terrified her.

He's going to murder me and drink my soul. They'd told her so, over and over, taking hideous delight in making her cry. So many questions, and always the threat of what they'd do to her if she didn't answer; not even hours of confessions satisfied them.

'All the magi deserters must die ... but we'll pardon you, Severine, if you tell us what we want to know,' they'd said, so she'd told them everything they wanted to hear – she *had* to, for Julietta's sake.

They all scared her: especially Ullyn Siburnius and his ugly threats; and vicious Alis Nytrasia and her repugnant shadow Perle . . . but worst of all was the Souldrinker, Delta. Just the sight of his shaven skull and hooded eyes was enough to set her limbs quivering. When she was a little girl, her mother always terrified her with stories of them, but seeing one up close was even more horrifying. He was outside now, prowling like a hungry lion.

Julietta whimpered in her sleep and Severine stroked her fine hair, murmuring, 'Papa will come,' to soothe her. 'Papa will save us.'

She didn't really believe that, of course. Ramon had never been good enough for her – and now, doubtless, he hated her. She would never be able tell him that looking back, every moment she'd ever spent with him felt golden.

As the light around the ill-fitting door faded, Julietta began to stir in her sleep, her little mouth quivering in anticipation of milk. Then Sevvie heard the thud of hooves and all her fears came flooding back.

But there was only one set of hoof-beats outside. She slowly sat up, mouth dry, heart thumping, holding Julietta to her breast. *They won't kill me if I hold her. They'll take pity. No one kills a mother.*

Someone spoke outside: a woman. The words were muted by the door, but Severine recognised the voice. Just hearing Alis Nytrasia made her bowels churn as her imagination dredged up all those horrible threats again.

'I said, *get up*,' Nytrasia rasped, just outside the door – not to her, though. She was using the tone she reserved for Delta. She heard the Dokken make a choking sound, and there was scrabbling in the sand. The lock rattled, a bolt was shot back and the door swung open, flooding the tiny cell with light and fresher air.

'Come out, Severine. Bring the brat with you.'

'Please,' Severine whispered. *If I stay in here she won't hurt me. If I hold Julietta, she'll remember that I'm a mother.* 'I can't.'

Something unseen seized her, like a hand around her throat, and pulled her towards the door. She clutched her child tight, trying to protect her as she was dragged bodily from the hut. Her foot caught the piss-pot, tipping it over, and the thin blanket she'd wrapped around them both snagged on the doorframe and tore, but Nytrasia, hand stretched towards her, was pitiless.

'Don't hurt me,' she begged.

'Are you a healer-mage?' Nytrasia demanded.

Severine looked at her blankly, then her eyes went past Nytrasia to her khurne. Lying on the ground beside it was a figure wrapped in bloody cloth. The face was covered, but the arms were bare and smoking in the last rays of sunset.

What in Hel?

'Can you heal him?' Nytrasia barked, and with a jolt Severine realised that the Inquisitor woman was frightened too, such that she might tip over into sudden violence at any moment. She clutched Julietta to her and shook her head fearfully.

'Then what use are you?' Nytrasia shouted, gnosis-fire kindling in her right hand.

'No!' Severine wrapped herself around Julietta, who woke and began to cry. She clung to the tiny newborn in desperation, her mantra running through her head: *She won't kill me if I'm holding her. I'm a mother – she can't! No one could kill a mother and baby . . .*

Then a voice rang out over the dell, crying, '*NYTRASIA!*'

Ramon's voice.

Severine heard a squeal escape her lips. *He's come for me!*

Ramon tethered his khurne outside the camp then ghosted in behind the rocks, sixty yards above and behind the Inquisitor, but he'd barely arrived when she raised her hand against Severine – he could see Nytrasia wasn't bluffing, and she was shielded, so the only way he could stop her harming Sevvie and Julietta was to distract her.

'*NYTRASIA!*' he shouted, and moved into view, showing his hands. '*WAIT!*'

The Inquisitor whirled, the shock on her face telling him she'd not known he was there. Then the shaven-haired Dokken, Delta, stepped from behind the small hut; for a moment Ramon wondered why he'd revealed himself, then he glimpsed a sliver of light running from Nytrasia to the man's throat, where a periapt pulsed.

Dokken don't use periapts – he's a slave! But that didn't explain why he'd stepped into view, unless her control was imperfect. Something to think about later; right now he had to stop her.

'You don't need to hurt them!' he shouted.

Nytrasia's face became calculating. 'I might *want* to,' she snarled.

'Well, let me put it like this, Nytrasia. If you touch Sevvie or Julietta, I'll kill Perle.'

'*No!*' Her panicked reaction told him he'd hit a very raw nerve indeed. Then the slyness crept back into her voice. 'Who are you to dictate to me, Silacian? Or should I say *half*-Silacian? Who's your father, Sensini?'

'Cut the pretence: you've spoken with the Treasury-men – you know exactly who I am.'

'You're right: I do. But what's interesting is that your own lover doesn't. Severine spilled everything else – every *single* thing – but you never told her that, did you? Sad to keep secrets from one you're so intimate with.' She peered about warily. 'Are you alone?'

'Don't you know?' Clearly Nytrasia wasn't a seer. Well and good if she thought he had support: he just wished he did.

Nytrasia edged closer to Perle, who looked barely alive, lying there in the sand. Her voice changed tone, becoming more reasonable. 'All right, Sensini. You win: you can have them both. I'm going to levitate Perle to the skiff and fly away with him and Delta. I'll leave you the woman and the child. No tricks, just a back-down on both sides. My pride can just about take that. Can yours?'

That sounds suspiciously sensible.

Perle moaned faintly and Nytrasia's face went ashen. The wounded Inquisitor had started writhing and muttering his partner's name softly, then he made a more chilling sound: a low snarl. Ramon remembered the impact of the two crossbow bolts, and him collapsing over his mount's back and rolling off with blood everywhere.

How is he still alive . . . ? Then he opened up his senses just a little and saw violet hues and smoking wounds and amended that question to: *Is he still alive at all?*

Then he realised Nytrasia was *waiting*, scarcely daring to move.

When he squinted, he could see that same violet light playing around her fingertips, barely visible in the glare of the setting sun.

Silence fell. Even Julietta's weeping stilled, as if she too felt the sudden tension, the palpable sense of impeding doom.

Muted red-orange light was streaming sideways across the clearing, lighting them all for a final few moments before the sun sank below the horizon and the desert night took over. Delta's pale face looked like a Lantric mask dipped in gold. Nytrasia was squinting into the light, her shadow long, her sword a ribbon of purple fire.

The sun's going down . . . and she's a Necromancer . . .

There wasn't time to think it through properly; he just burst into motion, yelling, 'Sevvie, *run*—!'

Severine was huddled into herself, clinging to her daughter for courage, when Ramon shouted, '*SEVVIE, RUN!*' The cry cut through her.

Ramon came roaring out of the shadows, his cloak rippling like bat wings. Perle was tearing at his dressing, revealing livid-white corpse-skin that immediately began to char as the necromantic-gnosis in his aura was corrupted by the sunlight.

He's dead – he's been reanimated! And when the sun goes down, he's going to be free to rip us apart—

Belatedly her brain interpreted what Ramon had shouted: *RUN!* To the left was the hut, behind it the skiff – but her gnosis was Chained, and the Dokken was there. So she went the other way, stumbling as the rocks gouged painfully through her thin sandals, as Nytrasia screamed, 'Delta! Get the baby! Kill the woman!'

She chanced a look over her shoulder and saw the Dokken turn his mask-face her way. His boots crunched on the sands as he followed her, getting closer and closer . . .

Ramon went for Perle, his blade raised, as the last few seconds of sunlight started vanishing and the night prepared to roll in like a giant boulder.

She's kept him alive through Necromancy, and that takes blood . . . But before he could think it through, Nytrasia stepped into his path and their swords hammered jarringly together and locked. Gnostic shields scraping against each other and setting off sparks, they both shoved and he was sent rolling head-over-heels. He jumped back up, circled right and came in again, slashing at her legs, but she parried, riposted and nearly skewered his thigh. He spun away, gasping, tried again, and came back bloodied across the left shoulder.

He backed up, blocking and shielding hard.

'You're still only a half-blood, "Dubrayle",' she jeered. 'I'm a pure-blood. You can't beat me.'

Behind her Perle whimpered, '*Mother!*' Then he cried out, '*I'm burning!*'

'Hold on!' she shouted over her shoulder. 'Just a few moments!'

'*Mother?*' Ah . . .

Ramon backed up a pace and glimpsed Delta pursuing Sevvie; he darted out of Nytrasia's reach and hurled a mage-bolt at the unshielded Dokken, blasting him off his feet. But Nytrasia used his inattention to strike back and he barely fended her first bolt and had to physically throw himself to one side to avoid the next. He came up even further from Perle, still writhing on the ground.

The sun slipped a little further; now it was half obscured by the horizon.

Severine heard Delta a heartbeat behind her, felt him reaching out . . . then Delta shrieked in agony and fell on his face – just as she, distracted, found herself running off the edge of a drop.

For a moment her legs flailed for purchase in the air and then she fell into darkness. She sheltered Julietta against her chest and shielded her as they tumbled over broken stones and slid, grazing skin and tearing flesh. Then her head struck a larger rock, right by her ear and she almost blacked out, and Julietta slipped from her grasp. She whimpered fearfully and groped around in the shadows, her voice echoing oddly. Above her was a line of pale sky, a narrow ribbon of light. She'd fallen into some kind of shallow cleft, only a dozen or so yards wide. Julietta was only a few yards below her, screaming and wriggling, half-free of her swaddling.

Then a head and shoulders appeared, silhouetted against the sky above. His features were lost in the shadow, but she could tell it was Delta. He began to slither face-first down the slope towards them.

She scooped up her child, then tried to scrabble up the far side of the cleft as the Dokken reached to the bottom. He straightened up, his smooth skull gleaming wetly from a fresh wound. His eyes were blank as he lunged towards her.

I shouldn't have come alone. Ramon circled to the right, trying to get a line of sight on the half-dead Perle, but Alis Nytrasia kept extending her shields to protect her son. The young man's body kept twitching into life. The most delicate necromantic-gnosis couldn't be completed while the sun was still up . . . but darkness was only a few more seconds away.

He backed away, moving towards where he'd seen Severine running, and called with his mind to the khurne he'd ridden here. The creature responded with a whinny, but it was at least a hundred yards away. Nytrasia let him retreat unmolested, focused on protecting her son.

He guessed she'd used a Revenant spell to bind soul to flesh to buy the young Inquisitor time until a healer could be found. The Arcanum tutors had called the spell a 'last resort', because each minute Perle spent in that state would be killing him in different ways. In a few hours he'd be so far gone that not even the Inquisition would take him back. Though Ramon wasn't sure Alis Nytrasia cared any more; she just wanted her son alive.

And I'm here for my daughter. At least she's not a ravenous corpse . . .

His khurne burst into view and he ran towards it, widening his shields to protect them both, easily deflecting the mage-bolt Nytrasia fired at his back. Behind her, Perle gave an eerie moan and slowly pulled himself upright. Bloodied blankets fell away from him, revealing a horribly damaged body: his midriff was swathed in filthy bandages that looked to be holding him together; what bare skin Ramon could make out was either corpse-pale, or seared black. His eyes now glowed with violet light, the same colour that pervaded his aura and crawled down his blade. He looked at Nytrasia questioningly, then his eyes went to Ramon and he howled with pure hunger.

Rukka!

He spun, calling to his khurne. *<Come to my left side!>* and the beast veered and swept towards him, slowing as he used kinesis to propel himself into the saddle. He almost came straight off again as the khurne powered him back towards his foes. Another mage-bolt hit his shields and they wavered, but he reset just as Nytrasia fired again, this one flying harmlessly over his shoulder as he veered, guiding the khurne to where he'd last seen Sevvie.

Then another mage-bolt slammed through the edges of his shields, far too powerful for him to stop, and blasted the khurne's forelegs to stumps. The construct screamed in anguish, and so did he as they both catapulted head over heels. Instinctive kinetic-gnosis was enough to break his fall, but he shredded his skin painfully as he skidded across the barren ground. The khurne's neck snapped horribly and it crashed into a heap a few yards away.

Then the night flowed over him as the sun's light dissipated and the purple glow of Perle's eyes closed in.

Severine fell on her back as the Dokken clambered towards her, all thoughts of resistance crumbling in the lurid glow of his face, lit from below by the giant crystal he wore. His shields faded as he pulled the thrashing child from her grasp. She wailed, her hands reaching for Julietta, her own terror momentarily eclipsed as she tried to wrench the baby from him. For a fraction of a second, the Dokken, with only one free hand and his shields lowered, was unable to ward her blows.

Her hand gripped the pulsing crystal—

— and light exploded all around, a noiseless convulsion that blew through her. For a moment she was alone in the starry night, adrift in a sea of stars, ghostly faces spinning towards her – then those faces were all Delta's face, crying out in agony as he fell away from her.

Stars . . . I'm floating . . . alone.

Ramon? Julietta?

Something like wind blew it all away.

An arrow hit the Revenant in the middle of the back, and Perle, half-dead and taken unawares, threw his arms in the air, his spine arching, as a web of light crackled about him. His cry was echoed by Alis Nytrasia as the pain transferred itself along the link sustained by her spell.

More arrows flew, thudding into Perle's shoulder and leg, and more crackled off Nytrasia's shields. The cord linking her to Perle glowed brighter as she poured more energy into him, seeking desperately to keep him alive.

Ramon dived for the space between her and her son, sent raw energy into his blade and severed the link, and both Revenant and Necromancer convulsed, momentarily dazed – then Ramon swung his sword and chopped with all his strength into the back of Perle's neck. The blade carved right through; his head rolled off and sluggish blood ran from the stump.

Nytrasia screamed and fell to her knees.

A dozen steps, taken in two heartbeats, and Ramon rammed his shortsword up under her chin and out through the top of her skull. She stared up at him, a grotesque vision he cut short by kicking her off the blade and punching it through her breastplate and into her heart. He still wasn't done, not until he had spotted the scarab that darted from her mouth and stamped on it until it was nothing more than a smear amidst the stones.

He looked up to see Silvio Anturo and Tomasi Fuldo and half a dozen other men rising from vantage points on the right. All were carrying bows, with arrows nocked and ready—

Fuldo raised a hand and they lowered their aim. 'Ramon, are you all right?'

'Si, Tomasi!' Then Ramon whirled about, crying, 'My daughter—?'

He found Severine down a small cleft. He thought at first she was alive, until he got close enough to see that the front of her chest had been blown open, her ribs laid bare. He fell to his knees, aghast, then turned with murderous intent. The Dokken, Delta, was lying on his back, also burned, but still alive and breathing raggedly. Behind him, whimpering blindly, was Julietta. Ramon swept her up, shaking, and hugged her to him.

Delta groaned and rolled over, looking up at him. In ruined hands he held a big, blackened chunk of crystal. He was staring at it, a drawn, haunted look on his face.

'Hold,' he whispered in Rondian. 'I surrender.'

'*Surrender?*' Ramon echoed, as a red flame roared in his heart. 'You don't get to *surrender*, bastido! You just killed the mother of my child!'

Delta looked up at him, his lugubrious eyes pleading. 'It was not me – I swear this! The crystal flared when she touched it—! It was none of my doing! Please, mercy ... When she touched the crystal, she broke the bindings on me. I am finally free of them!'

Ramon's desire to strike didn't abate, but he managed to rein it in and asked, 'What do you mean, *free?*'

'Free of the Inquisition! Please, mercy!' Delta's eyes narrowed with recognition. 'I remember you – from the camps.'

'Then you'll know why there can be no mercy. You've killed thousands of innocents, you *pezzi di merda*.' Ramon raised his hands. 'You leave me no choice.'

'No! No! You don't understand – I want to *help* you.'

'Help me what?'

'Help you fight the Inquisition!'

30

Ebensar Heights

The Moontide Economy

*Since the Ordo Costruo completed their bridge, a new phenomenon has entered
the empire: the boom-and-bust cycle of the Moontide. For two years in twelve,
money flows in rivers, the wealthy speculate madly on all manner of goods and
the prices of everything from grain to timber to gold itself spikes to insane levels.
Afterwards comes the fall, leaving new victors and new casualties in the eternal
struggle for wealth. It is in its way as devastating as any military action.*

TREASURER CALAN DUBRAYLE,
LETTER TO EMPEROR CONSTANT, PALLAS, 918

Ebensar Heights, Zhassi Valley, on the continent of Antiopia
Awwal (Martrois) 930
21ˢᵗ month of the Moontide

Kaltus Korion was a worried man, and those worries were mounting
by the day.

His army was dug in on the Ebensar Heights, a range of hills on
the western slopes of the Zhassi Valley. Ebensar was the westernmost
point he could safely occupy without risking inundation when the
Bridge was destroyed and the floods came. The position was secure
and his army was strong, but everything else was falling apart.

His main concern was feeding his men. The caravans from Hebusalim and the west had stopped far earlier than planned; those from
Javon had ceased as well – Tomas Betillon had been knifed in the
back, metaphorically or literally, it really didn't matter which – by

that snake Gurvon Gyle. The details were sketchy, but it was clear that Gyle had betrayed them. Unsurprising, but it couldn't have come at a worse time.

It got worse, though: something complicated had happened, the sort of shit Calan Dubrayle had prophesied, and as a result the traders would only accept gold ... but his army had none left. He'd had to commandeer the last three caravans and hang the traders who protested, but the result of that had been no more caravans. His army had about a month's food left, if they went on short rations, and then they'd be down to eating their mounts. Some units already were.

We're fucked. Invincible, and fucked.

It wasn't even as if his troubles ended there. That idiot Jongebeau's reports had arrived: the Inquisition and Kirkegarde men sent from Vida to crush the deserters led by his former son had been massacred.

My son has betrayed the empire.

For years, Seth had been a disappointment – no, worse, an embarrassment: timid, overly sensitive, prone to tears, despite everything he had done for him. *I tried to bring him up hard, to make him strong. It's his mother's fault.*

The boy had been ridiculously eager to please, and always overreaching – always trying to show off, by leaping a pond or rose-bush, and always ending up in a squalling pile, while Kaltus fumed and his friends tried not to titter.

The reports coming out of the south, of a trek across enemy territory, cunning ruses and daring manoeuvres, heroic attacks and steely defensive lines? Those weren't his son. Seth wasn't *capable*. And in any case, just like those stupid pratfalls of his childhood, these deeds brought no pride, no honour to the Korion name, just shame.

He's doing all this to spite me. People will think we're in collusion ... The Treasury Arch-Legate, Hestan Milius, was demanding that he bring Seth's people to heel, insisting that staggering amounts of gold were at stake. *I have to take a direct hand in this. I must be seen to serve the empire loyally.*

He turned to his aide, who frankly would have made a better son. 'Tonville, send in General Bergium.'

Tonville saluted, and a few seconds later he ushered in old Rhynus Bergium, who threw him a laconic salute and stumped over to a chair. Rhynus was permitted such laxity; he'd earned it.

'My friend, we have a crisis,' Kaltus told him. 'I have to deal with it myself.'

He quickly outlined what was required to pen the deserter legions and bring them to heel. Bergium was, quite understandably, concerned at being left behind with a weakened army, especially one which was about to go to starvation rations.

'You're going to leave me here and take our best men south? When the Moontide has only four months left to run?' Bergium shook his head in disbelief. 'Rashid Mubarak has a million Noories on the plains below!'

'Don't worry, my friend. We've got good men, well dug in, with plenty of magi and archers. You must hold these highlands against the Keshi – it's simple enough.'

'And you'll take all the strike units?'

'That's right: all the khurne cavalry, and most of the aerial units. I've got to prevent these deserters from seizing Bassaz: they're going to occupy the city and declare themselves independent.'

That was a fiction: but he needed an excuse to march out and grab that gold. No doubt the Imperial Court was wondering aloud why the sons of Kaltus Korion and Calan Dubrayle were leading the renegades – that spelled PLOT to anyone with half a brain. *I must be seen to deal with this threat myself*, he repeated to himself.

Bergium looked uncomfortable, but said, 'Do what you need to, Kaltus. An ugly business, no doubt, but you must do what is right.'

'Thank you, my friend. I knew I could rely on you.'

Once Bergium had gone, Kaltus sighed heavily. It made no sense to him, that someone with his blood could be such a *lesser* creature. Seth Korion – no, *Fetallink*. It had to be his mother's fault. That was the only thing that made sense. She'd never been worthy of him.

The next morning he took three fully mounted legions – fifteen thousand men, the teeth and claws of his army – and began the march south. The khurne cavalry were the least of the beasts. There were more than four thousand war-hounds, each as intelligent as the khurnes. Eighteen Inquisitor Fists, all mounted on venators. And even they were dwarfed by his newest weapon, just arrived at the front from the Pallas Animages: two Drakken, winged construct-reptiles bred with the power of Fire-gnosis. They'd flown for the first time at Mater-Imperia's sanctification two years ago. Now they were flying into battle.

My former son will see his deserters reduced to ash.

Three weeks after Kaltus Korion's force departed, Rhynus Bergium started awake from a semi-slumber. Ebensar Ridge lay quiet beneath a full moon so bright it glowed through the canvas like a giant eye through gauze. He'd nodded off at his desk and spilled red wine was soaking into a stack of unsigned orders. It took him a moment to realise that he'd been woken by a gnostic call.

<*General Korion?*>

The whisper was coming through the relay-stave on the table, Bergium realised blearily. The voice was unfamiliar, but only someone who knew the family sigil of the First Army's Commander could reach the staff Kaltus had left behind. So he composed himself, then grasped the wooden rod.

<*Yes?*>

<*General Kaltus Korion?*> the voice asked sharply. It was a male voice, young, assured, brimming with self-regard. His contact-sigil was of the Inquisition: the Eighteenth Fist, and his face was shrouded.

<*I am General Rhynus Bergium. Who is this?*>

The young man's voice became irritated. <*Who commands on Ebensar Ridge?*>

<*I do,*> Bergium replied tersely.

<*Then I guess you'll have to do.*>

Bergium scowled at this impertinence and almost broke the connection. <*I ask again: who is this?*>

<*Who do you think it is?*>

<*I don't play games,*> Bergium snapped. <*Speak, or be gone.*>

The other tutted. <*Oh dear. You're hardly making me feel welcome, are you? Especially considering that I have a maniple of your men at my mercy.*>

Bergium sat up, suddenly queasy and cold. <*Who the Hel are you?*>

A face appeared: young, but possessed of maturity and elegant disdain. It had a familiar stamp, confirmed when the young man said, <*My name is Malevorn Andevarion.*>

Andevarion. Everyone knew the name and the tale of disgrace. But gossip said this one was a prodigy. <*What do you want, Andevarion? Didn't you join the Inquisition?*>

But he doesn't look like an Inquisitor, the general thought. His hair and beard were unkempt, and his skin so dark he could have passed for a Noorie. <*What's this about?*>

Malevorn's shimmering face smiled coldly. <*I've already told you . . . Rhynus. You have a maniple stationed at a village called Sukkhil-wadi, at the northern end of your lines. There's a castle on the slopes above where your captains dice and drink, with a lot of trembling Noories scuttling around in their service. I'm looking down at it now, would you believe?*>

Bergium glanced at the map. *Sukkhil-wadi . . . ? There!* Guarding a road into the heights, not crucial, but important enough. Pallacios IV, a fine veteran legion, occupied that region: ten maniples spread over the key strategic points. It was likely that a maniple would be occupying the castle, certainly, but he'd need to read through the old despatches to verify that. <*What are you saying, Andevarion?*>

<*I'm saying that I wish to meet with you, General. You see, I need soldiers, men willing to march in my army against the empire. I'm offering you the chance to join my Holy Crusade to purge Rondelmar of the Sacrecours and establish a new dynasty. If you agree to meet, I will refrain from destroying the maniple below.*>

<*Is this some kind of joke? Who the Hel do you think you are—?*>

Malevorn Andevarion smirked. <*How very predictable. Well: think on it, General; you could have saved them all.*> He gave an ironic salute, and as suddenly as it had begun, the connection ended.

Bergium stared into the space where the young man's face had appeared, perplexed and disturbed. He wanted to put it down to drunkenness or some kind of prank, but something about the conversation had been unnerving. He looked again at the map, at that isolated dot. *Sukkhil-wadi*. He called his duty mage-adjutant with a sharp mental touch and the man shambled in a few moments later, slapping himself awake. 'Sir?'

'Contact the garrison commander at Sukkhil-wadi – tell him to be on his guard.'

The aide saluted again, puzzled, but not inclined to question, and set up a scrying bowl. Bergium poured himself another mug of wine and watched the young man cast his spells. Within a few minutes it was clear that the battle-mage stationed at Sukkhil-wadi wasn't responding. It took longer to establish enough of a fix on the location for someone to scry it – instant scrying usually required first-hand knowledge of a place. That took more time, and before it happened, a ripple of distant power rolled across all of their senses. Then they ran into wards the adjutant's scrying couldn't penetrate.

By then Bergium feared the worst.

It wasn't until dawn that a windskiff reached the fortress at Sukkhil-wadi. He reported that the keep and all the adjacent town, even the ancient Dom-al'Ahm on the ridge, had been destroyed as if melted from above. Every man, woman and child, Rondian and Noorie alike, had been incinerated.

The next contact from Malevorn Andevarion came soon after.

<So, Bergium: are you ready to talk yet?>

Mandira Khojana, Lokistan, on the continent of Antiopia
Awwal (Martrois) 930
21ˢᵗ month of the Moontide

The sails of the wind-dhou caught the breeze and Alaron stood with Ramita at the side, waving to Master Puravai. A young woman standing beside the old monk held Dasra, who was waving brightly, not understanding that this parting might be for weeks, even months . . . perhaps for ever.

Alongside the dhou, a trio of Keshi windskiffs rose, bearing their new Merozain Bhaicara and piloted by those most skilled in Air-gnosis. Despite their teachings, few of the young Brothers had gained more than a touch of anything outside the core disciplines – that was understandable: they'd had only a few months, not studied for years in the Arcanum like Alaron had, or spent eighteen months with the focused learning that Ramita had received. The subtleties might be beyond them – for months, years, even – but all of them had Ascendant-level strength, and they could shield, imbue destructive gnosis into their staff and throw a mage-bolt of considerable power. None could claim the title "Savant" yet, but they were already formidable, and their skill and knowledge were constantly growing.

But we're still hardly ready to take on Malevorn and his ilk . . .

When they felt concussive bursts of force in the aether from far to the northeast, they knew they'd run out of time.

Corinea, scrying at the time of the second explosion of force, recognised something in the gnostic signature. 'Your Enemy has acted,' she said confidently. 'I'm not sure where; the mountains have distorted the direction of those blasts – but he has done *something*. If he continues to use such force we will find him swiftly once we're clear of the mountains and can scry properly.'

She wouldn't say why, but she was now eager to go. Alaron and Ramita conferred with Master Puravai, who gave his permission to take the Merozain Bhaicara to war.

Ten Brothers shared the dhou with Alaron, Ramita, Corinea and Tegeda; all took their turn piloting, guided by Tegeda who knew more about how to fly a wind-vessel than any of them. Each of the three skiffs held three Brothers, bringing their party to twenty-three. This signified a return from isolation to a world the young Zains had renounced once, but their spirits were high. Even Corinea was alight with anticipation.

<Farewell Dasra! Farewell Puravai!> Ramita called, and the old monk and the young boy raised their hands and waved as the skiffs turned in the wind and headed for the pass leading out of the valley.

At long last, they were off to find their enemies.

31

Delta's Tale

Slave Uprisings

The most bloody slave uprising against the Rimoni Empire took place at Tetrusium, in Lantris. The Rimoni there had taken shipment of a whole tribe of Sydian nomads, underestimating their bloodthirsty sense of independence. At a hidden signal, the Sydian slaves rose against their masters, then fled into the wilds. Surrounded on a mountainside, they took their own lives rather than surrender.

ANNALS OF PALLAS, 498

Southern Kesh, on the continent of Antiopia
Thani (Aprafor) 930
22ⁿᵈ month (of 24) of the Moontide

A circle of magi sat around the Dokken, their faces rapt. The branded man displayed no fear – but then, he'd likely seen more fearsome foes than the magi of the Lost Legions. They'd been listening to the Souldrinker for more than an hour as he revealed what the Inquisition had been doing with the Keshi and Dhassans in the death-camps, and how the khurnes and other constructs came to be so intelligent.

They were all appalled by his tale.

Delta had a real name – Hul Vassar – but he preferred the name branded onto his forehead, almost as if he'd forgotten how to be that other person. He was of Schlessen descent, with the trace of a forest accent. Perhaps the most horrifying thing was that he'd been bred in captivity.

'But it was the Inquisition who decreed that all Dokken must die,' Lanna Jureigh repeated, still stunned by everything she'd heard.

'So they don't always play by their own rules,' Ramon replied. 'Who'd've thought?'

'Tell us about this,' Seth asked Delta, turning over the blackened but icy-cold lump of crystal the Dokken had worn about his neck. He held it gingerly in a gloved hand – it fit easily in his palm. Despite the scorched exterior, it glowed as if a galaxy swam inside it. Delta claimed to be attuned to it, though it was what had enslaved him.

'It's made of the same crystals that power the Leviathan Bridge,' Delta explained. 'An Ordo Costruo man called Ervyn Naxius brought them to the Imperial Arcanum and taught us how to use them.'

'Ervyn Naxius?' Ramon looked around, but the name meant nothing to anyone. Seth looked superstitiously scared, but resolved. Gerdhart was in the corner, as far from the avowed enemy of his Church as he could get and still hear him. Even Jelaska was on edge. Only Kip looked relaxed, but then, he had a beer in his hand.

'What does it do?' Seth asked. 'It feels *inordinately* powerful.'

'Like one hundred of your periapts,' Delta said, 'that's what we were told. But they are fatal to use.'

'You're alive,' Ramon noted.

'I'm Dokken,' Delta replied. 'We can trade a life for a life to sustain ourselves. I needed to take a soul every day I used it.'

Seth looked sick. 'We've been on this Crusade for nearly two years.'

'I dwelled in the Imperial Arcanum far longer. They brought us men and women sentenced to die for their crimes.' Delta's face was enigmatic. 'There were very many. Rondian society must be full of crime.'

Gerdhart could contain himself no longer. 'This creature must die!' he shouted suddenly, storming into the midst of the pavilion. 'He has forfeited his right to life a thousand times over, by his own admission! *He must die!*'

Seth raised a hand. 'Peace, Chaplain.'

'I cannot remain silent! He must—'

'I said *peace!*' Seth snapped, with a sudden crack of authority they'd never heard from him before. 'Kore's Blood! We'll learn all there is to know here, and then I will decide what happens!'

'But—'

'*Sit!*'

Gerdhart blinked, then backed to a seat and fell into it.

'Thank you,' Seth said with a touch of acid in his voice. 'So, "Delta", how many of you are there?'

'Attached to the Inquisition? Twenty-six.'

Ramon did a quick mental calculation and came up with a lot of corpses and khurnes. 'What are your affinities, Delta?'

'Sorcery and Earth, the same as all those of my Brethren assigned to this mission.'

A combination that is best for Necromancy: for the leeching and capture of the dead . . . That makes sense. 'You told me you want to fight the Inquisition. Do you still hold to that?'

'I most certainly do.'

'Neyn! He's lying,' Gerdhart snapped. 'He's a Souldrinker – he'd say anything to save his life!'

'Let him speak,' Seth said impatiently, glaring at Gerdhart until he fell silent.

'Thank you,' Delta said gratefully. 'Please, hearken. I know that you think us evil – think what you will! – but please know that killing was not a pleasure but something they forced us to do. Know also that we are strongly bonded, we of the Brethren: we live inside each other's minds, sharing thoughts and emotions. I have suffered, and even now I feel the suffering of those still enslaved. Your Inquisition *compelled* us to kill – but we do not want this. We want to be free.'

'Free to kill,' Lanna Jureigh breathed.

'Free to just *be*.'

'We all know what your freedom means: the death of others.'

'It need not – when a Rune of the Chain is applied. The hunger within us is subdued and we can live just like normal people. That was what we were, before the Inquisition found us, and that is all we want. Believe me. Let me help you.'

Ramon found the whole room was looking at him – except Kip,

who was looking for more ale. 'I think we would be foolish not to accept his aid,' he said.

That decided the matter.

The next morning Ramon led his cohort northwest towards Medishar to try and purchase supplies. There was no point going right into the city, because the garrison there had apparently rioted a week before, plundering the centre, then burning it to ashes before leaving. But gold was still gold, after all, and everyone, Keshi, Dhassan or Rondian, wanted it badly. Time was running short if they were to make the Bridge by the end of Maicin: it was Aprafor already, and they had only about three weeks of full rations left.

'How're your men doing?' he asked Lukaz as they picked their way through yet another dried-well village in the middle of nowhere. Broken-down houses, dried-out rice paddies and fields gone to brown weeds spoke of the ruin that always followed war. Dust coated everything – even the crows had lost interest and gone.

'We're down to ten of our original twenty,' Lukaz replied softly. 'It's Ferdi the lads miss most; he used to keep 'em laughing with his pranks. But we're not the kind to look back too far.'

'Tell me, that first javelin thrown at Siburnius . . . that was Bowe, wasn't it?'

'Might've been, sir.'

'He did right, whoever it was. I'd forgotten to signal. You all did well.' He clapped the cohort commander on the shoulder. 'Pilus, is there anything you need?'

'Well, I need more men, frankly: we're operating with four in the front rank, and only two in the second with the long spears, and only one flanker on either side. That means Baden or I have to help the second rank in a scrap – so we lose tactical oversight, and our flanks are exposed. Harmon can likely handle it, but Tolomon's not so good on his own.'

'I'll watch that if we're caught in the open,' Ramon said. 'And I'll talk to Seth about dispersing the under-strength cohorts, maybe having fewer, but each at full strength.'

'Fair enough, sir.' Lukaz dropped his voice and asked, 'What's with the Dokken?'

Delta had ended up riding with them because he was more forthcoming when talking to Ramon. To ordinary men like Lukaz and his rankers, the Dokken were a fairy tale, mythical bogeymen to frighten children – but this one was real, and *evil*: all the tales agreed on that.

'I think we can use him to hurt the Quizzies,' Ramon said.

Lukaz thought about that, then saluted. 'That's good enough for me, sir.' He glanced at the road ahead, where a dust-cloud was moving fast. 'Outrider, coming in hard: it looks like Coll.'

Ramon rode out alone to meet the scout; anyone going that fast had to be bearing bad news. The rough-faced outrider pulled a face. 'There's a "delegation" waitin', 'bout a mile up, wantin' to speak wi' yer. Man calls hisself "Arch-Legate Hestan Milius". Looks like Kore hisself – an' prob'ly thinks he is.'

Ramon whistled softly. He knew who Milius was: a *very* senior Imperial Treasury-man, sent to Antiopia to solve the promissory note issue. He'd already talked to Seth, and demanded Ramon's arrest. 'How many men did he have with him?'

'Half a dozen. They'd flown in, I'd warrant: I didn't see any horses. He an' this fat guy were the only magi.'

'Did the fat guy have a name?'

Coll shrugged. 'Din' share it wi' me.'

Ramon chuckled. 'All right. I need mage back-up – who's closest?'

'Kip's lot,' Coll replied, pointing out a column of men in the hazy distance.

Ramon exchanged salutes with the scout, waved Lukaz and his cohort into motion, and they all trotted off to see Fridryk Kippenegger.

An hour later they found them on a little-used track Coll had found for them, eyeing up a cluster of armed men about a hundred yards away. One heavily robed mage waited between them, sitting on a low bridge.

'Do I need to punch anyone?' Kip asked. 'Is it one of *those* meetings?'

'I wouldn't: they'll be pure-bloods. Just look threatening and pretend you're a half-blood.'

'Halb-blut? How do I do that?'

'I don't know. Just look competent.'

'I do that already,' Kip replied, in a hurt voice. He was clad in his battered leather jerkin and his bulging shoulders and arm muscles were horribly sunburned. He looked like a dragon-slaying hero of northern sagas. 'Should've brought my Bullheads. They look scarier than your men.'

'Your "Bullheads" dress like sheep-fuckers and can't fight for shit,' Kel Harmon replied coolly. 'And they en't real Schlessens, they's jus' playin'.'

'They are my Bullheads,' Kip rumbled. 'You say these things to their face, skinny, and see if they can fight.'

'Half o' 'em is from Kenside in Pallas,' Vidran sniffed. 'Dockers, mos'ly.'

'Cunnis, mostly,' little Bowe added. The hatred fostered between those of the different districts of Pallas was legendary; Lukaz's cohort were mostly from tough and insular Tockburn-on-Water. Bowe was an odd case: Ramon disliked his views on almost everything, but he was devoted to his cohort, and utterly irrepressible.

'The spirit of the Bullhead makes my men strong,' Kip sniffed. 'Not puny like you,' he added, eyeing the scrawny, rat-faced little man contemptuously.

'That's enough, you lot,' Ramon interjected. 'I'm going to go down there to talk with this mage. If his guards try anything, warn me and we'll take it from there.'

The cohort fanned out, finding the best vantage points, while Ramon swung from the saddle and walked down a gentle slope to where a thirty-foot-long stone bridge crossed a dry stream that at best could have been no more than twelve inches deep and three feet wide. It was perhaps the most pointless bridge in Creation.

Arch-Legate Hestan Milius looked just as Coll had described: like some vision of magi wisdom and majesty plucked from the Book of Kore, where all gnosis was wielded by Imperial Saints. He wore heavy purple robes lined in gold and was sucking in gnostic power, presumably to keep from perspiring or expiring in the desiccating heat.

His voice was impressively deep. 'Ramon Sensini, I presume?'

The Arch-Legate's guards were clustered on the opposite ridge, including the obese mage Coll had mentioned. Ramon stopped at the near end of the bridge. 'Si, I am he.'

Milius produced a sealed envelope, which he sent slowly towards Ramon using kinesis. 'It's from your father.'

Ramon had been expecting some kind of approach, but here it was and suddenly he was trembling slightly, especially in the wake of the news about the riot in Medishar. 'What does he want?'

'You'll have to read it yourself.'

The envelope hung before Ramon. He plucked it from the air, examined the seal – it was unbroken – then pulled it open. It contained an amulet bearing the seal of House Dubrayle, and a letter. He glanced at Milius to ensure he wasn't about to try something while he was distracted, then read the letter.

My Son,

It has come to my notice that you've misused my acknowledgment documentation, which is disappointing, but unsurprising. Nevertheless, I see silver linings to the dark clouds you've blown my way. No doubt you are aware that your little forgery business has exacerbated the usual over-inflation of investment, credit and gold prices that always occur at this stage of the Crusades. However, I understand that you have managed to protect much of the bullion poured into the Crusade, and have therefore become a potential agent for bolstering the Treasury.

You and I are in a unique position, my errant son, to forge an alliance that will be mutually beneficial. I'm sure you see no need to aid such a recovery, but I assure you that order must be maintained, and a small army in a desert isn't a secure place for wealth of this sort. The vultures are circling.

The amulet I have enclosed will act like a relay-stave and enable you to communicate with me directly and securely. I urge you to use it.

Your Acknowledged Father

Calan Dubrayle

Ramon was immediately struck by a number of things: there was no expectation of familial feeling, but considerable knowledge of his situation. That fit with the man he pictured. And his father dangled tangible benefits, not emotional ones. 'What else are you allowed to tell me?' he asked Milius.

'That the offer is genuine. I am authorised to protect you and yours, provided certain *baggage* accompanies you. That you will be conveyed to a place of guaranteed safety and an Imperial Pardon is authorised.' The Arch-Legate's voice conveyed his dislike of playing messenger-boy.

Ramon held up the amulet. 'You know about this?'

'Of course. You may be aware that there is an eight-hour difference in time between here and Pallas; bear that in mind when you choose to communicate.'

When, not if, Ramon noted. 'How long have I got?'

'Not long. Your name is now known in very high circles. I can tell you for free that other parties are aware of what you've done. You must chose a side, before it's chosen for you: Crown, Church, Army or Treasury. Your father can extend some protection, but not for ever.'

He'd hoped the powerful men and women who controlled the empire might have better things to do, but he wasn't really surprised. There probably wasn't anything left worth doing in the whole of Antiopia that was better than finding his gold.

'I'll speak to him soon,' he told Milius. 'Stay close, Arch-Legate. I might need you.'

Milius lowered his brows disapprovingly. 'You *will* need me, boy. This is no game.'

Ramon forced an impudent grin. 'Everything's a game, Milius. Arrivederci, for now.'

<Lord Dubrayle?>

There was a long silence as Ramon's call echoed out into the aether, during which he had a lot of time to question Dubrayle's motives, his own motives, and to simply stare out at the flat horizon. This latest campsite was a little-used road chosen to avoid the refugees streaming out of Medishar, and today was Holy Day – the only movement on the road was their own wagons, bearing rice and lentils purchased at outrageous prices from the locals.

After some consideration, Ramon had gone to Seth Korion and told him about the proposed meeting with Dubrayle. He wasn't used to confiding in others, but Seth knew most of the tale anyway, and they were likely going to have to cooperate to get out of this. Seth had even looked a little envious, being estranged from his own father. They'd had two days to discuss what they might do.

A cool mental voice interrupted his thoughts. <Ramon . . . 'Sensini', I suppose?> There was an echo, due to the three or four thousand miles between them.

<Si,> Ramon replied, deliberately using the Rimoni word, emphasising that he had another parent. <I've read your letter.>

<Obviously. Where are you currently situated? Who is with you?> Dubrayle spoke briskly, as if this were a conversation slipped in between much more important meetings – but Ramon doubted that was the case. He'd chosen the time deliberately – morning here; around midnight in Pallas – hoping Dubrayle would be tired or drunk or both. He didn't sound it, though.

<I'm alone. The army is southeast of Medishar. You could cook eggs on an upturned shield-boss here.>

<Ah, the legendary Antiopian heat. Here it is autumn, nothing but fog and rain.> Dubrayle tsked, already impatient with small-talk. <Listen, you don't know me, and I won't pretend I've followed your upbringing closely. Your mother was . . . a mistake. I was out of Pallas for the first time, and

disoriented. The culture of the occupying legions was distasteful, but one had to conform. I was glad to help her—>

<So long as it remained a secret,> Ramon concluded for him.

<It was a delicate time for me. I was new, and the Treasury doesn't like indiscretions.>

<Like raping thirteen-year-olds,> Ramon snarled. <That's so indiscreet.>

<I didn't know her age, and I didn't take anything not offered.>

<That's not what anyone I know says.>

Dubrayle's voice became distant, haughty. <Then they lied. Such people don't like to acknowledge truths that don't suit them. They'd rather lie about strangers. Regardless, she did well from our 'transaction'. And you were given life, which you've clearly seized with both fists.>

<You think it a transaction?>

<Life is a series of transactions. We all give to receive. Even that which we appear to get for free or take by force costs something. The art of success is to gain the most in each exchange. As I have. And as you – who are of my blood – have also done, otherwise you would not now have what so many others want.> His voice became more relaxed as the discussion became less personal. <Ramon, the reports I've received about your time on Crusade have proved a lot of things to me. The most important of those is that you are undoubtedly my son. You've displayed coolness under pressure, and the ability to think and act with dispassion and alacrity. These are the traits of a true Dubrayle. You belong under my wing: and frankly, under my protection is the only place you'll find safety now.>

Ramon bit at his lip. The offer wasn't unexpected. Bring the gold to Papa and you'll be safe. <Go on.>

<Well, I'm sure you don't really need to be told that right now the empire's finances are ... problematic. Yuros has been depleted significantly of hard currency and is trading on notes issued under the assumption of impossible returns from the Crusade. Our currency has appreciated far past its face-value, gold is trading at ridiculous prices and rumours of an impending 'correction' are rife. The plunder from the East has gone straight into the coffers of the generals, while many of the Pallas nobility are extended well beyond their means. In short, the empire is, technically, insolvent. Supplies and equipment have stopped flowing. There is nothing to pay the soldiers with except worthless

paper and already the first legion has mutinied – in Medishar as it happens; they've run amok and butchered Noories by the hundreds. More will follow in the coming days. Though it happens every time, this Crusade will be worse, and have deeper consequences . . . unless we can give the market confidence, and that will require the gold you have amassed.>

<What are you doing about all this?>

Dubrayle sighed ironically. <Expressing confidence that all will be well. Issuing new notes we can't cash. Working the goldmine slaves to death. In short, pretending there isn't a problem while working feverishly to prevent chaos. Otherwise there's going to be a Medishar in every city in Yuros.>

<You're exaggerating.>

<If only.> Dubrayle's mental voice softened, a stage actor's version of 'paternal'. <In any society, those in power are supported by a number of pillars: wealth, status, moral authority, and force. Disrupt any of those and they have to reassert themselves. The Pallas magi had all four of those pillars, but this Crusade – this botched, failed Crusade – is destroying their wealth, and they will react: with force. There will be chaos, and the millions who deserve it least will suffer most. That is why the status quo must be supported, and why those bred to rule must be permitted to do so. Elites must be sustained, for the alternatives are unthinkable.>

Ramon inhaled. It all sounded so *reasonable*, in Calan Dubrayle's matter-of-fact yet *caring* tones. Yet it also made him angry. *Elites must be sustained, must they? The alternatives are unthinkable, are they?* He wanted to lash out, but he had to admit to being captivated by hearing this giant of the empire – his natural father – speak. It was like being permitted to interview a deity. He wished Vann Mercer, Alaron's father, who'd been responsible for shaping his political beliefs to a large extent, was here to help him frame the questions he wanted to ask. But he was alone, and Dubrayle wanted answers too, and soon.

<What is it you are offering?> he asked, then added, <Father.>

Dubrayle's voice became warmer. <The chance of a lifetime, son.>

'So what happened next?' Seth Korion asked, leaning forward as Ramon paused and took a swallow of brackish, lukewarm water from his bottle. 'What did he say?'

They were watching their men tramp down a dusty road towards a flat horizon. The sun was its usual oppressive presence, but the rankers were singing, and so too the Khotri women riding with the baggage train: two songs merging into one.

Ramon laughed. 'He said that if I surrendered myself and all the gold I have to him, he'd pardon me, acknowledge me publically and give me a position as a Junior Legate in the Imperial Treasury.'

'Holy Kore! What did you say?'

'I told him to go and rukk himself with a sharp stick.'

Seth's jaw dropped. 'Seriously?'

'Well, no, actually. I told him I needed to think about it – if I can string him along, it might buy us some time. I told him that I've no longer got the gold, and said that it's been dumped in a series of marked sites on the Tigrates River, and that no one person, not even me, is aware of all the sites. I thought that way he might hold off trying to just snatch me from the column.'

'Do you think that will work?'

'Not for long. But he says your own loving ex-Papa has despatched men to intercept us, and the Imperial Volsai and the Church are converging on us too. He also said that Saint Lucia is terrified that whoever succeeds in snatching the gold will seize the throne, so she's trying to create alliances in each camp. This could buy us time.'

'To do what?'

'To come up with a better plan.' He winced. 'Sorry, I'm running out of ideas.'

They fell silent for a minute, then Seth said, 'So he would actually *acknowledge* you? And take you under his wing?' He was still in agony over being rejected by his own father.

'Dubrayle doesn't want *me*,' Ramon said. 'He wants to preserve the wealth of "his people" – the Elites. He'd be more than happy to have me executed as a traitor, provided he gets the gold first.'

Seth listened gloomily. 'Look at us: both illegitimate sons of powerful men who'd happily see us dead. And we even went through the Arcanum together. Incredible.'

'There aren't that many Arcanums,' Ramon replied. 'Don't invent coincidences, General Korion.'

'Fetallink,' Seth corrected.

'No, you're a Korion – sorry, but you really are. So, anyway, Dubrayle tried to scare me with all his "world will collapse unless we let rich pricks rule for the rest of eternity" shit. It just left me twice as determined to get our rankers home with gold in their pockets. Dubrayle can go to Hel.'

Seth listened, then solemnly shook his hand. 'So then. We've got the whole of the empire lining up to annihilate us. What are we going to do?'

'Honestly? I don't know.'

'Come on, you've always got a plan,' Seth teased, his voice light and his eyes fearful.

'Not this time. We need a miracle.'

'I thought you didn't believe in those?'

'I don't. But I'm thinking I better get praying.'

He didn't actually get around to praying; instead Ramon worried at his problems as the column wound west of Medishar, buying what food they could from a destitute rural populace. He insisted on paying – the Crusade had done enough damage here, and the exorbitant prices were easily affordable to him – and before long Dhassan merchants began to come to them, lining the roads to sell, knowing they'd get more than from the locals, not caring that their own people might starve. If he'd had a choice, he'd rather have hung them for profiteering. Instead, he made them rich.

Everywhere they went they saw the suffering the invasion had caused, and it affected the rankers especially, despite all they'd seen and been through, not to mention their own predicament. The best and worst of their natures came out: some of the men were foolishly generous to the locals; others were cruel and bullying – and sometimes it was the same man, just on a different day, when stress made him snap.

The time passed in a haze, the road like a burning dream.

On the last day of Aprafor, under the Darkmoon, they reached a place marked on the maps as 'Bassaz Junction'. They'd approached from the east; there was wilderness to the south and the city of Bassaz itself was fifteen miles further westward. But the northern route was the great road of the Dhassan kings, and it went all the way to Hebusalim.

Ramon was riding next to the Souldrinker Delta, who was quietly lugubrious company, and not unpleasant if you could ignore what he was. They crested a rise and found themselves overlooking a low valley. Coll and his fellow scouts were waiting for them, because the Lost Legions could go no further: above the crossroads, blocking the northern route, was another army, some fifteen thousand men or more, according to Coll's estimates. 'They're First Army, sir, with plenty of Inquisition and Kirkegarde – all cavalry, mounted on those damned khurnes.'

Ramon's spine stiffened at the thought of a whole lot more Siburniuses and Nytrasias and their ilk. He glanced at Delta. *His kind too, perhaps?*

'What else, Coll?' he asked, because the scout was almost bursting to go on.

'They've got hordes of war-hounds – I barely got out. And I saw venators . . . and worse.' Coll's voice dropped to a whisper. 'I was there in Pallas when Lucia Sacrecour got 'erself Sainted, sir. These two giant flyin' reptiles flew over the plaza, breathin' fire – Drakken, sir, jus' like the legends, come to life.'

Drakken? Oh . . . that's just rukking *wonderful . . .*

32

Limits of Power

The Elder Gods of Gatioch

Great Masters, I swear that this was the only way of inculcating these heathens with the Word of Ahm! They just could not conceive of the Prophet as being divine, yet not one of their pantheon. So yes, I allowed them to think that we regarded Aluq-Ahmed as a child of Markud, the king of their gods! Yes, this was a heresy! But it has brought them to the Faith! I beg you for clemency!

GODSPEAKER GULBRACH, AMTEH MISSIONARY TO GATIOCH,
AT HIS TRIAL FOR HERESY, Y132 (A586)

Valley of Tombs, Gatioch, on the continent of Antiopia
Thani (Aprafor) 930
22nd month (of 24) of the Moontide

The thrum of the Keshi windship was clear, even in the after-deck cabin, which told Alaron they were still making good speed. He, Ramita and Corinea were crammed together, poring over the map on the table dominating the tiny cabin. Coloured stones etched with runes covered the parchment.

They were somewhere over Gatioch, flying under a burning sun. Corinea had been scrying the route ahead so that they could narrow down where to find Malevorn and Huriya; it gave them something to do as they flew northeast, aided by the spring winds rolling across Ahmedhassa from the western seas. Free of the mountains, they'd come up against strong wards whenever they tried to scry Malevorn, Huriya or Nasatya directly. But Corinea was focusing on something else right now, what she referred to as a 'snail's trail' of gnostic echoes that apparently bore 'his taint'. Alaron wasn't sure if the 'his' referred to Malevorn any more.

'This is the position of the Crusade now,' Corinea said, indicating the map. 'Kaltus Korion's forces are arrayed north to south, facing Rashid from atop the Ebensar Heights, east of Galataz. They're only two months from Pontus if they march quickly. I presume they'll stay in Ebensar until the beginning of Maicin.'

'That's only a few weeks away,' Alaron mused.

'Indeed.' Corinea pointed to a number of markers in southern Dhassa. 'Here we have the southern Keshi army, led by the sultan himself. He seems to be moving into Dhassa, trailing a number of smaller Rondian forces: the former garrisons of the southern cities.' She tapped the marker for the sultan. 'The Keshi armies are huge.'

'Remind me about this one?' Alaron asked, pointing to a marker in the south of Kesh. They were Rondian, apparently marching from Medishar to Bassaz in good order. He'd been rather optimistically scrying for Ramon – more in hope than expectation – but if he was out there, he was warded too. He could have tried calling for him, but that was noisy and might have alerted unfriendly minds to their presence.

'A small Rondian force,' Corinea replied. She indicated another marker. 'They appear to be linking up with this force that's come south, very swiftly, from the First Army.' This was well out of their way – Corinea's 'snail's trail' began in Gatioch, far to the east.

'What about Huriya?' asked Ramita, who cared little of the Crusade's progress. 'What about my son?'

She knew the answer; they all did: Huriya was nowhere to be found, and nor was Nasatya. 'They're just warding too strongly for us to find them,' Corinea said soothingly, though the growing fear that the boy was dead gnawed at them all.

Ramita wasn't mollified. 'So: we know where all manner of people are: just not those we actually want to find.' She brushed Alaron's hand away irritably. She had a temper she seldom showed, but when she did, the world knew it.

Corinea smoothed back her long silver hair. 'I shall attempt another divination,' she said, as if only she could perform the really useful tasks. 'I'll need this cabin, of course.'

'Of course,' Ramita yawned wearily. 'I need fresh air.'

'There's plenty of it out here,' Alaron quipped as they left the sorceress and went out into the biting wind. The deck was exposed to all the elements and any of the Merozain Brothers who weren't actively working on trimming the sails were cowering in the shade. By now the young men were fed up with the miracle of flight. They'd crossed the great gulf of the Rakasarphal nonstop, then carried on flying through the daylight hours, keeping high up to minimise detection, only landing at dusk to sleep. The lack of success in finding their quarry was getting to them all.

Alaron and Ramita had barely settled into their customary nook on the fore-deck to doze the afternoon away when Gateem shouted excitedly, 'Look, *look*—!'

As everyone stood to see, Alaron exclaimed, 'Holy Kore! What an incredible place!'

They were flying into a valley that ran from east to west, where giant statues fifty feet tall or more of enthroned animal-headed men facing the dawn had been carved in weathered stone. There was a mass of stone and marble buildings, rows and rows of them, a great city, filled with palaces and monuments, broad streets and narrow alleys. But they were all utterly lifeless: more than five miles of empty stone, filling up with sand.

'It looks abandoned,' Ramita said.

'It's a city of the dead,' Gateem called from the rigging above. 'The Gatti used to build them for their kings. But when Gatioch declined, such places were abandoned. It was long ago, before the Prophet came.'

'Master Puravai isn't here to mark your work now,' Yash called, laughing. 'We learn the histories in our training,' he added to Alaron. 'Gatioch was a great empire, before Kesh conquered all.'

'Look!' Gateem shouted, pointing away to their right. 'There!'

Alaron followed his finger and saw a plaza on the south side of the valley where the tombs were blackened and broken, and in the midst was the blasted carcase of a large creature, slowly being pulled apart by a huge swarm of vultures and carrion crows. There was another one, a little further onwards, already reduced to bones and dried skin, and what looked like armoured human remains.

Holy Hel, what happened here?

After circling cautiously to ensure they were alone, they put down in the next plaza. Only the birds shrieked in fury at their passing. They left half the Brothers with the windships and then together went to investigate the fallen, using Animagery to drive the shrieking mass of birds away. What was revealed was the eerie sight of two dead venators. They spent an hour trying to piece together what had happened, using Clairvoyancy and other gnostic methods, which revealed traces of gnosis-use, powerful blasts of energy that had wrecked the tombs here. They also revealed that many of the bodies had distorted skeletons, warped by the gnosis, but still the details remained sketchy.

'They were Shapechangers, most of the dead,' Corinea said after examining them. She was holding one of their skulls, sniffing it occasionally. She pointed to the armoured corpses, and added, 'These were Inquisitors.'

'So the Inquisitors were victorious?' Ramita asked.

'I doubt it. Inquisitors don't leave their bodies unburied. It's part of their oath, to respect their fallen.'

'The bodies are weeks old, and there are fresher ones in the pits on the south side. Hundreds and hundreds of them,' Yash commented. He was holding Tegeda's hand, publically testing the limits. Alaron didn't care: they'd not put anything about chastity, or even not marrying, into their fledgling order's vows.

Then Aprek came running from a tomb shouting for Alaron and Ramita: he'd found the body of a small black-haired female, chained in manacles to the wall of a cell. When Ramita saw it she almost fainted.

'*It's Huriya!*' She sank to her knees in a torrent of tears.

Ramita let the ashes pour through her hands and merge with the sands. They said in Baranasi that every speck of sand marked a death, one grain for every person deceased since time began.

Goodbye, Huriya. Namaste and farewell. I thought of you as my sister, as my heart's companion, but you were someone else entirely. I'll not waste my life trying to understand; I've got more pressing things to do. But I'll never forget you. Perhaps in the end you saw the Light, and that's why they left you chained in the dark? I will pray that's the way it was. May all the gods forgive you.

She couldn't think of anything else to say so she stood up, dusted her hands on her kameez and turned away. The wind whispered wordlessly through the dunes and blew the ash away.

The cell next door to where Huriya had been found had contained a couple of discarded toys, just crude wooden figures, but they had filled her with hope. Huriya was dead, but perhaps Nasatya was still alive.

'I am ready,' she said quietly to Alaron. 'Let us go and find my son.'

They joined Corinea on the south side of the Valley of Tombs. She'd pulled a skull from a fresh grave and given it to Alaron to anchor the scrying-spells he was using to find Malevorn, even though it certainly wasn't his skull. It wasn't even human. But it must have had something to do with the Inquisitor, because it was definitely helping. Alaron had been able to penetrate Malevorn's shields enough to sense direction – somewhere northwest; meaning Malevorn was alive. That thought energised them all.

The old sorceress looked up as they approached. 'Have you finished your mourning?' she asked Ramita in a careless voice.

Ramita flinched. 'Huriya has been cremated and her ashes spread to the winds. She was my blood-sister, and once I loved her. Perhaps you remember such feelings?'

Corinea's grey eyes flashed. 'I've lost *everyone*,' she said in a hollow voice. She flung the skull against the wall in a sudden fit of violence – then abruptly she was calmness itself again. 'I have what we need here. I have powdered the skull of the dead shapechanger found near the cell where your Huriya was found: there is a gnostic trace burned into its very bones that links to the the very taint I've been tracing. The next time this Malevorn expends a significant amount of gnosis, I'll know precisely where he is.'

Zhassi Valley, on the continent of Antiopia
Thani (Aprafor) 930
22ⁿᵈ month (of 24) of the Moontide

Malevorn Andevarion knelt on his right knee, bending over the hilt of his sword. He'd used Earth- and Fire-gnosis to reshape the blade from the heathen curved blade to a good straight Rondian sword. The cross-piece, forming the Sacred Dagger of the Kore, provided him a focus for his worship.

Growing up as a mage was a strangely ironic position in Yuros society. All magi were descendants of the Blessed of Kore, with magical powers and sacred status – and yet the very learning of the gnosis gave insights that the common people never saw. Like stagehands in a theatre, magi saw the ropes and mirrors behind every performance; they more than anyone knew that they and their fellows were far from divine. Malevorn had despised his closest friends at the Arcanum, and had to admit that even he had sinned at times.

But now he'd been chosen by Corineus Himself, and that demanded higher standards: *I will institute a new Inquisition, one that is more deeply rooted upon the ideals of the Kore,* he decided. *I will return us to the fundamentals of Faith.*

He'd taken the Ablizians into the desert to refine their powers after destroying the garrison at Sukkhil-wadi. En route, he allowed them to slay an unwary group of Keshi refugees, replenishing their gnosis for the next step in the struggle.

The Struggle – for it was a struggle, a quest that only one such as he could attempt.

Yield and join me, or perish. Those will be the choices.

He'd been under sustained scrying attacks since the purging of Sukkhil-wadi, of course. But he was unsleeping, unstinting in his vigilance and enduring through the energies of his aetherial links and the blessing of his Saviour. *My faith sustains me.*

It was the presence of Corineus, so close to his thoughts that he felt himself a vessel, that gave him the courage for the next step. He grasped the relay-stave and reached out. The response was almost immediate, which pleased him; he imagined the recipient waiting anxiously, perhaps with beads of sweat dotting the upper lip, despite the chill of the Pallas air . . .

<*Who is this?*> a woman's voice asked quietly.

<*I am Malevorn Andevarion.*> He sensed apprehension in her. She'd know what he was capable of by now, for he'd bullied General Bergium into arranging this gnostic contact after Sukkhil-wadi.

<*This is Lucia Sacrecour, Malevorn. I'm delighted to make your acquaintance.*>

She didn't seek a visual contact, another hint that she feared him. <*You have been in contact with Bergium?*> he asked, not acknowledging her title.

<*Indeed,*> she replied, her voice growing in confidence as she spoke. <*I like to be direct and act with honour, Master Andevarion. It is a trait that has always served me well in a man's world. So I have this to say: you were part of a Fist sent on a secret mission. I know of the mission and its purpose: I ordered it. I know what's at stake.*>

Does she guess that I have the Scytale yet? Surely she must suspect . . .

<*So you know of my demonstration of power at Sukkhil-wadi?*>

<*I do – and I am unimpressed by such wasteful barbarism. You are an Inquisitor of the Holy Church. You have only to walk into any Imperial camp and you will be given a fair hearing.*>

<*I don't require a 'hearing' – I am above the judgement of others. I have a higher purpose, and I required an example to be made. You see, Mater-Imperia, where all others failed, I succeeded in that mission you ordered.*>

She inhaled sharply. <*You have the artefact?*>

<*Yes, right here.*> He sent a brief glimpse of it to whet her appetite.

Her voice intensified. <*You must return it to Pallas, Malevorn. It belongs here. You will be rewarded beyond your most extravagant desires.*>

<*Mater-Imperia, I have some very extravagant desires. I have spoken directly with Corineus Himself, and my soul resides in Him. I will not be*

coming to Pallas seeking reward and favour. I will be coming to institute a new rule of Divine Law, based upon the Book of Kore, with the powers of Emperor and the Grand Prelate combined in my hands. I do not come as a supplicant, but to rule.>

He wasn't sure what response he expected, but laughter wasn't it. She had the temerity to giggle, a tinkling sound that scratched at his dignity and infuriated him.

<Young man,> she said in a condescending voice, *<you are deluded! Do you really think you're the first Ascendant to believe himself ordained for the throne? There have been dozens, and they have all been dealt with by the Keepers! I strongly counsel you to rethink – after all, there is more to power than sheer gnostic strength.>*

<I am the Ordained of Corineus!> he roared. *<It's your duty to bow down before me!>*

<No, young Andevarion. My duty is to the empire. Listen: I've been told you were a single-minded student and acolyte of the Inquisition, dedicated to restoring your family's fortunes. That family presently reside in my care. Your mother and siblings would be pained to hear you rant and rave like this.>

That gave him pause. *My mother, my little sister . . .*

Who was he doing any of this for if not for them?

But who are they really, compared to the infinity that is Corineus?

He opened his mind to his Master and Corineus was with him, aware of all he did. *<The Sacrecours have their place,>* he suggested. Their reign meant stability for the empire – taking control while leaving them with a role might be an interim step. He would need someone to help him transition into power – why not this woman, who knew the stage and the ropes to pull?

Corineus gave him the words to use, and all but spoke through him: *<You are a Living Saint, Lucia Sacrecour. I know that Kore is in your heart.>*

She was silent a few moments, as if she realised just what power had touched her own in that moment. When she replied, she sounded far more conciliatory. *<Perhaps I should send an intermediary, Magister Andevarion? Someone to meet you face to face, to verify your claims? There is a man I trust, known for his learning: Ervyn Naxius.>*

Naxius. His Master immediately supplied the man's history: Ordo

Costruo, then treachery. So he served the empire now, did he? <Very well.> He looked at the map and picked a small town in the Zhassi Valley – if it was still inhabited, the better; his Ablizians could feed.

<Let this Naxius meet me in ... Zarrabadh ... in a week's time,> he suggested. <Let it be a matter of trust between us: that I let him meet me.>

He severed the link and sat back, basking in the glow of his God's presence. Then he felt something, a niggling sensation that had recently started to nibble at him: a scrying that was coming closer than he liked. He was unsettled, but Corineus answered before he had even framed the question.

<It is our enemy,> his Master told him. <Alaron Mercer.>

<Mercer?> Malevorn was incredulous. <He's not capable—>

<Nevertheless.>

It was puzzling, although it didn't scare him. Mercer was a fool, but somehow he'd found and held the Scytale, for a time at least, and made it across two continents. He had either grown, or he had powerful protectors ... yes, someone was helping him. <What should I do?>

<Whatever you wish,> Corineus replied. <Just know that when you expel power, he is aware: I feel his mind soon after any particularly strong use of the gnosis.>

<Then let him come,> Malevorn decided. <I'll be ready ...>

Afterwards, he cradled the Scytale and closed his eyes, to dream of his triumphant return to Pallas, with all of the court bowing down before him ...

Malevorn was awaiting Ervyn Naxius at the chosen rendezvous. Zarrabadh was virtually a ghost town, but the few remaining peasants on the outskirts had been handy fuel for his Ablizians, who needed to be strong for this encounter. He wanted to be able to demonstrate his full powers to this Erwyn Naxius, so that Mater-Imperia would know that he was everything he had claimed to be.

He wondered idly where Hessaz – or Huriya or Sabele or whoever she was now – had gone, but he found that, actually, he didn't overly care. Perhaps it rankled a little that she'd come so close to destroying him, but what she'd forced him to do, setting his soul apart from his body, had purified him, stripping away the last vestiges of human needs. He still needed to eat and drink, but lust, hate, greed . . . all receded in the Light of Him.

He was no longer pretending to himself that he was doing this for his family; Lucia could hold a knife to his mother's throat or his sister's heart and he'd care not a whit. His Master's victory was all that mattered.

I'm ascending the stairway to Kore Himself. I am Purpose Incarnate.

He'd waited a week to meet Ervyn Naxius, but he didn't have to wait much longer. A black-winged shape appeared in the darkening skies: a venator, with the man Malevorn had come to meet perched on its back, sitting between the wings on a strange-shaped saddle. Naxius was a disappointment: a hunched-over, wizened, vague-looking bald old man.

They exchanged greetings, both reserved, then Malevorn took him to the pavilion he'd had his Ablizians prepare in the middle of Zarrabadh's square. The old man was obviously rather taken with the Ablizians, for he was staring at them avidly. Malevorn had only a dozen in sight; the rest were surrounding the square, concealed in the ruined buildings. The twelve on view had jackal heads; they wore uniform loincloths and carried spears.

'I can feel the bonds between them,' Naxius marvelled. 'They are as one creature! We must speak of them in greater detail, because I must say that I find them fascinating. They are Souldrinkers, all? As are you: the mystery of Nasette, I take it?'

That Naxius was so comfortable in the presence of Dokken spoke of the man's familiarity with secrets most magi ran a mile from. Malevorn was grudgingly impressed. *Will Lucia be so sanguine when she learns that particular secret?* he wondered. He motioned the ancient mage to a seat, poured arak – plunder from the village – and pointedly tasted it first. Naxius still waved a hand over the arak, ensuring for himself it was not poisoned, then sipped it and winced.

'You've some knowledge of the Dokken, Magister Naxius?' Malevorn asked.

'I've studied the Souldrinkers for decades. You know, I believe we may have a cure.'

Hogshit. If he had a cure he'd be offering amnesties and displaying his success for all to see.

The meal was served by one of his Ablizians, a jackal-headed woman, bare-breasted and altogether magnificent. Naxius examined her with interest, not as a younger man might, but with dispassionate, analytical eyes. 'She is a possessed Souldrinker, yes? Housing a daemon you control?' His eyes narrowed. 'Yet I do not see binding spells in her aura.'

'My Ablizians serve me unfettered by conventional Wizardry: I have mastered them – with this,' he added, displaying the spear. The scarlet diamonds caught the light of the fire and reflected it back a thousand-fold. 'Their service is now entirely consensual.'

'Really? Consensual control of a daemon is regarded as impossible!' Naxius eyed the spear greedily, then scratched his nose. 'You said: "Ablizian"? From Bahil-Abliz, yes? I know that name: that is the daemon who claims to have snared the soul of Johan Corin.'

Malevorn felt a sudden rage, so virulent he realised that it came from His Master Himself. 'Lord Corineus' soul is most certainly not captive!' he shouted, only marginally in control of his own responses. 'He resides in the aether, watching over us until His return!'

Naxius raised his eyebrows and then held out his hand placatingly. 'As you say,' he said cautiously. 'Do you know the tale of Grand-Prelate Goetfreyd of Delph?'

<*A delusional fool who died spouting lies,*> Corineus growled, and Malevorn repeated the words aloud.

'Perhaps he was,' Naxius replied, sensing he'd touched a nerve and backing off. Their earlier cordiality frayed, and they stared at each other watchfully.

Malevorn brandished the Scytale. 'Do you recognise this?'

'Only by repute,' Naxius replied, as if the artefact didn't impress him. 'I was Ordo Costruo until recently, Magister Andevarion – we were not privy to Imperial secrets.'

'I suppose not.' Malevorn put the Scytale down again and leaned forward, impatient with the small-talk. 'I have shown you my creatures, and you know of the destruction they have wrought. Mater-Imperia says you speak for the emperor: will you hear my demands?'

Naxius leant back in his chair, his eyes hooded. 'State your desires, young man.'

'That I will be welcomed to court, and betrothed to Princess Coramore. I have no desire for your offer of a cure: the stigmatising of the Souldrinker nation will end and they will be invited to serve the emperor. In exchange I will return the Scytale and place myself and my Ablizians in the service of Emperor Constant.'

This was not *exactly* his true intent, but Corineus had counselled him to proceed slowly; the time to fully exert his will would be when he was ensconced in Pallas.

Naxius bowed his head. 'I must confer with Mater-Imperia, Master Andevarion.' He rose to his feet. 'I could do that here and now, if you will allow me to go outside?'

When Malevorn gestured in assent, they walked together back outside, under the gaze of his Ablizian guards again. Naxius walked away a few paces, then turned and clasped his hands together.

'Master Andevarion, it has been instructive to meet you, but I remain unconvinced of your powers. You speak of "mastery" over these creatures, but that is untried in real battle, and you have so few. I see little reason why I should trouble Mater-Imperia with your pathetic demands.' He smiled thinly. 'Only a fool bargains from a position of weakness, Andevarion.'

Malevorn drew his sword, then gripped the diamond spear tighter with the other hand, alerting his other Ablizians, lurking in the darkness beyond the cook-fires. 'Are you testing me, old man?'

Naxius raised a hand and a dozen figures in hooded purple cassocks and carrying ornate carved staves strode out of the darkness, with a line of soldiers dressed in fantastical armour at their backs. 'Think of it as the ultimate test.' He gestured expansively as he said, 'These men and women are Keepers: those raised to the Ascendancy by the Scytale before it was stolen. They are protected by men of the Eternal Guard. Mater-Imperia sent them to reclaim what belongs to Pallas.'

Malevorn was already raising the diamond spear when a deeper darkness loomed above. He dragged his eyes skywards: a massive Rondian warbird hung above, lit by gnostic shields and packed with archers and ballistae and Ahm knew what else. Then came another, and a third ...

He formed shields and summoned his creatures – light crystallised in the air about him an instant before the Keepers lifted their staves. Then the night exploded into fire as gnosis-blasts poured at him from all directions. Amidst it all, he could feel the insidious thrusts of mental assaults.

The first seconds were crucial: the Ablizians meshed their shields and threw them around Malevorn as he marshalled them into place. The Keepers and their guards poured from the western end of the plaza: a dozen magi and dozens of soldiers. He knew of the Eternal Guard: elite fighters devoted to the Rondian Empire, lavished with luxuries but brutalised in training, taught every dirty trick, including how to resist mental assault. But they were still just men. His dozen Ablizians still stood, despite the intial assault, and he could sense the consternation of the Keepers at that.

Silently, he ordered those positioned in the buildings to attack from the flanks.

Another wave of gnosis-fire, the concentrated power of a dozen Keepers, slammed into his creature's wards, which burned red, wavered and this time began to come apart. He gripped the spear, shouted aloud for Corineus to be with him and threw his own power into holding together the crumbling gnostic web binding the Ablizians to him.

His Saviour heard, and His righteous anger filled him, stiffening the Ablizians and drawing them into unity again. In his left hand, the spear began to blaze – the diamonds themselves appeared to be melting; something was happening to the spear, but he could feel the levels of power within it build and build.

<What's happening?>he cried.

<Open to Me and I will guide you,> Corineus thundered inside his skull. Every second of his life felt as if it had been leading to this moment:

to perish at the hands of the Keepers, or to submit to his Saviour and become one with Him! The universe demanded it!

... and yet ...

His sense of selfhood held ... just.

I am Your servant, Lord Corineus ... I am not Your vessel ...

Instead of submitting control of the gnostic web he'd built, he fought to guide it still. It was like riding a wild horse. Beyond the wall of light, he could sense the purple-robed figures renewing their assault, while above the warbirds kept pouring arrows and ballistae bolts into his shield-dome, trying to tear it down. But the power in the spear grew and grew, channelling power directly from the aether, from Corineus Himself. It was frightening him now – the diamonds were almost at the point of liquefying, and they were the basis of his control of the Ablizians.

With no time to consider his options; he gripped the energy and directed it upwards, at the hull of the closest warbird – and *unleashed*—

It was almost the last thing he did.

With a blinding flash, white light flashed from the spear to the hull of the warbird and engulfed it. The keel came apart as the sails, masts and hull went up in flames, and the whole craft was hurled away in a blazing fire ball, right into the second windship. They smashed together, and the fire leaped and went roaring through both craft as men dropped like fireflies towards the ground. Some struck his shield-dome and slid down the sides, clothing and skin aflame. The third craft lifted away, frantically pulling for safety, but Malevorn barely noticed. The instant of the release of the spear's energy had been overpowering: a sucking torrent of raw power that gripped and drew his own residual gnosis into its wake. He felt like a stick in flood-water, hurled about helplessly by forces so beyond him that he barely existed.

He was at the point of surrendering control to Corineus after all when suddenly the pressure eased and he staggered, blinking, back into awareness of his surroundings ...

... as, slowly, like falling stars, the two burning windships fell to earth, coming apart in a crash of blazing timbers. Those few who won free of the blazing wreckage immediately fell victim to his spear-wielding Ablizians as they poured in from all sides, slaughtering the fallen windshipmen before arraying against the Eternal Guard and the Keepers.

After that the night became a blur.

Malevorn watched himself as if from afar, his body glowing like molten metal. He could scarcely believe he was surviving any of this, then he realised what had happened, and laughed aloud . . .

His soul was contained elsewhere than his body – that condition wrought by Hessaz and her treachery had once again preserved him! The soul-gem he'd made for himself was one of those studding the spearhead, which meant he wielded . . . *himself*. There was no other way he would still have been alive.

This truly is destiny!

He salved his mortal form with healing-gnosis, numbing its pain before re-entering the scarred and charred flesh. His armour was twisted and blackened, but with each passing second his body was reforming. He searched the night skies for the third warbird and brought it down with another burst of energy from the spear.

Then at last he paused to take stock.

Firstly, he checked his grip on the minds of the Ablizians. He'd lost almost twenty, but the remainder were gathered about him. The beast-headed warriors were in the process of butchering the Eternal Guard; all eight Keepers had already been reduced to charred corpses by the combined mage-bolts of his Ascendant warriors fighting in unison. The much-vaunted Ascendants had failed to overcome his creatures! The implications were astounding. *No one can stop me!* He extended his awareness and found remnants of the Eternal Guard at the edge of the town, retreating into the wilderness.

Where's Naxius . . . ?

He cursed: the ancient mage had gone, or his wards were too strong to penetrate and find him.

So what about these . . . ?

He walked unsteadily to where the purple-robed Keepers were lying. They'd been burned to the bone; the few left with faces intact were filled with utter terror, confronting a power so great that even they, Ascendants all, had been rendered helpless. They were all ancient, he noticed: too old for the powers they wielded, perhaps, but this was still an incredible victory.

This spear . . . What have I wrought?

One of the Ablizians howled, calling him to a survivor: a young mage-noble, richly dressed, who'd fallen from one of the warbirds. His legs had been crushed by a falling mast and he was sustained only by self-administered healing-gnosis.

'Who are you?' Malevorn asked, crouching down and feigning sympathy.

'Oljan Fruleau – General Bergium's aide-de-camp,' the young man gasped. 'Oh Kore, it hurts!' He gripped Malevorn's forearm, wincing painfully. 'Please, save me . . . I don't want to die!'

'None of us want to die. Why are you here?'

'Naxius came . . . he commanded aid . . . in catching you.' He blinked back tears. 'General Bergium brought *everyone* . . .' He sobbed aloud. 'All the senior magi . . . were in the flagship . . .'

The senior magi! Great Kore, have I just crippled the Rondian First Army?

'Was Kaltus Korion up there?' he demanded.

'No . . . he went south . . . a month ago. We had orders to . . . destroy a traitor . . .'

Malevorn scowled, and hardened his heart. *Is this how you deal, Lucia? Is this your much-vaunted 'honour'?*

He straightened and addressed the nearest Ablizian. 'Find me a relay-stave. Identify the bodies of the dead magi where possible and let me see them. Replenish your gnosis from the survivors. We'll assault the main Rondian camp in three days.'

'Please . . .' Fruleau begged, reminding him that he existed.

Unwise. He spun the diamond spear theatrically, then plunged it through the young man's heart. Then he drank his soul.

A better place awaits you, Fruleau: with Corineus.

Pallas, Rondelmar, on the continent of Yuros
Aprafor (Thani) 930
22ⁿᵈ month of the Moontide

Lucia Sacrecour waited in a room with a domed ceiling decorated with a translucent mother-of-pearl mosaic which shimmered in the candlelight. A low divan faced a scrying-bowl filled with liquid silver. Using it she could reach as far as Antiopia, with clearer image and sound than a relay-stave.

In Pallas it was midday, but in Antiopia it was evening. Even now Ervyn Naxius, with a contingent of Keepers, was finally reclaiming the Scytale of Corineus for the Empire. Outside, rain and wind lashed the Imperial capital from Roidan Heights to Tockburn-on-Water, but in here was warmth and simple, elegant luxury – that had always been her trademark in a court where the garish and ostentatious so often held sway. It was something she took pride in.

I'm a tasteful woman: a beacon of culture.

The silver shimmered and the symbol of the First Army command formed in red and gold on the silver surface. She lifted her hands, conjured it from a flat image to three-dimensional and accepted the contact.

<*General Bergium, I trust?*> she said warmly, as anticipation thrilled through her. *We've recovered the Scytale! We've saved the Empire! And finally – FINALLY! – I will be permitted to Ascend!*

<*Wrong.*>

A dark and utterly unexpected visage formed before her. Her words of congratulation died in her throat as Malevorn Andevarion's burning eyes bored into her. <*What—? Is this some kind of—? Where is General Bergium?*>

<*Dead. All his retinue: dead. The Eternal Guard: dead. All your Keepers: dead. Anyone else you want to know about, your Imperial Holiness?*>

Her mouth was dry as ashes as she tried to comprehend. At last she managed, <*That's impossible,*> cringing at her own banal response.

<*Clearly not,*> the burnished silver image said mockingly. <*If it's any consolation, Ervyn Naxius is still alive, which is a shame because cockroaches*

should be crushed, but at least he can give you a first-hand description of what transpired when you betrayed me.>

<Naxius overstepped! I never intended—>

Malevorn held up his hand. *<Don't. Don't even try, Mater-Imperia. I was willing and eager to join your family and serve the empire. I offered you the return of its greatest treasure. I offered to place my immense power in your service. Yet in your greed and arrogance you tried to stab me in the back! I am one of you: I am a pure-blood of the Blessed! You should have been grateful for my service!>*

<I see that now,> she said meekly.

<Too late, Holiness. I'm coming for you now. I am going to take all of the things I asked for, and more. When I return as a hero to Pallas, as sole Keeper of the Scytale, I'm going to take your granddaughter as my wife. Your idiot son will abdicate and I will be crowned emperor. And as for you . . .> He laughed and said, *<Let's just say that the punishment will fit the crime . . .>*

<You wouldn't dare—! The people will never let you! We are Sacrecour – we are beloved of the people! I'm revered! Revered!>

<No, Lucia, you're deluded. All I will need to do is shout: 'Down with the Sacrecours' and half of Yuros will rally to me. After my first victory, the rest will follow. And as for loving you? You're a lying Fasterius snake and no one cares two figs for you. Your so-called 'sainthood' is a sham, and everyone knows it. You've forgotten your place and a whole kingdom longs to remind you of it. Perhaps I'll chain you in the stocks at Justice Plaza and we can see how well you are loved.> He leered. *<Or rather, how often.>*

Kore, dear Kore, he means it . . . She realised she was shaking. *<Malevorn, please, think of the people! The empire needs stability – it needs its figureheads. We'll give you everything you want – everything, and more – but you must preserve at least the semblance of continuity or there will be chaos. By all means, join our family – rule us! Rule me! But don't . . . overthrow us.>*

I'm so selfless, she thought, regaining her poise as she spoke. *So dignified, even in this terrible moment.*

He laughed.

She swallowed all of her pride and waited, head bowed.

<Prepare for my coming as you will,> he told her. *<Nothing you can do will defeat me. I will be in Pallas inside a month. If I were you, I'd run.>*

She lifted her head. *<If you were me, you'd know that I've never run.>*

She broke the connection before he did, and only then did she allow herself the small luxury of tears, for her son, and for her grandchildren. *Not for myself, of course.* Then she stormed from the chamber, bellowing for her sleeping aides, barraging them with commands as they staggered in, rubbing at their eyes.

'Bring my council! Summon my generals! And the Keepers who are still here – I need them *all!* Rouse my son! Summon the Grand Prelate and the Treasurer! *Now!*'

As the bleary-eyed staff scattered she looked up at the twelve-foot-tall statue of Sertain, the first of the Sacrecours, in the centre of the courtyard. He bestrode the mountains with lightning in his grasp.

It was as if he spoke to her: *We are gods among men, superior beings set on this world to rule it – the gnosis is the least of our powers; we have the money, the influence – the lineage! We were born to rule – and I will tear down the world before I surrender it to an upstart.*

She thought on that, and a plan began to form.

Yes, we will tear it all down, starting with that damned bridge. If Malevorn Andevarion wants to cross the seas, he'll have to fly . . . and we will be waiting to meet him when he lands, exhausted and vulnerable.

Now . . . where in Hel is Naxius?

33

The Adversaries

Gnostic Trace

Just as every person looks and smells different, every mage has their own unique 'trace'. Often it is associated with their affinities, but it is also said to reflect personality. Reports indicate that the gnostic trace of Emperor Sertain was like rough granite and brandy, while Baramitius was akin to vellum and tallow. Disguising this trace appears to be impossible, although methods of concealing it have been discovered.

ENIK TAMBLYN, THE THEORY AND
PRACTISE OF THE GNOSIS, BRES, 913

*Ebensar Heights, Zhassi Valley, on the continent of Antiopia
Thani (Aprafor) 930
22nd month (of 24) of the Moontide*

Alaron slithered towards the top of the rise, ducked beneath the lip of a small crater gouged by a hurled boulder and rolled in. A ruined Dom-al'Ahm loomed on the crest of Ebensar Ridge, beside the wreckage of a destroyed legion camp smouldering like coals on a dying fire. Yash darted in behind him. He was grinning fiercely, as if this were the best game since Hoop.

They'd been flying northwest out of Gatioch four days ago when they sensed the massive expenditure of gnosis coming from the Zhassi Valley – every mage in Ahmedhassa must have felt it: a sensation like distant thunder, rolling on and on for several minutes, sending a current through their skin, then fading out. Corinea confirmed that it was the same gnostic-taint she'd been tracking: they'd found Malevorn. Their maps, and Corinea's best guesses at direction and distance, had him in the Zhassi Valley, in or near a town called Zarra-badh. They'd been making for there until last night, when another torrent of power had been unleashed further westward, at the fortress of Ebensar, which gave its name to the Ebensar Heights.

They landed the skiffs several miles away, behind a line of hills, and come in on foot. Far down the valley, at the edge of sight, was a sea of cooking-fires: the Keshi army. Finding the site where the power had been expended had been easy because the aether was still reverberating. That trace was like a cloud over the fortress and small town which crowned the ridge. Every building was shattered, blackened and smoking.

Alaron realised with a start that there was someone lying in the crater he'd slithered into, a bloodied, dust-caked Rondian ranker. He was clutching his side, a wet rattling sound accompanying every breath. Alaron crept to his side, kindling a gentle stream of heal-ing-gnosis. A trickle of added Water-gnosis cleansed the wound and then sealed it, then he roused the man softly, a hand over his mouth.

'Stay quiet,' he whispered. 'We're friends.'

The soldier took in Alaron's glowing periapt and pale skin and his eyes lit with relief. 'Lor'ship, am I that glad t'see you! I thought I was a goner, see.' His accent evoked the alleys of the northern cities of Rondelmar.

'What happened here?'

'Lor'ship, I wish I knew. The camp were already a mess, because all the gen'rals ran out on us three days back. They left some junior battle-magi in charge, like, but they was all at sea. Then this bloody Inquisitor rides in at dawn, like 'e owns the place an' tells us to sur-render or he'll let loose 'is "Ablizians". Well, the magi told 'im to be off, and 'e just laughs . . .' The soldier started to shake and Alaron laid a hand on his shoulder until he'd calmed a little.

At last he went on, his voice fading in and out, 'Then these ani-mal-headed barstards – 'is *Ablizians* – they come outta nowhere, swear to Kore, an' they bloody well ripped our battle-magi to shreds. Then they started on the rest of us, killing anyone they could find. I been playing dead, been 'ere all day an' night. Not dared t'move . . .'

We're too late . . . Or no, maybe not . . . 'Are they still here?'

'Lor'ship, I dunno; it's gone quiet. But I been too scared to call out, 'cause these Ablizian things . . . they're *Souldrinkers*, like in the stories! They been killing for sport. I saw 'em, but they en't seen me yet.' He clutched at Alaron's arm fearfully. 'Don' bring 'em down on me, please – just get me out of 'ere!'

'Hush. Don't worry, we'll see you safe.' Alaron doubted the man would last many more minutes; he certainly couldn't be moved, not without using so much gnosis that their enemies would know. 'Tell me about the Inquisitor.'

'That one – 'e's a black-haired prick, and 'e carries this spear that glows like the sun.' The man gasped, and blood bubbled from his mouth. He looked as scared as a child facing monsters in the dark.

Alaron glanced anxiously at Yash. 'What spear?'

'I saw it, Lor'ship: there was this great bolt o' light, an' it fried them battle-magi right up! You 'ave to watch out!' He clutched weakly at Alaron's arm and Alaron started to increase the healing-gnosis that was just about keeping the man alive – then a thin, ululating sound rang through the ruins above and he froze.

By the time the sound had faded, the ranker was dead.

Yash hissed in anger, while Alaron closed the man's eyelids.

What are we facing? Malevorn's destroyed an entire army . . .

Yash had crept to the lip of the crater and was peering into the ruined Dom-al'Ahm. 'There is something moving on the takiya.' When Alaron looked puzzled he added, 'The takiya is the open space where the worshippers kneel and pray.' The young Merozain huddled lower. 'What if it's them?'

'We've got to face them sometime,' Alaron replied grimly. 'Go and tell everyone what we've just learned – use words, not the gnosis; these "Ablizians" might be able to sense gnosis-use. Bring everyone to the rear of the Dom-al'Ahm above, quietly as you can. I'm going to scout ahead.'

Once Yash had slipped away, Alaron climbed to the Dom-al'Ahm.

The dome had been blasted open as if from within, leaving a ragged hole blackened by fire. Beyond the ruined shrine the takiya was strewn with dead bodies – Keshi slaves perhaps, and many armoured men. Beyond the prayer platform was a debris-strewn plaza in front of a broken-walled castle which looked to have been used by the Rondian high command, judging by the banners still hanging there. The ruins were smoking. The close-packed buildings of the town west of the fort looked lifeless. Whatever was left of the army itself was gone; the stench and wreckage of a hastily abandoned camp stretched away to the south.

The Rondians have been attacked and fled, but the Keshi don't know that yet . . . Or maybe they do know something's happened, but they aren't coming near until they know it's safe . . .

He re-entered the ruined Dom-al'Ahm, making his way through the halls to see what lay on the north side of the shrine. The edifice still echoed with recently discharged gnosis, prickling Alaron's skin as he crept through deserted corridors strewn with fallen plaster and broken mudbricks. He found another plaza on the north side, scattered with more corpses and a pair of smouldering windskiffs; beyond that was a storm-tossed sea of tents, many burnt out. He couldn't see anyone, but hooting noises could be heard in the distance – the sounds were too bestial to be human, but there were words in the calls, he was sure of it.

What's an Ablizian? he wondered. *Is that their call?*

He heard Yash and the others and was heading back inside to the central dome when he glanced backwards, through the open doors, and froze. There was a figure on the takiya, a man-shaped silhouette with a lean waist and broad shoulders, carrying a spear. It walked slowly about, prodding at the bodies with the butt of its spear. Firelight illuminated its face, and Alaron stared.

So that's an Ablizian . . .

The creature was, just as the soldier had described: animal-headed – this one had an eagle's skull, man-sized and rising from a thick neck and muscular shoulders, a feathered crest reaching all the way to the small of the back. It had a human torso with arms and legs, though, and walked upright. It was naked but for a loincloth, and its aura was a disturbing swirl of dark gnosis.

And it saw Alaron, even in the shadows and shrouded by illusion.

They stared at each other, and Alaron caught the sense of an encounter unplanned. With his inner eye engaged, he could feel the hum of communication. He reached out with mystic-gnosis to tune into the creature's mind and isolate it, but touching its mind was like bumping into a hornet's nest: the buzz increased and he caught an image of himself as seen through the eyes of the creature, projected to dozens of others. Unseen eyes blinked and turned his way from all over the smouldering ruins of the camp. Within a few seconds another Ablizian appeared, this one lizard-headed; it came gliding over a tangled pile of charred bodies and wrecked wagons some sixty yards away, and others followed. Their movements were eerily coordinated, as if the same mind was animating them all, as they closed in from all sides.

Alaron sent a warning to his group: <*Come quickly. I've run into an Ablizian, and he's not alone.*>

<*Abliz was a Demon-Prince of pre-Amteh Kesh and Gatioch,*> Corinea commented as she and Ramita emerged from within the shrine, along with Yash, Gateem and Meero. The air thrummed as more Ablizians strode into view or floated over the top of the broken buildings, looking down at them with bright, curious eyes.

Corinea had an intent look on her face. 'Don't engage with them mentally. You're not ready for that, any of you. Strengthen your shielding. Do you see the colours in the aura? They have access to every affinity and at great strength, just like you.'

Alaron gulped. More of his Merozains were arriving as the Ablizians formed a ragged line facing them across the corpse-strewn plaza. Beyond them were the smashed walls of the castle. There were now twenty beast-men before them, and even without engaging his gnosis he could sense more arriving; there was a *thrum* of combined might, growing as their numbers increased.

Corinea obviously sensed it too. 'They're building to something . . .'

'Then we must interrupt them,' Ramita said. She gathered gnosis-fire in her hands as the young monks formed their own defensive line on the edge of the takiya.

<Pick your targets,> Alaron told his brother Merozains. <Await my signal.>

He pulled down his hood to open up his peripheral vision, then addressed the beastmen, calling, 'Who are you?'

The closest of the Ablizians, the hawk-headed one he'd first seen, looked squarely at him, then blinked. A single incredulous word escaped its beak, a reedy, piping sound: 'Mercer?'

The sound didn't come from a human mouth; it didn't even form his name properly. But the tone of contemptuous disbelief told him all he needed.

Malevorn can see through these things' eyes . . .

'Watch out!' he shouted as each of the Ablizians raised their left hands in identical gestures and blazed at him with gnosis-fire. He hurled himself to the ground.

The Ablizians struck at exactly the same instant, with more power than Alaron had ever faced – more than he had ever even conceived – and the only thing that saved him was that he was already halfway to the ground before the coruscating light struck. His shields were torn apart and totally destroyed by the concussive force of that energy, which struck as one, in the exact same spot – but they had aimed for his heart, and he had already been moving. If even one of them had been out of true, or aimed lower, he would have been cut in half.

Instead, he found himself lying in the dust, twenty yards behind his fellows, winded and shaken, as the twilight lit up with molten violence.

Anger pulls the bowstring, Ramita's family's guru had been fond of saying. Since they'd stolen her child, Ramita's anger had been close to the surface whenever she thought of Huriya Makani and Malevorn Andevarion. Her control had snapped when Alyssa Dulayne attacked the monastery. When Alaron vanished in a livid blast of fire, her instant thought was that no one could survive such a thing, not even her new husband – and that kindled fury and terror in her.

As the Ablizians reeled in the wake of their own strike, she and the Merozains lashed out in response; unlike their attackers, however, their return fire was ragged and ineffective and sprayed off their shields – except for Ramita's. She sent twinned kinesis-blows at the hawk-headed creature who'd spoken: a savage double-punch from thirty yards away, with all the unique strength that Antonin Meiros had bred into her. The first blow slammed into the Ablizian's shields with overwhelming force and tore them open. The second, unopposed, shattered the creature's face, driving the shards of bone and break back into its brain cavity. It dropped, and the rest of the Ablizians staggered, as if they'd all felt the blow.

They are joined somehow, the practical part of her brain reported. The enraged part shrieked in glee and sought another target as her aura blazed with light . . . and began to pull her body into a form that could contain and control her fury.

Dar-Kana-ji, be with me!

Behind her the Merozains gripped their staves; before her the Ablizians turned and sent a coordinated blast of energy – at *her*. The air before her blazed like sunlight through coloured glass, both brilliant and blinding, and her shields went rose and gold at the stresses – but Ramita was already in motion, blurring forward, so the blasts shredded layers of shielding, but never quite reached her. Her second blows crushed another Ablizian and they all recoiled again, but before they could properly regroup, Yash and his brothers charged into them, picking out individual foes and forcing them to fight one-on-one, preventing further united strikes. Alone, the Ablizians immediately proved less effective, and half were bludgeoned down in seconds – but now more were pouring in from all sides.

Dar-Kana howled inside Ramita's heart and she let that wave of fury launch her forwards, through a storm of mage-fire that never quite touched her.

Then her heart lurched with savage exultation and the beast inside her roared. She had heard a voice she loved: Alaron had re-entered the fight, battered, but running freely.

590

Malevorn Andevarion had been waiting in a tower of the ruined castle, watching the net closing on the small group of intruders: a mere twenty to his eighty. Then he saw them: young men in grey robes with wooden staves – *wooden staves! And they have the gnosis?* He hesitated, not quite crediting what he saw.

<*Zain monks?*> Corineus exclaimed inside his brain, and if there was any emotion in his voice at all, it was incredulity, if a god could feel such a thing.

The peace-worshippers? Malevorn didn't know what to make of it, but as the Zains and his Ablizians closed, he realised there was nothing peaceful in the blows these monks were striking, and nothing ineffectual in their shielding, either. Alaron Mercer was lying in a crumpled heap – *ha!* – but there was a Lakh woman among them: *Ramita Ankesharan.*

Did Mercer somehow unravel the Scytale before I took it off him? Surely he didn't waste the Ascendancy on a handful of Zains? It sounded inconceivable, but already he'd lost half a dozen or more of his Ablizians. He shouted through his links for the rest to converge, and flowed through the air himself to join the fray.

Alaron might look dazed, but the Lakh wasn't: when she saw him coming the air about her shimmered, her aura becoming a dark shroud. Within that darkness she grew arms that held flame and lightning and big, crude blades. She had four arms, then six, looking like a giant spider rearing on hind-legs, her face flashing through bestial to monstrous.

What is she?

At the Isle of Glass he'd seen her hurl a mast through the shields of a pure-blood Inquisitor. In Teshwallabad she'd overcome wards designed to prevent gnosis-use by anyone up to pure-blood in power.

Kore's Light! he cried to himself, *she's been an Ascendant all along!*

But so was he, now – and he had another weapon. He bared his teeth and lifted the gleaming spear. Ruby light shimmered as he readied its blast, waiting unflinching as the thing that Ramita Ankesharan had become stormed towards him, shrieking at him in a voice like thunder, '*WHERE IS MY SON?*'

Lillea Selene Sorades drifted almost unnoticed through the chaos of the battle, like a knot of smoke amidst a conflagration. She had no desire to fight, only to keep her charges alive – for much to her surprise, that was how she felt about them now. She hadn't thought of herself as a caring person, not for centuries, but somehow when she saw them in danger, she realised that she was invested emotionally after all, despite the distance she'd tried to maintain.

When the battle was joined, she wound illusion about herself and did nothing to draw while everyone else was consumed by ferocity and bloodlust – even little Ramita, overcome by the urge to destroy those who'd stolen her child and threatened her lover.

Her own objective was quite different.

She'd had an ulterior motive in getting Alaron to do the scrying to find Malevorn Andevarion – she could have done it herself, and probably quicker – but she hadn't wanted her gnostic touch detected, because now she knew who she was *really* trailing. His touch, so achingly familiar though she'd not felt it in more than five hundred years, had been all over Malevorn's gnostic trace, and all through the Ablizian remains in Gatioch.

You're somewhere near, my love. I know you are . . .

She pulled out her dagger, that same blade she'd plunged into his heart nearly six hundred years ago, and chose a foe. She permitted a goat-headed Ablizian with a narrow skull and winding horns to see her; it snarled and charged. She didn't flinch, but gripped it in a kinetic fist. The beastman struggled frantically, almost pulling free, then she closed in, and as their eyes met she raised her left hand and plunged her thumb and forefinger into either eye-socket. She threw her awareness into its skull, and they both went rigid as the network of gnostic bindings that tied him to his fellows engulfed her too: a livid blaze of shifting light that throbbed with information.

Then she adjusted her perceptions. Overlaying the world of flesh and stone was the aether, the world of light and energy. The Ablizians were linked to each other, but they were also joined to a glowing scarlet ball of light in the hands of Malevorn Andevarion, only a few dozen yards from her, preparing to confront Ramita. The light at that nexus-point was growing with every second, a conflagration beyond any she'd ever seen.

Beyond her experience – but not beyond her reach.

She tightened her grip on the Ablizian's skull, her fingers gouging out its eyes as it flailed helplessly, then with a wrench she threw a link at Ramita, shouting a warning to *shield*, while she pulled at the energy of Malevorn's spear, diverting some of its power to herself. A flash of crimson light forked from the spear in an eye-blink; half poured over Ramita, and the remainder gushed over the Ablizian she was holding.

She let it go as it immolated then crumbled to ash in an eye-blink.

The fire washing over her shields momentarily set her robes alight. Every Ablizian was yowling, and all round her the plaza was blackened, but she was unharmed. She flashed to the next creature, a cobra-headed woman with a scimitar; before the daemon could react she had rammed her left hand down its throat, twisted her wrist and forced her hand upwards, plunging her fingers into its brain. The web of light was throbbing, the spearhead nexus half as bright as it had been. This time she didn't try to manipulate it: instead, she threw her own spiratus into the link.

The Ablizian woman fell twitching and Corinea collapsed on top, her awareness no longer in her body. But her spiratus flashed along the skeins of light and into the spearhead . . .

. . . and out the other side, into another place entirely.

Ramita was focused entirely on the man who had stolen her child, standing before her. She bounded towards him, cleaving a bull-headed Ablizian in two with one of her blades in passing, blasting another with lightning, overloading his shields then turning him to a blackened and shrivelled twig, clearing the path to Malevorn Andevarion.

She felt indestructible; barely registering the glowing red light coalescing around the Inquisitor's spearhead as she closed the distance.

But at the last second, a cool voice spoke inside her skull: <*Shield, Ramita.*>

At the same time, something else gripped her, something from the aether that found her and fuelled her, and she shielded a bare instant before a blast of incandescent light engulfed her, a wave of heat and flame that washed over not just her, but everything within twenty yards. Two of the Merozains and four Ablizians just ceased to be: ripped from life and blasted to dust. Another Ablizian standing beside Corinea – who'd suddenly appeared amidst the fighting not twenty yards away – was torched too, but the ancient sorceress looked unharmed.

Ramita's shields bowed inwards, her clothes shrivelled and caught alight and the blades in her hands went red-hot. The skin on her face and the front of her body seared and she screamed in agony, but the beast inside her snarled and she staggered on. A curtain of fire parted and she saw Malevorn Andevarion staring at her in disbelief. The scarlet light of his spear was lessened, as if it had exhausted its power. He shouted furiously as he lifted it to protect himself, and her first blow, with a sword whose hilt had fused with the flesh in her hand, slammed into the spear-haft.

The wooden shaft snapped.

Something hammered into them both, an explosion of energy that tore them apart. She glimpsed Malevorn as he went spiralling head over heels, but she too flew backwards, the spear-head landing beside her thigh, still blazing with light. She thumped to the ground on her back, winded and dazed, but Andevarion was on his feet, while she was still groaning and fighting for breath.

Then the pain hit her like a bolt of lightning.

Her whole body was burned, her shields were folding up – and Malevorn appeared above her, face blazing. He cast about for the spear-head and when he spotted it on the ground beside her he brandished his sword and it burst into blue fire.

But before he could stab down, he was slammed backwards by a kinetic blow. Then Alaron leapt over her and went after his old college nemesis like a man possessed.

The spear-head pulsed again, and began to move – towards Andevarion – and she grabbed it instinctively. Light blazed agonisingly in her head and she almost passed out, but she clung on grimly, somehow maintaining her grip as she fell into a spider-web of stars.

Malevorn hadn't seen Alaron's blow coming, but as he spun through the air his well-honed combat instincts took over, he gripped the earth with kinesis and landed on one knee, sword still in hand. He raised it just in time to parry Alaron Mercer's stupid wooden staff. Then he threw Mercer off with a savage riposte while his mind sought the link to the diamond spear-head. His Ablizians fought on, still guided by Corineus through the spear-link, even though Malevorn was no longer holding it. He tried to draw it to him, but it wouldn't come –it was gripped in the Noorie woman's hand. He snarled in frustration, then Mercer came at him again.

Mercer was in grey robes, and his wooden staff was lit up with gnosis-light. The kinetic push he had used had been Ascendant-strong, and his shielding gleamed about him.

Well, well . . . so Mercer did crack the Scytale . . . But Malevorn could taste victory – Mater-Imperia herself had quailed before him. *How dare these imbeciles interfere? I am destined for a seat at Corineus' right hand – gutting Mercer will be the cherry on the cake!*

<*Kill the monks,*> he told his slaves. <*Leave this one to me!*>

He squared up to Mercer, then went at him with all his skill and fury.

Alaron's staff smashed into Malevorn's sword and sparks flew as he parried desperately against a battering of kinesis and steel. Fighting Malevorn Andevarion had always been a harrowing experience: his old enemy was bigger, stronger, more ruthless, and with a deadly instinct for picking out a weakness. But this was worse, because Ramita had slumped to the ground, and Alaron was in a delirium of fear for her.

Malevorn kept coming at him, with savage intensity, raining in blows, pushing Alaron to continually defend, all the while sending bursts of mage-fire at Ramita's body too, forcing Alaron to spread his shielding, preventing him from countering.

Is she even alive? What happened to her? Alaron prayed silently as he fought, wanting only to throw himself over her, but he couldn't take his eyes from Malevorn for an instant.

All about them the Merozain Brothers and the animal-headed shapeshifters hammered at each other, spread across the plaza, with the Zains in a ragged circle in the middle, and almost double their number of Ablizians pressing inwards beneath the shadow of the broken castle and the shattered Dom-al'Ahm. They were holding their own, perhaps even winning more of the duels, but Alaron sensed that his people were tiring. With Ramita lying motionless, unable to lend her power, they were beginning to waver.

Caught in a losing fight, he tasted desperation, realising that he must break the evolving pattern of this fight before all was lost. He blocked another combination, parried and countered.

Try this, bastard!

He sent one image of himself left while darting right and jabbing at Malevorn's midriff. Malevorn half-turned the wrong way for a moment and his staff slammed through his foe's shielding. The shield flared red, he kicked and caught Malevorn on his booted ankle, sent him off-balance. For a moment Malevorn was vulnerable, but he recovered with a blaze of fire and an impossible twist, flipping over, his face a mask of concentration. Alaron circled, keeping himself between Ramita and Malevorn, praying that hadn't been his last chance. Beside him, another of his Merozains – Meero with the pug-nose and steely eyes, who'd liked to joke that the new order was really named after him – fell, his throat torn out. The Merozain Brothers tightened ranks, fully on the defensive now.

'You've been practising, Mercer,' Malevorn acknowledged with a curl of the lip. 'But you're using a *stick*.' He lunged, struck the staff and flashed his blade along it, and he would have taken Alaron's fingers off if he hadn't yanked his hand back just in time: an action that he turned into a jab to the head with the other end of the kon-staff. Malevorn's shield held, but he was again forced to back up.

'Useful things, sticks,' Alaron panted. 'Both ends can kill, you know?' His eyes flickered around the mêlée, saw that only half a dozen of his Merozains were down, but they were outnumbered and giving ground. Tegeda was in there, fighting like a Hadishah with whirling scimitar and slashing dagger. But one of the Ablizians stabbed Urfin through the chest and inhaled his soul and Alaron could almost see the energy coursing into its kindred. *Come on*, he berated himself, *do something!*

But Malevorn's blade and the need to protect Ramita kept him pinned in place. Then he saw Corinea, lying lifeless over the body of another Ablizian, her left hand buried past the wrist in its throat and its fangs embedded in her forearm.

Kore's Blood, we're not going to win this . . .

'You found someone who could decipher the Scytale?' Malevorn asked curiously, as if they weren't fighting for their lives. All his old arrogance was coming back. 'I can't ask you afterwards,' he added with a sneer, 'because you'll be dead.'

Alaron was silent for a moment, then he replied, more to buy time than anything else, 'I worked most of it out myself.' He needed a plan. He'd been fighting Malevorn half his life – he knew his strengths and could guess at the weaknesses; he'd just never been in a position to exploit them before. But perhaps there was a way . . . even if Malevorn did have access to all the gnosis, could he use it all . . . ?

He parried hard, seeking a respite, preparing a new attack.

'You worked it out? Never!' Malevorn sneered. 'You had help, surely!'

'Unlike you, I have friends,' Alaron replied.

'And where are they now, Mercer? Dead or dying.'

Stay cool . . . Malevorn had been a Thaumaturge, a Fire- and Earth-mage, practical, brutal but straightforward. Alaron sought the antithesis – Sorcery and Theurgy, based in Air and Water . . . *How about this?*

He kindled his full aura around him, watching Malevorn blink at the sudden display of power, a spiratus-blade appeared in his left hand and he thrust. The blade, too insubstantial to be entirely repelled by conventional shields, stabbed through and took Malevorn in the side as he desperately twisted away. He shouted in alarm and pain as his aura was slashed open and ghostly blood sprayed.

Not a fatal blow, but a wound to his aura is a drain on his gnosis, Alaron thought. *A good start . . .*

Malevorn backed away, eyes widening. 'You've *never* been able to do that, Mercer!' He adjusted his shields, which was obviously a strain; his aura was still bleeding. Though the old Malevorn wouldn't have even been able to do that . . .

He really does have all of the gnosis too. Alaron bit his lip: he had to land a serious blow soon, but he was running out of ideas. Malevorn now wore a look of absolute concentration on his face, and his blade had all its usual deadly grace.

Now what? How about . . .

Alaron released the spiratus blade and lunged with his staff again, throwing in a twist of illusion, so that Malevorn's parry went too high; he then jammed the lower end of the kon-staff into his foe's thigh and gnostic-fire seared flesh: not a dangerous wound, but one that might slow him. *Ha!* he shouted inwardly.

But Malevorn's flesh re-knit in seconds. 'Interesting,' the Inquisitor grimaced, bounding back and unleashing a flurry of blows, his own blade flashing in six directions at once, as a torrent of air and fire gusted through the air between them. It was Alaron's turn to blanch as the unexpected attacks carved up the space between them. Only a frantic dart backwards prevented the Inquisitor's blade from plunging into his stomach. He beat the blade away, lunging and retreating, still buying time.

Malevorn's face was confident once more. 'Corineus Himself has blessed me, Mercer. I can do *anything* I want with the gnosis when He is with me.' He lunged again, another combination of illusory blades and one deadly and very real sword, thrusting straight for Alaron's throat – only a flash of divining-gnosis anticipated precisely where the real blow was intended and he jerked aside, the blades drawing a line of sparks through his shields.

Malevorn growled in frustration as he circled again, but his confidence had clearly been restored. It was beginning to feel like only a matter of time.

Alaron's spirits sagged. *He can do anything I can . . . Hel, he's always been better than me, and he still is . . .*

It was a crushing blow, after all he'd been through, to find his rival had somehow managed to match him.

But how? How he has he gained what I have? Why is his aura different? It's as if he's pulling his powers from another place . . .

Then Malevorn came at him again in a whirl of gnosis that pummelled every facet of his defences, and all he could do was block, shield and give ground, until a sight-defying slash pierced his defences . . .

Corinea had fallen through some gateway into another world. Though her body lay in the midst of battle, her awareness of it was gone. She was pure spirit here, still holding the spiratus of her dagger in her right hand. The memory of Johan's blood made the blade glisten scarlet.

Before her was a vast plain. In the middle rose a mountain that grew in size as she flashed towards it. The peak was shaped as a throne, and seated on it was a being who looked just like the Rondians pictured Kore: a white-robed man with lightning grasped in his fists. She felt like an insect before him.

The giant figure was Johan Corin. This was *his* world, *his* reality.

She cried aloud to see him, but he appeared to be intent on a scene playing out in a bubble of light floating before him. As she drew closer she saw that it was the battle between Alaron and Ramita's monks and Malevorn Andevarion's beastmen.

Then he caught sight of her own body, lying stricken amid the tangled corpses, and he turned . . . *and he saw her.*

His eyes bulged, his jaw dropped and he rose to his feet. '*SELENE!*' he thundered, in a voice that managed to convey rage and fear and a thousand other emotions. His cry struck her like a blow, almost ripping her out of his world. A thousand other voices gibbered around her, each individual but somehow part of him, and for a moment he wasn't a man at all, but a giant blob of eyes and mouths and deformed spiratus bodies, all horribly melted into each other in a hideous tangle of limbs and faces. Then he was himself again, terrified and furious to have his sanctum penetrated. He lifted one hand to a phantom sun and it blazed like a weapon.

'HOW DARE YOU BE HERE!'

Johan, what have you become? She found herself filled with horror and pity, but there was no time; he threw the lightning-bolt in his hand, glowing with the power from the sun, and her hand rose in reflex, holding the spell-encrusted dagger before her. He recognised it, and his fear outweighed all else: the weapon – his nemesis and bane when he had lived – caught the blaze of power and shielded her, sending reflected bolts sparkling off into the skies.

A chorus of dismay rose from his throat, and again came the hints of other faces. He flinched from her and his voice fragmented as different facets cried simultenously:

'HOW CAN YOU BE HERE—?'

'YOU SLEW ME—!'

'BUT I LIVED—!'

'SUBMIT TO ME!'

She didn't immediately understand, wanting so badly to see only him, but there were so many others—

Then she remembered and finally understood: Corineus had risen a Souldrinker, and when he died, he'd entered the aether, as all spirits did – but he was a drinker of souls, so he must have become a predator in the aether too. The more spirits he consumed, the more he *needed:* he had become *more than* a daemon: he was a web of souls, the sum of every part that formed him. No wonder his Ablizians were able to use every form of the gnosis: everyone whose soul he swallowed became another tool in his massive armoury.

How the dead souls must have flocked to him – he'd scarcely have needed to hunt, she thought. *'Be as one with your Saviour!' – that would have been all the lure he needed. If gods existed, they would be like this. Like* him . . .

'Oh my love,' she breathed, because she had never forgotten their great love; she wanted only to save him.

He saw that, and his face changed. '*Corinea?*' he said, the special name he'd given her long before it became a curse, and he smiled *that* smile, the special one, the wild, intoxicating look that had stolen her heart when he'd been a young man aflame with mad ideas and determined to change the world. That was the face he'd worn as he seduced her, won her body, her heart and her soul.

He reached down to her, his voice changing, becoming his alone. 'My darling,' he breathed. 'You've come back to me.'

His face appeared, and then Lillea Sorades was that young woman again, the one who'd been enraptured, in love and loved by the most wonderful, most charismatic man she'd ever dreamed of, travelling Yuros, free and enlightened – in love with ideas; in love with love, and about to change the world . . .

Tipping points can be tiny things, little details that nudge giant forces a fraction from their path and cause consequences that might never have been to suddenly appear inevitable. If the spear-head hadn't landed next to Ramita's thigh, she would never have picked it up; she would never have been holding it as disaster loomed.

But she was.

She had spent months under Master Puravai's training, learning with Alaron and Corinea, and she could now wield at least a fragment of every aspect of the gnosis. She held onto the spear-head, intending only to keep it from Malevorn, anything to give her lover a chance of victory, but it pulled her psyche from her body with terrifying ease and she found herself *whooshing* along a path of light, flying through the minds of bewildered and terrified Ablizians, seeing ghostly shadows of the Zains and the Ablizians still fighting, visible to her through their auras. She'd barely begun to take that in, when she fell through a blaze of fire, into another place . . .

. . . to see Corinea had got there before her. She was young again, a dreamy, blissful look on her face as a glorious blond man, the most handsome man Ramita had ever seen, bent over her, one hand tilting her head to his, their lips straining towards a kiss . . . while the hand behind his back became a giant claw with razor-tipped nails . . .

She screamed a warning . . .

*

. . . and Lillea recoiled, the scales falling from her eyes.

The last time she'd seen Johan, they'd been locked in a shared dream, her newly formed gnostic aura entwining their minds – until he pulled out a dagger and tried to kill her.

That same dagger she held in her hand.

She stabbed him again . . .

. . . and Malevorn's senses were overwhelmed by the most horrendous of screams, from a man's voice that echoed through the link that joined him to the spear-head, and to every one of the Ablizians, to the thing in the aether that was Bahil-Abliz, that was Corineus.

He fell to his knees, and as his god howled inside his skull, he sensed his Ablizians collapsing all around him.

Somehow, even through Corineus' agony, he was dimly aware that Mercer had rolled away from him and was using healing-gnosis to seal the slash to his belly.

His chance to administer the fatal blow had slipped away, but he just couldn't move, couldn't *think*.

Then the whole tapestry of gnosis he'd wrought was torn apart with a whirling rush, leaving him alone inside his skull. They staggered to their feet at the same time, but Mercer was healed and moving freely, while Malevorn was trying to cope with the realisation that Corineus was gone from inside him: his personal gnosis was all he had left again, and that was in tatters. He rebuilt his shields, pale shadows of what he'd had, and sought a way to run.

For a few seconds Mercer didn't appear to realise anything had changed; he still fought defensively with that *stupid stick* – then he coupled that with an Illusion which left Malevorn flailing, and the stick slammed into his chest and knocked him backwards ten yards or more, his shields stressed, his ribs cracked and his breath wheezing. He rose, panting, as Mercer closed in and blows came raining in.

I'm going to die . . .

He shouted with his mind, <*CORINEUS! COME BACK TO ME!*>

But there was only silence.

'*YOU HAVE SLAIN OUR GOD!*' he cried. Rage turned the world scarlet, and he went at Mercer in a berserk rage.

Something's happened to Malevorn. That was all Alaron registered; that somehow his foe had lost something, his shielding was now weak, his aura paler and earthen again, no longer multi-hued. So he attacked before his enemy could regain what he'd lost, throwing everything he had into it. He was using all facets of the gnosis, every trick he'd learned, and it was working; he was driving Malevorn backwards into the rubble surrounding the plaza, then he blasted him over backwards, took a breath and glanced left and right.

What the Hel?

The monks were surrounding them, blocking wherever Malevorn might have wanted to run, their faces blood-spattered and grim as executioners. All of the Ablizians were either down, or standing motionless with vacant expressions on their faces.

'*YOU HAVE SLAIN OUR GOD!*' Malevorn shouted, and launched himself at Alaron like a madman, blasting away with no vestige of control, all restraint gone – and all that much-vaunted technique lost as well.

Alaron felt like he was at the eye of a storm, calm and aware, able to deal with whatever was coming: deflecting, parrying, even preparing his counter-attack. He started with Necromancy, a Study he'd never been able to grasp at the Arcanum, and a withering blast of death-energy crackled through Malevorn's shields.

The Inquisitor staggered and his face, always older than his years, visibly aged and his temples turned to silver.

'Surrender,' Alaron said, though he knew yielding wasn't in Malevorn's nature.

The Inquisitor roared like a rabid beast, gripped his sword in two hands and hurled himself at Alaron, not even bothering to defend himself.

Alaron darted sideways and slammed down his kon-staff, breaking Malevorn's grip on his sword, then he infused it with raw energy and rammed it through Malevorn's guard. The metal heel broke the frayed shields and plunged into Malevorn's chest like a spear-thrust.

The concussion of force smashed his ribs and flayed the vital organs, and his old nemesis pitched onto his back.

Malevorn sighed heavily, as if this was all just too tiring. One word fell from his lips: 'Corineus . . .'

Then he died.

Alaron had thought he would feel pity, or triumph, but he felt neither. He closed his burning eyes and just stood there, afraid of what he might do if he allowed the anger in his heart free rein. He'd been beaten, bullied and tormented by Malevorn Andevarion for too many years to be able to take his death with total equanimity – but in the end his vision and his brain cleared.

Then he sprinted to Ramita's side and rolled her over. Her clothes were burned away at the front, her hair too, and the skin of her face and chest was blackened, cracked and weeping. But she was alive, and for a mage with healing-gnosis, those were not serious wounds.

At the first touch of his gnosis, Ramita convulsed, and her eyes flew open.

He was scared to pull her to him in case it hurt her, but she held up a hand and stared at it, and the skin reformed perfectly, new skin flowing over the wounded flesh like water; the most sudden and incredible healing-gnosis he'd ever seen. *I wonder if there are any limits to her strength?*

Not that he cared. He threw his arms around her and pushed the rest of the world away.

A moment – *a lifetime* – later, he kissed her, drank in her face, then disentangled, dreading to think who might be dead from among his friends.

A spear-head encrusted with diamonds caught his eye first, lying in the dust at Ramita's side. But the diamonds were blackened and fading into lifelessness even as he went to pick it up. As his fingers touched the spear, he glimpsed something so massive and chilling that his brain couldn't take it in: *immensity*, like a sea of stars or a flood of eyeballs the size of worlds, but they were all flying in different directions, silently shrieking.

Then Corinea was inside his skull: looking young and beautiful and wild, a knife as bright as suns in her hand. She turned to look at him, her eyes wet with helpless grief and wonder.

I killed him again, she whispered. *I had to kill him again.*

Like a starburst, the ocean of eyes burst apart and there was only her.

He dropped the artefact and his vision cleared in time to hear the last of the remaining Ablizians scream as one. The inside of their skulls blazed with light exploding from eye sockets and open mouths, and then they all collapsed.

The battlefield fell utterly silent.

Alaron felt hollowed out, empty. He wanted to be alone, to process all he'd seen and done, to curl up in a bundle under a blanket with Ramita's head resting on his chest, to sleep for a week, a month, a year . . .

But there were tasks to be done, first and foremost of which was the burning of their dead. He joined the surviving Merozains, only seven still on their feet, and together they used Fire-gnosis to immolate their fallen.

Yash said the words of farewell: for Meero, and Urfin, and brave Kedak who'd been cut down and Alaron never knew until afterwards, and five other young men he'd trained with and seen wake from the ambrosia eager to embrace a new life.

I led them to this end, he reflected, angry and sad and proud at once. It was easy for others to say, 'Blame our enemies', but Malevorn and his creatures hadn't been the enemy of these young men until Alaron drew them into the struggle.

There were tears on the survivors' faces, but thankfully – because he didn't think he could have borne it – no reproach. He couldn't have blamed them if there had been. But after the prayers had been spoken, each brother went down the line, hugging each survivor tightly, and they all thanked him for the skills he'd imparted.

'You kept me alive, Pahali,' they said.

It was daunting, to have so many lives depending on him, but it didn't fill him with fear as once it might. It made him feel brave.

Afterwards, Alaron went looking for Ramita. He found his wife huddled on a stone bench overlooking a blasted courtyard that was still strewn with Ablizian bodies. He sank to his knees as she turned to him, and they hugged fiercely, each clasping the other as if they were the only solid things left in a shifting, untrustworthy world.

'Nasatya isn't here,' Ramita whispered, tears streaming down her face. 'I can't find him *anywhere*.'

He just held her, unable to find any words that might help.

Finally, when she'd cried herself out, she stroked his face. 'Are you all right, husband?'

Alaron thought about that. 'I'm fine, I suppose. We've lost ... Kedak, Meero, Jharaad ... eight dead in all, and four badly wounded. But we won,' he added proudly. 'All the training, all the work ... It was enough. Just.'

'My father would say that hard work brings rewards.'

'So would mine.' Alaron smiled fondly, wondering where his father was. 'Malevorn and those creatures – they stole their powers from somewhere. They never learned all that we did, so when whatever it was that was fuelling them disappeared, they didn't have the skills to cope ...'

'Huriya was like that. I worked to make things; she charmed others into giving them to her.' Ramita's eyes were bright with tears and vindication. 'Al'Rhon, why isn't Nasatya here?'

'I don't know. But we won't stop looking, I promise.'

She squeezed this hands. 'So your enemy is dead?'

'He is. You know, at the Arcanum, Malevorn Andevarion was considered the epitome of the perfect pure-blood mage. The tutors all held him up as a role-model. And truly, he wasn't lazy – he worked harder than anyone – but he was vindictive and cruel, a bully, *and they didn't care*. He lorded it over us all in the name of his precious *honour*. He hurt people for pleasure and broke things for fun. He didn't even believe in the church he claimed to serve. So I'm glad he's gone and I never want to speak of him again.'

'Then let us forget him,' Ramita replied. 'Did you find the Scytale?'

Alaron looked down at the bundles beside his feet. 'He had it on him. And that spear-head ... I don't understand what it does, but it's too dangerous to touch.'

Ramita looked at the wrapped artefacts. 'I honestly don't know how I survived when he used it against me – but the Goddess upheld me: she warned me, and fed me strength, enough to survive and reach him.'

'The Goddess?' he enquired, gently sceptical.

'Yes! I felt her touch me, in the throes of battle. She warned me to shield from the spear, then upheld me through his attack.' She looked up. 'I saw inside the heads of those Ablizians: their god was with them, giving them their power; so why not mine?'

'I don't think what was in their heads was a god,' he replied, but his mind was going over what Malevorn had said during the fight, about being the chosen of Corineus, some rot like that. 'Some daemons pretend to be gods to help them possess stupid people.'

'*Stupid people?*'

'I meant Malevorn,' he said quickly. 'Not you! *Never* you!'

She gave him a very hard look. 'I can well imagine that what was in Malevorn's creatures was a daemon, because *his* god doesn't exist. But I also know what I felt.'

Alaron swallowed apologetically and they fell silent until Corinea appeared, wandering out of an alley as if this were a garden she was strolling in, a glazed look on her face.

I had to kill him again, she'd said. He stood and walked to the ancient mage-woman, offering an embrace that she accepted wordlessly. He couldn't imagine how she must be feeling.

'I'm sorry,' he whispered, feeling helpless.

'Life is a circle,' she said, hugging him in return, then stepped away and glanced over his shoulder at Ramita. 'That was me, inside her mind,' she said softly. 'She'd forgotten to shield – she wouldn't have survived. I lent her strength through a mystic link until she reached him. But I'm not going to tell her, and nor should you. She needs her beliefs.'

Alaron nodded mutely. 'Is Corineus ... is he truly dead now?'

'I don't know. But I think so. I hope so.' She hugged him again, then sighed wearily and went and sat with Ramita, laying her head in the Lakh girl's lap and closing her eyes. Ramita looked up at Alaron, puzzled, then cradled the Queen of Evil and whispered something Alaron couldn't hear.

We're all damaged, every one of us. Images of the battle returned, and he found himself trembling at the eye-blink luck that had kept them all alive. *Please, let this be the end of the war . . . if wars ever truly end.*

Ebensar Heights, Zhassi Valley, on the continent of Antiopia
Thani (Aprafor) 930
22nd month of the Moontide

Alaron found a relay-stave wrapped up with the Scytale. He kept it close, because it seemed inevitable someone would use it. That contact came the evening after the destruction of Malevorn's creatures, as he and Ramita sat on a salvaged Mirobezian carpet in one of the less damaged houses surrounding Ebensar Plaza. A half-eaten meal was spread between them. Corinea was eating with the Brothers, and Yash and Tegeda were off together, doing what young lovers the world over did.

The house Alaron and Ramita found to sleep in had enough repairable furniture for them to be somewhat comfortable for a day or two, and from the eastern window they overlooked the valley below, where Rashid Mubarak's Keshi army were encamped. The Keshi army hadn't moved, but their scouts had been circling closer, obviously trying to work out if they were still facing an enemy army.

The answer to that question was 'barely'. The Rondian First Army, shorn of its generals and battle-magi, was camped two miles further south on the ridge, paralysed by indecision. Corinea had been scrying them and reported nightly desertions as individual men and even whole cohorts gave up and headed for the Leviathan Bridge.

When the relay-stave lit up and began to quiver, he touched Ramita's shoulder and put a finger to his lips, before grasping the stave.
<Hello?>

A frosty, fragrant mind like cold roses brushed his. *<Who is this?>* a female voice said, level and dispassionate: a Pallas accent, lordly and commanding – but there was a definite hint of uncertainty.

<You first,> he sent back; something in her tones had immediately set his teeth on edge. He tossed a cup of water into the air and bound it to the stave; a liquid image of the other person appeared, a pristine, bloodless face of regal dignity and disdain.

Her lips thinned as she regarded him in turn. *<My name is Lucia Sacrecour. You may address me as 'Your Holiness'.>*

His heart thudded. *Mater-Imperia herself.* He found himself tongue-tied, to his extreme annoyance, until she demanded, *<Where is Malevorn Andevarion? Are you one of his servants?>*

She's been talking to Malevorn? Holy Hel! But she clearly doesn't know what's happened here! That ignorance humanised her, and he pulled himself together. *<I'm sorry, he's indisposed, your Holiness.>*

<No one is indisposed if I ask for them, boy. Get him!>

Alaron glanced at Ramita, who looked distinctly unimpressed at this brush with Rondian royalty. *<I'm sorry, your Holiness, but it's really not possible.>*

Lucia's face radiated cold anger. *<Who are you?>*

<I'm the new bearer of the Scytale of Corineus,> he told her, and watched with interest as relief and confusion and greed flashed across Lucia Sacrecour's visage before she could control them.

<You have the Scytale? But Malevorn Andevarion—?>

<He's dead. I had to kill him.>

She recovered with remarkable celerity. *<Then the emperor himself yearns to greet you! You are his slayer? What's your name? All of Rondelmar is in your debt—!>*

<I very much doubt that,> Alaron responded. *<The Scytale won't be going anywhere near your realm, not ever again.>*

The Living Saint's face filled with barely repressed fury. *<You fool—! Do you comprehend my reach, boy? I have only to command a death and it happens, in Yuros or in Antiopia!>*

Alaron was about to retort when Ramita grabbed the stave and broke the connection. The globe of water hanging in the air sprayed

609

over him, soaking his grey robe. He threw his hands up in exasperation. 'What did you do that for? I was just getting warmed up!'

'You were getting angry,' Ramita said mildly. 'No one bargains
well in anger.'

He opened his mouth crossly, then closed it again.

'In Aruna Nagar we say you should reveal neither what you know,
nor what you don't know.'

'Rondian traders say the same,' he admitted. 'You were right; I
wasn't keeping my cool.' And her words reminded him of something
else too. 'As well as Nasatya, we have to find my father. I'm scared
someone will hold them both over us, like in Teshwallabad.'

She put her hands over his. 'Husband, at the Mughal's Dome in Teshwallabad you willingly exchanged the Scytale for the lives of my sons.
I love you for that. If you must do the same for your father, you must.'

'Best we remain a secret, then. If the emperor and his court don't
know who we are, then they don't know what they can hold over
us – which means you were right.'

'As always.'

They shared a grin, and the tension drained out of him. He sighed
tiredly. 'I suppose we should move on from here.'

'Yes, but not tonight.' Ramita looked up at him tiredly. 'Husband,
tonight I'm very proud of you. But I feel sad . . . and *awfully* tired,
and I wish to sleep.'

He gathered her to him, lifted her and carried her towards their
tent. She was asleep before he got her inside.

The next morning they all rose before the sunrise, returned to
their windcrafts and were gone before the sun kissed the ridge.

Ebensar Ridge, Zhassi Valley, on the continent of Antiopia
Thani (Aprafor) 930
22nd month of the Moontide

Salim Kabarakhi I, Sultan of Kesh, sat alone in his silken pavilion,
wondering if the time had come to abandon the shihad – not officially,

of course, never that. But the time for one battle was ending. Another bloody and fruitless assault on Ebensar Heights would be stupidity ittself. The scarlet tides were ebbing, flowing westwards towards the Bridge. The Moontide was almost done, and his armies – his *people* – were exhausted.

Wars needed manpower; they needed food, equipment and money. They also needed willpower, the emotional stamina to keep going. The victory at Shaliyah had given his people a great burst of vigour for the fray, but that was subsiding as the cease-less fighting took its toll. There had been no further successes to buoy their morale, just awful, grinding defeats. The hope of fresh victories was receding, overtaken by the recognition that this was all attritional now, grinding at the enemy to deter them from ever returning.

But have we done enough?

He'd reunited his army, joining forces again with Rashid, in part to reassert his authority: the emir's men had not seen their sultan for almost two years, and he wanted no confusion in their minds when it came to Rashid's position as his subordinate.

Recently there had been a terrifying new turn of events: a Gatti border-town called Vaqo, far behind the lines, had been completely razed, then a Rondian-held fortress at Sukkhil-wadi had been simi-larly destroyed. There were no survivors at either place; no reports of what had happened. It was as if some deadly storm were striking at random, taking lives on either side, without reason or explana-tion. Even Rashid was at a loss – he claimed the vast expenditure of magical energies was well beyond his own experience. There had been another such outpouring in a supposedly deserted town only twelves miles to the south, at Zarrabadh. Whatever was happening was coming closer and closer.

Then, two nights ago, there had been another gnostic-firestorm, centred around the castle of Ebensar itself. The fort was clearly dam-aged, and now he wasn't sure whether to advance or retreat. Scouts had been sent out; he awaited them impatiently.

There was a discreet chiming on the gong that hung outside his tent, followed by a servant entering, bowing and prostrated himself before declaring, 'Great Sultan, Emir Rashid begs audience.'

Salim pursed his lips. He'd issued instructions not to be disturbed unless the world ended – or the scouts were returned – and yet here was Rashid again, pushing boundaries others daren't.

He is a mage – he thinks himself above the rules. How will we contain him after this war?

'He may enter,' Salim told the servant, resigned.

But it wasn't the usual Rashid who entered the tent; that creature was almost serpentine in all his poised, glittering grace and complexity. This Rashid was someone else entirely: an excited student who had just graduated. He scampered into the pavilion, forgot to bow – forgot how to speak for a few seconds – and then blurted, 'Great Ahm on High! Salim, you must come—!'

Salim came to his feet, emotions racing through irritation to bewilderment to fear to excitement. 'Emir Rashid!' he snapped, to remind him of his standing, 'Stop! Tell me: what is it?'

Rashid dropped to his knees on the prayer mat facing Hebusalim and kissed the ground. 'Sal'Ahm!' he cried again, 'Sal'Ahm on High!'

Salim went over to him and laid a hand on his shoulder – a shocking breach of protocol – but Rashid's behaviour made *no* sense: all this awed excitement, as if the Prophet had returned. 'What is it, Rashid?'

Rashid lifted his head, clutched his hand and kissed it. 'Great Sultan – I bring you joyous tidings!'

'What? What has happened?' Salim demanded in exasperation.

Tears began to stream down Rashid's face. 'Great Sultan, the scouts have returned with a herald from the Rondian First Army. They wish to *surrender*.'

34

Jekuar

Magi and Battlefield Supremacy

After the Ascendancy, the magi were the dominant piece on the battlefield. But their role has changed over time. The first Ascendants used only Thaumaturgy, destroying legions with Fire- and energy-blasts. Since then the magi have learned other uses of the gnosis – but most now are of lower blood. Meanwhile, the legions have developed superior archery and siege-weapons, and better tactics for combating magi; no longer can one man with the gnosis easily vanquish hundreds of ordinary soldiers. The role of the mage on the battlefield is now more focused upon reconnaissance, coordinating attacks, disrupting the enemy with precision strikes and duelling each other.

GENERAL RHYNUS BERGIUM,
IMPERIAL LEGION COMMANDER, PALLAS, 908

Jekuar, Javon, on the continent of Antiopia
Thani (Aprafor) 930
22nd month of the Moontide

Gurvon Gyle looked across the plains and asked, 'Endus, my friend, how did it come to this?'

Endus Rykjard gave him a puzzled look. 'Well, after Forensa—'

'I was speaking rhetorically,' Gyle interrupted.

'You should have said.' The Hollenian looked irrepressibly cheery, exuding confidence: *Look like a winner, and you'll be one* was his mantra.

Gurvon couldn't say he felt the same. *The Nesti flags still fly over there. Rutt failed in his sacrifice, though he did at least kill Timori Nesti . . . but he hasn't destroyed the unity of our enemy.*

He knew who to blame. *I should have killed Cera and Elena when I had the chance. But this is still a battle we can win, especially if Aranio plays his part . . .*

Gyle and Rykjard were in the command position, at the centre of their lines. They'd set up along a low ridge facing east, straddling the main road near a tiny mud-brick village called Jekuar, eighty miles east of Brochena and twenty southwest of Riban. 'The Battle of Jekuar,' Gurvon murmured, trying out the sound of it. What songs would the bards compose to remember it? What lessons would it teach to history?

He really just wanted it to be over so he could retreat from the glare of visibility to the back stairs and shadowy alleys that were his natural habitat. *Even during the Noros Revolt, I fought behind the lines. I'm a spy, not a bloody king . . . I should've stuck to what I'm good at.*

He had a sudden urge to apologise to Rykjard. 'Endus, it wasn't supposed to be like this. Elena should have done her job – there'd be no rallying point without her; no Cera Nesti to unite them. We'd have occupied the whole of Javon without a fight.'

'Aw, where's the fun in that?' Rykjard grinned.

'I guess I'm just bitter, that's all. Elena's made it complicated – she's forced me to improvise, and now we're trapped in this bloody cycle. Even if we win here, we're going to have to re-conquer the whole damned country.'

'Victory here will knock the stuffing out of them,' Rykjard predicted. 'Chin up, Gurv. We've got the better ground, the better men, agents inside the enemy command tent and numbers on our side. What could go wrong?'

I know Endus is right . . . After all, he *did* have the better position – and something else up his sleeve that even Endus didn't know about.

They reviewed the order of battle together: Roland Heale's Dorobon legion, only about three thousand men since Forensa, were on the left. He could count on them: they had nowhere else to go. In the centre was Rykjard's legion, a little under-strength after losses at Lybis earlier that year, but loyal, no doubt of that. That was more than he could say about his right, where he'd placed Hans Frikter's Argundians; barely two thousand remained in fighting condition, and since Forensa they'd been positively mutinous. To bolster them, he'd quietly brought three thousand of Adi Paavus' men north from the Krak; he was risking losing the fortress to gain victory here. He really hoped Elena hadn't got wind of that.

Protecting both flanks and poised to sweep in were the Harkun, led by Ghujad iz'Kho, some six thousand riders in all – all of them survivors of the carnage at Forensa. They gave him little confidence; he doubted they'd stick if things began badly. Iz'Kho had sent most of his surviving riders to the Rift Forts, to try and capture them and so bring more men up, but so far the Forts were holding.

So: seventeen thousand men, roughly told. He thought about who they were matched against, trying to weigh the odds.

The enemy's right, facing the Dorobon, were the Aranio, Rimoni cavalry and footmen, just about a full legion, but unblooded – and more importantly, he was inside Stefan di Aranio's head: the Lord of Riban was primed to run at the first chance. But that could change if the Nesti had some early successes.

On the enemy left: the Kestrians. They'd fought at Forensa so more than likely they were depleted – but they were hardened soldiers. They'd be up against Adi Paavus' best, plus three thousand Harkun.

The enemy centre would be held by Rimoni of Forensa – only around two thousand of them, from what he could determine. Most of the Nesti fighting men were safely chained up in the Gorgio slave-mines, hundreds of miles away in Hytel. But they did have the Jhafi militia, five thousand or more ragged, poorly equipped Noories of the sort who'd somehow held up Hans Frikter at Forensa. They'd been defending their city then, fighting for their home; an exposed battlefield in the middle of nowhere was a different sort of fight entirely.

So he made it roughly seventeen thousand men each: too even for his liking, but his magi were fighting men, not scholars like the Ordo Costruo. *We should be victorious . . . especially with our little surprise . . .*

'What's your first move, Endus?'

The Hollenian wrinkled his nose. 'We've got the best of the ground, and we're dug in through the centre and left. We'd do best to defend initially, let 'em beat their heads against our shield wall until they've knocked themselves silly, then counter-charge.'

'If either flank gives way, the Harkun there will bolt,' Gyle warned.

'I know that, and so do Heale and Paavus.' Rykjard peered away toward the hazy southern flank. 'Adi's the key. We've tried to disguise his legion as Frikter's, and we're keeping most of the men behind the ridge so the Kestrians will think they're up against a weakened force. The plan is to lure 'em in, then once they're committed to the attack, I'll loose the Harkun at their flank.'

Gyle nodded approvingly. 'It sounds good. I'm taking our skiffs up to prevent Elena's magi from overflying us and spotting Adi's men.'

And that has the added advantage of me being in the air already if this goes badly.

'I love this moment, when everything's still perfect,' Rykjard said with a relaxed smile. 'From now on, it all gets messy.' He approximated a salute and walked back to the cluster of magi and tribunes, already beginning to gesticulate. Orders were scrawled and signed, messengers scattered. In the distance, the village bell in Jekuar chimed thrice: the third hour of daylight.

It was time go to war.

Cera Nesti wondered if she was going to be sick. Every man who marched past her was going into mortal danger: many would be crippled for life, or lie buried in an unmarked grave after a few hours of savagery. They'd hack at other men with sharpened metal until something vital was hurt beyond bearing, then collapse, only to be stabbed or trampled or simply ignored while they bled to death.

Dead, like Timori.

It was what she'd seen on the streets of Forensa and she was trying to steady herself to go through the same ordeal here. She'd thought she would be burning for vengeance, but instead she just felt ill. *Is anything worth this?* she asked herself for the hundredth time.

Everyone around her seemed to think it was. Even those who'd been through it before looked eager to get started, as if this were an unpleasant but necessary task, like digging a ditch or burning out a roach nest. Scouts and runners were coming in all the time, clamouring for attention if their news was urgent, or waiting patiently in line until Piero Inveglio was free. She had made the comte her battlefield commander, over the heads of Stefan di Aranio and Justiano di Kestria: the old Rimoni nobleman was the highest-ranked man with any expertise in battle left to the Nesti family. Justiano and Stefan hadn't been happy about it, but she'd told them to do their duty and win glory by contributing to victory.

Glory . . . what is it anyway? Isn't it enough to win?

'They've put what's left of Frikter's men on our left,' Justiano's messenger was explaining. 'We can cut through them – it's where they're weakest.'

Piero Inveglio was nodding, his sharp face taut with anxiety. He clearly didn't relish the role of commander, but no one else in Nesti colours had his experience. Thankfully, Theo Vernio-Nesti was still days away from joining them, something she was beginning to think might be deliberate. That line had always been a nest of cowards – the only members of the family who hadn't risen against the Dorobon during either occupation.

'I agree,' Stefan di Aranio announced. 'Let the Kestrians attack on the left.' He'd been chipping in nonstop all morning, suggesting anything that didn't involve his people taking risks. Cera trusted him less and less as battle approached.

Inveglio looked skywards. It was still early morning; the third bell had just chimed. He could delay a decision no longer. 'They are dug in. It will likely not be so easy as you believe.'

Cera turned to Odessa D'Ark. 'Odessa, is there some way we can end this swiftly?'

The expectant mother was plainly in discomfort, which only emphasised their desperate straits – Kazim had not regained consciousness and Elena could barely stand without him, so there was no way they could spare her.

Odessa grimaced. 'Of course. Kill Gurvon Gyle.'

'Is that possible?'

'Anything's possible. But he'll not be making himself obvious.'

'The stories say that in the early times, disputes between villages would be settled by heroes fighting on behalf of everyone, so that fewer people would suffer,' Cera suggested. 'Is there any such tradition in Yuros?'

'Not among magi,' Odessa replied drily. 'We've never been shy about letting others die in our stead. Anyway, Gyle would laugh in our faces.'

'What about this question of where to attack?'

'I'm not a general. Elena knows war, not me. I'm just here to keep you alive.'

'Attacking on the left is a stupid rukking idea,' rasped an unexpected voice, and Cera's heart leapt to her throat as she whirled.

'*Elena?*'

Her champion looked awful: sickly-faced, grey about the temples and not even clad in armour. Her breathing was laboured and she was using a wooden staff to compensate for her left knee; she couldn't put weight on it. But she was *here*. Cera choked up. At last she managed, 'You should be in bed!'

'I'll rest afterwards,' Elena croaked.

Cera swallowed. 'Is Kazim—?'

Elena's wounded eyes focused briefly on her. 'Asleep.' She looked away. Her lover hadn't regained consciousness since Timori's assassination, and Elena had quietly confided one night that without him, she had very little gnosis energy: all she had was going into keeping Kazim alive.

'You look like shit,' Odessa snapped. 'Go back to the healers' tent.'

'I can't.' Elena scowled at the clump of arguing men. 'We shouldn't attack on the left. The key advantage to the attacker in battle is the choice of where and how to strike; the art of the defender is to direct the attackers towards a point that is stronger than it looks.' She jabbed a finger at the Rondian right. 'Given we know that Frikter's men were mauled a month ago, they should be hiding them, not waving banners to help us find them.'

'So you're saying Gyle wants us to attack his right?'

'Exactly. But Aranio and Kestria seem to think otherwise and Inveglio doesn't have a clue. Who am I to say: I don't have a cock. But I had better try.' She grimaced at Cera, then hobbled into the argument.

'Send her to the rear,' Odessa muttered. 'She's going to get herself killed.'

From the air, it all looked different. Gurvon rejoiced to be above, detached by distance. His windskiff went whisking along the lines, flanked by two others piloted by Brossian and Veritia, as he got the shape of the battle from above. From up here, the units stopped being people, instead resembling tabula pieces, their individuality subsumed into the greater whole.

He pictured Elena in the lines opposite, giving terse advice and snapping at the knights and officers, cutting off their half-baked ideas with a withering comment. She'd always been more at home in such scenes: a player, not an observer.

But Endus is playing my pieces, and he's better versed than either of us.

He conjured a face in the air and reached out to make contact, to reassure himself. Gabrien Gorgio-Sintro appeared, Ricardo's older brother.

Ricardo had been left in Hytel to secure the city – and, of course, Portia Tolidi. *I'm not sure I'd trust any brother of mine with her.*

Gabrien was a swarthier man than Ricardo, with a cold, hard face. <*Lord Gabrien,*> Gurvon greeted him. <*When will you arrive?*>

'Inside two hours,' Gabrien responded, speaking aloud. 'My men are jogging.'

<*In this heat?*>

'This is not heat, Rondian,' Gabrien replied. 'You will see, in summer.'

<*Fair enough! But make sure you don't exhaust your men before the fight.*>

'We'll be ready, Magister Gyle. The Gorgio and the Nesti have a long history.'

He broke the contact and took his skiff on another circuit of the lines, quietly pleased with Gabrien Gorgio-Sintro's demeanour. He looked like a fighting man. He was equally pleased when he saw the Nesti massing to the south: the Kestrian knights were preparing to attack right where he wanted them to.

They're falling for it . . . I think they're falling for it.

His optimism grew as the pieces began to move exactly as Endus had foreseen.

Tabula. That's what we're playing here. Cera tried to tell herself that she had to be dispassionate about all this. Victories required sacrifices to achieve victory, they'd lose. She'd read the books, learned the lessons.

But it still made her belly churn to look to the south, her army's left: the Kestrian knights and their levies were marching forward, walking their mounts to the edge of arrow- and crossbow bolt-range, so they wouldn't blow the horses before they hit the enemy lines. She wondered how all those young men felt. Were they frightened rigid, or did their eyes shine with faith? Did they believe in their cause, or were they simply doing their duty? Or was it still just a game to them?

Pawns advance! Knights go forth!

The army was like a great organism, an anthill of movement, a confusion of motion that had an acrid smell of sweat and sickness and the tang of adrenalin and fear. The noise was constant: shouted orders, calls of encouragement, banter between men as they passed each other. Messengers, riders and runners came and went in a blur, men marched by, towards the rise where the Rondians were positioned. She caught her breath at the first volleys of arrows, but they were hers, flying from the Jhafi militia into a clump of distant Harkun horsemen on the left.

'What's happening?' she asked Elena, who was slumped beside her on a young mare, hunched over in the saddle, looking pale and sweaty.

'I couldn't persuade Inveglio not to attack on the left,' she growled. 'The Kestrians are moving forward, with Jhafi skirmishers screening their left to deter the Harkun from attacking their flank. The main body are marching towards Frikter's legionaries: see his banners? I don't know who's in charge of them now.

'Meanwhile we'll hold ground here in the middle, while Aranio pretends to attack on the right, to give Gurvon something else to worry about, so perhaps he won't reinforce Frikter in time.'

Cera peered northwards, almost a mile away, but it was all a blur, nothing more than dark stains on the dun sand. *Knights take mercenaries . . . Please, Pater Sol!*

'The Harkun nomads are returning fire,' Elena reported. 'They're massed to the south of our flank and they're shooting back at the skirmishers. But we've still got a clear run at Frikter's Argies.'

'Is that good?'

'Only if Gyle's an idiot. Or if his men aren't obeying him.'

'That could happen,' Cera said hopefully. 'Why don't we attack with everyone?'

'Stick to law books, Cera. If we over-commit, we've got nothing in reserve if anyone breaks. It's all about holding your line and not getting flanked, even when attacking. If you get flanked, you start losing men at three or four to one. If your line gets broken, same thing, and then it gets ugly, fast.'

The dark smudge of Kestrian footmen went forward first, advancing at a walk as the arrows began to fall among them. They recoiled at a line of undefended trenches, then poured through, while the men coming in behind began ripping out the stakes the Rondians had laid. It looked all very professional, but it was horribly slow when they were under fire.

'Why are they only walking?' Cera asked, appalled.

'You've got to move in a line if you don't want the lead men to be hacked apart before the rest arrive. So you move in an orderly fashion,' Elena replied matter-of-factly. 'Those obstacles slow the advance, give more time for the archers. They'll reform on the other side of the trenches then you'll see them charging at speed. But first – *oh, shit!*'

A blast of flames had erupted from a line of secondary trenches, and even across the distance and above the noise all round them, they could hear the screams of the tiny human torches lurching about blindly. A dismayed cry erupted and the advance stalled, until more men poured through: plumed officers, shouting orders. A robed battle-mage, an Ordo Costruo man, appeared and started dousing a ten-yard-wide area of trench before coming under mage-bolt fire himself. Taking heart, the Rimoni advanced again up the slope, finally reaching the Argundian lines.

The noise rose as Cera jiggled with frightened excitement. For several minutes all she could see was a thick press at the base of the low ridge, slowly bulging at three or four points as the enemy lines gave way and the Rimoni pushed forward, and the Argundians wavered. But the cheers of her men were stifled as the enemy counter-surged, reserves pouring to the breach from behind the ridge the Argundians defended. The distant noise grew more shrill, and then the Kestrians began to retreat down the slope, back to where the next wave were gathering. Further south, a large line of mounted men wheeled towards the Harkun, pennants fluttering on lances.

'Justiano's ordered his knights to drive off the Harkun horse-archers,' Elena reported. She shook her head. 'They won't get near them. And he's making another push against the Argundians.'

More minutes crawled by that must have been hellish in the middle of that press, but from her vantage Cera could only imagine. Every few minutes the front line boiled back or forth as a weak spot was made or found, then it would close. Little waves of momentum built then dissipated, breaking down in the morass of men. Above, six Rondian skiffs were now engaging five Ordo Costruo windcraft – one of the Rondian ones almost immediately burst into flame, and the whole army cheered.

It was almost a half an hour since the engagement began, and it was going well, Cera thought. The Kestrian knights had driven off the Harkun, and the footmen were steadily pushing to the old front line and driving the Rondians back. 'Are we winning?'

'It's too early to say,' Elena replied. 'Frikter's lot aren't breaking, just getting pushed. It's almost got to the point where reinforcements might break them.' She didn't sound like she thought that would happen, though.

Cera glanced to the north and saw that the Aranio were milling well short of the enemy lines. Clouds of arrows were flying. 'What's happening up there?'

'Not enough,' Elena muttered. 'Just archery practise. Aranio is supposed to be advancing, not trading shots.'

Enemy trumpets droned into life, a haunting wail emanating from the southwest, behind the Argundians, and suddenly new banners rose from a point behind the ridgeline, a forest of black and yellow, which poured forward onto Justiano's left flank. Bursts of lightning shot across the gap between the forces, and gouts of flame.

Elena cursed aloud. 'Rukka! It's Adi Paavus' boys! See the yellow serpent? Gyle's brought Adi's boys up from the Krak!' She swore furiously. 'And look at the Harkun— They're wheeling back onto the Kestrian knights – they've been hiding their full numbers too.'

Cera clutched at her heart. 'What's Justiano doing?'

'He's deployed footmen at a fallback position, while trying to counter-charge Adi's lads. It's rukking suicide.' Elena broke off into a coughing fit and almost fell out of the saddle.

The Kestrian knights were indeed on the move: they suddenly kicked into motion, and the ground rippled as the heavy horses lumbered forward, building in momentum as they plunged towards the line of yellow banners. It looked irresistible, until fire and crossbow bolts flew all at once, ripping apart the front riders and cutting deep into those beyond. Cera cried and clutched her stomach as the whole force wavered. Then with a howl, the Harkun blades flashed in the sun and the nomads poured towards the stricken assault. The two forces careered into each other and the Kestrians dissolved.

'I knew this would rukking happen,' Elena muttered, then raised her voice. 'Piero, reinforce the left!'

Piero Inveglio looked increasingly distressed, capering about snapping commands as another flock of runners shot in different directions. One of his aides ran towards her. 'Please, Lady! Retire to the baggage area!'

Cera glared at the boy until he fled.

Queen to the rear. Never!

Her reserve infantry came to life as the army struggled to respond to the unfolding crisis. This was more frightening even than Forensa, where you couldn't see more than a few dozen yards. This was panoramic and all the worse for it.

Pater Sol, be with us. Mater Lune, bring confusion to our enemies! It can't end here – not after all we've been through: it can't!

35

The Last Betrayal

Gods and Daemons

It is intriguing that many of the daemons of the aether have names that can be equated with the names of pagan deities in both continents. The questions raised are obvious.

SAKITA MUBARAK, ORDO COSTRUO, HEBUSALIM, 916

Jekuar, Javon, on the continent of Antiopia
Thani (Aprafor) 930
22ⁿᵈ month of the Moontide

Cera Nesti sipped from her water-flask, trying to quench her parched throat and settle her stomach. Beside her, Elena Anborn was hunched in the saddle, sweating and haggard. A few yards away Comte Piero Inveglio looked little better as he issued orders and missives to the runners, all the while keeping one eye on what was before him. He was forming a new defensive line on the left, sending in reserves to anchor it, to give the Kestrians something to retreat to as they came streaming back from the Rondian lines – they were not quite fleeing, but they were being heavily pursued. The initiative was now clearly held by Gyle's men.

'What about the north?' Cera asked anxiously.

Elena was glaring across the battlefield. 'Aranio was supposed to attack, but he's clearly not going to. All he's done is form a defensive line and let the Harkun pepper him with arrows. Did Piero change his orders, or did he ignore them?' Her rasping voice couldn't conceal her tension. 'The next half hour will decide this.'

A blast of trumpets to the west, in the middle of the Rondian lines, drew their attention back to the centre as the Rondians began to pour over their own barricades in ordered ranks, banners flying. 'Are they attacking our centre?'

Elena's expression grew grimmer. 'Yes, they're attacking here too.'

Cera's mind raced. 'They know something . . . they must do, to feel so confident.' The sick feeling in her belly congealed. She strained her eyes first north, then south, could see nothing, but still the Rondians came forward, leaving their ridge and fortifications and setting up the charge in full view.

This is the end!

Except it wouldn't be: not for her. Gyle would make an example of her, something to be whispered of whenever anyone contemplated rebellion. 'Can we hold them?'

Elena threw her a sick look. 'We're about to find out.'

A mental communication fizzed into Gurvon Gyle's mind from Endus Rykjard. *<I've got ten thousand fucking Gorgio on my left flank!>* the Hollenian drawled. *<Where the Hel did they come from?>*

<All the way from Hytel,> Gurvon smirked. *<That, my friend, is what a long-term bet coming off feels like!>*

<You might have told me they were coming!> Endus grumped. *<I'm coordinating a bloody army here!>*

<I needed to keep it dark, Endus, so the Nesti wouldn't be able to guess they were coming from our deployments.>

<Sure – but I could have left the Harkun entirely on our right, so the Gorgio knights could enter unimpeded.>

<And Elena would've spotted it right off. Know thy enemy, Endus. I'll buy you a drink later and you can tell me what a prick I am.>

<I do that every day. But a free beer will be a novelty.>

Gurvon looked north and saw the arrays of men, both mounted and footmen, all in Gorgio white, pouring in behind the Dorobon legion: ten thousand men, enough to crush the Aranio flank, then pincer the Nesti centre and finish this war.

<All right, keep them coming in behind the Dorobon and push forward on all fronts. We've got to commit the Nesti to the battle now so they can't retreat. We're going to destroy this revolt, right now! Push forward!>

The Rondian assault struck the Nesti centre like a wave, battering at the lines of violet-tabarded Rimoni and rough-clad Jhafi, which reeled and shook and recoiled, barely holding. Rivulets of sweat were running down Elena's face as the fighting edged closer and closer: three hundred yards, then the last two hundred in a rush. Cera was staring motionless, completely caught up in the struggle as it boiled closer and closer to their position.

We're breaking, Elena thought anxiously. *We must hold longer!*

For a few minutes the push and shove staggered this way and that, then suddenly the Nesti ranks were blasted apart in a burst of flame and a wedge of Kirkegarde mage-knights thundered through the gap, footmen following them through like a flash-flood in the rainy season.

Dear Kore, I wish Kaz was here . . .

The emptiness where Kazim should be inside her awareness ached, sucking at her soul. She'd grown so used to having him with her, *in* her mind and heart, that his absence was defining her. She was a husk with a very telling lack of gnosis. She thought she could manage a shield and a few mage-bolts, but after that—

I'm going to last about six seconds against Kirkegarde magi. Some bloody royal champion I am . . .

'Hold them! Hold them!' she shouted, as the Nesti royal guards formed up in front of Cera and the commanders, presenting long spears and preparing to sell their lives dearly. Even Piero Inveglio had drawn his sword now, though his face was despairing.

We need more time . . .

But the Kirkegarde men were coming right for them, carving up the distance between in seconds. The Nesti army folded aside, unable to slow the charge as they thundered out of the middle distance, and suddenly they were *here*.

She blasted at the lead man, but his shields held, so she slammed kinesis at the horses' hooves; she mowed one beast down, sent it tumbling headlong and the rider slammed into the earth at full gallop. His neck snapped in a sickening wet crunch – but there were dozens behind him, lances low and fire blossoming all around them. They hit the ranks of Nesti footmen just as they presented pikes; the long spears skewered steeds and riders in a sudden, sickening tangle of colliding flesh. The whole line bulged backward, and Cera shouted in fright.

Then Elena herself came under attack, mage-bolts slashing at her shields as she made her horse dance, lurching in the saddle as she fought to stay mounted. A crowd of Nesti knights tried to form up to pull Cera away, but the Kirkegarde had punched through already and were streaming in from both flanks and engaging them.

The whole front was dissolving.

'Hold them!' she screamed. 'Hold the line!'

Then she saw, away to the northwest, line upon line of white-clad men marching out of the haze, entering the field behind the Dorobon banners on the extreme left of Gyle's lines. She sucked in a mouthful of air as she recognised the uniforms: *Gorgio of Hytel . . .*

'Hold! Hold!' she shrieked, projecting her voice towards the Kirkegarde commander. She recognised Lann Wilfort's heraldry: she'd not met him, but she knew his reputation as more morally flexible than most. 'Parley! A parley, Grandmaster!'

Wilfort's helmed head swivelled towards her. *<Anborn? A parley?>*

<We need to discuss surrender,> she sent plaintively.

Grandmaster Lann Wilfort reacted to the crackling voice in his mind by raising his bloodied sword, looking left and right, then he sent a stern command to his men to pull back a few paces.

The Nesti centre were broken open, just a thin line of footmen standing between him and the Nesti leaders. He could see Cera Nesti herself, just a bookish girl in violet on a pale horse. She certainly didn't look worthy of all the fuss, and Elena Anborn appeared to have crawled from her sickbed.

A glance to either side showed him that Gyle's army was advancing on all flanks, and victory looked inevitable: sixty minutes or so after the first major contact, which, in his experience, was about right. Unless two armies had vast reserves arriving in staggered groups onto the field, it usually took only an hour or two to crack a line and break it open. The rest of the day would be spent mopping up. The bards who sang of day-long battles were just dressing the ham.

<All right, Anborn,> he sent. *<Let's talk.>*

He knew of Elena Anborn, of course: one of Gyle's people, gone rogue. A veteran of the Noros Revolt, and an operative on the fringe of criminality since. She'd been given an amnesty after the Revolt – all Gyle's people had – as the empire wanted to use them in the Second Crusade, and since then she'd been mostly in the East, Wilfort understood – changing sides and cutting throats.

I don't care what else is agreed, he told himself, *there's no way in Hel she's escaping the noose.*

His men formed up again, facing the Nesti. There were enemy soldiers hurrying in, trying to interpose, but the convention of war said that once surrender was raised, it should not be abused. Not that he believed Anborn gave a shit about conventions, so he kept his sword in hand as he spurred forward.

'Grandmaster Wilfort?' Elena Anborn called.

'I'm Wilfort,' he replied. 'You look like shit.' She did too: she was sweating like a fever-bound child, and beneath her tan she was pallid and drawn. She looked closer to sixty than her reputed age of forty-odd. 'Are you wounded?' he asked, a little puzzled; he could see no blood nor distinctive bandages.

'Just unwell,' she replied, her raspy voice dry, ironic. 'Thanks for the concern.'

He smiled quietly at her off-hand manner, deciding he rather liked her. That wouldn't stop him hanging her, of course. He nudged his horse closer so they could negotiate out of earshot of the riff-raff. 'I could order the charge and you and your queen would be butchered in a few moments. But you offered surrender?'

'I did,' she acknowledged, cocking her head as though listening to something distant. 'I freely offer it.'

'Excellent. Wise, I'm sure. These are my terms: the Nesti girl and her senior aides will be surrendered to me immediately: including yourself and your pet Noorie. The Ordo Costruo may—'

'No, Grandmaster: you misunderstand,' Elena interrupted. 'I'm offering *you* the chance to surrender.'

'You're . . . *what?*'

Roland Heale had already formed his men up before the embankment, facing front and ordered, watching the Harkun wheeling and swirling as they fired their arrows at the massed Rimoni below. They were Aranio's men from Riban, bearing heavy shields and well-drilled: the arrow storm was cutting into them, but most of the shafts were striking shields or armour. They were withdrawing with shields aloft, and looked like any moment they'd simply turn and march away, which Heale understood was something Gyle and Aranio had arranged.

Gyle gets everywhere. The thought wasn't a comforting one: he'd done his own deals with that particular devil and felt good about none of them.

It looks like he's brought us a victory today, though . . .

In the centre the lines were dissolving into mêlée and the momentum was all with Rykjard. There were Kirkegarde banners well in advance of the assault, and the Nesti flags in the centre were down. Collapse was imminent, and the rout would begin.

'Sir,' his closest aide called in an excited voice, 'the Gorgio are here!'

He nodded in acknowledgement: Gyle had taken him aside and warned him to expect a surprise at some point in the day. This must be it. He turned to face the rear, watching the massed ranks of white tabards and green shields tramping towards them, led by a young man with drawn sword and bared teeth: Gabrien Gorgio-Sintro, he presumed from his plumage and shield insignia. He ran his practised eye over the ranks: some fifteen thousand, he estimated – a Hel of a lot of men to march across the land unseen, but Javon was a big place. They looked travel-worn, but eager to join the fray. He raised his hand to their captain: 'Lord Gabrien Gorgio-Sintro?'

The Gorgio lord – the late Alfredo's nephew, if Heale remembered correctly – raised his right hand in return, trotting closer. 'Sir Roland? I am he for whom you have been awaiting,' he said in passable Rondian.

They clasped hands, while the Gorgio officers moved closer, grim-looking men with bitter faces. 'You've marched all the way from Hytel? That's a Hel of a way!'

The young man was so deeply tanned he could almost be a Noorie. His teeth flashed brilliantly as he replied, 'A forced march, ten hours daily, without fortifying our camps – the Jhafi fear us too much to take us on.'

'I'd heard they had you all but locked up inside Hytel,' Heale noted.

'Then you heard wrong,' he replied. 'There was no way we were going to miss out on this!' He surveyed the battlefield. 'You are advancing?'

'We're about to – we've already driven them back in the south and the centre. You're just in time for the rout!'

'Indeed.' He licked his lips. 'Where do you want my men?'

'Put them in behind my ranks and follow us in. Rykjard wants us moving forward as swiftly as possible.'

'Excellent,' he purred and turned to his second, a giant Rimoni with a morose face and drooping moustaches. 'Move the men in behind our friends the Dorobon.' The giant growled some orders, then nudged his horse closer, joined by his fellow officers, who slid in among the half-dozen magi Heale had at his side, those kept back from the frontline. They reluctantly made room for the Gorgio men. 'Where are the Nesti?' the Gorgio lord asked eagerly. 'Show me their banners.' His voice positively dripped with hate.

Heale spent the next few minutes pointing out the enemy positions and explaining their own placements while the Gorgio formed up. 'Basically, the Harkun are pinning the Aranio down until we advance and sweep through them, then we'll swing south.' He waved an arm expansively. 'My front line is ready to move, if your men are?'

He inclined his head.

'Let's unleash Hel,' Heale said grandly.

The Gorgio leaned over and slapped him on the back.

Hard.

It was accompanied by a sharp pain, and a puzzling numbness in his chest. He went to tell the Gorgio boy not to be so forward, but instead, his whole body went into some odd state of disassociation, as if it wasn't his any more. He looked around in sudden alarm and saw the giant Rimoni sweep a greatsword across his chaplain's neck, lopping off his head almost effortlessly, then all about him, his healers and junior magi were stabbed from behind before they could shield. He looked at Gabrien, bewildered. There was a bloody dagger in the Rimoni knight's left hand, and a dark smile on his face.

'Damned Rondian scum,' the Gorgio snarled. 'I'll show you *Hel*.' He pushed the dagger into Heale's throat and wrenched viciously. Blood sprayed, and Sir Roland reeled in the saddle. His horse shrieked and tore loose of his grip, and the ground rose up like a dark wave . . .

Endus Rykjard turned his eyes from the centre where the aether was thrumming with whispers of a Nesti surrender, then north towards the white-clad Gorgio ranks formed up behind the Dorobon, ready to advance. He smiled in grim satisfaction and was turning back to order the centre to advance when an odd movement stayed his eye: there was some kind of a mêlée around Roland Heale's banner, a strange fracas – and then, quite suddenly, from a quarter of a mile away, too far to do anything but *watch*, he saw the unmistakeable sight of massed javelins, hurled from the Gorgio rear . . . *into the backs of the Dorobon legion.*

'*Shizen!*' he bellowed, staring wide-eyed in disbelief, like his aides and bodyguards, as the Gorgio newcomers followed up their thrown javelins with drawn swords, pounding forward into the back of the Dorobon legion, hacking down men who were barely aware they were in a fight. The whole line convulsed, and those at the front – now the rear – of the Dorobon line panicked as a wall of men thrice their number came roaring down the slopes towards them.

'What's happening?' someone gasped.

How the Hel would I know? Rykjard grabbed a relay-stave. *<Heale? Answer!>*

It wasn't Heale who responded, but a Jhafi-dark Gorgio, with bright eyes and a savage look on his face. *<Sir Roland is dead. Soon you too will die.>*

<What the Hel—?>

<My name is Emilio Gorgio and we are here to free Ja'afar from scum like you.>

The relay-stave went dark and the connection snapped. From across the sands came a new roar, pouring from the mouths of the advancing Gorgio. *'NESTI! NESTI! FORZA NESTI!'*

Elena watched the Grandmaster's face change as the aether and his natural senses told him of this last betrayal, the one she'd hoped and prayed for ever since Ivran Vostycka, the scholarly Ordo Costruo Air-mage she'd sent to Hytel in the wake of Forensa, had first reported the changing situation there.

After the Kirkegarde had pulled out of Hytel, Emilio Gorgio had struck. He was part-Jhafi, but an acknowledged bastard, son of Alfredo Gorgio's brother; he had many Jhafi adherents – and a strong Rimoni following as well. Being good-looking and charismatic certainly did no harm, but his popularity had a lot more to do with his natural intelligence and proficiency with arms. After Alfredo's unexpected demise, he'd rallied both peoples and destroyed the Gorgio-Sintro faction. With Gyle now effectively blind in Hytel, Ivran Vostycka's offer of alliance with the Nesti had gone unnoticed, and once Emilio had been given assurances that his marriage to Portia Tolidi would not be opposed, nor his claim on the Lordship in Hytel, he'd freed the Nesti mine-slaves and marched south himself.

Lann Wilfort brandished his sword. 'I could cut you in half with one hand tied behind my back, Anborn,' he sneered. 'You're out on your feet.'

She didn't try to deny it. 'To what avail, Grandmaster? The empire's adventure in Javon is over, either way. Gyle's lost this battle, and he's lost the war. If you fight on, in the end you'll be overwhelmed and die. Surrender, and save yourselves. Or just run – if you go like the wind, you might just get your men out.'

She gripped the faint amount of gnosis she still had, ready for whatever desperate sacrifice was required, because she was going to die before she let him by.

But she hadn't misjudged: Wilfort had always had a reputation for pragmatism. He pulled his warhorse's head around and faced southwest, then turned back and fixed his eyes on her. 'Well played, Anborn,' he said, grudgingly.

Then he shouted at his men to turn around and get the Hel out of here, at the double.

Elena wobbled in her saddle, feeling about to faint – but somehow she stayed upright. This was the culmination of so much, and even though she was utterly exhausted, she didn't want to miss a moment.

Cera Nesti watched in stunned disbelief as everything turned on its head.

At first everyone around her was in near panic as they watched the Gorgio arrive, trying to rearrange themselves into defensive lines. Elena and the Kirkegarde grandmaster were parleying, and that meant surrender.. *I'm only la Scrittoretta, but I know the rules here. You can't renege on an offer to yield* . . .

Then something Elena said made the Kirkegarde Grandmaster's head whip around to the North, and she saw his eyes widening. Everyone followed his glance, and at that moment there was a strange ripple in the enemy lines as the Dorobon and Gorgio blurred into each other.

Then a cry carried all the way across the plain, loud enough to make her heart explode: '*NESTI! NESTI! FORZA NESTI!*'

Tears leapt to her eyes, turning her sight liquid, while on every side men began to scream the praises of their favoured god, roaring their lungs out. Swords were shaken at the skies and trumpets blared, as everyone in her army expressed utter joy . . .

'*FORZA LA VIOLA! FORZA NESTI!*'

The cry was being taken up on all sides now, and the lines of men were straining. Piero Inveglio was in a shouting match with the knights around him, trying to restrain them from a headlong charge. 'The Rondian centre is unbroken!' he was yelling. 'Hold! *Hold!* Let the north take its course, and then let's see if—

'. . . *Oh, rukk it! Let's kill the bastidos!*' he bellowed, and spurred towards the enemy.

Her whole army began to surge forward in his wake, still disciplined, until the enemy ahead suddenly fell apart, their ranks collapsing even before contact was made. With a roar, the Rimoni centre threw itself into the pursuit.

'*NESTI! NESTI! FORZA NESTI!*'

No! That makes no sense! Endus conjured in the air to bring the sight closer, but that was far worse: it showed him so-called Gorgio ripping off their white outer tabards to reveal violet beneath. He shouted in denial, 'No! They can't be Nesti—! They can't! They were all killed – Gyle *ordered it!*'

We're betrayed by the Kore-bedamned Gorgio . . .

He kept scrying, realising the newcomers were both Nesti and Gorgio, fighting together, decades of rivalry and hate buried beneath something greater: Rimoni against Rondian, an older hatred by far. And beyond them he could see more Jhafi – men from the northern part of the country, who had always known who their enemy was – were swarming onto the battlefield. His own men, facing east, were now looking over their shoulders at the commotion to the north.

Suddenly the battlefield felt utterly different. Endus whirled on his aides and runners, all casualness shed as he looked to save what he could from this. 'Wheel left! Cancel the advance and pull back to the ridge! Defensive formations! Secure the baggage and put the horses to the wagons! We need to be able to move—!'

The runners scattered and five minutes lasted for ever while the

Harkun fled and between them, the Nesti and Gorgio at the rear and the Aranio from the front destroyed the Dorobon legion. Endus would have screamed his rage to the heavens, had he not been aware of the frightened eyes of his men fixed on him. *Don't panic the lads. Keep your head.* A mercenary crew always knew when to run, and this was turning into one of those times.

'Sir, they're advancing in the centre now!' an aide called, sounding worried.

It was true: the Nesti in the centre were countering now, and unbelievably, the Kirkegarde – *the Kirkegarde!* – were fleeing south. As his centre sensed the attack break down and the new threat behind them they began wavering, while the Nesti forces half a mile across the plain were rolling forward . . .

Can we still win this . . .? he wondered, then decided, *No.*

He turned to order a retreat when one of his men rashly plucked at his sleeve. 'Sir, look!' He followed the man's arm up into the sky to see a solitary windskiff was streaking away into the west.

It's fucking Gurvon, bailing on us!

'Damn this – retreat! *Pull back!* But keep it orderly! Hold together!'

He might as well have been shouting at the wind. At the first mention of the word *retreat*, the lines dissolved. His men didn't do defeats – they'd never had to before. Their money and plunder were in the baggage trains, together with their women and children. They didn't give a shit about Gurvon Gyle and his Mercenary Kingdom; they never had. They just wanted their stuff, and somewhere to hole up.

The Rondian centre disintegrated.

Cera rode forward, surrounded by her guards, to meet the newcomers. The men had been 'mopping up', which Elena had been taking pains to shield her from, but she'd still seen enough to haunt her for ever. *If this is victory, preserve me from defeat.* Over the last few hours she'd seen far too many bodies of men she'd liked or valued or both, and thousands more dead whom she'd not known at all, but who'd come here to fight for Javon, and for her. And there were thousands more injured, many maimed for life – and the greatest prize still eluded them: Gurvon Gyle was last seen flying west at high speed.

But she had to maintain the grave smile of the conqueror because her people expected it. They *needed* it. If she stopped to think how close they'd come to disaster, she started to shake again. It was hard to maintain her dignity when she so badly wanted to escape all this rack and ruin.

But there was also joy, enough to move her to tears, and chief in that was seeing thousands of Nesti men, taken prisoner by the Gorgio at Fishil Wadi almost two years ago, standing before her, armed and free. They were gaunt and sunburned, all showing signs of terrible privation, but they were *here*! And there at the fore was Paolo Castellini, his huge frame unbowed, but his eyes were wet and his bones shaking as she embraced him.

There was also a new ally to greet, one unlooked for: Emilio Gorgio, Alfredo's brother's bastard, a name barely known until now. He was dark, and had a feverish energy to him that made her glad he was on their side – and also made her wonder how he could be contained.

He greeted her with great reverence, however, prostrating himself in the most extravagant of supplications, which startled her. 'Sal'Ahm, Great Queen!'

'I'm not a queen,' she replied hurriedly, 'merely Autarch—' then his words and actions struck her. 'Lord Emilio – you're an *Amteh* worshipper?'

'My mother was a Jhafi servant. My father acknowledged me, to Lord Alfredo's great displeasure,' Emilio replied. 'It left me uniquely positioned when Lord Alfredo died to make alliance across lines previously uncrossed.'

'But Lord Alfredo's sons . . . the Sintro line . . . ?'

'. . . have met with unfortunate accidents. It was a time for swift blades. It was regrettable,' he added, without any hint of actual regret. 'I have powerful friends among the Northern Jhafi; I used them to gain control of my House and free your prisoners. I am betrothed to Portia Tolidi and have custody of the Dorobon child.' He met her eyes. 'Though of course they have no claim on the legitimate rule of our nation.'

Cera's first thoughts were for Portia as a pang of jealousy and loss speared through her, though of course she'd realised their fleeting relationship was over some time before. She looked at Emilio and saw him as a formidable man – adversary or ally, though? That would be the question. The Gorgio's mining interests had made them wealthy, but they had always been politically hamstrung by their refusal to embrace the Jhafi population. That was obviously not the case any more.

'I trust Lady Portia is satisfied with this new alliance?' she enquired.

He didn't look like he'd ever given that a thought. 'She knows her duty.'

'You *must* treat her well,' she said firmly. 'She has been through much.'

Emilio looked puzzled. 'Portia will be my *wife*, and the *centre* of my House.'

I suppose she'll be treated as well as any wife can hope to be. Like a caged bird.

'I must return to my men,' Emilio said, kissing her hand again. 'You are victorious, Lady. Javon belongs to you.' He looked at her frankly. 'For now . . . I understand soon you will be leaving us, and a new ruler will be elected.' He sounded like he thought himself a fair chance in that ballot.

'You understand correctly,' she told him. 'An Autarch may rule for ninety days only, and this crisis is over, Ahm willing. Soon the sultan will send for me.'

'I was sad to hear of the loss of your brother,' Emilio said. 'I am sure that he would have made a fine king.'

'Thank you, my lord. I believe so too.' She looked away. 'No victory can ever bring him back.'

36

The Bassaz Crossroads

Curses

*The earliest Lantric Myths are usually about some person suffering from a 'curse',
a common motif of 'magic'. Yet 'curses' are not a feature of the gnosis; there is
no spell which can subject another to ongoing, unspecified misfortune.*

Though you can be sure that someone in the Pallas Arcanum is working on it.

RENE CARDIEN, ORDO COSTRUO COLLEGIATE,

HEBUSALIM, 883

*Kesh, on the continent of Antiopia
Thani, (Aprafor) 930
22nd month of the Moontide*

'We've got out of worse situations,' Bowe remarked.

Serjant Vidran cuffed him around the ear. 'Shut up, Bowe. There
en't no worse situations than this.'

Ramon glanced down the line, measuring the men's reaction. He
thought he saw a tired fatalism in their eyes and got the sense that
they thought this would be the end of the road for them. That was
understandable; it really was difficult to see a path through the forces
arrayed against them.

The cohort made up part of the front line of the Lost Legions, in
their usual loose formation that could become attacking or defensive
in a few seconds. They were all gazing up at the mounted men on the
slopes opposite. A small dip in the land was all that lay between the
two armies. The banners opposite matched Seth's personal blazon:

House Korion. Seth himself was nearby, looking pale and agitated. Jelaska stood beside him, along with Evan Hale and Chaplain Gerdhart. Hale's left arm now ended at the elbow, but he'd already had a wooden arm fitted, with his bow nailed to a false hand. When Kip rode up, picking his nose, they just about had their full complement of magi.

'We should form up along the road, where the ditches and the embankments give us a little cover, and something to hold,' Hale was saying. He glanced at his ruined arm with haunted eyes. 'We can take a few of them down.'

'That's sound against ground forces,' Jelaska commented, her eyes on the distant swirl of venators and drakken. 'But how do we stop those damned beasts slaughtering us from above?'

No one had an answer to that, but some cover, something to anchor the lines, was a matter of urgency when faced by cavalry, so the orders were rapidly given and the army boiled into motion, flooding into the crossroads and planting their spears in the earthworks raised to stop the road from flooding during the rainy season. While the men marched and the wagons rolled by, the few cavalry of their own created a screen in the fields to deter enemy archers, but Kaltus Korion's forces left them alone, apparently content to let them form up however they willed.

Is that arrogance? Ramon wondered, *or are we doing just as they want us to?*

Runners began to come in, reporting when units were in place, requesting permission to adjust this or that, asking for orders concerning baggage and disposition of the women and children and a hundred other details. Seth fielded them with considerable composure, far more at ease in command than he'd been when they'd started this. He was growing into the role impressively.

Breeding? Ramon wondered. *No, I don't believe in that. Just a young man learning to do a job he's expected to perform since birth, despite being desperately unsuited to it. It takes practise, but we get there.*

What impressed Ramon most was the spirit shown. Though the

smallest child could see that they were ridiculously overmatched, there was no panic. It looked as though they were all watching him out of the corner of their eyes, waiting for some miracle to be pulled from his sleeve.

Sorry, people; there's just arms inside those sleeves today . . .

Seth sent his magi to direct their maniples into position, leaving only Jelaska and Ramon, with Delta waiting in the distance. 'Well?' Seth asked.

'If it's a straight fight, we'll be annihilated,' Jelaska said quietly. She and Seth turned to Ramon, as if waiting for him to say that he had it all in hand.

'Who the rukking Hel do you think I am?' Ramon complained. 'I've got no idea what to do either.' That Seth and Jelaska actually looked *disappointed* in him for not producing an instant miracle struck him as grossly unfair.

'Then what? Do we parley? Surrender?' Seth peered towards the Rondian forces lining the uplands. 'That's my father's personal banner. He's come all the way from the Zhassi Valley to stop us.'

'If we surrender they'll execute or enslave all the wives and children, then their husbands, then decimate the rest,' Jelaska said with a heavy voice. 'That's what Jongebeau said and I doubt Kaltus Korion will soften that sentence. But perhaps that's better than having them destroy us in battle, then letting his legionaries run amok. I've seen what even the most disciplined soldiers do when they're off the leash. They forget that they're human. Anyone who's been in northeast Argundy knows that.'

Ramon swallowed. 'The people of Silacia know this also.'

Seth's face was sickly. 'Perhaps I can beg some kind of concession?'

'Is your father famous for mercy?' Ramon asked. 'I don't think so.'

'Dubrayle and Milius must know that if Korion gets that gold, they won't – that must worry them. Perhaps there's some angle there? Some way of playing them off against each other?'

'It's good to hear you're thinking like that, Seth. Being around me is clearly rubbing off. But I really can't see a way out,' Ramon admitted. 'Honestly, the Treasury have no reach out here. We're so exposed: Kaltus thinks the gold is here, and he's not going to back off, not with a prize like that dangling in reach.'

'Then we have no choice. I'll just have to try and get the best terms of surrender I can. I'll send a herald.' Seth hung his head, close to tears. 'Thank you both. You've done your best, you and all the others – more than your best; you've performed bloody miracles. But this is the end.' He clicked his tongue, dug heels into his horse's flanks and kicked it into motion.

Ramon looked at Jelaska, who was staring away into space. She turned back to him, her long sorrowful face drawn with fear and resignation. 'So, the harlequin is out of tricks, then?'

'I'm sorry, *amica mia*. We're completely rukked.'

'Thought so.' The Argundian sorceress smiled sadly. 'All good things end, yar.'

'Si. They do indeed.'

Jelaska smiled sadly and rode towards her Argundians; she'd share the last moments with her own kind. Ramon watched her go, wondering why he was still here. For days he'd been thinking of running, to try and draw the pursuit away from the Lost Legions and onto him, but he'd rejected every plan – not because that mightn't have worked, but because increasingly he knew he *belonged* here. Tomasi Fuldo and Silvio Anturo were screaming at him via relay-staves every chance they got, but still he refused to go.

That hadn't stopped him accepting one of the phials of poison Lanna Jureigh and Carmina Phyl had brewed, in case they fell into Inquisition hands. The little glass bottle was clicking around his belt-pouch, a tiny reminder that not all escapes involved running.

With a sigh, he rejoined Delta. The Dokken was staring at the Rondian lines, a pained but wistful expression on his face. 'I can feel their presence,' he said softly.

'Do you mean your kin? Are they over there?'

'Yes, my kin are there; I can sense them, still enslaved to the Inquisitors. And all those construct-creatures, too. They're like a swarm of bees inside my skull, crying out in horror at what they'd become. I cannot shut them out of my head!'

Something germinated inside Ramon's skull, the flower of an idea. He dragged his eyes from Korion's majestic army to the Dokken slave. 'You can *sense* them,' he said breathlessly, 'can you *reach* them?'

'It's a white flag, sir!' one of Kaltus Korion's aides called eagerly.

Kaltus acknowledged impatiently. The whole army could see the parley flag, but there was always someone who felt the need to state the obvious. He looked for intelligent life; with Rhynus Bergium dead in the north, that wasn't easy to find among the cluster of sycophants and political appointees in his current entourage. Eventually he sighed and waved forward young Tonville. 'What would you do here?' he asked, pretending he was grooming the young man for higher things, when in fact he wasn't entirely sure how to proceed now they were here.

Tonville looked flattered. He bit his lip, considering. 'I think this is a situation that requires delicate handling, General,' he said carefully. 'It's not good for men of Yuros to fight each other on foreign soil. And . . .' Tonville hesitated, then to his credit ploughed on, 'well, that's your son down there.'

'My former son.'

'Yes, sir. But Seth Kor— Fetallink has been your acknowledged heir for a long time. That's not something a proclamation can erase overnight. It wounds your family name, I believe, for you to be in open conflict.'

'You think I should have stayed in the north, Tonville?'

Tonville swallowed. The news from the north, that some unknown group of magi had trapped and destroyed Rhynus Bergium's entire high command, had shocked them all. Barring the junior battle-magi, the First Army had been stripped of leadership. Although they were holding position on Ebensar Ridge, there were more desertions every day, a positive flood of them – and they were all living in dread of renewed assault by the sultan's army.

I should be there, not here, Kaltus thought. *But this situation must be resolved and the gold secured if I am to secure my future . . . and wrest the throne from Constant.*

'No sir, you were right to come south,' Tonville replied. 'But if you can resolve this peacefully, it would enhance the honour of your House.'

Kaltus mused on that. 'My thoughts exactly,' he replied eventually. 'The dirty laundry of a great House must be washed below-stairs, as my mother used to say. Make arrangements for the parley.'

Tonville saluted and hurried away, while all the courtiers gazed enviously at his back for having shared an intimate conversation with their noble commander. Kaltus gritted his teeth and looked up at the circling flock of drakken and venators, imagining how it would feel to unleash them.

Seth Korion trotted towards the enemy lines, flanked by Evan Hale and Jelaska Lyndrethuse. He'd asked for Ramon, but he'd been told that the Silacian was 'too busy' by a scruffy ranker from Ramon's personal cohort. He wasn't sure what to make of that, especially when the ranker had added in a low voice, 'He said on no account is you to surrender, gen'ral.'

Perhaps Ramon has a plan after all? Seth didn't enquire: best not to know when he was about to stand before his father like a recalcitrant child.

Three khurnes detached from the cluster of glittering mage-nobles in the centre of the Rondian lines and trotted down to meet them, stepping in unison and tossing their horns. He recognised the riders: his father had obviously decided to bring two young aides, both magi from renowned families.

His father saluted with casual condescension, as to a junior officer. 'General Fetallink,' Kaltus Korion drawled ironically. He made his introductions with a perfunctory air, then waited expectantly.

'This is Jelaska Lyndrethuse of Argundy, and Evan Hale of Andressea.'

'Magister Lyndrethuse is known to us,' Kaltus said, his voice suggesting she wasn't known in a good way. 'Not Magister Hale.'

'I'm related to House Korbriene,' Hale said nervously; the Korbriene line had been wiped out in one of Lucia's purges, but the Hale half-bloods of Andressea hadn't been implicated in anything. Yet.

Kaltus raised a faintly contemptuous eyebrow, glanced at Hale's wooden left arm, then fixed his predatory eyes on Seth. 'I think this is best resolved between you and me, don't you?'

Seth glanced at Jelaska; she gave him no sign, so he nodded. Kaltus dismounted silently and approached, and Seth did the same, very conscious of how very *unsafe* he felt. They stopped, almost close enough to touch, but Kaltus didn't offer his hand and Seth had to lower his, snubbed. Close up, he thought his father looked much older, his iron face showing deep fatigue, the sheer exhaustion of playing tabula with emperors and kings.

'Father,' he began, though, ironically, given what he was about to say, he'd never felt less akin to this man, 'you *are* my father. We both know that. I've got your face, your eyes, your build. Whatever you might have paid Mother to say otherwise, it doesn't change the truth.'

'Truth? What is truth?' Kaltus scoffed. 'Let me tell you: truth is what people believe, and they believe what they're told to. In a few months few will remember I ever had a son called Seth. In a few years, you'll have never existed. But my name will live on for eternity.'

'That won't make it true.'

'It's the only truth that matters: it's what the histories will say. In a few years' time, Arcanum students will hear of the destruction of a band of deserters led by someone called Fetallink and wonder how they could have been so foolish as to defy the great General Korion and the might of the Rondian Empire. Perhaps the only thing they will truly recall this moment for is the first combat deployment of drakken in Antiopia. Or perhaps you and your *rabble* will simply be forgotten.'

Seth bit his tongue, stifled his helpless anger. *I should have told someone else to do this.* But leadership included doing the unpleasant tasks too. 'My men have marched across Kesh and back,' he snapped. 'They deserve your respect.'

'They're deserters.'

'They fought their way out of a trap at Shaliyah, as I'm sure you know, given that you set it.'

His father made a dismissive gesture. 'Unprovable, even if it were true. Jongebeau read you the charges; they haven't changed. You and your magi will be arrested, tried and executed. Those of your men married to Noories will be executed, and the remainder decimated. The Noorie women and children will be sold as slaves. That is all irrevocably set down by the Imperial Judiciary.'

Before Seth could protest, Kaltus went on, 'You claim to be a Korion, Seth: then listen to me, the head of that House. If you were truly a Korion you would know that a Korion acts only for the good of his House. We must protect its reputation. Your mother understood this. That honour now requires of you the ultimate sacrifice. In time, I'm sure to be able to find a way to ensure that your sacrifice is marked in some way.'

'What? You'll cut me loose and let those bastards behead me, but if I keep my mouth shut, you'll give me a grave-stone? What the Hel kind of father are you?'

'I'm the Father of House Korion.' He bent closer, his voice an urgent whisper, 'Listen, Seth. There is some room for manoeuvre: I'm the commander in the field, and I set the rules here. Give us access to your command records and your baggage without resistance or deception and I will ensure that things go easier on you. I'm not unaware of the feats of your command. When the gold you have is mine, I will swiftly be answerable to no one, here or in Pallas. Justice will be what I say it is, and history could write something entirely different about you.'

'So if I let you have this gold to fund a coup, you might let me live? *That's* the honour of House Korion?'

'For Kore's sake, Seth, don't be such a damned *child*! There is only one rule in the eternal struggle for dominance: win by any means. Honour is just a cloak we wear to enlist the allegiance of the weak-minded. That's the world we live in. No one cares *how* the victory is won, only that it is! Freeing Rondelmar from the Sacrecour tyranny is worth *any* sacrifice.' He jabbed Seth in the chest with his forefinger. 'If you wish to be my son again, prove yourself a Korion!'

They stared hotly at each other, nose tips almost touching.

All I ever wanted was to be worthy of him . . . Holy Kore, is this what that means? 'Father,' he said thickly, 'I need to return to my men and make preparations.' He turned to go.

Kaltus swore under his breath. 'I need to know your purpose, Seth,' he said slowly, as if to a stupid child. 'I will destroy your forces if I don't have a clear indication that you will comply.'

'It's not just my decision.'

'What? You still can't make a decision on your own?'

'This decision is not mine to make. The lives of almost fourteen thousand human beings are at stake here. We will decide our fate, in our time.'

'Not *your* time, Seth. You've got until midday tomorrow. Any who seek to run will be hunted down – as you will have noticed, I rule the air here, and I can see everything you do.'

'It hasn't escaped me. Tomorrow then.' Seth saluted perfunctorily, and walked back to his mount.

'How did it go?' Jelaska whispered.

'Badly. I thought there were things worth dying for, but apparently there aren't.'

'Sure there are,' Jelaska told him. 'You just need to choose them carefully.' She pointed back to their lines and the faces of their people, anxiously watching. 'These reasons here will do for me.'

As they rode back, someone called out, 'Three cheers for General Korion!' The call was taken up, all along the line, a swell of noise that cracked the veneer of his composure. As he closed on them, he had tears running down his cheeks. They were met by men breaking ranks to shake his hand, pat his thighs, his calves, his horse, and Hale's too. The bravest kissed Jelaska's hands, then fled. It took an hour to get back to his pavilion and get his magi together.

Ramon Sensini arrived last, the look of suppressed excitement on his face enough to silence the room. He took in their gloomy despondency and exclaimed, 'Don't say we've already surrendered?'

'We're debating our options,' Seth replied. 'So far we've got three: surrender to save lives, fight to the death, or run like Hel and hope they can't catch us all. Do you have any better ones?'

They waited with bated breath as the Silacian pulled some

ambiguous faces, then struck a theatrical pose. '*Si!* I have found a way to fight them!'

'But there's no point unless we can win,' Evan Hale said tiredly.

'I only fight to win,' Ramon replied. A slow smile crept over his face. 'It's about the worst plan I've ever come up with, a hundred things could go wrong, but . . . there's a *chance* that come tomorrow it could be us accepting Daddy Korion's surrender instead.'

Seth stared. At best he'd hoped Ramon might have some way to escape, but *victory*?

Ramon slipped into the circle of cook-fires just after midnight, his brain fizzing, his body keyed up. The sentries were posted and three magi were watching the aether, but the Rondian camp, a mile away on the rise, was quiet.

'Anyways, why not go back east?' Bowe was saying, 'I've got nothin' left in Pallas anyway.'

'There's always the mercenary legions,' Harmon said, then he noticed Ramon's approach and fell silent. The whole cohort followed suit, watching his face to gauge his mood. Ramon looked for Pilus Lukaz, and found him sitting in the background with the dour Baden, the bannerman. Lukaz often did this, letting the men talk unimpeded, giving them a chance to blow off steam.

'Bowe's jus' tellin' us how 'e's only 'ere cos' you've got a plan, sir,' Vidran put in. 'Hope it's a fuckin' good one.'

'Lads,' Ramon began, 'Baby Korion asked us magi to go through the camp and gauge the mood. You've likely heard all sorts of stories about what we're going to do, but here's the truth: we're going to try something on, just before dawn, because that's when sneaky *bastidos* do their thing. If it works, we still mightn't win, but to my thinking, that's better than surrender. How do you lot feel?'

The men looked at each other, then Bowe put his hand up. 'Like I was jus' sayin' boss, some of us was thinkin' of headin' back to Ardijah, see if'n Bondeau might hire us. But it's a bloody long way, yeah?'

'An' Bondeau were always a wanker,' Vidran added, to general amusement.

'Mostly it's you, boss,' Harmon said to Ramon. 'We figure on seein' what you do and taggin' along. Seems best way to get out alive and flush.' There was a murmur of agreement around the cook-fire.

Ramon was oddly humbled by their faith. 'My plans don't always work out, and they can get people killed.' He grinned. 'I was thinkin' of Ardijah myself for a while. But I'm staying, because I think we've got a chance here. And let's face it: *anything's* better than crawling back to Renn rukking Bondeau.'

The men all laughed.

Lukaz called out, 'So what do you want from us, Magister?'

'To hold this piece of the line. I won't be here, but I'm placing you beside Kip's Bullheads.'

'Those mad fuckers?' Vidran grimaced. 'I'd feel safer tied up in the women's camp.'

'We've all 'ad that dream, Vid,' Manius chuckled. 'Why'dya put us alongside those nutters, boss?'

'Simple enough: Kip's a mage, an' you'll have Jelaska's Argundians on your left as well. The rest of my maniple are in the rear, but you men are rankers, and the line needs you. You're the best we've got.'

'Aw, pooty!' chuckled Bowe. 'We's the best! It's official now!'

'"Pooty"?' Ramon asked.

'Great. Fabulous,' Harmon clarified, giving Bowe a withering look. 'It's a baby's word.'

Bowe frowned. 'I've said it all me life—'

'Exactly.'

Lukaz waved for silence. 'So, we jus' hold the line, boss?'

Ramon nodded. 'Just until we can spring our surprise, then it'll be all about staying alive. I'm going to set something in motion and then I'll get back to you as soon as I can – but it relies on factors out of my control.'

'Plans don't always work.' Lukaz shrugged. 'We'll hold our lines. Tell those bastards flanking us to hold theirs.'

Ramon stood. 'Good on you, lads. I'd like to say you're the best men I've served with, but as you're the only ones I've served with, it's a bit hollow. But still true! Good luck tomorrow – I'll rejoin you as soon as I'm able.'

He took their salutes and offhand good wishes in return and walked away into the rear of the camp. The mood was quite different where the Khotri woman were gathered amongst the wagons. Most were pregnant or bearing newborns. They'd gathered in a large circle about a bonfire, and Ramon noticed many of their husbands had slipped from the lines to see them. They were singing a mournful song in their native tongue; it was both melancholic and longing, quite lovely, but very foreign. Then his ears pricked up as the Rondian men raised their own chorus, an old Brevian folk song:

> Under forest, under sky, walking home to you;
> Through winter snow, ice and rain, coming home to you.

The women's eerie voices wove around the song perfectly, enhancing the hoarse, ragged chorus of male voices. He wondered how many of the women had even seen ice or snow. This army was creating something new, born of both northern forests and eastern deserts, as fragile as any windblown weed, desperately thin and scrawny, struggling to take root, faced with the reaper's scythe and fire. The burden of responsibility bit him deeper. He'd brought these people together, however unwittingly, and they were his to see safe, if it could be done.

He moved on, beyond the sentries posted in case the Rondians were trying anything sneaky themselves, though Seth swore his father disliked what he always called 'chicanery', preferring 'victory with honour'. It was the sort of luxury a man who had always commanded the most powerful army could afford.

Delta slid impassively out of the darkness. 'Magister Sensini?'

'Call me Ramon. Are you ready?'

The shaven-headed man rubbed at the ugly brand on his forehead and set his jaw. 'Yes, Ramon. I'm ready.'

'You know most of my fellow magi believe you'll betray us, don't you?'

Delta smiled his lugubrious smile. 'Ramon, they can believe what they like. But you know what I am. My kindred and I have this "condition" that is inhuman. We have had that condition exploited by your "Holy" Inquisition. Your people might think us monsters, but we have consciences; we want it to stop. We desire revenge. I pray we can take this chance.'

Ramon clasped the Dokken's hand, the first time they'd made physical contact. His inner eye engaged and he got a queasy feeling watching the way their auras exchanged a *frisson* of energy. They both pulled away nervously. 'I've not seen that before,' Delta mused, 'though you are the first mage I have met in friendship.'

Ramon's hand still tingled. 'Interesting. If we get the chance later, let's talk.'

Later . . . as if there will be a later . . .

Jelaska appeared, wraithlike in her black robes and pallor. 'Are you ready?'

'Yeah, I'm pooty,' Ramon replied.

'Eh?'

'Never mind. Let's go.'

They skirted the dung-trenches and rubbish heaps and found their objective, a windskiff Chaplain Gerdhart was recharging. 'I don't like this,' he muttered in Ramon's ear. 'I don't trust that Dokken.' *Or you, entirely,* his eyes added.

'I do. He hates them more than we do. That's good enough for me.'

Gerdhart inclined his head. 'I'll pray for you, Sensini.'

'Tell the healers to look after my daughter,' he told him. He clambered in, taking the tiller, and Jelaska and Delta followed. Delta moved to the prow, where he could work unimpeded. They wrapped themselves in blankets to trap the heat and a minute later they were rising through the darkness. Delta went into a meditative trance, while Jelaska snuggled against Ramon's side and promptly began to snore.

Ramon's plan required elevation to widen the reach of Delta's spell-work, and to give themselves as much time as possible before any Rondian windcraft reached them. Initially they drifted on breezes from the northeast, quickly leaving the occupied areas behind them.

He worked the tiller gently, subtly extending his senses. There were Rondian skiffs patrolling above their lines, and venators too, although they were all far to the north.

By midnight they were some twenty miles south of the crossroads. Now the real work began. He found an updraft and slowly climbed into the sky whilst tacking across the wind, working his way steadily back towards the armies. His plan required them to return to the air above the Bassaz crossroads an hour before dawn, undetected, and high up, just below the point where altitude sickness and the freezing temperatures became deadly. Windcraft seldom went so high, and Ramon hoped that would mean the Rondian air-patrols wouldn't be looking upwards.

As they neared the crossroads again, it became apparent that Kaltus Korion's army were far from complacent. Ramon counted six pairs of windskiffs and venators aloft at a thousand yards or so, more than three thousand yards below them. The air up here was bitingly cold, even wrapped up as they were. All of their blankets were now coated in frost and their breath was streaming out in clouds.

Jelaska roused herself. 'Getting too old for this sort of shit,' she grumbled cheerily. 'My arse is frozen solid.'

'Then bring it here and I'll warm it for you.' Ramon winked.

She snorted tartly. 'Got your spirits back again, have you?'

'It's the danger, *amica*,' he replied, not entirely jesting. 'This is what it is to be alive.' He looked beyond her to Delta, whose fleshy face was impassive. 'Over to you,' he called softly.

The Dokken reached inside his robes and drew out the cluster-crystal he wore instead of a periapt. At once it kindled, but only dully; he wasn't yet fully exerting. He raised his hands from the blankets and began to call names, those of his kindred, and the air about him began to glow.

Kaltus Korion always slept poorly before engagements, though battle seemed unlikely today, and in any case would be brief and one-sided. He was a professional, and took nothing for granted. He'd ordered a full quarter of his magi to stay awake listening to the aether, scrying the enemy or on patrol above, or pre-enchanting ballistae shafts and crossbow bolts for use against important foes. He kept himself busy with correspondence, and dealing with a never-ending stream of gnostic contacts from far afield: nobles and courtiers wishing him well. After the disaster in the north they were anxious; rumours were flying of a renegade Inquisitor and a daemon army. It all sounded preposterous, but he couldn't make contact with anyone among the magi he'd left in the north, and all kinds of rumours were flying about. Clearly the sooner he returned to Ebensar and retook command the better.

Today's operation was complicated because of Seth's presence in the other army. It would be intolerable for anything to happen that his rivals could interpret as father-son collusion. The Imperial Court was full of mediocre men with clever, spiteful tongues: he refused to give them anything to work with. Victory had to be total.

After tomorrow, I'll have the only intact army in the field and all the gold for a march on Pallas . . . all unwittingly presented to me by my former son, and the bastard of one of my chief rivals. Perfect . . .

Eventually Kaltus went and lay down, drifting in and out of sleep. Mater-Imperia Lucia had contacted him in the evening, worried about the money again – she'd finally got wind of the bullion these 'Lost Legions' supposedly carried, and she wanted it, desperately. He was getting tired of swearing protestations of ignorance, but his army was filled with her spies and he didn't know what she believed. He'd begun to wonder if the pending destruction of the Bridge was designed to handicap him more than any other purpose.

Damn this. Realising he was wide awake and unlikely to sleep again that night, he clambered off his pallet, still the same fold-up cot he'd been issued as a junior tribune all those years ago – all part of the myth he cultivated, that he was just a common soldier at heart. The men liked it, and it was a small enough discomfort. He found a flask of strong Brician brandy and went looking for someone to share the vigil. There was light in the officers' mess, and inside he found Arch-Legate Hestan Milius of the Imperial Treasury, writing. The Arch-Legate looked up. 'Ah, General Korion. You too cannot sleep?'

The arch-legate wasn't the company Kaltus would have chosen, but he poured a couple of measures and sat with him. Milius looked as wise as Kore and he knew all the court gossip; perhaps he'd let something useful slip.

'So, Arch-Legate,' he began, 'what's going on inside the Treasury? And what's Dubrayle's bastard got to do with it?'

Milius took a sip of the brandy and purred, 'General, Lord Dubrayle is angry that his bastard is involved, like you are yourself. He is revoking his acknowledgment of the little ingrate, and is relying on you to be rid of him more permanently.'

'I want to see both bastards eliminated and forgotten, I assure you.'

'Then we're of one mind on that matter, at the least.'

'The harder question will be the alleged bullion,' Kaltus said carefully. 'It seems to me that whoever gains it will hold great power when this promissory note scandal collapses half the noble Houses, pushing them into penury.' He topped up Milius' cup. 'I have Inquisitors and Treasury-men hovering like vultures.'

'Many Inquisitors, perhaps,' Milius replied, 'but I'm the only Treasury-man who matters.'

'Hmm. Where does the Church sit in this matter? Would they use the bullion to stabilise the empire, or to shift its control from the palace to the prelature?'

'I rather think you can guess.' Milius raised his cup. 'This is good brandy, Kaltus.'

'I only deal in the best. And I think only of the empire's safety, which I feel is threatened most if the Church gains this bullion. Grand Prelate Wurther is an ignoble creature, and canonical rule would hurt us all.'

Milius stroked his white beard. 'The army is the Treasury's preferred partner. We would use this wealth to stabilise the empire, and ensure the Imperial Legions continue to be funded.'

I think I could work with this man, if not Dubrayle. I need allies in the Treasury, at the least. 'Do you speak for Lord Dubrayle in this?'

'Of course, as in all things.'

'He places great trust in you.'

'Rightly.' Milius looked mildly affronted. 'I'm an extremely loyal person.'

While it remains profitable, no doubt. 'It's my intention to hold the Inquisition Fists in reserve,' Kaltus said. 'My own men will be first into the deserters' baggage area. There's no guarantee that's where this mythic gold is though; we must react first once we know.' He fixed Milius with a firm eye. 'I know all there is to know about winning in battle, but I am not a money man. You are. Can we work together on this?'

Milius returned his gaze steadily. 'I believe we can.'

They toasted the agreement with more brandy, while outside dawn approached and the first stirrings of the army began. The cavalrymen were rising to ready their steeds: khurnes needed as much tending as any horse, and their heightened intellect meant they could be temperamental if neglected. Kaltus went to the flap of the tent and looked outside, savouring the pre-battle tension like the bouquet of a fine chardo.

It was still an hour till sunrise, and Luna was in the western skies. Staring up at her face always brought out the pagan in him, reminding him that Kore had once been a northern incarnation of the Sollan god, Pater Sol, before the rise of the magi, though Mater Lune had never been brought into the Rondian religion. There was something stirring about gazing up at that cratered, broken face, every shape on it alive in some myth or other. He toasted her silently.

Then the night shivered, and he heard a low, eerie sound. All over the camp, the warhounds began to bay, the khurnes whinnied and reared and the venators began to keen, as if every construct-beast in the army had suddenly woken and scented blood.

Pallas, Rondelmar, on the continent of Yuros
Aprafor 930
22nd month of the Moontide

One of the oldest rites of the Church of Kore was that of Absolution: the supplicant brought a coin for every sin they wished absolved, and then confessed it privately to the priest. The means of depositing the coin varied from region to region, from discreetly sliding it through the grille of the curtained booth, to placing it ostentatiously on the altar or into the font in the atrium. However, the need was universal: to lift the burden of guilt, and purify one's soul anew.

It was also an excellent source of revenue for the Church. But it came with responsibilities, and one of those was the very delicate matter of dealing with the Absolution of the noble House of Sacrecour. The role of Imperial Confessor was one of the duties of the Grand Prelate of the Kore, and on it hung the delicate relationship between Church and Throne. Grand Prelate Dominius Wurther had risen to the Arch-Prelature in early 921, just in time to marry young Constant Sacrecour to his ill-fated wife, Tarya, who'd borne him two children, then died. It had been a heady start to his tenure, but he'd enjoyed a long career in the Church prior to that; one didn't simply fall into the Arch-Prelature! One plotted and backstabbed and bribed, and whatever else it took. The struggle didn't stop then, either: it became a rearguard action against jealous rivals and the march of time.

The relationship with the Imperial Palace was the most decisive front on which Wurther fought. The Royal House and the Church were locked in an eternal struggle for the hearts and minds of the common people, but they had to maintain a front of unity, lest faith in either be shaken. So his mind was sharply focused as Lucia Sacrecour entered the Absolution Chamber in the Imperial Chapel at the appointed hour and knelt before the grille.

She slid a copper through the slats. 'Good morning, Grand Prelate!' she said cheerily. 'Or is it Arch-Prelate in this role? I can never remember the nuances.'

'Either title is perfectly acceptable,' he said, smiling. 'The Grand Prelate is the title of the foremost – and therefore "arch" – prelate in the land; I have almost as many titles as you, Sainted Lady.' They laughed together amiably. 'But what brings you here, dear Lucia? As a Saint it is theologically impossible for you to sin, so what need have you of a Confessor?'

'To abstain from Absolution would be the sin of Pride, would it not?'

'Holiness, you are Sancta Lucia. You are no longer burdened by the need to eat or drink or perform any other bodily function. That you choose to do so is a blessing upon those acts, done not out of need but choice.'

'So I shit because I wish to bless shitting?'

'Defecation is a very necessary thing for we lesser beings, Lady. That you choose to bless it no doubt eases the act for millions of grateful worshippers.'

'Dominius, you are funny,' Lucia chuckled. 'I do love you.'

'Then my soul is content, Holiness. But is yours? Why should a Living Saint seek out a lowly priest this day?' He drew his silk and velvet robes closer about him and listened with every fibre of his being.

Reading Lucia was an art form, one of the most delicate and rewarding, but beset with pitfalls. Some days she jested over serious things, sometimes it was the other way around. She could be in deadly earnest about matters she'd professed disinterest in just minutes ago. Cherished friends could become hated rivals overnight. Nothing was ever simple with Lucia Sacrecour.

'There is disturbing news from the Crusade, dear Dominius,' she said, her voice becoming serious.

'What news is this, Holiness?'

'Kaltus left Bergium in charge in the north and the old fool has got himself killed.'

Wurther knew this already; his own contacts said the First Army was falling apart, and if Kaltus Korion didn't get himself back into the north soon, they would collapse into a rabble and start fleeing for the Bridge . . . and into the mouth of the planned deluge.

'General Kaltus will reassert himself,' he said confidently, concealing his hope that he would fail to do so.

'Kaltus took his elite soldiers south to deal with deserters. You've heard the gossip, I take it: that the deserters are led by Korion's disavowed son, Seth? And this Seth is aided by an acknowledged bastard of Dubrayle's? That can't be coincidence!'

'Holiness, the Great Houses are small, and our connections are many. I warrant you could look at the magi of any army and see a

657

thousand conspiracies just by joining the family lines. Poorly connected and out-of-favour battle-magi always end up in one of a handful of punishment legions. It may well just be coincidence or opportunism on their part.' Wurther waited to see how she reacted to that. He liked to pretend to see only the bright side, then he would 'allow himself' to be convinced of conspiracies. It fit with his favoured persona: that of fat, trusting Dominius Wurther, a man whom no one need fear.

'You may be right, Dominius,' Lucia said, proving she wasn't immune. 'But my spies tell me Dubrayle's bastard might have been acting for Dubrayle. The promissory notes scandal can be traced to him – and no one could have escaped Shaliyah unless they were pre-warned. Who but Kaltus or Calan could have warned them?'

'I'm told this Seth Korion destroyed a force sent by Kaltus to arrest him, near Vida,' Wurther argued. 'That doesn't sound like collusion to me.'

'Among those slain was an Inquisition Fist,' she reminded him. 'Perhaps that was something father and son contrived to be rid of your own people, Dominius?'

It's not impossible . . . . But it didn't sound quite right. 'I have plenty of other Inquisitors still in Korion's army. But if Seth and Kaltus Korion are working together, why doesn't Seth simply hand Kaltus the money?'

'A charade,' Lucia replied instantly. 'At this point, we could still strand them both in Antiopia. But once the land-bridge is reformed and Kaltus is back in Yuros with the stolen gold, he is well positioned for a coup.'

Wurther sat up, considering. *Could that happen? Kaltus Korion is someone men flock to. He'd be a stronger ruler than Constant . . . and less pliable. He's never hidden his contempt for the Church, either.*

'Surely Korion knows he could never supplant your son in the hearts of the people,' he declared loyally, sure the opposite was true.

'Of course not – but if he tried, he could ruin us all,' Lucia replied darkly. 'If he lured Dubrayle in with the promise of more autonomy and a share of the gold, anything could happen. Some arrangement will be reached, mark my words. You and I will never see that gold

– until it shows up in Korion's hands as he marches on Pallas. I understand Kaltus will destroy the deserters tomorrow. This plot will unfold swiftly after that.'

It was frighteningly plausible. *My task is to make sure I come out of this on the right side of the ledger. The Church too, if I can manage it.* 'I see your fears, Holiness,' Wurther said gravely. 'These are difficult and perilous times, and we must stand together, as we always have: Throne and Mitre.'

'Thank you, Dominius. I knew I could count on you.' Lucia sat back, and her voice became clinical again. 'We'll accelerate our plans. Tomorrow, Constant and I will take windships to Pontus. I'm going to destroy the Leviathan Bridge as soon as possible. The Keepers stationed at the Bridge report that the solarus crystals in the towers are almost at full capacity – we'll have all the power we need.'

'Must you attend yourself, Holiness? Pallas sleeps better with you in its bed.'

'Of course I'm going! For one thing, this will be my son's great triumph over Antonin Meiros. Constant *must* be there, and so must I. Secondly, and this is purely selfish: I wouldn't miss such a sight for love nor money! It will be the spectacle of the age!' She laughed and pushed another copper through the grille. 'There: it must be that sin of selfishness I'm here to absolve!'

And not a thought for the millions of Noories and Pontic Yurosians who will die . . . But then, she's hardly going to hand me a million coppers, is she?

'Is there aught else that troubles you, Holiness?' he asked.

She'd been on the point of rising, then she stopped and knelt back down. Sounding unwontedly anxious, she said, 'Actually, Dominius, as a matter of fact there is. I know this might sound morbid of me . . . but should anything untoward happen, I charge you to do two things. Firstly, protect and raise my grandchildren, Cordan and Coramore. When we fly east, I will leave them in your care.'

I will control the royal heirs . . . He struggled to keep his voice solemn. 'Of course, Holiness. They will be safe with me.' Inside his heart, birds began singing joyously.

'There's no one I trust more than you,' Lucia replied, perhaps truthfully. 'Secondly, you must execute the prisoner at Saint Agnetta's.'

Ahhh. Wurther's heart now chorused. Saint Agnetta's was an abbey in the countryside where politically sensitive female prisoners were held, in secret: those too dangerous to let free but too damaging to execute. In particular it was where Natia Sacrecour, the emperor's elder half-sister, had been imprisoned since she was fifteen. She was now thirty-six. Wurther's people had been forbidden access in all that time, despite the abbey being legally his possession.

I'll have both the heirs of Constant, and their chief rival, in my grasp.

How he kept his demeanour humble he had no idea. 'Have no fear, Holiness,' he reassured Lucia. 'And I am sure that naught will happen at the Bridge, other than the destruction you intend. Pallas will rejoice at your triumphant return, with the throne stronger than ever, exactly as we've all planned.'

She pressed her face to the grille. 'Do you remember that meeting, Dominius, three years ago? Gyle's plan is still unfolding, despite all the twists and turns along the way! In a month, we'll destroy the Bridge and open up all of Antiopia to our rule.'

'It is fated, because we made it so.'

'It feels like such a long time ago now,' Lucia mused. 'Vult and Betillon are dead. Gyle has betrayed us, and Korion and Dubrayle are in the act of doing so. Only you have remained true.'

He bowed his head, not wanting to ruin such a perfect moment with words.

'I wonder whether I should move on Dubrayle tonight,' Lucia said softly.

Wurther shook his head. He still had investments that would need to be extricated. 'It would destabilise the empire at a crucial moment. But have your knives ready.' He stroked his smooth jowls, craving a cup of wine. This had been a most magnificent conversation, a pinnacle of his rule, in many ways.

It is almost a shame that Constant and Lucia will return from the Bridge hale and hearty as ever . . . Would it not better serve Mother Church best of all to have those two children in my power, to groom in the love and reverence of the Church? And Natia Sacrecour as an alternative, to raise up if they prove unruly . . .?

Suddenly the possibilities seemed endless.

Bassaz crossroads, Kesh, on the continent of Antiopia
Thani (Aprafor) 930
22nd month of the Moontide

Ramon kept the skiff moving in a slow circle high above the Bassaz crossroads. The shape of the land was hidden by shadow, the armies marked only by a faint twinkling from the largest fires. Mater Luna gazed down on them all from the western horizon, waning as the month passed. He shivered, not so much from the cold, or even the pre-battle tension, as from the immense power flowing from Delta. Possibly the magi far below could feel it too now: like a slowly exploding ball of fire.

This is it: Delta might save us all . . . but if he fails, or it's just not possible, we'll be annihilated.

The previous day Delta claimed that he and his fellow Souldrinkers shared a bond, a mental link that even magi didn't have, with which they all – unless they chose to shut each other out – could feel each other's emotions and surface thoughts.

Ramon had pondered that awhile, then asked, 'So could you reach the Dokken within the Inquisition in Korion's army?'

'I could try,' Delta had replied. 'Their minds aren't freed, like mine, but they're not Chained, as they need to be able to use the gnosis.'

'So if you could reach them . . . could you destroy the bindings on them?'

Delta had drawn out his solarus crystal and held it up. 'This crystal is very strong – it's used to trap souls, but it can also channel great power. Using it in such a way would be fatal, though, like a life-draining spell.'

'But you could . . .' Ramon was already hating the question, but he forced himself to ask, 'Would you . . . ?'

'To free my kindred?' Delta clarified. 'And wreak revenge on the Inquisition? Yes, indeed.' His lugubrious face had brightened. 'If I succeed, we would have unfettered control over these solarus crystals, and so many hated enemies about us we'd scarcely know where to strike first.'

37

Drawing Steel on the King

Drakken

The greatest beast of northern pagan mythology is the fire-breathing lizard known as the drakken. Some posit that they were dreamed up after early civilisations found the bones of giant reptiles, like those displayed in the Pallas Beastarium. The Animagi have been obsessed with the creature ever since, and have made literally hundreds of attempts to create them.

ORDO COSTRUO ARCANUM, PONTUS, 927

Kesh, on the continent of Antiopia
Thani (Aprafor) 930
22nd month of the Moontide

The old adage was that if you drew steel on the king, you got only one thrust. This was that blow; if it failed, the retaliation would be brutal. There would be no mere decimation of the Lost Legions; there would be a massacre.

Ramon lowered his sails and readied them for a swift release; staying motionless in the air would aid Delta's workings. Then he and Jelaska settled into the after-deck to wait, shielding themselves from the powers radiating from the Dokken and his solarus crystal and waiting to see what would happen. In the end, all of his schemes and plans had come down to this. He hated to have no control over events, but, galling as it was, all he could do now was watch, and hope.

Jelaska's lips brushed his cheek and she murmured, 'It's been a pleasure, Sensini. An adventure.'

He murmured a reply, a wordless appreciation of all she'd done, then they sent their awareness spiralling out into the pre-dawn skies to watch the show and deal with the inevitable counter-blows.

At first, all was dark, but dawn was coming, softening the blackness until shapes emerged. Kaltus' camp was directly below, lines of tents and earthen ramparts, the dim glow of cooling cook-fires blending with the pale auras of the guardsmen and the sleepers, and the thousands of beasts. People seldom realised how many beasts supported an army, and this one had more than most; thousands of warhounds and khurnes, over a hundred of the massive hulkas, and dozens of venators. And two drakken, smouldering mounds of heat. That was before you started counting the ordinary horses and mules. The soldiers were vastly outnumbered by their own beasts.

Ramon attuned himself to Delta's calls and felt him calling his fellow Dokken. All were bound, as he had been. And all bore one of the fatal solarus crystals. Delta was waking them one by one in the pre-dawn gloom. He sensed dim responses that became sharper, more alert and intense as the situation unfolded to them.

'During our captivity, we were gnostically conditioned to obey,' Delta had told him, 'but it was never complete, because it could never control the links we have with each other. We're all tethered, but we've not forgotten what it was like to be free.'

The notion of freedom was rekindled in the Dokken below by Delta's unexpected intrusion. He sent them information: the gist of the plan. Ramon sensed the pent-up rage of those Dokken, and felt them weigh that against the likelihood of death if they rose up. He caught their unanimous assent and exhaled in relief: the first hurdle of the night had been leapt.

The moment Delta snapped the gnostic bounds controlling his kindred, everything would happen with frightening rapidity – for good or ill.

Delta turned to him. 'Are you ready for this?'

When Ramon nodded wordlessly, the Dokken grinned fiercely and a pulse of energy surged along the links uniting Delta to his brethren, a powerful pulse that snapped the bonds of control. It was like a tear on a loom weft: suddenly hundreds of threads were blowing free. Below them, eighteen Souldrinkers woke from bondage in the camp of their enemies and reached for their deadly crystals.

The Souldrinker's name had been Edan Bretou, but the Inquisitors had shaved his head and branded him with the Lantric sigil 'Lambda'. They now called him *Lamb*. He was thin, and rather pretty for a young man – he had suffered abuses others of his kin hadn't. He hated certain of the Inquisitors with a transcendent passion.

When Brother Delta went missing, Lambda had mourned, as they all had. So when that same Brother Delta spoke into his mind that morning, his heart and head thudded with excitement as he announced, 'Our time has come, brothers and sisters. The abomination we suffer will end now.'

Brother Lambda trembled with the terror and enormity of what was required. It would end in death – his death, and all of his kindred here. It was clear none could survive the spell-work required.

'But what a toll we shall take in our passing,' said Sister Rho, bitter and angry, her words echoed by Brother Tau and Sister Zeta, equally enraptured at the notion.

What a conflagration we shall raise in our leaving! What a path we shall burn to Heaven on High!

Softly, gently, they all began to sing, a hymn to Kore, the *real* Kore, the God who loved even them. And as they sang, they gently, slowly, helped each other unlock the binding spells confining them to their tents, moving with patient precision to avoid detection. Then, robed and hooded, they slipped out into the shadows. Lambda looked up and saw that Heaven on High was strewn with stars. Somewhere up there was Brother Delta; he saluted him silently.

His senses were heightened, by adrenalin and the portending grace of freedom. It was as if every scent was new, every sound music. *Such a beautiful night. A shame to die before dawn.*

They flitted into position, utilising their gnosis freely for the first time in their lives, to conceal themselves from the sentries and the sleepless, until each was in position. Mentally they wished each other farewell, pledging to meet again beyond the skies. Then they turned away, to concentrate on their tasks.

For Lambda, that meant a tangle of giant reptile forms, thirty venators dreaming their bird-dreams amidst the gory remains of the cattle they'd feasted on the previous evening. The pen stank of rotting meat and hummed with flies, even at night. The mind of each flying reptile was tethered to their master . . . but each still, in some dim recess, remembered that once they'd been something else. Once they'd been free, living very different lives. Like Lamb and his kin, they were unwilling slaves. And they too could be freed – though the power to do it all at once would be beyond even the strongest pure-blood. But it wasn't beyond a Dokken wielding a solarus crystal, one who had no fear of whatever damage he might do to himself.

All around the camp, the freed Souldrinkers began their great task, to unleash freedom and devastation with the construct-beasts of Kaltus Korion's own army.

<Goodbye, Beloved Kindred,> they whispered through their links.

Lamb raised his crystal, and became a lion.

That eerie cry went on and on, growing, not fading. Kaltus Korion looked at Hestan Milius. <What's that sound?>

The camp was waking to a low hum, emanating from all sides. Voices cried out, the involuntary calls of frightened men pulled from a nightmare. Then came a rumble that set the sand beneath Kaltus' feet trembling, as if twenty thousand hooves had struck the bedrock at once, and that was followed by a rhythmic scraping and pawing and scratching. Behind that thumping heartbeat, thousands of mouths were panting, air gusting through bared teeth, the low growl of many, *many* beasts. It filled the air, at the edge of hearing, somehow maddening.

Suddenly apprehensive, Kaltus kindled shields and walked towards the nearest khurne-pen, where his own mount was housed. Three of his stable-hands were inside, facing a row of the creatures who'd torn loose from their pickets and were snarling, more like wolves than horses. Their deadly horns flashed.

Kaltus opened his mouth to warn them, but he was too late.

As one, the khurnes leaped forward with blinding speed, plunged their horns into the chests and bellies of the stable-boys and tossed them aside, then the whole herd of them, more than forty beasts, battered at the gates until they crashed down. They thundered out into the camp as screams and the sound of slaughter rose on all sides. He blasted down a khurne that came at him and leaped to evade another, which erupted in flames and went down screaming.

Kaltus whirled and found Milius at his side, blue gnosis-fire in his hands.

'General, what the—?'

Milius got no further. He was ripped almost in half from behind and tossed aside by another khurne that had flashed through the rear of the tent at full gallop, followed by more. They stamped on his carcase – deliberately, Kaltus thought, then as one, they turned on him.

He slammed fire into them, charred the front one and drove the rest away. But all around him, men and equipment were being torn apart. He had to roll aside as a madly out-of-control hulka slammed through a group of rankers, crushing three and scattering the rest like broken dolls. He shafted light into its skull and it collapsed, but now there were warhounds flooding in, tearing and ripping at the fallen, bearing down any who tried to fight.

Even as he thought, *I've got to get above this!* he was levitating above the tents and out of reach of the warhounds, then used kinesis to surge towards the venator pens, already in fear of what might be happening there. His elevation gave him a terrifying view of the night being torn apart by bestial shrieks and cries, of men panicking, running hither and thither, of fires raging out of control among the tents. It was a scene of Hel itself.

A dark shape flew out of the night, jaws wide open: a venator, as maddened as the beasts below. He blasted it backwards in a blaze of lightning, sending it plummeting into the chaos below, but other venators were rising, then peeling off into shallow dives, plucking men from the ground and biting them in two, spitting out the bloody pieces.

<Magi!> he bellowed into the aether. *<Magi! To me!>*

The responses came from all sides: his battle-magi, experienced men all of them, levitating out of the destruction below, many bloodied, some half-naked, torn from their beds into madness. But he took heart at the sight of the familiar faces. *<Call down the skiffs!>* he ordered. *<Someone scout the enemy, to see if they're behind this! Can anyone gain control of the beasts?>*

Young Tonville appeared, admirably cool in the face of chaos. *<Where are the damned Souldrinkers?>* he wondered aloud.

'Right here,' said a voice below, and they all looked down to see a slim figure in plain robes: a young woman with a shaven head and the Lantric sigil *Rho* branded onto her forehead. Between her breasts pulsed a blue light that was hard to look at, and her face was lined with veins, like the roots of redweed growing inside her.

Tonville raised a hand to send mage-fire at her, but she struck first.

Kaltus Korion had seen an Ascendant only once in his life: one of the Keepers had dealt with a rebel mage during the Noros Revolt. He'd been a withered old man, but the fire that had poured from him had turned stone to liquid.

That was as nothing to the explosion of energy that tore through the sky from the hands of the slight young woman below him.

It was directed at Tonville: a torrent of energy so pure it was like a fragment of the sun. It cut through the young man and he was gone, then it sprayed left and right as she spread her arms, engulfing his senior magi and plucking them from existence. Kaltus didn't stop to think; he fled, and only his speed saved him. As it was, the heat and the flame that burned through his shields were enough to send him spiralling though the air in agony. His elite magi, men and women who'd blazed through Noros and Argundy and Kesh like comets, winked out like fireflies.

He spun back, planning to try and assail the Souldrinker, when suddenly Rho combusted with a cry like a priestess in rapture and simply ceased to be. The concussion hurled blazing tents and weapons and debris into the air, sending him spinning away so hard that he ploughed into the ground beside a wagon.

Then the pain hit him, and he looked down to see his whole right side was burned away – to the bone in some places; the rest was a melted, weeping horror like a half-cooked chicken fallen from the spit. He almost blacked out, as much at the sight of it as the pain. Only the iron will of decades of command kept him conscious, kept him semi-sane, as he poured all the healing-gnosis he could into his tortured flesh, then began to crawl for the shadows beneath a wagon, to hide.

Ramon's scrying eyes were filled with images of horror as the giant living organism that was Kaltus Korion's army tore itself apart. Hulkas were rampaging through the wagons, stamping their handlers into pulp. Khurnes were spearing their riders, venators ripping the flesh of their Inquisitor masters. The warhounds were a seething mass of terror, hunting in giant packs, tearing ruthlessly into any prey they found. It was an awful, incredible insanity.

Here and there resistance formed: the remnants of a Fist regrouped, or a battle-mage found enough of a cohort able to form up and defend him. Crossbowmen gathered in small groups and managed to bring down a few of the raging construct-beasts. With courage and resourcefulness the common rankers sought ways to live, banding together to fight, or inching away to survive.

But the freed Dokken were stalking across the battlefield, blasting any functioning units apart using their diabolical crystals, even though they were tearing their own souls free of this life as they did. Ramon was attuned to Delta's mind and he felt each Souldrinker perish, one by one, in a roar of energy and release, until there were only two or three left still seeking prey. It was mesmerising, almost enticing, to watch a person wink out in self-immolation; he gripped Jelaska's hand to anchor him here, to remind him to *live*.

<*Up there! There's something*—>

The unknown mental shout drew him back to the here and now. He looked down and saw four skiffs and a pair of venators were spiralling up towards his skiff. Worse, a greater shape had risen from the darkness below: a mighty drakken, with a pair of armoured men

669

on its back – its riders must somehow have regained control, enough to get it aloft and keep it reined to their will.

'Here they come, Sensini,' Jelaska said. 'Now it's our turn.'

They readied their sails, working carefully around Delta. Now that he'd set the events below in motion, his role was largely done. They could see how badly the immensity of power required to break the controls on his kin had harmed him: his veins were engorged, glowing a deep radiant scarlet through his fragile skin. He was clearly dying, but holding off his last moments for as long as he could.

'Take me down,' he croaked.

Ramon looked at Jelaska, then shrugged. The Dokken had given *everything*. He began to power down the keel and began a controlled descent towards the skiffs and reptiles rising to meet them.

As they descended, Jelaska began her own workings, violet light creeping around her fingers, her lined face becoming even more drawn and withered as she drew on necromantic-gnosis. As the first enemy skiff came into range, a shaft of purple light flew from her hands and engulfed the pilot. An Air-mage, likely a Thaumaturge, his defences against the Earth- and sorcery-gnosis of the Necromancer were too weak; within seconds, a skeleton was piloting the skiff as it plummeted towards the ground. The shrieking mage in the prow wailed, then leaped free and went spinning away. A torrent of mage-bolts blasted against Jelaska's shields, turning the air around her brilliant with sparks ranging through blue to purple to red as her shields became stressed.

Ramon hauled on the tiller and turned with the wind to evade the skiff-borne magi . . . then swore as the drakken ate up the distance between them in one sudden swoop; it was almost upon them, fire spewing as it swung its head, and mage-light kindled on the lances of the riders.

Delta released the last of his reserves – not in a blast of energy, but Ramon sensed a *reaching out*, a struggle for control, and then—

The Dokken sagged quietly in the prow, as if the effort had been too much – but the drakken stalled mid-climb – then it turned its head and immolated itself, together with the riders on its back. The blast of its fire, as intense as any pure-blood Fire-mage could produce, charred the knights and its own wings and torso to ash, then it screamed as it lost the ability to fly. The blackened remains of the men on its back were already falling as it started to spin, head-over-tail, back down into the desert below.

Ramon stared awestruck at the falling beast, forgetting entirely that he was in the midst of a battle. Except that suddenly he wasn't: the surviving skiffs and venators had seen enough, and were frantically fleeing away. He watched them go in disbelief.

We did it. We're alive . . .

He blinked slowly at the scarred face of Mater Lune, Goddess of Insanity. The stars were fading and the few clouds turning pink and gold. Jelaska looked as shaken as he was. Wordlessly, they hugged, then turned to the slumped figure in the prow, huddled over a blackened crystal in his seared hands. Delta's morose, lifeless face held just the hint of a smile, but his eyes were empty.

May your god take you home, Ramon wished the Souldrinker silently, then he took up the tiller again and began to pilot them back towards the Lost Legions' camp.

They landed solemnly, to find their whole camp wide awake. Many of Kaltus Korion's rankers had fled in their direction, only to be taken captive; any of the wild constructs that'd come their way had been driven off.

The rising sun revealed the full extent of the devastation visited upon Kaltus Korion's army: his camp was not just wrecked; it was *devastated*, with construct-beasts still stalking the remains, seeking more men to kill. The tents and wagons had been mostly burned out and a pall of smoke hung over it all – ash, and the miasma of death.

Seth came to meet them and hugged them both hard, not even attempting to hide his emotion. The rest of the surviving Lost Legions magi – Fridryk Kippenegger, Lanna Jureigh, Carmina Phyl, Chaplain Gerdhart and Evan Hale – were not far behind, all lost for words as they gazed at the most destructive scene they'd ever seen: a battle won without a blow, through the sacrifice of others.

'What the Hel do we do now?' Evan Hale whispered, speaking for them all.

They all looked to Ramon, who looked to Seth.

'Well,' the general's son said, after collecting himself, 'I suppose we need to go over there and look around. There'll be injured, Lanna, so get ready for casualties. And some of those construct-beasts will still be hostile, so we'll need to move in groups. If anyone – or any-thing – resists, send for me or Jelaska. Remember, these people aren't our enemies any more. Tell the men.' He clapped his hands, a little dazedly. 'Well done, all of you.' He looked at Ramon. 'And three cheers, Bastidinio. You are a miracle-worker.'

Ramon raised a nonchalant, it-was-nothing hand. 'You should be cheering Delta. He did all that, not me.' He paused, then grinned. 'Though it was my idea. Si, you're right: I really am a genius.'

Seth Korion stared at the fallen drakken. The rear part of its body was charred through to the bone; he could see the ribs, broken by the fall from hundreds of feet above. The other drakken was gone, having eaten its handlers and destroyed two full Inquisition Fists as they slept, then driving off another before simply flying away. All the surviving magi were fled, and the Souldrinkers were all dead, immolated by their own powers. The aether still felt wounded from the immense energy expended here.

The camp was ghastly, a never-ending parade of the dead and the maimed, rent and shredded by wild beasts that had once been obedient constructs. Some were now padding about the camp as if wanting to resume their lives of servitude, but most of those still alive – the surviving legionaries had managed to slay a great many – were out in the desert now, and likely not coming back.

'We think around a third of Korion's men got away, but not many magi, sir,' said Tribune Storn, Ramon Sensini's senior logisti-calus, who was walking with him. 'Most of the survivors have fled along the northern road, but they've taken no supplies. We've man-aged to salvage enough food here to get us to Pontus, maybe even Verelon.'

'Incredible. I'd been wondering how we'd manage the supply situation.'

'Kore provides,' Storn said piously. 'Will they send more men to stop us, sir?'

'Perhaps. But the men who died here were the cream of the First Army. The rest must still be in the Zhassi Valley, facing Sultan Salim – so I don't know who they'd send.' Seth glanced at Storn. 'You've still got the gold, haven't you, Tribune?'

Storn ducked his head, then said reluctantly, 'Yessir.'

'Hmm. Look after it, Storn. A lot of men have died for that coin, and many more will if we mishandle it.' Storn saluted and Seth looked away, staring at the great bulk of the construct-drakken. 'I wonder if there were ever real drakken?'

'Sometimes folk dig up old bones in the wilds,' Storn replied. 'The Rimoni caravans show 'em off, for a price. Drakken bones, they say. But who knows?'

There were splintered shafts of timber protruding from beneath the monstrous carcase. Seth peered at them curiously. 'What did it land on?'

'We think it's a wagon. But the damn thing's too big to move, so we're not sure.'

'Then burn the carcase where it lies, Storn. I can't imagine it's good meat.' He saluted and started to walk on, then turned. 'Has there been any word of what befell my fa— er, General Korion?'

'No sir. Not a thing.'

Seth had felt his father's last few seconds; he'd been in utter agony, and his mind had bled his pain into the heavens, for those listening. There had been no remorse, no peace, just self-centred despair, the last roar of a dying predator, cut short abruptly.

In that moment, a weight had lifted from Seth's shoulders. It felt as if he could straighten his back for the first time in his life. He felt unfettered. *Free.*

An old ballad popped into his head and the melody formed in his mouth. He found himself singing as he walked away from the broken beast.

38

Kinship

The Duties of the Exalted

One of the key questions concerning the magi is their true role in society: are they, as the Rondian Empire posits, the natural leaders, divinely ordained and entitled to special privilege? Or should they be the nation's first servants, using their gifts for the betterment of those less fortunate?

And is the answer Pallas gives us the one we're prepared to accept?

LADY ODESSA D'ARK, ORDO COSTRUO, HEBUSALIM, 920

Brochena, Javon, on the continent of Antiopia
Thani (Aprafor) and Jumada (Maicin) 930
22nd and 23rd months of the Moontide

Before the magi and their systematic approach to the gnosis, the folklore of Lantris and Rimoni had been filled with 'magicians' – usually demigods of the Lantric pantheon – who could do the miraculous, the inexplicable. Their tales were replete with confounding subterfuges and trickery, like turning enemy soldiers into allies with a sweep of the cloak. Gurvon Gyle felt as if he were trapped in such a tale.

Damn you, Elena.

Either Gabrien Gorgio-Sintro had betrayed him, or another faction had triumphed, then marched south under false banners. No other explanation made sense. But Gurvon knew who to blame ultimately: himself.

I got too greedy. Chisel that on my tomb.

The sun was lowering, right in the line of his bowsprit, as he streaked towards Brochena in the aftermath of Jekuar. The winds were contrary, but that would slow anyone chasing him as well. There was no obvious sign of pursuit, but an illusion could hide a pursuer and at this range he'd not know.

I must reach Brochena before the news, otherwise the Jhafi will storm the palace and I'll end up with nothing.

He arrived at dusk, setting down in the inner courtyard where one of Endus Rykjard's messenger-pilots was working on her own skiff. His was almost drained; it wouldn't be ready to move again for hours. He waved the girl over as he disembarked. She was new and naïve, not someone who could be subverted in moments, and therefore of no use to him. He needed to empty the vaults and get out. Persuading her to help him in the time he had wasn't practical. Which meant . . .

She came to greet him, faint surprise on her face. 'Lord Gyle? I thought—'

'Hush, not here,' he told her. 'Come, there is an urgent situation unfolding. I need you to take a message to the Krak for me.' He ushered her towards a side room, away from the watching guardsmen, laying a friendly hand on her shoulders and flirting just a little with his eyes. 'Endus speaks highly of you,' he said, 'so I know I can trust you. Is your skiff fully powered up?'

'Of course. I—' She quivered, and her eyes flew wide as she looked down and saw the hilt of his knife jutting from her chest, just above her left breast. He grabbed her around the waist and put his other hand over her mouth, stifling her cries while his mind blocked her mental calls for help. She went gently, sagging against him as if grateful for his care, closing her eyes as if going to sleep.

Stupid bint . . .

He propped her up in one corner, pulled out the dagger and wiped it clean, then hurried up the stairs into the keep. The few servants he saw ducked from his path, which suited him fine. There was a watchful near-silence to the palace with all the decision-makers and most of the soldiers away, leaving a strange void here at the heart of power. He reached the royal suite unchallenged and co-opted the guards as labourers. He had his gold in eight chests hidden behind the walls in the old spy-tunnels. They broke them down, draped them in wall-hangings and carried them down to the girl's skiff below. Once they were done he sent them on their way with a generous tip each, none the wiser.

Within the hour he was gone, long before the news of Jekuar had every bell ringing, and every man, woman and child pouring into the streets.

Hebusalim, Dhassa, on the continent of Antiopia
Jumada (Maicin) 930
23rd month of the Moontide

Alaron Mercer strolled through the broken halls of the Ordo Costruo, wondering what it would take to restore the building. It had been burned out during riots in the wake of Antonin Meiros' murder, according to a grizzled grey-haired Dhassan who was squatting in a cellar below with a young wife and three half-clothed children.

The ruin was positioned atop a rise that gave views over all of Hebusalim. The city was dominated by the Bekira-Dome, the largest Dom-al'Ahm in Ahmedhassa, which had once been sheathed in gold – until the retreating Crusaders had scraped off the gilt as they fled. Huge city walls encompassed the inner city – this was the place where his parents had joined the assault on the city in the First Crusade, where his mother had been so badly burned that she never fully healed, and his father had once shared water with a Lakh trader named Ispal Ankesharan – Ramita's father. He was still getting his head around that coincidence. Ramita called it Fate.

The city was throbbing with movement in some parts, eerily deserted in others. Where there was life, it had a brittle feverishness to it, as if the normal mores of society had been put aside through the suffering and strangeness of war. Rondian traders, tolerated for the coin and supplies they brought, were pulling out now, cutting their losses and heading towards the Bridge. The Rondian army was in disarray, with outlying garrisons abandoning their posts and pouring northwards, strung out along the roads in little order.

Alaron and his Merozain brothers had flown here directly from the confrontation with Malevorn, intending only to see if there was anything salvageable in the Domus Costruo before returning to Mandira Khojana and collecting Dasra. They still had to agree how best to return the Hadishah prisoners to the Keshi, but he wasn't in any hurry to release them, especially Alyssa Dulayne, crippled or not.

A mental touch brought him to attention, and Yash spoke into his mind. *<Al'Rhon, you'll want to hear this. There are Rondian soldiers coming in from the south – what is left of an army. They've suffered another major defeat, near Bassaz.>* Yash's voice was full of suppressed triumph.

Alaron couldn't take the same pleasure in the news. Though most of the Crusaders might have acted like a gang of thieves, he knew that the legions from Noros were mostly just farmers and labourers, either unwillingly conscripted or seeking their fortunes when home offered little; most of the others legions were probably the same. *<I thought the sultan's armies were all in the Zhassi Valley?>* he sent back.

<They are. The soldiers are saying it wasn't Keshi who destroyed them but an army of Rondian deserters.>

<What? That's unbelievable!>

<I told you you'd want to hear it.>

An hour later he met Yash outside the stockade walls of a legion camp on the edge of the city, a dismal place full of hollow-eyed, exhausted men trudging gloomily past, or collapsed against the walls. The gates were wide open, the guards taking little notice of who came and went, and the lack of magi or even senior officers was striking. There were queues outside the cooking tents, and shorter ones to a row of semi-permanent huts housing a bedraggled line of Dhassan women with jaded bodies and sour faces, too tired even to call out to passers-by.

'Hey! Who're you?' a guard barked at Alaron, the first to even notice he existed. 'Stop there!'

Alaron was dressed in a cloak over his monk garb, but he was clearly Yurosian. He probably presented quite a puzzle to the guard.

He conjured gnosis-light in his periapt and the guard's eyes bulged. 'Magister! I'm sorry—'

'Who's in command here?' Alaron asked. 'May I see him?'

The guard looked blank and sent him to a pilus, a cohort leader, who found a lost-looking tribune, who pointed him towards a large tent that was almost empty, apart from a pile of broken wooden cases filled with all manner of Dhassan and Keshi carpets, cushions, and trinkets.

'I say!' a Brevian man exclaimed from among the bunks, 'who're you?'

'Alaron, Founder of the Merozain Brotherhood. And you?'

'Kendric Vitalis of Brevia IV.' He pulled a puzzled face. 'The Mero-what?'

Alaron shook Vitalis' sweaty hand and asked, 'Are you in charge?'

'Me? Kore's Blood, no! I don't think anyone is – I'm just trying to get some sleep before I go on. It's been a nightmare since Bassaz.'

'What happened in Bassaz?'

'You don't know? Hel's Belles, where have you been? It was a disaster! Worse than Shaliyah!' Vitalis poured Alaron a mug of wine and motioned him to a chair before giving him a vivid account of construct-beasts going mad and destroying the army. 'The worst is it was our own people who did it: deserter scum, men who ran at Shaliyah. Old Kaltus himself brought us south, all of us either riding or flying so we could move fast. Now Kaltus is missing and people are saying he's *dead*. And the men coming in from the Zhassi say the First Army has *surrendered*.'

Alaron blinked. 'Surrendered?'

'We're screwed, I tell you – I'm flying straight home! The only organised Rondian force left in the East are these damned deserters.' Vitalis leaned forward conspiratorially. 'They say Korion's disowned bastard leads them!'

Kaltus Korion had dozens of bastards, but to be disowned implied prior legitimacy. 'Who's this Korion bastard?' Alaron asked.

'Seth Fetallink.' Vitalis, clearly delighted to have an audience, explained. 'Fetallink had been presumed dead at Shaliyah; then the

Old Man disowned him after he'd re-emerged as commander of a band of deserters. We went south to put them in irons! Then, well . . . *chaos!* They must have done something to our construct-beasts to make them turn on us. I barely got out, I swear.'

'Seth Korion commanded the deserters?' Alaron asked. *Seth Korion?* His memories of a timid young man who was permanently out of his depth didn't align with any of this . . . except maybe the deserting part.

'Seth *Fetallink*,' Vitalis corrected him. 'Never met him, but they say he's a dirty cocksucker who sold his arse to buy his men's passage through enemy lines.' He dropped his voice. 'There was something going on, something involving Pallas, because the camp was crawling with Treasury legates and Inquisitor spies.'

'Where are these deserters now?'

Vitalis glanced nervously to the south. 'They're coming up the high road behind us, making for the Bridge. If Fetallink can destroy our army, what else can he do? I've heard he's going to march all the way to Pallas and make himself *emperor*.'

Alaron stifled a snort . . . *But then, I was thrown out of the Arcanum as a failure, and here I am as an Ascendant with the Scytale of Corineus in my bag. What's Seth been through?* 'His army is just a few days away, you say?'

'Maybe only a day,' Vitalis insisted. 'I tell you, I'm gone, first light!'

'Then who's going to get the men here home?'

'Not my problem. The damned garrison commander fled last week. It's every man for himself! Unless you're going to join Seth Fetallink and march on Pallas? Up to you: I don't give a shit! This city is going to go to the dogs, I tell you.'

Kendric Vitalis clearly wasn't going to be any further help; all he cared about was filling his skiff with plunder and flying away. *I hope his skiff runs out of gnosis-energy over the sea*, Alaron thought. But he thanked the mage and left, found Yash outside and went looking for Ramita.

He found her with Corinea in their small camp. The skiffs were almost fully primed and Ramita was anxious to return to Lokistan and Dasra.

Alaron took up a relay-stave. 'I've just found out something. There's

DAVID HAIR

a Rondian army marching up from the south, and I know the commander: someone from my college.'

'A friend?'

'Not really. Actually, he was only marginally less despicable than Malevorn Andevarion – but he's not the same sort of person. I think I can talk to him.'

Ramon Sensini was riding alongside his cohort, cradling Julietta, while the rankers grinned at the sight of 'Bastidinio' bouncing her on his knee.

When the domes of Hebusalim came into sight, he gave the baby to one of the many Khotri wet-nurses, ignored a string of speculative comments from the cohort as to why he didn't feed the child himself and nudged Lu into the more rarefied air around Seth Korion, who'd decided his legions would enter the environs of the Holy City looking as military as possible. So while correct uniforms were by now a rarity, their armour had been polished and the men were marching in more or less unison.

'You know this could be a trap?' he murmured to Seth.

The young general started. 'Really?' Then he laughed nervously. 'No, no, there are no ambushes here.' He threw an amused look at Ramon. 'Not really.'

For a couple of days now, Seth had been behaving like he was in the know on some giant joke. It was irritating, but Ramon refused to admit he didn't know what was going on. None of the other magi had let on either, leaving him with no choice but to grit his teeth and carry on.

They could afford to rest here for no more than a week if they were to cross the Bridge with enough time to beat the rising waves. But the men badly needed that down-time; they'd been on the march almost continuously for two months – and there were things to do here, lots of things. He needed to deal with the gold before they got to the Bridge. He needed to keep Tomasi Fuldo and Silvio Anturo onside. They had to resupply and re-equip, not to mention ensuring no nasty surprises awaited them in Pontus. So far the Rondian

680

Empire had been utterly silent about the destruction of the cream of the Northern Army; he doubted that would last.

The Rondian staging camp on the south side, where they'd camped almost two years ago, was a burnt-out wilderness, still smouldering. The only sounds were the distant yapping of wild dogs, the cawing of the crows and the crash of timbers as the city gates slammed in their faces.

'I guess all the talk about Hebb hospitality was just that,' Jelaska sighed.

Seth turned to an aide. 'Have the men make camp here. I want to have a look around.' He glanced at Ramon. 'Come on, Sensini.'

This was far enough outside the normal protocol – commanders never wandered off on their own – that Ramon was immediately wary. But Seth was so relaxed that he decided that whatever was going on probably wasn't dangerous, so he affected an air of normality as they wandered into a ruined legion camp which reeked of piss and ash. The local Dhassans had clearly waited until it was empty, then destroyed anything they couldn't salvage.

Seth turned to him, expectation all over his face. 'So, Sensini . . . Ramon . . . do you know why we're here? I keep thinking you've guessed—'

'Honestly, I have no idea.'

'Really?' Seth laughed aloud. 'Wonderful! Well, here we are, you and I: alumni of Turm Zauberin Arcanum, yet together on another continent entirely! Everything is so alien, yet some things remain familiar—'

'Si, si, I get it: skip the speech!'

Seth laughed again. 'Very well.' He raised his arms as if making a dramatic conjuring, and shouted, '*Khazza!*'

Khazza? A meaningless phrase used by stage performers portraying magi? Ramon poked his tongue into his cheek and wondered if he'd lost track and this was some kind of belated birthday surprise. Then on all sides gnosis-light shimmered and a dozen grey-robed young men appeared as if from nowhere. They looked like some monastic order, but they also looked like they'd faced death, and dealt it out too.

Ramon stiffened, staring. All carried staffs with ribbons knotted near one end, had long hair tied in top-knots, and clean-shaven faces. And all were Lakh – which was perplexing as well, especially as they all bore periapts and had managed to conceal their presence from him with Illusion. He'd always considered himself skilled enough that no one except perhaps a Keeper could do that to him.

He checked: their wards were impressive, not showy but very strong. The only badge they displayed was of a stylised winged man. It wasn't an insignia he knew.

Then another figure stepped from the shadows, taller, but dressed in the same grey robes, nothing ornate. He too had a staff, but his skin was white. Ramon peered, perplexed, as the newcomer dropped the hood.

'ALARON?'

A second later he was pounding on Alaron's back and hugging him until they were both breathless. 'Sol et Lune, it's really you! What in Hel, amici? What in Hel—?'

Ramon barely recognised his best friend – though he was still no more than average height, and leaner than most, everything else was different. His reddish-brown hair was in a topknot like the monks, and he'd filled out with strongly sculpted muscle. His face was different too: the puppy-fat had been winnowed away, along with his usual jumpiness and uncertainty. He had the look of someone who'd seen deadly combat, and the measured assurance of someone who'd prevailed. There was something *balanced* about Alaron, a grace that had never been there before.

Is it really two years since we hunted the Scytale together? Two years!

There was also that ineffable look on Alaron's face of someone in love, so it was no great surprise when a diminutive woman approached deferentially. She too was Lakh, very dark about the face, with trim, pleasantly determined features. Despite her size, she walked as if she were as solid as the stone beneath her feet. She had a gem-stone pasted to her forehead and long black hair in a tight ponytail, and wore one of the graceful saris he'd seen on some of the Lakh women in Khotri.

Alaron put a possessive arm about her – she just about came up to his ribcage – and beamed. 'This is my wife, Ramita,' he announced proudly.

'*Your wife?*' Ramon yelped.

Judging from Seth Korion's startled exclamation, this was news to him too.

'Congratulations, amici!' Ramon looked at her wide-eyed then spread his arms. 'May I greet the bride?'

While Ramon hugged Ramita, Alaron greeted Seth warmly; this was their first meeting too since their gnostic-contact a few days back.

'I'd heard Seth was still alive and hoped that meant you were too,' he told Ramon, 'but I didn't know, and I feared trying to scry you might put you in danger. But when Seth said you were with him, I was overjoyed.'

'But not so overjoyed you contacted me immediately,' Ramon said archly.

'And miss the chance to shock you?' Alaron laughed.

Ramon suddenly realised something. 'You used an *illusion* . . .' Alaron winked, and indicated the satchel on his shoulder.

Ramon stared. <*Is that the Scytale?*>

Alaron's smile broadened, and suddenly the monks and their gnosis became explicable. Ramon's mind froze at the need to ask a thousand things and not knowing where to start.

There was so much to explain, on both sides. Ramon let Alaron guide the Lost Legions magi to a vast palace, damaged but in reasonable state for all that: the abandoned Domus Costruo. 'We've been waiting for you,' Alaron said. 'We're supposed to fly south tomorrow – Ramita's son is waiting for us at the monastery.' That required more explanations, as everything did. He was still amazed at the confident maturity of his friend: clearly he'd been through immense changes.

The other monks – who Alaron called 'Merozain brothers' – were introduced to the Lost Legion magi, and after some initial tension, a cautious bonhomie broke out, aided by the wine Alaron's people had found behind gnostic locks in an unlooted cellar. They all settled down to a simple meal Ramita cooked, which the legion magi survived thanks to having their taste buds tempered by their time at Ardijah, and they all spoke of their travels, skirting the hard questions.

There was an old woman, clearly a mage, with Alaron's party. She was introduced as Lillea, an ill-omened name, and she had an unnerving manner, but she drifted, inevitably, towards Jelaska, and soon the two older women were deep in conversation in one corner with a bottle of passable merlo.

After dinner Ramon drew Alaron aside and found somewhere where they could *really* talk. There was so much to tell each other it was overwhelming, and characteristically, they both interrupted each other wildly, jumping from subject to subject. There were tears over Cymbellea di Regia; they'd both been in love with her, in their own ways. There were toasts for Julietta, and Alaron's stepsons, Dasra and Nasatya. They whispered grimly about the death-camps and the other atrocities they'd seen, and shared a satisfied look over the demise of Malevorn Andevarion. They shook their heads over the Scytale, and the new way to harness the gnosis that Master Puravai had shown Alaron.

'You should keep that to yourselves, *amici*,' Ramon advised. 'You're going to need an edge if you plan to face down the empire and keep the Scytale.'

Alaron rolled his eyes. 'Listen to us! Here we are, barely out of college and talking about facing down the empire!' He dropped his voice. 'But that's exactly what we've begun doing. The Scytale and Master Puravai's methods – both of these things are world-changing, in the right hands or the wrong ones.'

'Then all the more reason to be careful, *amici*,' Ramon told him.

The night vanished as they skipped from topic to topic without feeling they'd done any of it justice. But what was best was just being together: for six years they'd shared a room at Turm Zauberin, and talked about *everything*. Just seeing Alaron lifted Ramon's heart in ways he could barely express.

It was dawn before they even thought about yawning, and they realised they were both a little drunk. Everyone else had drifted off to sleep, except the mysterious Lillea and Jelaska who were still continuing their cool, detached discussion in the only unbroken cupola on the roof.

'Oh yeah,' Alaron threw in as if it were a minor oversight, 'Lillea? She's really Corinea, the Queen of Evil.'

Ramon fell off his seat, clambered back on and stared at him blearily. Then he refilled their cups, and the conversation began again.

Near Brochena, Javon, on the continent of Antiopia
Jumada (Maicin) 930
23rd month of the Moontide

Cera Nesti was under siege. Every moment, someone wanted something from her. The triumphal journey to Brochena felt like a funerary procession as she mourned her brother, and indeed her whole family. She was the last of her line, and the family name would die when she took a husband, as it was inevitable she must.

All week since the battle at Jekuar, Stefan di Aranio and Emilio Gorgio had been parading energetically before the commoners who lined the road home, but she was tired of the attention. Even more irksome was watching Theo Vernio-Nesti and Massimo di Kestria milking the crowds, when they'd not even been at the battles. Anger and resentment led her to vie with them, to show them what real popularity looked like – they might have earned praise for deeds they'd not even done, but she'd won the people's hearts, in the Beggars' Court, at the canals in Forensa, by being at Jekuar, and in cheating death by stoning. The adulation that came her way was frighteningly intense. *Mater-Javonesi*, they called her, and Ja'afar-mata chanting so loudly that it echoed from the buildings.

When Elena heard them, her nose wrinkled. 'It sounds far too much like Mater-Imperia, don't you think?' she said in an acid voice. Elena wasn't at her best, though: Kazim Makani was unconscious in the healers' wagon, utterly unchanged. It was tearing her apart, ageing her like a life-raining spell.

Cera's champion wasn't riding with her for this part of the journey, but there was no danger; instead, she had the Ordo Costruo protectors, soaking up the rare acclaim of the people, and showing solidarity with her: *Mater-Javonesi* . . .

There is no king. The enemy are in flight and we are marching back to take Brochena once more. The Moontide is ending and the Crusade has failed.

In such a world, anything seemed possible. Anything at all.

She felt as if she were tiptoeing on the very edge of a giant sword. A slip in either direction and she would fall – but right now she was balancing, and if she could only take the last few steps, she would be safe . . .

All these men wish to go back to ruling the world. They can't imagine the unimaginable: a woman ruling in her own right, not as a proxy for a man. In a crisis they could manage ninety days under a female Autarch, but now the crisis has passed, they're chaffing for Salim to send his ambassadors to claim me and take me away.

How dare *they?*

'MATER-JAVONESI! MATER-JAVONESI!' The words broke about her in rising crescendos as she passed and she waved her hand absently as she wondered what really was possible in this new world.

Her attention was called back to the present as Rene Cardien nudged his placid horse alongside hers. 'Milady Cera, a moment if you will? I have been contacted by someone I thought long dead: Lady Ramita Meiros, Lord Antonin's widow, has scryed me, through mountains and across five hundred miles.' He sounded awestruck. 'She wishes to meet with the surviving Ordo Costruo.'

Cera asked, 'Why?' *Are the Ordo Costruo to be tempted away from us?*

'I don't know. But she's remarried, to one Alaron *Mercer*.'

The name was vaguely familiar. 'Wasn't Elena's sister married to a Mercer?'

'Indeed: this Alaron is her nephew.' Cardien pulled a grim face. 'Cera, Kazim Makani slew Antonin Meiros when he served the Hadishah. Prior to that, it appears he was betrothed to this same Ramita Ankesharan.'

Sol et Lune . . .

'What did you tell her?' she asked.

'We urged her to come as soon as possible.'

Hebusalim, Dhassa, on the continent of Antiopia
Jumada (Maicin) 930
23rd month of the Moontide

Seth Korion's Lost Legions stayed at the Ordo Costruo palace grounds for another four days after Alaron's monks left – Ramita had apparently scryed all the way to Javon and located Elena Anborn, Alaron's aunt, and they had changed plans abruptly and gone to see her. Ramon was clearly disappointed to lose his friend again so quickly. Seth envied their bond: he wished he had old friends like that.

So Malevorn's dead, and Francis too, from what the couriers out of Javon say . . . Good riddance.

He'd liked Mercer's pert little wife, who was an odd mix of deference and boldness. Mercer wasn't yet fluent in Lakh, but she spoke Rondian well, and they clearly doted on each other. Another twinge of jealousy.

And then there was Lillea. *I bet she'd have been interesting to talk to.* But Jelaska had monopolised her, and now she was gone too. Afterwards, Ramon had retreated into a re-opened smithy with Storn and a clutch of the wagons and was doing something mysterious. Seth was curious, but decided he'd get nowhere barging in – and anyway, he had bigger tasks. There was another march to plan.

What will I do when this is over? he wondered briefly, before deciding that was a luxury he didn't have time to speculate on. The present was too complex without worrying about the future: like how to get his 'deserters' safely to Pontus. Their ranks were swollen daily by small units from the Zhassi Valley or garrison units coming in, often led by a solitary pilus or serjant, seeking someone to look after them. The Lost Legions were now sheltering hundreds of men seeking safety from an increasingly bold and hostile Dhassan populace.

He sought out Ramon and raised the matter. 'Listen, I think we have to speak with the empire to negotiate safe passage over the Bridge.'

Ramon gave him a knowing smile and produced a relay-stave. 'I wondered when you'd think of that. Alaron and I talked about it before he left – he found a bundle of these in a wrecked windship on Ebensar Ridge and he left me a few.'

'A wrecked windship?' Seth whistled. 'Are the Keshi destroying our warbirds now?' He tapped his fingers nervously against his lip, then took the stave. It had Imperial Seals – not just standard bureaucracy or army, but real, actual House Sacrecour seals. 'This is attuned to the Imperial household!'

'Si. Apparently it's attuned to Big Lulu herself,' Ramon said blithely.

'Lucia? Kore's Blood! We can't just contact Mater-Imperia—'

'Sure we can! Let's give the old tart a shout.' Ramon winked, then his face became somewhat more serious. 'I'm not joking now: if we want to cross the Bridge, we've got to convince Pallas to let us – otherwise there will be legions blocking our way.'

Seth stared, then said slowly, 'I suppose we have to.' Before he could change his mind, he held the stave aloft and kindled gnostic energy on the seal.

A woman's face appeared in the smoke of the cook-fire and Seth's heart double-thumped. Mater-Imperia Lucia Sacrecour herself was standing there, the wind whipping through her hair. 'Who is this?' her cool matronly voice asked, while she peered doubtfully at him.

Every relay-stave is unique: she'll know this one came from the First Army, which surrendered . . .

'Mater-Imperia,' he said, managing to make his voice sound resolute, 'my name is Seth . . . *Korion*. I'm the commander of the Second Army. I'm in Hebusalim, and I wish to bring my men home.'

The sick look on the woman's face told its own tale, as did the hurried glances, left and right, and the sudden retreat into the shadow of what looked like a windship's bowsprit. 'You're the disowned son . . .'

'I'm here too,' Ramon chipped in. 'Ramon Sensini-Dubrayle.'

Lucia clutched at a railing. 'General Kaltus . . .' It was two weeks since the slaughter at the crossroads at Bassaz; she must know of that disaster – but clearly she'd still hoped to hear from her invincible general.

'My father is missing, presumed dead,' Seth said, amazed at how calm his voice sounded when his heart was trying to burst through his ribs. 'His whole army perished, except for those few who ran.'

'*Kore's Blood!*' Clearly her worst fears were confirmed. 'What do you want?'

'To come home, of course. And to be absolved of the unjust charges of desertion made against us. It is the least we are owed, for all we've been through.'

'And that's all?' Lucia asked slowly. 'What is it you *really* want?'

'I swear: all I want is justice for my men,' Seth maintained. He noted that Ramon was frowning and scratching his head. He wished suddenly that they'd sat down and scripted this discussion a little, but it was too late now.

'Where are you flying to, Lady?' Ramon asked.

Lucia paused, then looked at them carefully. 'I'm flying to Pontus, with my court, to greet the heroes of the Third Crusade as they return.'

'One broken army, limping home,' Ramon jeered. 'That's what you've achieved this time, *your Holiness*.'

Lucia's face went stony, her voice defensive. 'You are angry, I see that. Perhaps with some justification. But I assure you, Kaltus Korion managed the war, not me. If there were ... bad decisions ... they were made by him and his staff.' She dropped her voice even lower. 'Tell me ... there are rumours of gold ... ?'

'All true,' Ramon drawled. 'I'm richer than your whole damned empire right now: though that isn't hard, because you're so bankrupt I expect you're melting down your plates for coppers.'

Lucia's mouth became a thin line. 'Then you are thrice welcome,' she spat between gritted teeth. 'Listen, if this is some plot between you and your father, young Dubrayle, I congratulate you. You'll earn a place at the highest table if you bring it to me. Both of you. Anyway, the Imperial Council needs new blood.'

'Then we'll see you at Pontus, my Lady,' Seth said, feeling surprisingly calm now. 'Do you guarantee my men a safe crossing?'

They watched her calculating . . . her hooded eyes were manifestly untrustworthy, but she exhaled heavily and said, 'Very well. Yes, I guarantee your crossing.'

39

The Crossing

The Great Flood

The legend of a Great Flood inundating lands and swallowing up cities is, unsurprisingly, part of the mythology of both Yuros and Ahmedhassa. Most philosophers explain it in terms of folklore explaining the Sunsurge, the twelve-yearly wet season affecting both lands. However, we believe it has deeper roots, concerning the drowning of an isthmus that once linked the two continents.

ORDO COSTRUO COLLEGIATE, HEBUSALIM, 678

The Leviathan Bridge
Akhira (Junesse) 930
24th and final month of the Moontide

The Lost Legions reached Southpoint on the first day of Junesse, which, by conventional wisdom, meant they were cutting it pretty damned fine if they were to clamber up the ramp at Northpoint before the waves came crashing over the barriers and the Bridge disappeared under the seas again. Seth Korion was a worried general.

'Can't we get these damned wagons moving faster?' he muttered to Jelaska Lyndrethuse as they hunched over the pommels of their saddles. 'We're an army, not a migration.'

'I think we stopped being just an army some time ago,' Jelaska replied drily. 'We're more of a refugee column.'

The Argundian sorceress wasn't wrong; over the last three weeks the march of the Lost Legions had become something quite different. More of the rankers had taken wives among the widowed Dhassan

women, and destitute natives whose homes were ruined and liveli-
hoods destroyed had started following them, and it looked like they
intended to do so all the way to Yuros. There were deserters from
the First Army too, and survivors of Kaltus Korion's forces who'd followed them from Bassaz. A lot of them were garrison troops who'd
seen little action until after Shaliyah, when the populace had turned
on them with ferocity. All had harrowing tales of murder at night
and treacherous servants, but Seth couldn't help feeling most had
brought their misfortunes on themselves. Keeping the groups from
turning on each other was a full-time mission, but they had the food
to feed them, and he couldn't turn them away.

'We've got to make ten miles a day without rest,' he reminded
Jelaska, 'and even that won't get us to Northpoint Tower before the
last day of the bloody Moontide! We've got no room for mischance.'

'I know. Don't fret, we can do this. We've got the supplies, and
we're used to marching. We've got a solid road with no bumps, and
the weather's good. We'll make it with days to spare.'

Seth grimaced and fell silent. Together they watched as their first
riders trotted down the ramp, leaving the stupendous coastal wall, and
took to the Bridge. The lead man – Coll, one of Sensini's scouts – waved
cheerily, then kicked his horse into a trot, and his mounted cohort
pounded ahead, then onto the Bridge marched Fridryk Kippenegger's
Bullheads. The giant Schlessen was resplendent in a bull's-horn helm,
and a sultry, long-haired Dhassan woman was mounted behind him
in the saddle, wrapped in a cloak and clinging to his back.

'Who the Hel's she?' Seth asked.

'I gather she's the first Dhassan whore he had when we arrived
in Hebusalim. When we got back he went looking, threw her over
his shoulder and brought her back to camp. Her pimp was furious,
but what do you do when a seven-foot Schlessen wants your girl?'

'Is she willing?'

Jelaska shrugged. 'I did confront him on that question. Now the
soldiers are leaving, her prospects are dismal, to say the least: she'll
be stoned by her own people, while the pimp flees with all the gold
she and her fellow whores earned him. She certainly hasn't tried to

run away – quite the opposite, if you're unfortunate enough to be trying to sleep near his tent.'

'This war . . . life . . the morality of it – it's too complicated. I'll never make sense of it all.'

'You think too much, Seth.' Jelaska peered down to the arches that decorated the entrance to the Bridge. 'What's going on down there?' She pointed at Ramon Sensini, who was standing beside the bridge entrance, shaking hands with every ranker, admonishing each one over something, then passing on to the next.

'Something Ramon's cooked up,' he replied tiredly. 'He says he's congratulating the men, but who knows? I've got too much else to do to worry about him.'

Jelaska grunted. 'So have I.' She threw Seth a casual salute. 'Best I get my maniple moving, General.' She began to move off, then turned and smiled. 'Well done, Seth. I didn't honestly think you'd last the distance, but blood will out, yar?'

'Not blood,' Seth told her. 'Never that.'

He watched the sorceress ride off, then dragged his mind back to the present. The men were cheering and whooping like children. The Leviathan Bridge, the greatest construction in the history of the Urte, extended straight as a spear towards the horizon. The seas were churning some two hundred yards below it, but in just thirty days' time, the high tide would be crashing over it, drowning the structure as it sank a mile below the surface for the next decade. They had some hard days ahead if they were to avoid being washed from its surface and into the ocean.

Above them all stood Southpoint Tower: hundreds of feet high, gleaming white with a bulbous turret at the pinnacle, glowing even in daylight. Solarus crystals: thousands of energy reservoirs like the one Delta had worn, gathering the power required to hold the Bridge together beneath the waves. It took Seth's breath away, but it made him fearful, too. There were magi up there, everyone knew that: Imperial Keepers, there to make sure the captive Ordo Costruo did their tasks and preserved the Bridge. They hadn't responded when he and Jelaska had knocked on their door.

He wished Alaron Mercer was here: somehow, he felt that Alaron might have been able to make even the Keepers take notice. He just oozed capability and certainty now, but without the arrogance that most magi had – and what he'd glimpsed of his gnosis now was extraordinary. Despite this, he was still humble and optimistic, as if he refused to be disappointed in the world around him. *I'd like to be his friend*, Seth decided, though they'd not heard from Alaron since he left.

He let his mind drift as unit after unit descended the ramp to the beat of the drums and the call-and-response chants that echoed over the cliffs, almost drowned by the crashing of the waves below. It was a still day and the spray was minimal, but it was still a frightening sight, especially for the Khotri and Dhassan women in the baggage train. They were singing too, their beautiful eastern songs with strange cadences, to keep their spirits up in the face of such strangeness.

Perhaps I should have married a Dhassan girl: someone obedient and quiet.

All that they were leaving behind came back to him. Bathed in a nostalgic glow, it was glorious: crossing the Leviathan, the escape from Shaliyah, the battles at Ardijah and Riverdown, and that terrifying night at the crossroads at Bassaz. *But what I'll remember most are days like this . . . the wonderful strangeness of it all. Different songs and languages. Haunting faces and landscapes. Conversations around the evening fires. The sight of Rondian rankers and Khotri civilians working in harmony. Reading eastern poetry with Latif.*

For half a gilden I'd turn around and do it all again.

The march across the Bridge slid into tedious routine, just as it had on the journey south two years ago. The land vanished within a day and then all was sea and one straight road, roughly three wagons in breadth. The march to Antiopia had been very different, though: then they'd been marching alongside giant hulkas hauling the wagons, and everyone had been full of brisk vigour, confident in their invincibility. Faces came back to Seth of those gone or left behind: rough-spoken Jonti Duprey, fire-breathing Rufus Marle, poor dear Tyron Frand, laughing Baltus Prenton, peppy Severine Tisseme, surly Renn Bondeau and the rest, marching into glory, or so they thought. *Look at us now.* They had mostly lost their uniforms, their faces were burned and hair sun-bleached, boots and sword-hilts were worn down to virtually nothing, and they were pulling a rag-tag baggage train filled with dusky Noorie women. And worse: they were deserters, according to the empire, with none of the promises of fame and fortune kept.

Well, of fortune, anyway. Of fame – perhaps we'll rate a song, one day?

He smiled at that. A ballad about a bunch of deserters destroying the empire's most powerful army while trafficking ill-gotten gold across the deserts would most likely earn the singer a noose.

A week slid by and now they were marching through sea-mists and the air was growing steadily colder. Still there was no news from Alaron Mercer, nor of what awaited them. Occasional windskiffs skimmed by, high above and aloof, and the feeling that they were under scrutiny grew. Sudden squalls lashed them, greeted with wonder at first by the Ahmedhassan women, but then with resigned misery as the cold and damp bit into them. Seth could see the beginnings of homesickness and felt sorry for them and the hard emotional journey they were on. His feeling of responsibility for the well-being of all of his small, battered army was growing.

Did you feel this too, Father? This overwhelming responsibility for everyone? Or did you only see the personal glory accruing? Were your men people to you, or just tools?

He suspected it had always been the latter. Regret that he'd never had one final parley with his father – that he'd never even found the body – gnawed at him, along with his own uncertain future. Mater-Imperia might be cowed into granting the promised pardons, but would he, the disowned commander of a renegade force, ever find a home again?

He spent his evenings wandering around, not quite sure what he was doing until he saw a woman in the sky-blue robes of a healer, leaning against the railing staring at the sea. He looked about and saw that no one was paying attention, then pretended he'd coincidentally decided to enjoy the view here too.

'Good evening, General,' the woman said, lowering her hood. It wasn't Lanna Jureigh, as he'd expected, but Carmina Phyl, the dour healer who was never seen except in the healing tents or on her knees praying in the chapel tent. He couldn't remember exchanging more than a greeting with her, and he'd spent more time helping in the healing tents than most.

'Lovely evening,' he said awkwardly. He peered at the railing before her, where she'd planted a candle and was shielding it from the wind. Lighting a birthday candle was a Brician tradition. 'Is it your birthday?'

Carmina ducked her head shyly. 'Twenty-third.'

His eyebrows shot up. Everyone assumed Carmina was forty-odd.

'I know,' she said placidly as if she had read his mind. 'Some girls are pretty. Some aren't.' She looked away. 'Only pretty boys care what their girls look like.'

Seth didn't know what to say to that. Carmina's olive-skinned face – he understood her to be at least part-Estellan – was lined, her hair was already going grey and her hands were aged from constant washing. She always looked worn-out and world-weary. Who'd have guessed she was so young?

'Um,' he started, 'so, you're from Bricia too?'

She pulled a somewhat exasperated face. 'Seth Korion, I grew up on your family's estates in Jenterholt.'

'Oh.' He was willing to swear he'd never seen her before in his life, not until this march. But then, Jenterholt had been for hunting and riding and the other 'manly pastimes' his father had loved and he loathed. 'Who's your family?'

'My father is Pastor Teodorus Phyl: he was an Estellan pastor who married a Brician and preached at the Kore Church in Jenterholt for thirty years.' She laughed wryly. 'I was born on a pew.'

Seth couldn't remember the church she spoke of, but she told him she remembered him riding through with his family on the way to the hunting lodge – 'you were a very serious young man, riding a fine white horse' – and they swapped a few reminiscences about Bres.

Carmina cast an eye back to the wagon she and Lanna shared. A lantern had just gone out. 'Ah, there's the signal.' When he frowned she explained, 'When Ramon's gone, Lanna lights the lamp, so I know it's safe to return.'

Seth coloured. 'Um, that's . . . I'll have a word with him . . .'

Carmina pulled a face. 'There's no point. They're both sinners: good people, but sinners.' She blew out her birthday candle and prized the wax base from the stone railing. 'It's just hard, when you love someone, to see them with another.'

Oh dear Kore, she's not enraptured with the little sneak too, is she?

'Well, goodnight,' he offered, and moped off towards his tent.

The following morning, Seth was trotting his horse down the column, calling out encouragement to those he passed, taking their salutes and cheers. The warmth of the men seemed genuine, which perpetually surprised and humbled him. *If they knew what a mess I am they'd jeer me.* It felt good, though, just to have some unshaven ranker call out a banal greeting. *Perhaps it's this sense of belonging I'll miss most?*

'Sir,' an aide called, 'the scouts are back! They've spotted the Midpoint beacon.'

'Thank Kore,' Seth called. He peered through the mists and saw it too: a faintest glimmer in the northwest quadrant. He understood the beacon was visible from forty miles away, so they were still a few days out: making steady progress, but still cutting it too close for comfort. He scryed ahead, on the Bridge and in the skies above . . .

. . . and found more than he expected.

What in Hel?

He kicked his heels to his horse's flanks and went seeking advice.

Such was his urgency, he entered the healers' wagon without warning those inside, which was a mistake, for Lanna was playing tabula with Ramon on the rear pallet – and both were naked. Lanna gave him a reproving stare, but appeared in little hurry to redeem her modesty, glancing at him sideways as she pulled up a blanket that barely covered her.

'A timely interruption!' Ramon indicated the tabula board. 'It's going poorly.'

Seth averted his eyes from Lanna's breasts with some difficulty.

He'd never really seen breasts before, and hers were full and creamy, with big pink nipples. But the matter at hand was more pressing. 'Ramon, we're three days from Midpoint and there's a fleet of Imperial windships hovering above it. What are we going to do?'

Ramon stopped smiling. 'We've got no choice: we have to go on.'

'But what if they try to stop us?'

'Then, Lesser Son, we'll have to come up with something, won't we?' the Silacian said irritably. He scowled and brushed the tabula board clear. 'Rukking Empire! The only thing you can trust is that they'll lie to you!'

Brochena, Javon, on the continent of Antiopia
Akhira (Junesse) 930
24th and final month of the Moontide

Cera Nesti was almost disappointed that the old palace in Brochena hadn't been stormed, looted and burned to the ground. Looking up at those towers brought a pang of anxiety; too many associations – those halls were where she'd had to grow up, and been forced to deal with far too much. Her father had been murdered here, and so had her sister Solinde. It was here she'd betrayed Elena, been forced into marriage to Francis Dorobon and found fleeting love with Portia Tolidi.

So many ghosts, it must be haunted.

But she forced a smile and waved to the crowds. Her people, the citizens of Brochena especially, deserved that from her, not this moroseness. The city was divided, with the Dorobon immigrants barricaded into one district, under siege in the houses they'd seized – although you'd never know that from the packed Jhafi and Rimoni crowding the streets and plazas on her route. There were only friends here, screaming in joy at the victory and the return of *La Scrittoretta*.

She'd ridden through such crowds before, when the Gorgio had been driven out back before the Moontide even began, but this was different: the enemies weren't simply gone, they were destroyed. Javon had faced its greatest test and endured. This was a carnival with no restraint. The wall of sound, the cacophony of voices and feet and music and drums, was a solid thing, a wind that shook her. She had been riding her placid mare at walking pace, unwilling to have the soldiers around her deny the people the chance to see her. Grown men and women were weeping as they reached out, and she tried to grip as many of their hands as she could. It was hugely moving, and queasily addictive.

Cera knew that this adulation of her worried the nobles. Stefan di Aranio had a stony smile on his face; Justiano di Kestria looked a little scared. Emilio Gorgio was playing up to the crowd, trying to compensate for the hatred his family had earned on their previous visits to the capital. And Theo Vernio-Nesti was parading in Nesti violet and full armour, as if he'd been at the battles that had gained him his new status.

For now, everyone was an ally, at least nominally. But they knew, as she knew, that very soon it would all end for her. Already Salim's ambassadors had been in contact; he would soon take her south: she would marry and live and die in a foreign land. And these men would renew the old rivalries of the Rimoni Houses.

It was late afternoon by the time she reached the steps of the palace. She made a point of firmly embracing Don Perdonello, the head of the bureaucracy, and kissing his cheeks, for she knew that many regarded him and his Grey Crows as traitors for the work they'd been forced to do by the Dorobon. She knew better; Dorobon secrets had flowed ceaselessly from the palace through his people, while legislation was cleverly skewed and delayed. These were thankless, dangerous tasks appreciated only by those who couldn't acknowledge their efforts until now.

She was thankful that such was her prestige now, when she kissed his cheeks, he would be accepted again.

'Have the windships arrived?' she asked him. Kazim Makani had been shipped here, as had Tarita, along with the Ordo Costruo healers.

'Si; the patients are already housed in the healers' suite.'

'There are other magi coming from Kesh,' she told him. 'They are kin of Kazim Makani.' *Well, sort of.* 'Perhaps they can do something.' She looked at him beseechingly. 'In the meantime, Francesco, if I cannot use a chamber-pot, I swear that something inside me will rupture.'

Perdonello's eyes twinkled. 'Then let us go inside.'

There was a fraught banquet in the evening, with prayers for the fallen and toasts to all the Houses. Even the Gorgio were cheered. Emir Mekmud of Lybis had ridden to the capital when he heard of the victory, and the lords of Intemsa and Baroz also: every great lord of the realm was present. They each gave a speech, congratulating her on the victory and looking forward to a time when *normality* was restored. She knew what that meant: a king on the throne and women returned to the boudoirs.

Nevertheless, as outgoing Autarch, it was still permitted that she speak, and she had no intention of passing up the chance for a few final words. 'My Lords, we are victorious. We give thanks, to Ahm and to the Sol et Lune, for our survival. Javon is free!' The court cheered this easy, obvious stuff. 'We have all lost so many. My whole family lie entombed, and only my dear cousin Theo can prevent the name of Nesti from being consigned to the history books—!'

'Never, Lady! You are immortal!' one of the Jhafi princes shouted, which didn't please the Rimoni lords at all.

'We have been victorious,' she went on, 'because when it mattered, on the streets of Forensa when we were set to be crushed, and again at Jekuar, when our army stood in peril, we Javonesi pulled together and became a whole nation: Jhafi and Rimoni, knight and militia, man and woman, human and magi, all set aside our differences and even our traditional roles to fight as one. Against cruelty we deployed courage; faced with might we were resourceful and tenacious. Faced with difficulties and complexities, we were persistent, diligent and tireless. In crisis we did not splinter, but sacrificed for each other. That is Javon as I wish her to be.'

More applause, which she indulged while collecting herself for the next salvo.

'Javon has endured because we embraced friendship where it was offered. We've fought side by side, rival Houses in alliance, feuds put aside! We've been aided by Rondian magi, though our own priests reviled them! We've fought shoulder to shoulder with Hadishah, lamiae and foreign mercenaries. They fought at our side, because Javon offered them friendship and inclusion, and we must continue to do so, for we are still at war!'

There was confusion at these words, so she pressed on, 'Yes, my lords, we're still at war: against the consequences of this ruinous conflict. The Yurosian enemy has gone, but others enemies remain: Hunger. Disease. Poverty. Ruined homes and workplaces. Burnt-out and abandoned farms. Religious conflict. Racial divides. These will tear us apart, unless we rise above them and seek out the same allies who fought with us in wartime: we must enlist them to help us win the peace! Enlightenment and tolerance is required for such unity: it makes us *strong*!' She raised her goblet, challenged them. 'Please *pledge* with me: to winning the peace!'

They were silent for a second, until those at the back with the least to lose and the most to gain by showing solidarity with her stood and raised their goblets. It shamed the lords at the front, who were calculating what they were gaining and losing, into rising too.

'*To winning the peace!*'

She drained her cup, applauded them all, making sure the lords at the front knew the words were marked, then walked out of the hall, head throbbing and limbs shaking. *I'm so tired of this stress.* She hurried to her room and slammed the door.

An hour later, she was in her armchair, sipping wine and half-dozing, when there was a knock at her door, and it opened a fraction. Elena Anborn's scratchy voice called through the crack. 'Cera? I know you're awake.'

She sat up, rubbed her eyes and stood. 'What is it?'

'You have visitors.'

She groaned internally, splashed rosewater from her basin on her face and turned to the door, wondering what was happening. Elena had barely come near her since their arrival in Brochena. *What's happening?*

The small cluster of men who entered her reception room did

little to allay her nerves. They were a mix of Rimoni and Jhafi, men she knew well and some she didn't. Emir Mekmud of Lybis was foremost, his hard, scarred face set in determination but his eyes flickering nervously. The head of the Crown bureaucracy, Don Francesco Perdonello was behind the emir, alongside Pita Rosco and Piero Inveglio. Saarif Jelmud, the young Jhafi prince who'd distinguished himself at Forensa, was among them, and a handful of armed guards. All were cloaked and only lowered their hoods once the door was closed behind them. Elena remained at the door, but the tingle of light at her fingers showed that she was kindling wards to lock the door and prevent scrying of the room.

Sol et Lune! A conspiracy . . . ? Her heart thumped as she confronted them. 'My Lords, what is it?'

Emir Mekmud spoke up. 'Lady Cera, we are here without the knowledge of the Lords of Loctis, Hytel and Riban. We wish to speak with you on a most urgent matter.' He gestured at Don Perdonello, who stepped forward.

She went utterly still, feeling as if she knew exactly what was about to be said already. 'Lady Cera, the constitution of Javon permits only men of land and wealth to vote for the king. The wealth of Javon lies in the Great Houses of Jhafi and Rimoni, in Forensa, Loctis, Hytel and Riban. Their votes will determine which of them will become our new king. The law does not permit a woman to put herself forward, nor would the men of wealth vote for one if the law permitted it. This is certain.'

'But we do not wish one of those men to rule us, Lady,' Saarif Jelmud burst out. 'We want *you*.'

Cera's skin went prickly, and her heart thumped. She had to fight not to go weak at the knees. 'I'm flattered,' she said hesitantly, 'but the law is the law.'

'A law that denies the people the ruler they crave is not a just law,' Piero Inveglio declared steadily. 'It is an impediment to justice. You have won this victory. You have guided us through these terrible Moontide years intact, and you are adored by the people. Surely their will should also be heard?'

That Inveglio, who she was certain had been quietly profiteering from the conflict behind her back, would say such things made her eyes sting. They were all nodding, adding their own emphatic endorsements.

'We are not saying the elective kingship should be abandoned, Cera,' Pita Rosco said. 'Just that the process must be changed.'

'But such a change can only be voted upon by those entitled to vote for the king, and thus it will never happen,' Perdonello added. 'Sometimes good laws require a nudge.'

A nudge. By which they mean a palace coup.

'We have more than enough men in place, Lady,' the emir told her. 'And the people will support you. They remember your Beggars' Court, and how you returned from the dead. Your victories at Forensa and Jekuar have made your legend eternal. You are our queen in all but name.'

'The Aranio, Kestria and Gorgio soldiers are encamped outside the city,' Piero Inveglio added. 'If we seize their leaders, they won't press the assault. The Ordo Costruo have intimated that they will stand aside. The loss of life will be minimal, I promise you.'

All of their eyes burned into hers, *willing* her, demanding she give assent. For a moment it was impossible to breathe. *I fought to preserve the Javon that is* . . . But her knees almost rebelled as the possibilities opened up. She could install the Ordo Costruo in the Krak, and defy Salim to claim her. The Keshi would quickly grasp the new reality and in a post-Crusade world, there would be no trade blockade. They desperately needed the grain she would control – they would make a deal with Shaitan himself to feed themselves. Meanwhile the imprisoned lords would be hostages against insurrection in their cities – things would be tense, but they would settle down; she could likely release them in a few years without fuss or fear of retaliation. Yes, she would be seizing power illegally, and there would be fighting, but she'd *win*. Then she could have her people make her actions retrospectively legal, and if she left the existing mechanism of elective monarchy in place, merely tweaked to widen the vote and permit women to hold the throne: she'd have done a great thing, and the Great Houses would fall into line with the new reality.

And I'd be queen . . . for life.

She swallowed again, looked at Elena, beside the door. The mage-woman's face was still expressionless, but neutral, withholding judgement. <*Well, 'Mater-Javonesi' – isn't this what you really want?*> Elena's voice asked quietly inside her head. Past conversations resurfaced, of warnings about power and what it did to people.

Yes, oh yes, it is what I want . . .

The old Rimoni saying played in her head: *You cannot turn a rock into a statue without taking a hammer and chisel to it.* These men would be her hammer . . .

But . . . what if it spiralled out of control, into another war . . . ?

She looked away from her protector, looked upwards instead, so she wouldn't have to meet their eyes.

'My lords,' she said, as levelly as she could, 'please hear me. I am flattered – beyond expression. Never has a woman been so honoured as I am.' She swallowed, thought about the future that could be, and the deeds that such a future would require. Her hands were trembling so much she had to bunch them at her midriff. She had to be stern now, had to be . . . *regal.*

'My lords, I have spoken many times of the Javon I fight for: a place of togetherness and freedom, where just laws are agreed in honour. A military coup has no place in that Javon, even for the best of reasons. So I must decline your offer, well-intentioned though it is. Please, go now, and never speak of this again, lest you draw the wrath of the Great Houses down upon you.'

The room fell utterly silent, and the crushing disappointment on the faces of Mekmud, Saarif, Piero and Pita and the rest, was painful to see. A couple of the men swallowed anger, but she stared at them until they all bowed their heads. Inside a minute they had all slunk away.

Elena stood at the door, saying nothing, and then she too was gone, without even an inkling of whether she approved.

Cera let her knees give way, collapsed to the rug and cried for all that she could have had.

<Kazim?>

The voice was familiar, nagging at Kazim Makani's awareness. It seemed to have been calling him for some time, and when he recognised the voice, he was taken back not moments but years, to rooftops on balmy nights in Aruna Nagar, when life was innocent and he was in love with a dark little girl with worldly eyes: his last days of innocence. It was as real as if he was really there.

Perhaps I can stay in this dream for ever, and never go on.

But then he'd miss out on all the terror and triumph that had followed, the great and awful moments that had marked him, changed him, and left him here . . .

And he'd miss out on *Elena* . . .

'Alhana?'

His voice was thin, so weak it scared him, so he immediately spoke again. 'Alhana?'

But when his eyes flickered open, the light was too blinding to see, and the hard little hand wasn't *hers* but the other's, the rooftop girl, and a name resurfaced from the sea of memory. *'Ramita?'*

It really was her, his first real love, holding his hand and weeping tears that she blinked at furiously. 'O Kazim! Namaste, namaste . . .' She hugged him, her head on his chest, weeping, but he couldn't really see her, just dark shapes and blurred light.

Then *she* spoke. 'Kaz! Thank every god—!' And his Alhana was there with him, nudging Ramita aside and filling his nostrils and his ears, holding and shaking him, and then other things came back: *'The assassin . . . Timori—?'*

Elena clutched him and sent soothing energies into him to soften her awful news. 'Timori is dead,' she whispered, 'but so is Sordell, and you saved Cera, and you so nearly saved Timi too. You're the hero of the kingdom.'

He moved weakly, not really caring about that *bok*. His happy-sad little prince was dead. For a few minutes all he could think of was that. Only Elena's arms kept his heart from ripping in half.

Then the rest of what had just happened finally struck him. '*Ramita?* Is that really you?' *I killed her husband* . . . 'I'm *so* sorry, Mita. I'm so sorry!'

He couldn't see her expression – perhaps that was a good thing – but her tough little hands gripped his and squeezed. 'You did what you believed right, Kazim,' she said. 'I can forgive you now.'

His vision blurred, and for a long time all he could do was weep. When he finally remembered how to think and speak, he asked, 'Where have you been, Mita?'

She took a couple of goes to reply, and then all she said was, 'I have been *very* busy.'

Alaron Mercer had to remind himself of all that he'd been doing recently: becoming an Ascendant mage, defeating an insane Malevorn Andevarion and his daemons, marrying Antonin Meiros' widow. Those were things to draw confidence from. It made it easier to face the intense, judgmental grey eyes of the woman on the stone bench opposite: his Aunty Elena.

'How did the Lakh girl wake him?' Elena asked. The silent addendum to that question was clear: how did Ramita, who Kazim supposedly no longer loved, wake him, when Elena couldn't?'

'Ramita is stronger even than an Ascendant. It took that to reach him.'

Elena swallowed tightly. 'Then I'm grateful.' Her eyes narrowed again. 'You have the Scytale of Corineus?' Elena's flat tones didn't quite convey the scepticism on her face.

He pulled it out and showed her. She stared, then slowly took it from him, turning it over in her hands. 'And you've *used* it?' He responded by conjuring his aura so that she could measure his strength and see just what his affinities were: *everything*. Her mouth dropped open. 'What the Hel? Are you even Alaron any more? And you're dressed as a Zain. Why?'

It took some telling, the hunt for the Scytale, and the trek from

Yuros to Antiopia, how he'd met Ramita, the formation of the Merozain Brotherhood, all the people he'd found and lost. Master Puravai's revolutionary gnostic training methods took a lot of explanation, and demonstration too, before she could take it all in.

'And you're married to the Lakh girl? Do Vann and Tesla know?'

He bit his lip. 'Aunty Ella, I'm really sorry . . . Mum's dead.'

Comforting his tough, quicksilver aunty was perhaps the most alien part of the whole evening.

They were still holding hands and trading reminiscences when a servant scurried up. 'Lady Ramita asks you to attend on her and Lord Kazim immediately,' he said breathlessly.

Elena looked put out to be interrupted, but Alaron knew Ramita didn't summon him through servants frivolously. They hurried to the infirmary to find Kazim lying propped up in bed, and Ramita holding his hands. Alaron had to quell a moment of jealousy, recalling that these two had history that predated him, but Ramita's face was all concern.

'Al'Rhon, Alhana – Kazim has remembered something!'

They all looked at the young Keshi Souldrinker, who spoke in a dazed manner, as if he didn't quite trust his recollection. 'During the fight . . . the assassin linked minds with me, while trying to break my mental defences . . . I read something in his thoughts, a memory of a conversation . . .' He grabbed Elena's hands. 'Alhana – *Gurvon Gyle . . . the emperor . . . they're going to destroy the Leviathan Bridge!*'

40

Changing Loyalties

House Fasterius

The House of Fasterius married into the Sacrecour Dynasty in what was the culmination of a multi-generational campaign. It reached its fulfilment in Lucia, who risked spinsterhood in her unwavering focus on winning the prized hand of Emperor Magnus. Lucia had been regarded as a prodigy, someone who could advance our understanding of the gnosis in unknowable ways, but she abandoned study for court intrigues, and was lauded for doing so.

What hope is there for female emancipation when she is our shining example of womanhood?

JUSTINA MEIROS, ORDO COSTRUO COLLEGIATE,
HEBUSALIM, 909

Midpoint, Leviathan Bridge, in the Pontic Sea
Akhira (Junesse) 930
24th and final month of the Moontide

Gurvon Gyle had not tasted failure since the Noros Revolt, and even that defeat had not been this bitter.

I lost, in a game even Cera Nesti played better than I. It was galling, and no matter how often he promised himself that he would exact revenge in time, the stink of defeat lingered.

Since escaping Jekuar and recovering his gold from Brochena, he'd been flying west, stopping where he'd laid his bolt-holes against potential disaster. He'd stayed in each for a week, enough to replenish supplies, pick up a few items and most of all, to think. This latest hidey-hole was a cave east of the Krak di Condotiori. It reeked of dead game, but it sufficed, for now, while he thought things through.

Only when he felt he was truly ready did he pick up a relay-stave and reach out. It was morning, and Veritia, who had escaped Jekuar and was now his eyes and ears in Pontus, said the Imperial Fleet was nearby. He kindled the gnosis and reached with his mind . . .

. . . Mater-Imperia Lucia looked as if she'd been interrupted while dressing. Her hair was down, and she had on no make-up. It made her look strange, unfocused and imperfect: matching him, in a way. Her eyes had a slightly alarmed, scared look, as if she too were unravelling. *<Gyle? What in Hel do you want?>*

<I can contact you another time, Holiness,> he offered, not wanting to speak with her if she was angry.

She scowled, but her eyes were flickering nervously. She hunched towards him. *<You've woken me, that's all. I'm in Pontus.>*

<Pontus? My sympathies.>

She didn't smile. *<I'm surprised you have the temerity to contact me, Magister. A survivor has just reported the disaster you've made of Javon! Your mercenaries are destroyed and the Dorobon legion is annihilated – you've lost the entire kingdom!>*

He didn't bother to deny any of that. *<Not all is lost, Mater-Imperia. I have recovered most of the gold you paid me when the Dorobon landed. Ten thousand auros, at a time the gold price is massively inflated. I imagine that you badly need it.>*

Her eyes narrowed. *<If you think my favour can be purchased, you're badly mistaken, Magister Gyle.>*

He ignored that as the posturing of a trader. *<Mater-Imperia, I could have run and used this money to vanish from view. But I believe I can still be of service to you.>*

<I'm not listening, Gyle! I'm about to reissue the warrant on your life!>

Lucia didn't break the connection, though. He could sense her mind calculating, indeed, *grasping* at this offer with more alacrity than he had anticipated. Veritia had advised that the empire's monetary crisis ran deeper than he could imagine. He pressed on. *<When we all met in Pallas in 928, Mater-Imperia, you reminded me that I could never aspire*

to your heights. That was my motivation for seizing Javon when it became apparent that the Dorobon were incapable.>

Her eyebrows shot up. <You blame me for your treachery?>

<Not blame, Holiness. I only emphasise the impact your words had on me. I soon learned that you were right: those bred to rule are far better equipped to the task! I should have known my place: as a servant of the ruler, with no higher ambitions than to serve well.>

<Playing the obsequious courtier doesn't suit you, Gyle.> Lucia replied. <A servant must be trusted, or they are worse than useless.>

<I know, Mater-Imperia. I understand loyalty. That is why I wish to renew mine to you.>

Even the fact that she was considering his words told him that she must be more than a little desperate. Veritia had told him that Kaltus Korion was missing or dead, and a deserter army was marching on Pontus, led by Korion's bastard, with Dhassa falling into chaos as the legions retreated across the Bridge. The details were sketchy, but he guessed that Lucia was feeling incredibly insecure.

She came to a decision: <Listen to me, Gurvon Gyle. I may be prepared, as thanks for past services, to grant you a reprieve. Prove your loyalty: deliver yourself and your gold to me, in Pontus. If you come to me willingly, and surrender your wealth, I will consider your offer. Fail in this, and I will hunt you down.>

Two weeks later, his rehabilitation had apparently been accomplished. Of course he hadn't given back all of his gold, and of course Lucia knew that, but they both pretended otherwise. She'd hidden his presence, but allowed him a secret audience, and to kiss her signet ring and swear allegiance to her – and her alone, he'd noted. She'd also given him a detachment of Volsai – although he only advised them, nominally, at least. No doubt their orders were to eliminate him at the first sign of betrayal, or maybe even as soon as his mission was complete. He was willing to take that risk, to be once again on the inside of the Sacrecours, the biggest gang in Yuros, with a mission that ranked higher in Lucia's mind than all else . . .

Recovery of the empire's gold from the remnants of the Second Army.

Now they were on windcraft south of Midpoint, tracking the deserters marching north across the bridge.

'You are right, Magister Gyle,' the woman beside him said, lowering her eyeglass. 'The gold will be in the central wagons.' Her name was Yrna Corloi, a Pallacian Volsai captain, and they were on the deck of a Rondian windcraft designed for two crew and six passengers. They had four more 'Owls' – warrior-magi of the Imperial Volsai – with them. Below, the column of deserters on the bridge were slogging towards Midpoint Tower. The Imperial Fleet was only days away, and the Keepers were readying the destruction of the Leviathan Bridge, just as planned.

His task was to recover the gold before they destroyed the span and sent all upon it into the sea. Corloi's people had been watching the column for weeks.

'They utilise all the wagons in the daily operation of the column,' Yna Corloi went on, 'but there are twenty that are always separate from the rest of the column and seldom entered, except by the same drivers. Which is exactly how one would treat an unmarked bullion caravan.'

Corloi had a businesslike manner Gyle liked; she was focused entirely on the result required and the most efficient way to deliver it. She was a comparative rarity as a woman in the circles she moved in, and displayed no hint of a softer side, from her cropped grey hair and lined face to her bony body. There was a touch of Elena to her, but he was utterly unmoved. He felt scarred from his brushes with woman of late.

'Have the Keepers confirmed when they propose to begin their task?' he asked.

'Three days hence,' Corloi replied in her flat voice. She knew exactly what was planned for the Bridge, and professed eagerness for the spectacle. 'Magister Naxius himself has gone to Midpoint, to ensure that the solarus crystals have reached the correct levels of energy.'

Naxius? Is that snake still involved? 'That doesn't leave us a lot of time to seize the gold.'

'The operation will take minutes if done well,' Corloi replied. 'We'll have three warbirds and twenty magi. That will suffice. My people are the best in the empire – and we will have surprise on our side. I'm confident we'll be successful.'

'It would be desirable to take the bastard sons of Dubrayle and Korion alive,' he suggested. He was rather fascinated by the notion that Dubrayle had a bastard; delivering the Treasurer's head in a basket might be a way to a more secure future for himself. 'There may be deeper levels to this that we're unaware of, and obtaining a confession from one or both might have further advantages.'

'That is a lesser priority than the gold, of course.' Corloi sniffed. 'But we'll make the attempt.'

Ramon hadn't intended to be awake at midnight, but he couldn't sleep. He decided to try and walk himself into exhaustion, pacing back and forth, wrapped up against the chill. The weather had turned cold and clouds obscured the sky, sometimes sending flurries of rain and hail to sting their faces.

His worries focused on the following day, which would see them pass beneath Midpoint Tower. The scouts had reported a lot of aerial activity, but no one on the ground. He was increasingly convinced that the empire was going to try and stop them crossing the Bridge, even though their scrying showed no signs of other legions on the Bridge, or in Pontus.

He paused, leaned against the parapet and looked away to the north, where Midpoint Beacon was shining out over the tumult of waves and spray. The moon was reduced to a faintly gleaming disc above, its outline lost in a wash of silver. He wasn't the only one awake: to the rear in the women's caravan, the new mothers tended their newborns, and there were guards about.

Then lightning flashed, tinged with the raw power of gnostic energy, searing his retinas as it blasted apart the Argundian cohorts slumbering on either side of the bullion wagons. Even as this happened, dark shapes dropped into view above, raining arrows down into the camp, while others leaped from the windcraft onto the Bridge, blazing light as they came. For a moment his tired mind refused to take it in, but then instinct took over, not least because he'd been expecting something of the sort. He'd not intended to be so close when it happened, though.

'*Wake up!*' he shouted, drawing his sword as he ran forward, as more and more bolts flashed down, scattering the soldiers. 'Get out! *Get out!*' he yelled, as dark shapes dropped all around him; all of them were wrapped in gnostic shields, more magi than the entire Lost Legions could deploy. He had a split-second as they converged in which he wrenched open his belt-pouch and fished for the glass vial.

A mage-bolt slammed into his shields and staggered him and he heard a grunt, not of surprise but satisfaction. A grey-clad figure drifted on Air-gnosis towards him, sword raised and another bolt prepared. <*Here's one of them!*> he heard the man call.

He flipped the stopper and tipped the fluid into his mouth, swallowed as he shielded another bolt. The unpleasant tang filled his mouth. Then he was fighting for his life, blade to blade. His attacker was dauntingly skilled, each bolt designed to unhinge his shields and allow the blade to slide through at another point. Firing off magebolts in the midst of a sword-fight duel took skill and concentration, but his attacker managed easily. Then their blades locked and the other man twisted with practised power while a dagger appeared in his other hand. It gouged into Ramon's shielding like a carving knife slowly slicing through meat, then Ramon caught the man's dagger arm by the wrist and tried to wrench it away.

The Imperial mage slammed his knee into Ramon's groin and he almost vomited up the contents of the vial, but he forcibly swallowed it back down as the dagger was pressed to his throat and the man snapped, 'Yield or die, Dubrayle.'

The startling fact that the man knew his father's name made Ramon slam down his mental shields even as his body went rigid. He repelled a sudden blast of mesmeric-gnosis designed to cripple his mind. Their eyes met – the other man's were a bleak grey – and they contended mentally before the dagger pricked his throat again. 'Either I cut your throat, or you let me Chain you, boy.'

He made the decision to relent as the venom he'd ingested began to take away his choice. As he lay on his back and the Chain-rune began to form about him, he had a close-up view of the slickness of the Imperial attack. Most of their magi had formed a perimeter around the bullion wagons and all the crates were hurriedly checked then moved with kinesis into the windcraft while Seth's Lost Legions were still trying to organise some kind of response amidst the confusion. Torches flared all along the lines, arrows whistled in, but the counter-fire was muted and sporadic. Then the pain of the Chain-rune left him in convulsions.

As he lay there, his awareness shrinking and his vision blurring, he realised that the grey-clad man was still kneeling over him, guiding in a windskiff. 'Get him aboard,' he ordered tersely.

'The gold's almost loaded, sir,' one of the windsailors called, grabbing Ramon's ankles. The Rondians dumped him like a sack of grain into the skiff and the craft rose, as with rising panic Ramon realised the enormity of what he'd just done to himself.

The grey-clad man vaulted over the sides of the windcraft nimbly, straddling him and looking down. He had lank brown hair and a ferret-like face, flushed with success. 'Master Dubrayle, I'm delighted to make your acquaintance,' he said cheerfully. 'My name is Gurvon Gyle, and you are my prisoner.' Then his face went from smug triumph to worry as he took in Ramon's slack features and glazed eyes. 'Shit! He's taken poison.'

41

Imperial Fleet

Leviathan

In northern Yurosian myth, the Leviathan is a giant sea-serpent who swims the ocean. It is one of the spawn of Shaitan, the universal figure of evil who features in both Yurosian and Antiopian religious myth. Massive beyond reckoning, Leviathan is said to be able to take bites out of the coastline, and whip up giant waves. One day, the sea-folk say, Leviathan will swallow the land, presaging the end of the world. But in Kore mythology, Corineus will slay the Leviathan, heralding the Days of Bliss.

ORDO COSTRUO ARCANUM, HEBUSALIM, 771

Midpoint, Leviathan Bridge
Akhira (Junesse) 930
24th and last month of the Moontide

Ramon Sensini woke in bleary waves of consciousness from a very strange and involved dream. He had dim recollections of questions, and a lot of punches to the belly. His stomach muscles were screaming. As more of his faculties returned, he realised that he was bound hand and foot and roped to a pair of metal rings screwed into a wall inside a small wooden room. From the sound of wind and the motion of the floor, he decided he was below-decks on a very large windship.

He wasn't alone; there was another man chained as he was and bound to a hook on the opposite wall. He was slumped over, looking at Ramon with grave, reserved eyes.

Ramon knew him: it was Alaron's father. '*Vann?*'

Vannaton Mercer winced, as though he'd hoped that Ramon would somehow prove to be a figment of his imagination. But the spell was broken now; the illusion had spoken. 'Ramon? It is truly you? Holy Kore, what are you doing here?'

'I was going to ask you the same thing,' Ramon groaned. 'You were supposed to be safe . . . we hoped—'

'Some hope! But you're alive – when Gyle brought you in here, he thought you were dying. They tried to neutralise the poison but they weren't at all certain they'd succeeded . . .'

'They must have done enough,' Ramon replied warily. 'We shouldn't speak. There may be listeners.'

Vann still wanted to talk, though. 'Why do the Volsai think I know anything about the Scytale of Corineus, for Kore's sake?' Pain flared in his eyes. 'Is Alaron . . . ?'

Ramon slowly rubbed a thumb to his palm: the Silacian hand-sign that all was well. Vann nodded faintly, just once. They fell silent as Ramon tested the Chain-rune; it was strong, and his gnostic senses were blinded, though he did wonder if . . .

Vann spoke again, interrupting his train of thought. 'Listen, I'll tell you my story anyway. I've already told them a hundred times: I was pulled off the road by Jean Benoit during the early months of the Crusade. He'd heard that Inquisitors were asking about me, and Alaron too. He put me in a safehouse in Pontus and kept me stocked up – wine, food and gossip. But a couple of weeks ago, with no explanation, I was handed over to the Owls. They've been questioning me, but I know nothing about what they keep asking.'

'So Benoit sold you out, or one of his underlings did.'

'Who knows? Anyway, they've not really hurt me yet: I think because they know I'm telling the truth. I think I'm just insurance. But the day before yesterday they rushed me here.'

'Yesterday? How long have I been out?'

'You've been in here with me for a day. This is the first time you've been awake in – well, perhaps two days?'

Ramon groaned. *What if I spoke . . . then they'd know all about Alaron and the Scytale . . . Which would explain why they'd rush Vann here.* 'Vann, they're going to use you to get Alaron to turn himself in. They'll already be trying to contact him.'

Vann looked ill. 'What's he done?'

'I can't say, but think about it and you'll work it out.'

Sol et Lune, we're screwed. Alaron will surrender the Scytale to save his father, and then Lucia will unleash all her rukking Volsai and Keepers and the rest on Seth.

Time passed in an agony of bitterness, that all he'd done – that *they'd* all done – was going to fall short.

Then the door opened and a pair of burly windsailors clambered in, wrenched them both from the metal rings, and hauled them out into a narrow below-decks corridor. They were permitted to piss in the privy, then manhandled up a flight of steps and into a small room, richly appointed by windship standards. The Imperial Sacred Heart was embossed on every fixture, in gilt and paint, and the timbers were polished walnut, exquisitely finished. The seats they were made to kneel before were cushioned in purple velvet with gold tassels, imperial colours.

Some rich bastard's ship . . . I guess we're about to find out whose.

The door opened and three people came through. The first was Gurvon Gyle. He was on his toes, quivering with nervous energy, wide-eyed and alert as he took in the room and the captives. Then he faded into the background as a far more arresting pair, a man and a woman, entered.

Ramon's eyes went wide.

The man was young, in his twenties, with smooth cheeks and a mousy beard, a weak chin and furrowed brow, slightly stooped beneath the weight of a heavy gold crown. He was clad in heavy velvets and ermine, purple and red with a Sacred Heart embroidered on the back of his cloak. He flinched at seeing Ramon and Vann, as if the sight of them was offensive.

'Mother, who are these men?'

'They're just a pair of common traitors,' the woman replied. She had a pleasant but subtly forbidding face, framed by perfectly styled honey-blonde hair set with a diamond tiara. Her dress was cream-coloured, with a matching gem-encrusted cloak, and like Gyle, her eyes were everywhere at once. 'I said you didn't need to be here.'

Sol et Lune . . . the emperor and his Sainted Mother . . .

Emperor Constant's mouth twisted sullenly. 'You never tell me what's really happening.' He grabbed Vann's hair and yanked it cruelly. 'Who are you?'

'I'm Vannaton Mercer,' Vann gritted. 'Widower of Tesla Anborn of Norostein.'

'Another Noroman cowpat!' Constant sneered. 'I'm sick of them!' Then his eyes narrowed. 'Anborn? *Berial's* line? Is this man related to that traitor-woman in Javon? What was her name?'

'Elena Anborn,' Gurvon Gyle replied, a touch reluctantly.

Constant snickered lewdly. 'That's right: the bint whose purse you were stuffing.' He flapped his hands disgustedly, then looked at Ramon. 'Who's the Rimoni?'

'He's Silacian,' Mater-Imperia Lucia said, with grim satisfaction. She stepped before Ramon and slapped him, a gnosis-strengthened blow that almost took his head off. He found himself up against one wall, his cheek throbbing scarlet and his brain rattling inside his skull. 'Not so cocky now, you filthy smear of slime!'

Ramon strained at his bonds with futile rage, biting back a retort.

'You know him, Mother?' Constant asked irritably. 'Who is he?'

'This is Ramon Sensini . . . the bastard son of Calan Dubrayle.' Lucia smiled in satisfaction. 'I've wondered whether these constant crises in the Treasury are being manufactured by Dubrayle to create opportunities for himself. Now we find his own bastard embroiled in his plots. A confession from this piece of filth will be enough to bring his father down.'

Constant grinned as comprehension hit him. 'I don't like Dubrayle. He's too smart. I don't like clever people.'

Ramon spat blood on the pristine floor. 'Luckily you're surrounded by idiots.'

Constant kicked him in the belly and his vision went white as his holders dropped him and he fell to the floor. 'Don't you dare insult my mother, you heathen scum.'

'Are you sure she's your mother?' He grinned recklessly.

The next kick cracked at least two ribs.

'Enough!' Lucia snapped. 'He's baiting you, dearest. He thinks that he's got nothing to lose.' Her voice became sly. 'He's quite wrong. I've seen the reports: he's got a daughter down there. Julietta, isn't it?' Mater-Imperia's reptilian eyes fixed on his. 'Her future promises to be very, *very* brief.'

No, not my daughter—

Constant smirked, then yawned. 'Then hand him over to the torturers. I've got better things to do than dirty my boots on him.' He sauntered out, whistling.

'The empire's in wonderful hands,' Ramon managed to gasp.

'It is,' Lucia replied. 'We've prepared a confession, to be despatched to Pallas. You will add any relevant names we've omitted to the list of conspirators before we shatter every bone in your body then drip acid over you. Believe me, the Master Torturer will keep you alive, conscious and able to feel for far longer than you imagine. You have mocked me; there is a price to pay for that.' She turned to Gyle. 'How long until the Keepers are ready?'

'About four hours,' Gyle replied. 'The power in the solarus crystals will reach their peak two hours after midday.'

Through the pain and the mental anguish, Ramon wondered what they meant.

'Excellent,' Lucia said smugly. 'We'll bring these two out to watch. I want the Silacian to see the deaths of his daughter and his entire deserter rabble.' She turned to Gyle again. 'How much gold was recovered?'

'Seventy crates of ingots, Holiness. I estimate two hundred thousand gilden, at pre-war prices. That's now worth millions at today's gold price.'

'Extraordinary.' She looked at Ramon, faintly impressed, then at Gyle. 'When he's dead, I want his skull dipped in gold, as a souvenir.' Her eyes went to Vann. 'As for this one: keep trying to make contact with his son and let him know that we have him. Tell him if he tries to intervene, his father dies.'

'My son will know that if I'm in your hands, I'm dead already,' Vann replied.

Lucia's hooded eyes narrowed. 'Your son will not defy me. No one does. The cataclysm to come will show him that.' She whirled and stalked out.

Ramon looked at Vann with widening eyes. *What cataclysm?*

Seth Korion stared at the blackened circle of wreckage in the midst of the column with a numbed heart. 'You say the bullion wagons are all gone?' he whispered hoarsely. 'All twenty of them?'

Tribune Storn, logisticalus of the tenth maniple of Pallacios Thirteen, nodded wanly. 'Entirely, sir.'

When the attack had come, he'd been asleep near the advance guard. By the time he'd arrived, the enemy windcraft were lifting away. Losses had been light – apparently Ramon had advised the cohort commanders to keep their men well away from the wagons – and the enemy had been mostly focused on the wagons.

Which is what matters most to them, after all. We're nothing, compared to that.

'They've *really* captured Sensini?' If he asked often enough, perhaps someone would say 'No'.

'I'm sorry, sir.' Storn looked stricken. 'He often spoke of the dangers. We've some contingencies in place.'

'Contingencies? I don't need those: I need Ramon!' He looked at Jelaska helplessly. The Argundian sorceress was glaring up into the night, but their one windskiff had been burned out in the raid so they had no way of striking back, and no protection from the air at all. 'We should have returned to Ardijah,' he moaned.

He realised he was shaking and sweating, standing alone in a circle of watching faces, and none of them was the person he needed. *Ramon was always in control of this army. I'm just a figurehead. What the Hel do I do?*

'Calmly, lad,' Jelaska murmured. 'The army draws inspiration from its commander.'

'But I don't know what to do.'

'Nor I. But we're on a three-hundred-mile-long piece of stone, and if we don't get off one end, we drown.' She sighed regretfully. 'We've always known we'd get to this point one day, Seth. Dreams end. We were dead the moment we were assigned to the Southern Army.' She didn't sound unhappy about it, but she was a Necromancer; maybe she was looking forward to death.

'Do we push on? Or do we run back to Southpoint?' He knew his men wanted to go home. They'd made that choice a long time ago, even knowing the empire might prevent them. But now even seeing Pontus looked impossible, with all those windships hanging in the skies above, like an affront to gravity.

He was about to go on when a gnostic contact came. It was Alaron Mercer, and Seth seized the link like a lifeline. *<Mercer? What's happening? Where are you?>*

Alaron sounded no less desperate. *<Seth? Where's Ramon? I can't reach him!>*

<The empire hit us from above. They've taken Ramon. We're at Midpoint, we have no windships and half the Imperial windfleet is in the skies above. I don't know whether to go on or go back.>

<It makes no difference,> Alaron told him. *<The empire is planning to destroy the whole thing.>*

Through Seth's feet, the Bridge suddenly felt as flimsy as straw. *They can't . . .*

They could though. *Could, and would.* There was more, information rammed into his brain by Alaron at a pace he could barely follow: plates of earth thousands of miles wide, the energy of the Bridge unleashed . . . enough power to destroy Dhassa, and Pontus too. He clutched the parapet and whispered a prayer. For a moment he just wanted to run screaming, but the practical – there was absolutely nowhere to run – caught up with the need to resist, in whatever way they could.

<What can we do?> he said at last.

<Attack! Seize that tower if you can! At worst, give them something to look at other than me.>

<Where will you be?> he asked, but Alaron was already gone.

He looked up at the towers of black clouds, tasted rain and salt on his tongue, inhaled the briny air, caught up in a sudden, vivid dream of life, all his senses intensified. Nothing felt real, everything was intensified. 'Jelaska, what is the hour?'

'About four bells: two hours to midday.'

'Thank you.' He turned to the rest of his battlemagi. 'Array for battle. We must take Midpoint, or die trying.'

Javon Seas, west of Midpoint
Akhira (Junesse) 930
24th and last month of the Moontide

'Al'Rhon, listen to me. We must go to Southpoint Tower.'

Alaron peered past the sail of the skiff, which was almost ripping from the stresses they were placing the craft under. Ramita was huddled in the fore-deck to add weight to the prow and keep the skiff low to the wind. They'd been en route when he'd contacted Seth and found they were too late: the empire had struck already, and Ramon had been snatched. Now they were off the Javon coast, tearing westwards across the ocean. He'd been making for Midpoint, but now Ramita wanted to veer hundreds of miles off-course. 'Why?'

She squirmed her way back towards him along the hull, crawled around the mast and under the boom and gripped his knee. Her face was devoutly forthright. It was an expression he knew: the one she used when she'd run out of rational explanations for anything and fell back on religion. 'It is Fated,' she said earnestly.

Kore's bollocks it is! 'There is no such thing as Fate!' he shouted, really angry at her for the first time in his life. 'Fate is coincidence masquerading as order! We've got to reach Seth at Midpoint!'

'No! Listen, husband: Lord Meiros foresaw this moment three years ago!'

'*What?*' he exclaimed. '*Three years ago?* That's impossible—! The number of variables involved are too many!'

'Please, Al'Rhon! A few days before he was murdered, he took me to Southpoint! He showed me a tunnel, a way into the tower that the Imperial Magi don't know about! He made me memorise the place!'

Alaron's mind reeled. *Kore's Blood, can I credit that? Could Antonin Meiros really have predicted this?*

What Kazim had seen in Rutt Sordell's mind was that Emperor Constant planned at the end of the Crusade for the Imperial Keepers – the Ascendant magi who'd been given control of the Bridge after the First Crusade – to destroy the Bridge. Not only that, but they would unleash a cataclysm that would trigger a vast earthquake, intended to raise a permanent land-bridge between Yuros and Antiopia, leaving the East open to permanent conquest.

I have no idea how to prevent that, but clearly we would need to storm one of the towers to even stand a chance. Logically that should be Midpoint . . . but what if Southpoint suffices, and old Antonin really did show Ramita a way in . . . ?

He met Ramita's eyes, trying to see past her fervent conviction that the world operated like some giant fable to the real matter: that Seth had told him the towers were fortified and nigh impregnable.

We're going to need a way in somehow . . . which is what this tunnel would be . . . But it adds at least two hours to the journey, while Ramon is in their hands . . .

'My father once told me that to love is to trust,' he said at last.

Her eyes shone.

A few hours later, the *Seeker* was hurtling under semi-control on a southwest tack, moving at speeds it could only have made – hyper-charged with spells as it was – with both Alaron and Ramita pouring energy into the keel and summoning a storm behind them. Below them, the waves roared as they streaked towards Southpoint's distant beacon.

Alaron was so deeply enmeshed in his gnosis-workings, he almost

723

didn't notice the gnostic contact; but it was persistent, and strong. <*Alaron Mercer! Speak to me!*>

It was Mater-Imperia's voice, well remembered from their brief contact after he'd slain Malevorn. He almost rejected the contact, but decided to allow it, while minimising the link so that she couldn't trace his position. <*Yes?*>

<*Ah, Master Mercer,*> she purred, the voice a cat might use while toying with a half-dead mouse. <*You and I need to come to an arrangement, boy. Where are you?*>

<*I'm in Javon,*> he lied.

<*Ah! Visiting your backstabbing Aunty Elena, no doubt. Tell her that we have unsettled business.*>

<*Do you have something to say?*>

<*Indeed I do. Does this voice sound familiar?*> She paused, then said, <*Say your son's name, Mercer.*>

There was a gasping sound, then a male voice. <*Alaron?*>

<*Father!*> he blurted, then thought of all the ways that this could be a trick and shut his mouth.

<*Alaron, in three hours – ugh!*>

<*Father!*> he shouted, while Ramita's eyes widened in comprehension.

Lucia's voice came back. <*We bought him from his merchant friends, which tells you about the morality of that scum. I have your friend Sensini too. He's gagged, because of his foul mouth, but I assure you he's right here.*>

He believed her. *Which means she's right there, at Midpoint! She's come to watch the spectacle!*

The surge of hatred he felt was most un-Zain-like. <*What do you want?*>

<*Let me just start the negotiations with my opening offer, boy. Your father's life, and that of your friend, for the Scytale and a day's head-start before I send my people after you and all you love.*> She paused, her voice filled with controlled relish, then she couldn't help but add, <*And be prepared for news that will validate the power of my empire in the eyes of all of Urte.*>

He had his mouth half-open to retort, to tell her that he would do all he could to prevent that 'news', when he remembered that surprise might be the only weapon he and Ramita had. He almost offered the Scytale to prevent the Bridge's destruction – but no, that would betray that he knew what she was up to, and anyway, he was sure that she was going to do it anyway, come what may.

Instead he broke the contact before he betrayed too much.

Three hours? Is that what Da said? They were still at least an hour from Southpoint. *We're running out of time . . .*

Southpoint Tower, Dhassa
Akhira (Junesse) 930
24th and final month of the Moontide

'This is the place,' Ramita said, finding the angles Antonin Meiros had told her to draw between the tower, the hill to the southeast and the hillock on the coastline.

Sea mist was drifting in from the north where the waves thundered, but the skies overhead were clear. She and Alaron were cloaked by Illusion, in case there were watchers on the tower piercing the skies some four hundred yards away – no distance at all, when it filled the sky. The beacon shone so bright it hurt to look up at it.

She raised her hands and gently blew the sand from the trap-door. Alaron made a small sound in the back of his throat, but there was no time for wonder. The bridge still stood, that much was clear, but the tower beacon was glowing like a fallen star, pulsing ever brighter.

She laid her hand on the door and it clicked open of its own accord, revealing a manmade hole in the ground. Alaron eschewed the ladder and dropped through, staff and gnosis ready. Ramita followed, finding a narrow tunnel, the walls made of brick and the ceiling low. It smelled dry, and the air was cool, and utterly lifeless, without rodents or lizards or even insects.

Alaron went to lead the way, but she pulled his arm. 'My Lord expected me to come here. I will lead the way.' She conjured light and took the lead. The tunnel was clear and straight, and they could see their destination, a wooden door far in the distance. She strode towards it as fast as her legs could carry her, with Alaron chafing behind her.

She'd heard those snatched words: *Three hours*. That was two hours ago . . .

They were within a stone-throw of the door when something shimmered in the air before them. She cried out as an image of her husband appeared. He looked just as he had the first time she'd met him, with lank grey hair and a full, wispy beard. He looked haggard and drawn, smitten with grief.

'Speak your name,' the image said in a reserved voice.

She felt a surge of fear and hope; she'd encountered a similar gnostic message at the Isle of Glass. 'Ramita Ankesharan-Meiros,' she replied in a clear voice.

The image flickered, and then Lord Meiros reappeared, looking exactly as he had the day they visited Southpoint, shaven-headed, with the bristly goatee she'd persuaded him to adopt.

'Dearest Ramita,' the image said. 'I leave you this message, not knowing if you will ever hear it, and also that if you do, it is likely at great need, and I will not be with you. The only reason you would come here that I can divine is to try and prevent the destruction of the Bridge, something I've long expected the empire to attempt.'

Alaron looked astonished at how accurate Meiros' message was, but Ramita wasn't surprised; her first husband had been the greatest mage in the world: of course he knew.

'I will therefore be brief and factual,' the image went on. 'The Leviathan Bridge is sustained whilst underwater by the accumulated gnostic power of the five Towers, which accumulate solarus energy and convert it to Earth-gnosis. The bridge is a self-repairing entity that can survive almost anything, provided the towers remain intact. The towers themselves are warded against all but the most overwhelming attacks.

'We've long known that the power of the solarus crystals can be misused, and therefore the method of constructing them is carefully guarded. To date it has suited the empire to leave the Bridge intact, but that has always been likely to change. To prevent them, you must first climb the tower to the highest room, the one beneath the solarus crystals themselves. Each of the Five Towers contributes equally to the control and flow of energy into the Bridge and they are manned at all times. Since the Bridge was seized, this has been performed by Imperial magi, with the cooperation of the Ordo Costruo. To destroy the Bridge requires the five magi manning each nexus-throne to collectively act to destroy the Bridge by disrupting the flow of energy. To prevent this requires one of the five to overcome the other four and wrest control.

'This is what you must do, my dearest: get to that nexus-throne, enter the link with the other four and prevent harm to the Bridge. They will try to stop you, and they'll be able to strike at you, even hundreds of miles away in the other towers. But you will be able to strike at them as well.'

The old mage's voice became low and earnest. 'My dearest, to achieve this you *must* have gained the gnosis in the strength I hoped, and learned to use it. You will be facing Keepers, cunning old Ascendant magi with vast experience. So I beg you: whatever need drove you here, go no further if you aren't the person required for this task. I'd rather lose the Bridge than lose you. If this task is beyond you, go home. Protect our children. And know that I care deeply for you.'

Meiros reached out, but his hand passed through her, flickered and then he was gone, leaving her tearful and shaken. She swallowed heavily, looking away when Alaron squeezed her shoulder. He looked overawed, as if he suddenly didn't think himself worthy of her.

'Am I ready?' she asked him. 'Can I do this?'

'I believe in you,' Alaron replied, with exactly the certainty she needed to hear. 'You're the strongest mage I've ever met, stronger even than an Ascendant. Your technique is improving all the time.' He bit his lip, then added, 'The key to fighting against many is to keep up a strong defensive screen, be mobile and to strike suddenly at the most vulnerable. We learned that in the Arcanum.'

'I'll remember. Thank you, my love.'

Alaron took a deep breath and flexed his shoulders. 'Then let's go.' They'd both been awake and active now for three days, and he looked exhausted, dark circles like bruises beneath his glazed eyes. She could feel him drawing on his reservoirs of energy to reinvigorate himself. She was doing the same.

The door before them wasn't locked. It opened onto a spiralling stair that led upwards, completely dark, and so narrow they were forced to go one at a time. Alaron went ahead and she let him: she had to take the throne, so his role was to get her there.

The stair led to a blank wall, with a touch-panel of carved stone: Ramita recognised the design from the panel used in Casa Meiros to allow only certain persons through. She put her palm to it, felt a faint tingle, then the door slid aside. Alaron peered left and right then stepped through, and she followed. The door, invisible from this side, closed silently. They were on a small landing in another spiral stair, this one well-lit with oil-lamps, floored in tiled sandstone with whitewashed walls. There was a musty, enclosed smell that hadn't been present in the tunnel, and distant noise. Moreover, there was the throb of powerful gnosis above them, pulsing like a giant heartbeat.

Alaron brandished his staff, while she drew a knife. She hadn't done a lot of fighting; instead, she'd applied herself to learning the gnosis with all the ferocity she could. She readied shields as they climbed higher and higher, still unseen and unchallenged, even passing doors from whence voices could be heard. Then another door loomed above, and the end of the stair. Before they could compose themselves, that door opened, and a redheaded woman wearing a silver sun and moon mask and deep blue robes stepped through, calling a farewell over her shoulder.

Then she saw them and froze, but not for long: mage-fire blossomed and flew.

42

A Storm at Midpoint

House Sacrecour

*The name Sacrecour means of course, 'Sacred Heart', a reference to Corineus'
heart that Corinea split with her dagger. Ironically, the image of the dagger
and heart is seen as a symbol of religious fidelity and purity by worshippers of
the Kore. The victims of the empire have another view: their dagger, our hearts.*

KING PHYLLIOS III OF NOROS, 910
(DURING THE NOROS REVOLT)

Midpoint, Leviathan Bridge
Junesse (Akhira) 930
24th and last month of the Moontide

The storm was rising, and so was the tide. Freezing winds from the
north were whipping spray from the churning seas below into their
faces, and lightning crackled on the horizon as Seth Korion strode
to the front of the lines.

It was the strangest battle he could ever have envisaged: with the
battlefield a ninety-foot-wide bridge, and the only visible enemies a
pair of large windships tethered to a platform just below the summit
of the tower. But he was under no illusions. *We must get inside, or we
drown.*

For the attack he'd summoned all his battle-magi, and the best
fighting men from among the rankers: the elite cohorts of Jelaska's Argundians and Kippenegger's Bullheads, and Ramon's personal
cohort, who'd refused to stay behind. For now, the unseen windfleet

somewhere in the clouds above had not reacted to his mustering, but he didn't doubt they were watching.

Mercer said two hours . . . that was nearly an hour and a half ago.

He'd not told anyone why they were doing this yet: he didn't want panic. If that was the wrong thing, he'd have about half an hour to live with it. But he did convey urgency.

'Listen, come in close,' he told the men and magi. He had Jelaska with him, Kip, Gerdhart and Hale. Lanna was here in case she could save anyone who fell. That left just Carmina with the rest of the column, though he doubted keeping her out of the fight would improve her survival chances much. *Virgins go straight to Paradise, according to the* Book of Kore. *I guess I'll see her there.*

He waved a hand for their attention as another rain-squall began. 'I'm going to keep this brief. After all we've been through, it comes down to this: the empire doesn't want us to go home. They're going to destroy the Bridge, with us on it, very soon. There is no time to save the column, and nowhere safe, even on this island. The only chance we have is to take this tower. So we're going to attack. If you've a question, make it a good one, because we've got about half an hour to do this.'

The looks on their faces were eloquent: initial surprise but not shock: they had probably all expected some act of treachery. Arguably not one as drastic as this, though. 'How do we get in?' asked one of Ramon's serjants, Vidran.

'Through the front door. We magi will kick it in, then it's up and up and up, and kill everyone you meet.' Seth was curiously unafraid. With so few options, there was no room for doubt. 'Any other questions?'

Jelaska shook her head, answering for everyone.

'Good, then let's go.'

They strode towards the huge tower, fanning out in case of fire from above, but the only resistance was the wind scouring their faces. Behind them the column lurched into motion again, moving everyone they could onto the island, in case the solid ground might offer some kind of protection from what was to come. Midpoint Island was a barren and pathless lump of rock only a mile or so wide, and being on it or the bridge probably wouldn't make the slightest difference. But there was no panic, and that was what gave him heart. They reached the steps unopposed, walked right to the door at the foot of the spire, glowing with its own light beneath the black clouds.

'Take us 'arf an hour jus' to walk up it,' Harmon, another of Ramon's men, commented. His flaxen hair was plastered to his face and his blade glistened with rain.

'That's cos yer a lazy Tocker,' Vidran grinned. 'Can't walk ten paces wi'out needin' a breather.'

Jelaska strode to the only entranceway, giant doors at the top of the stairs. At once they began to glow with pale tracery, curved webs of light hinting at the wards beneath. 'Locking wards, woven with protective spells,' she reported. She wiped strands of wet hair from her face. 'The Keepers set them . . . this won't be instant.'

They all watched anxiously as the sorceress drew on her gnosis and laid hands on the door.

'Holy shit! Lookit that!' half of the cohort exclaimed. In the stonework above, a carved face came to life, peering down at them. Seth prepared to counter whatever it did, but it merely observed as the energies around Jelaska grew.

'Shields up,' the cohort's pilus, the always calm Vereloni called Lukaz ordered. 'Rim to rim, lads.'

A locking spell was a simple binding enchantment made to hold two objects together; it was easy to cast – and to disrupt, though it took strength. An active counter-spell would usually triumph against a passive lock eventually, though other spells woven in made it more complex – harder and more dangerous to disrupt. He could tell just by the interplay of forces that this one was strongly wrought and multi-faceted.

Minutes crawled by as they sweated and worried. Seth glanced back down the Bridge; the rest of the army was slowly rolling into motion under the direction of their officers, crawling onto the solid rock of Midpoint.

Suddenly the air around Jelaska flashed scarlet and a torrent of fire poured from the handles, engulfing her. But she was well-warded, and absorbed the flame with no more cost than charring of the hems and sleeves of her robe. A few seconds later, the lock flashed blue and she stepped back to allow the doors to swing open.

They should have expected the crossbow bolts that sleeted out of the darkness inside.

Seth saw a hail of foot-long bolts pluck at Jelaska's shields, staggering her backwards as her shields were battered scarlet then torn apart. She screamed and doubled over, clutching her belly. The bolts that bypassed her battered the locked shields of Lukaz's cohort.

'Attack!' Seth shouted, and hurled himself forward.

A second volley slammed into his shields and tore them up, but the bolts only ripped his sleeves or grazed him as he ran forward onto a forest of spears. At his side Gerdhart, brandishing a big flanged mace, unleashed a torrent of blue mage-bolts into the massed Imperial Guardsmen shielding the archers. Then with a roar Lukaz's men poured in, and behind came the mass of Kippenegger's Bullheads, Kip at their head in his bull helm, zweihandle flashing as he hacked through a line of spearmen.

Seth followed them in, seeking magi enemies, but a pair of rankers at the side of the entrance lunged at him. He stabbed straight-armed through one's chest, but took a spear in the thigh; he numbed the pain with healing gnosis and wrenched it out, stabbed the spearman through the throat, then kicked him away. For another thirty seconds it was bewildering carnage, all hack and stab and blast. But men like Vidran and Harmon danced through it, two moves ahead of everyone else, carving paths that others widened and followed. Seth found space as a silver-masked mage on the stairs locked eyes with him, and for a moment they contested a mental link that left him staggered. He was gripped by immense power, Ascendant-strength, and was barely holding on, until Kip – unnoticed in the tumult – hacked at the masked man's leg and severed it. A second later the masked head rolled and Kip was roaring to his gods. Around him, his men were butchering the Imperial Guardsmen barbarically.

'"How thin the line between man and beast,"' Seth found himself quoting, adding reflexively, 'Sytrius the Younger.'

'The Elder, actually,' Lukaz corrected him, then shouted at his men, while Seth threw him a look of startled appreciation. 'Find the next doors! *Move it!*'

'He's right, we're done here,' Gerdhart panted, pulling his mace from the smashed helm of a spearman.

'Jelaska?'

The chaplain shook his head. 'I don't know.'

Holy Kore, we pray for our sister Jelaska . . . 'We go on!'

He took the lead as they pounded up the stairs.

'The deserters are attacking the tower,' Yrna Corloi remarked, staring from the side of the windship. 'Do they know what's happening?'

Gyle rubbed at his stubble and wondered. 'Does it matter? Can they do anything?'

Corloi scowled. 'Do I look like a Keeper?' She closed her eyes and muttered something through a gnostic-link, then turned back to him. 'Twenty minutes until destruction. The emperor is nervous.'

'Constant Sacrecour is always nervous. But does he have a right to be?'

'Not unless they reach the throne room. Should we help the defenders?'

'No! Why would we go down there? It's going to explode in twenty minutes.'

Corloi's look of contempt was more eloquent than any words. She stalked away to another vantage point, but he noticed she didn't go rushing off to defend Midpoint, either. He returned his gaze to the tower, focusing on the platform at the pinnacle, where four windsloops were now moored, ready to evacuate the Keepers once the destruction of the Bridge had been set in motion. The crystal cluster was now glowing so brightly no one could look straight at it. He'd heard those crystals were so debilitating the magi stationed there had to use special masks and garments to endure them and he understood that now: the air was growing hot and tainted.

He turned to see Vann Mercer and Ramon Sensini being marched onto the deck. He frowned, then looked at Mater-Imperia as she emerged from her cabin beneath the after-deck, alive with feverish triumph.

'What a day this is, Magister Gyle!' she called. 'Lightning, battle – and soon the greatest triumph of my son's reign. Are you ready for the spectacle?'

'Seth Korion's men are attacking the Tower.'

'There are twelve Keepers tending Naxius in the main chamber, and ten Volsai with five cohorts of rankers holding the lower levels. Within ten minutes, there is nothing anyone can do to prevent the release of the energy from the Bridge anyway. Korion's wasting his last breath.'

The stairs went on for ever, but they were still a blur as they stormed upwards. Seth pulled morphic-gnosis into his limbs to give him the strength, as did Gerdhart and Hale, behind him. They slammed into another ambush in a reception hall, with crossbowmen, spearmen and more silver-masked magi firing on them from the balcony above. A furious exchange of mage-fire presaged a blind charge by Kippenegger's Bullheads, who hurled themselves bodily into a withering volley of fire and shafts, then carved through the defenders. The stairs began to run with blood as Seth and Gerdhart led a second wave, Ramon's cohort, who were fighting with controlled professionalism.

The masked magi kept pulling out of reach, taking toll with mage-bolts and fire. They overmatched Seth's magi in power – they were pure- and half-bloods – but they were scholars and researchers, not battle-magi, and didn't fight well. Somewhat to his surprise, Seth found he could deal with them. Pilus Lukaz realised the squalor and chaos of battle confused their enemies, so he let Seth, Hale and Gerhardt distract the masked magi while he sent his men at them from unseen angles. Seth was struggling with a masked woman when the pilus himself darted in on her blindside and his shortsword skewered her beneath the armpit and into her heart. She sagged, and her mask slipped to reveal a middle-aged, bewildered face.

734

'Never liked killin' women,' Lukaz muttered.

'You had no choice,' Seth told him.

'Not this time,' the Vereloni said. 'Kill'd a woman I thought I loved in jealousy, years back. Should'a been hung, but got away. Been tryin' t'make up for it since.' He straightened. 'Old story.'

The hall was cleared. Harmon and Vidran had taken down another masked mage with a deadly double attack, though it cost Harmon a blast of flame in the side that had charred his flesh to the bared ribs. He was now slumped against a wall, unable to move or speak from the pain.

'Healer!' Lukaz shouted, but there was no time to do anything for him.

'Keep climbing,' Seth shouted. 'Kip, you're in front this time! Move!'

On they pounded, up and up. The only window they passed was blank and rain-lashed, and still the stair wound on, narrowing with every turn. Seth rounded a curve, then flung himself aside as a crossbow bolt pinged off the wall beside him and ricocheted against Kippenegger's shields, already broken. Half a dozen more bolts flew harmlessly; the shooters were not even visible. The part of him that was now inured to war thought, *They're panicky.* He looked over his shoulder and signed to Kip. 'Send in rankers to soak up the bolts, then go in.'

In other words, sacrifice the weak, and push on . . .

He hated himself, but Kippenegger nodded grimly and began reeling off names. 'Go! Go!' he finished, 'Minaus is watching!'

While they prepared, Seth closed his eyes and reached with his mind, found the crossbowmen, a dozen frightened men reloading under the eyes of three silver-masked magi. Then he reached further inside himself for something he'd never really used before: battle-divination. He had the training, but had never been able to use it, because fighting scared him.

I'm beyond scared now. So I may as well give it a try.

Using Divination to skim the subconscious minds of enemies as you fought them enabled the mage to read their intentions. Instinctive fighters – men like Harmon and Vidran – did it subconsciously, reading the way an opponent moved, anticipating their actions, but the gnosis offered advantages to those with the right affinities.

He shared a look with Kip. The giant Schlessen reached out, clasped his hand and said 'Bruder.' Then he bellowed his orders and the first of his Bullheads tore around the bend into a storm and were battered and thrown backwards in torn heaps – but Seth flung himself around the corner too, screaming 'A Korion! *A Korion!*'

The second rank of crossbowmen all fired at once, triggers jerked in reflex, and the bolts rained onto Seth's shields or against the wall, but by then he was already at the far wall, where his Divination showed fewer bolts would strike. One grazed his thigh, then his shields reformed and he fired off a mage-bolt. Someone howled and clattered to the stone. Then with a huge roar Kip led more Bullheads barrelling around the corner, driving Seth on into the ranks of crossbowmen. Mage-bolts flashed and a torrent of flames poured over the first men, charring the unprotected, and Kip, shielding to the edge of his ability and beyond, was flung backwards. Those who followed him screamed as if berserk, taking advantage of the respite won them by the front rank to reach their foes and start hacking them apart with axes.

'Kip?'

Seth hurried to the giant Schlessen. His whole face was burned raw, his leather armour charred brittle, but he grinned fiercely. Then he swore, launched himself at Seth and bore him backwards as the roof fell in.

Seth cried aloud as he felt the men above – from both sides – die, crushed by falling stone. Then the smoke and dust billowed and engulfed them, choking, so that they had to crawl lower, seeking air.

When they'd managed to find a place where they could breathe, their plight was revealed: the way forward was blocked with debris and crushed bodies, their blood bonding the dust like cement in the cracks. Seth looked up, then lowered his eyes, feeling as crushed as those beneath the rubble. Beside him, Kip sank to his knees.

There's no way forward. We can't go on.

'Ramon,' Vann Mercer said quietly, 'thank you for being a friend to Alaron.'

Nudged from his reverie, Ramon looked sideways. 'It was my privilege,' he replied. *At least Alaron's in Javon, out of the danger area.* He felt lightheaded, strangely disconnected, constantly distracted by strange perceptions. The aftermath of the poison made it an effort to just stay still and listen, even in this situation.

'Did Alaron know your parentage?' Vann asked. 'Your real father?'

'Sol et Lune, no!' Ramon snorted. 'I couldn't trust him not to blurt it out in class.'

They were chained to the rails of the Imperial Flagship by both wrists, so they couldn't turn away. He guessed closing his eyes was always an option, but when he did, faces swam into his mind: Julietta, Seth, Sevvie, Lanna, Kip, Lukaz, Jelaska and all the rest. It was easier to just watch the tiny shapes below and pretend he didn't know them. He'd been seeking some way to intervene, but nothing came to mind.

'We should have stayed in Dhassa,' he muttered.

'Gyle boasts that this will destroy all of Dhassa and Pontus,' Vann reminded him.

'Si. Well, we should have stayed in Ardijah then. We were welcome there.' He thought regretfully of Amiza al'Calipha. *I should have stayed with her and our child.*

Which of the tiny dots below was Julietta? Where was Seth? Was it possible some would survive? The Air- or Water-magi, perhaps? Was there *anything* he could do to help them?

Imperial windskiffs were swooping over the column, randomly blasting *his people* for the fun of it: a new variant of 'braffing' – shooting birds – for the young mage-nobles to play. Meanwhile, the whole Bridge appeared about to be engulfed by the storm waves. He felt so helpless it made him want to scream.

Pater Sol, I don't really pray, because you're just make-believe. But if you want to prove you are real, do something! Prove me wrong! Give me a chance here . . .

The solarus crystals gleamed brighter still, and suddenly beams of light shot out from four points of the compass and locked on Midpoint Tower, forming a horizontal 'X'. The countdown to destruction had begun.

'Ah!' a woman sighed, behind Ramon's ear. 'See that, Dubrayle?'

'My name is Sensini,' he retorted dully.

Mater-Imperia Lucia waved her hand in merry dismissal. 'Call yourself what you like.' She pointed at the bolts of light, visibly excited. 'It's irrevocable now: the Bridge is coming down.' She smiled musingly. 'My foolish son wanted to see it all from close up, but he'll be disembarking from the tower any moment now.' She turned to face Ramon. 'Enjoy the spectacle, *Sensini*.'

It was all he could do at that moment not to lash out, but this still wasn't the moment he sought . . .

She walked away towards the forecastle and its viewing platform, calling out to all aboard, the flocks of Imperial courtiers and churchmen on this and all the dozens of other windships in the sky, amplifying her voice into every mind in reach.

<PREPARE FOR THE GREATEST SIGHT YOU WILL EVER SEE!>

Southpoint Tower, Dhassa
Junesse (Akhira) 930
24th and last month of the Moontide

Alaron saw the blast coming; he was already ducking and weaving as his shields deflected the masked woman's mage-fire. He reached her, slammed his staff through her shields, battering her backwards into the room she'd left. He followed her through as she clutched at her blackened clothing and chest.

The large circular chamber was filled with rows of bunks and racks of weapons. Two dozen men turned at her cry, but Alaron was inside and moving. She kindled yellow light in her eyes, mesmeric-gnosis, trying to snare his gaze, and he let her, opening up his mental shields, then slamming them closed again: Ascendant-strength battled against her lesser pure-blood powers and she flailed blindly as he tore the linkages between her eyes and her brain, then drove the staff up under her chin, snapping her neck.

The men came at him from all sides, but he'd fallen into his state of trance-fighting where the gnosis came as easily as breathing. He threw the central weapons rack into a cluster of men with devastating power, spearing them with a wall of metal, then caught up a bunk bed with kinesis and sent it spinning into the next group, breaking bones and skulls. Thrown weapons spun from his shields and he spewed fire from the tip of his staff into the next group, dropping three and giving him a clear path to the left. Then Ramita entered, hurling the men on the right backwards against the wall, where they slumped, broken or dazed.

It was like bullying children, and left a nasty taste. He spoke to those still conscious. 'Here's the choice: stay in this room and don't come out until someone comes for you, or we'll have to deal with you.'

Please just stay out of our way.

To his relief, the remaining men who still could fled to the corner and turned their backs. He and Ramita passed, sealed the doors behind them, and found the stairs. They climbed, hurrying, but with heightened caution: there was a sense of gnostic pressure building above, and they felt little life here now that the armed men had been left behind. Southpoint probably didn't need a lot of guarding usually.

'What is this for?' Ramita wondered, brandishing the silver mask that the woman mage had worn.

'I don't know,' Alaron replied, 'but I've heard the solarus crystals are deadly, so perhaps it protects from that?'

Ramita frowned, then drew the cord over her head and left the face-piece perched on top of her hair. 'We will need one for you, then.'

They went onwards, through a deserted landing and up a narrow stair, then Alaron sensed life again. He reached ahead with his inner eye, then poked two fingers forwards. 'Guards,' he whispered. 'Give me a moment.'

He reached out and encountered shielded minds: *magi*. They were both young battle-magi, one dark-haired, the other bald, both tense and curious, their attention on what was happening behind the door they guarded. That would change the moment he came into view, of course.

Then Ramita walked past him, robed in black and wearing the silver mask over her face. The two young men turned to her, saw the mask and relaxed. A second later she'd gripped them with kinesis and slammed their heads together. She plucked a mask from one of the unconscious men and handed it to Alaron.

He put it on, then examined the door. The feeling of gnostic pressure beyond was immense. He took a deep breath, and faced her. 'Ramita, this is it.' He swallowed. 'I wish we'd had longer,' he blurted.

'We will, my love. Years and years.'

He stared into her eyes, drank her in. Then there was a sudden, hair-lifting shiver of power that radiated from the next room, dragging them back to the present. The realisation hit him that there might never be another shared look, another kiss, another morning waking in each other's arms. It almost took the strength from his legs.

He put a hand to the door, vaguely surprised but thankful to find it unlocked, because the three days of flight and the latest exertions had left him hollowed out.

All right. This is where we find out all the answers.

He took a moment to marshal his forces anew: the sixteen arms of the gnosis, waiting for him. He took stock: he wasn't the world's best mage or warrior. He'd stumbled into this place in time. But there were moments when he'd touched his potential and done things he'd never dreamed he was capable of. That fortified him, as did his purpose: he had a wife to protect and love, so they could grow old together.

He burst through into a blur of brilliant light, as a dozen masks turned his way, but his eyes went instantly to the centre of the dome, where a man was lying on a reclining throne, his mask upturned to the ceiling of crystals that glowed like clustered stars. His arms were raised and crackling with static lightning, gnosis energy spilling from eyes and mouth.

Alaron smashed his staff into the face of the first mask and it crumpled inwards, the skull of the black-robed wearer shattering. Lines of force linking him to the throne frayed and flashed, and every other masked mage in the chamber shrieked in unison.

Then all Hel was here.

Ramita Ankesharan could feel the presence of her gods: Vishnarayan the Protector's hand was on Al'Rhon now, his armour and his weapon, but Sivraman was there too, in his wild, graceful movements as he struck down one masked man, then another, spiralling around the room.

She waited a moment, letting these magi see her as another masked face and turn away again, their eyes instead drawn to Alaron's violence. She spent those seconds taking their measure, just as Corinea had taught her, until . . .

Now!

The first of the mages to strike at Alaron used fire: as he evaded, she conjured water inside that mage's mouth, then rammed it down his throat, leaving him choking for breath, drowning on the floor. She went into the centre, to the nexus, while all eyes were still on Alaron.

Alaron was moving in a blur, striking while the Keepers were still locked within the destructive spell and unable to give themselves wholly to defence. He cut down a middle-aged female with just an empowered staff blow, then another with fire. As one tried to change shape, Ramita intervened, ghosting a long spiratus arm through his shields and a finger into his skull. He screamed and collapsed, then she hurled another Keeper aside, a bent woman with a shrill, imperious voice who tried to conjure a daemon. On the far side of the circle, Alaron countered Necromancy with healing-gnosis, then zeroed in on weakness: drawing the air from the lungs of the Earth-sorcerer then slamming him against the wall, broken.

The throne swivelled, the Keeper in the seat flailing his arms as his helpers were slain or stunned, unable to intervene while he was in the throes of this web of powers. Ramita lit the dagger in her hand and sent it flying at him, impelled by kinesis and alive with energies. It pierced the enthroned Keeper's shields as if they were gauze and plunged to the hilt into his chest. He choked, bewildered, and in his agony lost control of the forces he wielded. Light blasted in every direction, along the threads of power that bound him to his fellows.

With a hideous, multi-voiced shriek, the remaining masked magi were thrown aside like toys, hammering into the walls and dropping, broken, to the stone floor. The man on the throne writhed and gibbered, sliding from the seat as he clawed at the knife. Healing-gnosis kindled and she snuffed it out, then Alaron slammed his staff across the man's throat.

'What do we do to stop this?' Alaron demanded.

The man on the ground looked up at him, bewildered. 'Who are you?'

'*How do we make it stop?*'

'You can't – you're too late. This tower's going to explode in five minutes and the whole Bridge is going down.' He coughed blood. 'Please, get me out of here! There's a windship moored to the outside, waiting! Please—' Then he fainted.

Alaron looked at Ramita, then the throne. 'We may be too late . . .'

'Or perhaps not,' Ramita said. *Parvasi, Mother of All, be with me.*

Above, the crystal ceiling was ablaze, tendrils of power reaching blindly downwards. She shared one final look with Alaron, then with deliberate movements, lowered herself into the throne and raised her hands to the heavens.

The first of the energy threads touched her fingers, then blazed through her.

At first Ramita was alone in a wilderness of stars and forked lightning. All awareness of Alaron, of the room, the tower, her own body even, fell away, and she was caught in a mesh of light, trying to make sense of a thousand sensations at once. The powers were too intense, too much. She floundered, began to panic . . .

. . . and then there was a presence with her: Antonin Meiros, his patient face smiling encouragingly. It was another gnostic message, set here on the throne, but it felt so real she almost believed he was truly present.

<You made it this far,> his image whispered into her mind. <That means that all is at stake and there is no time to lose. You must reach for the central core of energy above, dearest: hold it and tame it. Do you see the brightest crystal, at the apex of the dome? That is the one.> The image faded momentarily, then returned. <Well done, child, to come so far. Now is the final test.>

She did as he said, reached out with a spiratus arm for the apex crystal, jolting as energy coursed through her again, but she shielded her core and began to knot the threads together, weaving gnosis-energy. It was more power than she'd ever handled, but its nature was the same, and she was no longer bewildered. In seconds, she found that her strength was sufficient to control the flow – something that had taken the enthroned Keeper and a dozen others to do.

As she pulled the threads into one rope they fused, and suddenly the play of energy became clear. Southpoint Tower was revealed as a pillar of light, joined to a larger web of energy. Three cords of light shot away from her, two going diagonally left and right – to Sunset and Sunrise Isles, she guessed. But the thickest poured the energy of Southpoint into Midpoint, the centre.

She placed her awareness within those three flows.

For a few seconds there was only the rush of movement, but then she was *elsewhere*, or her spiratus was, seeing other chambers and other thrones: two men and a woman standing at the other points of the compass – Sunset and Sunrise; Northpoint and Midpoint. All of their faces turned towards her at once, and they knew her in the same instant she knew them.

In Northpoint, Grandmaster Lens Nauvoine of the Inquisition, raised to the Ascendancy sixty years ago, once a giant warrior and now a bloated, toad-like figure in cavernous robes, snarled in startled fury at her.

At Sunset Isle, vulturine Lady Delfinne de Tressot, staunch ally of the Sacrecours, raised fifty years ago, turned her head with diamond-like eyes flashing.

And Raneulf Fasterius, Ascendant and grandfather of Mater-Imperia Lucia Sacrecour, saw her all the way from Sunrise Isle and set his jaw.

On the central throne, Ervyn Naxius spun, his face unmasked, already so ruined that the solarus could do little more, and laughed savagely. 'Welcome to the end of your husband's creation, Lady Ramita,' he spat. He raised a hand, his power augmented by Nauvoine behind him in Northpoint; his gesture was mirrored by the others, then gnostic attacks blazed down the link towards her from three sides.

There were three principle goddesses in Omali theology and Ramita became each at once: in the same way that Alaron became a trance-mage, she found she could split her awareness and do several things at once. The concept that one being could encompass others had been inculcated into her from birth, and everything Puravai and Corinea had shown her at Mandira Khojana, how to reach and use all facets of the gnosis, combined with the core of who she was, an Omali Lakh, made this moment.

Sarisa-ji was Queen of Learning, associated with the Great River. Into her Ramita put her awareness of Water and Sorcery and faced the brutal flames that flowed along the direct link to Raneulf Fasterius at Sunrise Isle to the northeast.

Into Laksimi-ji, Goddess of Plenty, she poured her instincts for life and the physical, using hermetic-gnosis against the deathly power radiating towards her from Lady Delfinne on Sunset Isle.

But the greater part of her went into blocking the combined threats of Naxius, augmented by Grandmaster Nauvoine, that flowed the length of the Bridge aiming directly for her. She became, wholly in her heart, Parvasi-ji – but only for a moment, because she let the wilder spirit of Parvasi's darker incarnation flood through her, becoming the warrior-woman Darikha-ji, wielding Fire and Earth and all her anger.

Initially all she could do was defend, and she couldn't have survived without the raw power that Antonin Meiros had literally bred into her, or the hundreds of hours of training she had undergone. Even then, she felt like a candle in a rainstorm, flickering at the edge of extinction. Naxius' grip on her mind was like the claws of a bird of prey, gripping her naked brain and digging in, seeking an edge as he delved into her mind. He pulled up images of Antonin Meiros, dying ... Kazim, killing him ... Justina, dying with her throat torn out ... Nasatya, lost and crying ...

Showing her Nasatya was a mistake.

I will see him again! And to do that, I must do this! Her spiratus blazed in anger, and she swatted Naxius away as if he were nothing more than a fly. The energy flowing between her to these others suddenly was no longer a tether, but a *road*. With a growing sense of her own strength, she sent herself down those roads, fighting three at once.

Towards Sunrise Isle, pale-skinned Sarisa-ji, holding a sitar, floated on a lotus flower along the river of power towards the tall, haughty shape of Mater-Imperia's grandfather. Raneulf Fasterius snapped out runic words as he threw his spells at her, using Fire thaumaturgy with the intensity to melt stone. But she countered with Water, dousing the fires that burst about her, and poured onwards.

Raneulf Fasterius was a cunning fighter, but Ramita was more than an Ascendant and she overwhelmed him like a wave over a sea wall. He shrieked in agony as something like a steam-bath erupted around him, boiling his flesh on the bone, and his consciousness left him.

She stepped inside his fading mind and the silver-masked Keepers in the chamber at Sunrise Isle saw the dead Keeper's whole body change. The horribly burned corpse on the throne was engulfed by a loomy earthen fog, which cleared to reveal a woman in Lakh attire, crowned in flowers, with skin of the palest blue. She struck a note on a sitar that reverberated through their skulls, and they all collapsed.

Sarisa-ji turned her eyes to the other thrones, where her sisters still fought.

Midpoint Tower, Leviathan Bridge
Junesse (Akhira) 930
24th and last month of the Moontide

Emperor Constant Sacrecour stared at Ervyn Naxius through a glass wall a foot thick. The ancient mage was on the throne, his hands

745

ablaze with power and his face lit with rage as he hurled abuse at some unseen figure.

'What's going on?' Constant demanded. 'Has Naxius gone mad?'

One of the silver-masked Keepers, an ancient woman with the foulest breath he'd ever had the misfortune to inhale, was mewling with concern. 'Southpoint has been usurped,' she lisped.

'What? How—?' He had no idea what that meant, but it sounded bad. 'Who? Why—?'

'I don't know,' the old woman snapped. She was a former nun of Kore, an abbess who'd ingratiated herself into Imperial favour and gained the gift of the Ascendancy a century ago. 'Naxius contends with the intruder!'

This place no longer felt safe. 'Is he winning?'

'I don't know! I don't know anything!'

'Then what damned use are you?'

She looked at him with a puzzled exasperation. 'Use? I'm not here to be *useful*, boy, I'm here to bear witness to history. This is a great moment!'

Constant backed away. It didn't feel like a great moment. He signalled to his guards. 'Get me out of here.'

Southpoint Tower, Leviathan Bridge
Junesse (Akhira) 930
24th and last month of the Moontide

All Alaron could do was stare through the eyelets of his mask and pray. Ramita was deep in the link now and barely recognisable, not just because of the lurid colours swirling above her head, but for her own magical aura, which was blending with her body, turning her into a tall, regal being with multiple arms and deep blue skin. It was the aura shape she used when wielding the gnosis now, so it didn't surprise him, but this version was disturbing. It had three heads, looking away to the northeast, north and northwest, and there was a controlled ferocity and escalating rage about her he'd never seen before.

Abruptly she raised her left hand, pointing savagely into the north-west, along a track of light that appeared stretching towards Sunset Isle. His senses were pulled along the link and he saw a woman hunched like a skeletal bird on a throne. She was bathed in purple light, her hands so translucent they looked like bone. But she was howling with dread, and Alaron suddenly saw why: there were tree roots writhing towards her, withering as they touched the purple fires she wielded, but getting closer and closer . . .

. . . then suddenly the woman wailed in despair and tried to pull herself from the link. She never got the chance: the thickest tree-root struck like a snake, plunging through her abdomen like a thrown spear and impaling her. As blood soaked her dress, she convulsed, then more roots burst from her mouth and bloomed into leaves and a black flower, and more sprouted from her eyes, and she was engulfed.

Then the nightmare figure changed again, becoming a beautiful Lakh woman who lifted her head and turned to face Midpoint with burning eyes.

Holy Hel . . .

He turned his eyes back to Ramita and cried out in fear for her—
—and of her.

There was no sign of the Ramita he loved now, just a figure stream-ing dark light. The throne had vanished; it was now a tiger the size of a horse, and the dark goddess was astride the beast as it roared and swiped with claws like daggers. He pressed himself against the wall, fearful of approaching, scared to look away. Ramita radiated heat as if she were made of burning coals; her robes were smoulder-ing and falling apart, while the tiger seemed to be morphing with her, as if it was climbing into her soul. She became a dark giantess, giving voice to her anger.

His eyes followed the link to Midpoint Isle, where a cadaverous old man was seated, wreathed in energy. Behind him lurked another man, and after a moment Alaron understood instinctively that the second figure was far away in Northpoint, a bloated figure clutching the arms of his own throne, eyes bulging with stress. With a yowl like a great cat, Ramita hurled a spear of light that transfixed the fat man, pinned him to his throne. He deflated in a burst of blood that somehow splattered Ramita in Southpoint. She licked it from her face with relish.

<NOW!!!> the old man at Midpoint howled, and he threw a blast of fire into the crystal dome above him. The blast reverberated all along the link and staggered the giantess in the chamber with Alaron. She raged and tried to strike back, but the old man at Midpoint snarled vindictively and his rasping voice thundered down the link and filled the dome.

<It is done! The Bridge's energies are freed and directed. You're too late, Lady Ramita! The Bridge will fall!> Then he was gone, vanishing from the link, which began to collapse.

The giantess roared in fury as Alaron's energy wilted.

No – not when we came so far—! We can't have failed!

Midpoint Tower, Leviathan Bridge
Junesse (Akhira) 930
24th and last month of the Moontide

Emperor Constant had just reached the doors when there was a great roar behind him. He turned in time to see Ervyn Naxius launch a blast of scarlet gnosis into the dome above him. The entire crystal dome went a deep red and the tower quivered, sending Constant and his guards to their knees. Naxius stood, facing south, with his eyes blazing triumphantly, shouting, 'It is done! The Bridge's energies are freed and directed. You're too late, Lady Ramita! The Bridge will fall!'

Constant clutched at the arm of the nearest soldier. 'Thank Kore for that! Now get me out of here!'

Naxius hobbled from the central chamber and came towards him. 'I've taken all the energy I could, and disconnected the links. The energies are now channelled downwards at the remnants of the meteor, which is what this island is. She can't reach us to prevent that; only someone here can control the flow. So we must depart, my Lord. We have five minutes.'

'Then let's go! Take me away this instant.' He threw a glance back at Naxius, aware that some show of gratitude was warranted, but in truth the man was loathsome and he didn't want to spend another moment in his company. Nevertheless, forms must be kept. 'You will join us later this evening on the Royal Barge, Lord Naxius?'

The ancient mage bowed ironically. 'An honour, my Emperor.'

Constant's guards hurried him to the sloop hovering outside the tower. He glanced down and saw chaos below where soldiers in motley rags were milling, shouting with rage and fear. He waved down iron-ically, though he was probably too high to be seen. A shame. Then he was bundled safely onto the windcraft and they were rising and away as another came to collect Naxius and the others.

He looked skywards, exhaling in relief. The windfleet above circled or simply hovered, awaiting the great moment, and he wanted to be there, seated on his throne on the Royal Barge, when it happened. 'Fly like the wind!' he shouted to the pilot. 'Like the storm itself!'

Ramon saw the beacon atop Midpoint go scarlet, and he knew instinc-tively what it meant. The windships tethered to the tower hurriedly lifted away, and whatever lingering hope he had withered: the men below were all going to die. A few of the magi might escape, but the ordinary rankers and camp followers who'd crossed the continent with him were doomed. He blinked back tears.

On the forecastle, Mater-Imperia began some speech about how the Bridge was an affront to the traditions of society because it took the God-given rights of control from those bred to rule and handed it to bickering traders who cared only about gold. The hypocrisy enraged him. He looked around, rashly angry but still calculating, and spotted Gurvon Gyle nearby. The spymaster looked ill at ease among the glittering peacocks of Pallas. 'Hey, Gyle! Come here! I've got something to tell you!'

Vann looked at him warningly, but Ramon ignored him. He wanted to hurt someone, and Gyle was the only target he knew he could hit.

'What is it?' the Noroman asked, approaching quietly.

'What's happening down there?'

Gyle grunted indifferently. 'The Bridge's destruction is assured. Midpoint Beacon is now holding all the available gnostic power and will release it downwards into the island in less than five minutes.'

Good. Then I have nothing to lose . . .

'I suppose you're back in favour now?' Ramon asked.

'I'm the one who recovered the gold. I have a certain standing again.'

'That's nice. Have you checked the ingots?'

The spy blinked, his body tensing. 'Of course.'

'Deeper than the top level?'

Gyle went utterly still, and his voice fell to a whisper. *'What in Hel are you saying?'*

Ramon flashed his most irritating grin. 'Those wagons contained only about ten gilden of ingots: the top layer of each box. The rest is stone covered in gilt. You'd have discovered eventually, but I wanted you to know now.'

Gyle closed his eyes and breathed one word. *'Rukka . . .'*

'All the rest of the gold is still on the Bridge.'

'But – those were your only bullion wagons . . . We know they were full in Hebusalim, and you've been under surveillance ever since . . .'

'No doubt. But the gold has been turned to coin and distributed to the men. I paid them as they stepped onto the Bridge, each and every one: ten auros each, with bonuses for the officers and magi. So all of it is down there, on the Bridge you and your friends are destroying. It's all going into the sea.'

Gyle's face went grey as his tunic. *'You . . . rukking . . . dung-rat!'* He threw a panicked look over his shoulder at the clustered Pallas magi, who were clapping Emperor Constant as he stepped onto the barge and hurried to his throne, his mother resplendent beside him. No one was paying Ramon or Gyle any attention.

Gyle drew his dagger.

'Really?' Ramon asked. 'Right in front of everyone, with no explanation?'

Gyle gestured and Ramon's tongue and lips went numb. 'Silence, Silacian!' he snarled softly. He choked off Vann Mercer's cry with a flick of the hand, then cast about. There were plenty of vessels hovering alongside the royal barge, but all the skiffs were below, ferrying magi up from the tower, or skimming the Bridge, firing mage-bolts into random soldiers.

Except one.

Gyle waved and called mentally. Ramon couldn't hear the communication; he could sense little at all in his effort to breathe, but he saw the skiff respond. The pilot, swathed in imperial robes and barely distinguishable as female, swung her craft about and brought it alongside. Gyle surreptitiously unlocked his manacles, looked at Vann for a moment, then wordlessly unlocked his as well. He used kinesis to pull Ramon and Vann towards the skiff. Then as Constant made some remark and the whole court dutifully cheered and laughed, Gyle flung Ramon bodily through space to land roughly in the windskiff. He landed hard, and the skiff shuddered. Vann followed, then Gyle leapt, landing beside the mast. He flashed coin at the pilot.

'Pontus! Get me to Pontus as fast as you can. There's a fortune in it!'

The woman pilot, cowled and shadowy, sent her skiff dropping away from the royal barge and then began to speed through the clustered ships on a northeast tack. Vann and Ramon struggled to an upright position, but before they could contemplate jumping, ropes in the hull snaked out and grasped them.

'You're not going anywhere,' Gyle snarled. He fixed Ramon with a furious glare. 'I'm going to make you wish you'd never drawn breath.' Then he glanced at Vann. 'As for you – I want to know what your son has done with the Scytale. I've heard the rumours, and I want in.'

'Alaron knows better than to let anyone use my safety against him, Gurvon.'

While they glared at each other, the tip of Midpoint Tower flashed from red to indigo. Seth's army was massed below the tower and waiting to die, while the storm itself drew breath in expectation.

Ramon pictured Julietta and all the people he loved trapped down there, between fire and water.

Pater Sol, let their end be swift.

Seth Korion limped down the stairs, his arm around Kippenegger's massive shoulders for support. The scenes below were like a foretaste of Hel. The word was now out; his soldiers realised that something terrible was happening. They were reacting as men did, in a thousand different ways, all together and all alone, facing the end. Many were on their knees praying. Others were running, or even leaping into the sea. Several were rapidly getting drunk, and dozens had found their wives – or someone else's – and were holding them, taking and giving strength in these final moments.

As Seth stumbled from the tower, the whole army seemed to pause as one as they saw him. Their collective eyes struck him like a blow, but he set his shoulders and faced them. Behind him, Pilus Lukaz strode from the tower, followed by a straggle of wide-eyed men – the six other survivors of his cohort, all wounded. 'Present arms!' Lukaz shouted.

Seth watched dazedly as the tiny group of rankers formed up behind him.

'Bannerman Baden, raise the standard!' Lukaz shouted. A dour, stocky man who was so inexpressive he might have had no facial muscles, strode forward as if on parade. 'Soldiers of Pallacios Thirteen, salute your standard!'

Seth swallowed as the men lifted their heads and raised their hands, touching head and heart with their fists. Utterly at a loss, he followed suit, then all of the men in sight were saluting, whether they were of Pallacios Thirteen or any of the dozen other legions that had formed part of their trek.

Silence fell over the Bridge while the beacon went indigo. Seth found his voice, sensing the final seconds were here. 'Men of the Second Army, the emperor has seen fit to destroy this Bridge! I'm so sorry to have brought you so far, only to die here, of all places!'

'Good as any, Gen'ral!' someone shouted. A few men even laughed.

He blinked away a stinging tear. 'I'm so proud of you all!'

''Cept you, Bowe,' someone muttered, sotto voce, behind him. 'He en't proud o' you.'

'Fuck off, Harmon.'

The Bridge fell silent again, then someone slammed the butt of their spear into the stone, and began to chant, 'Korion! Korion! Korion!' In a few seconds they were all doing it, and the Bridge began to shake.

Then the beacon went brilliant white, and lit the entire sky ...

43

At the Last

The Rage of Dar-Kana

One of the most powerful myths of the Omali Faith is that of Dar-Kana. It is said that when in battle against demons threatening those she loves, the Lakh goddess Parvasi becomes her warrior-aspect, Darikha. But if the battle still goes badly, she becomes a ferocious creature called Dar-Kana. In this form, the goddess is so destructive that all creation is threatened.

Only her husband, the god Sivraman, can calm her, a curious inversion of the legend of the berserk god Minaus, whose destructive lust is slaked only by the kiss of his celestial lover, Fryffa.

LEONARDO DI KESTRIA, LETTER FROM LAKH, 926

The Leviathan Bridge
Junesse (Akhira) 930
24th and last month of the Moontide

Alaron did the only thing he could think of. He dropped his staff and walked, unarmed and slowly, towards the Lakh giantess as she poured her fury into the burning dome. She saw him coming and roared warningly, swiped at him though he was still out of reach.

'Ramita, it's me.'

But she was too far gone, lost in the persona of her Lakh goddess, overwhelmed by emotions loosened in the fight. He could recognise that anger, because it was the fury that she unleashed whenever she fought, the place she found in battle. But she was lost in it, when she needed to be doing something – *anything* – else. The world was falling apart and she was like a child smashing a toy that no longer worked.

'*Ramita!*'

But it was no good. He couldn't reach her. She wasn't even Ramita any more . . . just a channel for primaeval fury, unable to break from the prison of her own emotions, lost in the role she used to make sense of conflict.

So he followed her example . . .

Kindling his own gnosis, though exhausted and faint, he reached for the aura configuration Puravai had taught him: the image of Sivraman, holding tokens of the gnosis. He let it clothe him, made it visible, the image of the Lakh god clad in lion-skins, holding the elements like weapons.

'*Ramita!*' he called again, stepping right in front of her and reaching two hands for hers, her real ones, not those of the goddess.

She struck him with one of the goddess' clawed hands, and he staggered. Her tiger claws left four deep bloody furrows down his face and chest. He gasped at the pain. Then he reached again.

She raised another hand. She roared, beyond words, beyond reason, foetid meaty breath washing over him. Her eyes were bloody and her teeth jagged.

But this time she didn't strike. Her eyes finally saw him. 'Sivraman?'

He took her hands. 'No, Ramita. It's me: Alaron.'

Ramita waded waist-deep in blood and fire, swiping at phantoms that flittered in the scarlet fog. They shouted her name, praising her to the heavens above: 'Dar-Kana! Dar-Kana!' The sound coursed through her, fed her anger.

'Ramita!' someone said.

A man tried to grasp her and she lashed out. But he came back, kept returning, and he was speaking to someone, someone she remembered, and she knew him, from somewhere . . .

'Sivraman?' she asked uncertainly . . .

All at once, she *saw* him, truly and wholly. He was standing before her, four bloody wounds running parallel down his face and chest, right to left, his hands open, unthreatening, and a small voice in her head said, *This isn't your enemy.*

'No, Ramita,' he said. 'It's me: Alaron.'

'I am Dar-Kana!' she snarled, but with less conviction now. Someone else was surfacing, memories of sitting on her haunches in a packed square, surrounded by all the produce of the world, bartering for coppers, caught up in the cacophony and the life, with family around her. Then she was holding two boys to her chest, and then an old man was holding her, and then a younger man . . .

. . . this man.

'*Al-Rhon?*'

The gnosis-image fell from her hands, from her body, and she was just her and he was just him. She blanched at the wounds, but he healed them with a gesture, then pulled her to him. 'My love,' he murmured, 'you're back.'

She looked up. The dome was a swirl of light and the links to the other towers were gone. She heard again the final words Naxius had sent before the links went dead: '*It is done! The Bridge's energies are freed and directed. You're too late, Lady Ramita! The Bridge will fall!*'

She stifled a sob of despair. *I've failed.* Her late husband's great creation was doomed. The scattered bodies lying about the chamber were just a foretaste of what was to come. All Dhassa and Pontus were going to be shaken and torn apart. She looked at the throne, wondering . . . *I don't know what to do, but I have to try . . .*

He knew what she was thinking, knew all of her. And his friend's army was on the Bridge. He led her to the throne. 'It looks big enough for two,' he said. 'Let's do this together.'

Her heart lifted. They had joined their gnosis before, in much smaller ways. They'd found how to work together, and be stronger. *Perhaps . . .* She squeezed his hand and they clambered onto the seat, just wide enough to admit them both, clasped hands and auras and became something that was both of them, a single being of the gnosis, an Ardhanari statue, the type that combined the male and the female, wrought from their powers.

She knew the forces contained in Southpoint Tower now, and led

Alaron through the initial shock, then took hold of the remaining energies in the dome above. As she contemplated the destruction to come, her anger rose again, but he brought detachment and calmness, so that this time she remained clear-headed as she took up the reins. The path to Midpoint remained shut, but she could still feel the residue of the threads that led to the corpses on the thrones at Sunset and Sunrise isles. She sent energy into both . . .

Necromancy: they woke the dead Keepers on their thrones, Raneulf Fasterius and Delfinne de Tressot, woke them and clothed them in energy and awareness. All at once she was seeing through their eyes as well. Then she sent power back, strengthening the links, and brought in the dead man in Northpoint Tower also, Lens Nauvoine, lying amidst the corpses of his adherents while the dome above him blazed darkly.

We have to hurry, Alaron whispered.

Ramita knew, but still everything unfolded like a dream. Northpoint, Sunrise and Sunset Towers were all linked still to Midpoint and still feeding it with energy. She followed the channels of power into the nexus at Midpoint, she and Alaron together, moving as one.

Midpoint Tower opened to them, its energies swirling towards a climactic blast, directed downwards into the island itself. The nexus-throne Naxius had abandoned awaited, empty, and their spiratus form manifested in the chamber. They took the seat, feeling superaware, conscious of all the lives around them: above, where hundreds of windcraft circled to witness the end of an epoch, and below, where fifteen thousand men and women were saluting a banner and waiting to die.

The dome pulsed, the air shrieked and the channel opened to send the gathered might of the solarus crystals downwards, into the earth. This was what Kazim had warned of, and it was going to happen . . .

. . . *right now* . . .

Together they reached, wrenched, and tore the river of energy free, the instant before it lanced fire into the earth below. Then sent it elsewhere, because it had to go somewhere, and it was too much for them to contain.

As the windskiff bore Ramon and Vann Mercer and Gurvon Gyle away, a bolt of lightning burst from the pinnacle of Midpoint Tower, not down into the earth but upwards, into the skies, tearing a hole in the cluster of Rondian windships above. Ramon blinked at the blinding line carved across his retinas, unsure what he'd just seen. Beside him, Vann swore, and Gyle simply gaped, lost for words.

Then lightning flashed again, blasting another warbird into burning splinters.

'*HOLY KORE!*' Gyle shouted. He whirled on the pilot behind him. '*GET US THE FUCK OUT OF HERE!*'

Constant Sacrecour was caught up in a reverie of glory when the first bolt of light seared the skies. All round him, the courtiers *oohed* and *ahhed* uncertainly, then he looked at his mother for guidance.

Mater-Imperia Lucia Fasterius-Sacrecour, Living Saint, was standing apart, watching the tower avidly. Her face was lit with light, her aura bleeding through until she shone. An illusion, of course: Mother always tried to look like a divinity in public. But when that lightning flashed upwards, her expression became sickly.

'Er, what was that?' a fop from Pallas asked the silence.

'Oh, it's just a back-flash . . .' one of the prelates said knowledgeably. 'Happens often when . . . um—'

A second bolt tore sideways through the fleet and blasted a warbird apart. Someone squealed, then all the women and half the men were screaming. Constant leapt to his feet. '*Mother! Do something!*'

But for once his mother couldn't seem to react; she just stood there as her light faded, leaving just an overdressed woman with a vacant face. She looked back at him, paralysed, her lips moving helplessly, and that scared him more than anything else could have.

'*Mother!*' Constant lit his gnosis. '*We've to got shield!*' He shrieked spittle into the face of an old knight. '*SHIELDS!!*'

At first no one reacted as more blasts tore craft after craft from the sky all around them. A few courtiers mewled and milled, then someone yelled, 'To the skiffs!' and they all flooded for the lower decks. Constant cast about for Gurvon Gyle, but he was already gone.

His eyes went back to the tower as the Royal Barge's crew tried to raise sails. A giant figure was superimposed over Midpoint, something sculpted of smoke and sea-spray, a pagan thing with multiple arms and a blazing face. One arm stabbed upwards: at his barge.

He turned back to his mother. '*MOTHER!*'

Lucia jerked her eyes from the tower to him, and she seemed to rally. Her face lit with renewed determination and he took heart and stumbled towards her, opening his mouth to ask her what to do.

Then light and searing pain engulfed them both, and in a blaze of agony, everything vanished.

Seth Korion stared skywards as burning timbers began to drop from the skies. The beacon atop the tower blazed again, ripping another swathe through the windfleet, scything through shields as if they didn't exist, and skiffs and warbirds and frigates alike became balls of flame. The windships were scattering, calling the winds, and the skies became a whirl of craft seeking altitude and safety. The skiffs fared best, darting away in all directions, but the heavier craft were being systematically blasted apart as they rose, sluggish as drugged pheasants.

'Well *fuck* me,' Bowe breathed. 'I wanna worship whatever god done that.'

'Join the queue,' Vidran said in a stunned voice.

Lightning crackled as one or two of the warbirds tried to fight back, pelting the tower with gnosis, but they might as well have been throwing stones. Counter-blasts pulsed out, ripping through the fleet anew, concentrating on the fighting craft. Timber was raining down on them and Seth found his voice, amplifying his voice to all along the span, crying, 'Take cover, damn you! Protect yourselves!'

The men belatedly sought protection beneath wagons or raised shields. Seth tried to anticipate the worst of the debris and swat it aside, and the other magi did the same, but his eyes constantly went back to the tower, where the smoke was gathering into some giant form. For a moment it wore Alaron Mercer's face, then Mercer's wife's; and then it flew apart as lightning blazed upwards again and the last of the warbirds were blasted apart.

Enough.

The word hung in the air. Alaron wasn't sure if he said it, or Ramita, or whether at the moment it was spoken there was a difference.

We have to leave enough energy in the Bridge so that it can sustain immersion.

He looked upwards at the scattering windfleet. Riding the power of the Bridge, he could scry anywhere. *The emperor and his mother are dead, just vapour and ash. So is half the court and upper clergy.* He felt sickened by the destruction they'd wrought.

It's a good thing that we humans have human limitations. A god's wrath is too terrible . . .

Below, Seth's army looked more or less intact. They were safe. He sent them acknowledgment, and saw Seth Korion look up in wonder and wave.

He and Ramita slowly disentangled their gnosis and withdrew into themselves, back into their bodies . . .

He opened his eyes and found himself on the Southpoint nexus-throne, with Ramita tucked beneath his arm. She looked up at him, her eyes wide, the vestiges of what they'd seen clinging to her expression. He could still feel her inside his heart and mind; he suspected he always would.

It felt like a blessing.

As the skiff tore across the skies, Gurvon Gyle's eyes remained fixed on the chaos above Midpoint Tower. Each time the destructive fire belched forth, he was convinced it would take him, that he too would cease to exist in an eye-blink. But he couldn't take his eyes from it. In the foredeck, Ramon Sensini and Vann Mercer were similarly entranced, but the skiff-pilot behind him knew her business and was concentrating on flying them out of it.

Gurvon turned to her to finally ask her name.

And froze.

She held a small crossbow one-handed, aimed at his chest. As she pulled her hood back, her face changed.

'Elena . . .'

Her voice was dry and laconic. 'Alaron told me to stay in Brochena . . . but he's only my bloody nephew. Thinks 'cos he's an Ascendant now that he can tell me what to do . . .'

He could only stare. Behind him, in the foredeck, he heard Sensini and Mercer go still as they noticed. Then he began to fumble for words. 'Elena, there's so much we need to talk about! I've got your gold, so much more gold you'll be stunned. Just name your price and it's yours!'

If I shield I could jump and—

But before he could move, the bonds he'd wrapped round Ramon Sensini tore open, along with the Chain-rune that had supposedly been holding him. That wasn't possible – they'd been cast by a pure-blood. He didn't stop to wonder, though, instead readying himself to leap. Elena tried to fire and his shields caught the bolt and shattered it, then he was in motion, lunging towards the side, Air-gnosis flaring.

Then the air itself congealed around him and he was pinned in place by an impossibly strong grip. He felt his shields unpeel around him while Elena patiently reloaded her crossbow.

<It wasn't poison I drank,> Ramon whispered into his mind. <It was ambrosia. Alaron brewed it specially for me, just in case we ever met again. I guess that means it's you who's not going anywhere.>

Elena's finger twitched, and the crossbow jolted. The bolt slammed into the middle of his chest, driving the air from his lungs and filling his throat with blood. He tried to cry out, but only gurgled. 'Ella—!'

'Goodbye, Gurvon,' Elena said in a hollow voice.

He tried to marshal his thoughts through the pain, because there had to be an angle he could work . . . but the light was draining from the world and all he could do was stare at her and remember better days . . .

She's the only woman who ever mattered . . .

He tried to speak, to tell her that . . .

44

After the Storm

Crusades and Shihads

There have been two attacks launched by the Rondian Empire on Ahmedhassa, and a third is promised. The emperor calls them 'Crusades' – holy wars – to proselytise the Kore faith, as if this can only be done by force. A shihad – an Amteh holy war – is promised in retaliation. But war is not holy. Its nature is quintessentially unholy, and those who claim otherwise are themselves the most reprehensible of all. A plague on all their shrines.

ANTONIN MEIROS, HEBUSALIM, 925

The Leviathan Bridge
Junesse (Akhira) 930
24th and last month of the Moontide

Seth Korion nudged his horse along as he listened to Ramon Sensini's story. They'd found him – and Vann Mercer, of all people – waiting for them a mile along the Bridge. That was two weeks ago. The Lost Legions, scarcely believing they still lived, had been marching at full pace towards Yuros. The Bridge went on, straight as an arrow and apparently as solid as ever, towards Northpoint Tower. The tower beacon smouldered dully, pale blue against the afternoon sky. It was early summer, and for once the winds were still and the waves merely giant ridges and troughs, not massive monsters seeking to engulf them. The marker stone on the parapet read: *Northpoint, two miles.* They were so close to Yuros he could practically smell the mud.

'So,' Ramon said, continuing his story, 'Alaron's Aunty Elena shoots Gyle and watches him die, then she bursts into tears and I don't know what to think, except that no one's flying and we're in danger of tipping over in those insane winds. So I get her attention, she looks up, says, "We're flying a bit heavy, aren't we?". Then, cold as you like, she flips Gyle's corpse into the sea. The guy she's been crying over – whack and gone – and she forgets him, just like that. She sets us down on the Bridge – where you found us – and flies off without a backwards look.'

'Does she know what happened at the Tower?' Seth asked.

'Si: she said that Alaron had been in contact with her right after it happened. He and Ramita gained control of the towers and redirected the energy. She says half the Pallas Court were up there – Constant, Lucia: they're all dead.' He touched his heart in a Sollan blessing, then smirked. 'We'll miss them.'

'The whole world has changed,' Seth noted.

'Si, obviously! And you're marching an army back to Pontus, when all others have failed,' Ramon pointed out. 'I'm just saying, you know. You're a piece on the tabula board of power now, Seth Korion. If you choose to be.'

Seth thought about that. His father would have seized such a moment; he had possibly intended to. But he wasn't his father. *I'd settle for safety and peace.* 'Do we know what's waiting for us at Northpoint? Is your scout back?'

'Coll? No, but then, if I was him I'd be in a tavern, bouncing a young *cichita* on my lap and swigging warm beer.'

Seth winced at the thought. 'But you've scryed ahead?'

'Of course. There are a few soldiers, and many traders, setting up stalls. The Ordo Costruo are already in the tower, restoring it. All seems well.' Ramon cuffed him on the shoulder. 'You did it, General.'

'Me? We all did it. Especially *you*. We wouldn't have even got out of Shaliyah without you.'

'Si, si, you're right,' Ramon chuckled. 'But we've all done our part.'

Seth could only agree. The army felt like a brotherhood, and while he knew that no one wanted anything more than to get home, it was sad to think of them disbanding. Though they still had to cross half of Yuros, of course.

'Who's left?' he mused. 'You and me. Kippenegger, of all people. And Lanna. That's all the Thirteenth's magi, and we got off better than anyone. For the rest: Hel's Bells! Gerdhart's alive, and Carmina . . . Jelaska's only survived by some Necromancy spell that's probably illegal; and that's it . . . Dear Kore!'

'But we're here,' Ramon reminded him. 'We're alive, we'll reach Northpoint in an hour or so, and it's a beautiful day.' He indicated the columns of men behind them, bursting into cheers and songs as the land came into view through the coastal mists. 'Try telling them otherwise!'

Seth found himself smiling despite his worries. 'So, you're sure we can just march up the ramp without a fight?'

'Absolutely. In fact, I believe a party is planned.'

Ramon rode in behind his general, cradling Julietta and showing her the sea of cheering faces, though she was too young to appreciate it, much less remember. There were musicians and choirs bellowing hymns and folk songs as they rode through the crowds. Most of those who'd come to greet them were traders hoping against hope for something to buy and sell on, and local whores desperate for fresh pockets to empty. The Second Army marched in proudly, then just as proudly broke ranks and proceeded to get rotten drunk and dance until they fell over.

It was Darkmoon. When the next moon rose, it would herald the official end of the Moontide, though the Bridge was, according to reports, already almost engulfed when the tide was high.

It's over, Ramon thought, happy-sad. *Sol et Lune, it's over.*

At times during the night he glimpsed Kip, carousing among his Minaus worshippers, his Dhassan woman at his feet as he drank enough ale to float a Tigrates riverboat; and Gerdhart, preaching and giving thanks. He slipped into Jelaska's tent but she was sleeping, so he kissed her brow and left.

He went looking for the healers' tent, opened the flap, then stopped, smiling softly.

Seth Korion was asleep, cradling Carmina in his arms. The Brician woman signed at Ramon to go away. He winked at her, lowered the flap and slipped away.

He found Lanna Jureigh on a bench outside a doorway to a rented room, sipping brandy from a clay bottle and staring up at the stars. The doorway was packed with flowers and gifts of all sorts.

'Oh,' she said as he sat beside her. 'It's you.'

'You were expecting someone else?'

'Are you kidding?' She waved a hand at the piles of flowers and gifts. 'I've had serious marriage proposals from every man I nursed in the past two years.'

Julietta gurgled at the flowers, so Ramon put her down and let her crawl clumsily towards them. The healer watched the girl with wistful eyes. He kissed Lanna's cheek and neck. She smelled musky and sweet. 'Did you accept any of the proposals?'

'Of course not,' she laughed throatily. 'I have a higher calling. The army.'

'Would you accept a gift from me?'

She turned to face him. 'That depends what it is,' she replied, her voice non-committal.

He picked up Julietta and placed the girl in her lap. 'This is your daughter, Julietta.'

Lanna stared. 'That's not funny, Ramon.'

'It's not a joke. I'm not meant for fatherhood. I've got too much to do in Silacia. A mother and a half-sister to free. Vengeance to harvest. I don't have the time or energy to be a parent ... or even the heart for it. She deserves better: she deserves *you*.'

Lanna shook her head. 'I can't.' But she wrapped her arms around the little girl tightly, trembling.

'Of course you can.' He kissed the little girl's forehead, then Lanna's. 'You'll be perfect for each other.'

He left before she could find him a reason not to accept. It was like ripping himself in half.

DAVID HAIR

Out in the night, Silvio and Tomasi were waiting with a dozen men, fresh horses and the expectation of gold beyond their dreams. It was almost two thousand miles to Silacia.

Seth Korion woke with the sun, staring at the back of Carmina Phyl's shoulder. Her hair was tickling his nose and cheeks, and the air inside the tent was close and stale.

Well, that wasn't what I thought it would be.

Love poetry spoke of sweet honey and wine, of stars that exploded and dreams that came to life; of love forged eternal on the fires of passion. But it had been rather sweaty and fumbling and he doubted that she'd really been as enraptured as she pretended. He'd gone to sleep faintly disappointed, unsure what had been so important about spilling his seed inside this woman, or any woman, actually. It all seemed rather low, like something peasants and farmers might do but better-bred people should eschew.

'Better-bred'. Ha!

He must have snorted softly, because she was suddenly aware of him, casting a sleepy look back over her shoulder. 'Oh, you're still here.'

He wasn't sure what to make of that. 'Should I have gone?'

'No, no. It's just ... I understood men like to leave while the woman sleeps. At least, that's what I've heard.' She rolled over to face him. 'You can stay if you wish,' she offered.

'No. I need to be up. This is still an army, and we've a long way to go.'

She feigned protest, but not too hard. He dressed, kissed her mouth – sour from sleep – and left feeling little different to how he had going in. *Perhaps it will all feel more significant later.*

'Good morning, General!' Lanna Jureigh called. She was outside her the healing tent dandling a baby on her knee – Julietta Sensini, by the look.

'Good morning,' he called 'Is Ramon in there?'

'No,' she replied, with an odd timbre in her voice. 'He's gone.'

'Gone?'

She smiled, wet-eyed but happy. 'Gone away. He said he had things

766

to attend to in Silacia. But he left me with this little bundle.' She hugged Julietta to her chest, beaming and crying.

Seth swallowed, then blinked, saluted and walked away. For a few minutes he felt lost, wondering how on Urte he'd work out what to do without Sensini. Then the tyranny of logistics took over, all the obvious things that needed doing but wouldn't happen until he told someone so, and before long it was just another day of routes and supplies and equipment.

He cast Ramon from his mind, and Carmina too, and became a Korion again.

Hebusalim, Dhassa, on the continent of Antiopia
Rajab (Julsep) 930
One month after the end of the Moontide

Sultan Salim of Kesh knelt in the vast expanse of the Bekira-Dome, the greatest Amteh shrine of them all. The whole edifice had been emptied so that the Sultan could be alone to contemplate the wonders of Ahm. The inlaid marble shone in the brilliant sun, glistening words of the Kalistham rising from within the stone – a magic of the Ordo Costruo who'd built it, though they were largely Kore-worshippers or unbelievers.

Strange how much wealth we pour into such places, while the poor go without.

He'd been there for about an hour and it was about time he returned to the madness outside. He could hear the chanting masses gathered for a glimpse of him. He'd ridden into Hebusalim as a victor, exalted by the destruction of the Crusade. But there was so much that needed doing now; he had to repair the lives of his people.

Bare feet slapped on stone and another man dropped to his knees behind and to his left and made obeisance to Ahm. Salim let him finish, staying on his knees patiently in this vast place, which when full could hold twenty thousand but today held two.

'Sal'Ahm, Great Sultan,' Rashid Mubarak greeted him respectfully when his prayer was done.

'Sal'Ahm, Emir Rashid. Walk with me.' Salim got to his feet and together they went towards the fountain in the northward corner. They trod in silence until Salim asked, 'Who is your lord, Rashid?'

'You, Great Sultan,' Rashid responded instantly.

'Yet you keep secrets from me.'

'It seemed necessary, Great Sultan. If I have erred, I beg forgiveness.'

Salim regarded the other man: perfection in a male form, from his lean but muscular body to his haughty face with their piercing green eyes and perfectly styled hair and beard. A mage, a master swordsman and a ruler: the true architect of the shihad, in the eyes of most.

Who sent his lover off to find the Scytale of Corineus and hasn't spoken of it since.

'Where is Alyssa Dulayne?'

'I don't know. None of those with her have come back. There has been no contact, and I cannot find her through scrying. The last report from her, she was flying towards Lokistan, seeking a monastery.' Rashid sounded apprehensive. 'The same monastery that the "Merozain Bhaicara" appear to originate from.' He pulled a face. 'They have hinted that she is their prisoner.'

'And they have this "Sk'thali" also?'

'I believe so,' Rashid admitted, his worries even more clear now. 'But we don't know the purpose of these Merozains yet.'

'Ramita Ankesharan leads them, with a Rondian husband,' Salim reminded him. 'She has no reason to love you, Rashid, or our faith.' Rashid bowed his head at these indisputable facts. They reached the fountain and Salim sat on the edge and trailed his fingers in the pond. He didn't want to alienate Rashid; he needed him. 'Tell me of the oath you swore – and broke – to the Ordo Costruo.'

The emir's face became puzzled. 'I swore to place myself in service of the Order, who in turn were pledged to serve peace, and to build a better world for all.'

Salim nodded slowly, thinking of an idealistic dreamer with a predilection for poetry and wine who would've approved of the oath. 'If I asked you to create such an order – an Ahmedhassan order – dedicated to rebuilding our cities and towns, would you do so for me?'

'Of course . . .' Rashid licked his lips. 'But this is a time of huge opportunity, Great Sultan – the Rondians have been mortally wounded! If we moved agents into Sydia, inside ten years we would have friendly enclaves, ready to support a new shihad: the invasion of Yuros itself!'

'We do not need a new shihad, Rashid Mubarak. We need buildings and aqueducts and irrigation – we need roads and bridges! *That* is our need!'

Rashid bowed in reluctant acquiescence. 'As my Sultan commands.'

'Then I leave the formation of this order in your hands, but I desire close oversight. Your magi have been trained to kill and destroy; retrain them in the arts of healing and building.'

'As my Lord commands.'

'And Rashid: we will not put to death our Rondian prisoners. They will be a labour force for the rebuilding of Dhassa and Kesh – not slaves, but bonded workers. When the next Moontide comes they will be free to leave. I will keep a roster of them, and the fate of each will be accounted for.'

Rashid's eyes flashed. 'They are invaders!'

'They are men who followed orders.' Salim waited until Rashid bowed again. 'And what of my new bride?'

'Cera Nesti?' Rashid shrugged. 'Her value is less than it was, but she is still a strategic alliance. Place her in the zenana and plough her when her Moon is risen.'

'On that at least we agree.' Salim stood. 'Come, we must meet these "Merozain" magi and find out if they're any different to the other breeds.'

Alaron heaved a sigh of relief, and leaned on his elbows on the balcony. Beside him, Ramita held Dasra, showing him the newly risen moon. Nasatya remained elusive, and she had a resigned heaviness to her expression, the realisation that perhaps he would never be found.

'I'm sick of banquets,' Alaron said, watching the guests leave through the courtyard below. The evening had been spent with the Sultan of Kesh, a smooth and charming man who spoke of peace with apparent yearning.

'So am I,' Ramita replied. 'I want to go home, Al'Rhon, to Aruna Nagar. I want to see my parents and my brothers and sisters. I want to show them my husband and my son. Can we please, *please*, go home?'

He shared her longing, but his home was thousands of miles in the other direction. His father was at Pontus. Apparently Elena had him taken to her own skiff an hour after he and Ramita had left Brochena and had fished Father and Ramon from the mess at Midpoint Tower. He was so grateful he couldn't think how he could ever repay her. Not that she'd wanted to have that conversation anyway.

'There's so much to do.' Alaron sighed wearily. 'We have to work out what to do with the Scytale. We've got to find Nasatya. We've got to make sure the Bridge has enough energy to survive being underwater. We've got to make arrangements for Corinea, and we have to work something out with the Ordo Costruo – and this new order Rashid Mubarak is creating.'

Ramita glowered. 'I don't trust that snake.'

'Me neither.'

'Then let it all wait!' She took his hand, put it to her lips then her heart. 'Please, come to Baranasi. We'll marry under Omali rites: you will ride a white horse into my parents' yard to claim me, we'll walk thrice around the fire and exchange garlands, and be one in the eyes of the Gods.'

And it will mean everything to me, her eyes added. *Everything in the world.*

Brochena, Javon, on the continent of Antiopia
Rajab (Julsep) 930
One month after the end of the Moontide

The Scriptualist invoked the Ritual of Family, then the women present – Cera Nesti, Elena Anborn and Staria Canestos – unwound their scarves and removed their bekira-shrouds while the men looked on warily.

Cera concealed a smile. *What, too many girls in the room for you, boys?*

Cera surveyed them: the lords of Javon: Emir Mekmud of Lybis,

Stefan di Aranio of Riban, Justiano di Kestria of Loctis in proxy for his elder brother Massimo, and Emilio Gorgio of Hytel. The highest-ranking Jhafi nobles of Intemsa and Baroz were here too, and of course her own Nesti men. Posing on her left was Theo Vernio-Nesti, trying to pick up some reflected glory through kinship to her.

'My Lords, welcome,' she greeted them.

'Good morning, Autarch,' they murmured, clearly just wanting this over so they could get on with the voting for a new king. The day had come – her last council meeting. Outside, the ambassadors from Kesh were waiting, and these men would soon be rid of her again. And rid of Elena too, her role as her bodyguard being over. Despite all that the magi had done for Javon, and Elena in particular, they feared the powers they could never attain.

'My Lords, the ninety days of my emergency leadership are now behind us – by several weeks, in truth – but finally we are assembled together and can formalise my stepping down. It is with joy that I do so, knowing that I am passing the rule of Javon back into the hands of men born to rule.' She hoped her inner sarcasm didn't come through in her voice. She let her eyes drift around the room, looking at Stefan di Aranio, Justiano di Kestria and Emilio Gorgio as they fidgeted impatiently, keen for the real meeting to begin once she was gone. At Mekmud of Lybis, Saarif Jelmud and the other would-be conspirators, still seeing the disappointment and frustration they felt with her and what was to them an inexplicable decision. And finally she looked at Theo Vernio-Nesti, a pallid shadow of her father, or the man her brother could have been. 'May the gods smile upon your decisions.'

After that she couldn't get out fast enough, but she still had to endure a vote of thanks. Then there was nothing for it but to leave, Elena at her back, and hear the door close behind her. She'd put her last days as ruler to good use, working from dawn until midnight: ratifying land for the lamiae and restoring the legal code to what it had been before the Dorobon came – a secular code, administered collectively by the nobles and bureaucrats, with appeal to the Crown. Undoing the work of two years of Dorobon misrule, approving appeals for injustices perpetrated under their reign, and approving a rebuilding plan that would not be able to easily be cancelled by whoever became king. It had left her worn down and exhausted. She stumbled and paused, gripped the rail, breathing heavily and trying to pretend it was just tiredness, not the depression she could feel closing in on her.

How will I ever endure being nobody again . . . ?

'Cera,' Elena murmured, 'are you all right?'

'I don't know.' She blinked back tears. 'Did I do right? I could have been *queen*.'

'But you chose not to be. Do you regret that now?'

'No . . . and yes. I was afraid it would lead to civil war. So soon after the Moontide – it could have broken us.' She met the Noros woman's gaze. 'But all the things I could have done – good things, *right* things! Of course there are regrets.'

Elena's face softened a little. 'For what it's worth, I believe you did the right thing. Few people can resist such an opportunity, but you would have started a war that might have sent Javon spiralling into destruction. Sometimes change has to be gradual, even if that prolongs the suffering of those who should be protected. The reforms you would have passed would have alienated many, and made you a target for more than just hostile words.'

'Than perhaps it's a good thing I'm going to live the rest of my days in a box in Kesh,' Cera replied bitterly. She looked wearily up the stairs. 'Where are the ambassadors?'

'In the state rooms, waiting for me,' Elena said softly. 'They asked to see me while they await the Royal Election.'

Cera raised an eyebrow. 'Why?'

'I'm not sure. Maybe they just enjoyed my company last time they were here?'

While Cera trudged up to pack her bags, Elena strode through Brochena Palace to meet with the ambassadors in their guest rooms. They'd arrived the previous night and been banqueted and entertained with musical performances and dancers and a dozen courses of Jhafi delicacies conjured from the remains of war by some kitchen mage. Their mission here was to greet the new Javon king, whoever that might be, then tomorrow, their windship would take them and Cera south.

For some reason, they urgently wanted to speak to the dreaded Elena Anborn first.

She found them seated on cushioned stone benches in a viewing cupola overlooking the northern side of the city and the salt lake, idly studying the ceiling frescoes. They were guarded by young men in dark robes – clearly Hadishah – who despite their role were clearly reluctant to pat her down for weapons. She made it easy for them by handing them her blades before approaching the ambassadors. They exchanged the traditional greetings and reverences, then sat. A servant scuttled in, poured sharbat, offered the mezze platter around, then scurried away.

Salim of Kesh had sent the same pair of ambassadors he'd sent in 928, two years ago: the portly Faroukh of Maal, Salim's uncle, and the iron-bearded Godspeaker Barra Xuok. Then, Cera had been a young woman on a besieged throne and desperate for allies, enough to agree to wed one of her nation's traditional foes in exchange for guarantees about autonomy during the Moontide. She'd conceded a permanent Keshi embassy, with the ambassador permitted a seat on the Regency Council, and given herself in marriage so that Javon could keep its manpower and self-rule during the shihad. It was a poor deal, made at a time when her bargaining position was weak.

But now that young woman was a widow, after a not-quite forced marriage to a Rondian mage, as well as being a convicted murder-ess, smeared as a safian, and no longer the senior family member of her House.

The phrase 'damaged goods' barely covers it, Elena reflected.

'The world has changed greatly,' Faroukh said, to open discussions.

Godspeaker Barra Xuok lifted both hands skywards. 'Ahm has been generous in His blessings this Moontide. We have seen great victories, at Shaliyah and Ebensar, and here in Ja'afar also. The Rondians are gone, and we pray that the Third Crusade will be the last.'

'I hope so too.'

The Godspeaker's stony face softened just a little in remembrance. 'When last we talked, Lady, we had many – I think understandable – suspicions concerning you and your role here. But you have sacrificed much for your young protégé, fought long and well in the service of the Nesti and Ja'afar, and found love with a young man of the East. You have won our trust. Sultan Salim has hopes that you will continue to play a role in Ja'afar, even after the Princessa joins his court in Sagostabad.'

'Even after my freeing of the Ordo Costruo from the Hadishah?' she asked, arching an eyebrow.

'The Sultan regrets the loss of life, obviously, and Emir Rashid is not enamoured of the act. But Salim understands why a request for aid was not made to him first.'

'The Hadishah have raised documents of condemnation against both Kazim and me.'

'They will be asked to revoke them,' Faroukh replied soothingly. 'Salim rejoices that the Ordo Costruo have returned to society, and looks forward to welcoming their embassies to his court.'

'I suppose the status of magi in Keshi and Dhassan society will change somewhat, now that Salim and Rashid have them openly at court?'

'Indeed, Lady. As it has already in Ja'afar.'

'We do have more acceptance,' she agreed. 'And of course, the Ordo Costruo have agreed to help protect Javon by becoming custodians of the Krak di Condotiori.' *So you can't invade, even if you wanted to.*

'This is known, Lady,' Godspeaker Barra replied. 'And what of yourself?'

Elena glanced down at her stomach, now noticeably expanded. 'My future here in Brochena is uncertain at this stage. As you can see, I am with child. At the very least, I will be retiring from public life until I have recovered from the birthing.'

'We offer you our sincerest congratulations, Lady,' Faroukh said. 'A unique child, I am told.'

That's true. 'Every child is unique.' Not wanting to discuss it further, she changed the subject. 'Surely the sultan is concerned about Cera's changed circumstances?'

The two ambassadors glanced at each other, then nodded carefully. Barra Xuok spoke first. 'It is fair to say that a young virgin with some small experience in statecraft agreed to this betrothal; but Cera Nesti is no longer that girl. We have heard reports of a contentious woman administering mob justice from the zenana, convicted of regicide and perversion. The former charge is uncertain, perhaps, and the latter is denied, but we are given to understand that she has extended protection to the infamous Sacro Arcoyris Estellan, which does nothing to quell rumours about her . . .'

'Indeed: Staria's people have agreed to remain in the Rift Forts in return for autonomy from certain laws.'

'We will be watching them closely, Lady,' Godspeaker Xuok said dourly.

I bet you will. 'Staria's people aided the fight for freedom in Javon. All here know and are grateful.'

'But their predilections—'

'—did not prevent them from contributing nobly.' Elena met the Godspeaker's eyes steadily, until he waved a hand, letting the issue go. She took that as a sign that other concessions might be possible, but that Cera's reputation worried them.

What would Kesh make of a woman revered as a Saint in Javon? Especially one with a reputation for being independent of mind and tainted by all these associations? How does Salim really feel about it?

'Gentlemen, my understanding is that a sultan's betrothal is completely binding?'

Godspeaker Xuok nodded stiffly. 'The reason such alliances are made is to bind two nations in peace, so legally only a state of war can be invoked to break it. Of course, no such war is desired, but the history of Javon and Kesh is not peaceful, and Salim's honour does not permit him to allow any slight upon his name. Whether she fully understood that or not, Cera Nesti gave her vow irrevocably. Nor can Ja'afar easily ignore the snub if Salim breaks the betrothal:

DAVID HAIR

what that would say is that Ja'afar is beneath his notice. It would isolate your people in a hostile world.'

'So, will the old traditions of kidnapping the bride have to be resurrected?' Faroukh added drily.

'Cera understands her duty,' Elena replied. 'But there are some things you need to know first.'

The first act of Massimo di Kestria – now King Massimo I of Javon – was to welcome the Keshi ambassadors formally to his court and accept their congratulations. The election had been tight, but Emilio Gorgio and Theo Vernio-Nesti had swung in behind Massimo on the third ballot, leaving previous front-runner Stefan di Aranio gnashing his teeth in frustration. The crowning would be tomorrow, but for now, another matter took precedence: the formal claiming of a bride.

'The world has changed,' Faroukh of Maal proclaimed before the court, in reply to King Massimo's welcome. 'War came, and our Great Sultan was at the forefront of the struggle. Our losses were shocking, the destruction immense. Yet we have prevailed, here, as in Kesh and Dhassa.' He bowed to Cera. 'Ahm smiles upon your intended, Lady Cera.'

'I am blessed,' Cera replied dully. This feast would be her last taste of public life of Javon, or most likely anywhere else, bar her wedding in Kesh. She was struggling to hold back tears, but this moment was of her own making, so she had to bear it.

Better this than civil war ... She looked at Elena, but the Noros woman would not return her glance. She was clinging to Kazim's arm; both were recovering steadily from their wounds.

Faroukh raised his booming voice still further. 'Salim, mightiest pillar of our nation, lion of the deserts, has devoted himself to the crushing of his enemies! Yet now his sword is sheathed and the time for healing has come. Kesh will take years to banish the ghoulish visages of plague, famine and death that blight our sacred soil—'

'War was ever thus,' Massimo agreed, clearly puzzled at the direction Faroukh was taking.

Cera was wondering herself. These words weren't the ones she was expecting.

Faroukh smote his chest, staring tragically into the heavens. 'The years ahead will be full of labour. There will be no time for pleasure. No time for joy. Our noble sultan has pledged to revive his stricken land!'

A mutter ran about the court and the lords of Javon looked at each other in consternation. What was the ambassador saying? Cera looked at Elena suddenly. *Is Salim revoking our betrothal?*

Though her heart leaped, she knew the consequences would be dire. In the eyes of Ahmedhassa, such a snub would be a signal that Kesh saw Javon as beneath consideration. That would impact everything from border security, to terms of trade, to interest rates on the loans they required to rebuild. It could cripple Javon for years.

The court fell silent, straining their ears, as Faroukh went on, 'It is for these reasons that Salim feels that he must *defer* the wedding *indefinitely*.'

There was a collective intake of breath throughout the court.

'It is no light decision,' Godspeaker Barra Xuok put in. 'But there is a clear precedent, in the betrothal of the Prophet's son Tahmuhk to the Princess of Vida during the War of Black Stars.'

Cera's experience was that a skilled religious scholar could find whatever he liked in a big enough holy book, but she did recall the affair Xuok had invoked: Tahmuhk, in the end, *never* married the Princess of Vida. The betrothal was only formally ended by Tahmuhk's death fifty-four years later.

She looked sideways at Elena, realised her mouth had dropped open and shut it firmly. The Noros woman didn't smile, just gave the faintest lift of her chin. *Did she do this?*

'Lady Cera, I can only imagine the distress this must cause you,' Faroukh said gravely. 'For not only is this hoped-for union not currently possible, but you must retire to a preparatory zenana regardless, and live in solitude until he summons you. Public life is no longer open to you in such a role.'

Mater Lune, he doesn't want to wed me, just lock me away . . .

Did Elena arrange this as revenge?

By now the whispers about the court were audible, and the thunder on the brows of King Massimo and the other lords of Javon was clear. Everyone was looking about, unsure how to react.

'The sultan regrets that he is unsure when he may finally call upon you,' Faroukh said, raising his voice above the growing hubbub. 'However, Sultan Salim does retain the right to appoint an ambassador to Javon as agreed, with full council rights!' The courtiers narrowed their eyes, and Cera could feel the rebellious whispers at this. Salim was effectively rejecting Cera in all but name, but still reaping the benefits of the alliance.

Godspeaker Barra stepped forward, his harsh voice cutting through the noise. 'In token of your role in saving Ja'afar from the Crusaders, Lady Cera, our sultan prays that you will accept appointment as his ambassador, and the permanent place on the Javonesi Royal Council that it entails. He gives dispensation to attend the requisite duties, despite your seclusion.'

Cera had to put her hand to her mouth to stop from choking. She stared at the Godspeaker, then at Faroukh, who were watching her intently. She had enough prepossession to put her hand to her chest and groan in dismay. A few seconds later the smarter courtiers were doing the same.

One glance at King Massimo and the other lords told her they were shocked; but there was enough grim satisfaction and appreciation on the faces of men like Emir Mekmud, Saarif Jelmud and even Justiano di Kestria and the other fighting men that she knew she wouldn't lack support. And her loyal Nesti men looked like they'd just found a gold coin at the bottom of their cups.

Thank you, Pater Sol! She turned to Elena, saw a faint look of satisfaction. *And thank you, Elena Anborn!* She hung her head, dabbed at her eyes to imply that she wept, then nodded with apparent reluctance.

Ambassador for Kesh . . . ? In my own lands . . . ?

The opportunities would be infinite, and she would still be at the heart of events.

'A woman can only obey,' she managed, improvising desperately.

'Though obedience in this matter breaks my heart.' She stood suddenly, to the ambassador's visible alarm, left the dais and dropped to her knees before Barra Xuok. 'Bless me, Godspeaker! Absolve me! Give me the consolation that the Prophet still loves this poor handmaiden, adrift on the stormy seas of life!' She bowed her head expectantly.

The granite-faced Godspeaker looked totally put out, as well he might.

If a rumoured safian regicide once married to a heathen and now widowed, drops to her knees and demands your blessing, what's the precedent? Has your holy book got anything on that?

With a visible swallow, the Godspeaker looked about him, seeing a room full of people who either believed Cera Nesti was a living saint or a very clever ruler, and loved her either way. Then he showed exactly why he'd risen through the ranks of his calling.

'Lady Cera, it is known that the nephew of the Prophet's third son, Ul-haj II of Bindesh, once absolved his wife Sadah of adultery and stoning by deeming that the Harkun abducted her and took her unwillingly. The Godspeakers gave her their blessing, and she went on to devote her life to the poor.'

Cera had no idea whether this tale was true, or made up on the spot. Either way, it was just what she wanted. 'A praiseworthy example for any woman,' she said loudly. 'Let Sadah of Bindesh be my guide and inspiration!'

The Godspeaker blessed her, then helped her to her feet. She deliberately clung to him, to leave an indelible impression of royalty and clergy working together: an allegory of the relationship between spirituality and temporal power, perhaps. Something for the court painters to muse upon.

To cover his confusion, King Massimo told the musicians to play, and began drinking heavily with his inner circle, while well-wishers flooded towards Cera to congratulate or commiserate – not everyone had quite worked out which was the more appropriate yet.

She didn't get the chance to corner Elena until sometime later. 'How did you do it?' she murmured when Elena hobbled over.

Elena smirked. 'The solution wasn't hard to find, once I told them that you were indeed a safian, and that other young women find you utterly irresistible. I warned them that within weeks you'd have seduced all of Salim's other wives, and converted them to your desires.'

Cera stared queasily. *'You said that?'*

'Of course I didn't.' Elena cackled drily. 'It was the Beggars' Court they were worried about. They were frightened of you, Cera, and only too glad to find a compromise.' She fixed her with a hard look. 'You have a unique opportunity to make the lives of many, many people here in Javon better: women, children, people who are different and shunned, all will look to you for succour. I hope you take this chance and use it – *Mater-Javonesi.*'

'I will, I swear!' Cera promised fervently. *Oh yes, I will . . .*

That night, while the court celebrated – or in the case of the lords of Javon, huddled in corners and tried to make sense of this changed world – Elena Anborn slipped into the healers' ward. The patients were slumbering and their attendants looked as if they'd collapsed asleep in the midst of their duties, hunched over in chairs or on floors.

Her bags were packed and it was time to leave.

'Wear your gems,' a ghost whispered.

She found the curtained recess she sought and slipped inside. Tarita was awake, staring bleakly at the ceiling. She turned her head when she realised Elena was there, the only movement she was capable of herself. Elena sat on the bed and took Tarita's limp right hand in both hers. 'Hello Tarita. How are you?'

'Lady Alhana!' The maid tried to force a welcoming smile, but she couldn't hold onto it. 'Why am I still alive?' she asked in a despairing voice.

Elena looked at her squarely. 'Tarita, may I speak frankly of your condition?'

The maid swallowed, then nodded bravely.

'You're paralysed, beyond the skill of any healer, mage or otherwise. You will never be able to move again. You will live and die in a bed, with someone cleaning up your bodily wastes.' She stroked Tarita's cheek to soften her words. 'I don't say this to be cruel, but to be clear. The only way someone could heal your spine and reconnect the nerves would be to inhabit your head and make the connections from the inside. The only person who can do that is you, and you aren't a mage.'

'I can bear it,' Tarita whispered. 'Ahm will come for me soon.'

'Perhaps, but I've got a better offer.' Elena pulled out a small phial of liquid. 'This contains *ambrosia*. If you drink it, you might die. But if you don't die, you'll become an Ascendant mage with the power – though not the knowledge – to heal yourself. The knowledge will have to be acquired: it isn't a magical, instant fix; it is a slow and dangerous process. But if you are willing, this phial of ambrosia is the first step.'

Tarita's jaw dropped. 'How did you get this?'

'I called in some favours.' *From my nephew, of all people.* 'I take it that's a yes?'

'Yes! Yes-yes-yes!' Tarita's eyes began to shed tears of joy. 'Alhana, should I drink it now?'

'Not here. Kazim and I are going to take you away, somewhere safe.' She patted her stomach. 'Somewhere *all* of us can grow and learn in peace.'

By dawn, they were soaring over the city, Tarita wrapped in blankets on the fore-deck. Elena looked up at the rosy dawn kissing the sky, and then at kazim, the wind ruffling his tangled hair and light in his eyes as he piloted them. He set a course straight into the sun as it rose over Mount Tigrat, far away to the east, back to where she and Kazim had found each other. The only place left she regarded as home.

EPILOGUE

Moontide's End

A Naïve Optimism

*In Julsep 904, a Bridge my order built to promote peace was used to make war.
I had the opportunity to destroy the Bridge but didn't, for the sakes of tens of
thousands of innocent (a relative term, and many didn't remain so by any criteria) men marching across the span. I refuse to regret that decision, despite
the suffering I have seen unfold.*

*My defence is that conflict cannot be resolved without contact. Understanding
cannot be reached without interaction. It is an imperfect answer, that naïvely
assumes that some on both sides desire peace and fellowship. But that naïveté
has never been disappointed in the long term. Despite the prevalence of war,
the majority crave peace. Among that majority there is a sub-group who are
prepared to give their lives for the sake of that peace, and they are the true
heroes of any conflict. It is to them that I look, as the Third Crusade approaches.*

ANTONIN MEIROS, HEBUSALIM, 926

*Retia, Silacia, on the continent of Yuros
Julsep 930
One month after the end of the Moontide*

The window was open, like an invitation, but Ramon didn't enter; he
remained in the shadows, listening with all of his manifold senses.
There were guards, of course, but none had the eyes required to
detect him. A conversation in his own tongue floated to him on the
gentle breeze, like music after so many years away. He closed his
eyes and listened to the feelings behind the words.

782

His mother was arguing with Pater-Retiari about the bottle of wine they were drinking. It wasn't really an argument though, more like cook-fire banter. 'We opened it too soon, Vitor!'

'Too soon? Fanisia, this achantia is *perfect*, right now. It's a 924, it's been cellared six years, as the vintners say an achantia should. It is perfect!'

'Ha! Your palate died with your libido.'

'You bend over this table and I'll show you my libido isn't dead— I should have eloped with the gardener's wife!'

'Pah! As if she'd have you! She is half your age and frankly too good for you! Anyway, this 924 vintage needed longer, as all the growers warned! The season was wet, remember? They all said to give this vintage an extra year – but no, you *had* to open it now, when next year it would be divine!'

And on it went. They called each other names, laughed and thought up worse ones, then toasted their marriage: twenty years together. Then they toasted the vintners, the bottlers and everyone else they could think of while getting steadily more drunk. They rambled on about the weather and the news from the north, and the doings of the neighbouring familioso as if they were kin, not rivals in crime.

But what's crime here anyway but a job? The empire permits us little else . . .

They also spoke of their daughter, growing wild and free on country living.

My half-sister, Ramon thought, staring at Pater-Retiari from the darkness. *Damn it, I came to kill you, old man. I came to free my mother from you!* He'd thought to unlock a gaol, but here was a woman who'd grown fond of her chains. Perhaps she'd been so for years, but he'd not seen it.

At first it made him angry. *Did I peddle opium, issue fraudulent promissory notes and destroy the Crusade economy for this?* But then it made him somehow, strangely reassured. *Love can grow in strange places.* He drifted backwards, into the deeper shadows, and stood there, gnawing his lower lip.

She's not supposed to love him.

He closed his eyes, tried to think it through. Pater-Retia had taken her in, a rape victim – perhaps his motives were not entirely pure; her child would carry the prized mage's blood – but he had protected her and raised her son as his own.

All the way from Pontus to Silacia, he'd heard the rumours: the empire was in ferment, trade was breaking down, people suffering as shortages began to bite. The coinage was worthless and food increasingly scarce. The traders said that Estellayne and Argundy were about to rebel, and set the world aflame. The free city of Becchio, in South Rimoni, was the recruiting station for mercenary legions. Battle-magi could just about name their fee, and he now had a power none of his peers could match.

Yet here in Retia, his mother, his half-sister and his son by the maid were kept by a man he'd sworn to kill.

Is that what I really want to do?

Other futures offered themselves like Divination visions: *I could kill Pater-Retiari, certainly, and inherit his whole organisation. Or I could return as a loyal son and protect my family from the storms to come.* His thoughts went further afield as other options raised their hand. He felt the legion call him: Seth, Kip, Lanna, all of them. But the army was disbanding, the men returning to their civilian lives.

Lanna has my daughter: I could go back to them and learn to be a father.

Hel, I could even go and join Alaron's people and see if being a scholar and a peacekeeper suits me.

Or I could return to Ardijah, and duel Renn Bondeau for the calipha's hand.

He didn't move for a long, long time, watching the house settle to sleep while fondling the hilt of his dagger.

Or I could just let them all be . . .

He sighed, and slipped away.

Mounting his horse, he left Tomasi Fuldo and Silvio Arturo waiting in the copse to the north, still dreaming of gold they'd never see, and took the road towards Becchio.

House Korion, Bres, on the continent of Yuros
Augeite 930
Two months after the end of the Moontide

Seth Korion rode alone up a long carriageway lined with colonnades mounted with busts of his father. Most were stained with birdshit and moss, and a few were broken. The gardens and woods that surrounded the mansion looked unkempt, as if the gardeners and woodsmen had abandoned them.

He lost the sun before he even reached the manor, but he could have found his way blindfold. There was light in an upper window, and more shining from the servants' wing as he dismounted outside. Familiar faces poured out from all sides, calling uncertain greetings. In many ways the servants had been more of a family to him than either his mother or his father.

'Milord Seth,' the old gamesman Hobin kept shouting. 'You're back!' Others bowed and curtseyed, took his horse away, offered water or ale. He took a mug of the latter, and after greeting them all, asked at the state of disrepair that was so evident.

'Well, Milord,' the butler Taft drawled, 'It's a drimmy lay, and that's the truth of it. Your mother, Lady … ah, *Fetallink*, has shut herself in the top suite and won't come out, in case the bailiffs take her away. Not that they've come, but she's scared, Milord. Word came that you were disinherited.' The old man paused anxiously. 'Outraged, we were!'

Maybe they had been; he had, after all, been the heir apparent for twenty years, and their fate was uncertain if other families took over the manor. *How can I protect them, if I'm thrown out of here with Mother?*

'Go on,' he told Taft.

The butler smiled wryly. 'Well, the thing was: no papers have been brought to court. Several bastard sons *claimed* that they were to be legitimised, but no paperwork ever made it back here. So there's a legal dispute, y'see. Informal documents claim you're disowned, but there's nothing formal. So the estate's frozen, we en't been paid for months – we've been living off the cellars, begging yer pardon.

DAVID HAIR

An' yer mother won't come out of her rooms. You were supposedly dead,' – Taft raised a cautious eyebrow – 'then you were a traitor, according to reports—'

'Which we din' believe,' those listening chorused, 'not at all.'

'And now you're here!' Taft concluded heartily. 'Kore's blessings on ye, lad!'

'Well,' Seth said, mind racing. *The papers never made it back . . . so I'm still a Korion. And why the Hel not?* He took another sip of beer while they all waited on his word. 'It seems Mother and I must go to the Governor and put an end to these lies for good.' He raised his mug to them. 'Thank you all, my faithful friends, for keeping the old house so well, and making me welcome. There are a few soldiers a mile down the road, men from the Crusade who have no other life. I have promised them a home here. And my new wife also awaits word that she can join us. We have much work to do to make the old house ready for her.'

They raised a cheer at that, congratulating him, while he beamed and nodded. The new ring on his finger felt strange, as did the mere thought that he was now a married man. But Carmina would make a good wife, faithful and placid. He drained his mug, and then held it out for a refill, feeling light-hearted and lightheaded.

'My dear friends, it's so good to be home.'

Domus Costruo, Hebusalim, on the continent of Antiopia
Rami (Septinon) 930
Three months after the end of the Moontide

It was a state occasion – *another one.* Alaron Mercer sighed inwardly. He was getting used to them, but they were wearying. Ramita skipped most of them, but she was beside him tonight, because this one was special.

Today the Merozain Brotherhood formally stepped onto the tabula board of power.

East and West were here: Regis Sacrecour, Duke of Pontus, an obscure royal from a distant line unfortunate enough to fall out of favour at Pallas so thoroughly that they were sent to the far end of the continent, represented the Rondian Empire. Quite what that meant no one could say; Treasurer Dubrayle and Arch-Prelate Wurther were either preserving the Sacrecour dynasty or hastening its end, according to gossip. Some said Constant's young children would rule once they reached their majority; others that the infamously imprisoned Princess Natia was to be crowned. Or that she was already dead. It all stank of war. But Duke Regis was affable enough, and more importantly, he appeared to understand that without Alaron and Ramita, his palace in Pontus would be nothing but a smashed and sea-scoured boneyard.

The East was represented by Sultan Salim himself, who was smart enough not to bring Rashid Mubarak. Word was the emir had returned to Halli'kut to convene his new order of magi. He was trying to buy the freedom of Alyssa Dulayne and the other Hadishah prisoners, though a price was still to be agreed.

Building up the Merozain numbers was a priority. Alaron, Ramita and their Brothers numbered only a dozen now, but they planned to return soon to Mandira Khojana and see how amenable Master Puravai was to widening their net to other monasteries.

The Ordo Costruo themselves numbered only thirty, but Rene Cardien claimed that many more must still be prisoners of the Hadishah breeding-houses, a subject Alaron would shortly be raising with Salim.

Alaron didn't see the Ordo Costruo as rivals, and of course, they were at pains to befriend him: he had the Scytale, after all. Cardien argued that only the Ordo Costruo could protect the artefact from the Rondian Empire. Alliance or even merger was possible, but there were many, many issues to be resolved first. In the meantime, the Ordo Costruo's main concern was the Leviathan Bridge. In the wake of the damage done by the Sacrecours' attempts to destroy it, the Towers were all depleted, and the Bridge was unlikely to survive being submerged. But Cardien had plans to recover the situation, and Alaron and Ramita were eager to help.

After the speeches – Alaron got through his by pretending he was talking to his father with whom he'd been joyously reunited, and to Ramita in the front row – he introduced one final speaker, knowing that her words would be the one thing this night would be remembered for in the decades to come. The speaker was a willowy, silver-haired woman with a timeless face who took to the podium unidentified and waited for silence before her gentle, distant voice filled the room.

'My name is Lillea Selene Sorades.'

She paused as the whole room went silent with the accursed name resounding in their ears. Everywhere faces suddenly were attentive, confused, or stunned. Some shook their heads in denial. And in their seats on the right-hand side of the central aisles, the Kore clergy who'd come went white.

'Most of you know me by another name: Corinea. All your lives you've been told stories about me, but I'm here to tell you the truth. This is my story . . .'

Mount Tigrat, Javon, on the continent of Antiopia
Shawwal (Octen) 930
Four months after the end of the Moontide

The sun rose, sending hazy slabs of light through the pillars of the gallery on the east side of the monastery. The robed woman closed her eyes momentarily and soaked in the warmth. Her firm, rounded belly weighed on her as she trod the walkway, looking out over the plains below as they emerged misty and moist from the night.

I do love this land. Despite all it's taken from me. Elena stroked her stomach. *Feel that heat, little Serena? It's the warmth of your homeland.*

She found a stone seat where at times she used to sit with Kazim in the afternoon, sweating from their training bouts, still a little hostile and wary, but slowly feeling their way towards each other through the maze of prejudices and circumstance that lay between. This was where they'd really fallen in love.

One day you'll leave here and find your place in the world, Serena. But I don't know if I will ever leave again.

Kazim joined her, dressed in work clothes and ready to clear the lower levels of all the debris from their hurried abandonment last year. He'd made coffee, and they shared a cup, savouring the tang.

'We could house fifty people down there, easily,' he commented.

'What a horrible thought,' she replied.

They grinned, each knowing the other would unbend at some point. Communication crackled between them, wordless, intimate and endlessly loving. Time slipped past. 'Molmar's bringing timber from Brochena tomorrow,' Kazim told her. 'He says your Queen Cera – sorry, *Ambassador* Cera – is running rings around the Royal Council. Massimo relies on her for guidance, and his liking for her grows. She has been put in charge of Justice and the Courts.'

'That didn't take long,' she remarked. 'Not that I thought it would.'

The click of wood on stone caught their ears and a small figure with stick-like arms and legs, clad in thin cotton, shoved a wooden frame through the door and leaned on it, panting heavily. Then she thrust it a few inches forward, and lurched in its wake. Several times she almost fell, but caught herself with a nudge of gnostic force. When Tarita sensed their eyes on her, she called out, 'Look, Alhana! See! I can walk! I can do it!'

Elena wiped at her eyes.

I have two beautiful daughters: my adopted one, and Serena inside me. She stroked her belly. *Dokken or mage – what are you, little one? No matter: I'll love you, and so will your father.*

The child inside her kicked as if she heard.

Baranasi, Lakh, on the continent of Antiopia
Zulqeda (Noveleve) 930
Five months after the end of the Moontide

The streets of Aruna Nagar were teeming with noise and movement, the rich tang of spice and heat and sweat forming a heady brew. The alleys were at shuffling pace only, the buildings garlanded with brightly coloured ribbons of ochre and red: auspicious colours for the marriage season. Pandits read the stars to determine the optimal dates for the betrothed couples, and somehow managed to squeeze them all into autumn when the weather was cool but the nights warm: the best weather for such celebrations.

There were at least seven such festivals that afternoon within a stone's throw of each other around Aruna Nagar Square, where the market brought together buyers and sellers. Most residents were going to all of the weddings, even if just for a few minutes, because everyone was related to everyone else around here in some way. Family matriarchs felt honour-bound to see them all and pass judgement on the food, on the clothing, on the gifts, on the beauty of the couple and every other aspect. Families' social standings rose and fell on such things.

Ramita Ankesharan felt like a stranger in her homeland today. Half-familiar faces flashed by, girls she'd schooled with who were now young mothers, boys who'd once run riot with Kazim now labouring for their father's businesses, while a new generation of youths tore through the market like a whirlwind, stealing handfuls of roasted nuts and sweets and waving kalikiti bats.

'You grew up here?' Alaron muttered incredulously, holding her hand and buffeting his way through the press.

'I did,' she replied. 'Isn't it wonderful?'

'That's not the word I was thinking.' He pulled her from the flow and stared about him. His pale face was discernible beneath his hood, but Rondian traders were not wholly unknown here, so while his pale skin didn't trigger panic, he did attract curious glances and beggars: because *everyone* knew that Rondians were both inexplicably rich *and* stupid with money. 'But it is *amazing*,' he added fervently, which made her proud. 'I like it, I do.'

'If you like it now, then soon you will love it,' she said.

'Where do your family live?'

Ramita had to think for half a second. 'That way.'

Once back in Mandira Khojana, Ramita had finally had the opportunity to scry her family, and to her faint surprise, they were back in Baranasi. She supposed that once the money stopped flowing, they'd decided that there was no other place they would rather be. They were in a different house, of course: the money might have stopped but even the initial payment Meiros had made for her had been *lifetimes* of wealth. Their new house overlooked the river, among the well-to-do, and there were servants and house-guards.

My sacrifice did that.

They arrived unheralded at the gatehouse and with a touch of mischief told the doorman that Lady Ramita Meiros was here to see Master Ispal. The doorman looked at her strangely, then at Alaron's pale face, and fled, shouting 'Master! Master!'

I suppose he knows who I am, then . . .

Father and Mother came together, Ispal's face wide-eyed and his whole body shaking, her mother Tanuva pale and weeping. She didn't feel that she was home until she was enveloped in her mother's arms and pressing Dasra into Father's grasp. Then Jai sprinted in and lifted her and swung her around and around, and Keita waddled in with their toddler and her belly large again, then the twins exploded through the middle of them, the two surviving triplets arrived to see what the fuss was, and all was the merry chaos she'd grown up in.

Welcoming Alaron into the family required explanations and assurances, but he spoke Lakh credibly by now, enough that they could work out what was intended. Fear of ferang magi was not easily overcome, but her family was made of love and they drew him in. She skirted the details of what had befallen Kazim and Huriya and said little of her own transformation. Her parents weren't blind: they'd realised within minutes that this was a visit, not a homecoming. They made no demands, and she loved them all the more for that.

'Did I do wrong, Daughter?' her father whispered, much later, before she went to join Alaron in their room. 'I sold you to a stranger. I've been haunted ever since.'

'I don't know, Father. There is no way of knowing how things might otherwise have been. But the gods have been kind to us all. Our family is safe, and better off. And I now have another fine husband and two beautiful children. I cannot say you did wrong.'

'Makheera-ji was merciful,' her mother said.

Ramita smiled at what Alaron would think of that. 'We can only do our best with what is put before us. When is anything ever perfect?' She looked away, thinking of Nasatya, lost somewhere in the world. *We will see you again, little one, if the Goddess wills.*

It was night in Baranasi, but it wasn't dark. Holy Imuna was basted in silver by the moon hanging above like a giant eye. Alaron stood on a balcony and stared out at the river. Thousands of tiny leaf-boats bobbed past, each bearing a candle lit in prayer for remembrance of the dead, by the thousands of worshippers who came to the banks every evening. He'd lit one for Cym earlier and set it in the current.

We're all just candles floating on the river of life. He wondered if they were lines of a poem he'd once read.

Ramita slipped into the crook of his arm. She was carrying a drowsy Dasra. 'It's lovely, isn't it? This is Imuna at her most beautiful.' She giggled. 'It's too dark to see how filthy the water is, and it's too far away to smell it.'

'It's wonderful,' Alaron told her, sincerely. He plucked Dasra from her and pointed to the river. 'Look, little man. This is your mother's home. Maybe yours one day too.'

Ramita took his free hand. 'Husband,' she said seriously. 'My parents approve of you. They think you will make a fine father for our daughters.'

Phew. He grinned, then stared. '*Daughters?* Are you . . . Have we—?' She drew his hand to her stomach, smiling widely.

THE END OF THE MOONTIDE

APPENDICES

Timeline of Urte History

Year Y500BV[*]:	Approximate beginning of the Rimoni conquest of Yuros.
Year Y1:	Rimoni republics unite as Rimoni Empire, and new calendar adopted.
Year Y380:	The dissident Corineus and his followers engage in 'The Ascension of Corineus'. Corineus dies, but three hundred survivors led by Sertain gain the gnosis and begin the conquest of Yuros. Another hundred under Meiros forgo war and journey eastwards into the wilderness, and a further hundred 'Souldrinkers' survivors go into hiding.
Year Y382:	Sertain is crowned first Rondian Emperor in Pallas and establishes Sacrecour Dynasty that still rules in Pallas. In time Rondian rule extends across almost entire continent of Yuros.
Year Y697:	First wind-ships from Pontus 'discover' Antiopia and its ancient and thriving civilisations. Trade-links develop, and eventually, plans for a linking bridge are developed by Meiros and his order of peaceful magi, the Ordo Costruo.

* (BV = Before Victory)

Year Y808:	The First Moontide: the Leviathan Bridge is completed by Meiros and opens for the first time.
Year Y820+:	The Second Moontide sees Rimoni natives flood into Ja'afar (Javon) in large numbers, where they buy land and establish themselves. As they gain political control, civil war develops, but is averted by the 'Javon Settlement' formally adopted in 836. The monarchy of Javon becomes democratic and is legally tied to the necessity for mixed racial background.
Year Y834:	A Keshi invasion of northern Lakh establishes the Amteh in Lakh, and a dynasty subservient to Kesh (the 'Mughal' is a Keshi ruler of Lakh territories).
Year Y880/881:	The Seventh Moontide: the most successful Moontide trading season in Hebusalim, and the revelation that the Pallas debt exceeds revenues. Crown credit crisis resolved by underwriting of crown debt by merchant bankers Jusst & Holsen.
Year Y892/893:	The Eighth Moontide: trading is disrupted by a series of atrocities by both Amteh fanatics and Kirkegarde knights.
Year Y902:	'The Year of Bloody Knives': Emperor Hiltius is murdered and his son Magnus (and second wife Lucia) take over; they have a son, Constant in Y905, but the heir is still Natia (daughter of Magnus' first wife).
Year Y904/905:	The Ninth Moontide and the First Crusade: the Rondian Emperor Magnus

sends his legions into Hebusalim. His armies are permitted to cross the Bridge by the Ordo Costruo; they defeat the armies of Dhassa and Kesh. The Rondians establish the Dorobon monarchy in Javon and plunder Sagostabad. The Rondians leave a garrison in Hebusalim to resist re-occupation.

Years Y909/910: Emporor Magnus dies; his widow Lucia ensures her son Constant (aged 5) succeeds, with her as regent, imprisoning Natia. This triggers instability in the vassal-states including serious uprising in Noros. Despite initial successes, Noros is isolated and defeated in 910.

Years Y916/917: The Second Crusade: Rondian legions are reinforced in Hebusalim. They defeat the Sultans of Dhassa and Kesh and plunder as far east as Istabad. Again they withdraw to Hebb Valley as the Bridge closes.

Year Y921: Rebellion in Javon results in the Dorobon monarchs fleeing into exile and the establishment of the Nesti monarchy. Olfuss Nesti becomes king.

Year Y926: The Eighth Convocation of Amteh declares shihad upon the Rondian invaders.

Year Y927: The next Moontide will begin in 928. The Third Crusade is declared by Emperor Constant, and preparations for war accelerate in both continents.

Note: Antiopian chronology is counted from 454 years earlier than Yuros, so Y927 is A1381.

Time and Dates in Urte

The world of Urte uses a lunar calendar, and due to the size and influence that the moon has on both continents (or perhaps because they were once joined) they have essentially the same calendar, though they use different names for the months. There are twelve moon-cycles in a year, each 30 days long, making the lunar year 360 days. The solar calendar is a few hours longer, meaning that every few years an out-of-calendar day is recommended by the Ordo Costruo to the Emperor of Yuros and the rulers of Kesh, which is widely observed. The months are as follows:

Month of Year	Season	Yuros Name	Antiopian name
1st month	Spring	Janune	Moharram
2nd month	Spring	Febreux	Safar
3rd month	Spring	Martrois	Awwal
4th month	Summer	Aprafor	Thani
5th month	Summer	Maicin	Jumada
6th month	Summer	Junesse	Akhira
7th month	Autumn	Julsep	Rajab
8th month	Autumn	Augeite	Shaban
9th month	Autumn	Septinon	Rami
10th month	Winter	Octen	Shawwal
11th month	Winter	Noveleve	Zulqeda
12th month	Winter	Decore	Zulhijja

There are five parts to the lunar cycle, each roughly six days long, creating five six-day weeks. They are: New Moon, Waxing Moon, Full Moon, Waning Moon and Dark Moon. The weekly holy day is usually the last (or first) day of the six-day week; generally no commercial work is done and the day is divided between religious observance and relaxation.

The days of the week are as follows:

Day of Week	Yuros Name	Kesh name	Lakh name
1st day	Minasdai	Shambe	Somvaar
2nd day	Tydai	Doshambe	Mangalvaar
3rd day	Wotendai	Seshambe	Budhvaar
4th day	Torsdai	Chaharshambe	Viirvaar
5th day	Freyadai	Panjshambe	Shukravaar
6th (holy) day	Sabbadai	Jome	Shanivaar

The time is measured using sand-timers, and the hours are rung by a man assigned to staff the tallest tower of every city, town and village. There are varying numbers of hours to the day and night: at the instant of dawn, a bell is struck, and then again every hour until sunset, when a different (lower-toned) bell commences. Depending upon the season and latitude, a day might contain as many as sixteen daylight or night-time hours or as few as eight, but a day always totals twenty-four hours. Due to variability in quality of timing devices and vigilance of timekeepers, the time-keeping can be quite variable. The hours of the day are named as follows:

- Sunrise is the first hour: Day-Bell One
- Midday is typically Day-Bell Six
- Sunset would normally be considered Day-Bell Twelve, or Night-Bell One.
- Midnight is typically Night-Bell Six.

The Primary Religions of Yuros and Antiopia

Sollan (Yuros):

The Sollan Faith was the dominant religion of the Rimoni Empire and evolved from the sun and moon cults of the Yothic peoples that spread from the northeast prior to the formation of the Empire. Sol is the male deity and progenitor of mankind, together with his wayward wife Dara, or Luna, who is associated with the moon. The Sollan faith is kept by priests known as *drui* whose primary function is to keep records, advise communities and observe the seasonal rituals. The Sollan faith was outlawed by the Rondian Empire in 411 following the establishment of the Kore. It still thrives in parts of Sydia, Schlessen, Rimoni and Pontus, and also among the Rimoni of Javon.

Kore (Yuros):

The Church of Kore was established alongside the conquest of Rimoni by the Rondian magi. It believes that Corineus, the leader of the group who discovered and consumed ambrosia and gained the gnosis, was the son of God (or 'Kore'). The Church elevates people of mage-blood (i.e. related to one of the 300 Ascendants who led the conquest of Yuros by the Rondians) and holds that Kore gave the gnosis through the death of his Son. The Kore is the prime religion of Yuros, except where Rondelmar does not hold sway (parts of Sydia, Schlessen, Rimoni and Pontus). The Kore is male-dominated and places religion and the magi above secular society.

The Kore promises eternal life in Heaven for the faithful, a status that magi automatically gain, but ordinary men can aspire to. The wicked burn in Hel, a fiery underworld ruled by an evil spirit called Jasid (which is also one of the names of the Shaitan of the Amteh Faith).

Amteh (Antiopia): The Amteh Faith developed in the deserts of northern Antiopia and is principally associated with the Prophet Aluq-Ahmed of Hebb, who rose to importance in approximately A100 (Y450BV). His new teachings, collected in the *Kalistham*, superseded preceding religions based upon propitiation of gods that may have been related to the Omali faith. It is highly male-dominated and demanding of both time and conspicuous worship. The only deity is Ahm, a male Supreme Being. He reigns in Paradise where only the faithful go. The wicked are condemned to a place of Ice ruled by Shaitan, the eternal enemy.

The modern (Y900+) Amteh Faith has its centre in Sagostabad (Kesh) and holds sway in all of the northern lands of Antiopia and even parts of Lakh following the Keshi invasion and establishment of the Mughal line in Y834. There are some breakaway sects, notably the Ja'arathi, a more liberal sect that does not follow the more restrictive practices of Amteh (it separates secular and religious jurisdiction, does not require women to wear a bekira-shroud and allows widows to remarry without consequences). It has a following among the wealthy and the intellectual élite. The Ja'arathi claim their path to be a more accurate reading of the original teachings of Aluq-Ahmed.

There are also several fanatic Amteh sects, the most notable being the infamous Hadishah, outlawed by the Sultans of Dhassa and Kesh but harboured in Mirobez and Gatioch and widespread in the north.

Omali (Antiopia): Founded in Lakh in pre-history, the Omali faith posits one Supreme Being (Aum), who is both male and female and can manifest in many ways, but principally as the gods and goddesses of the Oma. The Omali assign specific virtues to the different Oma, and there are at least fifteen major deities and hundreds of minor ones.

The Omali believe in a cycle of death and rebirth called *samsara*, in which the same souls are reborn time and again into new lives, until they perfect themselves, attain a state called *moksha* and become at one with Aum. The prime deities are collectively known as the Trimurthi and encompass three male deities, the spirits of creation, preservation and destruction.

The Omali religion is the dominant faith of Lakh, despite the military conquest of northern Lakh by the Amteh-worshipping Mughal dynasty 100 years ago (around Y834).

Zainism (Antiopia): Zainism is believed to be derived from Omali and the teachings of Attiya Zai of Baranasi (whom the Omali believe to be an incarnation of Vishnarayan the Preserver). He preached removing oneself from worldly forces to seek spiritual, intellectual and physical perfection. Zainism's tenets still include the cycle of *samsara* and the seeking of *moksha*, but renounces worldliness. Zainism remains a fringe cult, but due to its liberal attitudes to gender equality, sexuality and the arts and its martial techniques, it has a following among élites.

The Gnostic Arts

Basic Theory: The Magi teach that when a person dies, their soul leaves their body. This disembodied spirit usually lingers for some time in our world and therefore has powers of movement and communication. The Scytale of Corineus enabled the magi to tap into these powers without having first to die, giving the mage 'magical' powers in life.

Mage's 'Blood': The child of a mage inherits powers equal to the average power of their parents: so a full-blooded mage and a non-mage would produce a half-blood with one-quarter the basic gnostic strength of the pure-blood. The 'blood-rank' of magi is therefore determined by their percentage of mage-blood.

Note that the children of Ascendants are not as powerful as their parents: consuming ambrosia generates greater power than can be inherited genetically.

Ascendants: Those who survive drinking ambrosia are Ascendants, and they wield the highest powers of the magi. The ambrosia is risky, however: not everyone who drinks the potion is strong enough to take the mental and physical strains; there is a strong likelihood of dying, or becoming insane.

Souldrinkers: Magi descended from 'God's Rejects' can access and maintain the gnosis only by using the energy of consumed souls. They are a secret sect that are held by the Kore to be wholly evil.

Magi and Society: Magi are prominent in Yuros society, and because of their skills, they generally do well financially, as well as acquiring great status and influence. They have special status in religious worship. They are expected to set the moral example and personify Kore's teachings.

Both male and female magi have fertility problems. There is great stigma should a female mage bear a child to a man considered beneath her and/or out of wedlock. Males have more licence and father many mixed-blood magi out of wedlock, but this is limited by their poor fertility.

Gnosis and Law: The use of gnosis is carefully controlled by the Church and the Arcanum (the fellowship of magi who control education and policy). Some Studies (especially within Theurgy and Sorcery) are closely monitored, but all gnosis is capable of misuse.

The Facets of the Gnosis

There are three facets to the gnosis: Magic, Runes and Studies.

Magic: Magic is the use of basic magical energies, such as discharging energy at an enemy (a 'mage-bolt'), lifting or moving an object with gnosis (kinesis), mind-to-mind communication, or protecting oneself with gnosis (shielding).

Runes:	These are a series of symbols from the old Yothic alphabet (the 'runes'), assigned for convenience to specific gnostic abilities. The symbols don't have intrinsic power; they are merely a form of shorthand for magical abilities. Some are assigned to general-use powers (like the Chain-rune, or wardings), and others represent powers accessed only through Studies (see below).
Studies:	These are the most sophisticated applications of gnosis, and even the best and most talented magi are usually only capable of using two-thirds of them, as their minds are conditioned to perform some tasks better than others. There are four Classes (or Fields) of gnosis and within each Class, four specific Studies (meaning there are sixteen Studies in all). The combination of Studies that a mage finds himself able to use is determined largely by personality (or 'affinity').
Class Affinity:	There are four Classes of gnosis; a mage will normally find they have more affinity to one than others, and therefore antipathy towards the opposing Study: for example, Thaumaturgy is the antithesis of Theurgy, and Hermetic the antithesis of Sorcery.
Elemental Affinity:	Each mage will also have an affinity to an element that will shape how they operate. This combined with Class-affinity will determine the abilities that mage will excel at, those they will merely be functional at, and those they cannot perform at all.

A mage who has an 'absolute affinity' has supreme mastery over a Study. It requires single-minded devotion to one Study for which they already have a strong affinity (in both Class and element). A mage with absolute affinity often has a narrower selection of Studies at which they are proficient.

The Classes (or Fields): Thaumaturgy: the manipulation of the prime elemental forces: earth, water, fire and air. Earth and Air are held as antithetical, as are Water and Fire. This is the simplest Class.

Hermetic: use of gnosis on living organisms, divided into Healing (restoring someone to normal), Morphic (altering 'normal' forms), Animism (emulating and controlling creatures) and Sylvanism (manipulating plant-matter).

Theurgy: use of the gnosis to affect the mind; divided into Mesmerism (influencing other minds), Illusion (deceiving the senses), Mysticism (communion of minds), and Spiritualism (projecting of the spirit).

Sorcery: dealing with other spirits; divided into Clairvoyance (using the 'eyes' of the spirits to observe other places), Divination (using the 'eyes' and knowledge of spirits to predict the future), Wizardry (control and use of spirits), and Necromancy (communion with the recently dead).

The Studies

Thaumaturgy: Fire: an aggressive Study; gives a resistance to fire and an ability to douse flame. This Study is primarily used by the military, as well as in metal-working.
Air: a versatile Study that gives the ability to fly and also to manipulate weather. It is widely used in commerce and by the military.

Water: the ability to shape water, to purify water, to breathe water and to use water as a weapon at times (the more skilful have been known to drown a man on dry land).

Earth: the ability to shape stone is valuable in construction. Earth-gnosis is also widely used in mining, hunting (tracking) and smithing, and has even been used to create or still earthquakes.

Hermetic:

Healing (Water-linked): restoring flesh to its normal undamaged state. It can be applied against illnesses and viruses as well. It is regarded as unglamorous.

Morphism (Fire-linked): the manipulation of the human form can be used to enhance (or deplete) musculature or appearance, right up to taking on the appearance of another person. Often used to gain special endurance for a task. The most feared use – to disguise oneself as another person – is illegal. It cannot be sustained for long periods.

Animism (Air-linked): can be used to enhance the senses, to command the behaviour of other creatures and even to take on beast-form oneself. Many applications, both in civilian and military context.

Sylvanism (Earth-linked): can be used to enhance or deplete wood and plant material. Often used in construction of buildings, tools and transport, in both peace and wartime. Wide use of potions and unguents for temporary gnostic affects.

Theurgy:

Mesmerism (Fire-linked): this is the use of mind-to-mind interaction to aid, dominate or mislead another. Can be used to strengthen another's determination or sense of purpose, but more infamously used to manipulate and mislead.

Illusion (Air-linked): the ability to produce false

sights, smells, tastes or sounds to deceive others. Can also be used for protection from the same, to deceive attackers, and to entertain.

Mysticism (Water-linked): the communion of minds, permitting rapid teaching, deep-probing of minds to restore lost memories and to heal mental disorders or calm anxiety. Can be used to link the minds of magi to enhance the power of gnosis-workings by sharing energy.

Spiritualism (Earth-linked): the ability to send one's spirit out of the body, where it can then travel long distance and use limited gnosis once there. Used in communication, also in scouting and similar.

Sorcery:

Clairvoyance (Water-linked): the ability to see other places, the distances being determined by the skill and power of the mage. It can be blocked by concentrated layers of earth or water, and certain other restrictions.

Divination (Air-linked): questions can be asked of the spirit world, which will then give information (often captured in visual symbols) and will allow the mage to predict a probable outcome based on the known information. Unreliable and subject to distortion by personal bias and knowledge gaps.

Wizardry (Fire-linked): the ability to summon a spirit and control it, either in its natural spirit form or within a body supplied by the caster. Perilous, due to hostility of spirits, and considered theologically dubious. Can give access to all other Studies second-hand, so widely used to achieve indirectly effects provided by other Studies.

Necromancy (Earth-linked): the ability to deal death through forcing the spirit to depart; can also be used to communicate with the recently dead, and even

ASCENDANT'S RITE

to bring a spirit back to reanimate a dead body. Its acceptable uses are to question the recently dead on crimes related to their deaths or to help a spirit 'pass on' (exorcism), but reanimation especially is illegal and other uses are morally and theologically dubious.

Gnosis Affinity Table

Below is a Mage Affinity table.

STUDIES	EARTH (element)	FIRE (element)	AIR (element)	WATER (element)
THAUMATURGY (The manipulation of inanimate matter)	Earth-gnosis	Fire-gnosis	Air-gnosis	Water-gnosis
HERMETIC (The manipulation of living matter)	Sylvanism	Morphism	Animism	Healing
SORCERY (the manipulation of spirit beings)	Necromancy	Wizardry	Divination	Clairvoyance
THEURGY (the manipulation of mind and spirit)	Spiritualism	Mesmerism	Illusion	Mysticism

How to use the table:

- All magi have a primary affinity to a Study, and/or to an Element. Most have an affinity to both, and many have a weaker secondary affinity.
- Any affinity creates a blind spot to its opposite:

FIRE	EARTH
AIR	WATER

THAUMATURGY	THEURGY
HERMETIC	SORCERY

Fire and Water are opposites
Air and Earth are opposites

Thaumaturgy and Sorcery are opposites
Hermetic and Theurgy are opposites

- So a person with affinities to Fire and Sorcery will be strongest at Wizardry and most vulnerable against Water-gnosis.

Glossary

Rukk/rukka!:	Fuck! (obscenity)
Rukka mio!:	Fuck me! (obscenity)
Safian:	Homosexual woman
Si:	Yes
Signor/i:	Gentleman/gentlemen
Silencio:	Silence
Stronzo:	Arsehole (also with connotations of stupidity)

Keshi/Dhassan/Jhafi

Afreet:	Evil spirit of the air in Kesh mythology
Bekira-shroud:	Loose-fitting black over-robe worn by Amteh women
Dom-al'Ahm:	Amteh place of worship.
Eyeed:	The three-day festival after the Holy month of Rami
Fatwah:	A religious death sentence decreed against those who have offended Ahm
Godsinger:	A person assigned to call the faithful to prayer
Godspeaker:	A senior Amteh priest and scholar
Raki:	Rice-based spirit, known in Lakh as arak
Scriptualist:	An Amteh priest
Shihad:	A holy war decreed against a people or place for religious reasons
Souk:	Market
Tribaddi:	Homosexual woman
Wadi:	Dried riverbed

Lakh

Achaa:	Okay or Yes or Very well
Arak:	Rice-based spirit, known in Kesh and Dhassa as Raki
Babu:	'Big man', a word for a local community leader
Baksheesh:	A tip or a bribe or a gift, depending upon the context
Father:	Father

Bhai:	Brother
Chai:	Tea, usually heavily spiced with cardamom, cinnamon, mint and other herbs and spices
Chapatti:	Flat bread
Chela:	A trainee Omali priest or sadhu
Chod!:	Fuck! (obscenity)
Chodia!:	Fucker! (obscenity)
Dalit:	An 'untouchable'; the lowest, most menial class of Lakh society
Didi:	Sister
Dodi Manghal:	The pre-dawn meal before wedding
Dom-al'Ahm:	Lakh (originally Gatioch) word for an Amteh temple
Dupatta:	A scarf worn by women with a salwar, and often used to veil the face from the sun or for modesty
Fenni:	A rough and cheap spirit distilled from wheat
Ferang:	Foreigner
Ganga:	Marijuana
Garud:	A bird-deity; the steed of the God Vishnarayan
Ghat:	Terraced steps leading down to water, used for worship and washing in Lakh
Gopi:	A milkmaid
Guru:	Teacher or wise person
Havan Kund:	Part of the wedding ritual, where the couple separately and together circle a fire, performing ritual words and actions
Haveli:	Walled style of house with an inner courtyard common among the well-off of Lakh
Jadugara:	A witch or wizard
Jhuggi:	Slums, shanty towns where the poor dwell
Kutti:	A woman's genitals (obscenity)
Lingam:	Male sexual organs
Mandap:	The holiest place in a shrine, and the consecrated place where wedding vows are exchanged in a person's house (which is blessed to become a temporary shrine)

Mandir:	Omali Shrine
Mata:	Mother
Mata-choda:	Motherfucker
Mela:	A fair
Nehin:	No
Pandit or Purohit:	Omali Priest
Pooja:	Prayer
Pratta:	A religious ban; e.g. the Blood-pratta that bars a menstruating woman from male company
Rangoli:	Decorative floor-paintings
Sadhu:	Itinerant Omali holy man
Salwar Kameez:	A pull-over one-piece dress worn with drawstring baggy pants and a scarf (dupatta)
Siv-lingam:	Religious icon representing the penis of the God Sivraman and his consort's yoni.
Tilak	A prayer-mark on the forehead
Vridhi Pooja:	Ancestor prayers
Walla:	'Fellow', usually associated with a job, e.g. a chai-walla is a tea-boy
Yoni:	Female sexual organs

Ascendant's Rite

As at Septinon 929

In Yuros
Imperial Court, Pallas

- Emperor Constant Sacrecour: Emperor of Rondelmar and all Yuros
- Mater-Imperia Lucia Fasterius: the emperor's mother, a Living Saint
- Cordan: son of Constant, heir to the throne
- Coramore: daughter of Constant
- Regis Sacrecour: Lord of Pontus
- Lord Calan Dubrayle: Imperial Treasurer
- Grand Prelate Dominius Wurther: Head of the Church of Kore
- Natia Sacrecour: Constant's imprisoned elder sister
- Ervyn Naxius: former Ordo Costruo mage
- Lady Delfinne de Tressot: A Keeper and Ascendant mage
- Grandmaster Lens Nauvoine: A Keeper and Ascendant mage
- Raneulf Fasterius: A Keeper and Ascendant mage
- Jean Benoit: Merchant Guildmaster
- Hestan Milius: an Arch-Legate of the Imperial Treasury
- Yrna Corloi: female Volsai agent

Eighteenth Fist of Kore's Holy Inquisition

- Elath Dranid: Fist Second [deceased]
- Raine Caladryn: an Acolyte [deceased]
- Dominic Rysen: an Acolyte [deceased]

Thirty-Second Fist of Kore's Holy Inquisition

- Fronck Quintius: Commandant
- Artus Leblanc: an Acolyte
- Geoffram: an Acolyte
- Nayland: an Acolyte
- Magrenius: an Acolyte
- Adamus Crozier: a bishop of the Kore

Twenty-Third Fist of Kore's Holy Inquisition

- Ullyn Siburnius: Inquisitor and Fist Commander
- Alis Nytrasia: Fist Third
- Einar Perle: an Acolyte
- Delta: a Souldrinker mage and prisoner of the Inquisition
- Lambda: a Souldrinker mage and prisoner of the Inquisition
- Rho: a female Souldrinker mage and prisoner of the Inquisition
- Tau: a Souldrinker mage and prisoner of the Inquisition
- Zeta: a female Souldrinker mage and prisoner of the Inquisition

Bricia

- Lady Laeticia Korion-Fetallink: mother of Seth Korion
- Hobin: gamesman of the Korion estates
- Taft: butler of the Korion estates

Norostein, Noros

- King Phyllios III: King of Noros
- Vannaton Mercer: a trader
- Tesla Anborn-Mercer: mage, wife of Vannaton Mercer [deceased]
- Captain Jeris Muhren: Watch Captain [deceased]

Silacia

- Vitor Mori: Pater-Retiari: a criminal clan-lord
- Fanisia Sensini: wife of Vitor; mother of Ramon
- Tomasi Fuldo: a Retiari familioso agent
- Isabella Petrossi: a criminal clan-lady
- Silvio Anturo: a Petrossi familioso agent

Gurvon Gyle's Grey Foxes (based in Noros)

- Gurvon Gyle: a mage-spy
- Rutt Sordell: a mage, whose soul is currently in the body of Guy Lassaigne
- Mayten Drexel: mage-assassin
- Veritia: female mage
- Sylas: mage
- Luc Brossian: mage

Ordo Costruo (Mage Order based in Hebusalim)

- Antonin Meiros: Arch-Magus and founder [deceased]
- Justina Meiros: Antonin's daughter [deceased]

Crusaders
The First Army (Northern)

- General Kaltus Korion: Commander of the Armies of Rondelmar
- Tonville: aide to General Korion
- General Rhynus Bergium: Korion's second-in-command
- Oljan Fruleau: aide to General Bergium
- Kendric Vitalis: Brevian battlemage

The 'Lost Legions' of the Southern Crusade

- Seth Korion: Commander of the Lost Legions
- Ramon Sensini: a battle-mage of Pallacios XXIII

- Severine Tiseme: Legion Farseer of Pallacios XXIII
- Julietta: newborn daughter of Ramon and Severine
- Baltus Prenton: Windmaster of Pallacios XXIII
- Lanna Jureigh: Healer of Pallacios XXIII
- Hugh Gerant: a battle-mage of Pallacios XXIII
- Evan Hale: a battle-mage of Pallacios XXIII
- Fridryk Kippenegger: a battle-mage of Pallacios XXIII
- Jelaska Lyndrethuse: Argundian battlemage
- Carmina Phyl: Argundian healer-mage
- Gerdhart: Argundian chaplain and mage
- Lysart: Noroman battlemage
- Sordan: Noroman battlemage
- Mylde: Noroman battlemage
- Runsald: Brevian battlemage
- Hulbert: Hollenian battlemage
- Nacallas: Brevian battlemage
- Til ven Lascen: Brician battlemage
- Barendyne: Brician battlemage
- Deceased battle-magi of the Pallacios XXIII legion: Legate Jonti Duprey, Secundus Rufus Marle, Coulder, Fenn, Lewen, Chaplain Tyron Frand
- Storn: Tribune of the Tenth Maniple of Pallacios XXIII
- Coll: a scout of the Tenth Maniple of Pallacios XXIII
- Gylf: commander of the Argundian contingent

Lukaz's cohort; Pallacios XXIII (Ramon's guards)

- Lukaz: pilus (commander)
- Baden: bannerman
- The Front Rank: Serjant Manius, Dolman, Ferdi, Trefeld, Hedman, Gannoval
- The Second Rank: Serjant Vidran, Bowe, Ilwyn, Holdyne, Gal Herde, Jan Herde
- The Flankman: Kel Harmon, Briggan, Kent, Ollyd, Neubeau, Tolomon

Rondian Garrisons

- Sir Bann Herbreux: Garrison commander of Vida
- Monrel Jongebeau: Rondian general

In Javon
In Forensa

- Cera Nesti: co-Queen of Javon
- Timori Nesti: Crown Prince and rightful King of Javon
- Harshal ali-Assam: brother of the Emir of Forensa
- Camlad a'Luki: Jhafi kinsman to Harshal
- Saarif Jelmud: Jhafi kinsman to Camlad and Harshal
- Pita Rosco: Master of the Royal Purse
- Luigi Ginovisi: Master of Revenues
- Comte Piero Inveglio: a Rimoni nobleman
- Seir Ionus Mardium: Nesti knight-commander
- Luca Conte: Nesti noble [deceased]
- Nehlan: Jhafi Scriptualist and royal soul-guide
- Tavis: Sollan drui
- Luqeef: Jhafi Godspeaker
- Borsa: Nesti family nursemaid
- Seir Delfin: Nesti knight
- Genas: a Nesti ranker
- Benirio: Nesti house guard
- Tello: Nesti house guard
- Jerid: Nesti house guard
- Drus: Jhafi maid
- Paolo Castellini: a Nesti guard commander [currently missing]
- Elena Anborn: mage, former Grey Fox and Nesti champion
- Kazim Makani: a Souldrinker and assassin
- Theo Vernio-Nesti: cousin of Cera Nesti; commander of Viola Fort

In Brochena

- Tomas Betillon: Imperial Governor of Hebusalim and Javon
- Lann Wilfort: Kirkegarde Grandmaster
- Blan Remikson: Kirkegarde Seer-mage
- Kinnaught: Betillon's spy master
- Mikals: aide to Governor Betillon
- Pendris: aide to Governor Betillon, son of Mikals
- Francesco Perdonello: Don (Chief) of Royal Bureaucracy
- Tarita: Cera's personal maid
- Mustaq al'Madhi: a criminal lord [deceased]

The Dorobon settlers

- Francis Dorobon: King of Javon [deceased]
- Craith Margham: mage-knight
- Roland Heale: mage-knight
- Guy Lassaigne: mage (possessed by Rutt Sordell)

Other Javonesi/Harkun

- Alfredo Gorgio: a Rimoni lord of Hytel
- Portia Tolidi: former Queen of Javon
- Seir Lorenzo di Kestria: a Rimoni knight [deceased]
- Seir Justiano di Kestria: Rimoni knight, younger brother of Lorenzo
- Lord Massimo di Kestria: Lord of Loctis, elder brother of Lorenzo and Justiano
- Lord Stefan di Aranio of Riban
- Emir Ilan Tamadhi of Riban [deceased]
- Marid Tamadhi: son and heir of Ilan Tamadhi, Emir of Riban
- Emir Mekmud bin al'Azhir of Lybis
- Gabrien Gorgio-Sintro: Rimoni bastard son of Alfredo
- Ricardo Gorgio-Sintro: Rimoni bastard son of Alfredo, younger brother of Gabrien

- Emilio Gorgio: half-Jhafi bastard of Alfredo Gorgio's brother
- Ghujad iz'Kho: Harkun chieftain
- Cabruhil: nephew of Ghujad
- Lekutto iz'Fal: Harkun scout

Gyle's Mercenaries

- Endus Rykjard: a mercenary commander
- Adi Paavus: a mercenary commander
- Hans Frikter: Argundian mercenary commander
- Ogdi: nephew of Hans Frikter
- Hullyn: Argundian battlemage
- Eafyd: Argundian battelmage
- Staria Canestos: female mercenary commander of the Sacro Arcoyris Estellan legion
- Leopollo Canestos: Staria's nephew and adopted son
- Kordea Canestos: Staria's adopted daughter
- Capolio: spymaster of the Sacro Arcoyris Estellan legion
- Marklyn: pilot-mage of Rykjard's legion
- Jesset: pilot-mage of Rykjard's legion

Among the Lamiae

- Kekropius: an Elder male
- Kessa: mate of Kekropius and Elder [deceased]
- Simou: an Elder male

In Kesh
Sagostabad

- Salim Kabarakhi I: Sultan of Kesh
- Latif: one of the Sultan's impersonators
- Faroukh of Maal: uncle of Sultan Salim
- Barra Xuok: Godspeaker
- Rashid Mubarak: Emir of Halli'kut and Ordo Costruo renegade

- Alyssa Dulayne: renegade Ordo Costruo mage, Rashid's mistress
- Narukhan Mubarak: younger brother of Rashid Mubarak, and mage
- Lesharri Dulayne: Alyssa's younger sister and servant
- Pashil: a Hadishah captain
- Qanaroz: Hadishah, second-in-command under Pashil
- Dashimel: Emir of Baraka; a Keshi general
- Darhus: a Keshi general
- Barzin: Mirobezan eunuch; aide and slave to Keshi royal house
- Selmir: a Hadishah captain

Among the Hadishah

- Molmar: a Hadishah skiff-pilot
- Jamil: a mage assassin [deceased]
- Gatoz: Hadishah mage and commander [deceased]
- Megradh: a Hadishah captain
- Tegeda: female Hadishah
- Satravim: Hadishah skiff-pilot
- Tahir: Hadishah breeding house overseer and Scriptualist
- Sadikh: Hadishah breeding-house supervisor and mage
- Yimat: Hadishah breeding-house mage
- Gulbahar: female Hadishah breeding house mage

Prisoners of the Hadishah

- Rene Cardien: Ordo Costruo mage
- Odessa D'Ark: female Ordo Costruo mage
- Clematia: female Ordo Costruo mage
- Lunetta: female Ordo Costruo mage
- Perdionus: Ordo Costruo healer-mage
- Valdyr: Mollachian bannerman
- Sir Beglyn: Pallacian knight

Huriya's Souldrinkers

- Huriya Makani: a Souldrinker, sister of Kazim
- Malevorn Andevarion: former Inquisition Acolyte, now Souldrinker
- Hessaz: a Souldrinker female
- Tkwir: a Souldrinker male
- Toljin: a Souldrinker male
- Sabele: a Souldrinker seer [deceased and soul taken by Huriya]

Renegades

- Zaqri: a Souldrinker male; deposed packleader
- Cymbellea di Regia: Rimoni gypsy and mage

Souldrinkers in the Sultan's army

- Prandello: a Souldrinker clanleader
- Maddeoni: Prandello's Vereloni consort

Souldrinkers of Gatioch

- Xymoch: Souldrinker and packleader

In Rural Kesh

- Bunima: a female Keshi refugee

In Khotriawal
Ardijah

- Amiza al'Ardijah: Calipha of Ardijah
- Renn Bondeau: Rondian former-battlemage, now Caliph of Ardijah

In Lokistan
Mandira Khojana monastery

- Puravai: a Zain master
- Yash: a Zain acolyte
- Gateem: a Zain acolyte
- Aprek: a Zain acolyte
- Kedak: a Zain acolyte
- Haddo: a Zain acolyte
- Sindar: a Zain acolyte
- Fenan: a Zain acolyte
- Bhati: a Zain acolyte
- Joa: a Zain acolyte
- Vekati: a Zain acolyte
- Meero: a Zain acolyte
- Urfin: a Zain acolyte
- Felakan: a Zain monk
- Alaron Mercer: mage, son of Vann and Tesla
- Ramita Ankesharan: Lakh widow of Antonin Meiros
- Dasra and Nasatya: twin newborn sons of Ramita and Antonin Meiros

In Lakh
Baranasi

- Vikash Nooradin: market trader [deceased]
- Ram Sankar: market trader
- Sunita Sankar: Ram's wife

In southern Lakh

- Ispal Ankesharan: trader; Ramita's father
- Tanuva Ankesharan: Ispal's wife; Ramita's mother
- Jai: Ispal's son
- Keita: Jai's wife

From the Past

- Johan Corin ('Corineus'): Messiah of the Kore
- Selene Corin ('Corinea') also known as Lillea Selene Sorades: sister (allegedly), lover and murderer of Johan Corin; personification of feminine evil
- Olfuss Nesti: a deceased King of Javon
- Jarius Langstrit: deceased Noros general
- Echor Borodium: Duke of Argundy (deceased)
- Belonius Vult: Governor of Norostein (deceased)
- Nasette Ledoc: only person in history known to have been transformed from a mage into a Souldrinker
- Attiya Zai: Omali holy man, founder of the Zain order of monasticism

The Blessed Three Hundred

- Sertain: First Emperor of the Rondian Empire
- Baramitius: Ascendant mage and creator of ambrosia, and the Scytale of Corineus
- Berial: Brician Ascendant; mage-ancestor of Alaron Mercer and Elena Anborn

ACKNOWLEDGEMENTS

There have been a lot of people involved in placing this book in your hands, and I'm very grateful to all of them. It *really* wouldn't have happened without them. First off, thanks to the wonderful Jo Fletcher for all the skill, experience and wisdom she's brought to bear; these books are a product of her faith in the ideas and vision of this occasionally errant writer, and it's impossible for me to express enough gratitude to her!

Thanks also to the rest of the team at Jo Fletcher Books, especially Nicola Budd and Andrew Turner; and to the US team, especially Eric Price and Olivia Taussig; and the wonderful publicists at Wunderkind led by Elena Stokes. Also big thanks (and apologies for the mishmash of languages and accents in the story) to Ryan Neuschafer and the team assembling the audio books. And thanks again to Emily Faccini for the cool maps.

Then there are the regular Moontide team: the test readers; Paul Linton, Kerry Greig and Heather Adams. I've said it before but these are the people who keep these books up to snuff and fit for consumption, kind of like a World Health Organisation Special Unit assigned to the Moontide Quartet. Sampling, testing and improving are just some of the duties they perform so well. Thanks so much!

It's very hard for a story to go from being a file in a computer to a book in a shop without someone to fight its corner and get it noticed by publishers. I'm lucky to be represented by the aforementioned Heather, who runs HMA Literary Agency UK (alongside her husband Mike Bryan). Thank you both once more for opening the doors for me and my dreams, and for being perfect hosts on our last visit to the UK.

As always, my greatest thanks is to my lovely wife Kerry, who has to put up with weird conversation at all hours about imaginary people and their deeds. Her willingness to test-read, edit and proof was massively important to the series, as well as her own imagination in contributing ideas and feedback. I literally crossed half the globe to be with her, and I've never regretted a moment.

Finally, shout-outs to my children Brendan and Melissa; my parents Cliff and Biddy, and all my friends, especially Mark, Felix and Stefania, Raj and Hina, Andrew and Brenda, my rakhi-sisters Tanuva and Vidhi, and Keith and Kathryn.

And hello to Jason Isaacs and the Doctors of Wittertainment, of course.

EMPRESS OF THE
FALL

THE SUNSURGE QUARTET BOOK I
DAVID HAIR

THE EMPEROR IS DEAD.
LONG LIVE THE EMPRESS!

Emperor Constant is dead and his rivals are scrabbling for power – but any misstep could plunge the land, already devastated by the shocking outcome of the Third Crusade, into a calamitous civil war.

The Imperial throne is not the only one in jeopardy. Two brothers, imprisoned veterans of the Crusades, finally return home to find their father's kingdom being plundered – but the price of regaining their birthright will have far-reaching implications for the entire empire.

In the East, Sultan Salim, peacemaker and visionary ruler, faces his greatest challenge as his people demand an invasion of the West in retribution for the Rondian Crusades

Jo Fletcher
BOOKS

MAGE'S BLOOD

THE MOONTIDE QUARTET
BOOK I

DAVID HAIR

**THE MOONTIDE BRIDGE IS ABOUT TO OPEN
AND DECIDE THE FATE OF THE WORLD.**

Most of the time the Moontide Bridge lies deep below
the sea, but every 12 years the tides sink and the bridge
is revealed, its gates open for trade.

The Magi are hell-bent on ruling this new world, and for
the last two Moontides they have led armies across the
bridge on crusades of conquest. Now the third Moontide
is almost here and, this time, the people of the East are
ready for a fight... but it is three seemingly ordinary
people who will decide the fate of the world.

Jo Fletcher
BOOKS

THE
SCARLET
TIDES

THE MOONTIDE QUARTET
BOOK II

DAVID HAIR

**RETURN TO URTE, A LAND IN CHAOS,
WHERE THE SMALLEST CHOICE MAY SAVE OR
DAMN THE WORLD.**

The Moontide has come, a scarlet tide of Rondian legions
is flooding into the East, and the Scytale of Corineus, the
source of ultimate magical power, is missing.

But there are some who have pledged to end the cycle of
war and restore peace to Urte. They are the unlikeliest of
heroes: a failed mage, a gypsy and a lowly market-girl.

As East and West clash more violently than ever before,
Urte will discover that love, loyalty and truth can be
forged into weapons as deadly as swords and magic.

Jo Fletcher
BOOKS

UNHOLY WAR

THE MOONTIDE QUARTET BOOK III

DAVID HAIR

THE MOONTIDE IS HERE, AND IN THIS KIND OF WAR, NOTHING IS HOLY.

The Moontide has arrived, the Leviathan Bridge has risen from the waves and the armies of the Third Crusade are battling to conquer the continent of Antiopia once and for all. But the East is rising against them, bringing equal measures of hope and despair to the magical world of Urte.

And while the armies of east and west clash in ever-more-bloody conflict, emperors, Inquisitors, Souldrinkers and assassins all have their attention turned elsewhere as they hunt the Scytale of Corineus: the key to ultimate power.

Jo Fletcher
BOOKS